The Crow Girl

Erik Axl Sund

Translated by Neil Smith

Harvill *Secker*

LONDON

1 3 5 7 9 10 8 6 4 2

Harvill Secker, an imprint of Vintage,
20 Vauxhall Bridge Road,
London SW1V 2SA

Harvill Secker is part of the Penguin Random House group of companies whose addresses can be found at global.penguinrandomhouse.com.

www.vintage-books.co.uk

A CIP catalogue record for this book is available from the British Library

ISBN 9781846557569 (hardback)
9781846557576 (trade paperback)
9781448161737 (ebook)

Printed and bound by Clays Ltd, St Ives plc

Penguin Random House is committed to a sustainable future for our business, our readers and our planet. This book is made from Forest Stewardship Council® certified paper.

In memory of

a sister, those of us who failed,

and those of you who forgave

Our lives are opaque. Great our innate disappointment – which is why so many stories blossom in the forests of Scandinavia – mournfully the fiery hunger in our hearts turns to embers. Many end up as charcoal-burners beside the stack of their own heart; in a crippled dreamlike state they set their ears to listen and hear the flames dying with a sigh.

– from *Flowering Nettles* by Harry Martinson

Part I

The house

was over a hundred years old, and the solid stone walls were at least a metre thick, which meant that she probably didn't need to insulate them, but she wanted to be absolutely sure.

To the left of the living room was a small corner room that she had been using as a combination workroom and guest bedroom.

Leading off it were a small toilet and a fair-sized closet.

The room was perfect, with its single window and nothing but the unused attic above.

No more nonchalance, no more taking anything for granted.

Nothing would be left to chance. Fate was a dangerously unreliable accomplice. Sometimes your friend, but just as often an unpredictable enemy.

The dining table and chairs ended up shoved against one wall, which opened up a large space in the middle of the living room.

Then it was just a matter of waiting.

The first sheets of polystyrene arrived at ten o'clock, as arranged, carried in by four men. Three of them were in their fifties, but the fourth couldn't have been more than twenty. His head was shaved and he wore a black T-shirt with two crossed Swedish flags on the chest, under the words 'My Fatherland'. He had tattoos of spiderwebs on his elbows, and some sort of Stone Age design on his wrists.

When she was alone again she settled onto the sofa to plan her work. She decided to start with the floor, since that was the only thing that was likely to be a problem. The old couple downstairs might have been almost deaf, and she herself had never heard a single sound from them over the years, but it still felt like an important detail.

She went into the bedroom.

The little boy was still sound asleep.

It had been so odd when she met him on the local train. He had simply taken her hand, stood up and obediently gone with her, without her having to say a single word.

She had acquired the pupil she had been seeking, the child she had never been able to have.

She put her hand to his forehead; his temperature had gone down. Then she felt his pulse.

Everything was as it should be.

She had used the right dose of morphine.

The workroom had a thick, white, wall-to-wall carpet that she had always thought ugly and unhygienic, even if it was nice to walk on. But right now it was ideal for her purpose.

Using a sharp knife, she cut up the polystyrene and stuck the pieces together with a thick layer of flooring adhesive.

The strong smell soon made her feel dizzy, and she had to open the window onto the street. It was triple-glazed, and the outer pane had an extra layer of soundproofing.

Fate as a friend.

Work on the floor took all day. Every so often she would go and check on the boy.

When the whole floor was done she covered all the cracks with silver duct tape.

She spent the following three days dealing with the walls. By Friday there was just the ceiling left, and that took a bit longer because she had to glue the polystyrene first, and then wedge the blocks up against the ceiling with planks.

While the glue was drying she nailed up some old blankets in place of the doors she had removed earlier. She glued four layers of polystyrene onto the door to the living room.

She covered the only window with an old sheet. Just to be sure, she used a double layer of insulation to block the window alcove. When the room was ready, she covered the floor and walls with a waterproof tarpaulin.

There was something meditative about the work, and when at last she looked at what she had accomplished she felt a sense of pride.

The room was further refined during the following week. She bought four small rubber wheels, a hasp, ten metres of electric cable, several metres of wooden skirting, a basic light fitting and a box of light bulbs. She also had a set of dumb-bells, some weights and an exercise bike delivered.

She took all the books out of one of the bookcases in the living room, tipped it onto its side, and screwed the wheels under each corner. She attached a length of skirting board to the front to conceal the fact that it could now be moved, then placed the bookcase in front of the door to the hidden room.

She screwed the bookcase to the door and tested it.

The door glided soundlessly open on its little rubber wheels. It all worked perfectly. She attached the hasp and shut the door, concealing the simple locking mechanism with a carefully positioned lamp.

Finally she put all the books back and fetched a thin mattress from one of the two beds in the bedroom.

That evening she carried the sleeping boy into his new home.

Gamla Enskede – Kihlberg House

The strangest thing about the young boy wasn't the fact that he was dead, but that he had stayed alive so long. Something had kept him alive where a normal human being would long since have given up.

Detective Superintendent Jeanette Kihlberg knew nothing of this as she backed her car out of the garage. And she was unaware that this case would be the first in a series of events that would change her life.

She saw Åke in the window and waved, but he was on the phone and didn't see her. He would spend the morning washing that week's accumulation of sweaty tops, muddy socks and dirty underwear. With a wife and a son who were mad about football, it was a constant feature of daily life, this business of thrashing the old washing machine almost to the breaking point at least five times a week.

While he was waiting for the machine to finish, she knew he would go into the little studio they'd set up in the attic, and continue with one of the many unfinished oil paintings he was always working on. He was a romantic, a dreamer who had trouble finishing what he started. Jeanette had nagged him several times about getting in touch with one of the gallery owners who had shown an interest in his work, but he always said the pictures weren't quite ready. Not yet, but soon.

And when they were, everything would change.

He would finally make his big breakthrough, and the money would start to pour in, and they could finally do everything they had dreamed of. Everything from fixing the house to travelling anywhere they liked.

After almost twenty years she was starting to doubt it was ever going to happen.

As she swung out onto the Nynäshamn road she heard a worrying rattle somewhere down by the left front wheel. Even though she was an imbecile when it came to cars, it was obvious that something was wrong with their old Audi and that she was going to have to get it fixed again soon. From past experience she knew it wouldn't be cheap, even if the Serbian mechanic she went to out at Bolidenplan was both reliable and competitively priced.

The day before, she had emptied their savings account to pay the latest instalment of the mortgage, something that happened every three months with sadistic punctuality. She hoped she would be able to get the car fixed on credit. That had worked before.

Jeanette's jacket pocket started to vibrate violently, as Beethoven's Ninth Symphony almost drove her off the road and onto the pavement.

'Yep, Kihlberg here.'

'Hi, Jan, we've got something out at the Thorildsplan metro,' replied the voice of her colleague Jens Hurtig. 'We need to get there at once. Where are you?' There was a loud screech on the line, and she held the phone away from her ear to protect her hearing.

She hated being called Jan, and could feel herself getting annoyed. It had started off as a joke at a staff party three years earlier, but since then the nickname had spread through the whole of the police headquarters on Kungsholmen.

'I'm in Årsta, heading onto the Essinge bypass. What's happened?'

'They've found a young dead male in some bushes by the metro station, near the teacher-training college, and Billing wants you there as soon as possible. He sounded pretty agitated. Everything points to murder.'

Jeanette Kihlberg could hear the rattle getting worse, and wondered if she ought to pull over and call a tow truck, then get a lift into town.

'If this bastard car holds together I'll be there in five, ten minutes. I want you there as well.' The car lurched, and Jeanette pulled into the right-hand lane just in case.

'OK, I'll get going – I'll probably be there before you.'

A dead man's body found in some bushes sounded to Jeanette like a fight that had got out of hand. It would probably end up as a manslaughter charge.

Murder, she thought, as the steering wheel juddered, is a woman killed in her own home by her jealous husband after she tells him she wants a divorce.

More often than not, anyway.

But the fact was that times had changed, and what she had once learned at police training college was now not only open to question, but just plain wrong. Working methods had changed, and policing was in many respects much harder today than it had been twenty years ago.

Jeanette remembered the first time she was out on the beat, around normal people. How the public would offer to help, even had confidence in the police. The only reason anyone reports a crime today, she thought, is that the insurance companies demand it. Not because people have any expectation of the crime being solved.

But what had she been expecting when she quit her social-work course and decided to join the police? The opportunity to make a difference? To help people? That was what she told her dad when she proudly showed him her letter of acceptance. Yes, that was it. She wanted to be the sort of person who stood between people who did bad things and people who had bad things done to them. She wanted to be a real person.

And that was what being in the police meant.

She had spent her whole childhood listening in awe as her father and grandfather talked about their work in the police. No matter whether it was Midsummer or Good Friday, conversation around the dining table would always revert to ruthless bank robbers, good-natured pickpockets and clever con men. Anecdotes and memories from the darker side of life.

Just as the smell of the Christmas ham used to conjure up a whole roomful of expectation, the men's talk in the living room provided a backdrop of security.

She smiled at the memory of her grandfather's lack of interest and scepticism about new technological tools. Nowadays handcuffs had been replaced by self-locking plastic ties, to make things easier. He had once told her that DNA analysis was just a passing fad.

Police work was about making a difference, she thought. Not about making things easier. And their work had to adapt to keep pace with changes in society.

Being in the police means that you want to help, that you care. It's not about sitting in an armoured police van, staring out helplessly through tinted windows.

The airport

had been as grey and as cold as the winter's morning. He arrived on Air China in a country he had never heard of before. He knew that several hundred children before him had made the same journey, and like them he had a well-rehearsed story to tell the border police at passport control.

Without hesitating over a single syllable he delivered the story he had spent months repeating until he knew it by heart.

During the construction of one of the big Olympic venues he had got work carrying bricks and mortar. His uncle, a poor labourer, organised somewhere for him to live, but when his uncle was badly injured and ended up in hospital he had no one to look after him. His parents were dead and he had no brothers or sisters or other relatives he could turn to.

In his interview with the border police he explained how he and his uncle had been treated like slaves, in circumstances that could only be compared to apartheid. He told them how he had spent five months working on the construction site, but had never dared hope he might ever become an equal citizen of the city.

According to the old *hukou* system, he was registered in his home village far away from the city, and therefore had almost no rights at all in the place where he lived and worked.

That was why he had been forced to make his way to Sweden, where his only remaining relative lived. He didn't know where, but according to his uncle they had promised to get in touch with him as soon as he arrived.

He came to this new country with nothing but the clothes he was wearing, a mobile phone and fifty American dollars. The mobile's contact list was empty, and there were no texts or pictures that could reveal anything about him.

In actual fact, it was new and completely unused.

What he didn't reveal to the police was the telephone number he had written down on a scrap of paper hidden in his left shoe. A number he was going to call as soon as he had escaped from the camp.

The country he had come to wasn't like China at all. Everything was so clean and empty. When the interview was over and he was being led by two policemen through the deserted corridors of the airport, he wondered if this was what Europe looked like.

The man who had constructed his background, given him the phone number, and provided him with the money and phone had told him that over the past four years he had successfully sent more than seventy children to different parts of Europe.

He had said he had the most contacts in a country called Belgium, where you could earn big money. The work involved serving rich people, and if you were discreet and loyal, you could get rich yourself. But Belgium was risky, and you had to stay out of sight.

Never be seen outside.

Sweden was safer. There you would work mainly in restaurants and could move about more freely. It wasn't as well paid, but if you were lucky you could earn a lot of money there too, depending on which services were in particular demand.

There were people in Sweden who wanted the same thing as the people in Belgium.

The camp wasn't very far from the airport, and he was driven there in an unmarked police car. He stayed overnight, sharing a room with a black boy who could speak neither Chinese nor English.

The mattress he slept on was clean, but it smelled musty.

On only his second day there he called the number on the piece of paper, and a female voice explained how to get to the station in order to catch the train to Stockholm. Once he got there he was to call again for further instructions.

The train was warm and comfortable. It carried him quickly and almost soundlessly through a city where everything was white with snow. But by coincidence or fate, he never reached Central Station in Stockholm.

After a few stations a beautiful blonde woman sat down in the seat opposite him. She looked at him for a long time, and he realised that she knew he was alone. Not just alone on the train, but alone in the whole world.

The next time the train stopped the blonde woman stood up and took his hand. She nodded towards the door. He didn't protest, and went with her like he was in a trance.

They got a taxi and drove through the city. He saw that it was surrounded by water, and he thought it was beautiful. There wasn't as much traffic as there was at home. It was cleaner, and the air was easier to breathe.

He thought about fate and about coincidence, and wondered for a moment why he was sitting there with her. But when she turned to him and smiled, he stopped wondering.

At home they used to ask what he was good at, squeezing his arms to see if he was strong enough. Asking questions he pretended to understand.

They always had their doubts. Then sometimes they picked him.

But she had chosen him without him having done anything for her, and no one had ever done that before.

The room she led him into was white, and there was a big, wide bed. She put him in it and gave him something hot to drink. It tasted almost like the tea at home, and he fell asleep before the cup was empty.

When he woke up he didn't know how long he'd been asleep, but he saw that he was in a different room. The new room had no windows and was completely covered in plastic.

When he got up to go over to the door he discovered that the floor was soft and yielding. He tried the door handle, but the door was locked. His clothes were gone, as was the mobile phone.

Naked, he lay back down on the mattress and went to sleep again.

This room was going to be his new world.

Thorildsplan Metro Station – Crime Scene

Jeanette could feel the wheel pulling to the right, and the car seemed to be heading along the road at an odd angle. She crawled the last kilometre at sixty, and by the time she turned off onto the Drottningholm road towards the metro station, she was beginning to think the fifteen-year-old car was finished.

She parked and walked over to the cordon, where she caught sight of Hurtig. He was a head taller than all the others, Scandinavian blond and thickset, without actually being fat.

After working with him for four years Jeanette had learned how to read his body language.

He looked worried. Almost pained.

But when he caught sight of her he brightened, came over and held the cordon tape up for her.

'I see the car made it.' He grinned. 'I don't know how you put up with driving around in that old crate.'

'Me neither, and if you can get me a raise I'll go and get a little convertible Mercedes to cruise about in.'

If only Åke would get a decent job with a decent wage, she could get herself a decent car, she thought as she followed Hurtig into the cordoned-off area.

'Any tyre tracks?' she asked one of the two female forensics officers crouched over the path.

'Yes, several different ones,' one of them replied, looking up at Jeanette. 'I think some of them are from the lorries that come down here to empty the bins. But there are some other tracks from narrower wheels.'

Now that Jeanette had arrived at the scene she was the most senior officer present, and therefore in charge.

That evening she would report to her boss, Commissioner Dennis Billing, who in turn would inform Prosecutor von Kwist. Together the pair of them would decide what should be done, regardless of what she might think.

Jeanette turned to Hurtig.

'OK, let's hear it. Who found him?'

Hurtig shrugged. 'We don't know.'

'What do you mean, don't know?'

'The emergency line got an anonymous phone call, about' – he looked at his watch – 'about three hours ago, and the caller said there was a boy's body lying here, close to the entrance to the station. That's all.'

'But the call was recorded?'

'Of course.'

'So why did it take so long for us to be told?' Jeanette felt a pang of irritation.

'The dispatcher got the location wrong and sent a patrol to Boliden-plan instead of Thorildsplan.'

'Have they traced the call?'

Hurtig raised his eyebrows. 'Unregistered pay-as-you-go mobile phone.'

'Shit.'

'But we'll soon know where the call was made from.'

'OK, good. We'll listen to the recording when we get back. What about witnesses, then? Did anyone see or hear anything?' She looked around hopefully, but her subordinates just shook their heads.

'Someone must have driven the boy here,' Jeanette went on, with an increasing sense of desperation. She knew their work would be much harder if they couldn't identify any leads within the next few hours. 'It's pretty unlikely that anyone moved a corpse on the metro, but I still want copies of the security camera recordings.'

Hurtig came up beside her.

'I've already got someone on that. We'll have them by this evening.'

'Good. Seeing as the body was probably brought here by road, I want lists of all vehicles that have passed through the road tolls in the last few days.'

'Of course,' Hurtig said, pulling out his mobile phone and moving away. 'I'll make sure we get them as soon as possible.'

'Hold on a minute, I'm not done yet. Obviously, there's a chance the body was carried here, or brought on a bike or something like that. Check with the college to see if they have surveillance cameras.'

Hurtig nodded and lumbered off.

Jeanette sighed and turned to one of the forensics officers who was examining the grass by the bushes.

'Anything useful?'

The woman shook her head. 'Not yet. Obviously there are a lot of footprints; we'll take impressions of some of the best ones. But don't get your hopes up.'

Jeanette slowly approached the bushes where the body had been found, wrapped in a black garbage bag. The boy, a young adolescent, was naked, and had stiffened in a sitting position with his arms around his knees. His hands had been bound with duct tape. The skin on his face had turned a yellow-brown colour, and looked almost leathery, like old parchment.

His hands, in contrast, were almost black.

'Any signs of sexual violence?' She turned to Ivo Andrić, who was crouched down in front of her.

Ivo Andrić was a specialist in unusual and extreme cases of death.

The Stockholm police had called him early that morning. Because they didn't want to cordon off the area around the metro station any longer than necessary, he had to work fast.

'I can't tell yet. But it can't be ruled out. I don't want to jump to any hasty conclusions, but from my experience you don't usually see this sort of extreme injury without there being evidence of sexual violence as well.'

Jeanette nodded.

She leaned closer and noted that the dead boy looked foreign. Arabic, Palestinian, maybe even Indian or Pakistani.

The body was visible in some bushes just a few metres from the entrance to the Thorildsplan metro station on Kungsholmen, and Jeanette realised that it couldn't have remained unseen for very long.

The police had done their best to protect the site with screens and tarpaulins, but the terrain was hilly, which meant it was possible to see the crime scene from above if you were standing some distance away.

There were several photographers with telephoto lenses standing outside the cordon, and Jeanette almost felt sorry for them. They spent twenty-four hours a day listening to police-band radio and waiting in case something spectacular happened.

But she couldn't see any actual journalists. The papers probably didn't have the staff to send these days.

'What the hell, Andrić,' one of the police officers said, shaking his head at the sight. 'How can something like this happen?'

The body was practically mummified, which told Ivo Andrić that it had been kept in a very dry place for a long time. Not outside in a wet Stockholm winter.

'Well, Schwarz,' he said, looking up, 'that's what we're going to try to find out.'

'Yes, but the boy's been mummified, for fuck's sake. Like some damn pharaoh. That's not the sort of thing that happens during a coffee break, is it?'

Ivo Andrić nodded in agreement. He was a hardened man who was originally from Bosnia, and had been a doctor in Sarajevo during the almost four years of the Serbian siege. He had witnessed a great many unpleasant things throughout his long and eventful career, but he had never seen anything like this before.

There was no doubt at all that the victim had been severely abused, but the odd thing was that there were none of the usual self-defence injuries. All the bruises and haematomas looked more like the sort of thing you'd see on a boxer. A boxer who had gone twelve rounds and been so badly beaten that he eventually passed out.

On his arms and across his torso the boy had hundreds of marks, harder than the surrounding tissue, which, when taken as a whole, meant that he had been subjected to an astonishing number of blows while he was still alive. From the indentations on the boy's knuckles, it seemed likely that he had not only received but had also dealt out a fair number of punches.

But the most troubling thing was the fact that the boy's genitals were missing.

He noted that they had been removed with a very sharp knife.

A scalpel or razor blade, perhaps?

An examination of the mummified boy's back revealed a large number of deeper wounds, the sort a whip would make.

Ivo Andrić tried to picture in his mind's eye what had happened. A boy fighting for his life, and when he no longer wanted to fight someone had whipped him. He knew that illegal dogfights still happened in the immigrant communities. This might be something similar, but with the difference that it wasn't dogs fighting for their lives but young boys.

Well, one of them at least had been a young boy.

Who his opponent might have been was a matter of speculation.

Then there was the fact that the boy hadn't died when he really should have. Hopefully the post-mortem would reveal information about any traces of drugs or chemicals, Rohypnol, maybe phencyclidine. Ivo Andrić realised that his real work would begin once the body was in the pathology lab back at the hospital in Solna.

At noon they were able to put the body in a grey plastic bag and lift it into an ambulance for transportation to Solna. Jeanette Kihlberg's work here was done, and she could go on to headquarters, at the other end of Kungsholmen. As she walked towards the car park a gentle rain started to fall.

'Fuck!' she swore loudly to herself, and Åhlund, one of her younger colleagues, turned and gave her a questioning look.

'My car. It had slipped my mind, but it broke down on the way here and now I'm stranded. I'll have to call a tow truck.'

'Where is it?' her colleague asked.

'Over there.' She pointed at the red, rusty, filthy Audi twenty metres away from them. 'Why? Do you know anything about cars?'

'It's a hobby of mine. There isn't a car on the planet that I couldn't get going. Give me the keys and I'll tell you what's wrong with it.'

Åhlund started the car and pulled out onto the road. The creaking and screeching sounded even louder from outside, and she assumed she would have to call her dad and ask for a small loan. He would ask her if Åke had found a job yet, and she would explain that it wasn't easy being an unemployed artist, but all that would probably change soon.

The same routine every time. She had to eat humble pie and act as Åke's safety net.

It could all be so easy, she thought. If he could just swallow his pride and take a temporary job. If for no other reason than to show that he cared about her and realised how worried she was. She sometimes had trouble sleeping at night before the bills were paid.

After a quick drive around the block the young police officer jumped out of the car and smiled triumphantly.

'The ball joint, the steering column, or both. If I take it now I can start on it this evening. You can have it back in a few days, but you'll have to pay for parts and a bottle of whisky. How does that sound?'

'You're an angel, Åhlund. Take it and do whatever the hell you like with it. If you can get it working, you can have two bottles and a decent reference when you go for promotion.'

Jeanette Kihlberg walked off towards the police van.

Esprit de corps, she thought.

Kronoberg – Police Headquarters

During the first meeting Jeanette delegated the preliminary steps in the investigation.

A group of recently graduated officers had spent the afternoon knocking on doors in the area, and Jeanette was hopeful that they'd come up with something.

Schwarz was given the thankless task of going through the lists of vehicles that had passed the road tolls, almost eight hundred thousand in total, while Åhlund checked the surveillance footage they had secured from the teacher-training college and the metro station.

Jeanette certainly didn't miss the monotony of the sort of investigative work that usually got dumped on less experienced officers.

The main priority was getting the boy's identity confirmed, and Hurtig was given the job of contacting refugee centres around Stockholm. Jeanette herself was going to talk to Ivo Andrić.

After the meeting she went back to her office and called home. It was already after six o'clock, and it was her night to cook.

'Hi! How's your day been?' She made an effort to sound cheerful.

As a couple, Jeanette and Åke were fairly equal. They shared the everyday chores: Åke was responsible for the laundry and Jeanette for the vacuuming. Cooking was done according to a rota that involved their son, Johan, as well. But she was the one who did all the heavy lifting when it came to the family finances.

'I finished the laundry an hour ago. Otherwise pretty good. Johan just got home. He said you promised to give him a lift to the match tonight. Are you going to make it in time?'

'No, I can't,' Jeanette sighed. 'The car broke down on the way into the city. Johan will have to take his bike, it's not that far.' Jeanette glanced at the family photograph she'd pinned up on her bulletin board. Johan looked so young in the picture, and she could hardly bear to look at herself.

'I'm going to be here for a few more hours. I'll take the metro home if I can't get a lift from someone. You'll have to phone for a pizza. Have you got any money?'

'Yeah, yeah.' Åke sighed. 'If not, there's probably some in the jar.'

Jeanette thought for a moment. 'There should be. I put five hundred in yesterday. See you later.'

Åke didn't reply, so she hung up and leaned back.

Five minutes of rest.

She closed her eyes.

Hurtig came into Jeanette's office with the recording of that morning's anonymous phone call to the emergency call room. He handed her the CD and sat down.

Jeanette rubbed her tired eyes. 'Have you spoken to whoever found the boy?'

'Yep. Two of our officers – according to the report, they arrived on the scene a couple of hours after the call was received. Like I said, they took a while to respond because the emergency operator got the address wrong.'

Jeanette took the CD out of its case and put it in her computer.

The call lasted twenty seconds.

'One-one-two, what's the nature of the emergency?'

There was a crackle, but no sound of a voice.

'Hello? One-one-two, what's the nature of the emergency?' The operator sounded more circumspect now, and there was the sound of laboured breathing.

'I just wanted to let you know there's a dead body in the bushes near Thorildsplan.'

The man was slurring his words, and Jeanette thought he sounded drunk. Drunk or on drugs.

'What's your name?' the operator asked.

'Doesn't matter. Did you hear what I said?'

'Yes, I heard that you said there's a dead body near Bolidenplan.'

The man sounded annoyed. 'A dead body in the bushes near the entrance to the *Thorildsplan* metro station.'

Then silence.

Just the operator's hesitant 'Hello?'

Jeanette frowned. 'You don't have to be Einstein to assume that the call was made somewhere near the station, do you?'

'No, of course. But if –'

'If what?' She could hear how irritated she sounded, but she had been hoping that the recording of the call would answer at least some of her questions. Give her something to throw at the commissioner and the prosecutor.

'Sorry,' she said, but Hurtig just shrugged.

'Let's continue tomorrow.' He stood up and headed for the door. 'Go home to Johan and Åke instead.'

Jeanette smiled gratefully. 'Goodnight, see you in the morning.'

Once Hurtig had shut the door she called her boss, Commissioner Dennis Billing.

The chief of the criminal investigation department answered after four rings.

Jeanette told him about the dead, mummified boy, the anonymous phone call, and the other things they'd found out during the afternoon and evening.

In other words, she didn't have much of any significance to tell him.

'We'll have to see what the door-to-door inquiries come up with, and I'm waiting to hear what Ivo Andrić has discovered. Hurtig's talking to Violent Crime, and, well – all the usual, really.'

'Obviously it would be best, as I'm sure you realise, if we could solve this as quickly as possible. As much for you as for me.'

Jeanette had a problem with his arrogant attitude, which she knew was entirely due to the fact that she was a woman. He had been among those who didn't think Jeanette should have been promoted to detective superintendent. With the unofficial backing of Prosecutor von Kwist, he had suggested another name: a man, obviously.

In spite of his explicit disapproval she had been given the job, but his unfavourable attitude towards her had tainted their relationship ever since.

'Of course, we'll do all we can. I'll get back to you tomorrow when we know more.'

Dennis Billing cleared his throat.

'Hmm. There's something else I'd like to talk to you about.'

'Oh?'

'Well, this is supposed to be confidential, but I dare say I can bend the rules slightly. I'm going to have to borrow your team.'

'No, that's not possible. This is an important murder investigation.'

'Twenty-four hours, starting tomorrow evening. Then you can have them back. In spite of the situation that's arisen, I'm afraid it can't be avoided.'

Jeanette was too tired to protest further.

Dennis Billing went on. 'Mikkelsen needs them. They're mounting a series of raids against people suspected of child pornography offences, and he needs reinforcements. I've already spoken to Hurtig, Åhlund and Schwarz. They'll do their usual work tomorrow, then join up with Mikkelsen. Just so you know.'

There was nothing more for her to say.

Mariatorget – Sofia Zetterlund's Office

Towards the end of the blood-soaked eighteenth century, King Adolf Fredrik lent his name to the square now known as Mariatorget, on the condition that it never be used for executions. Since then no fewer than one hundred and forty-eight people have lost their lives there in circumstances more or less comparable to an execution. In that respect it hasn't really made much difference whether the square was known as Adolf Fredriks torg or Mariatorget.

Numerous of these one hundred and forty-eight murders occurred less than twenty metres from the building in which Sofia Zetterlund had her private psychotherapy practice, on the top floor of an old building on Sankt Paulsgatan, next to Tvålpalatset. The three residential apartments on that floor had been rebuilt as offices, and were rented out to two dentists, a plastic surgeon, a lawyer and another psychotherapist.

The decor of the shared waiting room was cool and modern, and the interior designer had chosen to buy a couple of large paintings by Adam Diesel-Frank, in the same shade of grey as the sofa and two armchairs.

In one corner stood a bronze sculpture by the German-born artist Nadya Ushakova, of a large vase of roses that were on the point of wilting. Around one of the stems was a small engraved plaque bearing the inscription DIE MYTHEN SIND GREIFBAR.

At the opening ceremony people had discussed the meaning of the quote, but no one managed to come up with a plausible explanation.

Myths are tangible.

The pale walls, expensive carpet and exclusive works of art, taken as a whole, breathed discretion and money.

After a series of interviews a former medical secretary, Ann-Britt Eriksson, had been employed to serve as the shared receptionist. She organised appointments and took care of certain administrative duties.

'Has anything happened that I should know about?' Sofia Zetterlund asked when she arrived that morning, on the dot of eight o'clock as usual.

Ann-Britt looked up from the newspaper spread out in front of her.

'Yes, Huddinge Hospital called, they want to bring forward your appointment with Tyra Mäkelä to eleven o'clock. I told them you'd call back to confirm.'

'OK, I'll call them at once.' Sofia headed towards her office. 'Anything else?'

'Yes,' Ann-Britt said. 'Mikael just called to say he probably won't make the afternoon flight, but should be at Arlanda first thing tomorrow morning. He asked me to say that he'd like it if you stayed at his apartment tonight. So you have time to see each other tomorrow.'

Sofia stopped with her hand on the door frame.

'Hmm, when's my first appointment today?' She felt annoyed at having to change her plans. She had been thinking of surprising Mikael with dinner at the Gondolen restaurant, but as usual he had upset her plans.

'Nine o'clock, then you've got two more this afternoon.'

'Who's first?'

'Carolina Glanz. According to the papers she's just got a job as a presenter, travelling around the world interviewing celebrities. Isn't that funny?'

Ann-Britt shook her head and let out a deep sigh.

Carolina Glanz had crashed into the nation's consciousness on one of the many talent shows that filled the television schedules. She may not have had much of a singing voice, but according to the jury she had the necessary star quality. She had spent the winter and spring appearing at small nightclubs, lip-syncing to a song that a less beautiful girl with a stronger voice had recorded. Carolina had got a lot of exposure in the evening tabloids, and the scandals had followed, one after another.

Now that the media's interest was focused elsewhere she had started to question herself and her choice of career.

Sofia didn't like coaching pseudo-celebrities, and had trouble motivating herself for the sessions, even if she needed the money. She felt she was wasting her time. Her talents were better employed seeing clients who were seriously in need of help.

She'd much rather deal with real people.

Sofia sat down at her desk and called Huddinge straight away. Bringing forward the appointment would mean that Sofia only had an hour or so to prepare, and when she put the phone down she pulled out her files on Tyra Mäkelä.

All in all, almost five hundred pages, a bundle of paper that would at least double in size before the case was finished.

She had read everything twice from cover to cover, and now concentrated on the central aspects. Tyra Mäkelä's mental state.

Expert opinion was divided. The psychiatrist in charge of the investigation, along with the counsellors and one of the psychologists, was in favour of imprisonment. But two psychologists were opposed to this, and advocated secure psychiatric care.

Sofia's task was to get them to unite around a final verdict, and she realised it wasn't going to be easy.

Together with her husband, Tyra Mäkelä had been found guilty of the murder of their eleven-year-old adopted son. The boy had been diagnosed with fragile X syndrome, a disability that led to both physical and mental problems. The family had lived an isolated existence in a house out in the country. The forensic evidence was conclusive, and documented the cruelty the boy had been subjected to. Traces of excrement were found in his lungs and stomach, he had cigarette burns, and he had been beaten with the hose of a vacuum cleaner.

The body had been found in a patch of woodland not far from the house.

The case had got a lot of media coverage, not least because the boy's mother was involved. An almost unanimous general public, led by several vociferous and influential politicians and journalists, was demanding the harshest punishment available under the law. Tyra Mäkelä should be sent to Hinseberg Prison for as long as was legally possible.

But Sofia knew that secure psychiatric care often meant that the prisoner ended up being locked away for longer than if they served a prison sentence.

Could Tyra Mäkelä be regarded as mentally competent at the time of the abuse? The evidence suggested that the boy had suffered at least three years of torture.

Real people's problems.

Sofia wrote a list of questions that she wanted to discuss with the convicted murderer, but then was interrupted when Carolina Glanz swept into the office in a pair of thigh-high red boots, a short, red, vinyl skirt, and a black leather jacket.

Huddinge Hospital

Sofia arrived at Huddinge just after half past ten and parked in front of the vast complex.

The entire building was clad in grey and blue panelling, in sharp contrast to the surrounding houses, which were painted in a range of bright colours. She had heard that during the Second World War this was meant to confuse any potential bombing raid on the hospital. The intention had been to make it look from above as if the hospital were a lake, and the buildings around it were supposed to look like fields and meadows.

She stopped in the cafeteria and bought coffee, a sandwich and the evening papers, before heading towards the main entrance.

She left her things in a locker, then went through the metal detector and on into the long corridor. She walked past Ward 113, and as usual heard shouting and fighting inside. That was where they kept the most difficult patients, under heavy medication, while they were waiting to go to one of the other care facilities around the country.

She walked along the corridor, then turned right into Ward 112 and made her way to the consulting room that the psychologists shared. She glanced at the time and noted that she was fifteen minutes early.

She closed the door, sat down at the desk and compared the front pages of the two evening papers.

MACABRE FIND IN CENTRAL STOCKHOLM and MUMMY FOUND IN BUSHES!

She took a bite of the sandwich and sipped the hot coffee. The mummified body of a young boy had been found out at Thorildsplan.

More dead children, she thought with a heavy heart.

The door was opened by a thickset psychiatric nurse. 'I've got someone out here that I gather you're supposed to talk to. Nasty piece of work, with a load of shit on her conscience.' He gestured over his shoulder.

She didn't like the language the nurses used among themselves. Even if they were dealing with serious criminals, there was no reason to be offensive or condescending.

'Show her in, please, then you can leave us alone.'

Mariatorget – Sofia Zetterlund's Office

At two o'clock Sofia Zetterlund was back in her office in the city. She still had two appointments left before the day's work was over, and she realised it was going to be hard to stay focused after her visit to Huddinge.

Sofia sat down at her desk to formulate a recommendation that Tyra Mäkelä be sentenced to secure psychiatric care. The meeting of the members of the consultative team had led to the lead psychiatrist moderating his position somewhat, and Sofia was hopeful that they would soon be able to make a final decision.

If nothing else, then for Tyra Mäkelä's sake.

The woman needed treatment.

Sofia had presented a summary of the woman's background and character. Tyra Mäkelä had two suicide attempts behind her: as a fourteen-year-old she had taken an intentional overdose of pills, and she was put on disability benefit at the age of twenty as a result of persistent depression. The fifteen years she had spent with the sadistic Harri Mäkelä had led to another suicide attempt, then the murder of their adopted son.

Sofia believed that the time she had spent with her husband, who had been deemed sufficiently sane to be sentenced to prison, had exacerbated the woman's condition.

Sofia's conclusion was that Tyra Mäkelä had in all likelihood suffered repeated psychotic episodes during the years in which the abuse took place. There were two documented visits to a psychiatric clinic during the past year that supported her thesis. In both cases she had been found wandering the streets and had to be hospitalised for several days before she could be discharged.

Sofia also saw other mitigating factors regarding Tyra Mäkelä's culpability in the case. Her IQ was so low that it meant she could hardly be held responsible for murder, a fact that the court had more or less ignored. Sofia saw a woman who, under the ever-present influence of alcohol, idealised her man. Her passivity might mean that she could be regarded as complicit in the abuse, but at the same time she was incapable of intervention because of her mental state.

The verdict had been upheld at the highest level, and all that remained now was the sentence.

Tyra Mäkelä needed treatment. Her crimes could never be undone, but a prison sentence wouldn't help anyone.

The cruelty of the case mustn't be allowed to cloud their judgement.

During the afternoon Sofia completed her statement about Tyra Mäkelä, and got through her three and four o'clock appointments. A burned-out businessman and an ageing actress who was no longer getting any parts and had fallen into a deep depression as a result.

When she was on her way out at five o'clock, Ann-Britt stopped her in reception.

'You haven't forgotten that you're going to Gothenburg next Saturday? I've got the train tickets here, and you're booked into the Hotel Scandic.'

Ann-Britt put a folder on the counter.

'Of course not,' Sofia said.

She was going to see a publisher who was planning to print a Swedish translation of the former child soldier Ishmael Beah's *A Long Way Gone*. The publisher was hoping that Sofia could use her experience with traumatised children to help them check some of the facts.

'What time am I going?'

'Early. The departure time's on the ticket.'

'Five-twelve?'

Sofia sighed and went back into her office to dig out the report she had written for UNICEF seven years before.

When she sat down at her desk again and opened the file, she couldn't help wondering if she was actually ready to return to her memories from that time. She still dreamed about the child soldiers in Port Loko. The two boys by the truck, one with no arms, the other with no legs. The UNICEF paediatrician, murdered by the same children it was his calling to help. Victims turned perpetrators. The sounds of singing, '*Mambaa manyani . . . Mamani manyimi.*' Seven years, she thought.

Was it really that long ago?

Kronoberg – Police Headquarters

The following day Jeanette systematically worked her way through the documents Hurtig had given her. Interviews, reports from investigations and judgements, all of them dealing with abuse or murders involving an element of sadism. Jeanette noted that in every case but one the perpetrator was male.

The exception's name was Tyra Mäkelä, and she and her husband had recently been found guilty of the murder of their adopted son.

Nothing she had seen at the crime scene out at Thorildsplan reminded her of anything she had experienced before, and she felt she needed assistance.

She picked up the phone and called Lars Mikkelsen at National Crime: he was responsible for violent and sexual offences against children. She decided to give as brief an outline of the case as possible. If Mikkelsen was in a position to help her, she could go into more detail later.

What a fucking awful job, she thought as she waited for him to answer.

Interviewing and investigating paedophiles. How strong did you have to be to cope with watching thousands of hours of filmed abuse and several million pictures of violated children?

Could you actually have children of your own?

After her conversation with Mikkelsen, Jeanette Kihlberg called another meeting of the investigating team, where they attempted to piece the facts together. They didn't have that many lines of inquiry to follow up at the moment.

'The call to the emergency operator was made from an area close to the DN Tower.' Åhlund held a sheet of paper in the air. 'We should know where, soon.'

Jeanette nodded. She went over to the whiteboard, where a dozen photographs of the dead boy had been pinned up.

'So, what do we know?' She turned to Hurtig.

'On the grass and in the dirt where he was found we've secured tracks from a pushchair, as well as others from a small vehicle. The tyre tracks belong to a lorry, and we've already spoken to the refuse collector driving it, so we can write that off.'

'So someone could have used a pushchair or shopping trolley to get the body there?'

'Yes, definitely.'

'Could the boy have been carried there?' Åhlund asked.

'If you're strong enough it wouldn't be a problem. The boy didn't weigh more than forty-five kilos.'

The room fell silent, and Jeanette presumed that like her the others were imagining someone walking around carrying a dead boy wrapped in a black garbage bag.

Åhlund broke the silence. 'When I saw how badly abused the boy was, I immediately thought of Harri Mäkelä, and if it weren't for the fact that I know he's locked up in Kumla, well –'

'Well, what?' Schwarz interrupted with a grin.

'Well, I'd have said he was the man we are looking for.'

'You reckon? And you don't think that thought's already occurred to the rest of us?'

'Stop squabbling!' Jeanette leafed through her papers. 'Forget Mäkelä. I've got information from Lars Mikkelsen at National Crime about a Jimmie Furugård.'

'So who's this Furugård?' Hurtig asked.

'A former UN soldier. First two years in Kosovo, then one in Afghanistan. He last served with the UN three years ago, and left with decidedly mixed references.'

'What makes him of interest to us?' Hurtig opened his notebook and leafed through to a fresh page.

'Jimmie Furugård has several convictions for rape and violent assault. Most of the people he assaulted were either immigrants or homosexual men, but it looks as if Furugård also has a habit of beating up his girlfriends. Three rape charges. Found guilty twice, cleared once.'

Hurtig, Schwarz and Åhlund looked at one another, nodding slowly.

They're interested, Jeanette thought, but not really convinced.

'OK, so why did our little hothead stop working for the UN?' Åhlund asked. Schwarz glared at him.

'From what I can see, it came shortly after he was reprimanded for using prostitutes in Kabul on several occasions. No other details.'

'And he's not locked up at the moment?' Schwarz asked.

'No, he was released from Hall Prison at the end of September last year.'

'But are we really looking for a rapist?' Hurtig said. 'Anyway, how come Mikkelsen mentioned him? I mean, he works with crimes against children, doesn't he?'

'Calm down,' Jeanette said. 'Any sort of sexual violence could be of interest to our investigation. This Jimmie Furugård seems to be a pretty unpleasant character who's not above attacking children. On at least one occasion he was suspected of assaulting and attempting to rape a young boy.'

Hurtig turned to look at Jeanette. 'Where is he now?'

'According to Mikkelsen he's disappeared without a trace, so I've emailed von Kwist about issuing an arrest warrant, but he hasn't replied yet. I imagine he wants more to go on.'

'Unfortunately, we don't have much to go on from Thorildsplan, and von Kwist isn't the smartest prosecutor we've got –' Hurtig sighed.

'Well,' Jeanette interrupted, 'for the time being we go through the usual routine while forensics do their thing. We work methodically, and without any preconceptions. Any questions?'

They all shook their heads.

'Good. OK, everyone back to work.'

She thought for a moment, tapping her pen on the desk.

Jimmie Furugård, she thought. Evidently something of a split personality. Doesn't seem to regard himself as gay, and struggles with his desires. Full of self-loathing and guilt.

There was something that didn't make sense.

She opened one of the two evening papers she'd bought on the way to work but hadn't had time to read. She'd already noticed that they had pretty much the same front page, apart from the headlines.

She closed her eyes and sat completely still as she counted to one hundred, then picked up the phone and called Prosecutor von Kwist.

'Hello. Have you read my email?' she began.

'Yes, I'm afraid I have, and I'm still trying to work out your thinking.'

'What do you mean?'

'What I mean is that it looks like you've completely lost your mind!'

Jeanette could hear how upset he was.

'I don't understand . . .'

'Jimmie Furugård isn't your man. That's all you need to know!'

'So . . . ?' Jeanette was starting to get angry.

'Jimmie Furugård is a dedicated and well-regarded UN soldier. He's received a number of commendations, and –'

'I do know how to read,' Jeanette interrupted. 'But he's also a neo-Nazi and has several convictions for rape and violent assault. He used prostitutes in Afghanistan and –'

Jeanette stopped herself. She realised that the prosecutor wasn't going to listen to her opinion. No matter how badly mistaken she thought he was.

'I have to go now.' Jeanette regained control of her voice. 'We'll have to pursue other lines of inquiry. Thanks for your time.'

She hung up, then put her hands down on the table and closed her eyes.

Over the years she had learned that people could be raped, abused, humiliated and murdered in countless different ways. Clenching her hands in front of her, she realised that there were just as many ways to mismanage an investigation, and that a prosecutor could obstruct the work of an investigation for reasons that were anything but clear.

She got up and went out into the corridor, heading for Hurtig's office. He was on the phone, and gestured to her to sit down. She looked around.

Hurtig's office was the antithesis of her own. Numbered box files on the bookshelves, folders in neat piles on the desk. Even the plants in the window looked well cared for.

Hurtig ended the call and put down the phone.

'What did von Kwist say?'

'That Furugård isn't our man.' Jeanette sat down.

'Maybe he's right.'

Jeanette didn't answer, and Hurtig pushed a pile of papers aside before he went on.

'You know we're going to be a bit late starting tomorrow?'

Jeanette thought Hurtig looked rather embarrassed. 'Don't worry. You're only going to help bring in a few computers full of child porn, then you'll be back.'

Hurtig smiled.

Gamla Enskede – Kihlberg House

Jeanette Kihlberg left police headquarters just after eight in the evening of the day after the body was found at Thorildsplan.

Hurtig had offered to give her a lift home, and she had thanked him but declined, on the pretext of wanting to walk down to Central Station before catching the train out to Enskede.

She needed to be alone for a while. Just let her mind float.

As she was heading down the steps to Kungsbro strand her mobile buzzed to say she'd got a text. It was from her dad.

'Hi,' he wrote. 'Are you OK?'

By the time she approached Klarabergsviadukten her thoughts were back on the job again.

One family with three generations of police officers. Grandad, Dad and now her. Grandma and Mum had been housewives.

And Åke, she thought. Artist, and housewife.

Once her dad had realised she was thinking of following in his footsteps, he had told her plenty of stories intended to put her off. About broken people. Drug addicts and alcoholics. Pointless violence. The idea that people never used to kick someone when they were down was a myth. People had always done that, and would go on doing it.

But there was one particular part of the job that he hated.

Stationed in a suburb south of Stockholm, close to both the metro and the commuter rail lines, at least once a year he would have to force himself to go down onto one of the tracks to pick up the remnants of a person.

A head. An arm. A leg. A torso.

It left him a complete wreck each time it happened.

He didn't want her to have to see everything he had had to see, and his message to her could be summarised in one sentence: 'Whatever you do, don't join the police.'

But nothing he said made her change her mind. On the contrary, his stories only made her feel more motivated.

The first hurdle to being accepted into the police academy had been a problem with the sight in her left eye. The operation had cost all her savings, and she had to work overtime pretty much every weekend for six months to be able to afford it.

The second hurdle was when she found out that she was too short.

A chiropractor provided the solution to that, and after twelve weeks of treatment on her back he had managed to stretch her height by the two missing centimetres.

She had lain flat in the car on the way to the medical evaluation, because she knew that the body could shrink if you sat down for any length of time.

What happens if I lose my motivation? she thought.

That simply mustn't happen, she thought. You just keep going. She walked through the bus station towards Central Station, down the escalator, and through the crowded passageway between the commuter trains and the metro.

She opened her purse. Two crumpled hundred-kronor bills left, thirty of which would go to her ticket home. She hoped Åke still had some of the money she had given him for household expenses at the start of the week. Even if Åhlund was able to fix the car, she guessed it was still going to cost a couple of thousand.

Work and money, she thought.

How the hell do you escape from that?

Once Johan had gone to bed, Jeanette and Åke settled down with cups of tea in the living room. The European Football Championships were about to start, and this pre-game show was providing a detailed analysis of the Swedish national team's chances. As usual, there was talk of at least the quarter-finals, hopefully a semi-final and maybe even gold.

'Your dad rang, by the way,' Åke said, without looking away from the screen.

'Did he want anything special?'

'The usual. He asked how you were, then about Johan and school. Then he asked me if I'd managed to find a job yet.'

Jeanette knew her dad had trouble with Åke. He had once called him a slacker. On another occasion, a dreamer. Lazy. A couch potato. The list of negative epithets was as varied as it was comprehensive. Occasionally he came out with them in front of Åke.

Usually when that happened she felt sorry for Åke and immediately sprang to his defence, but recently she had found herself agreeing more and more with the criticism.

He often said he was happy being her housewife, but in reality she was just as much of a housewife as he was. It would have been OK if he actually did something with his paintings, but to be honest there wasn't much sign of activity there.

'Åke . . .'

He didn't hear her. He was deeply absorbed in a report about Swedish team captains over the years.

'Our finances are completely fucked,' she said. 'I'm ashamed of having to call Dad again.'

He didn't respond.

'Åke?' she said tentatively. 'Are you listening?'

He sighed. 'Yeah, yeah,' he said, still staring at the screen. 'But at least you've got a good reason to call him.'

'How do you mean?'

'Well, Bosse called here earlier.' Åke sounded annoyed. 'He's probably expecting you to call back, isn't he?'

Fucking incredible, Jeanette thought.

She wanted to avoid an argument, so she got up from the sofa and went out to the kitchen.

A mountain of washing-up. Åke and Johan had made pancakes, and the evidence was still there.

No, she wasn't going to do the washing-up. It could sit there until he dealt with it. She sat down at the kitchen table and dialled her parents' number.

This is the last time, I swear, she thought.

After the call Jeanette went back into the living room, sat down on the sofa again, and waited patiently for the programme to end. She liked football a lot, probably more than Åke, but this type of programme didn't interest her at all. Too much empty talk.

'I called Dad,' she said when the credits started to roll. 'He's putting five thousand in my account so we can get through the rest of the month.'

Åke nodded distractedly.

'But it's not going to happen again,' she went on. 'I mean it this time. Do you understand?'

He squirmed. 'Yeah, yeah. I understand.'

Vita Bergen – Sofia Zetterlund's Apartment

Sofia and her former partner, Lasse, had landed the apartment through a complicated triangular sale, in which Sofia sold her small two-room apartment on Lundagatan and Lasse sold his three-room apartment near Mosebacke and they bought this spacious five-room apartment on Åsöberget, not far from Nytorget and the park at Vita bergen.

She walked into the hall, hung up her coat and went into the living room. She put the bag containing the Indian takeaway on the table and went into the kitchen to get cutlery and a glass of water.

She turned on the television, settled down on the sofa and began to eat.

The body needs fuel, she thought.

Eating dinner alone depressed her, and she ate quickly, surfing through the channels. Children's programmes, an American sitcom, ads, something educational.

She looked at the time and saw that the evening news was about to start, and put the remote down just as her mobile phone buzzed.

A text from Mikael.

'How are you? Miss you . . . ' he wrote.

She swallowed the last mouthful of food and replied.

'Bored. I'll probably spend the evening working at home. Hugs.'

For a while now one particular person had commanded more and more of her interest, and Sofia had got into the habit of pulling out some of her notes each evening. Every time she hoped she was going to see something new, something conclusive.

Sofia got up and went into the kitchen, and scraped the last of the food into the bin. She heard the news start in the living room, and the lead story for the second day in a row was the murder at Thorildsplan.

The anchor said that the police had gone public with a phone call made to the emergency call centre the previous morning.

Sofia thought the caller sounded drunk.

She took her USB memory stick out of her bag, plugged it into her computer and opened the folder about Victoria Bergman.

It was as if there were several bits missing from Victoria Bergman's personality. During their conversations it had become clear that there were a lot of traumatic experiences in Victoria's youth. A lot of their sessions had developed into long monologues that couldn't be called conversations in any real sense.

Often Sofia actually came close to falling asleep from the sound of Victoria's monotonous, droning voice. Her monologues acted as a sort of self-hypnosis that encouraged drowsiness in Sofia as well, and she had difficulty remembering all the details of what Victoria said. When she mentioned this to her fellow psychotherapist at the office he had reminded her about the option of recording the sessions, and had lent her his pocket tape recorder in exchange for a decent bottle of wine.

She had marked the cassettes with the time and date, and now she had twenty-five little tapes locked away in the cabinet at work. Anything she had found particularly interesting she typed up and saved onto the USB stick.

Sofia opened the folder she had labelled VB, which contained a number of text files.

She double-clicked on one of the files, and read on the screen:

> Some days were better than others. It was like my stomach had a way of telling me in advance when they were going to start fighting.

Sofia saw from her notes that the conversation was about Victoria's childhood summers in Dalarna. Almost every weekend the Bergman family would get in the car and drive the two hundred and fifty kilometres up to the little cottage in Dala-Floda, and Victoria had told her that they often spent four full weeks there during the holidays.

She carried on reading:

> My stomach was never wrong and several hours before the shouting started I would take refuge in my secret den.
>
> I used to make sandwiches for myself. I never knew how long they were going to fight and when Mum would have time to make food.
>
> Once I watched through the gaps between the planks as he

chased her across the field. Mum was running for her life but Dad was quicker and brought her down with a blow to the back of the neck. When they came back across the yard later on she had a big cut above her eye and he was sobbing in despair.

Mum felt sorry for him.

It was his unjust fate to have been burdened with the difficult work of educating his two women.

If only Mum and I could just listen to him instead of being so obstinate.

Sofia made a few notes about what needed to be followed up, then closed the document.

She opened another of the files at random, and realised at once that it was one of the encounters in which Victoria had disappeared inside herself.

The conversation had begun as usual: Sofia would ask a question, and Victoria would answer.

With each question the answers got longer and longer, and less and less coherent. Victoria would talk about one thing, which would lead her to something completely different, and so on, at an ever increasing rate.

Sofia dug out the recording of the conversation, put it into the tape player, pressed play, leaned back in her chair and closed her eyes.

Victoria Bergman's voice.

Then I started to eat to put a stop to their bloody cackling and they fell silent at once because they saw what I was prepared to do to be their friend. Not that I was prepared to kiss their backsides. Pretending to like them. Getting them to respect me. Getting them to realise that I actually had a brain and could think.

Sofia opened her eyes, read the label on the cassette case, and saw that the conversation had been recorded a couple of months ago. Victoria had been talking about her time at boarding school in Sigtuna, and a particularly extreme incidence of bullying.

The voice went on.

Victoria changed the subject.

When the treehouse was ready I didn't think it was any fun any more, I wasn't interested in lying in there reading comics with him, so when he fell asleep I left the treehouse, went down to the boat, got one of the wooden planks, leaned it up against the entrance, and hammered some nails in until he woke up inside, wondering what I was doing. Just you stay there, I said, and carried on hammering until the box was empty . . .

The voice faded away, and Sofia realised she was on the verge of falling asleep.

. . . and the window was too small to crawl through, but while he sat inside crying I fetched more planks and nailed them across it. Maybe I'd let him out later, maybe not, but in the darkness he'd be able to think about how much he liked me . . .

Sofia switched off the tape player, got up from her chair and looked at the time.

An hour?

No, that can't be right, she thought. I must have dozed off.

Monument – Mikael's Apartment

At nine o'clock Sofia decided to do as Mikael wanted and go round to his apartment on Ölandsgatan, in the block known as Monument. On the way she bought things for breakfast, because she knew there'd be nothing in his fridge.

Once she got to Mikael's apartment she fell asleep on his sofa, exhausted, only waking up when he kissed her on the forehead.

'Hello, darling, surprise!' he said quietly.

She looked around, startled, scratching herself where his coarse black beard had tickled her.

'Hello. What are you doing here? What time is it?'

'Half past twelve. I managed to catch the last flight.'

He lay a big bouquet of red roses on the table and went into the kitchen. She looked at the flowers with distaste, then got up and followed him over the expanse of the living-room floor. He'd already taken butter, bread and cheese out of the fridge.

'Do you want some?' he asked. 'A cup of a tea and a sandwich?'

Sofia nodded and sat down at the kitchen table.

'How's your week been?' he went on. 'Mine's been awful! Some journalist's got it into his head that our products have dangerous side effects, and there's been a huge fuss on television and in the press. Has there been anything about it here?'

He put down two plates of sandwiches and went over to the stove, where the water was already boiling.

'Not as far as I know. There might have been.' She was still feeling drowsy and taken aback by his sudden appearance. 'I've had to listen to a woman who thinks she's been abused by the mass media –'

'I understand. Doesn't sound great,' he interrupted, handing her a cup of steaming blueberry tea. 'But I dare say it'll pass. We've discovered that the journalist is some sort of environmental activist who once took part in a protest at a mink farm. When that comes out . . .' He laughed and ran his hand across his neck to indicate what was going to happen to anyone setting themselves up against the big pharmaceutical company.

Sofia didn't like his arrogance, but she didn't feel up to having a debate. It was far too late for that. She stood, cleared the table and rinsed their cups before going into the bathroom to brush her teeth.

Mikael fell asleep beside her for the first time in a week, and Sofia realised that she had missed him, in spite of everything.

He reminded her of Lasse.

Sofia woke up when a car's headlights swept across the ceiling. At first she didn't know where she was, but as she sat up in bed she recognised Mikael's bedroom, and saw from the clock radio that she'd been asleep for little more than an hour.

Carefully she closed the bedroom door and went into the living room. She opened a window and lit a cigarette. A mild breeze blew into the room and the smoke disappeared into the darkness behind her. As she smoked she watched a white plastic bag drifting with the wind along the street below her, until it got stranded in a puddle of water on the opposite pavement.

I need to start from the beginning again with Victoria Bergman, she thought. There's something I've missed.

Her bag was beside the sofa and she sat down, took out her laptop and set it up on the table in front of her.

She opened the document in which she had gathered some brief notes together to compile a short overview of Victoria Bergman's case.

Born 1970.

Unmarried. No children.

Conversational therapy, focusing on traumatic childhood experiences.

Childhood: only child of Bengt Bergman, investigator for SIDA, the Swedish International Development Cooperation Agency, and Birgitta Bergman, housewife. Earliest memories the smell of her father's perspiration, and summers in Dalarna.

Prepuberty: raised in Grisslinge, in Värmdö outside Stockholm. Summer cottage in Dala-Floda in Dalarna. Highly intelligent. Private school from the age of nine. Started school a year early and was moved up from year eight to year nine. Subjected to sexual abuse from early puberty (father? other men?). Memories fragmentary, recounted as uncontextualised associations.

Youth: highly prone to risk-taking, suicidal thoughts (from the age of 14–15?). Early teenage years described as 'weak'. Once again, memories recounted in fragments. High school years at Sigtuna boarding school. Recurrent self-destructive behaviour.

Sofia realised that her time in high school was a conflicted period for Victoria Bergman. When she started there she was two years younger than her classmates, and was considerably less developed both physically and emotionally.

Sofia knew from experience how mean teenage girls could be in the changing room after gym classes. And Victoria had basically been entirely at the mercy of her peers for her upbringing. But there was something missing.

Adult life: career success described as 'unimportant'. Limited social life. Few interests.

Central themes/questions: trauma. What has Victoria Bergman been through? What's her relationship with her father? Fragmented memories. Dissociative disorder?

Sofia realised that there was one more central question that needed work, and added a new note.

What does 'weak' mean? she wrote.

She could see great angst, a profound guilt in Victoria Bergman.

Over time perhaps together they would be able to dig deeper and find a way to unravel some of the knots.

But that was far from certain.

There was a lot that suggested Victoria Bergman was suffering from a dissociative disorder, and Sofia knew that problems of that sort were, in ninety-nine per cent of cases, the result of sexual abuse or similar recurrent traumas. Sofia had met people before who had been through traumatic experiences yet had apparently been entirely incapable of remembering them. On some occasions Victoria Bergman would talk about terrible abuse yet on others appear to have no memory of the events at all.

Which was actually a perfectly logical reaction, Sofia thought. The psyche protects itself from what it regards as disturbing, and, in order for her normal life to function, Victoria Bergman suppresses her memory of events and creates alternative recollections instead.

But what did Victoria mean when she talked about her weakness?

Was it the person who had been subjected to the abuse who had been weak?

She closed the document and switched off the computer.

On one occasion she had given Victoria Bergman one of her own boxes of paroxetine, even though that was beyond her authority. It wasn't just illegal, but also unethical and unprofessional. Yet she had still managed to persuade herself to ignore the regulations. And the medication hadn't done any damage. On the contrary, Victoria Bergman had seemed much better for a while, and Sofia concluded that what she had done had been OK. Victoria needed medication, that was the bottom line.

Alongside the dissociative tendencies there were also signs of compulsive behaviour, and Sofia had even made notes hinting at savant syndrome. Once Victoria Bergman had commented on Sofia's smoking.

'You've smoked almost two packs,' she had said, pointing at the ashtray. 'Thirty-nine butts.' When Sofia was alone she had counted just to make sure, and found that Victoria had been right. But that could have been a coincidence, of course.

All in all, Victoria Bergman's personality was undoubtedly the most complex Sofia had encountered in her ten years as an independent therapist.

Sofia woke up first, stretched, and ran her fingers through Mikael's hair, then down through his beard. She saw that it was starting to go grey and smiled to herself.

According to the clock radio it was half past six. Mikael moved and turned towards her, put his arm across her breasts and took hold of her hand.

She had no appointments that morning, so decided to give herself permission to arrive late.

Mikael was in an excellent mood, and explained how, as well as digging up unflattering facts about the journalist, he had spent the week setting up a big account with a large hospital in Berlin. The bonus he was expecting could pay for a luxury holiday to anywhere.

She thought about it, but couldn't think of a single place she wanted to go.

'How about New York? A bit of shopping in the big department stores. Breakfast at Tiffany's and all that, you know?'

New York, she thought, and shuddered at the memory. She and Lasse had visited New York less than a month before everything fell apart.

It would be far too traumatic for her to tear open those old wounds.

'Or would you rather go somewhere sunny? A package holiday?'

She could see how eager he was, but no matter how she tried, she couldn't match his enthusiasm. She felt heavy as stone.

Suddenly she thought of Victoria Bergman.

The way Victoria had slid into an apathetic state during their last conversation, not showing the slightest sign of any emotional response. Right now she felt the same, and thought that she'd have to ask her doctor to increase the dose of paroxetine the next time she saw him.

'I don't know what's wrong with me, darling.' She kissed him on the lips. 'I'd really like to, but right now it feels like I haven't got the energy to do anything. Maybe it's because I've got so much to think about at work.'

'Well, in that case a holiday would be perfect. We wouldn't have to be gone for long. A weekend, or so?'

He rolled over to face her, letting his hand slide up over her stomach.

'I love you,' he said.

Sofia was somewhere else entirely and didn't reply, but she sensed his irritation when he suddenly threw the duvet off and stood up. She wasn't keeping up with him. He reacted so quickly, so impulsively.

Mikael sighed, pulled on his briefs and went out into the kitchen.

Why was she feeling guilty? Why should she feel guilty about him? What gave him that right? Guilt must be the most repulsive of all human inventions, Sofia thought.

She swallowed her anger and went after him. He was loading up the coffee machine, and glared sullenly at her over his shoulder. She was suddenly overcome with tenderness towards him. After all, it wasn't his fault he was the way he was.

She slid up behind him, kissed his neck and let her dressing gown fall to the floor. She'd let him take her against the kitchen worktop before she went into the shower.

It's not the end of the world, she thought.

Mariatorget – Sofia Zetterlund's Office

Just as Sofia Zetterlund was done for the day and was ready to leave for home, the phone rang.

'Hello, my name's Rose-Marie Bjöörn, I'm calling from social services in Hässelby. Have you got a minute?' The woman sounded friendly. 'I was just wondering, is it true that you've had experience dealing with children suffering from war trauma?'

Sofia cleared her throat. 'Yes, that's right. What do you want to know?'

'Well, we've got a family out here in Hässelby and the son could do with seeing someone who has a deeper insight into his experiences. And when I happened to hear about you, I thought it might be a good idea to get in touch.'

Sofia could feel how tired she was. Most of all she just wanted to end the call.

'I have to say, I'm fairly booked up. How old is he?'

'He's sixteen, his name's Samuel. Samuel Bai. From Sierra Leone.'

Sofia reflected for a moment.

That's an odd coincidence, she thought. I haven't thought about Sierra Leone for several years, and suddenly I've got two offers of work connected to the country.

'Well, it might be possible,' she said eventually. 'How soon would you like me to see him?'

They agreed that he would come for a preliminary evaluation in a week's time, and, after the social worker had promised to send Sofia the boy's file, they hung up.

Before she left the office for the day she changed into a pair of red Jimmy Choos. She knew the scars on her heels would start to bleed before she even got in the lift.

Village of Dala-Floda, 1980

She inhales from the bag she has filled with glue. First her head starts to spin, then every sound around her becomes twice as loud. Finally Crow Girl sees herself from above.

On the outskirts of Bålsta he pulls off the motorway. All morning she has been dreading the moment when he would pull over to the side of the road and turn off the engine. She closes her eyes and tries not to think as he takes her hand, puts it on that place, and she notices that he's already hard.

'You know I have my needs, Victoria,' he says. 'There's nothing strange about that. All men do, and it's only natural for you to help me relax so we can continue with the journey afterwards.'

She doesn't answer, and keeps her eyes shut as he strokes her cheek with one hand and opens his fly with the other.

'Help me out and don't look so sulky. It won't take long.'

His body smells of sweat, and his breath of sour milk.

She does as he has taught her.

Over time she has become better at it, and when he praises her she almost feels proud. For knowing how to do something, and being good at it.

When he's done she picks up the roll of toilet paper beside the gear-stick and wipes her hands.

'How about stopping at the shopping centre in Enköping and buying something nice for you?' he says with a smile, giving her a tender look.

'OK,' she mutters, because she always mutters her replies to his suggestions. She never knows what they really mean.

They're on their way to the cottage in Dala-Floda.

They're going to be there on their own for a whole weekend.

Him and her.

She didn't want to go.

At breakfast she had said she didn't want to go with him, and would rather stay at home. Then he had got up from the table, opened the fridge and taken out an unopened carton of milk.

He had stood behind her and opened the carton, then slowly poured the chilled liquid all over her. It ran over her head, through her hair, over her face and down into her lap. A big, white puddle formed on the floor.

Mum hadn't said anything, just looked away, and he had gone out into the garage without a word to pack the Volvo.

And now she's sitting here, driving through the summer green of western Dalarna, with a big black knot of anxiety inside.

He doesn't touch her all weekend.

He may have looked at her as she changed into her nightgown, but he hasn't crept in beside her.

As she lies there sleepless, listening for his footsteps, she pretends that she is a clock. She lies in bed on her stomach for six o'clock, then she turns clockwise and lies on her left side for nine o'clock.

Another quarter turn and she's lying on her back for twelve o'clock.

Then her right side, three o'clock.

Then onto her stomach again and six o'clock.

Left side, nine, on her back, midnight.

If she can control time, he'll be fooled by it and won't come in to her.

She doesn't know if that's why, but he stays away from her.

On Sunday morning, when they're due to drive back to Värmdö, he is making porridge as she presents her idea. It's the summer holidays, and she tells him she thinks it would be nice to stay a bit longer.

At first he says she's too little to manage on her own for a whole week. She tells him she's already asked Aunt Elsa next door if she could stay with her, and Elsa had been really happy.

When she sits down at the kitchen table the porridge is stone cold. The thought of the grey mass swelling in her mouth makes her feel sick, and as if it wasn't sweet enough to start with, he's stirred in loads of sugar.

To dilute the taste of the swollen, disintegrating, cold oats, she takes a sip of milk and tries to swallow. But it's hard, the porridge seems to want to come back up again.

He stares at her across the table.

They sit each other out, he and she.

'OK. Let's say that, then. You can stay. You know you're always going to be Daddy's little girl,' he says, ruffling her hair.

She realises that he's never going to let her grow up.

She will always be his.

He promises to drive to the shop and buy supplies so she doesn't run out of anything. When he comes back they unload the goods at Aunt Elsa's before he drives her the fifty metres back to the cottage to pick up her bag of clothes, and when he stops by the gate she hurries to give him a peck on his unshaven cheek before quickly jumping out. She had seen his hands on their way towards her and wanted to forestall him.

Maybe he'll make do with a kiss.

'Take care of yourself, now,' he says before shutting the car door.

He just sits there in the car for what must be a couple of minutes. She takes the bag and sits down on the little step up into the house. Only then does he look away and the car start to move.

The swallows are swooping above the yard and Tupp-Anders's dairy cows are grazing in the meadow beyond the red-painted outhouse.

She watches him drive out onto the main road, then off through the forest, and she knows that he'll soon be back on the pretext of having forgotten something.

She also knows with the same absolute certainty what he's going to want her to do.

It's all so predictable, and the whole procedure will be repeated at least twice before he leaves for real. Maybe he'll have to come back three times before he feels properly relaxed.

She clenches her teeth and peers off towards the edge of the forest, where you can just make out the lake through the trees. Three minutes later she sees the white Volvo approaching and goes back into the kitchen.

This time it's over in ten minutes. Afterwards he settles himself heavily in the car, says goodbye and turns the key in the ignition.

Victoria watches the car disappear behind the trees again. The sound of the engine grows ever more distant, but she sits and waits with the big lump still in her stomach, so as not to celebrate victory in advance. She knows how severe the disappointment is if you do that.

But he doesn't come back again.

When she realises he won't return, she goes off to the well to wash. With some difficulty she hauls up a bucket of ice-cold water and shivers as she scrubs herself clean, before going to Aunt Elsa's to eat lunch and play cards.

Now she can start to breathe.

After eating she decides to go down to the lake for a swim. The path is narrow and covered in pine needles. It feels soft under her bare feet. From within the forest she can hear a persistent peeping sound, and realises that it's coming from hungry chicks waiting for their parents to come back with something edible. The peeping is very close, and she stops and looks.

A tiny hole reveals the bird's nest, no more than two metres up in an old pine tree.

When she reaches the lake she lies on her back in the rowing boat and stares up into the sky.

It's the middle of June, and the air still feels fairly chilly.

Cold water rolls up and down beneath her back in time with the waves. The sky is like dirty milk with a splash of fire, and a black-throated loon is calling from the edge of the forest.

She wonders about letting the waves carry her out, off to unlimited freedom, away from everything. She feels sleepy, but deep down she realised long ago that she can never sleep deeply enough to get away. Her head is like a lamp that has been left on in a silent, dark house. There are always moths fluttering around the naked electric light, their dry wings in her eyes.

As usual, she swims four lengths between the jetty and the big rock fifty metres out in the lake before spreading her blanket and lying down on the grass a short distance from the narrow strip of white sand. The fish are lying in wait, and midges are buzzing across the water, along with dragonflies and pond skaters.

She shuts her eyes, enjoying an isolation that no one can disturb, when suddenly she hears voices from inside the forest.

A man and a woman are walking down the path, and a little boy is running ahead of them, with long, fair curls.

They say hello and ask if this is a private beach. She replies that she isn't really sure, but as far as she knows anyone's allowed to come here. She's always swum here, anyway.

'Ah, so you've lived here for a while, then?' the man says with a smile.

The little boy is running excitedly towards the water and the woman hurries after him.

'Is that your house over there?' the man asks, pointing. The cottage is just visible through the trees in the distance.

'That's right. Mum and Dad are working in the city, so I'm staying here on my own for a week.'

She lies to see how he will react. She has an idea that she wants to check out.

'I see. So you're an independent young lady?' the man says.

She watches as the woman helps the little boy out of his clothes down by the water.

'Suppose so,' she replies, turning towards the man.

He looks amused.

'How old are you, then?'

'Ten.'

He smiles and starts to take off his shirt.

'Ten years old and on your own for a week. Just like Pippi Longstocking.'

She leans back and runs her fingers through her hair. Then she looks him right in the eyes.

'So?'

To her disappointment, the man doesn't seem at all taken aback. He doesn't reply, and turns to look at his family instead.

The boy is on his way out into the water, and the woman follows him with her jeans rolled up to her knees.

'Well done, Martin!' he cries proudly.

Then he pulls off his shoes and begins to undo his trousers. Under his jeans he's wearing a pair of tight swimming trunks with the pattern of the American flag. He's tanned all over, and she thinks he's handsome. Not like her dad, who's got a pot belly and is always white as chalk.

He looks her up and down.

'You seem like a girl who knows her own mind.'

She doesn't reply, but for a moment she thinks she can see something she recognises. Something she doesn't like.

'Well, time for a swim,' he says, and turns his back on her.

He goes down to the water and tests the temperature. Victoria stands up and gathers her things together.

'See you another day, maybe,' the man says, waving to her. 'Bye!'

'Bye,' she replies, suddenly troubled by her solitude.

As she walks along the path leading through the forest towards the cottage, she tries to work out how long it will be before he comes to visit her.

He'll probably come tomorrow, she thinks, and he'll want to borrow the lawnmower.

Her sense of security is gone.

Gamla Enskede – Kihlberg House

Stockholm is as faithless as an old whore. Since the thirteenth century she's been lying there in the unquiet water, tempting with her islands and islets, with her innocent appearance. She is as beautiful as she is treacherous, and her history is coloured with bloodbaths, fires and expulsions.

And broken dreams.

As Jeanette walked to the metro station at Enskede gård that morning there was a chill mist in the air, almost like fog, and the lawns around the villas were wet with night dew.

Late spring in Sweden, she thought. Long, light nights and greenery, capricious lurches between heat and cold. She actually liked this time of year, but right now it made her feel lonely. There was a collective demand to make the most of this short period. Be happy, live your life, seize the day. Late spring in this city is hazardous, she thought.

It was the morning rush hour, and the train was almost full. There was reduced service because of signalling work, and a technical fault was causing further delays. She had to stand, squeezed into a corner by one of the doors.

Technical fault? She presumed that meant someone had jumped in front of a train.

She looked around.

An unusual amount of smiling. Presumably because most people were just a week or two away from their holiday.

She wondered how people at work thought of her. As a miserable cow sometimes, she assumed. Bossy. Domineering, maybe. Hot-tempered at times.

She wasn't really any different from the other senior detectives. The work demanded a certain authority and decisiveness, and the responsibility meant that you sometimes asked too much of your subordinates. And cost you your sense of humour as well as your patience. Did the people she worked with actually like her?

Jens Hurtig liked her, she knew that. And Åhlund respected her. Schwarz did neither. The others were probably somewhere in between.

But there was one thing that bothered her.

Most of them called her Jan, and she was sure they all knew she didn't like it.

That showed a lack of respect.

They could be split into two groups. Schwarz was at the forefront of the Jan team, followed by a long list of other officers. The Jeanette team consisted of Hurtig and Åhlund, but even they slipped up occasionally, along with a handful of other officers and recent recruits who had only ever seen her name written down.

Why didn't she get the same level of respect as the other senior officers? She was better qualified and had a higher rate of closed cases than most of them. Each year, when their rates of pay were adjusted, she received black-and-white evidence that she was still below the average salary for someone of her level. Ten years of experience were forgotten while new officers were promoted and others advanced.

Could the lack of respect really be because she was a woman?

The train stopped at Gullmarsplan. A lot of passengers got off and she sat down on an empty seat at the end of the carriage before it filled up with new passengers.

She was a woman in a position where most of her colleagues were men. Women weren't senior officers in the police. They didn't take command, not at work, and not on the football pitch. They weren't decisive, bossy or dominant like her.

The train shuddered, left Gullmarsplan and pulled out onto the Skanstull Bridge.

Jan, she thought. One of the guys.

Kronoberg – Police Headquarters

By the third day after the discovery on Kungsholmen nothing new had come to light that could lead the investigation forward, and Jeanette was feeling frustrated. In the register of missing children there was no one who, at first glance at least, matched the dead boy. Of course there were hundreds, possibly thousands of undocumented children in Sweden, but unofficial contacts within the church and the Salvation Army had indicated that they weren't aware of anyone who might match the victim.

The City Mission in Gamlastan had no information to offer either. But someone who worked for their nightly outreach programme told them that a number of children usually gathered beneath the Central Bridge.

'They're incredibly elusive, those kids,' the male charity worker lamented. 'When we're there they come out and grab a sandwich and a mug of soup, then disappear again. It's perfectly obvious that they don't really want to have anything to do with us.'

'Isn't there anything social services can do?' Jeanette asked, even though she already knew the answer.

'I doubt it. I know they were down there a month or so ago, and all the kids scattered and didn't come back for a couple of weeks.'

Jeanette Kihlberg thanked him for the information and wondered if a visit to the bridge might turn something up, if she could manage to persuade one of the kids to talk to her.

The door-to-door inquiries around the teacher-training college had been completely useless, and the time-consuming work of contacting refugee centres had now been expanded to cover the whole of central Sweden.

But no one was missing a child who might match the mummified boy who'd been found in the bushes by the metro station. Åhlund had been through hours of security camera footage from the station and the neighbouring college, but hadn't found anything unusual.

At half past ten she called Ivo Andrić at the Institute of Pathology in Solna.

'Tell me you've got something for me! We've ground to a halt here.'

'Well.' Andrić took a deep breath. 'Here's what I've got. The first thing is that all his teeth have been removed, so there's no point calling in a forensic orthodontist to check his dental records. Secondly, the body's completely desiccated, mummified, in fact . . .'

He fell silent, and Jeanette waited for him to go on.

'I'll start again. How do you want it? Technical terminology or something more comprehensible?'

'Whatever you think best. If there's anything I don't understand I'll ask, and you can explain.'

'OK. Well, if a dead body is left in a dry environment at a high temperature, with relatively good ventilation, it dries out fairly quickly. Which means that there's basically no decay. And in extreme cases of drying – such as this one – it's difficult, not to say impossible, to remove the skin, especially from the skull. The facial skin has dried out completely and can't be removed from the underlying –'

'Sorry to interrupt,' Jeanette said impatiently. 'I don't want to seem unfriendly, but I'm mainly interested in how he died and when it might have happened. Even I could see that he was dried out.'

'Of course. Maybe I got a bit sidetracked. You have to appreciate that it's practically impossible to say when death occurred, but I can tell you that he hasn't been dead for longer than six months. The process of mummification also takes time, so I'd guess he died somewhere between November and January.'

'OK, but that's still a fairly broad period of time, isn't it? Have you managed to get any DNA?'

'Yes, we've taken DNA from the victim, as well as urine from the bag.'

'What? You mean someone pissed on the bag?'

'Yes, but that doesn't necessarily have to be the killer, does it?'

'No, that's true.'

'But it might take another week before we get back comprehensive results about the DNA and can build up a more extensive profile. It's a tricky job.'

'OK. Have you got any ideas about where the body might have been kept?'

'Well . . . like I said, somewhere dry.'

The line fell silent, and Jeanette thought for a moment before going on.

'So pretty much anywhere, then? Could I have done it at home?'

She saw the disgusting and utterly absurd image in her mind's eye. A dead boy at home in the house in Enskede, getting drier and more mummified by the week.

An indescribably terrifying picture was developing. What Ivo Andrić was explaining had a purpose.

'I don't know what your home's like, but even an ordinary apartment might do. It might smell a bit to start with, but if you had access to a hot-air ventilator and put the corpse in an enclosed space, it would certainly be possible to do it before the neighbours started to complain.'

'A wardrobe, you mean?'

'Maybe not as small as that. A closet, a bathroom, something like that.'

'That's not much to go on.' She could feel her frustration growing.

'No, I realise that. But there is something that might be able to help you.'

Jeanette listened intently.

'The preliminary chemical analysis indicates that the body is full of chemicals.'

Something, at last, she thought.

'To start with, there's amphetamines. We've found traces in the stomach and in the veins. So he's either eaten or drunk a lot, but there's also evidence to suggest that it had been injected as well.'

'A drug addict?' She hoped he was going to say yes, because everything would be a whole lot simpler if they were looking for an addict who had died in some drug den, then dried out over the passage of time. They'd be able to write off the case and draw the conclusion that one of the young boy's drugged-up friends had dumped the body in the bushes in a state of confusion.

'No, I don't think so. He was probably injected against his will. The needle marks are fairly random, and most of them wouldn't even have hit a vein.'

'Oh, fuck.'

'Yes, I'm inclined to agree with you there.'

'And you're quite sure he wasn't shooting up himself?'

'As sure as I can be. But the amphetamines aren't the most interesting thing. What's really strange is that he's also got traces of anaesthetic in his body. More precisely, a substance known as Xylocain adrenalin, which is a Swedish invention from the forties. To start with, AstraZeneca marketed Xylocain as a luxury medicine: Pope Pius XII took it for hiccups, and President Eisenhower was treated with it for hypochondria. These days it's a standard painkiller, the stuff you get injected into your gums if you ask the dentist for anaesthetic.'

'OK . . . I'm not following you now.'

'Well, this boy hasn't got it in his mouth, of course, but throughout his body. Bloody weird, if you ask me.'

'And he's been severely abused as well?'

'Yes, he's taken a lot of beatings, but the anaesthetic would have kept him going. Eventually, after hours of suffering, the drugs would have paralysed his heart and lungs. A slow and horribly painful death. Poor kid . . .'

Jeanette was feeling dizzy.

'But why?' she asked, in the vain hope that Ivo had some sort of reasonable explanation.

'If you'll permit me to speculate . . . ?'

'By all means.'

'The first thing that came to mind were organised dogfights. You know, two prize dogs fighting until one of them is killed. The sort of thing that sometimes goes on in the suburbs.'

'That sounds like a hell of a long shot,' Jeanette said instinctively, repulsed by the macabre thought. But she wasn't entirely sure that it was. Over the years she had learned not to dismiss even the most unlikely ideas. On many occasions, once the truth was revealed it turned out to be far stranger than any fiction. She thought of the German cannibal who had used the Internet to find a man who was prepared to let himself be eaten.

'Well, I'm just speculating,' Ivo Andrić went on. 'Another idea might sound more plausible.'

'What's that?'

'That he's been beaten beyond recognition by someone who didn't stop even though the boy was dying. Someone who dosed him up with drugs and then carried on with the abuse.'

Jeanette felt a memory flicker.

'Do you remember that ice-hockey player in Västerås, the one who was stabbed about a hundred times?'

'No, I can't say that I do. Maybe it was before I came to Sweden.'

'Yes, it was a while back now. Mid-nineties. It was a skinhead off his head on Rohypnol. The hockey player was openly homosexual, and you know what neo-Nazis think of gays. The skinhead carried on stabbing the dead body way beyond the point when his arm should have cramped up.'

'Yes, that's more or less what I'm suggesting. A merciless lunatic full of hate and, well . . . Rohypnol or anabolic steroids, maybe?'

Jeanette hung up. She was feeling hungry and looked at the time. She decided to give herself a long lunch down in the police headquarters canteen. She'd grab the booth at the far end of the room so she had a chance of being left in peace. The restaurant would be full of people soon, and she wanted to be alone.

Before she sat down with her tray she snatched up a discarded copy of one of the evening papers. Almost at once she realised that the paper's source in the police department was someone close to her, seeing as the article was based on facts that only someone intimately connected to the case could know. Since she was sure it wasn't Hurtig, that only left Åhlund or Schwarz.

'So you're down here already?'

Jeanette looked up from the paper.

Hurtig was standing beside her, grinning.

'Is it OK if I join you?' He nodded to the empty seat opposite her.

'Are you back already?' Jeanette gestured to him to sit down.

'Yes, we got finished an hour or so ago. Danderyd. Some rich bastard in construction with a hard drive full of child porn. Bloody awful.' Hurtig walked round the table, put his tray down, then sat. 'The wife went to pieces, and their fourteen-year-old daughter just stood and stared as we arrested him.'

'Otherwise?' she asked.

'Mum called this morning,' he said between mouthfuls. 'Dad's not well, he's in the hospital up in Gällivare.'

Jeanette put her knife and fork down and stared at him. 'Is it serious?'

Hurtig shook his head. 'More like unbelievable. Looks like he got his right hand caught in the circular saw, but Mum said they can probably save most of his fingers. She managed to find them and put them in a bag of ice cubes.'

'Damn.'

'But she couldn't find his thumb.' Hurtig grinned. 'The cat probably got it. It's OK, the right hand would be the best one for this to happen to for Dad. He likes carving and playing the fiddle, and for both of those his left hand is more important.'

Jeanette thought about what she actually knew of her colleague, and had to concede that it wasn't much.

Hurtig grew up in Kvikkjokk, went to school in Jokkmokk, then high school in Boden. He spent a few years working after that – she couldn't remember what he did – then, when Umeå University started training police officers, he was in the first group of students. After doing work experience with the police in Luleå he applied for a transfer to Stockholm. Nothing but facts, she thought, nothing more personal than the fact that he lived alone in an apartment on Södermalm. Girlfriend? Maybe.

'Why's he in the hospital in Gällivare?' she said. 'They still live in Kvikkjokk, don't they?'

He stopped eating and looked at her. 'Do you seriously think there's a hospital there, in a village with about fifty inhabitants?'

'Is it that small? In that case I get it. So your mum had to drive your dad to the hospital in Gällivare? But that must be a hell of a way.'

'It's about two hundred kilometres to the hospital, it usually takes about four hours by car.'

'Wow,' Jeanette said, feeling embarrassed at her poor grasp of geography.

'Yes, it's not easy. Lapland's big. Fucking big.'

Hurtig sat in silence for a moment before going on.

'Do you think it was any good?'

'What do you mean?' Jeanette gave him a quizzical look.

'Dad's thumb.' He grinned again. 'Do you think the cat appreciated it? There can't be that much meat on an old Lapp bastard's thumb. What do you think?'

Hurtig is Sami, she thought. Something else I had no idea about. She decided to say yes next time he asked if she wanted to go for a beer. If she was going to be a good boss and not just pretend to be one, it was time she got to know her subordinates.

Jeanette picked up her tray, stood and went to get two cups of coffee. She grabbed a few biscuits and went back. 'Anything new about the phone call?'

Hurtig swallowed. 'Yes, I got a report just before I came down here.'

'And?' Jeanette sipped at the hot coffee.

Hurtig put his knife and fork down. 'As we suspected. The call was made from the vicinity of the DN Tower. To be more precise, from Rålambsvägen. How about you?' Hurtig picked up a biscuit and dunked it in his coffee. 'What have you been doing this morning?'

'I had an interesting conversation with Ivo Andrić. Looks like the boy was full of chemicals.'

'What?' Hurtig looked curious.

'Large amounts of anaesthetic. Injected.' Jeanette took a deep breath. 'Probably against his will.'

'Oh, fuck.'

That afternoon she tried to get hold of Prosecutor von Kwist, but his secretary told her that he was currently in Gothenburg to take part in a debate on television, and that he wouldn't be back until the next day.

Jeanette went onto the programme's website and read that the debate was going to be about escalating levels of violence in the suburbs. Kenneth von Kwist, who advocated firm measures and longer sentencing, was expected to attack the previous minister of justice.

On her way out Jeanette stopped off to see Hurtig, and arranged to meet him at ten o'clock at Central Station. They needed to try to talk to some of the children who hung out beneath the bridge as soon as possible.

Gamla Enskede – Kihlberg House

At half past four the traffic on St Eriksgatan was complete chaos. The old Audi had cost Jeanette eight hundred kronor for parts and two bottles of Jameson, but she thought it was worth every öre. The car was running like clockwork after Åhlund repaired it.

Tourists from the country, unused to the frantic pace of the capital, were doing their best to share the limited space with the more experienced locals. It wasn't going terribly well.

Stockholm's roadways had been constructed during an age when there were far fewer cars, and to be honest it was more suitable for a small town the size of Härnösand than a city with a million inhabitants. The fact that one of the lanes on the Western Bridge was closed for roadworks did nothing to help the situation, and it took Jeanette over an hour to get home to Gamla Enskede. Under more favourable circumstances it took less than fifteen minutes.

As she stepped through the door she almost bumped into Johan and Åke. They were going off to a football match, and were wearing identical shirts and carrying matching green-and-white scarves. They looked confident and expectant, but Jeanette knew from experience that they'd be back in a few hours with all their hopes in ruins.

'We're going to win today!' Åke gave her a quick peck on the cheek, and herded Johan out of the door. 'See you later.'

'I probably won't be here when you get back.' Jeanette saw Åke's mood change. 'I need to go out on a job, I should be back sometime after midnight.'

He shrugged, looked up at the ceiling, then went out to join Johan.

This wasn't the first time they had met briefly in the doorway, only to part a moment later. Two entirely separate lives under the same roof, she thought. Smiles transformed into looks of disappointment and irritation.

She and Åke. On their way in different directions, with different dreams. More friends than lovers.

Jeanette shut the door after them, kicked off her shoes, and went into the living room, where she threw herself down on the sofa in the hope of getting some rest. In about three hours she'd have to set off again, and hoped she might manage a short nap at least.

Thoughts drifted aimlessly in her head, aspects of the case blurring into practical matters. Grass that needed cutting, letters to be written, interviews to be arranged. She was supposed to be a mum who kept an eye on her child. A woman with the capacity to love and feel desire.

And alongside that she was supposed to have time for her life. Dreamless sleep without any real respite. A short break in the otherwise perpetual motion. A brief period of calm in the lifelong business of moving her body from one place to another.

Sisyphus, she thought.

Central Bridge

The traffic had thinned out, and as she parked the car she could see from the clock above the entrance to Central Station that it was twenty to ten. She got out of the car, shut the door and locked it. Hurtig was standing by a fast-food stall with a hot dog in each hand. When he caught sight of Jeanette he gave her an almost embarrassed smile. As if he were doing something forbidden.

'Dinner?' Jeanette nodded at the impressively large sausages.

'Here, have one.'

'Have you seen if there are any of them here?' Jeanette took the proffered hot dog and gestured towards the Central Bridge.

'When I got here I saw one of the City Mission's vans. Let's go over and have a word.' He wiped a dribble of sauce from his cheek with a napkin.

They walked past the car park beneath the slip road from Klarastrandsleden, with Tegelbacken and the Sheraton Hotel on the other side of the street. Two different worlds in an area no bigger than a football pitch, Jeanette thought as she caught sight of a group of people in the darkness beside one of the grey concrete pillars.

Twenty or so young people, some of them no more than children, gathered around a van with the City Mission logo on its side.

Some of the children pulled back when they noticed the two new arrivals, vanishing under the bridge.

The two volunteers from the City Mission had nothing useful to tell them. Children came and went, and even though they were there almost every evening, very few of them ever opened up. Just a succession of nameless faces. Some of them went back home, some moved on elsewhere, and a not inconsiderable number of them died.

That was just fact.

Overdoses or suicide.

Money was one problem all the youngsters shared, or rather the lack of it. One of the volunteers told them there were restaurants where the children were occasionally allowed to do the dishes. For a whole day's work, twelve hours, they got a warm meal and one hundred kronor. The fact that several of the children also provided sexual services came as no surprise to Jeanette.

A girl of about fifteen ventured forward and asked who they were. The girl smiled and Jeanette saw that she had several teeth missing.

Jeanette wondered what to say. Lying about what they were doing there wasn't a good idea. If she was going to stand any chance of gaining the girl's trust, it was just as well to say it straight out.

'My name's Jeanette, and I'm a police officer,' she began. 'This is my colleague Jens.'

Hurtig smiled and held out his hand.

'Oh. And what do you want?' The girl looked Jeanette straight in the eyes, giving no indication that she'd noticed Hurtig's outstretched hand.

Jeanette told her about the murder of the young boy, and said they needed help identifying him. She showed a picture that one of the police artists had drawn.

The girl, whose name was Aatifa, said she usually hung out in the city centre. According to the volunteers, she was in no way atypical. Her parents had fled from Eritrea and were both unemployed. She lived in an apartment in Huvudsta with her parents and six siblings. Four rooms and a kitchen.

Neither Aatifa nor any of the others recognised or knew anything about the dead boy. After two hours they gave up and walked back towards the car park.

'Little adults.' Hurtig shook his head as he took out his car keys. 'Christ, they're no more than children. They ought to be playing, making forts.'

Jeanette could see how upset he was.

'Yes. And evidently they can just disappear without anyone missing them.'

An ambulance flew past, blue lights flashing, but with no siren. At Tegelbacken it turned left and vanished into the Klara Tunnel.

Jeanette pulled her jacket more tightly around her.

Åke was snoring on the sofa, and she wrapped a blanket around him before going to the bedroom, getting undressed and curling up naked under the duvet. She switched the light off and lay there in the dark with her eyes open.

She could hear the wind against the window, the sound of the trees in the garden rustling and the distant rumble from the motorway.

She felt sad. She didn't want to sleep.

She wanted to understand.

Mariatorget – Sofia Zetterlund's Office

Sofia felt drained as she left Huddinge. Her conversation with Tyra Mäkelä had taken its toll, and Sofia had also agreed to take on another job, which looked likely to be fairly demanding. Lars Mikkelsen at National Crime had asked her to join the investigation into a paedophile who was going to be charged with the abuse of his own daughter and dissemination of child pornography. The man had confessed when he was arrested.

There's never any end to it, she thought with a heavy heart as she pulled out onto Huddingevägen.

It was as if she were being forced to bear Tyra Mäkelä's experiences. Memories of humiliation, the scarring inside her that really just wanted to break out and reveal its own feebleness. The awareness of how much pain a person can cause someone else becomes a sort of impenetrable armour.

Armour that can't let anything out.

Her despondency followed her all the way back to her office and the meeting she had arranged with social services in Hässelby. The meeting with Samuel Bai, the former child soldier from Sierra Leone.

A conversation she knew would revolve around insane violence and appalling abuse.

On days like this there was no chance of lunch. Just a short period of silence in the break room. Eyes closed, lying down, trying to regain some sort of equilibrium.

Samuel Bai was a tall, muscular young man who at first seemed reserved and uninterested. But when Sofia suggested that they talk in Krio instead of English, he opened up and immediately became more communicative.

During her three months in Sierra Leone she had learned the West African language, and they spent a long time talking about life in Freetown, and about places and buildings they both knew. As the conversation progressed, Samuel began to trust her as he realised that she could understand something of what he had been through.

After twenty minutes she began to hope that she might be able to contribute something positive.

Samuel Bai's problems with focus and concentration, his inability to sit still for more than thirty seconds, and his difficulty holding back sudden impulses and emotional outbursts were all reminiscent of ADHD, with a strong element of hyperactivity and lack of impulse control.

But it wasn't as simple as that.

She noted that Samuel's tone of voice, intonation and body language changed with the subject of conversation. Sometimes he would suddenly begin to speak English instead of Krio, and would occasionally break into a version of Krio she'd never heard before. His eyes also changed as he shifted language and posture. He would switch from sitting bolt upright, with an intense look in his eyes as he spoke loudly and clearly about wanting to open a restaurant some day, to sitting slumped, his eyes dull, muttering in that strange dialect.

If Sofia had discerned dissociative tendencies in Victoria Bergman, they seemed to have reached full fruition in Samuel Bai. Sofia suspected that Samuel was suffering from post-traumatic stress as a result of the terrible things he had experienced as a child, and that this had provoked a personality disorder. He showed signs of having several different personalities, which he seemed to switch between unconsciously.

The phenomenon was sometimes called multiple personality disorder, but Sofia preferred the term 'dissociative identity disorder'.

She also knew that people like that were very difficult to treat.

To start with, treatment of that sort was very time-consuming, both in terms of each individual conversation and the total length of the treatment. Sofia realised that her usual forty-five- or sixty-minute sessions wouldn't be enough. She'd have to try to increase each session with Samuel to ninety minutes, and suggest to social services that she see him at least three times a week.

But the treatment was also difficult because the sessions demanded utter concentration from the therapist.

During that first conversation with Samuel Bai she felt the same thing she had experienced during Victoria Bergman's monologues. Samuel, like Victoria, was a talented self-hypnotist, and his sleep-like state began to affect Sofia.

She knew she was going to have to be at the very top of her game if she was to stand any chance of helping Samuel.

Unlike her work for the criminal justice system, which ultimately had nothing to do with care of the people she met, she actually felt that she could be of some help here.

They talked for over an hour, and when Samuel left her office Sofia felt that the image of his wounded psyche had become slightly clearer.

She was tired, but knew that her day's work wasn't over, because she still had to conclude her file on Tyra Mäkelä, and also needed to prepare for her fact-check of the child soldier's book. The story of what happens when children are given the power to kill.

She pulled out all the material she had and leafed through the English version. The publishers had sent her a list of questions that they were hoping she could answer during their meeting in Gothenburg, but she quickly realised that she couldn't give them any straight answers.

It was too complicated.

The book had already been translated, and her contribution was mainly going to consist of technicalities.

But Samuel Bai's book wasn't finished yet. It was right in front of her.

Screw this, she thought.

Sofia asked Ann-Britt to cancel the train tickets and hotel in Gothenburg. The publishers could think whatever they liked.

Sometimes acting on impulse is the best decision.

Before she left for the day she put an end to the Tyra Mäkelä case by emailing the members of the investigative group in Huddinge her final conclusions.

That was really just another technicality.

They had agreed that Tyra Mäkelä should be sentenced to secure psychiatric care, just as Sofia had proposed.

She felt she had been able to make a difference.

Monument – Mikael's Apartment

After dinner Sofia and Mikael cleared the table together and put the plates in the dishwasher. Mikael said he just wanted to relax in front of the television, which Sofia thought sounded like a good idea, since she had work to do. She went into his office and sat down at the desk. It had started to rain again, and she shut the little window and opened her laptop.

She took a cassette marked 'Victoria Bergman 14' from her bag and inserted it into the tape player.

Sofia recalled that Victoria Bergman had been sad during that particular meeting, and that something had happened, but when she had asked about it Victoria had merely shaken her head.

She heard her own voice.

'Tell me exactly what you want to do. We can sit in silence if you'd rather.'

'Mmm, maybe, if only silence weren't so horribly unsettling. So incredibly intimate.'

Victoria Bergman's voice turned darker, and Sofia leaned back in her chair and shut her eyes.

I have a memory from when I was ten years old. It was in Dalarna. I was looking for a bird's nest, and when I found a little hole I crept slowly up to the tree. When I got there I banged hard on the trunk and the chirping inside stopped. I don't know why I did it, but it felt right. Then I took a few steps back and sat down in the blueberry scrub and waited. After a while a little bird appeared, and sat in the opening. It crept inside and the chirping started up again. I remember getting annoyed. Then the bird flew off again and I found an old stump that I leaned up against the tree. I got hold of a decent-sized stick and climbed on top of the stump. Then I rammed it in hard, aiming it downward, and continued until the chirping had stopped. I climbed down again and waited for the bird to come back. I wanted to see how it would react when it discovered its dead chicks.

Sofia felt her mouth go dry, and got up and went out into the kitchen. She filled a glass with water and drank it.

There was something in Victoria's story that felt familiar.

It reminded her of something.

A dream, maybe? She went back into the study. The tape player was still running. She'd forgotten to switch it off.

Victoria Bergman's voice was eerily rasping. Dry.

Sofia jerked as the tape came to an end. She looked around, bleary-eyed. It was past midnight.

Outside the window Ölandsgatan lay silent and deserted. The rain had stopped, but the street was still wet and the street lamps were twinkling.

She switched off her computer and went out into the living room. Mikael had gone to bed, and she carefully slid in beside him.

She lay awake for a long time, thinking about Victoria Bergman.

The strangest thing was that after her monologues, Victoria immediately went back to being her normal, focused self.

It was as if she changed the channel to a different programme. A quick press of the remote, and she was on another channel. Another voice.

Was it like that with Samuel Bai? Different voices talking in turns? Probably.

Sofia realised that Mikael wasn't asleep, and kissed him on the shoulder.

'I didn't want to wake you,' he said. 'You looked so peaceful sitting there. You were talking in your sleep.'

At three o'clock she got out of bed, pulled out one of the cassettes, turned on the tape player and leaned back, letting herself be swallowed up by the voice.

The pieces of Victoria Bergman's personality began to fall into place, and Sofia thought that she was beginning to understand. And could sympathise.

She could see the images Victoria Bergman painted with her words as clearly as if they were a film. It was far too immense to comprehend. But Victoria's dark sadness frightened her.

In all likelihood she had nurtured her memories, day after day, over the years creating a world in her mind where she sometimes consoled herself, and sometimes blamed herself for what had happened.

Sofia shuddered at the sound of Victoria Bergman's growling voice.

Sometimes whispering. Sometimes so agitated her mouth sprayed saliva.

Sofia fell asleep, and didn't wake up until Mikael knocked on the door and said it was morning.

'Have you been sitting here all night?'

'Yes, almost, I'm seeing a client today and I need to work out how I'm going to approach her.'

'OK. Look, I've got to go. See you tonight?'

'Yes. I'll call.'

He shut the door, and Sofia decided to continue listening, and turned the cassette over. She could hear her own breathing when Victoria Bergman stopped for breath. When she began to speak again it was in an authoritative voice.

. . . he was sweaty and wanted to hug me, even though it was so hot, and he went on sprinkling water on the stove. I could see the bag between his legs when he leaned over to get water from the wooden bucket, and I felt like pushing him over so he fell onto the hot rocks. The rocks that never seemed to cool down.

Warmed up every Wednesday with a heat that never managed to penetrate all the way to my bones. I just sat there quietly, quiet as a little mouse, and all the while I could see the way he was looking at me. The way his eyes went strange and he started to breathe heavily, then I would go out to the shower and scrub myself clean after the game. Although I knew I could never be clean. I ought to be grateful to him for showing me so many secrets, so that I'd be prepared for the day when I met boys, who could be really clumsy and pushy, and he certainly wasn't, because he'd been practising all his life, and had been trained by Grandma and her brother and no harm had come to anyone, it had just made him strong and resilient. He'd done the Vasaloppet ski race a hundred times, even with cracked ribs and bad knees, without a word of complaint, though he did throw up in Evertsberg. The chafe marks I got down there when he'd finished playing on the sauna benches and pulled his fingers out weren't worth making a fuss of. When he was done with me and closed the door of the sauna, I thought about the female spider who eats the smaller males after they've mated . . .

Sofia jerked. She felt sick.

She must have fallen asleep again, and in her sleep she'd dreamed a load of terrible things, and she realised it was just because the tape player had been running. The monotonous voice had directed her thoughts and dreams.

Victoria Bergman's monologue had forced its way into her subconscious.

Village of Dala-Floda, 1980

T*he fly's wings are stuck fast in the chewing gum. There's no point in you trying to flap them, Crow Girl thinks. You'll never fly again. Tomorrow the sun will be shining as usual, but it won't be shining on you.*

When Martin's dad touches her she flinches instinctively. They're standing on the gravel outside Aunt Elsa's house and he's just got off his bicycle.

'Martin's been asking for you. I think he misses having someone to play with.'

He reaches out a hand and strokes her cheek. 'I'd like it if you came down to swim with us one day.'

Victoria looks away. She's used to being touched, and knows exactly what it leads to.

She sees it in his eyes as he nods, says goodbye and continues down towards the road. Just as she suspected, he stops the bike and turns back.

'By the way, you haven't got a lawnmower I could borrow, have you?'

He's just like the others, she thinks.

'It's by the outhouse,' she says, and waves goodbye.

She wonders when he's going to come and get it.

Her chest feels tight as she thinks about it, because she knows that's when he's going to touch her again.

She knows it, but she still can't stay away from the beach.

In a way she doesn't quite understand, she finds herself enjoying spending time with the family, and with Martin in particular.

His language is undeveloped, but his terse and occasionally hard to understand declarations of love are among the nicest things anyone has ever said to her. His eyes shine every time he sees her again, and he runs towards her and hugs her tight.

They play and swim and go for walks through the forest together. Martin stumbles uncertainly over the uneven ground, pointing at things, and Victoria patiently explains what they are.

'Mushroom,' she says, and 'pine tree', and 'woodlouse', and Martin tries to imitate the sounds.

She teaches him the forest.

First she takes off her shoes, and feels the sand creep between her toes, trying to tickle her. She takes off her top and feels the sun warm her skin. The waves lap coolly against her legs before she jumps in.

She stays in the water so long her skin goes wrinkly, and she wishes it could split or fall off so she could get new skin, untouched.

She hears the family approaching along the path. Martin lets out a squeal of delight when he sees her. He runs towards the water and she hurries to meet him so he doesn't continue into the water and get his clothes wet.

'My Pippi,' he says, hugging her.

'Martin, you know we've decided to stay until the start of the autumn term,' his dad says, looking at Victoria. 'So you don't have to squeeze her to bits today.'

Victoria returns Martin's hug and suddenly feels the insight strike her.

So little time.

'If only it was just you and me,' she whispers in Martin's ear.

'You and me,' he repeats.

He needs her, and she needs him more and more. She promises herself to nag Dad as hard as she can to let her stay up here as much as possible.

Victoria pulls her top on over her wet swimming costume, and slips her sandals on. She takes Martin by the hand and leads him along the shore. Under the mirror-like surface she sees a crayfish crawling along the bottom.

'Do you remember what that plant is called?' she asks, to get Martin to look at a fern while she reaches for the crayfish. She grips it and hides it behind her back.

'Firm?' Martin says, giving her a questioning look.

She bursts out laughing, and Martin joins in. 'Firm,' he repeats.

While he's still laughing she pulls out the crayfish and holds it up in front of his face. She sees it contort with horror and he bursts into hysterical crying. As if in apology she throws the crayfish on the ground and stomps on it hard until the claws stop moving. She puts her arms around him, but his sobbing is inconsolable.

She feels she's lost control of him, it's no longer enough just to be herself for him.

Losing control of him is like losing control of herself.

It's the first time his faith in her has been shaken. He thought she wanted to hurt him, that she was one of the others, the ones who want to hurt you.

She doesn't want her time with Martin to end, but she knows Dad's coming to get her on Sunday.

She wants to stay in the cottage forever.

She wants to be with Martin.

Always.

He absorbs her totally. She can sit and watch him sleeping, see how his eyes play under his closed eyelids, listen to the little whimpering sounds he makes. Calm sleep. He has shown her what it looks like, shown her that it exists.

But Saturday comes, relentlessly.

As usual, they are down on the beach. Martin is sitting on the edge of the blanket at his dozing parents' feet, playing idly with the two Dala horses they bought in a shop in Gagnef.

The sky has been clouding over gradually, and the afternoon sun is only intermittently visible.

'Well, it's probably time to head for home now,' Martin's mother says.

His father shakes the blanket and folds it up. In the grass the faint shadow of bent blades of grass indicates where their bodies had lain. Soon the grass would reach up towards the sky, and the next time she saw the place it would be as if the family had never existed.

'Victoria, perhaps you'd like to come and eat with us this evening?' the mum says. 'We can try that new croquet game as well. You and Martin could make up one team.'

She starts. More time, she thinks. I can have more time.

She thinks that Aunt Elsa will be sad if she doesn't spend her last evening with her, but in spite of that she can't bring herself to say no. It's impossible.

When the family heads off along the path she is filled with a calm sense of anticipation.

She carefully packs her beach bag, but doesn't go straight home. Instead, she stays close to the timber shacks by the lake, enjoying the calm and solitude.

She rubs her hands over the smooth wood and thinks about all the ages the timbers have seen, all the hands that have touched them, polishing them smooth, removing any resistance. It's as if nothing can affect them any more.

She wants to become like them, just as untouchable.

She spends several hours wandering around in the forest, observing how the trunks have curved so their leaves can reach the sun, or how they have been bent by the wind, how they have been attacked by moss or parasites. But deep inside each trunk is a perfect piece of timber. You just have to know how to find it, she thinks.

Then she steps out from the forest and into a clearing.

In the midst of the forest's dense growth is a place where the light filters through the treetops and shines down on the slender pines and soft moss.

It's like a dream.

Later she would spend several days trying to find that glade again, but no matter how she searched, she would never find her way back and, as time passed, she would begin to question whether it had ever existed.

But now she is there, and the place is just as tangible as she is.

When Victoria reaches the steps to Aunt Elsa's porch she is struck with anxiety again. Disappointed people can hurt you, even though they don't really mean to. That's one of the things she has learned.

She opens the door and hears the shuffling sound of Aunt Elsa's slippers approaching. When the figure appears in the hall, Victoria can see that Elsa's back is a little more bent and her face a little paler than usual.

'Hello, my dear,' Elsa says, but Victoria says nothing.

'Come in, and we'll go and sit down and have a talk,' Elsa goes on, heading into the kitchen.

Victoria can see the tiredness in Elsa's eyes, her jaw is set, and the corners of her mouth are turned down.

'My little Victoria,' she begins, and tries to smile.

Victoria sees that her eyes are shiny, as if she's been crying.

'I know this is your last evening,' she continues, 'and I'd like to have made you a really nice meal and spend the evening playing cards . . . but I'm not feeling terribly well, you see.'

Victoria breathes a sigh of relief before seeing the guilt in Elsa's eyes. She recognises it, as if it were her own. As if Elsa too had the same fear of having cold milk poured over her head, of being forced to eat lentils until she throws up, of not getting birthday presents because she's spoken out of turn, of being punished every time she does anything wrong.

In Aunt Elsa's eyes Victoria imagines she can see that she too has learned that it's never enough to do your best.

'I can make tea,' Victoria says cheerily. 'And tuck you in and maybe read something to you until you fall asleep.'

Elsa's face softens, her mouth curls up into a smile, and she lets out a laugh.

'You're a sweet child,' she says, stroking Victoria's cheek. 'But there won't be a nice meal to send you off, and what will you do once I've fallen asleep? It won't be much fun for you, sitting here all alone in the dark.'

'Don't worry,' Victoria says. 'Martin's parents said I could help put him to bed, and that I could have some food there. So first I can put you to bed, then Martin, and I'll end up with a full tummy as well.'

Elsa laughs and nods.

'We'll make a salad for you to take.'

They sit down by the kitchen worktop together and chop vegetables.

Every time Victoria gets too close to Elsa she detects an acrid smell of urine. It makes her think of Dad.

Hard Dad.

The smell makes her feel nauseous. She knows all too well what it tastes like.

Aunt Elsa has a tin of orange sweets on the kitchen table. Victoria opens the tin whenever she wants to fend off thoughts of him. She never knows in advance when the memory of him is going to creep up on her, so she never chews the sweets, not even when there's only a sharp little sliver left.

She sucks the sweet as she slices the cucumber into good-sized pieces. Even though Elsa has rinsed them carefully there's a little soil left on the lettuce leaves, but Victoria doesn't say anything because she realises that Elsa's eyes are too old to see such small details.

She tucks Elsa in, as she promised, but she's thinking of Martin.

'You're a very sweet girl. Never forget that,' Elsa says before Victoria shuts the door. She gets the salad and sets off with a feeling of tense anticipation towards Martin's cottage with the bowl in her hands.

She thinks about how nice it would be if she could persuade Dad to let her stay another week. It would be good for everyone. And she's got so many exciting things left to show Martin.

The only thing that spoils the fairy tale in her thoughts is Martin's dad. She thinks the way he looks at her has become more intense, his laugh louder, and that his hands stay on her shoulders a little longer. But she's prepared to accept that in order to escape her own father for another week. It isn't usually so bad the first few times, she thinks. It's only when they start taking her for granted that they dare to be less careful.

As she goes up the drive towards the cottage she can hear someone shouting inside. It sounds like Martin's dad, and she slows down. The door is half open and she can hear splashing from inside the house.

She goes up to the door, opens it wide, and happens to hit the old doorbell that's hanging there. It lets out a few muffled rings.

'Is that you, Pippi?' the father calls from the kitchen. 'Come right on in.'

There's a nice smell in the hall.

Victoria steps into the kitchen. Martin is in a bathtub on the floor. His mum's sitting in a rocking chair over by the window, and is busy knitting. She's facing away from the others, but turns her head to greet Victoria. Martin's dad is sitting with his top off in just a pair of shorts beside the bathtub.

Victoria goes completely cold when she sees what he's doing.

Martin is covered in soap, and his dad gives her a broad smile. He's got one arm wrapped around Martin's bottom, and is washing him with the other.

Victoria just stares.

'We had a bit of an accident,' Martin's father says. 'Martin messed his trousers while we were playing up in the forest.'

He gently rubs the boy's genitals. 'We need to get you properly clean, don't we?' he says.

Victoria watches as the man takes hold of the little penis with his thumb and forefinger. With his other hand he carefully rubs the pink bit at the end.

She recognises the scene. The dad with the child, the mum in the same room but looking the other way.

Suddenly the bowl feels so heavy that it slips from her hands. There's an explosion of tomatoes, cucumber, onion and lettuce all over the floor. Martin starts crying. His mum puts her knitting down and gets up from the rocking chair.

Victoria backs away towards the door.

She starts running as soon as she's in the hall.

She runs down the steps, stumbles and falls head first onto the gravel but gets up at once and continues running. She heads down the drive, out through the gate, along the road and home. In tears she shoves the door of the cottage open and throws herself down on her bed.

She's in complete torment. She realises that Martin will be ruined, he'll get big, he'll become a man, he'll be like all the others. She had hoped to protect him from that, give herself to save him. But she was too late.

Everything nice was gone, and it was her fault.

There's a gentle knock on the door. She hears Martin's dad's voice outside. She crawls over to the door and locks it.

'Is something wrong, Victoria? Why did you get so upset?'

She realises she can't open the door now. It would be far too embarrassing.

Instead she creeps into the bedroom, opens the window at the back and climbs out. She walks in a wide curve around the outhouse and out to the road. When they hear her coming they turn round and walk towards her.

'Ah, there you are, we thought you were inside. Where did you take off to?'

She feels she's on the verge of laughter.

Mum, Dad, with the child in their arms, wrapped in a blanket.

They look so ridiculous. So scared.

'I needed the toilet,' she lies, not knowing where the words came from, but they sound good.

The mum carries her back to their cottage, and there's nothing odd at all.

Her arms are safe, like arms usually are when everything's OK again.

Her legs hit Martin's mum's thigh with each step she takes, but it doesn't seem to bother her. She walks on, focused. As if Victoria belonged with them.

'Will you be coming back next summer?' she asks, feeling the woman's cheek against hers.

'Yes, we will,' she whispers. 'We'll come back to you every summer.'

That summer Martin has six years left to live.

Huddinge Hospital

Karl Lundström was going to be charged with child pornography offences, as well as the sexual abuse of his daughter, Linnea. As Sofia Zetterlund turned off towards Huddinge Hospital she reflected on what she knew of his background.

Karl Lundström was forty-four years old and had a senior position at Skanska, where he was responsible for a number of the largest construction projects in the country. His wife, Annette, was forty-one, and their daughter, Linnea, fourteen. Over the past ten years the family had moved half a dozen times, between Umeå in the north and Malmö in the south, and were currently living in a large turn-of-the-century villa at Edsviken in Danderyd. At the moment there was an extensive police investigation trying to identify whether or not he was actually part of a larger paedophile ring.

Always on the move, she thought as she turned into the car park. Typical behaviour for paedophiles. Moving to escape discovery and to get away from suspicions about odd behaviour within the family.

Neither Annette Lundström nor their daughter Linnea wanted to admit what had happened. The mother was in despair and denied everything, whereas the daughter had retreated into an apathetic state of complete silence.

She parked outside the main entrance and went in. On the way she decided to take one last look at her notes.

From what had emerged from police interviews, it was clear that Karl Lundström was an extremely complex individual. In the transcripts he talked about how he and the other members of the suspected paedophile ring behaved. He spoke of a physical attraction to children that was seldom noticed by other people, but which paedophiles instinctively recognised in one another. Sometimes, in the right circumstances, they could identify one another's inclinations simply by their body language or the way they looked around them.

On the surface, at least, he matched well with Sofia's previous experiences of a certain sort of man with paedophile or ephebophile personality disorders.

Their main weapon was the ability to control, manipulate and build up trust and implant guilt and subordination in their victims. In the end there was often a form of mutual dependency between victims and perpetrators.

Their interest in children wasn't the only thing they had in common. They also shared the same view of women. Their wives were under their control. They knew what was going on, but never intervened.

'Well, we may as well get this out of the way. You're here to evaluate whether or not I can be held responsible for my actions. What do you want to know?'

Sofia looked at the man seated in front of her.

Karl Lundström had thin, fair hair that was starting to go grey. His eyes were tired and slightly swollen, and she thought they expressed a sort of mournful solemnity.

'I'd like us to talk about your relationship with your daughter,' she said. It was just as well to get straight to the point.

He ran his hand through his stubble.

'I love Linnea, but she doesn't love me. I have abused her, and I'm admitting that to make things easier for all of us. For my family, I mean. I love my family.'

His voice sounded weary and disengaged, and his apathetic tone made what he said sound false.

He had been arrested after a lengthy period of surveillance, and the child pornography found on his computer included several images and video clips of his daughter. What option did he have but to confess?

'In what way do you think it will make things easier for them?'

'They need protection. From me and from others.'

His claim was so peculiar that she felt it demanded a follow-up question.

'Protection from others? Who do you mean?'

'The sort of people only I can protect them from.'

He made a sweeping gesture with his arm, and she could smell his body odour. He probably hadn't washed for several days.

'If I tell the police what this is all about, Annette and Linnea can have their personal details made confidential. Because they know too much. There are dangerous people out there. A human life is nothing to them. Believe me, I know. God has nothing to do with these people, they aren't His children.'

She realised that Karl Lundström was referring to the players in the child sex trade. In interviews with the police he had explicitly claimed that Organizatsiya, the Russian mafia, had threatened him repeatedly, and that he feared for his family's lives. Sofia had spoken to Lars Mikkelsen, who thought Karl Lundström was lying. The Russian mafia didn't work the way he had described, and his claims were full of contradictions. Besides, he hadn't been able to provide the police with a single concrete piece of evidence suggesting any threat.

Mikkelsen had said he thought Karl Lundström wanted his family's identities protected for the simple reason of saving them from any shame.

Sofia suspected that Karl Lundström might be trying to construct something that could be seen as extenuating circumstances for himself. Taking on some sort of heroic role, in marked contrast to what had actually happened.

'Do you regret what you've done?' Sooner or later she had to ask.

He looked oddly distant.

'Do I regret it?' he said after a moment's silence. 'It's complicated . . . Sorry, what was your name? Sofia?'

'Sofia Zetterlund.'

'Of course. Sofia means wisdom. A good name for a psychologist . . . Sorry. OK, well . . .' He took a deep breath. 'We . . . I mean, me and the others, we were free to swap wives and children with each other. And I think this happened with Annette's tacit consent. And the other wives' as well . . . In the same way that we men instinctively found each other, we were also careful in our choice of wives. We met in the home of shadows, if you get what I mean?'

The home of shadows? Sofia thought. She recognised the phrase from the preliminary report.

'Annette's brain is switched off, somehow,' he went on without waiting for her to reply. 'She isn't stupid, but she chooses not to see things she doesn't like. It's her self-defence mechanism.'

Sofia knew this phenomenon wasn't unusual. There was often a degree of passivity in those close to the events that allowed this sort of abuse to continue.

But Karl Lundström's answer was evasive. She had asked if he regretted what he had done.

'Did you never realise that what you were doing was wrong?' she tried instead.

'You'll have to define the word "wrong" if I'm going to understand what you mean. Culturally wrong, socially wrong or wrong in some other way?'

'Karl, try to tell me about what's wrong in your own way rather than anyone else's.'

'I've never claimed to have done anything wrong. I've merely acted from an impulse that all men actually have, but suppress.'

Sofia realised that the defence speech had begun.

'Don't you read books?' he went on. 'There's a clear line from antiquity to today. Read Archilochus . . . "A spray of myrtle she bore joyfully in her hand, and glorious roses in her hair, my shadow fell upon her shoulders, and the virgin's body awoke the flame of love in old men . . ." The Greeks wrote about it. Alcman's lyric poetry praises the sensuality of children. "Childless the lonely man lives his life and misses them bitterly. And devoured by his longing he goes to the home of shadows . . ." In the twentieth century Nabokov and Pasolini wrote the same things, to mention just two. Although Pasolini wrote about boys.'

Sofia recognised further phrases from his interviews with the police.

'What did you mean when you said that you met in the home of shadows?' she asked.

He smiled at her.

'It's just an image. A metaphor for a secret, forbidden place. There's plenty of poetry, psychology, ethnology and philosophy to console yourself with if you want to feel understood. I'm not alone, of course, but it feels as though I'm alone in my time. Why is what I desire wrong now?'

Sofia could tell that this was a question he had been wrestling with for a long time. She knew that paedophile desires couldn't really be cured. It was more a matter of getting the paedophile to recognise that their perversion was unacceptable and that it harmed others. But she didn't interrupt, she wanted to hear more about his reasoning.

'It isn't fundamentally wrong, it isn't wrong for me, and I don't actually think it's wrong for Linnea either. It's a constructed social or cultural wrong. Ergo, it isn't wrong in the true sense of the word. The same thoughts and feelings were current two thousand years ago, but what was culturally right then has become culturally wrong. We've simply been taught that it's wrong.'

Sofia thought his reasoning was provocatively irrational.

'So according to you, it isn't possible to re-evaluate an old assumption?'

He looked confident.

'No. Not if it goes against nature.'

Karl Lundström folded his arms and suddenly looked hostile. 'God is nature . . .' he muttered.

Sofia sat in silence and waited for him to go on, but when nothing came she decided to shift the focus of the conversation.

Back to shame.

'You say there are people you want to protect your family from. I've read your interviews with the police, where you say you were threatened by the Russian mafia.'

He nodded.

'Are there any other reasons why you want Annette's and Linnea's identities to be kept confidential?'

'No,' came the short answer.

She wasn't convinced by his self-assured attitude. On the contrary, his unwillingness to discuss the matter indicated doubt. There was shame in this man, even if it was buried deep within him.

He leaned forward over the desk. The intensity in his eyes had returned, and she backed away when she caught his odour.

It wasn't just sweat. His breath smelled of acetone.

'I'm going to tell you something,' he went on. 'Something I haven't told the police . . .'

His mood swings were starting to concern Sofia. The stench of acetone could be a sign of a lack of calories and nutrition, an indication that he wasn't eating. Was he on any medication?

'There are men, perfectly ordinary men around us, maybe one of your colleagues, a relative, I don't know. I've never bought a child, but these men have . . .'

His pupils seemed normal, but her experience of psychoactive medication told her something was wrong.

'What do you mean?'

He leaned back and seemed to relax slightly.

'The police have found things that are compromising on my computer, but if they want to find the real stuff, they ought to be looking in a cottage up in Ånge. There's a man called Anders Wikström. The police ought to take a look in his cellar.'

Lundström's eyes were darting about, and Sofia doubted the truth of what he was saying.

'Anders Wikström bought children from a man from Organizatsiya. The third brigade or whatever they call it. Solntsevskaya Bratva. There are two videotapes in a cupboard. On the first one there's a four-year-old boy and the man is a paediatrician from the south of Sweden. You never see his face in the film, but he's got a birthmark on his thigh, like a clover leaf. On the second film there's a seven-year-old girl with Anders, two other men and a Thai woman. From last summer. It's the worst of the films.'

Karl Lundström was breathing shallowly through his nose, and his Adam's apple was bobbing up and down as he spoke. Sofia felt physical disgust looking at him. She wasn't sure she wanted to hear more, and she realised she was having difficulty maintaining an objective attitude to what he was saying.

But no matter how she looked at it, it was her duty to listen and try to understand him.

'Last summer?'

'Yes . . . Anders Wikström and the fat man in the film. The others who were there didn't want to say what their names were, and you can see the Thai woman doesn't really want to be there. She was drinking a lot, and on one occasion when she didn't do as Anders said, he hit her.'

Sofia didn't know what to think.

'I understand that you've seen the films,' she tried. 'But how do you know all the details about the recording?'

'I was there when they were filmed,' he said.

Sofia knew she'd have to tell the police what he had just told her.

'Had you had other experiences of this sort of abuse?'

Karl Lundström looked sad. 'I'll tell you how it works,' he said. 'Right now something like five hundred thousand people are hooked up on the Net swapping pictures and films of child pornography with each other. To take part you have to produce your own material. It isn't hard if you've got the right contacts. Then you can even order children online. For a hundred and fifty thousand you can have a Latin American boy. Officially he doesn't exist, you own him. It goes without saying that you can do what you like with him, and the way it usually ends is that he disappears. You have to pay for that as well if you can't handle killing him yourself. That often costs more than the hundred and fifty thousand, and you don't haggle with people like that.'

None of this was new to Sofia. It was in the interview transcripts. Yet she still felt nausea rising. As a pressure in her stomach, a dryness in her throat.

'Are you saying that you yourself have actually *bought* a child?'

Karl Lundström smiled distantly. 'No. But, like I said, I know people who have. Anders Wikström bought the children who were in the films I told you about.'

Sofia swallowed. Her throat was burning and her hands were trembling.

'How did it feel to witness all that?'

He smiled again. 'I got excited. What do you think?'

'Did you participate?'

He let out a laugh. 'No, I just watched . . . As God is my witness.'

Sofia looked at him. His mouth was still smiling, but his eyes looked mournful and empty.

'You often mention God. Would you like to tell me more about your faith?'

He shrugged his shoulders and raised his eyebrows quizzically.

'My faith?'

'Yes.'

Another sigh. He sounded resigned when he went on. 'I believe in a divine truth. A God who exists beyond our understanding. A God who was close to man at the beginning of time, but whose voice within us has faded away over the centuries. The more God has been institutionalised by human inventions like churches and the priesthood, the less remains of what was there at the start.'

'And what was there at the start?'

'Gnosis. Purity and wisdom. I used to think that God existed in Linnea when she was little, and . . . I thought I'd found Him. I don't know, I was probably wrong. A child today is less pure at birth. It's already been contaminated in the womb by the noise of the world outside. A stupid chatter of human lies and petty distractions, meaningless words and thoughts about material concerns . . .'

They sat in silence for a moment as Sofia reflected on what he had said.

She wondered if Karl Lundström's religious thoughts might somehow explain why he had abused his daughter, and felt that she was going to have to approach the core of what the conversation was about.

'When did you first subject Linnea to sexual abuse?'

His answer came without reflection.

'When? Well . . . she was three. I ought to have waited another year or so, but it was just too . . . It just happened, I suppose.'

'Tell me how you felt that first time. And tell me how you look back on that occasion now.'

'Well . . . I don't know. It's difficult.' Lundström squirmed in his chair and made several attempts to start talking. 'It was . . . well, like I said, it just happened,' he eventually said. 'It wasn't actually a good occasion because we were living in a house in Kristianstad at the time. In the centre of town, everyone could see what went on there.'

He paused and seemed to think.

'I was giving her a wash out in the garden. She had a paddling pool and I asked her if I could get in as well, and she said yes. The water was a bit cold, so I fixed up the hose to add some hot water. It had one of those old, rounded metal spouts on the end. It had been in the sun all day and was nice and warm to the touch. Then she said it looked like a willy . . .'

He looked embarrassed. Sofia nodded to him to go on.

'Then I realised that she was thinking of mine. Well, I don't know . . .'

'And how did you feel?'

'I, I just felt sort of giddy . . . I had the taste of iron in my mouth, a bit like blood. Maybe it comes from the heart? That's where all the blood comes from.' He fell silent.

'So you stuck the end of the hose inside her, and you don't think you did anything wrong?' Sofia was feeling sick, and was having difficulty suppressing her revulsion.

Karl Lundström looked weary, and didn't answer.

She decided to go on. 'You said before that you thought you'd found God in Linnea. Did that have anything to do with what happened in Kristianstad? With your ideas about right and wrong?'

He shook his head slowly. 'You don't understand . . .'

Then he looked Sofia straight in the eye and carefully explained his reasoning.

'Our society is based on a moral construct . . . Why isn't mankind perfect if it's a reflection of God?'

He thrust his arm out and answered his own question.

'Because God isn't the one who wrote the Bible, people did . . . The true God is beyond feelings about right and wrong, beyond the Bible . . .'

Sofia realised that he was likely to carry on a circular argument on the issue of right and wrong.

Perhaps she'd asked the wrong question to start with?

'The Old Testament God is unpredictable and jealous because He's basically a human being. There's an original truth about the nature of humanity that the Bible's God knows nothing about.'

She saw that their time was almost up, and let him go on.

'Gnosis. Truth and wisdom. You ought to know that, if you're called Sofia. It's Greek, it means wisdom. In Gnosticism, Sofia is the female emanation who is responsible for the Fall.'

Once Lundström had been collected and driven back to the cells, Sofia remained seated, deep in thought. She couldn't stop thinking about Lundström's daughter, Linnea. Only just into her teens, but already so badly damaged that it would affect her for the rest of her life. What would happen to her? Would Linnea herself, like Tyra Mäkelä, become an abuser? How much can a human being withstand before they break and turn into a monster?

Sofia leafed through her papers, trying to find any facts about the daughter. All that was there were scant details of the girl's schooling. She was in her first year at boarding school in Sigtuna. Good grades. And very good at sports. School champion at 800 metres.

A girl who can outrun most people, Sofia thought.

Town of Sigtuna, 1984

The old man could have been anyone, she's never seen him before. Yet he evidently thinks it's OK to comment on how she's dressed. As for her, Crow Girl thinks his pea coat looks all right, so it's perfectly justifiable to spit in his face instead.

On the western hill in Sigtuna stand the ten student blocks that belong to the boarding school. The school, whose previous pupils have included King Karl XVI Gustaf, Olof Palme and the Wallenberg cousins, Peter and Marcus, positively drips tradition.

The grand yellow main building is impregnable against scandal for the same reason.

The first thing Victoria Bergman will have to learn is that everything that happens here stays here, but she's already very familiar with that particular rule. She's lived the whole of her childhood in a bubble of mute terror. That's her clearest memory, much clearer than any individual recollection.

Compared to that, the closed ranks at Sigtuna are nothing.

As soon as she steps out of the car she feels a liberation that she hasn't felt since she was on her own in Dala-Floda. Immediately she feels she can breathe. She knows she'll be able to stop listening for footsteps outside the bedroom door.

At reception she is introduced to the two girls with whom she'll be sharing a room for the coming term.

Their names are Hannah and Jessica. They're from the Stockholm region as well, and she gets the impression that they're quiet and orderly, not to say boring. They're keen to tell her that their parents have senior positions in the Stockholm court system, and suggest that it's already been decided that they will follow in their parents' footsteps and train as lawyers.

Victoria looks into their naive blue eyes and realises that they could never be a threat to her.

They're too weak.

She sees them as two passive dolls who always let other people think and plan things for them. They're like shadows of people. Scarcely interested in anything. It's almost impossible to pin them down at all.

During the first week Victoria realises that some of the girls in the top year are planning something. She picks up amused glances across the dinner tables, exaggerated politeness, and a constant tendency to want to be near her and the other new pupils. All of this makes her suspicious.

Justifiably so, as it turns out.

From careful observation of their glances and movements, Victoria soon works out who the group's informal leader is. Her name is Fredrika Grünewald, a tall, dark-haired girl. Victoria thinks that Fredrika's long face combined with her large front teeth make her look like a horse.

During one lunch break Victoria makes her move.

She sees Fredrika go into the toilets and discreetly follows her in.

'I know all about the initiation,' she lies right in the face of a surprised Fredrika. 'There's no way I'm going to agree to it.' She folds her arms over her chest and tilts her head nonchalantly. 'Not without a fight, that is.'

Fredrika is clearly impressed by Victoria's cockiness and self-assured style. They each smoke a sneaky cigarette during the ensuing conspiratorial conversation, as Victoria presents a plan that she says will raise the bar for all forthcoming initiation rites.

There's no question that it will cause a scandal, and Fredrika Grünewald is particularly taken by Victoria's dramatic vision of what the evening papers would say: SCANDAL AT KING'S SCHOOL! YOUNG GIRLS HUMILIATED IN RITUAL.

During the following week she gets a bit closer to her room-mates, Hannah and Jessica. She lures them into revealing their secrets, and in a short space of time manages to make them her friends.

'Take a look at this,' she says.

Hannah and Jessica stare wide-eyed at the three bottles of Aurora wine that Victoria has managed to smuggle in with her.

'Who'd like to share some?'

Hannah and Jessica both laugh uncertainly and exchange anxious glances with each other before eagerly nodding their assent.

Victoria serves the girls large glasses, convinced that they haven't got a clue what their tolerance levels are.

They drink quickly and curiously, talking loudly.

The initial giggling is soon replaced by slurring and tiredness. By two o'clock the bottles are empty. Hannah has already fallen asleep on the floor, and, with a great deal of effort, Jessica manages to get to her bed, where she promptly loses consciousness.

Victoria has drunk just a couple of sips, and goes to bed tingling with anticipation.

She lies there awake, waiting.

As agreed, the older girls show up at four o'clock in the morning. Hannah and Jessica wake up as they are being carried through the corridor, down the stairs and across the yard towards the tool shed next to the caretaker's house, but are so drowsy they can't put up any resistance.

Inside the shed the girls get changed and put on pink capes and pig masks. They've made the masks themselves out of plastic cups and pink cloth that they've cut eyeholes in. They've drawn on grinning mouths with a black marker, and the nostrils in the snout are marked by two big black dots.

The cups are full of shredded aluminium foil, and they fasten the masks around their heads with rubber bands. Once they've changed, one of the girls produces a video camera, and another one begins to speak. The sound that emerges from her jutting snout is more like a rustling, metallic hiss than real words.

Victoria sees one of the older girls leave the shed.

'Tie them up,' another one hisses.

The masked girls throw themselves on Hannah, Jessica and Victoria, putting each of them on a chair, tying their arms behind them and blindfolding them.

Victoria leans back contentedly, and hears the girl who left the shed return.

Victoria is taken aback by the smell of what the girl brings in with her.

Later that morning Victoria is trying to scrub the smell from her skin, but it seems to be ingrained.

It had been worse than she could have imagined.

At dawn she picks the lock to Fredrika's room and when the girl wakes up Victoria is sitting astride her.

'Give me the tape,' she hisses quietly so as not to wake Fredrika's room-mates, while Fredrika tries to defend herself.

Victoria has a firm grip on her hands.

'No way,' Fredrika says, but Victoria can hear how frightened she is.

'You seem to be forgetting that I know who you are. I'm the only person who knows who was behind those masks. Do you really want Daddy to know what you did to us?'

Fredrika realises that she has no choice.

Victoria goes upstairs to the media room and makes two copies of the tape. She's going to drop one of them in the postbox at the bus station, addressed to herself out in Värmdö. She's planning to keep the other copy in reserve to send to the papers in case they ever try anything with her again.

Svartsjölandet – Crime Scene

For the second time in two weeks, Jeanette Kihlberg was having to investigate the murder of a young boy.

Hurtig had called that morning, and she had driven straight out to Svartsjölandet to lead the investigation. The body had been found by an elderly couple who were out exercising.

Unlike the boy at Thorildsplan, this time they had a good idea of the boy's identity. His name was Yuri Krylov, a Belarussian boy who had been reported missing in early March when he disappeared from an immigration centre outside Upplands Väsby. According to the migration board he had no relatives, either in Sweden or back home.

Jeanette walked down to the jetty where the boy's body lay. The stench caught in her nose. After a long period in the water, his body fat had transformed into a rancid, stinking, almost putty-like consistency. She knew the body had been attacked by flies after just a few hours in the water, and there were yellowish-red beads around the corners of his eyes, nose and mouth. Fly eggs that had hatched into larvae after a few days, so-called corpse maggots. The skin of the boy's hands and feet had absorbed so much water that it had come loose and looked like gloves and socks.

'Damn it' was all she managed to say, before leaving the jetty and walking over to Ivo Andrić.

'Can you tell me what you've got so far?' she asked, even though she knew that he wouldn't be able to give her all the relevant information until after the post-mortem examination.

The prosecutor, von Kwist, had that morning consented to a detailed forensic post-mortem in the Yuri Krylov case, the most elaborate type of post-mortem conducted in Sweden, reserved for the most serious crimes.

Ivo Andrić scratched his head. 'Bodies left lying in water assume a characteristic pose, with their head, arms and legs hanging down and their back raised. That means that the head decays most rapidly, because of the amount of blood that gathers there.'

Jeanette nodded.

'And when I pressed the ribcage, I discovered that there wasn't enough water in the lungs to indicate that he'd drowned, which –'

'– means he was already dead when he was put into the water,' Jeanette concluded.

Ivo Andrić smiled. 'And it isn't unusual for bodies that have decayed in water to show signs of attack from fish. As you must have noticed, that's what's happened in this instance. The boy's eyes have been partially eaten. And his face has large haematomas around the edges of the jaw and chin.'

'What about the genitals?'

'This boy's genitals have also been removed.'

Ivo Andrić went on to explain that this had been done with the same precision as before. And, once again, the body showed evidence of extreme violence. There was extensive subcutaneous bleeding on the back that suggested that this boy, too, had been whipped.

'It wouldn't surprise me if the body also contains high quantities of Xylocain adrenalin,' the medical officer concluded. Jeanette hoped the forensic chemistry lab would be able to analyse the samples quickly.

She realised that they were probably dealing with the same perpetrator, and so were investigating a double murder.

How many more boys would die before this was over?

The only significant evidence they had found were two shoe prints, one large and one much smaller, almost a child's, and some tyre tracks from a vehicle of some sort. Forensics had taken casts, but these would only be useful when they had something to compare them with.

Some hundred metres from the place where the body had been found, Åhlund had noted that the same vehicle had scraped a tree, so if it was the perpetrator's car, the car was blue.

Someone out there was abducting children no one would miss, then abusing them so severely that they died. Even though there had been a lot of coverage in the press, and they had asked the public for help identifying the boy from Thorildsplan, the tip-off lines had remained silent.

But an item on TV3's *Crimewatch* programme had led to a considerable number of disturbed individuals claiming responsibility for the crime. Often that sort of coverage could assist a case that had ground to a halt, but on this occasion it had only wasted valuable time. All of the callers were men who, were it not for various political decisions, ought to have been in psychiatric institutions and receiving professional help. But instead they were wandering the streets of Stockholm, suppressing their demons with drink and drugs.

Welfare state – yeah, right! she thought.

Kronoberg – Police Headquarters

'Forget Furugård!' was all von Kwist said on the phone.

'What? What do you mean?' Jeanette Kihlberg got up and went over to the window. 'But the guy's extremely . . . I don't understand this at all.'

'Furugård has an alibi and has nothing to do with this. I told you we should steer clear of him. It was a serious mistake on my part to listen to you.'

Jeanette could hear how upset the prosecutor was, and could see his bright red face before her.

'Furugård's in the clear,' he went on. 'He has an alibi.'

'Really? So what is it?'

Von Kwist said nothing for a moment, then went on.

'What I'm about to tell you is confidential and must stay between you and me. I am merely conveying a fact. Is that understood?'

'Yes. Of course.'

'The Swedish international force in Sudan, that's all I can say.'

'And?'

'Furugård was recruited in Afghanistan, and has been stationed in Sudan all spring. He's innocent.'

Jeanette didn't know what to say.

'Sudan?' was all she managed to get out. She felt utterly impotent.

Back to square one. No suspect for the murders, and only one victim identified.

How and why Yuri Krylov, the boy out in Svartsjölandet, had come to Sweden was anyone's guess. The Belarussian embassy on Lidingö hadn't been particularly helpful.

The mummified boy in the bushes next to the Thorildsplan metro station was still unidentified, and Jeanette had contacted Europol in The Hague in the hope of getting some help. But it wouldn't do any good. Europe was crawling with illegal refugee children who had no contact with any authorities. There were children coming and going everywhere without anyone ever knowing where they'd disappeared to. And even if they did know, no one did anything.

After all, they were only children.

Ivo Andrić out in Solna had told her that it looked likely that Yuri Krylov had been castrated while he was alive.

She wondered what she could deduce from that. From experience, the extreme brutality, the torture, suggested that the perpetrator was male.

But there was also something almost ritualistic about it all, so the possibility that it had been carried out by more than one person couldn't be dismissed. Could they be dealing with human traffickers?

Right now she had to concentrate on the likeliest explanation. A lone, violent male who was probably already in their database. The difficulty with working from that presumption was that there were so many men like that.

She stared at the heaps of files on her desk.

Thousands of pages, covering about a hundred potential perpetrators.

Three hours later she found something interesting. She stood up, went out into the corridor, and knocked on the door of Jens Hurtig's room.

'Have you got a moment?'

He turned towards her, and she smiled at his quizzical expression.

'Follow me,' she said.

They sat down on either side of her desk, and Jeanette handed Hurtig a file.

He opened it, then looked up in surprise.

'Karl Lundström? But he's the one we raided. The one with a computer full of child porn. What about him?'

'Let me explain. Karl Lundström has been questioned by National Crime, and in the transcript you've got there Lundström goes into detail about how to go about buying a child.'

He looked interested. 'Buying a child?'

'Yes. And Lundström seems to have detailed knowledge. He mentions precise figures, but claims he's never had any direct involvement, although he knows people who have.'

Hurtig leaned back and took a deep breath.

'Damn, this could be interesting. Any names?'

'No. But Lundström's file isn't complete yet. In parallel with the police interviews he's been undergoing an evaluation by forensic psychiatry. Perhaps the psychologists who've been talking to him can tell us a bit more.'

Hurtig leafed through the file. 'Anything else?'

'Yes, a few more things. Karl Lundström advocates castration of paedophiles and rapists. But reading between the lines you can tell he doesn't think that's enough. All men ought to be castrated.'

Hurtig looked up at the ceiling. 'Isn't that a bit far-fetched? I mean, we're talking about little boys in these cases.'

'Maybe, but there are a couple more things that tell me we should still check him out,' Jeanette went on. 'There's a case that was dropped, into the abduction, sexual abuse and rape of a child. Seven years ago. The girl who reported him was fourteen at the time, name Ulrika Wendin. Guess who dropped the case.'

He grinned. 'Prosecutor Kenneth von Kwist, I presume?'

Jeanette nodded.

'Ulrika Wendin is listed at an address in Hammarbyhöjden, and I suggest we get out there as soon as we can.'

'OK . . . what else?'

He looked at her inquisitively, and she couldn't help pausing before she answered.

'Karl Lundström's wife is a dentist.'

He looked uncomprehending.

'A dentist?'

'Yes. Lundström's wife is a dentist, meaning that he could have had access to medication. We know that at least one of our victims was given an anaesthetic used by dentists. Xylocain adrenalin. Two plus two. I wouldn't be surprised if the test results show that Krylov's blood contains traces of it as well. In other words, it's not out of the question that all this is connected.'

Hurtig put the file down and stood up.

'OK, you've convinced me. Lundström sounds worth investigating.'

'I'll call Billing,' Jeanette said. 'Let's hope he can persuade the prosecutor to arrange an interview.'

Hurtig paused in the doorway and turned back.

'Is it absolutely necessary to involve von Kwist, when it's just a first, exploratory interview?'

'I'm afraid so,' Jeanette said. 'Seeing as Lundström's already facing one charge, we have to inform von Kwist at least.'

Hurtig sighed and walked away.

She called Commissioner Dennis Billing, and to her surprise he was unusually helpful and promised to do what he could to persuade the prosecutor. Then she called the lead interviewer at National Crime, Lars Mikkelsen.

She explained why she was calling, but when she mentioned the name Karl Lundström he laughed.

'I don't think so,' Mikkelsen said, clearing his throat. 'He's no murderer. I've dealt with a lot of murderers over the years, and I recognise them. This man is sick. But he's not a murderer.'

'That's possible,' Jeanette said. 'But I'm interested in finding out more about his contact with child trafficking.'

'Lundström is making out that he knows a lot about how it all works, but I'm not sure you'd get much out of him. That's an international business, I doubt you'd get much help even if you turned to Interpol. Believe me, I've worked with this crap for twenty years, and we're constantly trying.'

'How can you be so sure that Lundström isn't a killer?' she asked.

He cleared his throat again. 'Well, anything's possible, I suppose, but you'd understand if you met him. You should probably talk to the forensic psychologist instead. A woman called Sofia Zetterlund has been brought in to offer an expert opinion. But the investigation's hardly got going yet, so you might want to wait a few days before heading out to Huddinge.'

They ended the call.

Jeanette had nothing to lose, and maybe the psychologist would be able to give her something, even if it was just a small detail. That sort of thing had happened before. The way things looked, she had every reason to call this Sofia Zetterlund.

But it was long past office hours, and Jeanette decided to hold off making the phone call. Right now she just wanted to go home.

Gamla Enskede – Kihlberg House

She called Åke from the car to see if there was any food in the house, but they'd had pizza and the fridge was bare, so she stopped at the Statoil garage near the Globe and ate a couple of hot dogs.

The air inside the car was warm and she wound down the window and let the fresh breeze caress her face. As she parked the car in front of the house and walked through the garden she could smell freshly cut grass, and when she went round the corner she caught sight of Åke sitting on the terrace with a beer. He was sweaty and dirty from working in the rocky, steep garden. She went up to him and kissed his stubbly cheek.

'Hello, handsome,' she said out of habit. 'You've made it look great. It needed it! I've seen the way they were sneering over the fence.' She nodded towards the neighbours' house and pretended to throw up. Åke laughed and nodded.

'Where's Johan?'

'He's over at the football pitch with some friends.'

He looked at her with a smile and tilted his head.

'You're beautiful, even if you do look tired.' He grabbed her around the waist and pulled her down into his lap. She ran her hand over his cropped hair, pulled free and got up, and went towards the terrace door into the kitchen.

'Is there any wine in the house? I could really use a glass right now.'

'There's an unopened box on the worktop, and there are some slices of pizza in the fridge. But seeing as we're on our own for an hour or so, maybe we should go in for a bit?'

They hadn't made love for several weeks, and she knew he took care of himself in the bathroom, but she felt far too tired. She turned and saw he was coming after her.

'OK,' she said, without any enthusiasm.

She heard how it sounded, but didn't have the energy to pretend otherwise.

'Forget it, then, if that's how you feel.'

She turned round and saw that he'd gone back to his chair and opened another beer.

'Sorry,' she said. 'But I'm completely exhausted, all I want to do is change into something more comfortable and relax for a bit until Johan comes home. Can't we do it before we go to sleep?'

He looked away and muttered, 'Sure.'

She drew a deep sigh, overwhelmed by a sense of inadequacy.

She strode purposefully back out to Åke and stood in front of him, legs spread.

'No, that's not good enough! I want you to shut up and come inside and give me a good seeing-to! No fucking about with foreplay!' She took his hand and pulled him up from his chair. 'The kitchen floor will do just fine!'

'God, you're so damn provocative all the time!' Åke pulled free of her grip and walked off towards the corner of the house. 'I'm going to fetch Johan on the bike.'

All these men, she thought, all thinking they had the right to make demands and try to make her feel guilty. Her bosses, Åke and all the bastards she spent her days trying to catch.

All of them men who had some sort of influence over her life, and without whom life would often be a hell of a lot simpler.

Huddinge Hospital

Once Karl Lundström had left the room Sofia felt exhausted. Although he denied it, she could see he was consumed with shame. It was there in his eyes when he talked about the episode in Kristianstad, and was lurking behind his religious reflections and his stories about the child sex trade.

In the last of these, it was mainly about suppressing it.

The guilt and shame weren't his, they belonged to all of humanity, or possibly the Russian mafia.

Were the stories unconscious inventions?

Sofia decided to share with Lars Mikkelsen the information that had emerged from the conversation, even if she doubted that the police would find an Anders Wikström in Norrland, let alone any videotapes in a cupboard under the stairs in his cellar.

She dialled police headquarters, got put through to Mikkelsen, and gave him a short summary of what Karl Lundström had told her.

She ended the phone call with a rhetorical question.

'Is it really so impossible not to administer anxiety-suppressing medication in one of the largest hospitals in Sweden?'

'Lundström was drowsy?'

'Yes, and if I'm going to be able to do my job in the future, I really would prefer that the person I'm talking to has had a bath.'

As Sofia left Ward 112 of Huddinge Hospital she reflected on her attitude to her work.

What sort of clients did she really want to work with? How and where did she do the most good? And how much should it cost her in terms of poor sleep and an unsettled stomach?

She wanted to work with clients like Samuel Bai and Victoria Bergman, but there she had shown that she wasn't up to the job.

In Victoria Bergman's case she had simply become far too involved and had lost her judgement.

Otherwise?

She walked into the car park, pulled out her keys and took a quick look at the hospital complex.

On the one hand there was her work out here, with men like Karl Lundström. She wasn't able to make decisions unilaterally. She gave recommendations to investigations. At best, her conclusions were adopted and passed on to the court.

It felt to her like a game of Chinese whispers.

She whispered her opinion into someone else's ear, the whisper was passed on to the next person, and the next, and eventually reached a judge who made a final decision that was usually completely different, and quite possibly influenced by some important adviser.

She unlocked the car door and sank into the seat.

On the other hand there was her work at the practice, with clients like Carolina Glanz, where she was paid by the hour.

The client pays for an agreed period of time, and uses the therapist, who gets paid to allow themselves to be used by the client.

A rather sad way of looking at things, she thought as she pulled out of the car park.

I'm like a prostitute.

Klara Sjö – Public Prosecution Authority

Prosecutor Kenneth von Kwist's office was a restrained and very male room, with black leather seats, a large desk, and plenty of naturalistic art.

His stomach ached, but in spite of that he poured himself a stiff whisky and offered the bottle to the lawyer Viggo Dürer, who shook his head.

Von Kwist raised his glass, took a cautious sip and enjoyed the powerfully smoky aroma.

The meeting with Viggo Dürer hadn't yet changed anything, for either better or worse. Although Dürer had admitted that he was more than superficially acquainted with the Lundström family.

'Viggo . . .' Prosecutor Kenneth von Kwist said, letting out a long breath. 'We've known each other a long time, and I've always stood up for you, just like you've always been there when I've needed your help.'

Viggo Dürer nodded. 'That's true enough.'

'But right now I don't know if I can help you. The fact is, I don't even know if I want to.'

'What are you saying?' Viggo Dürer looked at him uncomprehendingly.

'Karl landed himself in hot water when he confessed to abusing Linnea.'

'Yes, that was a terrible business.' Viggo Dürer shuddered and attempted a not wholly successful look of distaste. 'But what does that have to do with me?'

'Linnea has confirmed what he said.'

Viggo Dürer looked surprised. 'But I thought Annette . . .' He fell silent, and Kenneth von Kwist was struck by the fact that he had stopped himself.

'Annette, what?'

His eyes flitted about. 'Well, that she'd put it behind her.'

There was something in Viggo Dürer's attitude that strengthened Kenneth von Kwist's suspicion that the girl had been right.

'Linnea is also suggesting that you were involved in Karl's . . . how should I put this . . . activities.'

Viggo Dürer went white as a ghost and put a hand to his chest. 'Damn it.'

'What is it – are you all right?'

The lawyer groaned and took several deep breaths before raising one hand. 'I'm OK,' he eventually said. 'But what you're saying sounds extremely troubling.'

'I know. So you have to be pragmatic. If you understand my meaning?'

Mariatorget – Sofia Zetterlund's Office

When Sofia got back to the office she felt completely empty. She had an hour before her next client, a middle-aged woman she'd seen twice before, whose main problem was that she had problems.

A conversation that would be devoted to understanding a problem that wasn't a problem to start with, but which became a problem because it turned into one, more or less unnoticed, during the course of the conversation.

After that she would be seeing Samuel Bai.

Real people's problems, she thought.

One hour.

Victoria Bergman.

She put her headphones on.

Victoria's voice sounded amused.

It was so easy you almost couldn't help laughing at their serious expressions when I bought a toffee for ten öre and had my jacket full of goodies that I could sell to everyone competing to see who dared touch me on the breast or between the legs, and then laugh when I got cross and squirted glue in the lock so they were late and the old guy with the beard hit me over the head with the book so hard my teeth shook, and forced me to spit out the chewing gum that had already lost its taste anyway, and later on I stuck a fly to it . . .

Sofia was amazed at how the voice changed with the different associations. It was as if the memories belonged to different people who were competing for control of a medium. Mid-sentence, Victoria's voice took on a melancholy strain.

. . . and of course I had more chewing gum in reserve, and could sneak another piece in while he was sitting and reading and checking to see if I was cheating using the answers on my hand, but they got smeared with sweat and I only got the spelling wrong because I was nervous and not because I was stupid like the other poor bastards who could do endless tricks with a ball but knew nothing about capital cities or wars but who ought to know because it was people like them who started wars the whole time and never realised when enough was enough, but kept on picking on anyone who stood out, whose trousers were the wrong label, or who had an ugly haircut or was too fat . . .

The voice got sharper. Sofia recalled that Victoria had been angry.

. . . like that big fat girl who always rode around on her tricycle, and whose face looked odd, she was always drooling, and once they told her to take her clothes off, but she didn't understand until they started pulling her pants off. They had always thought she was just a big baby, so they got a surprise when they saw she was all grown up down there, and you would end up getting beaten up just because you didn't cry when they thumped you in the stomach and you just laughed and carried on without telling anyone or complaining, and were just tough and focused . . .

Then the voice fell silent. Sofia could hear the sound of her own breathing. Why hadn't she asked Victoria to continue?

She pressed fast-forward. Almost three minutes of silence. Four, five, six minutes. Why had she recorded this? All she could hear was breathing and the sound of paper rustling.

After seven minutes Sofia heard the sound of her pen clicking. Then Victoria broke the silence.

I never hit Martin. Never!

Victoria was almost screaming, and Sofia had to turn the volume down.

Never. I don't let people down. I ate a load of shit for them. Dog shit. Fuck, I'm used to shit! Fucking Sigtuna snobs! I ate shit for their sake!

Sofia took off the headphones.

She knew that Victoria got her memories mixed up, and that she often forgot what she'd said just a few minutes before.

But were these gaps ordinary memory lapses?

She felt nervous before her session with Samuel. The conversation mustn't get diverted into a dead end the way it had seemed to when they last met.

She had to get close to him before it was too late, before he slipped out of her hands completely. She knew she was going to need all her wits about her if she was going to be able to cope with the conversation.

As usual, Samuel Bai turned up punctually with a social worker from Hässelby.

'Half past two?'

'I thought we might have a longer chat this time,' Sofia said. 'You can pick him up at three o'clock.'

The social worker disappeared off towards the lift. Sofia looked at Samuel Bai, who let out a whistle. 'Nice meeting you, ma'am,' he said, and fired off a broad smile.

Sofia was relieved when she realised which of Samuel's personalities was standing in front of her.

This was Frankly Samuel, as Sofia had described him in her notes, the polite, extroverted, pleasant Samuel who prefaced every other sentence with 'Frankly, ma'am, I have to tell ya . . .' He always spoke in a kind of homespun English that Sofia found faintly amusing.

Last time Samuel had assumed this personality as soon as the social worker disappeared and they shook hands.

Interesting that he chooses his polite persona when he sees me, she thought as she showed him in.

Frankly Samuel's polite manner made him the most interesting of the various Samuels that Sofia had observed in their meetings so far. The 'normal' Samuel, whom she called Common Samuel, the one that was his dominant personality, was withdrawn, correct and not particularly expressive.

Frankly Samuel was the part of his personality who talked about the terrible things he had done as a child. It was fairly odd to see him smiling constantly and giving Sofia charming compliments on her beautiful eyes and well-formed bust, then going on to explain how he had sat in a dark shack on Lumley Beach outside Freetown, cutting a little girl's ears off. Occasionally he would burst into infectious laughter that she thought reminded her of the football player Zlatan Ibrahimovíc. A deep, cheerful 'ho-ho' that lit up his whole face.

But several times his eyes had flashed, making her wonder if there wasn't another Samuel in there, one who hadn't shown himself yet.

Sofia's aim with the therapy was to collect all the various personalities into one coherent person. But she was also aware that you shouldn't move too fast in cases like this. The client has to be able to deal with the material he or she has to absorb.

With Victoria Bergman everything had happened of its own accord.

Victoria was like a sewage treatment plant in human form, using her droning monologues as a mechanism to filter out the evil.

But with Samuel Bai it was different.

She had to be careful with him, but without being unproductive.

Frankly Samuel exhibited no deep scars when he told her about the terrible things he had experienced. But she was more and more convinced that he was a ticking bomb.

She invited him to have a seat, and Frankly Samuel sat down on the chair in a snake-like movement. This personality was accompanied by an elastic, slippery type of body language.

Sofia looked at him and gave him a cautious smile.

'So . . . how do you do, Samuel?'

He tapped his big silver ring on the edge of the table and looked at her with cheerful eyes. Then he made a movement, as if a wave were passing through him from one shoulder to the other.

'Ma'am, it has never been better . . . And frankly, I must tell ya . . .'

Frankly Samuel liked talking. He showed a genuine interest in Sofia, asked personal questions, and asked her outright for her opinions on various matters. That was good, because it meant she could lead the conversation towards the things she felt were important if there was to be any breakthrough in the treatment.

The session had been going on for about half an hour when Samuel, to Sofia's disappointment, suddenly switched to Common Samuel. What had she done wrong?

They had been talking about segregation, a subject that interested Frankly Samuel, and he had asked where she lived and which metro station was closest for anyone wanting to pay her a visit. When she replied that she lived on Södermalm, and that Skanstull or Medborgarplatsen stations were closest, the open, polite smile faded and he became more reserved.

'Close to Monumental, oh, fuck . . .' he said in broken Swedish.

'Samuel?'

'What d'you want? He spat in my face . . . spiders on arms. Tattoos . . .'

Sofia knew what he was referring to. Hässelby social services had informed her that he had been beaten up in a doorway on Ölandsgatan. By Monumental, he meant the Monument block close to the exit from the Skanstull metro station.

Close to Mikael's flat, she thought.

'See my tattoo: *R* for Revolution, *U* for United, *F* for Front. See!'

He pulled his top down to reveal a tattoo on his chest.

RUF in jagged letters, a symbol whose loaded meaning she was all too aware of.

Was it the memory of the attack that had summoned Common Samuel?

She pondered this for a moment while he sat there in silence staring at the table.

Perhaps Frankly Samuel hadn't been able to bear the humiliation of being beaten up, and had left the whole thing to Common Samuel, who was the one who seemed to handle contact with the police and social services. That could have been why Frankly Samuel disappeared as soon as the Monument block had been mentioned.

That had to be it, she thought. Language is a carrier of psychological symbolism.

All of a sudden she realised how to get Frankly Samuel to come back.

'Will you excuse me a moment, Samuel?'

'What?'

She smiled at him. 'There's something I want to show you. I'll be back in a minute.'

She left the room and went straight into the waiting room belonging to Johansson, the dentist, just to the right of her own office.

Without knocking she walked into the dentist's treatment room. She apologised to the startled Johansson, who was busy rinsing an elderly woman's mouth, and asked if she could borrow the model of an old motorcycle from the bookcase behind him.

'I only need it for an hour. I know you're very fond of it, but I promise to be careful.'

She smiled ingratiatingly at the sixty-year-old dentist. She knew he had a soft spot for her. He was probably a bit lonely, she thought.

'Psychologists, always psychologists . . .' He chuckled beneath his mask. He stood up and took the little metal motorcycle down from the shelf.

It was a red-lacquered model of an old Harley-Davidson. It was very skilfully done; Johansson had said it was made in the States in 1959, using metal and rubber from a real HD.

Perfect, Sofia thought.

Johansson handed her the motorcycle and reminded her of how valuable it was. At least two thousand kronor on one of the online auction sites, and probably more if you sold it to someone in Japan or the US.

It must weigh at least a kilo, she thought as she walked back to her room. She apologised again to Samuel and put the motorcycle down on the windowsill to the left of the table.

'Jeesus, ma'am!' he exclaimed.

She hadn't expected the transformation to be so rapid.

Frankly Samuel's eyes were shining with excitement. He rushed over to the window, and Sofia watched with amusement as he very carefully turned the motorcycle around, all the while letting out small whistles and cries of delight.

'Jeesus, beautiful . . .'

During her previous conversations with Frankly Samuel she had detected a particular passion in him. On several occasions he had mentioned the motorcycle club in Freetown, where he would hang out and admire the long rows of bikes. When he was fourteen temptation got the better of him and he stole a Harley and rode it along the wide beaches outside the city.

Now Samuel sat in the chair with the motorcycle in his arms, patting it as if it were a little dog. His eyes were radiant and his face had cracked into a broad smile.

'Freedom, ma'am. That is freedom . . . Them bikes are for me like momma-boobies are for the little children.'

He began to talk about his interest. Owning a motorcycle didn't just mean freedom to him, it also impressed girls and got him a lot of friends.

'Tell me more about them. Your friends.'

'Which friends? Da cool sick or da cool fresh? Myself prefer da cool freshies! Frankly, I have lots off dem in Freetown . . . start with da cool fresh Collin . . .'

Sofia smiled discreetly and let him talk about Collin and his other friends, each one cooler than the last. She realised after ten, fifteen minutes that he would probably use up the rest of their time telling anecdotes about his friends in impressive detail, sometimes admiring, sometimes boastful.

She knew she had to be on her guard. Frankly Samuel's rolling torrent of words and body language were making her lose her concentration.

She had to try to steer the conversation onto something else.

Then something happened that she had actually considered before, but wasn't expecting at that precise moment.

Another Samuel revealed himself to her.

The living room

was bathed in the flickering light of the television. The Discovery Channel had been on all night, and at half past five in the morning she woke up on the sofa to the narrator's monotonous voice.

'*Pla Kat* is Thai, and means 'plagiarism', but it's also the name of the large, aggressive species of fighting fish bred in Thailand for use in spectacular contests. Two males are set loose in a small aquarium, where their innate territorial instincts lead them to attack each other immediately. The brutal and bloody trial of strength doesn't end until one of the fish is dead.'

She smiled and sat up, then went out into the kitchen to switch on the coffee machine.

While she waited for it to be ready she stood at the kitchen window looking out onto the street.

The park and the leafy trees, the parked cars and the thawed-out people.

Stockholm.

Södermalm.

Home?

No, home was something completely different.

It was a state of being. A feeling that she would never experience. Not ever.

Gradually, piece by piece, an idea began to take shape.

She drank her coffee, cleaned up and went back into the living room.

She moved the floor lamp, lifted the catch and opened the door behind the bookcase.

She saw that the boy was sleeping heavily.

The table in the living room was full of newspapers from the past week. She had expected at least a mention of a missing child, and more likely screaming headlines.

A child vanishing into thin air was surely big news?

Something that could keep the sales of the evening tabloids up for at least a week.

That was usually the way.

But she hadn't found any indication that he was missing. There were no announcements on the radio, and she began to realise that he was even more perfect than she could have hoped.

If there wasn't anyone looking for him, it meant he would turn to her for protection as long as she fulfilled his basic needs, and she knew she was going to do that.

She would more than fulfil them.

She would refine his desires so that they matched hers, and the two of them would become one. She would be the intelligent brain of the new being, and he its muscles.

Right now, as he lay knocked out on the mattress, he was just an embryo. But once he had learned to think like her, only one truth would exist for them.

When she had taught him how it feels to be victim and perpetrator at the same time, he would understand.

He would be the beast, and she the one who decided if the beast should give in to its urges. Together they would be a perfect person, one whose freedom of will was governed by one consciousness, and whose physical desires by another.

Her desires could be fulfilled through him, and he would enjoy it.

Neither of them could be held responsible for what the other did.

The body would be made up of two beings, one beast and one human being.

One victim and one perpetrator.

One perpetrator and one victim.

Free will united with physical instinct.

Two antipodes in one body.

The room was gloomy, and she turned on the light in the ceiling. The boy came round, and she gave him a drink. Bathed his sweating brow.

In the little bathroom she filled the sink with warm water. She washed him with a small facecloth, soap and water. Then she dried him carefully.

Before she went back out into the apartment she gave him another injection of tranquilliser, and waited for him to sink back into unconsciousness.

He fell asleep with his head against her chest.

Harvest Home Restaurant

As usual, the clientele was a mixture of local artists, a few semi-famous musicians and actors, and passing tourists who wanted to experience the supposedly bohemian Södermalm.

In fact these blocks were the most middle class and ethnically homogeneous in the entire country. It was also one of the most crime-ridden neighbourhoods, but was always portrayed in the media as trendy and intellectual instead of violent and dangerous.

Weakness, Victoria Bergman thought with a snort. She had been going to therapy with Sofia Zetterlund for six months, and what had they come up with so far?

To begin with she had felt the conversations were giving her something; she got a chance to air her feelings and thoughts, and Sofia Zetterlund had been good at listening. Then she began to think she wasn't getting anything back. Sofia Zetterlund just sat there, looking like she was asleep. While Victoria was genuinely opening up, Sofia sat opposite her nodding coolly, making notes, shuffling her papers, fiddling with her little tape recorder and generally looking rather distant.

She took a packet of cigarettes from her bag and put it on the table, drumming her fingers nervously on the tabletop. A feeling of discomfort weighed heavy on her chest.

It had been there a long time.

Far too long to be able to bear it.

Victoria was sitting at a pavement table on Bondegatan. Since she'd moved to Södermalm she often went there to have a glass of wine or two.

The staff were friendly, without being too personal. She hated bartenders who started calling you by your first name after just a few visits.

Victoria Bergman could see Sofia Zetterlund's sleepy, uninterested face in front of her, and a thought struck her. She took a pen from her jacket pocket and lined up three cigarettes on the table in front of her.

On one she wrote the name SOFIA, on the second WEAK and on the third SLEEPY.

Then she scrawled SOFIA ZZZZZZZZZZ . . . across the front of the packet.

She lit the cigarette with SOFIA on it.

To hell with it, she thought. No more of those sessions. Why should she go any more? Sofia Zetterlund called herself a psychotherapist, but she was a weak person.

She thought about Gao. She and Gao weren't weak.

Recent events were still fresh in her mind, and she felt almost euphoric. But in spite of her excitement, something unsatisfactory, some sort of discontent was still gnawing away at her. As if she needed something more.

She realised she had to set Gao a test that he couldn't succeed at. Then maybe she'd feel the way she had at the start. She understood that she wanted to see the look in Gao's eyes, not anyone else's. The look in his eyes when he realised she'd betrayed him.

She knew she used betrayal as a drug, and that she told lies to make herself feel good. Having two people in her power, and deciding for herself who to embrace and who to strike. If you kept mixing it up, randomly switching victims, you could make them hate each other and do anything to get approval.

Once they were sufficiently insecure, you could make them want to kill each other.

Gao was her child. Her responsibility, her everything.

Only one person before him had been that. Martin.

She sipped the wine and wondered if it had been her fault that he had disappeared. No, she thought. It wasn't her fault, she had been just a child then.

The fault lay with her dad. He had ruined her faith in adults, and Martin's dad had had to bear the collective guilt of all men.

He simply liked me, and I misinterpreted the way he touched me, Victoria thought.

I was just a confused child.

She took a deep gulp of wine and looked idly through the menu, even though she wasn't planning to eat anything.

Bondegatan – Commercial District

Sofia Zetterlund had gone to the Tjallamalla boutique on Bondegatan in the hope of finding something nice to add to her wardrobe, but walked out instead with a small painting of the Velvet Underground, Lou Reed's former group. She'd listened to them a lot when she was a teenager.

She had been surprised to find that the shop sold art as well; it never used to. But she hadn't hesitated for a moment; she thought the picture was a bargain.

She sat down at one of the tables along the pavement outside Harvest Home, just a stone's throw away, resting the painting on the next chair.

She ordered a half-carafe of house white. The waitress smiled in recognition, and she smiled back and lit a cigarette.

She was thinking about Samuel Bai and their therapy session a few hours earlier. She shuddered at the thought of what she had unleashed, and how she herself had reacted.

When he was angry he was unpredictable, with an impenetrable facade, totally divorced from any sort of rationality. Sofia recalled how she had tried to cut right into a noisy, chaotic consciousness, taking root there and becoming something for him to cling to. But she had failed.

She loosened her scarf and felt her sore neck. She had been lucky to survive.

Everything had been going fine until the moment when the new Samuel showed himself.

Without any warning, she had witnessed a terrifying transformation. Almost in an aside about one of his childhood friends, Samuel had mentioned something called the Pademba Road Prison.

When he reached the third word his voice changed and the word came out as a muffled hiss.

'Prissson . . .'

She knew that dissociative personalities could switch very rapidly. A single word or gesture could be enough to change Samuel's personality.

He had let out a loud laugh that had scared the life out of her. His broad smile was still in place, but it was completely empty, and the look in his eyes quite blank.

Her memory of what followed was unclear.

She remembered Samuel getting up from his chair, knocking the desk as he rose and tipping the jar of pens into her lap.

And she remembered what he had snarled at her.

'I redi, an a de foyo. If yu ple wit faya yugo soori!'

I'm ready, and am here to get you. If you play with fire, you'll be sorry.

'*Mambaa manyani . . . Mamani manyimi . . .*'

It had sounded like baby talk, and the grammar was odd, but there was no doubting the words' meaning. She had heard them before.

Then he had picked her up with a firm grip around her neck, like she was a doll.

Then everything had gone black.

As Sofia lifted her wine glass to her lips with a trembling hand, she discovered that she was crying. She wiped her eyes with the sleeve of her blouse and realised that she had to try to make sense of her memories.

The social worker arrived to collect him, she thought.

Sofia remembered that she had smiled as she handed Samuel over to his contact from social services. As if nothing unusual had happened. But what about before that?

The strange thing was that her only memory was of a perfume she recognised.

The one Victoria Bergman usually wore.

I can't keep my clients apart, she concluded numbly as she took a few sips. That's the real reason I can't cope with this.

Samuel Bai and Victoria Bergman.

Along with the shock and the lack of oxygen, her judgement wasn't working properly, which was why her only memory of what had happened with Samuel at the practice was of Victoria Bergman instead.

I can't do this, she repeated silently to herself. It's not enough just to postpone my next session with him, I'll have to cancel the whole lot. I can't help him right now. Sometimes you have to be allowed to be weak.

Her thoughts were interrupted by her mobile phone. It was a number she didn't recognise.

'Yes?' she said warily.

'My name's Jeanette Kihlberg, I'm calling from the Stockholm police. Am I talking to Sofia Zetterlund?'

'Yes.'

'It's about one of your patients, Karl Lundström. We believe he might be involved in a case I'm investigating, and Lars Mikkelsen suggested I contact you about your conversations with Lundström. I'm interested in finding out if Karl Lundström has said anything to you that might help us.'

'Obviously, that depends. As I'm sure you know, I've got a duty of confidentiality, and unless I'm mistaken there has to be a court order authorising me to discuss a patient.'

'It's on its way. I'm investigating the murders of two boys who were tortured before they died. I presume you read the papers or watch the news, so I doubt you could have missed it. I'd be very grateful if you had anything to tell me about Lundström, no matter how insignificant it might seem.'

Sofia didn't like the tone of the woman's voice. It was ingratiating and patronising at the same time. It looked like the woman was trying to pull a fast one and milk her for information she had no right to divulge. 'Like I said, I can't discuss anything until you have a court order. Besides, I haven't got access to my notes on Karl Lundström at the moment.'

She could hear the disappointment in the woman's voice. 'I understand. Well, feel free to get in touch if you change your mind. I'd be grateful for anything.'

Monument – Mikael's Apartment

That evening Sofia and Mikael were chatting in front of the television, and as usual he was mainly preoccupied with telling her about his successes at work. She knew he was self-obsessed, and most of the time she liked listening to his voice. But that evening she felt a need to talk about what she had been through.

'I was attacked by a patient today.'

'What?' Mikael looked at her in surprise.

'Nothing serious, he just hit me, but . . . well, I'm thinking of saying I can't see that patient again.'

'But surely that sort of thing must happen all the time?' Mikael said, stroking her arm. 'Of course you can't keep seeing a patient who's dangerous.'

She said she needed a hug.

Later, as she was lying against Mikael's shoulder, she could see the shadow of his profile close to her in the dim light of the bedroom.

'A few weeks ago you asked if I wanted to go to New York with you. Do you remember?' She stroked his cheek, and he turned towards her.

She saw how keen he looked, and for a moment regretted mentioning it. But, on the other hand, it was probably time to tell him.

'Lasse and I were there last year, and . . .'

'Are you sure this is something you want me to hear?'

'I don't know. But what happened is important to me. I wanted to have children with him, and . . .'

'I see . . . And this is something I want to hear?' Mikael sighed.

She switched on the light and sat up in bed. 'I want you to listen,' she said. 'For once, I've got something to say to you that actually means something.'

Mikael pulled the duvet around him and turned away.

'I wanted to have children with him,' she began. 'We were together ten years, but nothing ever happened, because he didn't want it to. But during that trip things happened, and made him change his mind.'

'The light's in my eyes, can't you turn it off?'

She was hurt by his lack of interest, but turned the light out and curled up against his back.

'Do you want to have children, Mikael?' she asked after a while.

He took her arm and wrapped it around him.

'Mmm . . . maybe not right now'.

She thought about what Lasse had always said. He spent ten years saying 'not right now'. But in New York he had changed his mind.

She was sure he had meant it, even if things were different when they got home.

What had happened after that was something she'd rather not think about. How people change, and how it sometimes seems as if everyone contains different versions of the same person. Lasse had been very close to her, he had chosen her. But at the same time there was another Lasse, one who pushed her away. It's really just basic psychology, she thought. But that didn't make any difference, it still scared her.

'Is there anything you're frightened of, Mikael?' she asked quietly. 'Something that really frightens you?'

He didn't reply, and she realised he'd fallen asleep.

She lay awake for a while thinking about Mikael.

What had she seen in him?

He was handsome.

He looked like Lasse.

He had caught her interest, in spite of the fact that he seemed so friendly, or possibly precisely because of that.

Classic middle-class background. Raised in Saltsjöbaden with Mum, Dad and one younger sister. Safe and secure. No money worries. School and football and following in Daddy's footsteps. Done and dusted.

Daddy had committed suicide just before they met, but Mikael never wanted to talk about it. Every time she tried to raise the subject he left the room.

His father's death was an open wound. She realised they had been close. She'd only met his mother and sister once.

She fell asleep behind his back.

She woke up at four in the morning, bathed in sweat. For the third night in a row she had dreamed about Sierra Leone, and was far too agitated to get back to sleep. Mikael was sleeping soundly beside her, and she got out of bed carefully so as not to wake him.

He didn't like her smoking indoors, but she switched on the exhaust fan in the kitchen, sat down and lit a cigarette.

She thought about Sierra Leone, and wondered if she'd made a mistake in turning down the job of checking facts for that book.

It would have been a wiser and more cautious way of starting to deal with her experiences there than by coming face-to-face with a child soldier the way she had with Samuel Bai.

In many ways Sierra Leone had been a disappointment. She never quite managed to get close to the children she had imagined she might be able to help find a better life. She remembered their blank faces and their wary attitude towards aid workers. She had soon realised that she was one of the others. An adult white stranger who had probably scared them more than she had helped them. The children had thrown stones at her. Their trust in adults was gone. She had never felt so impotent.

And now she had failed with Samuel Bai.

Disappointment, she thought. If Sierra Leone had been a disappointment, then her life now, seven years later, was just as much of a disappointment.

She made herself a sandwich and drank a glass of juice, thinking about Lasse and Mikael.

Lasse had let her down.

But was Mikael a disappointment too? It had all started out so well.

Were they already starting to slide apart, before they even got properly close to each other?

There wasn't really any difference between her work and her private life. The faces blurred together. Lasse. Samuel Bai. Mikael. Tyra Mäkelä. Karl Lundström.

Everyone around her was a stranger.

Slipping away from her, beyond her control.

She sat down beside the stove again, lit another cigarette, and watched the smoke disappear up into the exhaust fan. The little tape recorder was on the table, and she reached for it.

It was late, and she ought to try to get some sleep, but she couldn't resist the temptation and switched it on.

. . . always been afraid of heights, but he really wanted to go on the big wheel. If it hadn't been for him, it would never have happened, and he would have been speaking with a Skåne accent by now, he'd be grown up and know how to tie his laces properly. God, it's so hard to remember. But he was horribly spoiled and always had to have his own way.

Sofia could feel herself relaxing.

Just before she fell asleep her thoughts roamed free.

The door

opened and the fair woman came into his room. She was naked too, and it was the first time he'd seen a woman without clothes. Not even his mother had revealed herself to him like that.

He shut his eyes.

She curled up beside him and lay there completely quiet as she smelled his hair and gently stroked his chest. She wasn't his real mother, but she had chosen him. Just looked at him and took his hand with a smile.

No one had ever caressed him like that before, and never had he felt so safe.

The others had always doubted. They pinched him rather than felt. Testing his strength.

But the fair woman had no doubts.

He shut his eyes again and let her do whatever she wanted with him.

The mattress got wet from their exertions. For several days they did nothing but stay in bed, practising and sleeping in turn.

When he wasn't sure what she wanted him to do, she would show him exactly what she meant. Even if all this was new to him, he was a quick learner, and as time passed he got more and more adept.

What he had the most trouble learning to handle was the claw-like object.

He often pulled it too gently and she was forced to show him how to scratch her until she started to bleed.

When he pulled hard she groaned, but showed no sign of punishing him, and he realised that the harder he pulled, the better, even if he didn't really understand why.

Maybe it was because she was an angel and couldn't feel pain.

The ceiling and walls, the floor and mattress, the squeaking plastic under his feet, and the little room with the shower and toilet. All this was his.

His days were filled with lifting weights, doing painful stomach crunches, and spending hours on the exercise bicycle she had installed in one corner of the room.

Inside the bathroom was a little cupboard. It was full of oils and creams that she rubbed into him every evening. Some had a strong smell, but they helped his aches and pains go away. Others smelled wonderful, and made his skin soft and elastic.

He saw himself in the mirror, tensed his muscles and smiled.

The room was like a miniature version of the country he had come to. Silent, safe and clean.

He remembered what the great Chinese philosopher had said about people's ability to learn.

I hear and forget, I see and remember, I do and learn.

Words were superfluous.

He just had to look at her and learn what she wanted him to do. Then he would do it, and understand.

The room was silent.

Every time he made an effort to speak she put her hand over his mouth and shushed him, and when he communicated with her it was via small, precise and muffled grunts, or with sign language. After a while he didn't utter a single word.

He could see how pleased she was when she looked at him. When he put his head in her lap and she stroked his cropped hair, he felt calm. He showed her he was happy by quietly humming.

The room was safe.

He watched her and he learned, memorising what she wanted him to do, and as time passed he went from thinking in words and sentences to relating his experiences to his own body. Happiness became a warmth in his stomach, and anxiety a tension in his neck.

The room was clean.

He merely did, and understood. Pure feeling.

He never said a word. When he thought, he did so in pictures.

He would be a body, and nothing else.

Words were meaningless. Words must not exist even in thoughts.

But they were there now, and he couldn't help it.

Gao, he thought. My name is Gao Lian.

Kronoberg – Police Headquarters

Jeanette Kihlberg felt deflated as she ended her call to Sofia Zetterlund. She knew there'd be problems getting hold of a court order. Von Kwist would raise objections, she was convinced of that.

And then there was Sofia Zetterlund.

Jeanette didn't like how cool she had been. She was far too rational and unemotional. They were dealing with two dead children, after all, and if she could be of any help, why wouldn't she want to? Was it really just a matter of professional ethics and her oath of confidentiality?

It felt like they weren't getting anywhere.

That morning she and Hurtig had tried in vain to track down Ulrika Wendin, the girl who had reported Karl Lundström for rape and sexual abuse seven years ago. The phone number in the directory was no longer in use, and there was no answer when they drove out to the address in Hammarbyhöjden. Jeanette hoped that the note she had put through the letter box would encourage the girl to get in touch as soon as she got home. But so far the phone had remained silent.

This case had turned into a real uphill struggle. It had been two weeks, they had no leads, and one boy was still unidentified.

She felt she needed a change. A new challenge.

If she wanted to go any further up the police hierarchy it would mean being deskbound or taking on more administrative responsibilities.

Was that what she wanted?

While she was reading an internal memo about a three-week-long training course on how to interview children, there was a knock on the door.

Hurtig came in, followed by Åhlund.

'We're thinking of going for a beer. Do you want to come?'

She looked at the time. Half past four. Åke would be busy making dinner. Macaroni and meatballs in front of the television. Silence and a suggestion that boredom was all they had in common these days. Change, she thought.

She balled up the memo and threw it in the waste bin. Three weeks in a classroom.

'No, I can't. Maybe another time,' she said, remembering that she had promised herself that she would say yes.

Hurtig nodded and smiled. 'Sure. See you tomorrow. Don't work too hard.' He shut the door behind him.

Just before she packed her things to go home, she made up her mind.

A quick call to Johan to ask if he could see if it was all right for him to sleep over at David's before she called and booked two cinema tickets for the early screening. Not exactly a massive change, admittedly, but at least it was a small attempt to shake up their grey, everyday life. The cinema, then dinner. Maybe a drink after that.

Åke sounded annoyed when he picked up the phone.

'What are you doing?' she asked.

'What I usually do at this time of day. What are you doing?'

'I'm about to leave, but I thought maybe we could meet in the city instead.'

'Oh, something special going on?'

'Not really, I just thought it's been a while since we did anything nice together.'

'Johan's on his way home, and I'm standing –'

'Johan's staying over at David's,' she interrupted.

'Oh, OK then. Where shall we meet?'

'Medborgarplatsen, outside the market hall. Quarter past six.'

They hung up, and Jeanette dropped her phone in her jacket pocket. She had been hoping he would be pleased, but he had sounded fairly cool. But, on the other hand, it was just a trip to the cinema. Even so, he could have tried to sound enthusiastic, she thought as she switched off her computer.

As Jeanette walked past the steps of Medborgarhuset and the Anna Lindh memorial, she caught sight of Åke. He looked tense, and she stopped to look at him. Twenty years together. Two decades.

She went up to him. 'Seven thousand, give or take,' she said with a smile.

'What?' Åke looked quizzical.

'Might be a bit more. I'm not good at maths.'

'What are you talking about?'

'We've been together for more than seven thousand days. Get it? Twenty years.'

'Mmm . . .'

Indira – Restaurant

An outstanding study of human degradation, the first feature-length film made using a mobile phone. Possibly not the best film Jeanette had ever seen, but definitely not as bad as Åke seemed to think.

'Are you hungry?' Jeanette turned towards Åke. 'Or shall we just go and have a beer somewhere?'

'A bit peckish, maybe.' Åke was looking straight ahead. 'A bit of food wouldn't hurt.'

Jeanette thought it sounded like a sacrifice. That it was an effort to have to endure a couple of hours in her company.

The Indian restaurant was full, and they had to wait ten minutes for a free table. She wondered how long it had been since they last had an

Indian meal. Five years? Or any meal in a restaurant, come to that? Two years, maybe.

Jeanette ordered a simple palak paneer, Åke a strongly spiced chicken dish.

'Yes, you always have the same thing,' Åke said.

Always the same thing? Jeanette knew he was just as predictable. He always picked the hottest dish, explained to her why you ought to eat heavily spiced food, and ended the meal feeling unwell and insisting on going home.

What he said next gave her an odd sense of déjà vu.

'To start with, it's good for you. The spices kill stomach bacteria and make you sweat. The body's cooling system kicks in. That's why people eat strongly spiced food in hot countries. But it's also a hell of a kick. It sends the endorphins flying around your head, almost like being high.'

Jeanette realised with sadness that he was boring her. She tried to change the subject, but he didn't seem interested, and she realised that she was probably boring him as well.

Our entire relationship is stagnant, she thought with a sense of defeat, looking at Åke, who was immersed in his mobile phone.

'Who are you writing to?'

He looked up at her. 'Oh . . . it's a new art project. A new contact.'

Jeanette started to get interested. Had something finally happened?

Åke tried to smile but failed. He stood up and disappeared off to the toilet.

A new art project, she thought. She wondered who this new contact was.

Five minutes later he came back to the table and grabbed his jacket from the chair without sitting down. Outside the restaurant they hailed an empty taxi. Jeanette opened the car door and got in the front passenger seat. She reflected on how much the evening had cost. And for what? she thought as Åke slumped into the back seat.

She turned to the driver. 'Gamla Enskede.'

Jeanette was good at faces, and it only took her a couple of seconds to place him.

He'd been at the same middle school as she had. The eyes and nose were the same, but his lips were no longer as full. It was like seeing a child's face hidden under a layer of fat and loose skin, and she couldn't help laughing.

'Damn! Is that you?'

He laughed back, and ran his hand over his almost-bald scalp, as if to hide the ravages of age.

'Jeanette?'

She nodded.

'So . . .' he said as they pulled out onto Ringvägen towards Skanstull. 'What are you up to these days?'

'I'm a police officer.'

He turned towards the Skanstull Bridge. 'I can't say I'm too surprised to hear you joined the police.'

'No? Why not?'

'It's obvious.' He looked at her. 'You were the class police officer back then.'

Was she that predictable?

Probably.

Palak paneer.

Already the classroom cop back in middle school.

City of Uppsala, 1986

She's the only girl at the place she's working that summer. Fifteen teen boys goading each other on, and the shack isn't very big, especially not when it's raining all the time and they can't sit outside. They play rummy to work out who gets to go with Crow Girl into the other room.

The large area of grass in front of the old barracks at Polacksbacken is covered with rides, carnival booths and food stalls. It's early August, and a travelling fair is in Uppsala for a week.

She's going to take Martin around while his parents go into the centre for dinner.

Martin is at his most charming, and she can see how much he's enjoying being there on his own with her. After the summers they have spent together she has become his best friend, and she's the one he turns to if he wants to talk about something important. If he's sad or if he wants to do something exciting, something forbidden.

She is assuming that this summer will be the last they spend together, because Martin's dad has been offered a new job with a better salary down in Skåne. The family will be moving in the middle of August, and Martin's mum has just said that they've already found an au pair for him, a very conscientious, responsible girl.

Victoria has promised to meet his parents at eight o'clock by the big wheel, where Martin will finish his evening by getting to see the immense view across the Uppsala plain. Apparently they'll be able to see all the way home to Bergsbrunna from up there.

All afternoon Martin has been looking forward to going up in the Ferris wheel. No matter where you are in the fair, you can see the big wheel with its gondolas almost thirty metres above the ground.

As for her, she isn't looking forward to the ride, because it won't just mean the end of their evening, but might possibly be the last thing they ever do together.

There won't be any more after that.

And she doesn't want the grown-ups to come along. So she suggests that they go on the Ferris wheel now, and then again when his mum and dad come back. Then he can point out different places to them before they work out what they're looking at.

He thinks that's a great idea, and before they go and stand in the queue they each buy a drink. When they're standing immediately beneath the wheel and look up, they feel dizzy. It's so incredibly high. She puts her arm around him and asks if he's scared.

'Just a bit,' he replies, but she looks at him and can see that that's not entirely true.

She ruffles his hair and looks him in the eye.

'It's nothing to be scared of, Martin,' she says, trying to sound convincing. 'I'll be with you. And that means nothing bad can happen.'

He smiles at her and clutches her hand as they take their seats in one of the gondolas. As new passengers get on and they rotate higher and higher, Martin's grip on her arm gets progressively tighter. When the gondola sways and stops for a while almost at the very top, while the last gondola is filled down below, he says he doesn't want to continue.

'I want to go down.'

'But, Martin,' she tries, 'now that we've got to the top we can see all the way to Bergsbrunna – you want to see that, don't you?' She points across the countryside, in the way she used to when she was showing him things in the forest. 'Look over there,' she says. 'That's the jetty where we go swimming, and over there's the factory.'

But Martin doesn't want to look.

She is seized by an impulse to give him a good shake, but resists when she sees that he's started to cry.

When the wheel begins to turn again he looks at her and wipes his eyes on his sleeve. By the third revolution his fears seem to have vanished, and he now seems curious about the views opening up all around them.

'You're the best in the world,' she whispers in his ear, and they giggle and hug each other.

A row of houseboats is visible along the river through the trees. There are children swimming by one of the jetties and their laughter is audible all the way to the gondola they're sitting in.

'I want to go swimming too,' he says.

She knows it can smell down there if the wind is in the wrong direction, bringing with it the cloying, heavy whiff of dirt and excrement from the sewage plant in the distance.

When their ride on the big wheel is over he makes a fuss about wanting to go to the river.

They leave the crowds at the fair, walk round the main barrack building, and follow the path leading down the ravine-like slope towards the Fyris River.

The jetty where the children were swimming a short while ago is empty now, except for a forgotten towel draped on one of the posts. The houseboats are bobbing, dark and empty, on the murky water of the river.

She strides out along the jetty, bends over and feels the water.

Afterwards she couldn't understand how she had managed to lose him.

All of a sudden he's just gone.

She calls for him. She hunts desperately among the bushes and reeds along the shore. She falls and cuts herself on a sharp stone, but Martin is nowhere to be found.

She runs back out onto the jetty but sees that the water is completely still. Nothing. Not a single movement.

It feels like she's inside a watery bubble that shuts out all sound, all sensory impressions.

When she realises she can't find him she runs back to the fairground on weak legs, and wanders helplessly around the stalls and carousels until she finally sits down in the middle of one of the busiest paths.

Legs and feet, and a suffocating smell of popcorn. Flashing lights, all different colours.

She gets the feeling that someone has hurt Martin. And that's when the tears come.

When Martin's parents find her she's beyond reach. Her sobbing is bottomless, and she's wet herself.

'Martin's gone,' she keeps repeating. In the background she hears Martin's dad call for first aid, and feels someone wrap a blanket around her. Someone takes her by the shoulders and puts her in the recovery position.

To begin with they aren't particularly worried about Martin, seeing as the fairground covers a large area and there are plenty of people who could look after a child on his own.

But after half an hour or so of looking their anxiety starts to grow. Martin isn't in the fairground, and after another thirty minutes his dad calls the police. Then they start searching the area closest to the fair more systematically.

But Martin isn't found that evening. It's only when they start to drag the river the following day that they find his body.

To judge by his injuries, he seems to have drowned, possibly after hitting his head against a rock. What is most remarkable is that the body has been very badly damaged, presumably during the evening or night. The conclusion is that the injuries were caused by boat propellers.

Victoria is admitted to University Hospital for observation for a few days. During the first twenty-four hours she doesn't say a word, and the doctors declare that she is in a state of severe shock.

It isn't until the second day that she can be questioned by the police, but she suffers an attack of hysterics lasting over twenty minutes.

She tells the police interviewing her that Martin disappeared after they had been on the big wheel, and that she panicked when she couldn't find him.

During her third day in the hospital Victoria wakes up in the middle of the night. She feels like she's being watched, and the room stinks. When her eyes get used to the darkness she can see there's no one there, but can't shake the feeling that someone's watching her. And there's still that nauseating smell, like excrement.

She creeps carefully out of bed, leaves her room and goes out into the corridor. It's lit up, but silent.

She looks around to find the source of her anxiety. Then she sees it. A flashing red light. The realisation is brutal and hits her like a punch in the stomach.

'Shut it off!' she screams. 'You've got no damn right to film me!'

Three of the night staff appear simultaneously.

'What's the matter?' one of them asks as the other two take hold of her arms.

'Fuck off!' she yells. 'Let go of me, and stop filming! I haven't done anything!'

The care workers don't let go, and when she struggles they take a firmer grip.

'OK now, time to calm down,' one of them tries.

She hears them talking behind her back, ganging up on her. Their scheming is so obvious that it's laughable.

'Stop talking in damn code and stop whispering!' she says firmly. 'Tell me what's going on. And don't try lying, I haven't done anything, it wasn't me who smeared shit on the window.'

'No, we know it wasn't,' one of them says.

They try to calm her down. They lie to her face, and she's got no one she can call out to, no one who can help her. She's at their mercy.

'Stop it!' she cries when she sees one of them preparing a syringe. 'Let go of my arms!'

Then she falls into a deep sleep.

Rest.

In the morning the psychiatrist comes to see her. He asks how she is.

'What do you mean?' she says. 'There's nothing wrong with me.'

The psychiatrist explains to Victoria that she's been having hallucinations because she feels responsible for what happened to Martin. Psychosis, paranoia, post-traumatic stress.

Victoria listens to him in silence, but inside her a mute, solid resistance is rising up, like a coming storm.

The kitchen

was set up like a basic autopsy room. The shelves in the pantry no longer contained jars and tins of food, but bottles of glycerine and potassium acetate and a whole load of other chemicals.

On the clinically clean worktop lay a range of common tools. There was an axe, a saw, and various pairs of pliers, some flat-nosed, some for cutting, and a large pair of pincers.

The smaller instruments were laid out on a towel. A scalpel, tweezers, needle and thread, as well as a long tool with a hook at one end.

When she was finished she wrapped the body in a clean white towel. She placed the jar containing the amputated genitals beside the other containers in the kitchen cupboard.

Using a bit of powder she dusted his face, then carefully applied eyeliner and some pale lipstick.

The last thing she did was to shave all the fine, downy hair from his body, because she had discovered that formalin made the body stiffen slightly, and the skin swell. Now the hair would be pulled in, and the skin would end up smoother.

When she was finished the boy looked almost alive.

As if he were asleep.

Danvikstull – Crime Scene

The third boy was found four weeks after the first at the boules club below Danvikstull, and was, according to the experts, a good example of successful embalmment.

Jeanette Kihlberg was in a terrible mood. Not only because her football team had lost their match against Gröndal, but also because she was now on her way to yet another murder scene instead of going home for a shower. She arrived at the scene sweaty and still wearing her football gear. She said hi to Schwarz and Åhlund, then went over to Hurtig, who was having a smoke next to the cordon.

'How was the match?' Åhlund asked.

'Lost three to two. One bad penalty decision, one own goal and one torn knee ligament for our goalie.'

'You see, just like I've always said,' Schwarz said with a grin. 'Girls shouldn't play football. You always get knee trouble. You're just not built for it.'

She could feel herself getting wound up, but couldn't face having the same argument again. It was the standard comment from her colleagues whenever her football matches were mentioned. But she still thought it odd that someone as young as Schwarz could have such tired, obsolete opinions.

'I know all that. What's it look like here? Do we know who it is?'

'Not yet,' Hurtig said. 'But I'm afraid it looks alarmingly similar to our previous cases. The boy's been embalmed; he looks alive, if a bit pale. Someone laid him out on a blanket so it looked like he was sunbathing.'

Åhlund pointed towards the clump of trees beside the boules club.

'Anything else?'

'According to Andrić, the body could have been there for a couple of days, in theory, anyway,' Hurtig replied. 'I think that's pretty unlikely, myself. I mean, he's out in the open. And I'd certainly think it was a bit weird if I saw someone lying on a blanket in the middle of the night.'

'Maybe no one walked past last night.'

'Maybe, but all the same . . .'

Jeanette Kihlberg did what was expected of her, then asked Andrić to call her as soon as he finished his report.

Two hours after she first arrived at the crime scene she got back in the car to drive home, and realised how sore she was after the match.

As she was passing the Sickla roundabout she called Dennis Billing.

The commissioner sounded breathless. 'I'm on my way home. How did things look out there?'

'Another dead boy. How's it going with Lundström and von Kwist?'

'I'm afraid von Kwist is unwilling to let us interview Lundström. There's not much more I can do right now.'

'I see. Why's he being so fucking unhelpful? Do they play golf together?'

'Be careful, Jeanette. We both know that von Kwist is a very talented – '

'Bullshit!'

'Well, that's just the way it is. I have to go now. Let's talk tomorrow.' Dennis Billing hung up.

As she turned right into Enskedevägen and pulled up at a red light beyond the roundabout, her mobile rang.

'Um . . . hello, my name's Ulrika. You were looking for me?'

The voice sounded brittle. Jeanette realised it must be Ulrika Wendin.

'Ulrika? Thanks for getting back to me.'

'What was it you wanted?'

'Karl Lundström,' Jeanette said.

There was silence on the line. 'OK,' the girl said eventually. 'Why?'

'I'd like to talk to you about what he did to you, and I was hoping you might be able to help me with that.'

'Shit . . .' Ulrika sighed. 'I don't know if I can bear to go through all that again.'

'I understand that it's difficult for you. But it's for a good cause. You can help other people by telling me what you know. If he gets put away for what he's been accused of, you'll get some sort of justice.'

'What's he accused of?'

'I can tell you all about it tomorrow, if you could see me then? Is it OK if I come by your place?'

Another silence, and Jeanette listened to the girl's heavy breathing for a few seconds.

'That's probably OK . . . What time?'

Gamla Enskede – Kihlberg House

It was way past midnight when Jeanette was woken by the phone.

It was Ivo Andrić.

He told her that by coincidence it turned out that one of the night cleaners at the pathology institute was a Ukrainian who had studied medicine at the University of Kharkov. As soon as the cleaner caught sight of the body he said it reminded him of Lenin. Ivo Andrić had asked him to elaborate, and the cleaner said he remembered reading something about a Professor Vorobyov who had been given the task of embalming Lenin's corpse in the 1920s.

'I checked online,' Ivo said. Jeanette could hear the tiredness in his voice. 'One week after Lenin's death his body had started to show signs of decay. The skin was starting to turn darker, more yellow, and was getting mottled, with signs of fungal growth. The person charged with preserving the body was Vladimir Vorobyov, a professor at the Kharkov University Institute of Anatomy.'

Jeanette listened with fascination as Ivo Andrić explained the process.

'First they removed the internal organs, washed the corpse with acetic acid, then injected the soft tissues with formaldehyde. After several days of intensive work they put Lenin into a glass bath and covered the body with a mixture of water and chemicals, among them glycerine and potassium acetate. I realised at once that whoever had embalmed the boy could have been following Vorobyov's notes.'

The medical officer admitted that his initial assumption that it must have been done by someone with specialist knowledge had been overly hasty.

'Nowadays it's enough to have access to the Internet,' he said, and sighed. 'And, seeing as we can probably assume that the person responsible was also the perpetrator in the earlier cases, and that that person had access to large quantities of anaesthetic, it shouldn't have been too difficult for them to get hold of the chemicals needed to embalm a body.'

The injuries were the same as on the two other boys. More than a hundred bruises, needle marks and wounds to his back.

As Jeanette expected, this boy's genitals had also been removed. With a similarly sharp knife, and with the same precision.

Andrić concluded by saying that he had made a plaster cast of the boy's teeth, which – miraculously enough – were intact, and was going to send it to the forensic odontologists for identification.

It was half past two by the time they hung up.

Someone out there has now committed three murders, Jeanette thought.

And they were unlikely to stop at that.

She felt frozen as she finally closed her eyes to get some more much-needed sleep. Åke's snoring wasn't making it any easier, but she'd learned how to deal with that. She gave him a nudge, and he rolled over onto his side with a murmur.

By half past four Jeanette couldn't bear lying there awake, twisting and turning, any longer, and went quietly down to the kitchen and put some coffee on.

While the machine was brewing she went down into the basement and filled the washing machine. She made herself a couple of sandwiches, got a cup of coffee, and went out into the garden.

Before sitting down she walked to the mailbox and got the newspaper.

Obviously the main story was the news about the boy at Danvikstull, and Jeanette almost felt like she was being stalked.

On the other side of the road, next to one of her neighbours' mailboxes, stood an abandoned pram.

The morning sun coming through the hedge was blinding her, and she raised a hand to her eyes to see what was going on.

Movement from the bushes. A young man hurried across the street, doing his trousers up, and she realised he'd just had a pee in her hedge.

He went up to the pram, took out a newspaper and put it in her neighbour's mailbox. Then he moved on to the next house.

A pram, she thought, as an idea occurred to her.

Kronoberg – Police Headquarters

The first thing Jeanette Kihlberg did when she got to the office was to call the main company responsible for delivering newspapers.

'Hello, my name's Jeanette Kihlberg, I'm calling from the Stockholm police. I need to find out who was on duty in the area around the teacher-training college on Kungsholmen on the morning of 9 May.'

The operator sounded nervous.

'OK . . . that ought to be possible. What's this about?'

'Murder.'

While Jeanette waited for them to call her back, she called Hurtig into her office.

'Did you know that people delivering papers sometimes use prams instead of bikes with trailers?' she said when Hurtig had come in and was sitting opposite her.

'No, I didn't. How do you mean?' He looked at her questioningly.

'Do you remember that we found the tracks from a pram at Thorildsplan?'

'Sure.'

'And who's out and about early in the morning?'

Hurtig smiled and nodded. 'People delivering papers . . .'

'The phone should be ringing shortly,' Jeanette said. 'Why don't you answer it?'

They sat in silence for a minute or so until the phone rang and Jeanette pressed the speaker button.

'Jens Hurtig, Stockholm police.'

The girl from the delivery company introduced herself. 'I was just talking to a female police officer who wanted to know who was on duty in western Kungsholmen on 9 May?'

'Yes, that's right.'

Jeanette could see that Hurtig had worked it out.

'His name is Martin Thelin, but he no longer works for us.'

'Have you got a number we can reach him?'

'Yes, there's a mobile number.'

He made a note of the number, then asked the operator if she had any other information about the former employee.

'Yes, I've got his personal details. Do you want them?'

'If you wouldn't mind.'

Hurtig wrote down Martin Thelin's ID number and ended the call.

'Well, what do you think?' Jeanette asked. 'A suspect?'

'Either that or a witness. It would be perfectly possible to transport a body in a pram, wouldn't it?'

Jeanette nodded. 'Or else it was Martin Thelin who found the body at Thorildsplan when he was delivering papers. And called the police.'

She gave Åhlund a ring and asked him to try to track down Thelin. She gave him the phone number.

'OK, quick run-through,' she said afterwards. 'Tell me which name you think is hottest right now.'

'Karl Lundström,' Hurtig replied, without hesitation.

'Right,' she said. 'Why?'

Hurtig seemed bemused by the situation.

'Paedophile. Knows how to buy children from the Third World. Thinks castration's a good idea. And has access to anaesthetics because his wife is a dentist.'

'I agree,' Jeanette said. 'So, let's concentrate our fire on him. I got hold of the file from the preliminary investigation into the Ulrika Wendin case this morning, so I suggest we do a bit of homework before driving over to see her.'

Hammarbyhöjden – a Suburb

The girl who opened the door was short and thin, and didn't look a day over eighteen.

'Hello, I'm Jeanette Kihlberg. My colleague here is Jens Hurtig.'

The girl avoided eye contact, nodded and led the way into a small kitchen.

Jeanette sat down opposite her while Hurtig remained standing in the doorway.

'There was a different name on the door,' Jeanette said.

'Yes, I'm renting third- or fourth-hand.'

'I know what it's like. Stockholm's completely hopeless. It's impossible to find somewhere to live if you're not a millionaire.' Jeanette smiled.

The girl no longer looked quite as scared, and risked a small smile back.

'Ulrika, I'll get straight to the point, so you don't have to put up with us for longer than necessary.'

Ulrika Wendin nodded, fiddling nervously with the tablecloth.

Jeanette gave her a short summary of the case against Karl Lundström, and the girl seemed to relax a bit when she realised that the evidence against the paedophile was so strong that it was likely to lead to a conviction.

'Seven years ago you reported him for rape. Your case could be reopened, and I think you'd stand a good chance of winning.'

'Winning?' Ulrika Wendin shrugged her shoulders. 'I don't want to start that up again . . .'

'Do you feel like telling us what happened?'

The girl sat there silently staring down at the tablecloth while Jeanette studied her face. What she could see were fear and bewilderment.

'I don't know where to start . . .'

'Start at the beginning,' Jeanette said.

'It was . . .' she attempted. 'It was when me and a friend answered an Internet ad . . .' Ulrika Wendin fell silent and glanced at Hurtig.

Jeanette realised his presence was putting Ulrika off, and with a discreet gesture let him know that it would be best if he left the room.

'To begin with it was just for fun,' the girl went on when Hurtig had gone out into the hall. 'But soon we realised we would earn money. The man who placed the ad wanted to sleep with two girls at the same time. And we'd get five thousand . . .'

Jeanette could see how hard it was for the girl to tell her story.

'OK. What happened after that?'

Ulrika Wendin was still looking down at the table. 'I was a bit out of control in those days . . . We got drunk and agreed to meet him, and he picked us up in his car.'

'Karl Lundström?'

'Yes.'

'OK. Go on.'

'We went to a bar somewhere. He paid for all the drinks, and my friend legged it. He was angry at first, but I promised to go with him for half the price . . .'

Jeanette could see that the girl felt ashamed.

'I don't know why . . .'

Her voice was getting thinner. 'Everything was so fuzzy, and he led me back to the car. Then there's a blank. The next time I woke up I was in a hotel room.'

Jeanette guessed she'd been drugged.

'Do you know which hotel?'

For the first time Ulrika Wendin met Jeanette's gaze.

'No.'

To begin with, the girl's story had been tentative and fragmented, but from now on it became more clear and factual. She explained how she had been forced to have sex with three men while Karl Lundström stood and filmed it. In the end he too had forced himself on her.

'How did you know it was Karl Lundström?'

'I didn't know who he was until I happened to see his picture in the paper.'

'And that's when you reported him?'

'Yes.'

'And you were able to identify him in a line-up?'

Ulrika Wendin looked tired. 'Yes. But he had an alibi.'

'Is there any chance that you were mistaken?'

There was a flash of contempt in the girl's eyes.

'Like fuck is there! It was him.'

Ulrika Wendin sighed and stared blankly down at the table.

Jeanette nodded. 'I believe you.'

When Jeanette and Hurtig had left the apartment and were walking across the car park, Hurtig opened his mouth for the first time since they had arrived.

'What do you think?' he said.

Jeanette unlocked the car and opened the door. 'That von Kwist is going to have to reopen her case. Anything else would be a dereliction of duty.'

'And our case?'

'Pretty doubtful.' They got in the car, and Jeanette started the engine.

'Doubtful?' Hurtig let out a laugh.

Jeanette shook her head. 'For God's sake, Jens, it was seven years ago. She was drunk, and drugged. And besides, there aren't many similarities with the crimes we're looking at.'

As she pulled up at an intersection her mobile rang. Who the hell is it now? she thought.

It was Åhlund.

'Where are you?' he asked.

'Hammarbyhöjden, heading back into the city,' Jeanette replied.

'You might as well turn round. Our newspaper boy, Martin Thelin, lives out in Kärrtorp.'

Kärrtorp – a Suburb

The former newspaper deliveryman Martin Thelin looked hung-over when he opened the door wearing a pair of black tracksuit bottoms and an unbuttoned shirt. He was unshaven, his hair was sticking up, and his breath could have brought down an elephant.

'What do you want?' Martin Thelin cleared his throat, and Jeanette took a step back, fearing that he was about to throw up.

'Can we come in?' Hurtig held up his police ID and gestured inside the flat.

'OK, but it's a bit of a mess.' Martin Thelin shrugged and let them in.

Jeanette was struck by the fact that he seemed so unconcerned by their presence, but reasoned that he had probably been expecting them to find him sooner or later.

The apartment stank of spilled beer and rubbish, and Jeanette tried to remember to breathe through her mouth. Thelin showed them into the living room, sat down in the only armchair, and gestured to Jeanette and Hurtig to sit on the sofa.

'Is it OK if I open a window?' Jeanette looked around, and when the badly hung-over man nodded, she went and opened one of the windows wide before settling down next to Hurtig.

'Tell us what happened at Thorildsplan.' Jeanette took out her notebook. 'Yes, we know you were there.'

'Take your time,' Hurtig said. 'We want you to be as detailed as possible.'

Martin Thelin rocked back and forth, and Jeanette realised he was searching his drink-sodden, fragmented memory.

'Well, I wasn't on top form that morning,' he began, reaching for a packet of cigarettes and shaking one out. 'I'd been drinking all the previous evening, and a good part of the night, so . . .'

'But you still went to work?' Jeanette made a note in her pad.

'That's right. And when I was finished I stopped outside the metro station to have a piss, and that's when I saw the bag.'

Even though he had been half drunk, his account was detailed and without any gaps. He had gone into the bushes to the left of the station, pissed and then discovered the black bin bag. He had opened it, and been shocked by what he found.

Confused, he had backed away onto the path, grabbed the pram he used to carry his papers, and quickly headed off through the park towards Rålambsvägen.

When he reached the DN Tower he called the police.

That was all.

He hadn't seen anything else.

Hurtig was looking at him intently. 'Really, we ought to pull you in for not getting in touch with us. But if you come to the station and leave a saliva sample, we might be able to overlook that.'

'Saliva sample?'

'Yes, so we can exclude your DNA from the investigation,' Jeanette explained. 'After all, your urine was on the plastic bag.'

The plastic

rustled whenever the other boy moved in his sleep. He had been asleep for a long time. Gao had counted almost twelve hours, since he had worked out that the clock he could hear faintly in the distance struck once every hour.

Then the clock struck again, and he wondered if it was a church.

He thought in words, even though he didn't want to.

Maria, he thought. Peter, James, Magdalena.

Gao Lian. From Wuhan.

He heard the other boy waking up.

The darkness made the sounds the other boy was making louder. The sobbing, the rattle when he pulled at the chain, the groaning, and the plaintive, unfamiliar words.

Gao had no chains. He was free to do what he liked with the other boy. Perhaps she'd come back if he did something to the boy? He was longing for her, and didn't understand why she didn't come.

He noticed that the other boy kept feeling around in the darkness, as if he were searching for something. And sometimes he called out in his odd language. *Chto, chto, chto*, it sounded like.

He wanted the boy to go away. He hated him, and his presence in the room made Gao feel alone.

Eventually she came.

He had been in the dark so long that the light streaming in hurt his eyes. The other boy screamed and cried and kicked out. Then, when he saw Gao in the light, he calmed down a bit, and stared at him aggressively. Perhaps the boy was just jealous because Gao didn't have to wear chains?

The fair woman stepped into the room and went up to Gao with a bowl in her hands. She put the steaming soup on the floor, then kissed him on the forehead and ran her hand through his hair, and he was reminded of how much he liked it when she touched him.

After a while she returned with another bowl that she gave to the other boy. He began to eat greedily, but Gao waited until she had shut the door and it was dark again. He didn't want her to see how hungry he was.

Just an hour later she came into the room. She was carrying a bag over her shoulder, and in her hand she had a black object that looked like a big beetle.

The ceiling had lit up with bright flashes when the other boy died. Gao no longer felt alone; he could move freely in the room and didn't have to hide from the other boy. She came in to see him more often now, and that was good as well.

But there was one thing he didn't like.

His feet had started to ache. His nails had grown long and had curled down and inward, and he was having trouble walking without it hurting.

One night when he was sleeping she came in without him noticing. When he woke up his hands were tied behind his back and his feet were bound. She was sitting astride him and he could see the shadow of her back.

He understood at once what she wanted to do. Only one person had done it before, and that had been at the children's home outside Wuhan where he had grown up. On more than one occasion the old man with the scar had chased him down the corridors. He always got caught in the end, and then the old man took out his knife. He had held Gao's feet so hard he started to cry, and as he took out his knife from the little wooden sheath he would laugh through his toothless smile.

It wasn't good that she, whom he liked so much, was doing this to him.

Afterwards she loosened the ropes and gave him something to eat and drink. He refused to touch the food, and when she got tired of stroking his forehead and left, he lay awake for a long time thinking about what she had done.

Right then he hated her, and no longer wanted to be there. Why did she hurt him when he had so clearly shown that he didn't want it? She hadn't done that before, and it didn't feel good.

But a bit later, when she came in again and he realised she had been crying, he could feel that his feet no longer hurt, and they weren't bleeding either, like they always did when the old man had cut them.

Then he spoke to her for the first time.

'Gao,' he said. 'Gao Lian.'

Gamla Enskede – Kihlberg House

The sun had been up for several hours and had dried the morning dew from the lawn.

Jeanette Kihlberg looked out of the kitchen window and realised that it was going to be a hot June day. No wind, and already ripples of heat from the roof tiles on the other side of the road.

The deliveryman with the pram full of newspapers went past at seven exactly.

Martin Thelin, she thought. Just like Jimmie Furugård's, Thelin's alibi was difficult to doubt. While Furugård had been on a secret mission in Sudan, Thelin had been in rehab. Six months in Hälsingland. Hurtig had double-checked the record of his absences from the clinic. Martin Thelin wasn't involved.

It was now half past seven and she was sitting eating breakfast alone at the kitchen table.

Johan was still snoring in bed. Where Åke was she had no idea. He'd gone out with some friend of his the previous evening. He hadn't come home, and hadn't answered when she'd called him half an hour before.

How the hell can he go to the pub when we haven't got any money? she thought.

Out of the five thousand kronor she had got from her dad, she had given two to Åke. My buddies are paying, he had said. Sure. She knew perfectly well how he behaved after a few glasses. Last of the big spenders, rounds for everyone. Åke the generous friend. Their money. No, her money, which she'd borrowed from her dad, and which was also supposed to support Johan.

She and Åke had hardly seen each other for several days, and she reflected on the failed evening out at the cinema and restaurant.

What was the point in trying to resuscitate a relationship that had stagnated? Why struggle to find your way back to something that may no longer even exist?

It would probably be better to move on. Go in different directions.

The thought of splitting up didn't scare her. It mostly felt like a nuisance.

Uncomfortable, like an uninvited guest.

How different they had become.

The change hadn't happened overnight, it had slowly crept up on them, and it was impossible to identify when. Five years ago, two years, six months? She couldn't say.

All she knew was that she missed the way they used to communicate. Even if they had had different opinions on loads of things, they had discussed them, talked, been curious, surprised each other. The dialogue had slowly developed into two silent monologues. Work and finances were their main topics of conversation, and even then they were unable to conduct a proper dialogue, even though it ought to be so easy.

She felt like she was nagging, and that he was irritable and uninterested.

Jeanette drank the last of her coffee and cleared the table. Then she went into the bathroom, brushed her teeth and got in the shower.

It was easy to communicate with the girls on the football team. Not always, but often enough for her to miss them if there was too big a gap between games or training sessions.

Ten, fifteen different individuals with different opinions, preferences and backgrounds, making up a community. Obviously they didn't all get along with one another, but at least you could talk openly to pretty much all of them. Laughing and joking, arguing, it didn't matter.

Two players who worked together out on the field could become friends even if they were completely different as people.

Yet she didn't have any close friendships with any of them away from the football pitch. They had all known one another for several years, saw one another at parties, went to the pub together. But she had never asked any of them over.

She knew why. She didn't have the energy, it was as simple as that. She needed all her energy for work, and knew that as long as she was doing this job, that had to be the priority.

Jeanette got out of the shower, dried herself and began to get dressed. She glanced at the time and realised she was on the verge of being late.

She left the bathroom, nudged the door of Johan's room open and saw that he was still asleep. Then she went into the kitchen and wrote him a short note.

'Good morning. Home late tonight. Dinner in the freezer, just heat it up. Have a good day. Love, Mum.'

It was almost eighty-five degrees out in the sun, and she'd much rather have been lying on a beach somewhere with Johan. But she knew it would be a while before she could think about taking a holiday.

Kronoberg – Police Headquarters

Half an hour later she was at her desk on Kungsholmen, and had already had a short, depressing run-through with Hurtig, Schwarz and Åhlund.

During the morning Jeanette had found out that she would have to continue with her investigation for the simple reason that it would look bad if it was dropped so soon.

Reading between the lines, no one cared about the three boys. Jeanette realised that the sole purpose of her work right now was to gather information that might turn out to be important if another dead boy turned up, one who was actually missed. A dead, tortured Swedish boy with a family who might go to the press and accuse the police of not doing enough.

Jeanette didn't think that was likely to happen, because she was convinced that the perpetrator wasn't picking victims at random. The cruelty and modus operandi were so similar that they were surely dealing with one and the same perpetrator. But she couldn't be sure. Sometimes coincidence stepped in to confuse everything.

She had ruled out all the usual types of murder. Here they were dealing with torture and sophisticated, protracted violence in which the perpetrator had both access to and knowledge of anesthetics. The victims were young boys and their genitals had been removed. If there was such a thing as normal murders, these were the opposite.

There was a cautious knock on the door, and Hurtig came in. He sat down opposite her with a look of resignation.

'So? What do we do?' he asked.

'I honestly don't know,' she replied. It was as if his listlessness were infectious.

'How much time have we got? I presume this isn't exactly the highest priority?'

'A few weeks, nothing exact, but if we don't find something soon we'll have to move on.'

'OK. I suggest we have another go with Interpol, then trawl the refugee centres again. And if that doesn't work, we can always try the Central Bridge again. I refuse to believe that children can simply vanish without anyone missing them.'

'I agree, but this is actually the exact opposite,' Jeanette said, looking Hurtig in the eye.

'What do you mean?'

'I mean that these children seem to have appeared rather than vanished.'

Åke called at half past two. At first she couldn't understand what he was saying because he was so excited, but once he'd calmed down a bit she managed to grasp what had actually happened.

'Don't you see? I'm getting an exhibition. The gallery's fucking brilliant, and she's already sold three pictures for me.'

Who's this she? Jeanette wondered.

'It's bang in the middle of the city, in Östermalm! Fuck, I can hardly believe this is happening!'

'Åke, calm down. Why haven't you said anything?'

Admittedly, he had hinted that something was in the works during that meal after the film, but at the same time she couldn't help thinking how he had spent twenty years meandering about at home, how she'd supported him and encouraged him in his art. And now he'd taken his paintings to a gallery without saying a word.

She could hear him breathing down the phone, but he wasn't saying anything.

'Åke?'

He came back after a few moments. 'Yes . . . I don't know. It was just an idea I had. I read an article in *Perspectives on Art* and decided to go and talk to her. Everything seemed to match what she said in the article. I was scared at first, but I probably knew all along that it was the right move to make. It was time, basically.'

So that's why he didn't come home last night, Jeanette thought.

'Åke, you're talking in riddles. Who did you go to?'

He explained that the woman representing one of Stockholm's biggest art galleries had been completely bowled over by his work. Using her contacts she'd already managed to sell paintings worth almost forty-five thousand kronor before the exhibition had even opened.

The curator reckoned they could reach four times that, and had promised him another exhibition at her Copenhagen branch.

'Almost the Louisiana Museum of Modern Art.' Åke laughed. 'Even if it is just a small gallery in Nyhavn.'

Jeanette felt warm inside, but while she was glad something was finally happening, she had a gut feeling that something wasn't right.

Was his art really his alone?

She'd lost count of the number of nights they'd sat up discussing his work. It usually ended with him in tears, saying it wasn't working, and she'd have to comfort him and encourage him to continue along the path he'd chosen. She had believed in him.

She knew he had talent, even if she was hardly an authority on the subject.

'Åke, you never cease to surprise me. But this really takes the biscuit.' She couldn't help laughing, although she would rather have asked him why he'd kept all this secret from her. This was what they'd been talking about for years, after all.

'I suppose I was scared of failure,' he eventually admitted. 'I mean, you've always supported me. Hell, you've basically been paying for me to keep going. Like a patron. I really appreciate everything you've done for me.'

Jeanette didn't know what to say. A patron? Was that how he saw her? Like a personal cash machine?

'And do you know what? Do you know who's exhibiting in Copenhagen at the same time as me? At the same place?'

He spelled it out: 'D-i-e-s-e-l–F-r-a-n-k,' then laughed out loud. 'Adam Diesel-Frank! Look, I've got to go now. I'm meeting Alexandra to go through a few details. See you this evening!'

So her name was Alexandra.

Gamla Enskede – Kihlberg House

As Jeanette turned into the drive of the house she had to slam the brakes on to avoid running into the unfamiliar car that was parked in front of the garage door. The red sports car's number plate revealed who owned it. Kowalska was the name of the gallery Åke had contacted, and Jeanette concluded that the car's owner must be Alexandra Kowalska.

She opened the door and went into the house.

'Hello?'

There was no answer, so she went upstairs. She could hear voices and laughter from Åke's studio, and knocked on the door.

The voices fell silent, and she went in. Several of Åke's paintings were spread out on the floor, and at the table sat Åke and a strikingly beautiful blonde woman in her forties. She was wearing a tight black dress and discreet make-up. So this is Alexandra, Jeanette thought.

'Do you want to celebrate with us?' Åke pointed at the bottle of wine on the table. 'You'll have to get a glass, though,' he added when he realised there wasn't one there for her.

What the hell is this? Jeanette thought as she saw the bread, cheese and olives laid out.

Alexandra laughed and looked at her. Jeanette didn't like the woman's laugh. It sounded false.

'Maybe we should introduce ourselves?' Alexandra pointedly raised an eyebrow and stood up. She was tall, considerably taller than Jeanette. She walked over and held out her hand.

'Alex Kowalska,' she said, and Jeanette could tell from her accent that she wasn't Swedish.

'Jeanette . . . I'll get another glass.'

Alexandra – or Alex, as she evidently preferred to be called – stayed until almost midnight before calling for a taxi. Åke had fallen asleep on the sofa in the living room and Jeanette was left alone in the kitchen with a glass of whisky.

It hadn't taken Jeanette long to realise that Alex Kowalska was a manipulative person.

During the course of the evening Alex had promised Åke another exhibition. In Kraków, where she appeared to have not only her roots but also significant contacts. An awful lot of what she said about breakthroughs and success struck Jeanette as blatantly provocative. Her superlatives about Åke's work and her grand plans for the future were one thing. But then there were the compliments. Alex described Åke as a uniquely social person, and she regarded him as an incredibly talented and exciting artist. His eyes were clear, intense and intelligent, and so on. Alexandra had even said that his wrists were beautiful, and as Åke had looked down at them with a smile, she had run her finger over the veins on the back of his hand and called them the lines of a painter. Jeanette was appalled. Had this woman no shame? She thought that most of what Alex had said during the evening was pathetic, but Åke had obviously been delighted by her flattery.

This woman is a snake, Jeanette thought, already beginning to suspect the disappointment Åke would feel when his hopes weren't completely realised.

How had the relationship come to this? Was this the beginning of the end?

She turned out the kitchen light and went into the living room to wake Åke from his snoring. But it was impossible to shake any life into him, and she went up to bed on her own.

Jeanette slept badly, having nightmares, and when she woke up she felt pretty low. The sheets were wet with sweat, and she had no desire whatever to get up. But she couldn't just lie there.

It would be so nice to have a normal job, she thought. The sort of work where you could have a day off if you called in sick. A workplace where you could be replaced and your responsibilities postponed for a day or two.

She stretched, shivered and pulled back the covers. Without really knowing how it had happened, she was up. Her body had instinctively made the decision for her. Take responsibility, it had said. Do your duty and don't give in.

After a shower she got dressed and went downstairs to the kitchen, where Johan was sitting eating breakfast. Her lethargy had faded and she felt ready for a new day at work.

'Are you up already? It's only eight o'clock.' She filled the coffee machine.

'Yes, I couldn't sleep. We've got a match tonight.' He leafed through the paper, found the sports pages and began to read.

'Is it a big match?' Jeanette got out a cup and bowl, put them on the table, and took the milk and yogurt out of the fridge.

Johan didn't answer.

Jeanette got the coffee pot, filled her mug, then sat down opposite him and repeated the question.

'It's a cup match,' he muttered, without looking up from the paper.

Once again Jeanette felt the impotence of not knowing anything. Not having any idea of what her son's everyday life looked like. It occurred to her that she hadn't been to his school at all last term, except on the final day of the school year.

'Who are you playing, and what cup is it?'

'Give it a rest!' He folded the paper and stood up. 'You're not really interested.'

'Johan! Of course I'm interested, but right now you know I've got a lot going on at work . . .' She lost her thread and thought about what she was saying. Were poor excuses the best she could come up with? She felt ashamed.

'We're playing Djurgården.' He picked up his plate and put it in the sink. 'It's the final tonight, I think Dad's going to come and watch.' He went out into the hall.

'You're bound to win,' she called after him. 'Djurgården sucks.'

He didn't reply, just went into his room and shut the door.

When she was about to leave she heard Åke moving around on the sofa. She went into the living room. He had just woken up, and was sitting there rubbing his face. His hair was all over the place and his eyes were bloodshot.

'I'm off now,' she said. 'I don't know what time I'll be home. It might be late.'

'Yeah, yeah.' He looked at her, and from the weary look on his face Jeanette realised that right now he didn't care if she came home or not.

'Don't forget that Johan's got a match this evening. He's hoping you're going to be there.'

'We'll have to see.' He stood up. 'I'll go if I've got time, but I don't know if I will. I'm meeting Alex to put together an exhibition catalogue, and that might take a while. Why don't you go instead?' He smiled sarcastically.

'Let it go. You know I can't.' She turned round, went out into the hall and walked towards the door. Their shoes and boots were in a big heap, surrounded by bits of grit and dust balls.

Inadequate, she thought. Worthless and self-obsessed.

'I'll call later to hear how it went.'

She opened the door, stepped out onto the porch and shut the door before he could answer.

Kronoberg – Police Headquarters

The traffic heading into the city was sluggish as usual, but eased up slightly beyond Gullmarsplan, and as she parked the car she realised it had only just turned nine. She decided to start her working day with a long walk around Kungsholmen to clear her head.

When she got to her office Hurtig was sitting behind her desk waiting for her.

'The best people always show up late.' He grinned.

'What are you doing here?' She walked over, leaving no room for doubt that she wanted him to move.

'Correct me if I'm wrong, Jeanette,' he began. 'But we're in a pretty lousy position right now, aren't we?'

Jeanette nodded. 'What are you getting at?'

'I took the liberty of looking at a number of old cases featuring extreme violence . . .'

'OK, I'm with you.' She suddenly felt excited, because she knew Hurtig wouldn't be bothering her if he hadn't come up with something.

'By chance I came across this.' He tossed her a brown document file. On the front were the words 'Bengt Bergman. Case closed.'

'Bergman has been here for interviews seven times over the years, most recently on Monday.'

'On Monday? What for?'

'A Tatiana Achatova reported him for rape. She's a prostitute, and –' Hurtig stopped himself. 'Well, never mind her, that isn't what made me suspicious. It was the brutality. And when I compared it with the earlier reports, it was the same there.'

'Violence?'

'Yes. The girls were badly beaten up, some had been whipped with a belt, and they'd all been anally raped with an object of some sort. Probably a bottle.'

'I presume he was never convicted of anything, since he's not in the register.'

'Exactly. The evidence has always been too weak, and most of the victims have been prostitutes. His word against theirs, and if I'm not mistaken his wife's given him an alibi for every occasion.'

'So you think we should bring him in?'

Hurtig smiled, and Jeanette realised he'd been saving the best till last.

'Two of the reports concern sexual abuse of minors. One girl, one boy. Brother and sister, born in Eritrea. And there was violence there as well . . .'

Jeanette picked up the file at once and began to leaf through it. 'Damn, Hurtig. I'm glad I work with you. Let's see . . . Here it is!'

She pulled out a thin document and glanced through it.

'June 1999. The girl twelve, the boy ten. Extreme violence, wounds from being whipped, sexual assault, children with a foreign background. Case dropped because of . . . what does it say? The children weren't thought to be credible because their testimonies didn't match. And his wife gave him an alibi once again. It might be hard to link him to our cases. We need more than this.'

Hurtig had already thought of that.

'We could take a chance,' he said. 'In Bergman's file I found the name of his daughter. Maybe we could try giving her a call?'

'I'm not with you. How do you think she could help?'

'Who knows, maybe she isn't as willing to give her father an alibi as his wife seems to be. OK, it's a shot in the dark, but it's worked before, hasn't it? What do you say?'

'OK. But you make the call.' Jeanette passed him the phone. 'Have you got her number?'

'It wasn't in the file, but . . .' Hurtig said, turning to a page of his notebook with an extravagant gesture before dialling the number. 'It's a mobile phone, no address, sadly.'

Jeanette chuckled. 'You knew I'd agree to this.'

Hurtig smiled at her as he waited in silence.

'Yes, hello . . . I'm trying to get in touch with a Victoria Bergman. Is this the right number?' Hurtig looked surprised. 'Hello?' He frowned. 'She hung up,' he said.

They looked at each other.

'We'll leave it a while, then I'll try talking to her.' Jeanette stood up. 'Maybe she'd rather talk to a woman. Anyway, I could do with a coffee now.'

They went out into the corridor and off towards the kitchen.

Just as Jeanette had taken the hot plastic cup from the machine, Schwarz came racing in, closely followed by Åhlund.

'Have you heard about the security van robbery on Folkungagatan?' Schwarz adjusted his holster. 'Billing wants us to head over and help out. Looks like they're short of people.'

'Yeah, yeah. If that's what he says, then you'd better get going.' Jeanette shrugged.

Ten minutes later Hurtig passed Jeanette the phone, and she glanced at the time on her computer, then made a note: TEL BENGT BERGMAN'S DAUGHTER.

After three rings a woman answered.

'Bergman.' The voice was deep, almost like a man's.

'Victoria Bergman? Bengt Bergman's daughter?'

'That's right.'

'Right, hello, my name's Jeanette Kihlberg, I'm calling from the Stockholm police.'

'I see. So how can I help you?'

'Well . . . I've actually been given your phone number by your father's lawyer, who's wondering if you'd be able to act as a character witness for your father in a forthcoming trial.'

Hurtig nodded and smiled in approval at her lie. 'Smart,' he whispered.

There was silence on the line before the woman answered.

'I see. So you're calling me for that?'

'I understand if you think it's uncomfortable, but according to what I've been told you have things to say about your father that might help him. Presumably you know what he's been accused of?'

Hurtig shook his head. 'Christ, you're crazy!'

Jeanette held up a hand to shut him up, and heard the woman sigh.

'No, I'm sorry, but I haven't spoken to either him or Mum for over twenty years, and to be honest I'm surprised he thinks I'd want anything to do with him.'

The woman's reply made Jeanette wonder if Hurtig had been right.

'Ah, that doesn't quite fit what I've heard,' she lied.

'No, but there's nothing I can do about that, is there? If you're interested, I could tell you instead that he's bound to be guilty. Especially if it's got anything to do with what's between his legs. He forced that on me from when I was three or four years old.'

The candour of the woman's response left Jeanette speechless, and she had to clear her throat.

'If what you're saying is true, I can't help wondering why you never reported him.'

What the hell is this? she wondered, as Hurtig gave her a thumbs up and smiled in triumph.

'That's something I prefer to keep to myself. You've got no right to call this number and ask questions about him. He's dead to me.'

'OK, I understand. I won't disturb you again.'

There was a click, and Jeanette put the phone down.

Hurtig sat in silence waiting for her to say something.

'We bring him in,' she eventually said.

'Yes.' Hurtig stood up. 'Do you want to interview him, or do you want me to do it?'

'I'll take it, but you can sit in if you like.'

Her phone rang just as Hurtig shut the door behind him, and Jeanette saw that it was her boss.

'Where the hell are you?' Billing sounded cross.

'In my office. Why?'

'I've been waiting for you for almost fifteen minutes. Had you forgotten that we've got a steering-group meeting?'

Jeanette put a hand to her forehead. 'No, not at all. I'm on my way.'

She hung up and, as she half ran to the conference room, thought that it was going to be a long day.

Gamla Enskede – Kihlberg House

When Jeanette was having breakfast the next morning and opened the paper and saw the picture, she felt ashamed for the second time in as many days.

In the sports section of the morning paper was a photograph of Johan's team.

Hammarby had won the final against Djurgården 4–1, and Johan had scored two of the goals.

Jeanette was mortified that she'd forgotten to call the previous evening to ask how the match had gone, even though he had said it was a cup final and everything.

The steering-group meeting had dragged on, because Billing was so long-winded, then the rest of the afternoon had been spent trying to get hold of Bengt Bergman and interviewing the prostitute who had reported him. She had been very terse, and merely repeated what she had said in her original report. It was eight in the evening by the time Jeanette left police headquarters. She fell asleep on the sofa in front of the television before Åke and Johan came home, and by the time she woke up after midnight they had already gone to bed.

Jeanette realised that the dead boys she was working on were getting more of her attention than her own living son. But at the same time there was nothing she could do about that. Even if he was upset today, and was justified in thinking that she was neglecting him, hopefully one day he would realise that that wasn't the case. And understand that things hadn't been so bad for him. A roof over his head, food on the table, and parents who might have been absorbed in their own affairs but still loved him more than anything else.

But what if he grew up not seeing it like that, and only remembering the things he thought were wrong?

She heard Johan emerge from his room and go into the bathroom as Åke came down the stairs. Jeanette stood up and got two more plates and mugs out.

'Good morning,' Åke said, getting the orange juice out of the fridge and drinking a few mouthfuls straight from the carton. 'Have you spoken to him?'

He pulled out a chair, sat down and looked out the window. The sun was shining and the sky was clear blue. A few swallows were swooping over the lawn, and Jeanette was thinking of suggesting they have breakfast in the garden.

'No, he's only just up. He's in the shower at the moment.'

'He's very disappointed in us.'

'Us?' Jeanette tried to catch his eye, but he went on staring out the window. 'I thought I was the only one he was pissed off with?'

'No.' Åke turned round.

'So what have you done to make him pissed off with you?'

Åke put his mug down with a bang, pushed his chair back and stood up abruptly.

'Pissed off?' He leaned across the table. 'Is that what you think it is? That Johan's pissed off with us?'

Jeanette was taken aback by the sudden outburst.

'But –'

'He's not angry, and he's not pissed off. He's sad and disappointed in us. He thinks we don't care about him, and that we argue all the time.'

'Weren't you at the match yesterday?'

'No, I couldn't make it.'

'What do you mean, you couldn't make it?' Jeanette realised she was about to transfer her own shortcomings onto Åke. At the same time she still thought it was his responsibility to make sure that everything functioned at home. She worked as hard as she could, and when that wasn't enough she called her parents and asked them for money. All he had to do was sort out the dishes, occasionally do some laundry, and make sure that Johan did his homework.

'No, I couldn't make it! As simple as that!'

Jeanette saw that he was seriously upset now.

'I have work to do, you know,' he went on, throwing his arms out. 'God, you're suffocating.'

Jeanette could feel herself getting angry. 'So do something about it then!' she yelled. 'Get yourself a proper job instead of lazing about at home!'

'What are you fighting about?' Johan was standing in the doorway. He was dressed, but his hair was still wet. Jeanette could see how sad he was.

'We're not fighting.' Åke went over to the coffee machine. 'Your mum and I were just talking.'

'It didn't sound like it.' Johan turned to go back to his room.

'Come and sit down, Johan.' Jeanette let out a heavy sigh and glanced at her watch. 'Dad and I are sorry we missed the match yesterday. I see you won. Congratulations!' Jeanette held up the paper and pointed to the picture.

'Oh,' Johan said, and sighed, sitting down at the breakfast table.

'You know,' Jeanette began, 'we've both got a lot on our minds at the moment, your dad and I, with work and . . .' She started to make a sandwich as she searched for words that weren't there. They had let him down, and there were no good excuses.

She put the sandwich in front of Johan, who looked at it with distaste.

'Everyone else's parents were there, and they all have jobs as well.'

Jeanette looked at Åke for some support, but he was still standing and looking out the window.

Unconditional love, she thought. She was the one who was supposed to be the bearer of that, but without noticing it she had somehow shifted the burden to her son's shoulders.

'But you know,' she said, giving Johan a beseeching look, 'Mum goes out catching bad guys so you and your friends and their parents can sleep soundly at night.'

Johan glared at her, and in his eyes was a flash of fury that she'd never seen before.

'You've been telling me that since I was five years old!' he yelled, getting up from the table. 'I'm not a bloody child any more!'

The door to Johan's room slammed.

Jeanette sat with her cup of coffee between her hands. It was warm. The only thing that was warm at that moment.

'How did it come to this?'

Åke turned and looked at her thoughtfully. 'I can't remember it being any other way,' he said, and looked away, then glanced back at her. 'I'm going to start the washing machine.'

He turned his back on her and walked out.

Jeanette buried her face in her hands. Tears were burning behind her eyelids. She could feel the ground giving way beneath her feet. Everything she had taken for granted was being shaken to its foundations. Who was she really, without them?

She pulled herself together, went out into the hall, grabbed her jacket and left without saying goodbye. They didn't want her there.

She got in the car and drove off to what was left of her life.

Kronoberg – Police Headquarters

While she was waiting to get hold of von Kwist she read everything she could find about anaesthetics in general, and Xylocain in particular.

At half past ten she finally managed to reach the prosecutor by phone.

'Why are you so insistent?' he began. 'As far as I'm aware, you've got nothing to do with that case. It's one of Mikkelsen's, isn't it?'

Jeanette felt herself getting annoyed at his authoritarian tone.

'Yes, that's true, but there are a number of things I'd like to get clear. Things he said in his interviews that I've been wondering about.'

'I see – like what?'

'The most important is that he claims to know how to go about buying a child. A child that no one would miss, which you can later pay to get rid of. Then there's a couple of other things I'd like to get clear with him.'

'Such as?'

'The dead boys had been castrated, and their bodies contain an anaesthetic used by dentists. Karl Lundström has fairly extreme views about castration, and, as I'm sure you're aware, his wife is a dentist. In short, I believe he's of interest to my investigation.'

'Excuse me . . .' Von Kwist cleared his throat. 'But I think it sounds very hazy. Nothing concrete. And there's also something you don't know.' He fell silent.

'Really? What is it I don't know?'

'That he was under the influence of strong medication during those interviews.'

'OK, but surely that doesn't explain –'

'My dear,' he interrupted her, 'you don't know which medication we're talking about.'

The prosecutor's patronising arrogance made her boil with rage, but she realised she had to keep her cool.

'No, that's true. Which medication are we talking about?'

She heard him rustle some papers.

'Does the name Xanor ring any bells?'

Jeanette thought.

'No, I can't say –'

'I thought as much. Because if it did you wouldn't be taking Lundström's claims seriously.'

'What do you mean?'

'Xanor is the same drug that made Thomas Quick confess to pretty much every murder that's ever been committed. If they'd asked him, he'd probably have taken responsibility for Palme's murder and the Kennedy assassination as well. Maybe even the Rwandan genocide.' Von Kwist chuckled at his own joke.

'So you mean –'

'That there's no point in you taking this any further. Let me put it this way: I forbid you to take this any further.'

'Can you do that?'

'Of course I can. I've already spoken to Billing.'

Jeanette was shaking with anger. If it hadn't been for the prosecutor's arrogant tone, she might have been able to accept his decision, but right now it just strengthened her determination to defy him. She didn't care how many drugs Lundström was on, what he had said was far too interesting to dismiss.

She wasn't about to give up.

Mariatorget – Sofia Zetterlund's Office

Thunder-black rain was pattering on the copper roof of the München Brewery, and every now and then the water of Riddarfjärden Bay was lit up by sharp lightning.

Sofia's headache had got worse, and she went into the toilets, rinsed her face and took three aspirin. She hoped that would be enough to get a bit of strength back.

She unlocked the cupboard under her desk, took out the file on Karl Lundström, and read it through to refresh her memory.

Her recommendation was based on the fact that nothing had emerged during their conversations that would justify secure psychiatric care. She had explained her decision by saying that Karl Lundström's opinions were based on ideological conviction, and that as a result she recommended prison.

That was unlikely, however.

Every indication was that the district court would decide to put Karl Lundström in a mental health facility. Because he had been under the influence of Xanor in his interviews and during their sessions in Huddinge, her conclusions weren't regarded as valid for the basis of a court judgment.

In other words, her conversations with him were being dismissed as useless.

The district court had just seen a pathetic, confused man, but Sofia had realised that what Karl Lundström had told her wasn't concocted under the influence of any drug.

Karl Lundström's view was that only he could see the truth. He was convinced that strength was what mattered, and, by extension, justified his own privilege to abuse weaker individuals. He had a very high regard for his own character, was proud of it.

She remembered what he had said.

It had been one long self-justification.

'I don't consider what I've done to be wrong,' he had said. 'It's only wrong in today's society. Your morality is sullied. The urge is ancient. The word of God doesn't forbid incest. All men have the same desires as me, an ancient urge that comes down to gender. It was expressed long ago in pentameter form. I am God's creation and am acting on the mission He has given me.'

Moral-philosophical and quasi-religious excuses.

She could only conclude that Karl Lundström's belief in his own greatness made him an extremely dangerous person.

One who believes himself to be highly intelligent.

And shows a severe lack of empathy.

Karl Lundström's skill at manipulation would probably mean that after a while he'd end up on day release from Säter or some other secure psychiatric unit, and every moment he spent at liberty would put other people in danger.

She made up her mind to call Detective Superintendent Jeanette Kihlberg.

In this case it was her duty to ignore legal niceties.

Jeanette Kihlberg sounded extremely surprised when Sofia explained that she wanted to book a meeting to tell her what she knew about Karl Lundström.

'How come you've changed your mind?'

'I don't know if there's any connection to your case, but I think Lundström might be involved in something bigger. Has Mikkelsen followed up Lundström's story about Anders Wikström and the video recordings?'

'As far as I'm aware, they're looking into it right now. But Mikkelsen believes that Anders Wikström is a product of Lundström's imagination, and that they aren't going to find anything. I understand that you were invited to give a recommendation? He certainly seems to be sick.'

'Yes, but not sick enough to be able to abdicate responsibility for what he's done.'

'No? OK . . . But isn't there a sliding scale for illness?'

'Yes, with a range of punishments.'

'Which means that someone can have sick values and be punished for them?' Jeanette said.

'Exactly. But the punishment has to be suited to the perpetrator, and in this particular case I recommended imprisonment. It's my belief that Lundström can't be helped by psychiatric treatment.'

'I agree,' Jeanette said. 'But what do you make of the fact that he may have been under the influence of medication?'

Sofia smiled. 'From what I've read, the dose wasn't high enough to make any decisive difference. We're talking about very small doses of Xanor.'

'The same drug that Thomas Quick was given.'

'Yes, but Quick's dosage was of an entirely different order.'

'So you don't think I should let that worry me?'

'Exactly. I think it would be worth questioning Lundström about the dead boys. A draught from one open door can sometimes push another one open.'

Jeanette laughed.

'The draught from an open door?'

'Yes. If what he's said about buying a child has a grain of truth in it, maybe there's more you could find out from him.'

'I see. Well, thanks for taking the time to call.'

'Don't mention it. When can we meet up?'

'I'll call tomorrow morning, and we can meet over lunch. Does that sound OK?'

'That sounds fine.'

They hung up, and Sofia looked out the window. The sun was shining.

Monument – Mikael's Apartment

That evening it started to rain, and everything suddenly looked dirtier. Sofia Zetterlund packed up her things and left her office.

If the weather was a disaster, then her dinner with Mikael wasn't far behind. She had made a genuine effort, since this was going to be their last meal together for a while. Mikael had been invited to work at his firm's head office in Germany and was going to be away for a couple of months. But after some desultory conversation he had fallen asleep on the sofa after the dessert Sofia had spent almost an hour and a half making, carrot cake with cheese curd and raisins, and, as she stood at the sink rinsing their glasses to the sound of his snoring from the living room, she had to admit that she wasn't happy.

Things weren't going well at work. She was annoyed with everyone involved in the Lundström case. Social workers, psychologists and the forensic psychiatrist. And she was annoyed with her patients at the practice. At least she wouldn't have to see Carolina Glanz for a while, seeing as she'd cancelled her latest appointments and Sofia knew from the evening tabloids that she was making her living these days from performing in erotic films.

Victoria Bergman was no longer coming to see her either. That felt like a loss. Now her days were filled with coaching company bosses in leadership skills and giving presentations. Most of it was routine stuff, and required practically no preparation at all. But when it came down to it, this was so incredibly dull that she was starting to wonder if it was worth doing.

She decided to give up on the rest of the cleaning and went into the study instead with a cup of coffee, and switched on the computer. She took her memory stick from her bag and put it on the table.

Victoria Bergman was struggling with a little girl who gave every appearance of being her younger self.

Had a single event had a decisive impact?

Victoria kept returning to one particular incident in her first year at high school, but Sofia still didn't know exactly what it was, since Victoria always rushed her narrative when she got to that part.

But it could also be more than one single event. A feeling of exposure that had lasted years, possibly throughout her entire childhood.

Being a pariah, being the weaker party?

Sofia was inclined to believe that Victoria detested weakness.

She leafed through to a fresh page and made a mental note always to have her notepad in front of her when she listened to their recorded conversations.

She saw from the label on the tape that this particular conversation had taken place scarcely a month before.

Victoria's dry voice:

. . . and then just standing there one day with my hands tied behind my back while everyone else's hands were free to do whatever they liked, even if I

didn't want to. Didn't want to cry when they weren't crying because that could have been really embarrassing, especially when they'd come such a long way to sleep with me and not their wives. They probably thought it was nice not to have to pay the bill for being at home and pottering about all day instead of getting their arms and legs scratched from all the dragging . . .

She felt confused, tired and reluctant. A physical tiredness, as if she'd been exercising.

The noise of the television. The rain against the window.

And then that relentless voice. Should she stop listening?

. . . the old guys wanted to go off in the morning of course and then come back to food that was always good and nutritious and filling even if it tasted of sex and wasn't spiced . . .

Sofia could hear Victoria start to cry, and thought it odd that she herself had no memory of it happening.

When no one was looking of course you could let your mouth drip over the saucepans and fill them up with things you really ought to flush away. And then I got left with Grandma and Grandad. That was nice because I got away from all the arguments with Dad and without him it got easier to sleep without the wine or pills that you could have a go at if you wanted to get a nice feeling in your head. Just getting that voice to shut up, and stop going on and on, asking if today was going to be the day when you were going to dare . . .

Sofia woke up in front of the computer at half past midnight, feeling very uncomfortable.

She closed the document and went out into the kitchen to get a glass of water, but changed her mind and went back into the hall to get the packet of cigarettes from her coat pocket.

As she smoked under the exhaust fan she thought about Victoria's story.

Everything fitted together, more or less, and even though it seemed incoherent to start with, there weren't actually any gaps. It was one long, single story. An hour stretched out to a lifetime like a piece of chewing gum.

How far could it stretch before it broke? she thought, putting the burning cigarette down in the ashtray.

She went back into the study and got her notes. They said: SAUNA, BABY BIRDS, CLOTH DOG, GRANDMA, RUN, TAPE, VOICE,

COPENHAGEN. The words were written in her handwriting, even if it was scruffier and more jagged than usual.

Interesting, she thought, taking the pocket tape recorder back to the kitchen. She pulled a chair up against the stove.

While she rewound the tape she picked the cigarette out of the ashtray. She stopped the tape halfway and pressed play. The first thing she heard was her own voice.

'Where did you go when you went far away like that?'

She could see in her mind's eye how Victoria changed position, adjusting the skirt that had ridden up around her thighs.

'Well, I wasn't very old then, of course, but I think we used to go up to Dorotea and Vilhelmina in southern Lapland. But we might have gone even further. I got to sit in the front for the first time, and I felt like a grown-up. He told me loads of things, then tested me to see if I remembered them. Once he had an encyclopedia on the steering wheel and tested me on all the world's capital cities. In the book it said that Quezon City was the capital of the Philippines, but I said it was actually Manila, and nothing else. He got cross and we took bets on a pair of new slalom boots. When it later turned out that I was right I got a second-hand pair made of leather that he'd bought from a flea market and that I never used.'

'How long were you away? And did your mum go with you?'

She heard Victoria laugh.

'God, no, she never came along.'

They sat in silence for almost a minute before she heard herself point out that Victoria had said something about a voice.

'What sort of voice was it? Do you often hear voices?'

Sofia was annoyed at her repetition.

'Yes, sometimes when I was little,' Victoria replied. 'But to start with it was more like an intense noise that gradually increased in volume and tone. Sort of like a constantly rising hum.'

'Do you still hear it?'

'No, that was a long time ago. But when I was sixteen, seventeen, the monotonous noise turned into a voice.'

'And what did the voice say?'

'Most of the time it wondered if I was going to dare today. Dare you? Dare you? Dare you, today? Yes, it was pretty annoying sometimes.'

'What do you think the voice meant about daring?'

'Easy – daring to kill myself! Christ, if you only knew how I've struggled with that voice. So when I finally did it, it stopped.'

'You mean you tried to commit suicide?'

'Yes, when I was seventeen and had been off travelling with some friends. We were coming back from somewhere in France, I think, and when I got to Copenhagen I was completely wrecked, and tried to hang myself in the hotel room.'

'You tried to hang yourself?'

When she heard her own voice she thought it sounded unsteady.

'Yes . . . I woke up on the bathroom floor with the belt around my neck. The hook in the ceiling had come loose and I'd hit my mouth and nose on the tiles. There was blood everywhere, and I'd chipped one of my front teeth.'

She had opened her mouth to show Sofia a crown on her right front tooth. It was a slightly different colour from the one on the left.

'And that's when the voice stopped?'

'Yes, seems like it. I'd proved that I dared, so I don't suppose there was any point in it carrying on nagging.'

Victoria laughed.

Sofia heard them sit there in silence, just breathing, for what must have been a couple of minutes. Then the sound of Victoria pushing her chair back, picking up her coat and leaving.

Sofia stubbed out her third cigarette, switched off the fan and went to bed. It was almost three in the morning, and it had stopped raining.

What had happened that had made Victoria stop their sessions? They were finally getting somewhere.

She realised that she missed her conversations with Victoria Bergman.

The road

meandering across Svartsjölandet was empty for a long time, but eventually she found a boy.

Alone at the side of the road with a broken bicycle.

In need of a lift.

Trusting everyone.

Had never learned to recognise people who have been let down.

The room was lit up by a bulb in the ceiling, and she watched the performance from a chair in one corner.

In the wall opposite the hidden door to the living room she had mounted a sturdy iron boathook.

They had undressed the boy, put a choker chain around his neck, and tied him to the hook using a two-metre-long chain.

He had four square metres to move around in, but had no chance of reaching her.

On the floor beside her lay the electric cable, and in her lap she had the taser that, if necessary, could fire two metal projectiles. When they hit the boy, fifty thousand volts would pulse through his body for five seconds. His muscles would cramp and he would be rendered completely harmless.

She gave Gao the signal that the performance could begin.

He had used the morning to purify himself and, through hour after hour of meditation, to minimise his thought processes. There must be no logic left to distract him from doing what he had been trained to do.

Now, in the seconds before the performance began, he needed to eradicate the very last remnants of thought.

He must be a body, with only four life-sustaining requirements.

Oxygen.

Water.

Food.
Sleep.
Nothing else.
He is a machine, she thought.

The plastic on the floor rustled when the boy began to move. He was still confused and bewildered from being unconscious, and looked around uncertainly. He tugged rather feebly at the chain around his neck, but he had already realised that it was pointless trying to get loose, and therefore crept backwards warily, getting to his feet and standing with his back to the wall.

Gao moved to and fro in front of the naked, helpless boy.

With a carefully aimed kick to his stomach he made him sink to his knees, gasping for breath. Then he kicked him hard on one ear and the boy collapsed, whimpering.

There was a cracking sound and blood ran from the boy's nose.

She realised that the fight was too uneven and loosened the boy's chains.

The bulb was swaying gently from the ceiling and the shadows played over the back of the crawling boy. Gao had read the situation and knew immediately what was expected of him. But the other boy thought that his begging and sobbing would save him, and so never realised the gravity of the situation.

He lay on the floor kicking his legs, like a submissive puppy.

She wondered if it was because this was the first time he had ever felt real physical pain, and therefore had no access to the necessary survival instincts. Perhaps he had been raised to believe in people's innate goodness? That delusion meant that he never had a chance to defend himself.

Gao was raining down blows and kicks on him.

In the end she tried to even the odds by giving the boy a knife, but he just threw it away and howled in horror.

She got up from her chair and gave Gao the water bottle containing the amphetamine. He was sweaty and the muscles of his torso rippled with his deep breathing.

She and he would become something perfect, something whole.

In the shadows they were one being.

Openings and closings.

Blood and pain. Electrical impulses.

Slowly she began to whip the boy's back with the electric cable, gradually increasing the pace and hitting him with growing fury.

The boy's back was bleeding badly.

She picked up one of the syringes, but as she was about to inject the anaesthetic into his neck, she realised that he was no longer alive.

It was over.

Kronoberg – Police Headquarters

Karl Lundström was the only interesting name on the list of suspects at the moment. Jeanette Kihlberg was both surprised and grateful that Sofia Zetterlund had got in touch. Maybe she could bring something new to the investigation?

It was desperately needed. Everything had ground to a halt.

Thelin and Furugård had long since been written off, and questioning the suspected rapist Bengt Bergman had been pointless.

Jeanette had found Bergman a particularly unpleasant individual. Emotionally unpredictable, but at the same time cold and calculating. He had talked about his great powers of empathy several times, while simultaneously demonstrating the exact opposite.

She couldn't help seeing the similarities to what she had read about Karl Lundström.

It was Bergman's wife who had given him an alibi each time he had been suspected of anything. Jeanette had angrily pointed this out to von Kwist when she suggested they should talk to him again. She had also mentioned the similarities with Karl Lundström and his wife, Annette, who had taken his side even when they were dealing with the abuse of their own daughter.

As usual, the prosecutor had been immovable, and Jeanette had to admit to herself that she'd been taking a chance with Bengt Bergman anyway.

A gamble that hadn't paid off.

But it was clear to Jeanette from the short telephone conversation she'd had with his daughter that Bengt Bergman had a lot on his conscience.

Jeanette realised wearily that she wouldn't be at all surprised if the prosecutor decided to drop the case relating to the aggravated rape of Tatiana Achatova, the prostitute.

What chance did a middle-aged prostitute with several drug convictions behind her stand against a senior official from the Swedish International Development Cooperation Agency? Her word against his. And it didn't take much to work out who Prosecutor von Kwist was going to believe.

No, Tatiana Achatova didn't stand a chance, Jeanette thought.

Once again she felt tired, and would much rather be taking a break from work, to enjoy the summer and the heat. But Åke had gone to Kraków with Alexandra Kowalska, and Johan was up in Dalarna with some friends. She realised she'd only end up feeling lonely if she took her holiday now.

'You've got a visitor.' Hurtig stepped into the room. 'Ulrika Wendin is sitting down in reception. She doesn't want to come up, but says she wants to see you.'

The young woman was standing out in the street smoking. In spite of the heat she was wearing a thick black padded jacket, black jeans and a pair of heavy, military-style boots. She had her hood pulled up, and beneath it was wearing a large pair of black sunglasses. Jeanette went up to her.

'I want my case to be reopened,' Ulrika said, stubbing out her cigarette.

'OK . . . Let's go somewhere we can talk. I'll buy you a coffee.'

They walked down Hantverkargatan in silence, and Ulrika managed to fit in another cigarette before they reached the cafe. They each ordered coffee and a sandwich before sitting down on the outdoor terrace.

Ulrika took off the big sunglasses and Jeanette realised why she'd been wearing them. Her right eye was swollen and blackish purple in colour. A black eye as big as a fist and, to judge by the colour, no more than a couple of days old.

'What the hell is that?' Jeanette exclaimed. 'Who did that to you?'

'Don't worry about that. Just a guy I know. Pretty nice guy, actually. When he's not drinking, I mean.' She smiled awkwardly. 'I was the one offering booze, and we had an argument when I wanted to turn down the volume of the stereo.'

'Damn it, Ulrika. That hardly makes it your fault! What sort of people are you hanging out with? Some guy who hits you because you don't want the music so loud that the neighbours complain?'

Ulrika Wendin shrugged her shoulders, and Jeanette realised she wasn't going to get any further.

'So . . .' she said instead. 'I can help you organise the legal side if you want to petition for a new trial against Lundström.' She assumed that von Kwist was unlikely to take the initiative. 'What made you change your mind?'

'Well, after we talked,' she began, 'I realised I'm not done with this. I want to explain everything.'

'Everything?'

'Yes, it was so hard back then. I felt ashamed . . .'

Jeanette studied the young woman and was struck by how fragile she looked.

'Ashamed? What for?'

Ulrika squirmed. 'They didn't just rape me.'

'What haven't you told us?'

'It was so humiliating,' Ulrika eventually said. 'They did something that made me lose all feeling below my waist, and when they raped me . . .' She fell silent again.

Jeanette jumped in. 'What?'

Ulrika stubbed out her cigarette and immediately lit another.

'It just poured out of me. Shit, I mean. Like a fucking baby.'

Jeanette could see that Ulrika was close to bursting into tears. Her eyes were shining and her voice trembling.

'It was like some sort of ritual. They were enjoying it. It was so fucking humiliating, I never told the police.'

Ulrika wiped her eyes on the sleeve of her jacket.

'You mean they drugged you with some sort of anaesthetic?'

'Yes, something like that.'

She looked at Ulrika's bruise. From her right eye the almost black broken blood vessels formed a network leading down towards her ear.

Recently beaten by a so-called boyfriend. And raped and humiliated seven years ago by four men – one of them Karl Lundström.

'Let's go up to my office, then you can give me a detailed statement.'

Ulrika Wendin nodded.

Anaesthetic? Jeanette thought. No one outside the investigation could know that the bodies of the dead boys contained anaesthetic. That couldn't be a coincidence.

Jeanette felt her pulse rate increase.

Mariatorget – Sofia Zetterlund's Office

When the phone rang Sofia Zetterlund was deep in thought. The shrill ringing tone almost made her spill her coffee. She had been thinking about Lasse.

'Jeanette Kihlberg here. Is there any chance you could take an early lunch, to give us a bit longer to talk? I can get some Chinese on the way and see you down at the Zinkensdamm sports complex. Do you like Chinese, by the way?'

Two questions and one presumption, all in the same breath. Jeanette Kihlberg didn't mince her words.

'That sounds good. The Olympics are in Beijing this year, and I could use the practice,' Sofia joked.

Jeanette laughed, and they hung up.

Sofia found it hard to concentrate. Lasse was still on her mind.

She opened the desk drawer and took out his photograph.

Tall and dark, with intense eyes. But what she remembered most clearly were his hands. Even though he worked in an office, it was as if nature had equipped him with a pair of sturdy, gnarled hands made for manual labour.

She was also grateful that she had managed to suppress any sense of missing him and replaced it with ambivalence. He didn't deserve to be missed.

She recalled what she had said to him in the hotel room in New York before everything collapsed.

I'm giving myself to you, Lasse. You get me, all of me, and I trust you to take care of me.

So naive. She'd never make that mistake again. No one would get that close.

Sofia pulled her jacket on and walked out.

Zinkensdamm Sports Complex

'Ah, so I can put a face to the voice at last,' Jeanette Kihlberg said, holding out her hand in greeting.

Smile.

'Indeed,' Sofia Zetterlund replied with a smile. The detective was in her forties, and considerably shorter than Sofia had been expecting.

Jeanette turned, and Sofia followed in her lithe, confident steps. They sat down on the big, new concrete stand at the Zinkensdamm sports complex and looked out across the artificial turf.

'An unusual place for lunch,' Sofia said.

'Zinken's classic territory,' Jeanette said, returning her smile. 'It would be hard to find a nicer place. Maybe Kanalplan, I suppose.'

'Kanalplan?'

'Yes, Nacka used to play there, back in the day. These days the Hammarby women's team plays there. Sorry, I'm getting sidetracked, we'd better start. You've probably got an appointment booked?'

'No problem, we can sit here all day if necessary.'

Jeanette concentrated on chewing a chicken wing. 'Good, this might take a while. Lundström isn't an easy man to understand. And there are also a number of things that aren't quite clear in the facts that have emerged.'

Sofia put her bag down on the next seat.

'Have you managed to find that Wikström, Lundström's friend in Ånge?'

'No, I talked to Mikkelsen this morning. There does appear to be an Anders Wikström in Ånge. Or rather an Anders Efraim Wikström. But he's over eighty and he's been living in an old people's home outside

Timrå for the past five years. He's never heard of a Karl Lundström, and can hardly have anything to do with this.'

Sofia wasn't surprised by what Jeanette had said. It matched what she had thought all along. Anders Wikström was a product of Karl Lundström's imagination.

'OK. Anything else you've found out?'

Jeanette dropped the last of her food in the bag.

'Lundström's got plenty more baggage. Yesterday evening a young woman gave a statement that could be of interest to my case. I can't say any more at the moment, but there's a connection to the murders I'm investigating.'

Jeanette lit a cigarette and coughed.

'God, I really should quit . . . Would you like one, by the way?'

'Thanks, I would . . .'

Jeanette passed her the lighter.

'Have you asked his wife if she knew about the films?'

Jeanette was silent for a moment before she replied.

'When Mikkelsen asked her, he only got a very confused reply. She doesn't know, she can't remember, she wasn't there, and so on. She's lying to protect him. As for Karl Lundström's story, I'm having trouble getting it to fit together. All that talk about Anders Wikström and the Russian mafia. Mikkelsen thinks it's all a pack of lies.'

'I'm not convinced that Karl Lundström is simply lying,' Sofia said, taking a deep drag on the cigarette. 'That's one of the reasons why I called you.'

'How do you mean?'

'I think it's more complicated than that.'

'Really? In what way?'

'I mean it's possible that he sometimes tells the truth, but that his imagination takes over. Or rather his delusions, his self-deceptions. He's done something that is strictly taboo: he's abused his own daughter.'

'And you mean he needs to find a way to handle the guilt?'

'Yes. He's starting to loathe himself to a point where he feels responsible for a series of other assaults that he never actually committed.'

Sofia blew several smoke rings.

'During our conversations he addressed the concept of wrong several times, in the context of male attraction to young girls, and it's clear that he regards that attraction as natural. In order to convince himself beyond any doubt, he has invented a series of events so extreme that they can't be dismissed.' Sofia put her cigarette out. 'How's Linnea?'

Jeanette looked thoughtful. 'Apart from what they found on Lundström's computer, they also found a number of VHS cassettes in the basement.'

'At their home, you mean?'

'Yes, and on those cassettes they found not only Lundström's fingerprints, but Linnea's as well.'

Sofia shuddered. 'So she's seen the films too?'

'Yes, that's what we're assuming. According to our analysis they are, if you'll pardon the phrase, classic child pornography. As far as we've been able to determine, they were filmed in Brazil in the late eighties. They've been circulating in paedophile circles for a long time, and have – again, sorry about this – legendary status among collectors . . .'

'So they're nothing to do with the Russian mafia?'

'No, the Russian mafia seems to be entirely innocent in this case, just like Lundström's imaginary Anders Wikström. But the things that happen in the films do fit with what he said during your conversation with him, with the significant difference that they were actually filmed in Brazil twenty years ago.'

'That sounds plausible. So his lies about Anders Wikström were inspired by existing child porn films. That would explain why the lies were so detailed.'

'In one of the drawers of Lundström's desk they also found a lock of hair and a pair of pants belonging to his daughter. Can you explain what that's all about?'

'Well, I recognise the behaviour. He's collecting trophies,' Sofia said. 'The aim is to exercise control over the victim. Using those objects, he can return to the assaults in his imagination, and relive them.'

They sat in silence for a while. Possibly because it was all just so grotesque.

Sofia was thinking about Linnea Lundström and everything she had been through. Victoria Bergman resurfaced in her mind, and Sofia wondered how Linnea was handling her experiences. Victoria had learned to channel what she had been through. How was Linnea dealing with it?

'How's the girl now?'

Jeanette held out her hands and looked baffled.

'Mikkelsen says he recognises her reaction from other kids he's met. They're angry, but so incredibly let down. They don't trust anyone. When she's not crying, she's screaming that she hates her father, but at the same time there's no doubt that she's missing him.'

Sofia thought about Victoria Bergman again. A grown woman who was still a child.

'I understand,' she said.

Jeanette looked out over the artificial turf. 'Do you have any children?' she asked, lighting another cigarette.

Sofia was surprised by the question.

'No . . . It's never been the right time. You?'

'Yep, one boy.' Sofia noted that Jeanette looked thoughtful. 'He . . .' Jeanette turned serious. 'He's the same age as Linnea. They're so incredibly fragile at that age, if you know what I mean . . .'

'I know.'

'Anyway, according to Mikkelsen this is your specialist area? Traumatised children . . .' Jeanette held up her hands and added, 'To be honest, I have real trouble understanding this sort of criminal. What the hell is it that drives them?'

The question was blunt, and Sofia felt that a similarly blunt answer was required, but didn't know what to say at first. Jeanette's intensity and presence both interested and distracted her.

'It's not always easy to say,' she said after a pause. 'But there were a couple of things that struck me as odd with Karl Lundström.'

'What?'

'I don't know if it means anything, but he kept coming back to castration. Once he asked me if I knew how to castrate a reindeer, then went on to explain that you crush the testicles by biting them. On another occasion he went so far as to say he thought all men ought to be castrated at birth.'

Jeanette sat in silence for several seconds.

'Everything we discuss here has to stay between us. But what you've just said definitely strengthens my suspicions. Because each of the three murdered boys had been mutilated.'

'Damn . . .'

Jeanette looked reproachfully at Sofia. 'Shame you didn't tell me that the first time we spoke.'

'There was no reason for me to give up my oath of confidentiality when you first contacted me. I simply couldn't see a direct connection to your case.'

Jeanette made an apologetic gesture with her hands.

Sofia realised that Jeanette had a fiery temper and, to her surprise, found that she quite liked that.

Jeanette Kihlberg's face didn't mask her emotions, and Sofia saw the reproachful look in her eyes fade, to be replaced by melancholy.

'Well, it's not worth arguing about. Have you got anything else useful?'

'Xylocain adrenalin,' Sofia said.

The smoke from Jeanette's cigarette caught in her throat, and she was seized with a coughing fit.

Sofia was taken aback by the strength of her reaction, and wasn't sure at first how to continue, but Jeanette pre-empted her in between coughs.

'What the hell are you saying?'

'Well . . . Karl Lundström said that Anders Wikström usually injected his victims with Xylocain adrenalin. It's not a substance I'm familiar with. I don't know if it induces intoxication.'

Jeanette shook her head and took a deep breath. 'It's not the sort of thing you take to get high,' she said in a tone of resignation. 'It's an anaesthetic. The same anaesthetic we found in the dead boys. Xylocain adrenalin is used by dentists, and Annette Lundström is a dentist, of course. Need I say more?'

Silence fell once again.

'That sounds pretty incriminating, I must say,' Sofia said after a while.

They were interrupted when Jeanette's mobile phone rang. She excused herself.

Sofia couldn't hear what was being said at the other end, but it was evidently something that upset Jeanette.

'Fucking hell. OK . . . what else?'

Jeanette stood up and began to walk up and down between the rows of seats in the stand.

'OK, I can see that. But how the hell could it happen?'

She sat down again. 'OK. I'm on my way . . .' Then she snapped her phone shut and sighed in despair. 'Fuck.'

'What's happened?'

'Well, we were talking about him . . .'

'What do you mean?'

Jeanette Kihlberg leaned back and swore silently between drags on the cigarette. Her face was like an open book. Disappointment. Anger. Resignation.

Sofia didn't know what to say.

'There won't be any more conversations with Lundström,' Jeanette Kihlberg muttered. 'He's hanged himself in prison. Anything to say about that?'

Toronto, 2007

The snowstorm over the eastern seaboard means that Flight 4592 has been diverted to Toronto instead of landing at John F. Kennedy Airport as planned. As a result the airline books them into a four-star hotel and they get allocated seats on the morning flight the next day.

After taking a shower, they decide to stay in the hotel room and share a bottle of champagne.

'God, how wonderful! Some time off at last!'

Lasse leans back and stretches out on the bed. Sofia, who's standing in just her underwear and putting her make-up on in front of the mirror next to the bed, picks up a damp towel and throws it at him.

'Come here and make a child with me,' he suddenly says, still with the towel over his face. 'I want to have a child with you,' he repeats, and Sofia stiffens.

'What did you say?'

'I said I want us to have a child.'

'You mean it? Seriously?' Sofia can't tell if he's joking with her.

Sometimes he says things, only to take back what he's just said a moment later. But there's something different in his voice this time.

'Yeah, what the hell! You're getting close to forty and it's starting to get a bit late. Not for me, but for you. And I've got a feeling we could keep on . . . Oh, you know what I mean.' He removes the towel, and she can see that he's being completely serious.

Maybe it's the alcohol or the long, tiring flight that gets to her and makes her start crying. Probably a combination of everything.

'Hey, are you crying?' He gets up from the bed and comes over to her. 'Is something wrong?'

'No, no, no. I'm just so incredibly happy. Of course I want to have a child with you. You know that's what I've always wanted.' She looks him in the eye in the mirror.

'OK, let's do it then! Now or never!'

She goes over to the bed. He embraces her, kisses the back of her neck, and begins to undo her bra.

His eyes are sparkling the way they used to, and she feels her insides quiver.

Afterwards they go to a nightclub down on Nassau Street. One of the few places along the road where the queue isn't too long.

The club is dimly lit and consists of a series of different rooms separated by red velvet curtains. In the first one is a small stage, empty when they arrive.

There aren't many people there, and they take a seat at the bar and order a drink. A couple of hours pass as she gets slowly more intoxicated, more people arrive, and the music from the stage gets louder.

A man and a woman sit down next to them at the bar.

Afterwards she can't even remember their names, but she'll never forget what happens next.

To begin with they just exchange looks and smiles. The woman compliments Sofia on some detail of her outfit.

The drinks mount up, and soon the four of them move to some more comfortable seats in a quieter part of the club.

A big room.

Subdued lighting, to match the music. The sofa shaped like a heart.

Then she realises what sort of place Lasse has taken her to.

It had been his idea to go to a club. And hadn't he seemed to be directing their steps straight to Nassau Street?

She feels rather foolish for taking so long to realise where they are.

Then everything goes so quickly and so easily.

And not just because of the alcohol. But because something happens between her and Lasse in the presence of the two strangers.

He introduces her as his life partner. His body language says they belong together, and she realises that's because he wants her to feel secure in this situation.

She leaves the table to go to the toilet, and when she returns the woman is sitting next to Lasse, and the seat beside the man is free. She feels her excitement mount at once, and her pulse is racing in her temples as she sits down.

She looks at Lasse and realises that he has worked out that she knows what's going on, and that she doesn't have anything against it.

She can certainly imagine sharing him with someone else. After all, she's there, and she knows he'd never do anything without her consent.

There are no secrets any longer. They will love each other just as much, no matter what happens.

And they're going to have a child together.

When Sofia wakes up the next morning she has a terrible headache. Even yawning leaves her seeing stars.

'Wake up, Sofia . . . Our flight leaves in just over an hour.'

She glances at the clock on the bedside table.

'Shit, quarter to six . . . How long have I been asleep?'

'Half an hour or so,' Lasse laughs. 'You should have seen yourself yesterday.'

'Yesterday?'

She smiles at him, even though her headache makes smiling a painful effort. 'Just now, you mean? Come here!'

She's naked, and lets the covers slide off. She lies on her stomach and pulls one leg up beneath her. 'Come on!'

Lasse laughs again. 'God, you're so beautiful lying there like that . . . You haven't forgotten that we've got visitors?'

She hears the shower running in the bathroom. She can see naked bodies through the gap in the door when she rolls over to kiss him.

'Is that supposed to put me off?'

Had they done the right thing? Either way, it feels good to her, and he seems happy as well.

'It'll have to be a quickie,' he whispers. 'Aeroplanes don't wait for crazy people.'

Her headache now merely feels pleasantly giddy.

'Sofia? You've got to see this. It looks kind of futuristic . . .'

She's dozed off against his shoulder, and straightens up stiffly to look out of the plane window. New York, white with snow, split in two by the Hudson River, which cuts like a black line across the view. The street networks of the Bronx and Brooklyn look like narrow lines on a sheet of white paper. The shadows of the skyscrapers look like diagrams.

She feels safe having him there beside her.

When they arrive at the hotel on Manhattan's Upper West Side, the sun is shining from a clear blue sky. Sofia has been to New York a couple of times before, but her last visit was almost ten years ago and she's forgotten how beautiful the city can be.

She and Lasse are standing entwined by the window of their hotel room. From the fifteenth floor they have a magnificent view of Central Park, which is lying cocooned in the thick blanket of snow that's fallen overnight.

She turns and kisses him on the lips.

'I can feel that I'm giving myself to you, Lasse. You get me, all of me, and I trust you to take care of me.'

'I . . .' He stops himself and gives her a long, hard hug. She gets the feeling that he's about to tell her something.

'I love you too,' he says after a pause, but she can't help thinking that he had been about to say something else.

In the mirror she can see the window he's facing. His face is visible in the glass and it looks to her as if he's crying. She thinks about how she felt just a few weeks ago. It feels like another world. Now he wants to have a child with her and everything is going to be different.

Then he lets go and looks at her again. Yes, he has been crying. But his whole face is lit up in a smile. 'Do you know what I think we should do now?'

'No . . . What should we do? You've been here hundreds of times, so you ought to know,' she says, smiling back.

'First we'll have lunch in the hotel restaurant. The food's excellent – at least it was when I was here last year. Then I'm going to take you somewhere. To a place that's very special at this time of year.'

When it's time for dessert he suddenly gets a mischievous look in his eye, and he excuses himself and goes over to the bar, where he leans over to give something to the man behind it. They exchange a few quiet words, then he returns to the table with a smile.

Suddenly the loudspeaker system begins to echo with the sound of a guitar and snare drum. Sofia recognises the song immediately, but can't think where she first heard it.

'Oh my God, Lasse! I love this song . . . how did you know?'

Then she remembers where she knows the music from.

A year or so ago. It had been in an Asian film she'd watched. She hadn't been that impressed by the film, but couldn't forget the song, which had been played over and over again.

By the time she got home she'd already forgotten what the film was called, but she remembers saying to Lasse that there was a song in it she liked. He had laughed at her when she tried to sing it to him, but evidently he had understood exactly what she meant.

'Who's singing? This is from that film . . . but you haven't even seen it?'

He leans over. 'No, but I've heard you sing it. Let's drink a toast, then I'll explain.'

He fills their glasses and goes on. 'The girl in the song actually comes from the place we're going to. And the record must have been in the cupboard under the stereo for at least ten years, but you've never wanted to listen all the way through on the few occasions you've let me play it. Old man's music, you usually say. This is the last track on the album.'

They drink a toast, then Lasse just sits there quietly in front of her. She waits, deep in thought and listening to the lyrics. And soon she understands.

And the straightest dude I ever knew was standing right for me all the time . . . Oh, my Coney Island baby, now. I'm a Coney Island baby, now.

She sighs and leans back in her chair with a smile. 'Coney Island? We're going to Coney Island? In the middle of winter?'

'Believe me, it's a great place,' he says, looking serious. 'You'll love it.'

She strokes the back of his hand. 'Beaches, carousels, slushy snow, wind, and utterly deserted? Junkies and stray dogs? I'd love that? Who's this idiot singing, anyway?'

They share a long kiss, then he tells her it's Lou Reed.

'Lou Reed? We haven't got any Lou Reed albums . . . ?' she says uncertainly.

He smiles. 'Don't you remember the cover? Lou Reed in a suit and bow tie, his face half hidden under a black hat?'

She laughs. 'Lasse, you're teasing me. I know we haven't got the album at home. I actually clean that cupboard from time to time, unlike certain other people.'

He looks bewildered. 'But of course we've got the album, haven't we?'

His doubt amuses her. 'I'm absolutely certain we haven't, and you've never played it for me. Not that it matters. What you just did makes up for your absent-mindedness.'

'What I just did?'

'Yes, getting the song played, silly.' She laughs again. 'You remembered that I liked it.'

He looks relieved, and the uncertainty vanishes from his face.

'Right . . . Well, drink up, then!'

They clink glasses again, and she thinks about how much she loves him.

When she sang the song for him after she came home from the cinema, he showed no sign of recognising it. But he'd actually been waiting for the right moment to play it for her.

He had waited a whole year for the opportunity, he had waited, and he had remembered.

It's only a detail, but it's a detail that she takes very seriously. He cares about her, even if he never says so in so many words.

They spend the last day shopping and relaxing in the hotel room.

Coney Island had been wonderful, just like he'd said.

During the flight home Sofia thinks about how long it had been since they had been able to relax like this. She feels like she's just rediscovered a Lasse she knew was there, but hasn't seen for several years.

Suddenly he's back again, the Lasse she once fell in love with.

But back in Stockholm everything pales. After just a few weeks Sofia realises that, no matter how hard she may want to believe the opposite, he's always going to pull the rug out from under her.

Just as suddenly as he came back to her, he disappears again.

They're sitting at the breakfast table reading the paper.

'Lasse?'

'Mmm . . .' He's absorbed in his reading.

'The pregnancy test . . .'

He doesn't even look up from the paper.

'It was negative.'

Now he looks up. Surprised.

'What?'

'I'm not pregnant, Lasse.'

He sits in silence for a few seconds. 'Sorry, I'd forgotten about that . . .' He smiles awkwardly and goes back to the paper.

His absent-mindedness is no longer so attractive.

'Forgotten? You've forgotten what we talked about in New York?'

'No, of course not.' He looks tired. 'I've just had a lot going on at work. I hardly know what day it is any more.'

The paper rustles.

He looks down at it, but she can see he isn't reading. His eyes aren't moving, and they don't seem to be focused. He sighs and looks even more tired.

Their days in New York are starting to feel like indistinct memories of a dream. His closeness, the understanding between them, the day they spent at Coney Island, it's all gone.

The dream has been replaced by a grey, predictable daily grind where she and Lasse walk past each other like shadows.

It's obvious to her that he takes her for granted. And he's also managed to forget the child they had decided to have together. She can't understand it.

She can feel that she's about to explode.

'By the way, Sofia, there was something,' he says, finally pushing the newspaper aside. 'They called from Hamburg to say that things have got snarled up there. They need me to go down, and I couldn't say no.'

He reaches for the juice, looking at her uncertainly, first pouring some for her, then himself.

'You know Germans never rest. Not even over the holidays.'

She snaps.

'For fuck's sake! You've got to be kidding!' she yells, and throws the newspaper at him. 'You were away for Midsummer. You were away for Lucia. And now Christmas and New Year as well! This is ridiculous.

You're supposed to be the boss, for God's sake! Surely there's some way to delegate your damn work over public holidays?'

'Please, Sofia, calm down.'

He holds his arms out and shakes his head.

She thinks she can detect a smirk. He doesn't even take her seriously when she's angry.

'It's not as easy as you'd think. If I turn my back, everything just collapses behind me. OK, the Germans are smart, but they're not very independent. You know, they like rules and regulations, marching in straight lines.'

He laughs and tries to approach her with a smile. But she's still furious.

'It might not just be in Germany that things collapse behind your back when you aren't there.'

He looks suddenly worried. 'What do you mean, collapse? Has something happened?'

His reaction isn't what she was expecting, and her anger dissipates slightly.

'I don't know what I meant, I'm just fucking angry and disappointed about being left on my own over another holiday.'

'I realise that, but there's not much I can do about it,' he says, getting up and turning his back on her as he puts the breakfast things in the fridge. He feels a very long way away all of a sudden.

Later, while he's in the shower, she does something she's never done before in the ten years they've been together.

She goes into the hall and gets his work phone from his jacket pocket. The one he always has on silent when he's at home and not working. She types in the pass code and clicks through to the list of dialled numbers.

The first four are German numbers, but the fifth has a Stockholm dialling code.

More German numbers. Then the same Stockholm number again.

She scrolls down and the same number reappears at regular intervals. She sees from the dates that he's been calling someone in the Stockholm region several times a day.

She pulls up the unknown number and calls it, glancing at the bathroom door as she listens to it ring.

A soft woman's voice answers.

'Hello, darling! I thought you were going to be busy?'

Sofia ends the call.

She sits down at the kitchen table.

Behind his back? Everything's collapsing behind *my* back.

Lasse comes out with a towel wrapped around his waist. He smiles at her and goes into the bedroom to get dressed. When he's done, she knows he'll come in and make coffee.

She opens the fridge, takes out the carton of milk and empties it down the sink. Then she crumples up the empty packet and pushes it down into the rubbish bin.

He comes out into the kitchen.

'If you want coffee you'll have to go and get some milk. It's all gone.'

'OK, I'll go to the shop and you can make the coffee in the meantime.'

When she hears the front door close she goes out into the hall and sees that he's gone out without a coat. His jacket is still there.

She takes the mobile phone out again and sees that he's got two missed calls.

Presumably the unknown woman has called back, but she daren't look, because then the missed calls will disappear from the screen.

She finds her way to his messages instead, and opens the inbox.

Once she's read the thirty or so text messages Lasse has exchanged with the unknown woman over the past few months, it feels like she's just slammed into a wall.

Kronoberg – Police Headquarters

A passage of sighs connects the Stockholm police headquarters with the city courts, through which people under arrest are led to their trials. It meanders through the tunnels belowground, and is said to have been the scene of several suicides.

Karl Lundström was currently in a coma, after he had tried to hang himself in his cell.

Jeanette Kihlberg realised that meant that the question of his guilt might never be cleared up properly.

The evening after the suicide attempt it was on the television news, and several of the usual suspects were lamenting the security failures within the criminal justice system. Even the psychologists got it in the neck for failing to identify that Lundström was a suicide risk.

Jeanette leaned back on her shabby office chair and looked out of the window.

At least she had done all she could.

Now she would have to call Ulrika Wendin and inform her that the situation had changed.

The girl didn't sound surprised when Jeanette told her what had happened and explained that there wouldn't be any new trial for as long as Karl Lundström was in a coma.

Åhlund and Schwarz had been given the job of finding out if Karl Lundström's blue Volvo might be the same vehicle that had scraped a tree out in Svartsjölandet, but initial analysis didn't seem to support that idea.

The colour of the paint didn't match. Different shades of blue.

Outside the window the afternoon sun was blazing down.

Then the phone rang, with news of another body.

At roughly the same time that Karl Lundström had been knotting a sheet around his neck in Kronoberg Prison, another dead boy had been discovered in an attic on Södermalm.

Monument – Crime Scene

There wasn't actually much to suggest that the boy, who had been found in an attic in the Monument block close to Skanstull, was a victim of the same perpetrator as the earlier bodies.

Two empty holes showed where the eyes had once been, and you could just about make out what had once been his nose and lips. The whole face was covered with large, liquid-filled blisters, and there were only a few tufts of hair left.

The heavy iron door to the attic opened and Ivo Andrić walked in, together with the forensic medical officer, Rydén.

'Hi, Rydén. Everything's under control, I hope?' Jeanette said, then turned towards Ivo Andrić. 'So you've ended up here as well.'

'Coincidence. Someone else is on holiday and I volunteered.' Ivo Andrić scratched his head.

At first glance the blisters looked like burn injuries, but since the rest of the body was intact and the clothes showed no traces of either ash or soot, another explanation was most likely.

'Looks like acid,' Ivo Andrić said, and Rydén nodded in agreement.

The floor beneath the boy and the walls closest to him showed splash marks, and Rydén took out a swab and pressed it against one of the dried yellow stains. He sniffed the swab and looked thoughtful.

'Off the top of my head this seems to be hydrochloric acid – fairly strong considering what happened when it hit his face. I wonder if whoever did this realised the risk they were taking? The chances of getting hurt in the process are pretty high.'

Ivo Andrić rubbed his chin. 'That wall looks new.' He pointed at the left-hand wall, and went on. 'Builders often use some sort of acid. I believe they wash down the old brickwork so that the plaster sticks.'

'That sounds plausible,' Rydén said.

'Do we know who he is?' Jeanette turned to face them.

'I thought that was your job,' Rydén replied. 'Ivo and I are only here to work out how. Not who did it, and definitely not why. But the kid was wearing a bloody weird necklace. We took pictures before we removed it. Not that I know anything about ethnology, but I'm pretty sure it was African.'

Jeanette went over to Schwarz and Åhlund, who were talking at the other end of the attic.

'So Chip and Dale are here?' She grinned. 'Who found him?'

Åhlund laughed. 'A junkie who lives in the building; he claimed he came up here to get a box of old records he was going to sell. But since several of the storage areas further down the corridor have been broken open, that's probably what he was up to when he discovered the boy hanging from the ceiling. Must have been one hell of a shock, if you ask me.' Then he added that the man who had found the boy was on his way to Kungsholmen for questioning. There was no indication that he had anything to do with it, but it couldn't be ruled out.

Over the next few hours the crime scene was secured, and a mass of different objects sealed in plastic bags and numbered. The noose was an ordinary clothes line, tied with a granny knot. The boy had the typical noose marks in his neck, like an upside-down V, with the apex marked by the knot, which had cut about a centimetre into the skin. The mark left by the cord was reddish brown, dry and leathery. At the edge of the wound Jeanette noted some discreet signs of bleeding.

On the floor below where the body had been hanging were signs of urine and excrement.

'Well, there can't be anyone who thinks he committed suicide.' Rydén pointed towards what had once been the boy's face.

'Unless he fixed the cord to the roof, tied a knot around his neck and then tipped a bucket of hydrochloric acid over himself, which, frankly, seems pretty fucking unlikely to me. There's also the fact that if a young and mentally unstable young man decides to take his own life, however sick it might seem, there's usually no reason to suspect a crime unless, as in this instance, it seems to have been physically impossible.'

'What do you mean?' Jeanette asked.

'The rope the boy was hanging from is at least ten centimetres too short.'

'Too short?'

'Exactly. The rope isn't long enough for him to have been able to fasten it to the ceiling even if he was standing on a bench. Elementary, my dear Watson.' Rydén pointed to the ceiling.

'Besides, he was strung up alive. His bowels emptied, and we're probably going to discover that he ejaculated as well.'

'You mean he shot his load while he was being strangled?' Schwarz turned towards Rydén, and Jeanette thought he looked like he was going to laugh.

'Yes, that usually happens. Well, as I was saying. Someone strung him up from the ceiling, probably using that ladder over there.' Rydén indicated a ladder leaning against the wall a short distance away. 'Then they arranged the bench to make it look like he'd been standing on it, and then they threw acid in his face. And why would anyone do that?'

'Good question . . .'

'My initial thought is that it was to conceal his identity.' Ivo Andrić turned to Jeanette. 'But of course that's not our job. Then you've got the fact that the rope was too short. Something to get your teeth into.'

'The funny thing is that this is the second time I've come across this in a fairly short period.' Rydén looked inexplicably pleased with himself.

'What do you mean?'

'Well, not the acid, but the bit about the rope being too short.'

'Really?' Jeanette was curious.

'Yes, it was the same thing there. A middle-aged man who'd been deceiving his partner, and had two families. The only thing that made us suspicious was the fact that the rope was too short. Everything else suggested suicide.'

'You were never in any doubt?'

'No, his partner claimed she'd got back from a trip and found him. She was the person who called the police. There was a pile of phone directories beside the chair.'

'So you thought he'd put the phone books on the chair and stood on top to tie the rope?'

'Yes, that was the conclusion we came to. His partner said she'd been in shock when she moved the directories to get him down, and there was no reason to question that. There was no sign that anyone else had been there, and, if I remember rightly, she had an alibi. Her story was confirmed by a car park attendant and a train conductor.'

'Did you analyse his blood?'

Jeanette had a nagging feeling that there was something right in front of her that she wasn't seeing. A connection she couldn't put her finger on.

'No, not as far as I know. It never came up. It was written off as suicide.'

'So you don't think there's any connection to this, then?'

'You're clutching at straws, Jan,' Rydén said. 'These cases are completely different.'

'OK, maybe. But get the boy to Solna and let forensics check if there are any signs of anaesthetic.'

Rydén looked affronted. Ivo Andrić, who realised what Jeanette was thinking, explained.

'We've got three bodies in the pathology lab. Young men who we think fell victim to the same killer. Admittedly, there are plenty of differences between them and this boy. They'd all been badly abused and castrated. But they'd also been anaesthetised and had traces of drugs in their blood, so if we check out this boy, well . . .' With a gesture he invited Jeanette to continue.

'Well, I don't know. It's just a feeling.' She smiled gratefully at Ivo.

Kronoberg – Police Headquarters

In the boy's pockets they had found a letter from social services in Hässelby, calling him to a meeting. So now they had a name. Schwarz and Åhlund picked up his parents and drove them to Solna to identify the body.

The necklace found on the boy turned out to be a family heirloom that had been passed down the generations.

Admittedly, it wasn't possible to confirm his identity beyond all doubt, because of the damage to the boy's face, but when the parents saw his tattoo they were convinced it was their son. RUF, carved into his chest with a shard of glass, wasn't exactly a common motif in Stockholm, and at 11.22 the papers giving the boy his identity back had been signed.

As far as the acid was concerned, Rydén was proved right. Ninety-five per cent hydrochloric acid.

Jeanette Kihlberg called Ivo Andrić, and the forensic medical officer gave her a brief summary of his findings.

'There are some similarities with the other boys,' he began. 'But I haven't had the results back to say if he'd been given Xylocain adrenalin. So far we've only found traces of amphetamines, but in this case they weren't injected.'

'They weren't?'

'No, there were no needle holes, so he must have absorbed them some other way. But I did find two small marks on his chest.'

'What sort of marks?'

'Looks like he was hit by a taser, but I can't be sure.'

'And you're absolutely certain there were no similar marks on the other boys?'

'Not absolutely certain, because of the state the bodies were in. But I'll take them out again and have another look. I'll be in touch.'

They ended the call.

A taser, Jeanette Kihlberg thought. Someone's seriously out of control.

The boy who had been found hanged in the Monument block was called Samuel Bai; he was sixteen years old, and had been reported missing after running away from home. Social services in Hässelby had forwarded his case notes, detailing instances of drug abuse, theft and violence.

His parents had fled the war in Sierra Leone and had been the subject of numerous investigations. The family's biggest problem had been the eldest son, Samuel, who showed signs of trauma from the war, and who had at intervals been treated at the centre for childhood psychiatry on Maria Prästgårdsgata, as well as by a private therapist named Sofia Zetterlund.

Jeanette started. Sofia again. First Lundström, and now Samuel Bai. If the world was a small place, then Stockholm was even smaller.

Odd that her name keeps cropping up, Jeanette thought. But maybe not. The Swedish police could muster all of five officers specialising in sex crimes against children. How many psychologists specialised in traumatised children?

Two or three, maybe.

She picked up the phone and dialled Sofia Zetterlund's number.

'Hello, Sofia, Jeanette Kihlberg again. This time I'm calling about Samuel Bai from Sierra Leone. You treated him, I understand. He's been found dead.'

'Dead?'

'Yes. Murdered. Can we meet this afternoon?'

'You can come straight away. I was on my way home, but I can wait.'

'OK, see you soon. I'll be with you in fifteen minutes.'

Mariatorget – Sofia Zetterlund's Office

Jeanette had to drive around the streets of Mariatorget twice before finding somewhere to park.

She took the lift up and was met by a woman who introduced herself as Ann-Britt, Sofia's secretary.

Jeanette explained why she was there, and while the woman went to get Sofia she looked around the room. The exclusive decor, with its genuine artworks and obviously expensive furniture, made her think that this was what you should be doing if you wanted to make serious money. Not sitting on Kungsholmen working like a slave.

The secretary returned with Sofia, who asked if Jeanette would like a drink.

'No, I'm fine. I don't want to take up too much of your time, so maybe we should get down to it straight away.'

'It's really not a problem,' Sofia said. 'I'm happy to help if I can. It feels good to be useful.'

Jeanette looked at Sofia, and felt instinctively that she liked her. During their previous meeting there had been a distance between them, but now, after just a minute or so, Jeanette detected real warmth in Sofia's eyes.

'I'll try to avoid making any Freudian slips,' Jeanette joked.

Sofia smiled back. 'That's sweet of you.'

Jeanette didn't understand how it had happened, or where the intimate tone came from, but it was there. She let it sink in, enjoying it for a moment.

In Sofia's office they sat down on either side of the desk and looked at each other curiously. There was something about Sofia that felt different from the last time they'd met. She's attractive, Jeanette admitted quietly to herself, before shrugging the thought aside.

'So, what would you like to know?' Sofia asked.

'I'm here because of Samuel Bai and . . . well, he's dead. He was found hanged in an attic.'

'Suicide?' Sofia asked.

'No, not at all. He was murdered, and –'

'But you just said –'

'I know. But he was strung up by someone else. Possibly in a failed attempt to make it look like suicide, but . . . actually, no, it wasn't an attempt to hide the fact that it was murder.'

'I'm not sure I'm with you now. Either it was suicide, or it wasn't.' Sofia shook her head in confusion and lit a cigarette.

'I think we can skip the details. Samuel was murdered. That's all. Maybe we could discuss that on another occasion, but right now I need to know a bit more about him. Anything that can give me an idea of who he was.'

'OK. But, more specifically, what do you want to know?'

She could tell that Sofia was disappointed, but there was no time to explain all the details.

'To start with, how did you come to meet him?'

'I'm not actually trained in child psychology, but I worked in Sierra Leone and that was why we made an exception.'

'OK, that sounds pretty heavy,' Jeanette said sympathetically. 'You said we? There were other people involved in the decision?'

'Yes, I was asked by social services in Hässelby if I would consider taking on Samuel's case. He's from Sierra Leone, of course, but you probably already know that?'

'We do.' Jeanette thought for a moment before she went on. 'What do you know about his experiences down in . . .'

'Freetown,' Sofia added. 'Among other things, he told me he was part of a criminal gang, and used to make his living from robberies and break-ins. Every so often they'd frighten the life out of people on the orders of some local mafia boss.' Sofia paused for breath. 'I don't know if you're aware of it, but Sierra Leone is a country in total chaos. Paramilitary groups use children to carry out tasks that adults can barely imagine doing. Children are easily led, and . . .'

Jeanette noticed that Sofia was finding this a difficult subject to talk about, but didn't try to help. However much she would have liked to spare Sofia, she needed to know more.

'How old was Samuel then?'

'He told me he first killed someone when he was seven. By the time he was ten he'd lost count of how many people he'd murdered and raped. All under the influence of hash or alcohol.'

'God, that's awful. What the hell has humanity come to?'

'Not humanity. Just men . . . you can strike everyone else off the list.'

They sat in silence, and Jeanette wondered what Sofia herself might have been through during her time in Africa. She was having trouble imagining her there. Those shoes, that hair.

She was so clean.

'Do you mind if I bum one?' Jeanette pointed at the packet of cigarettes on the desk next to the phone.

Sofia slowly pushed the pack over and looked Jeanette in the eye as she did so. She put the ashtray in the middle of the desk between them.

'For Samuel, the readjustment it took to live in Swedish society was extremely difficult, and he had problems adjusting from day one.'

'Well, who wouldn't?' She was thinking about Johan, who had had his own problems with concentration. And he hadn't been through anything even close to what Samuel had experienced.

'No, quite.' Sofia nodded. 'He had trouble sitting still at school. He was noisy and disruptive. On more than one occasion he got angry and violent because he felt insulted or misunderstood.'

'What do you know about how he spent his free time? I mean, when he wasn't at school or at home? Did you get the feeling he was scared of anyone?'

'Samuel's restlessness, combined with his great experience of violence, meant that he was often in trouble with the police and other authorities. As recently as this spring he was himself attacked and robbed.' Sofia reached for the ashtray.

'Why do you think he ran away from home?'

'When he disappeared, he and his family had just been informed that he was going to be taken into local authority care. I think that was why he decided to take off.' Sofia stood up. 'Well, I don't know about you, but I could do with a cup of coffee now. Can I get you one as well?'

'Please.'

Sofia went out to reception, and Jeanette heard the whirr of the coffee machine.

Jeanette thought about how peculiar the situation was.

Two fully functional, intelligent adult women discussing the murder of a violent and dysfunctional young man.

They had absolutely nothing in common with his world, yet here they sat.

What was it that was expected of them? That they should find a truth that didn't exist? Understand something that couldn't be understood?

Sofia came back with two cups of steaming black coffee and put them down on the desk.

'I'm sorry I can't be of more help, but if you give me a few days to look through my files, maybe we could meet again?'

Strange woman, Jeanette thought. It was as if Sofia could read her thoughts. It was both fascinating and – although Jeanette couldn't quite understand why – frightening.

'Would you like to? I'd be extremely grateful.' She smiled and felt how her faith in Sofia just kept growing. 'If you wouldn't mind, maybe we could combine business with pleasure and go out for dinner together?'

Jeanette listened to her own words in surprise. Where did the idea of dinner come from? It could easily be misinterpreted as an invitation to intimacy, and that wasn't the point. Was it?

What am I doing? she thought.

She didn't usually get this personal. She'd never even asked the girls from her football team to her house, even though she'd known them for ages.

But instead of declining, Sofia leaned forward and looked her in the eye. 'I think that sounds like an excellent idea. It's been ages since I had dinner with anyone but myself.' Sofia paused before going on, still without taking her eyes from Jeanette. 'Mind you, I am in the middle of renovating the kitchen. But if you haven't got anything against having a takeaway, I'd be happy for you to come round to my place.'

Jeanette nodded. 'Shall we say Friday?'

Mariatorget – Sofia Zetterlund's Office

After showing Jeanette Kihlberg to the lift Sofia went back into her office. She felt excited, almost happy, and reflected on the fact that she had actually invited Jeanette over to her place for dinner. Was that really such a smart move?

Just because she had felt something for Jeanette didn't mean that her feelings were reciprocated. And what exactly had she felt? It had been some sort of connection, that much was obvious. A sense of affinity.

But was she actually longing for physical contact with Jeanette?

Sofia thought for a while before concluding that she was. Although she wasn't sure that that meant anything more than a hug.

Either way, at least she and Jeanette were going to meet in private, and only the future knew if anything was likely to happen. Sofia's experience of intimacy with women, or men, for that matter, told her it was best to wait and see. Let it happen if it happened.

Like when she was in New York with Lasse.

Enough of that, she thought. Back to work.

She took out her cassettes of Victoria Bergman, put one of them into the tape player and pressed play. As she heard Victoria's voice she put her notepad in her lap, leaned back and closed her eyes.

. . . so the cowardly bitch must have known all along, even though she pretended there was nothing funny about waking up alone and finding him in my room with his pants on the floor and yellow stains that smelled.

Sofia tried to harden herself against the intrusive images conveyed by Victoria's voice. I have to be professional, she thought, I mustn't let it become personal. Even so, she had a mental image of a father creeping into his daughter's room.

Getting into her bed.

Sofia could imagine the smell of sex, had trouble breathing and started to feel sick.

Everywhere, the smell of defilement, the sort that could never be washed off.

. . . and of course I couldn't shout out because then I'd get a beating and end up crying. The pickled gherkins on the liver pâté were already salty enough without my tears so it was better to keep quiet and go along with it and answer the questions. And it was nice to get through and say hello to my cousin who lived in Östersund, or Borgholm, or anywhere at all. Dad said there were more than enough stupid people to go round, and I always agreed. I went along with it and sat there with skin on my chocolate milk and his hand was there again when Mum wasn't looking . . .

Sofia felt that she wasn't up to hearing any more, but something was stopping her from switching off the tape player.

. . . and you could run even further and faster but never enough to get a prize to put on the bookshelf next to the picture of the boy who didn't want to swim once he'd seen the view . . .

The voice was getting more intense, louder, but it was still just as monotonous.

The frequency and colour changed.

Bass to begin with.

. . . and only wanted to have a hug but he'd already found someone new to go on holiday with . . .

Then alto.

. . . and making a fuss of him when she was going to be allowed to go all the way up to Padjelanta . . .

Mezzo-soprano, soprano, lighter and lighter.

. . . and walking twenty kilometres a day and smelling the roseroot which was the only thing that felt exciting because there was something underneath that wasn't ugly . . .

Still with her eyes closed she felt across the desk, found the tape player and knocked it to the floor.

Silence.

She opened her eyes and looked down at her notepad.

Two words.

PADJELANTA, ROSEROOT.

What was Victoria talking about?

About the violation of being wrenched from her life when she was least expecting it?

About seeking solace in integrity, becoming untouchable?

Sofia could feel herself fumbling in the dark. She wanted to understand, but it was as if Victoria were in a state of complete disintegration. No matter where Victoria looked, she kept coming eye-to-eye with herself, and if she tried to find herself, she found only a stranger.

Sofia closed her notebook and got ready to go home. She looked at the time. It was twenty to ten, so she must have slept for almost five hours. That would explain why she had a headache.

Gamla Enskede – Kihlberg House

After her meeting with Sofia Zetterlund, Jeanette had trouble concentrating on work. She felt shaken, but couldn't put her finger on why. But she was looking forward to seeing her again. In fact, she was almost longing for Friday to come.

As she turned off the Nynäshamn road she nearly collided with a little red sports car pulling out from the right, and which ought to have given way. Just as she hit the horn angrily she realised it was Alexandra Kowalska.

Fucking moron, she thought as she gave a cheery wave. Alexandra waved back and shook her head apologetically.

She parked the car in the drive and went in, where she found Åke standing in the kitchen frying meatballs. He was in an exuberant mood.

Jeanette sat down at the table, which was already set.

'Do you know what this means?' he said out of the blue. 'Alex was here to say that the Copenhagen exhibition has been hung and that I've already sold two pictures. Look!' He pulled a piece of paper from his pocket and slapped it down on the table. She could see it was a cheque for eighty thousand Swedish kronor.

'This is only the beginning,' he said in delight, as he stirred the frying pan and got two beers from the fridge.

Jeanette sat there silently. So this is how it feels when things change fundamentally, she thought. That morning she had been worried whether they had enough money to get through to the end of the month, and now, just a few hours later, she was sitting here with a cheque worth more than two months' salary.

'OK, what's wrong now, then?' Åke was standing in front of her, holding out an opened can of beer. 'Don't you think it's good that I'm finally earning a bit of money from something you thought was a hobby for all these years?' She could hear the disappointment in his voice.

'Oh, Åke, why are you saying that? You know I've always believed in you.' She was about to put her hand on his arm, but he pulled away and went back to the stove.

'Yeah, you say that now. But just a couple of weeks ago you were moaning at me and saying I was irresponsible.'

He turned and smiled at her. But it wasn't his usual smile, more like an arrogant one.

She could feel herself getting angry as she noticed how smug he was. Hadn't they made this journey together? Was he totally blind to the fact that throughout their time together she had been the one making sure there was food on the table and paint on his palette?

Åke came over and gave her a hug.

'Sorry. That was a stupid thing to say,' he said, but she thought it sounded hollow. 'Alex says there's going to be a review in *Dagens Nyheter* on Sunday, and they want to do an interview for the Saturday supplement. God, I so deserve this.'

He held his arms up in the air as if he'd scored a goal.

Vita Bergen – Sofia Zetterlund's Apartment

'Like I said, the kitchen's uninhabitable for the time being, so we'll have to stick to the living room,' Sofia said as she opened the door.

Jeanette went in and detected an unfamiliar smell. At home there was always a smell of turpentine and old sports clothes, but here the air was tainted by something sharp, almost chemically pure, mixed with a faint scent of Sofia's perfume.

'All right for some,' Jeanette said, looking around the large, sparsely furnished living room. 'I mean living in the middle of the city like this, and on your own.' She sat down on the sofa with a deep sigh of relief. 'Sometimes I'd give anything to get home and be able to just sit.' She leaned her head back against the cushion and looked through the door at Sofia. 'How wonderful to escape all the obligations, all the running around, all the meal plans, all the excruciating conversations in front of the television.'

'Maybe,' Sofia said with a pointed smile. 'But it can get quite lonely too.' She came into the room. 'There are times when I just want to sell the apartment and move.' She got two wine glasses from the glass-fronted cupboard and poured the wine before sitting down next to Jeanette.

'Are you very hungry, or shall we wait a while? It's going to be Italian.'

'I can certainly wait.'

They looked at each other.

'So where would you like to move?' Jeanette went on.

'Good question! If I knew that, I'd sell it tomorrow, but I've got absolutely no idea. Abroad, maybe.'

Sofia raised her glass in a toast.

'That sounds exciting,' Jeanette said, raising her glass towards Sofia. 'But I'm not sure it sounds any less lonely.'

Sofia laughed. 'I've probably fallen for the myth of the reserved Swede, who imagines everything will be nice and lively the minute I reach the Continent.'

Jeanette laughed back, but picked up the serious tone behind the airy words. The coolness. As if she herself hadn't felt the same. 'I'm more tempted by the thought of avoiding understanding what people are saying.'

Sofia's smile faded. 'Really? Do you mean that?'

'No, not really, but sometimes it would nice to be able to blame language when you don't want to listen to all the chatter . . .' Jeanette paused and took a fresh breath. 'OK, you and I don't really know each other that well yet.' She looked deep into Sofia's eyes and took a sip of her wine. 'Can you keep a secret?'

She immediately regretted the dramatic tension caused by her choice of words. Like they were sitting in a teenage bedroom and were exploring the world together, as if words were the only guarantee you needed to feel safe.

She might just as well have asked if they could be best friends. The same naive desire to control a chaotic reality with words, instead of letting actual circumstances dictate what was said.

Words in place of action.

Words instead of security.

'That depends on whether it's anything criminal. But at the same time, you know I'm under an oath of confidentiality.' Sofia smiled.

Jeanette was grateful for the way Sofia handled the adolescent question.

Sofia looked at her as if she wanted to see. Listened to her as if she wanted to understand.

'If you were a Christian Democrat, you'd probably think it was criminal.'

Sofia threw her head back and laughed. Her neck was long and sinuous, simultaneously vulnerable and strong.

Jeanette giggled as well, moved a bit closer and pulled her knees up onto the sofa. She felt at home. She wondered if it could really be as straightforward as she had thought: that her friends had disappeared over the years because she had always prioritised work.

This was something else.

Something obvious.

'I've been married to Åke for twenty years, and I'm starting to get the hang of it.' She turned so she was facing Sofia again. 'And sometimes I'm so damn tired of knowing in advance exactly what he's going to say.'

'Some people would call that security,' Sofia said, with an undertone of professional curiosity.

'Of course it feels secure having someone so close, but even so . . . It's like living with your own brother. Oh, I don't know what closeness is . . . It can't just be purely a question of geography. God, I feel like I'm being really mean.' Jeanette shrugged helplessly, even though she knew Sofia wasn't likely to judge her.

'It's OK.' Sofia smiled gently, and Jeanette smiled back. 'I'm happy to listen, as long as you'd like me to do so as a friend.'

'OK, so I love Åke, but I don't think I want to live with him. Actually, I know I don't want to. The only thing keeping me there is Johan, my son. He's thirteen. I don't know if he could cope with a divorce. Well, maybe "cope" is the wrong word. He's probably big enough to realise that things like that happen.'

'Does Åke know you feel this way?'

'He probably suspects that I'm not one hundred per cent engaged in the relationship any more.'

'But you've never talked about it?'

'I . . . not really. It's more of an atmosphere between us. I do my thing, he does his.'

'Constantly present and constantly absent?' Sofia said sarcastically.

'And I think he's having an affair with a gallery owner,' Jeanette heard herself say.

Was it the fact that Sofia was a psychologist that made it so easy to talk to her?

'To feel secure you also have to feel that someone understands you.' Sofia took a sip of wine. 'But that's a fundamental failing in most human relationships. People forget to pay attention to each other, to appreciate what the other person does, because the only path that seems worth following is your own path. I blame individualism. It's become a sort of religion. It's actually damn weird that people despise security and loyalty in a world so full of war and suffering. It's one hell of a paradox!'

Jeanette saw that something had changed in Sofia, and her voice had got darker and harder. She couldn't quite keep up with the sudden mood swing. 'Sorry, I didn't mean to upset you.'

'Never mind, it's just that I've had personal experience of being taken for granted.' Sofia stood up. 'Well, what do you say? Shall we have some food?'

Jeanette could hear even more clearly that Sofia's voice had got deeper and significantly less melodious, and realised she'd touched a very raw nerve.

Sofia put out the dishes, filled their glasses and sat down. 'Have you told him how you feel? Financial stress is one of the most common causes of tension in a marriage.'

'Of course we've had the occasional fight, but it's like . . . I don't know, sometimes it feels like he can't imagine what I go through when we can't pay the bills and I have to call my parents to borrow money. As if that's just my responsibility.'

Sofia was looking at her seriously.

'It sounds to me as if he's never needed to take responsibility. As if he's always had someone to take care of everything for him.'

Jeanette nodded mutely. It felt like the pieces were falling into place.

'Oh, enough of all that,' she said, putting her hand on Sofia's shoulder. 'We were going to meet to talk about Samuel, weren't we?'

'I dare say we'll have time for that, even if it doesn't happen tonight.'

'Do you know,' Jeanette whispered, 'I'm really pleased I've met you. I like you.'

Sofia moved closer and put her hand on Jeanette's knee. Jeanette heard a rushing sound in her head when she looked into Sofia's eyes.

In there I might be able to find everything I've ever looked for, she thought.

At the same moment she heard one of the neighbours putting up a picture.

Someone was hammering.

Stockholm, 2007

When you look back sometimes you can identify the birth of a new age, even if at the time it merely seemed that one day was following on from another, just like normal.

For Sofia Zetterlund this starts after the trip to New York. By the time Christmas arrives, her private life is occupying more and more of her consciousness.

The first day after the holiday she decides to call the tax office to get detailed information about the person she had once thought she knew everything about.

The tax office needs just an ID number for everything they have on Lars Magnus Pettersson to be sent to her.

Why has she waited?

Has she not wanted to know?

Has she already realised?

At the pharmaceutical company they don't know who she means when she asks for Lars Pettersson, but when she insists they put her through to the sales department.

The receptionist is helpful, and does all she can to assist Sofia. After a bit of searching she locates a Magnus Pettersson, but he left over eight years ago, and only worked for a very short time at the German office in Hamburg.

The most recent address they have for him is out in Saltsjöbaden. Pålnäsvägen.

She hangs up without saying goodbye, and pulls out the piece of paper where she wrote down the unknown number she found in Lasse's phone. According to directory enquiries, the number belongs to a Mia Pettersson, listed at Pålnäsvägen in Saltsjöbaden. Below that address is another number, for a Pettersson's Flowers in Fisksätra, and even though she is starting to realise that she is sharing Lasse with someone else, she still wants to believe that it is all just a huge mistake.

Not Lasse.

It's as if she's standing in a corridor where one door after the other is opening up ahead of her. In a fraction of a second all the doors have been thrown open and she can see that the corridor stretches into infinity, and there, right in the distance, she can see the truth.

At one and the same moment she sees everything, understands everything, and everything becomes crystal clear.

Lasse has had his hands full with two families. One in Saltsjöbaden, and one with her in the apartment on Södermalm.

Obviously she should have realised much sooner.

His gnarled hands that suggested physical labour, even though he claimed to work in an office.

Insecurity and jealousy are gnawing away at her, and she realises that she has stopped thinking logically. Is she the only person who doesn't understand how everything fits together?

He needs help, she thinks. But not from her.

She can't save someone like him, if there is any salvation to be had.

She gets up and goes into the study, and starts looking through his drawers. Not that she knows what she's hoping to find, but there ought to be something there that could cast some light on who the man she has been living with really is.

Beneath some brochures with the logo of the pharmaceutical company she finds an envelope from Södermalm Hospital. She pulls out the contents and reads.

It's an appointment notification, dated nine years earlier, saying that Lars Magnus Pettersson had been given an appointment in the urology clinic for a vasectomy.

At first she understands nothing, then she realises that Lasse had himself sterilised. Nine years ago.

So for all these years he hasn't been capable of giving her the child she has longed for. What he had said in New York about having a baby wasn't just a lie, it was also an impossibility.

It's as if someone has tied a rope around her chest and is slowly pulling it tighter, and she thinks she's going to faint. Her experience of patients suffering panic attacks means that she knows she's going through the same thing.

But no matter how rationally she looks at herself, she can't help feeling scared.

Am I going to die now? she thinks just before everything goes black.

On Friday the 28th she travels out to Fisksätra. There's sleet in the air and the thermometer on the side of the Hammarby works says it's just above freezing.

She parks down by the marina and walks up towards the city centre.

What is it she wants to know that she doesn't already know?

She presumes it's something as simple as just wanting to put a face to the unknown woman.

But now that she's standing alone in the square she no longer feels so sure. She hesitates, but if she were to go home with her mission unaccomplished, it would only go on gnawing away at her.

She walks decisively into the shop, but finds to her disappointment that the person behind the counter is a young girl between twenty and twenty-five.

'Hello, happy Christmas!' The girl walks round the counter and comes over to Sofia. 'Are you looking for anything in particular?'

Sofia hesitates and turns round to leave, but at that moment the door to the back of the premises opens and a beautiful brunette in her fifties comes into the shop. On her left breast is a badge with the name Mia on it.

The woman is almost the same height as Sofia, and she has big, dark eyes. Sofia can't stop staring at the two women, who are strikingly similar.

Mother and daughter.

In the young woman she can also see clear traces of Lasse. His slightly crooked nose.

The oval face.

'Sorry, were you looking for anything in particular?' The younger woman breaks the awkward silence, and Sofia turns towards her.

'A bouquet for my . . .' Sofia gulps. 'For my parents. Yes, today's their wedding anniversary.'

The woman goes over to the glass cabinet containing cut flowers.

'Then I think these might be appropriate?'

Five minutes later Sofia goes into the newsagent's next to Pettersson's Flowers and buys a large mug of coffee and a cinnamon bun. She sits down on a bench with a view of the square and sips the coffee.

Nothing is as she expected.

The young woman had put together a bouquet while Mia went back into the storeroom. Then nothing. Sofia assumes she must have paid, but isn't entirely sure. She must have. No one has come after her. She remembers the sound of the little bell above the door, then the crunch of the snow. She thinks about Lasse, and the more she thinks about him, the more unreal he becomes for her.

She crumples up the bouquet and presses it into a bin outside the bank. The coffee follows; it tastes of nothing. It didn't even manage to warm her up.

Stupid tears are on their way, and she does her best to hold them back. She hides her face in her hands and tries to think about something other than Lasse and Mia.

Mia, who has been making love to him the whole time. And the girl, Lasse's daughter? His child. What he didn't want to have with her. She thinks about the Lou Reed album, which he had played for her in the hotel bar in New York. It dawns on her that it must be in his record collection in Saltsjöbaden, and that it was with Mia that he had listened to it.

Sofia leans her head back to stop her tears running down her cheeks. She realises that she has to end things with Lasse. Then nothing more. No thoughts, no worrying, nothing. Let him look after himself as best he can, but he will be dead to her.

Some things you just have to cut out of your life in order to survive. She's done it before.

But there's one thing she needs to do first. However much it's going to hurt.

She has to see them together, Lasse, Mia and their daughter.

She knows she has to see that, otherwise she will never be able to stop thinking about them. The image of the happy family all together. It will haunt her, she understands that. She needs to confront it.

During the remaining days leading up to New Year's Eve, Sofia Zetterlund doesn't do much. She only talks to Lasse once, and the conversation lasts no more than thirty seconds.

At eleven o'clock on New Year's Eve Sofia drives the car out to Saltsjöbaden. It doesn't take her long to find Pålnäsvägen.

She parks the car a hundred metres away from the large house and walks back to the drive. It's a yellow two-storey villa with white bargeboards and a large, well-kept garden. Lasse's car is parked in front of the carport.

She walks round the carport to the rear of the house. Under cover of some trees she has a perfect view in through the large picture window. The yellow light is cosy and welcoming.

She sees Lasse come into the living room with a bottle of champagne, calling back into the house behind him.

The beautiful brunette from the florist's comes in with a tray of champagne glasses. From an adjacent room the daughter comes in, together with a young man who looks like Lasse.

He has a son as well? Two children? Even if they are grown up now.

They sit down on the large sofa and Lasse pours champagne for them all and they smile and they drink a toast.

For thirty minutes Sofia stands as if paralysed, and watches the laughable performance.

It's real and at the same time so false.

She remembers once being shown round the Chinese Theatre. It had been a disconcerting experience, seeing the stage scenery from behind. From the front there had been a bar or restaurant, and outside the windows a sea and a sunset. It had all looked so genuine.

But when she was allowed behind the scenery everything seemed so tawdry. It was built of sheets of chipboard and held together with duct tape and clamps. The contrast with the cosy room onstage had been so great that she felt practically deceived.

What she is watching now is similar. Inviting on the surface, but false inside.

Immediately before midnight, as she sees the happy family stand up for another toast, she takes out her mobile and calls his number. She sees him flinch and realises he's got his phone on vibrate.

He says something and goes upstairs. She sees a light go on in one of the windows, and a few seconds later her mobile rings.

'Hello, darling. Happy New Year! What are you doing?' She can hear how hard he's trying to sound stressed. Because of course he's still in the office in Germany, and is having to work even though it's New Year's Eve.

Before she can say anything she has to hold the phone aside so she can throw up in one of the bushes.

'Hello, what are you doing? I can hardly hear you. Can I call you a bit later? It's a little chaotic here right now.'

She hears him running water in the sink so his lovely family downstairs can't hear the conversation.

A dam breaks, and out floods a torrent of ugly betrayal. There's no way she's going to accept being the second woman.

She ends the call and walks back to the car.

She cries all the way home, and a snowy sleet whips the windscreen and merges with her tears. She can taste her mascara, acrid and bitter. In the end she's crying so much she has to pull over.

She has spent ten years playing ball by herself, and all the time she thought he was throwing the ball back to her, he had just been standing there with his arms by his sides.

'What do you think, Lasse, shall we treat ourselves to four weeks off in the summer and rent a house in Italy?'

'Lasse, what do you think about me stopping taking the pill?'

'I was thinking . . .'

'I'd like . . .'

Ten years of suggestions and ideas, revealing herself and her dreams. Just as many years of hesitation and excuses.

'I don't know . . .'

'There's a lot going on at work . . .'

'Now isn't a good time, but soon . . .'

In one single, slow moment, he's taken everything away from her.

Everything that just a few days ago was true and tangible has turned out to be an illusion, a conjuring trick.

Is she supposed to look on passively while her life is dismantled?

A lorry goes past, blowing its horn, with scarcely any room to spare. She switches on the car's hazard lights. If she's going to die, it's going to happen in style, not in some shitty ditch on an industrial estate in Västberga.

Victoria Bergman, her new patient, would never put up with being treated like something you can throw away when you get tired of it, she thinks.

Even though they haven't seen each other particularly often yet, Sofia has realised that Victoria possesses a strength that she can only dream of. In spite of everything, Victoria has survived and transformed her experiences into awareness.

Acting on a sudden impulse, Sofia decides to call Victoria. Then she sees that she's missed a text from Lasse. 'Darling. I'm getting the plane home. We need to talk.' She clicks the message away and dials Victoria's number, then waits for the phone to ring. To her disappointment she gets the busy signal. Then she laughs when she realises what she was about to do. Victoria Bergman? Victoria's the one coming to her for treatment, and not vice versa.

She thinks about Lasse's message. Home? What's that? And getting the plane? He'll be driving in from Saltsjöbaden, nothing more. But perhaps he's starting to suspect that she knows. Something must have made him want to leave his real family all of a sudden like that. After all, it is New Year's Eve.

Without warning she feels sick again, and only just manages to get the car door open in time to throw up on the grey slush.

She starts the car, turns up the heater and drives towards Årsta, down into the tunnel and on towards Hammarby Sjöstad.

She stops at the Statoil garage to fill up, and when she's done she goes into the shop. She wanders around the shelves, wondering where to go, and curses the fact that she's allowed herself to become so isolated that she's now so pathetically alone.

When she goes up to the counter she looks down in her basket and discovers that she's picked up a pair of windscreen-wiper blades, an air freshener and six packets of Ballerina biscuits.

She pays and is walking towards the exit when she passes a display of cheap reading glasses. Mechanically she tries a few with the weakest lenses available. Finally she finds a pair with a black frame that makes her look thinner, stricter and a bit older. Sofia sees that the cashier has his back to her and quickly puts them in her pocket. What's going on? She's never stolen anything before.

When she's back in the car she takes out her mobile phone, brings up Lasse's last message and clicks reply.

'OK. See you at home. Wait for me if I'm not there.'

Then she drives into the city centre and parks the car in the multi-storey on Olof Palmes gata. She uses her credit card to get a ticket covering the next twenty-four hours.

That will be more than enough.

However, she doesn't leave the ticket on the dashboard, but puts it in her purse instead.

The time is now half past five on New Year's morning. When she reaches Central Station she goes into the departure hall and stands in front of the large screen announcing the next trains. Västerås, Gothenburg, Sundsvall, Uppsala, and so on. She goes up to one of the automated ticket machines, takes out her credit card again, and buys a return ticket to Gothenburg, leaving at eight o'clock.

She buys two packs of cigarettes from the newsagent's before settling down at a cafe to wait for the train.

Gothenburg? she thinks.

Suddenly, she realises what she is about to do.

Gamla Enskede – Kihlberg House

Sunday morning was gloriously beautiful, and Jeanette woke up early. For the first time in a very long time, she felt properly rested.

The weekend had passed without any significant trials. Åke's parents had come to visit, and even that had gone surprisingly painlessly, even if his mum had thought the pork was a little dry and that you really weren't supposed to buy potato salad from ICA.

Apart from that they had had a nice time. Watching television and playing games.

Her parents-in-law would be leaving on the morning train, giving her the rest of the day to herself. She lay in bed, planning what to do with the time.

Definitely no work.

Pottering about, a bit of reading, maybe a long walk.

She heard Åke wake up. He took several deep breaths and squirmed in the bed.

'Is everyone else up?' He sounded tired as he pulled the covers over his head.

'I don't think so. It's only half past seven, so we can lie here a bit longer. We'll hear when your mum starts banging around in the kitchen.'

Åke got up and began to get dressed.

Oh, just go, there's nothing left here anyway, she thought, and saw Sofia's pale face in front of her.

'When does their train leave?'

'Just before midday. Do you want me to give them a lift?' Jeanette said, trying to sound disinterested.

'We can do it together, can't we?' he replied, in an obvious attempt to sound friendly.

Half an hour later she went down to the kitchen and had breakfast with the others. When they were finished and the table was cleared, she took a mug of coffee out into the garden.

In spite of everything, she was feeling pretty happy.

Her meeting with Sofia had developed into something utterly different to what she had been expecting, and she hoped that it was the same for Sofia. For the first time she had felt something for a woman that she had previously only felt with men.

Perhaps sexuality doesn't actually have to be connected to gender? she wondered, feeling confused. Maybe the banal truth is that it's the person who matters. Man or woman really doesn't make any difference.

How simple everything could be. And simultaneously how complicated.

When it was time to head off to Central Station, Jeanette carried the suitcases out to the car because she didn't want to be in the way when her in-laws gathered the last of their things and said an emotional goodbye to Johan.

Jeanette parked between two taxis in front of the station. They got the luggage out together, then waved goodbye on the platform after another tear-soaked farewell. Jeanette suddenly found it easier to breathe. She took Åke's hand and walked back to the car.

The troubling thoughts she had had during the day seemed to have blown away. She belonged with Åke, in spite of everything, and he with her.

What could Sofia offer her that she couldn't get from Åke? she thought.

Excitement and curiosity aren't everything.

Grit your teeth and bear it.

On the way home they stopped at a kiosk and bought a copy of *Dagens Nyheter.* It was supposed to contain a review of Åke's exhibition. He would rather have got hold of a copy before breakfast, but had held off because he didn't want his parents reading a review that slaughtered him.

Once they were home they sat down together at the kitchen table and spread the paper out in front of them. Jeanette could see he was more nervous than she had ever seen him.

He was laughing and pretending to be unconcerned.

'Here it is,' he said, folding the paper and putting it in between them.

They sat and read in silence. When Jeanette realised she was reading about her Åke, she started to feel dizzy.

The male reviewer was utterly lyrical. According to him, Åke's paintings were the most important thing that had happened in the Swedish art world in the past decade, and he predicted a brilliant future for Åke. There was no doubt that he was going to be the next great Swedish cultural export, and in comparison artists such as Ernst Billgren and Max Book looked like pale imitations.

'I have to call Alex.' Åke got up and went into the hall to fetch his mobile. 'Then I have to go into the city. Can you give me a lift?'

Jeanette sat where she was, not sure how she should feel.

'Sure,' she replied, understanding that from now on nothing was going to stay the same.

Allhelgonagatan – a Neighbourhood

The familiar strains of accordion music were drowning out the noisy traffic on Dalslandsgatan. 'The Ballad of the Brig Blue Bird of Hull' was blasting out of an open window, and Sofia Zetterlund stopped to listen before carrying on towards Mariatorget.

A few other passers-by stopped and smiled, and a woman began to sing along with the mournful lyrics about the ship's lad who was lashed to the mast and forgotten when the ship sank. The music created an unexpected spiritual space, and functioned as a verbal catalyst in a country where no one talks to anyone else without good reason. Everyone knows their Evert Taube, as they're given him along with herring and mother's milk.

When she came to Allhelgonagatan she stopped, took the little tape machine from her bag and put the earphones in. On the cassette case she read that the recording had been made four months earlier.

Sofia pressed play and carried on walking.

. . . so I got the ferry to Denmark with Hannah and Jessica, that pair of hypocritical cows I got to know in Sigtuna, and obviously they had to go to the

Roskilde Festival and left me alone in the tent with those four awful German guys who kept at it all night, fiddling and rubbing and pushing and grunting, while I could hear Sonic Youth and Iggy Pop in the distance, and couldn't move because they took turns holding me down . . .

Completely cut off, she wandered into a dreamlike state where she neither saw nor heard anyone around her.

. . . knew that my so-called friends were right at the front by the stage and didn't give a shit about the fact that I was lying there knocked out by their sweet dessert wine getting raped and then didn't want to tell them why I was so upset and just wanted to get away from there . . .

Magnus Ladulåsgatan. Her body was moving automatically.

Timmermansgatan. The words became images she had never seen before, yet were still familiar.

. . . and continue on to Berlin where I emptied their backpacks and lied and said we'd been robbed while I was lying there asleep when they were out buying even more wine as if we hadn't drunk enough already. But they were making the most of it because their parents weren't there, and were back home in Danderyd working to earn the money they sent down to Germany so we could keep interrailing . . .

Then she realises what Victoria Bergman is talking about and remembers that she's actually listened to this particular tape several times before. She must have heard the story of Victoria's journey through Europe at least ten times.

How could she have forgotten?

. . . to Greece and got stuck at the border and sniffer dogs checked our luggage and we had full-body searches by randy old men in uniforms who stared at our breasts as if they'd never seen breasts before, and thought it was a good idea to use plastic gloves when they stuck their fingers in you. Then the bad stuff passed as we drank vodka and ended up with a big memory gap covering pretty much all of Italy and France and woke up somewhere in Holland. Then those two cows had had enough and said they were going home and I left them and ended up with a guy in Amsterdam and he couldn't keep his fingers to himself either and that's why he got a flowerpot on his head. It was only right to steal his wallet and the money was more than enough for a hotel room in Copenhagen, where everything was supposed to end and the voice fell silent when I finally showed that I dared to do it. But the belt snapped and I fell to the floor and my tooth broke and . . .

Suddenly she feels someone grab hold of her and she jerks awake.

She stumbles, takes a step to the side.

Someone pulls out the earphones, and for a moment everything is completely silent.

She ceases to exist and becomes calm.

It's like being in water, and coming back up to the surface after diving too deep, and finally being able to fill your lungs with fresh air.

Then she hears the cars and the shouting and looks around, dazed.

'Are you OK?'

She turns round and stares into a wall of people on the pavement and realises that she is standing in the middle of Hornsgatan.

Eyes watching her, inspecting her critically. Beside her a car. The driver is blowing his horn angrily, shaking his fist and revving the engine.

'Do you need help?'

She hears the voice but can't work out who in the crowd it belongs to.

It's hard to focus.

She walks quickly back to the pavement and on towards Mariatorget.

She pulls out the cassette player to remove the tape and put it in its case. She presses eject.

Astonished, she stares at the empty space where the cassette should be.

Earlier, Vita Bergen – Sofia Zetterlund's Apartment

Mambaa manyani . . . Mamani manyimi . . .

Sofia Zetterlund wakes up with a throbbing headache.

She was dreaming that she was hiking in the mountains with an older man. They were looking for something, but she can't remember what. The man had shown her an insignificant little flower and told her to dig it up. The ground was stony and hurt her hands. When she finally manages to get the whole plant out the man told her to smell the roots.

It had smelled like an entire bouquet of roses.

Roseroot, she thinks, and goes out into the kitchen.

She's been getting headaches sporadically recently, but they usually pass after an hour or so. This time she feels it's here to stay.

It's part of her.

While the coffee machine hisses Sofia leafs through the pad of notes from her conversations with Victoria Bergman.

She reads: SAUNA, BABY BIRDS, CLOTH DOG, GRANDMA, RUN, TAPE, VOICE, COPENHAGEN, PADJELANTA, ROSE-ROOT.

Why has she written down those particular words?

Presumably because they were details that she felt were important for Victoria.

She lights a cigarette and leafs a bit further through the pad. On the penultimate page she sees some new notes, written upside down, as if she had started to write in the pad from the other direction: BURN DOWN, WHIP, SEEK GOODNESS IN FLESH . . .

At first she doesn't recognise the handwriting. It's jagged, childish, almost illegible. She takes a pen from her bag and tries writing the words with the wrong hand.

She realises that she wrote the words, but with her left hand.

Burn down? Whip? Seek goodness?

Sofia feels giddy and can hear a faint buzzing inside her head, behind the headache. She wonders about going for a walk. Maybe a bit of fresh air would clear her thoughts.

The buzzing gets louder, and she's having trouble concentrating.

The sound of children shouting out in the street penetrates the windows, and an acrid smell stings her nose. Her own sweat.

She gets up to switch the coffee machine on, but when she sees that it's already on she gets a mug out of the cupboard instead. She fills it and goes back to the kitchen table.

There are already four mugs on the table.

One is empty, but the other three are full to the brim.

She can feel that she's having trouble remembering.

As if she's repeating herself, and has got caught in a loop. How long has she been awake? she wonders. Did she actually go to bed at all?

She tries to pull herself together, think about it, but it's as if her memory can be divided into two parts.

First the past, all about Lasse and the trip to New York. But what happened after they got home?

Her memories from Sierra Leone are just as tangible as her conversations with Samuel, but what happened after that?

The noise from out in the street is loud, and Sofia starts to walk anxiously up and down in the kitchen.

The other part of her memory is more like frozen images, impressions. Places she's been to. People she's met.

But no broad panoramas, no faces. Just quick excerpts. A moon that looks like a light bulb, unless it was the other way round?

She goes out into the hall and puts her coat on, then looks at herself in the mirror. The bruising caused by Samuel's hands has started to fade. She loops the scarf around her neck once more to conceal it.

It's not quite ten o'clock, and the summer outside is hot, but it's as if it can't reach her. Her eyes are focused inward as she tries to understand what's happening to her.

Thoughts she doesn't recognise are flashing like lightning.

Victoria Bergman's speech about exposing her body to violence. Her thoughts about who decides when an individual's fantasies, impulses and desires pass the boundary of social acceptability and become destructive.

Victoria's talk about good and evil, where evil, like cancer, can live and grow inside an apparently healthy organism. Unless it was Karl Lundström who said that?

When she reaches Björns Trädgård she sits down on a bench under the trees. The buzzing is now deafening and she doesn't know if she's going to be able to make it home.

Victoria's monotonous voice.

Dare you? Dare you? Dare you today, you weak fucker?

No, she needs to get home and go to bed. Take a pill and get some sleep. She's probably just been overdoing it at work, and she longs for the solitary darkness of her apartment.

When did she last eat? She can't remember.

She's malnourished. Yes, that must be it. Even though she has no appetite she'll force herself to eat, then do her best to keep it down. She won't vomit.

Just as she gets up a number of police cars go speeding past, sirens blaring. They're followed by three big SUVs with dark tinted windows and flashing lights. Sofia realises that something big must have happened.

At the McDonald's near Medborgarplatsen Sofia buys two bags of food, and understands from the excited chatter of the other customers that there's been a raid on an armoured car further down Folkungagatan.

Someone mentions gunshots, and someone else says several people have been injured.

Sofia takes her food and leaves.

She doesn't see Samuel Bai when she emerges onto the street and starts to walk home.

But he sees her, and follows.

She passes the police cordon and turns right down Östgötagatan, over Kocksgatan, and then left into Åsögatan.

At the little park Samuel catches up with her and slaps her on the back.

Startled, she turns round.

He darts quickly past her, and she has to turn right round before she sees who it is.

'Hi! Long time no seen, ma'am!' Samuel smiles his dazzling smile and takes a step back. 'Hav'em burgers enuff 'or me? Saw ya goin' donall for two.'

It's like she's stopped breathing.

Calm, she thinks. Calm.

Her hand reaches instinctively to her throat.

Calm.

She recognises Frankly Samuel's English and realises that he has been watching her for a while.

Smile.

She smiles and says there's enough food for him too, and suggests that they eat at her place.

He smiles back.

Strangely, her fear vanishes as quickly as it appeared.

Suddenly she knows what to do.

Samuel takes one bag and they walk on, cross Renstiernas gata and turn onto Borgmästargatan.

She puts the bag of burgers on the living-room table. He asks if he can use the shower to freshen up before they eat, and she gets a clean towel out for him.

He shuts the door behind him.

What's going on?

Sauna, baby birds, run, tape, voice, Copenhagen, roseroot, burn down, whip.

The pipes rumble.

'Sofia, Sofia, calm down, Sofia,' she whispers to herself, and tries to take deep, calm breaths.

Baby birds, run, tape.

She waits a while before going back into the living room. A rancid smell of burnt meat is coming from the hamburgers.

Burn down, whip.

Nausea overwhelms her, and she sits down heavily on the sofa with her face in her hands.

Sauna.

The shower is running and her head is full of Victoria's voice. It's as if it's eating its way into her, gnawing at the tissue of her brain.

It's a voice she's been listening to her whole life, but never got used to.

Dare you, dare you today?

She gets up on unsteady legs and goes into the kitchen to get a glass of water. Come on, she thinks, I've got to calm down.

She sees her reflection in the hall mirror and realises how tired she looks. Tired, down to her very marrow.

She turns on the kitchen tap, but it's as if the water doesn't want to get cold enough, and in her mind's eye she sees it being drawn from ancient rocks, deep beneath her, where it's hot as hell.

She burns herself on the jet of water and she can see flames before her eyes.

Children in front of a campfire.

Mambaa manyani . . . Mamani manyimi . . .

Sofia shudders at the memory of the childish song.

She goes out into the hall and rifles through her bag, looking for the box of paroxetine.

She tries to gather enough saliva to swallow the pill. Her throat is dry, but she still pops a tablet in her mouth. Its bitterness takes her by surprise, and when she tries to swallow, it catches in her throat. She swallows over and over again, and feels it move jerkily down her throat.

Dare you today? Dare you?

'No, I dare not,' she mutters quietly, and slumps halfway down the wall of the hall. 'I'm petrified.'

She curls up there, waiting for the medication to take effect. Trying to rock herself to a state of calmness.

Waiting. The rumbling noise she can't get away from.

Sauna, baby birds, cloth dog.

She clings to the thought of the cloth dog, calmness. 'Cloth dog, cloth dog,' she repeats to herself to get the voice to shut up and to regain control over her thoughts.

Suddenly her mobile rings, but it's as if the sound comes from another world.

A world she no longer has access to.

With an effort she gets up to answer the ringtone that fate has thrown her just as she is losing her grip. The phone call is the way back, the link between her and reality.

As long as she can manage to answer it, she can come back down and find her way home. She knows that's how it is, and that conviction gives her the strength to grab her phone.

'Hello,' she mutters, sliding down the wall again. She managed it. She managed to catch the lifeline.

'Hello? Is anyone there?'

'Yes, I'm here,' Sofia Zetterlund replies, and believes she's home again. Safe.

'Yes, hello . . . I'm trying to get in touch with a Victoria Bergman. Is this the right number?'

She hangs up and bursts out laughing.

Mambaa manyani . . . Mamani manyimi . . .

Suddenly she recognises Victoria's voice, gets to her feet and looks around.

Do you think I don't know what you're up to, you weak fucker.

Sofia follows the sound into the living room, but the room is empty.

She feels she needs a cigarette and reaches for the packet. She fumbles but manages to get hold of one, sticks it in her mouth, lights it and inhales deeply while she waits for Victoria to make herself known.

She hears Samuel clattering about in the bathroom.

So you're not smoking under the exhaust fan today?

Sofia jerks. How the hell can Victoria know that that's what she usually does? How long has she been here? No, she tries to calm herself. It's impossible.

What's really going on in your kitchen?

'Victoria, what do you mean by that?' Sofia makes an effort to resume her professional role. Whatever happens, she mustn't show that she's afraid, she has to stay calm, regain control.

The bathroom door opens.

'Talkin' to ya'self?'

Sofia turns round and sees Samuel standing naked in the doorway. He observes her, dripping with water from the shower. He smiles.

'Who you talking to?' He looks around the room. 'Nobody here.' Samuel takes a few steps out into the hall and walks over to the doorway. 'Who's there?'

'Forget about her,' Sofia says. 'We're playing hide-and-seek.' She takes Samuel's arm.

He looks surprised and raises his hand to her face.

'What's happened to ya' face, ma'am? Look strange . . .'

'Get dressed and eat before it gets cold.' She opens a drawer of the dresser and passes him yet another towel. He wraps it around himself and goes back into the bathroom.

She closes the door behind him, gets the box of pentobarbitone from her handbag and empties it into the mug of Coca-Cola.

Are you going to lock him up as well?

'Victoria, please,' Sofia pleads. 'I don't understand what you're talking about. What do you mean?'

You've got a little boy locked up here in the apartment. In the room behind the bookcase.

Sofia understands nothing, and her unease is growing stronger and stronger.

Then she remembers the significance of the song the first time she heard it, when she was sitting tied up in a pit in the jungle.

Mambaa manyani . . . Mamani manyimi . . .

Scarecrow fuck children . . . Must have a dirty cunt . . .

You disgusting fat whore. Didn't it do any good, cutting your arms with a razor blade?

Sofia thinks how she used to sit behind Aunt Elsa's house cutting herself.

Hiding the bleeding wounds with long-sleeved tops.

And now you buy shoes that are too small instead. To remind yourself of the pain.

Sofia looks down at her feet. On her heels she has terrible calluses from years of tormenting herself. On her arms pale scars from razor blades, shards of glass and knives.

Suddenly the other part of her memory opens up, and what have previously been fuzzy still images become fragments of film.

What was past becomes present, and everything falls into place.

Dad's hands, and the judgemental look in Mum's eyes. Martin on the Ferris wheel, the jetty down by the Fyris River, then the shame at having lost him. University Hospital in Uppsala, the medication and therapy.

Memories of Sigtuna and the masked girls in a ring around her.

The humiliation.

The boys who raped her at Roskilde, then her flight to Copenhagen and the failed suicide attempt.

Sierra Leone and the children who didn't know what they hated.

A tool shed in Sigtuna, a hard earth floor and a light bulb through a blindfold.

The same image.

Sofia has dug into Victoria's internal world and occasionally seen things Victoria has spent her whole life trying to forget. Now Victoria is walking around in her home, in her private space. She is everywhere and nowhere.

And the tape player that you spend hours with, talking and talking and talking. No wonder Lasse left you. He probably couldn't bear you banging on about your horrible childhood. It was you who wanted to go to a sex club in Toronto, you who wanted group sex. Thank fuck he didn't want to have children with you.

Sofia makes an attempt to protest, but can't make a sound. But he'd been sterilised, she thinks.

You're perverted. You tried to steal his children. Mikael is Lasse's son! Have you forgotten that?!

The voice is so loud that she flinches away and sinks onto the sofa. It feels like her temples are about to burst.

Mikael? Lasse's son? That can't be right . . .

The image of the happy family at home in Saltsjöbaden that New Year's Eve. Sofia sees Lasse drink a toast with Mikael.

Once you'd killed Lasse you picked up Mikael. Don't you remember? The phone books you scattered across the floor to make it look like suicide? The rope was too short, that was it, wasn't it?

Distantly Sofia hears Samuel emerge from the bathroom and hazily sees him sit down at the coffee table. He opens the bag of food and starts to eat as she sits there in silence and watches him.

Samuel gulps down the Coke.

'Who ya talking to, lady?' He shakes his head.

Sofia gets up and goes out into the hall. 'Shut up and eat,' she snarls at him, but he doesn't react and she can't work out if he heard her or not.

She sees her own face in the mirror above the dresser in the hall. It's as if one side is paralysed. She doesn't recognise herself. How old she looks.

'What the hell?' she mutters to the reflection, and takes a step closer and smiles, raising a finger to her mouth and touching the front tooth that broke when she tried to hang herself in a hotel room in Copenhagen twenty years ago.

Mimesis.

The relationship between what she sees and what she is is unquestionable.

Now she remembers everything.

Then her mobile rings again.

She looks at the screen.

10.22.

'Bergman,' she answers.

'Victoria Bergman? Bengt Bergman's daughter?'

She looks back into the living room. The sleeping pills have left Samuel knocked out on the sofa. His eyes are moving slowly even though he's unconscious.

'That's right.'

My father is Bengt Bergman, Sofia Zetterlund thinks.

I am Victoria, Sofia, and everything in between.

A voice she seems to recognise asks her questions about her father and she answers mechanically, but when she hangs up she can't remember any of what she said.

However, she is perfectly aware that she made a big mistake the time she called home to her mum and dad. They must have kept her number. And now, somehow, it's ended up with the police.

The number can't be traced, but she's still going to have to get rid of the phone.

She clutches the phone and looks at Samuel. So much on his conscience, yet still so innocent, she thinks, then goes over to the bookcase and unfastens the catch holding it in place. As she opens the hidden door she is hit by the stale, fetid air.

Gao is sitting in one corner with his arms around his knees. He squints towards the light forcing its way in through the doorway. Everything is under control, and she goes out, rolls the bookcase back into place and begins to undress. After a quick shower she wraps a large, red towel around her and airs the apartment by opening all the windows for a few minutes. She lights an incense stick, pours a glass of wine and sits down on the sofa next to Samuel. His breathing is deep and regular, and she gently strokes his head.

Of all the terrible things he did as a child soldier in Sierra Leone, he is guilty of none, she thinks. He is a victim.

His intentions had been pure, unblemished by feelings like revenge or jealousy.

Feelings that have been her driving force.

The sun starts to go down, dusk falls outside the windows and the room is bathed in a grey gloom. Samuel moves, yawns and sits up. He looks at her and smiles his dazzling smile. She loosens her towel and moves so she's sitting in front of him. His eyes move up her calves and in under the towel.

You have freedom of choice now, she thinks. Either you follow your instincts, or you resist.

Your choice.

She returns his smile.

'What's this?' she says, pointing at his necklace. 'Where did you get that?'

He lights up, takes off the necklace and holds it up in front of him.

'Evidence of big stuff.'

She pretends to be impressed, and when she leans forward to inspect the necklace more closely she notices that he is looking at her breasts. 'So, what did you do to deserve something as nice as that?'

Now she leans back and pulls the towel up a bit further so he can see that she isn't wearing any underwear. He gulps and moves closer to her.

'Killed a monkey.'

He smiles and puts his hand on her naked thigh.

Because his eyes are focused elsewhere, he doesn't see her take out the hammer she had hidden under a cushion.

Can you be evil if you don't feel guilt? she wonders, and brings the hammer down with full force on Samuel's right eye.

Or are feelings of guilt a precondition for evil?

Kronoberg – Police Headquarters

Sofia Zetterlund hangs up and wonders what has happened. Jeanette said she needed to talk, and it had sounded urgent. She had said some new facts had emerged in the Samuel Bai case.

What does Jeanette need to talk to her about, and could she have found something out?

Had someone seen her with Samuel?

Sofia goes into the living room and checks that the bookcase is in its place. Now there's only Gao left in there, and he's no problem.

Back in the hall she checks her make-up before picking up her handbag and heading down to the street. Folkungagatan, four blocks, then the metro. Far too short a walk to have time to think.

To change her mind.

She's got used to Victoria's voice, but the headache is still new and grates behind her forehead.

Her insecurity increases the closer she gets to police headquarters, but it's as if Victoria is pushing her forward. Telling her what to do.

One foot at a time. One in front of the other. Repeat. Pedestrian crossing. Stop. Look left, then right, then left again.

Sofia Zetterlund tells the receptionist who she is and, after a brief security check, is allowed through to the lifts.

Open the door. Go straight ahead.

After a couple of minutes waiting she is fetched by a beaming Jeanette.

'Great that you could come so quickly,' she says when they are alone in the lift. 'I've been thinking about you a lot. I was so pleased to have a reason to call you.'

Sofia feels uncertain. She doesn't know how to react.

Inside her head two voices are competing for her attention. One is telling her to give Jeanette a hug and tell her who she really is. Give up, the voice says. Put an end to this. See the fact that you've met Jeanette as a sign.

No, no, no! Not yet. You can't trust her. She's like all the others, she'll betray you as soon as you reveal your weakness.

'There's been a lot going on . . .' Jeanette looks at Sofia. 'We're under pressure from all sides, and this business with Samuel is just getting weirder and weirder. But we can talk about that later. Coffee?'

They each get a cup from the machine, then head down a long corridor together until they reach the right door.

'Well, this is me,' Jeanette says.

The room is small, full of files and piles of paper. In the narrow window a dried-out plant is drooping next to a photograph of a man and a boy. Sofia realises they must be Åke and Johan.

'Do you remember if Samuel told you he got beaten up? About a year ago?'

Remember the details, Sofia.

Sofia thinks. 'Yes, he said he'd been attacked somewhere near Ölandsgatan –'

'Close to Monument,' Jeanette fills in. 'He was beaten up in the Monument block. The same place he was later found hanged.'

'Yes, maybe it is. I remember him saying that one of the men who attacked him had snakes tattooed on his arms.'

'Not snakes. Spiderwebs.' Jeanette tosses her empty cup in the bin. 'The guy was a neo-Nazi in his teens, and in those circles it's a status symbol to have spiderwebs on your elbows. It's supposed to mean that you've killed someone, although in his case I seriously doubt that. But that's not really relevant.'

Jeanette gets up and opens the window.

They can hear children playing in Kronoberg Park.

In her mind's eye Sofia can see Gao mercilessly attacking Samuel, who had been far too badly hurt to put up any resistance. Samuel had staggered around and only made feeble attempts to shield himself from Gao's kicks and punches.

Sofia looks out of the window and considers how the blood loss from his crushed eye eventually led to him losing consciousness. He must have realised that that was as good as dying.

The moment he passed out the insane creature facing him would jump on him and tear him to pieces. He had seen it happen back home in Sierra Leone, and knew this was a cat-and-mouse game with a predetermined outcome.

The phone on the desk rings, and Jeanette apologises before answering.

'Sure, she's sitting right next to me, we'll be there as soon as we can.'

Jeanette hangs up and looks intently at Sofia.

'The man with the spiderweb tattoos is Petter Christoffersson, and we've got him in the building. He's being held for grievous bodily harm, and seems to think he can bargain with us by revealing something. He's probably seen too many bad American films and thinks it works the same way here.'

Sofia's head is spinning and she's starting to sweat.

'I was thinking you could come with me and listen to him. He says he's got something to say about Samuel. He reckons he saw him the day before he was found dead. Outside McDonald's at Medborgarplatsen, with a woman. Apparently he knows who the woman is, and . . .' Jeanette falls silent. 'Well, you get it.'

Sofia thinks how easily Gao dismembered the little boy they found by the side of the road out in Svartsjölandet.

While Jeanette had been visiting her, Gao had been smashing his skull to pieces with a hammer. Later they had thrown the fragments of bone away, along with the remnants of a roast chicken.

Lie. Make something up. Go on the offensive.

'Well, I'm not sure that would be appropriate. I don't know if it's really allowed . . . But sure, I'll come along.'

Sofia sees that Jeanette is watching her reaction carefully. It's as if she's testing her.

'You're right. It isn't allowed. But you could sit outside and watch. Listen to what he has to say.'

They get up and go out into the corridor.

The interview room is on the floor below, and Jeanette shows Sofia into a small room alongside. They can see through a window into the interview room, where Petter Christoffersson is leaning back in a chair, seeming fairly relaxed. Sofia looks at his tattoos and remembers.

It's him.

The last time she saw him he was wearing a T-shirt with two Swedish flags across the chest. He delivered the building material for the room she constructed behind the bookcase. Polystyrene, planks, nails, glue, a tarpaulin and duct tape.

How could she be the victim of such a ridiculous coincidence? She feels sweat trickling down her back.

'One-way mirror.' Jeanette points at the window. 'You can see him, but he can't see you.'

Sofia feels in the pocket of her coat, finds a paper napkin and wipes her clammy hands. She isn't feeling well.

Her shoes are chafing, and her throat feels tight.

'Are you OK, Sofia?' Jeanette is looking at her.

'I feel horribly ill all of a sudden. It feels like I'm going to be sick.'

Jeanette looks concerned. 'Do you want to go back to my office?'

Sofia nods.

She goes back out into the corridor.

She's made it.

Back in Jeanette's office she goes over to the bookcase and almost immediately finds a thick folder labelled THORILDSPLAN – UNKNOWN. After a bit more searching she finds the others: SVARTSJÖLANDET – YURI KRYLOV and DANVIKSTULL – UNKNOWN.

She turns round and looks at the messy desk. Beside the phone is a stack of CDs, and when she picks them up she sees that they are recordings of interviews.

She looks through them without really registering what the labels say, but when she reaches the last disc she suddenly stiffens.

At first she thinks she's seen it wrong, but when she checks again she finds a disc marked BENGT BERGMAN.

Quickly she looks for the stack of blank CDs that she assumes ought to be here somewhere, and finds it on top of the bookcase, next to a glass jar of rubber bands and paper clips.

She goes round the desk, sits down in front of the computer, then inserts the original disc and the blank one, and when the computer asks if she wants to copy the contents, she clicks yes.

The seconds grind past, and she thinks about how she and Gao drove Samuel's body to Mikael's building in the Monument block.

How they carried him up to the attic, and how their work united them as they strung the body up from the ceiling.

After less than two minutes the computer spits out both discs, and she puts the original back where she found it. She puts the copy in her handbag.

Sofia sits down and picks up a newspaper.

It had been Gao who found the acid, and emptied the bucket over Samuel's face.

Jeanette comes back ten minutes later. Sofia is reading an old copy of *Swedish Police*.

'Anything interesting?' she wonders, looking thoughtful.

It's as if Jeanette is looking at Sofia with a new awareness, and she feels her insecurity returning.

'I was going to do the crossword,' Sofia replies, 'but I couldn't find one, so I looked at the pictures instead. How did you get on with Spider-Man? Did you find out anything interesting?'

Jeanette is still looking thoughtful.

'How long have you lived in Borgmästargatan?' she suddenly says, and Sofia starts.

'Since '95 . . . I've lived there thirteen years. God, time really does fly.'

'Have you noticed anything odd while you've been there? Especially in the last six months?'

It's like this is an interrogation and she's suspected of something.

'How do you mean, odd?' Sofia gulps. 'I mean, we're talking about Södermalm, with all that implies in terms of drunks, fights, weirdos talking to themselves, vandalised cars, and –'

'Missing boys –'

'Yes, that too. And dead boys in attics. So you'll probably have to be a bit more precise if I'm going to be able to tell you anything interesting.'

Sofia feels Victoria taking over. The lies pop up by themselves, without her having to think about them. The whole thing is an act, and she knows her role by heart.

'Petter Christoffersson was at Fredell's Building Supplies out in Sickla working last winter. He says he remembers driving a load of insulation material to an apartment on Södermalm just after New Year. He doesn't remember exactly where, but it was somewhere in the area of SoFo. He claims that the woman they delivered the supplies to was the same woman Samuel was with the day before his body was found.'

Sofia clears her throat.

'Can you trust that he's telling the truth and not just trying to make himself look important? Didn't you say he was trying to bargain?'

Jeanette folds her arms and rocks on her chair. She doesn't take her eyes off Sofia's.

'That's exactly what I'm wondering. But there's something believable about his story. Details that make it sound credible.'

She leans forward and lowers her voice slightly.

'Admittedly, his description is extremely vague. A fair-haired woman, a bit above average height, blue eyes. He said he thought she was attractive, maybe a bit more attractive than most, he said. But otherwise that could describe any number of people. I mean, it could even be you.'

Smile.

Sofia laughs and pulls a face to show what a ridiculous idea she thinks that is.

'I can see you're not feeling too good,' Jeanette says. 'Maybe it would be best if you went home.'

'Yes . . . I think so.'

'Get some rest. I can come over to your place after work.'

'Do you want to?'

'Definitely. Go home to bed now. I'll bring some wine. Does that sound OK?'

Jeanette gives Sofia a long look.

Vita Bergen – Sofia Zetterlund's Apartment

The metro from Rådhuset to Central Station, then change to the green line to Medborgarplatsen. Then the same walk as a couple of hours before, just the opposite direction. Folkungagatan, four blocks, then home. One hundred and twelve steps.

When she gets home she puts the CD she'd copied into her laptop.

'First interview with Bengt Bergman. The time is 13.12. Lead interviewer Jeanette Kihlberg, assisted by Jens Hurtig. Bengt, you're a suspect in a number of crimes, but this interview is primarily concerned with rape and/or aggravated rape, as well as bodily harm and/or grievous bodily harm, which carries a minimum sentence of two years in prison. Shall we begin?'

'Hmm . . .'

'Can I ask you to speak clearly into the microphone from now on? Obviously if you nod it can't be heard on the recording. We want you to express yourself as clearly as possible. OK. Let's begin.'

There's a brief pause, and Sofia can hear someone drinking, then putting a glass down on the table.

'How does it feel, Bengt?'

'To begin with, I'm wondering what sort of formal training you've had?'

She recognises her dad's voice immediately.

'What makes you competent to question me? I've done more than eight years of higher education, I've got a degree, and I've studied a fair bit of psychology on my own. Do you know Alice Miller?'

His voice makes Sofia start, and she pulls back automatically, raising her arms to shield herself.

Even as an adult her body is so primed that it reacts instinctively. The adrenalin is pumping, and her body is ready for flight.

'Bengt, you have to understand that I'm the one leading this interview, not you. Is that clear?'

'I don't really know –'

Jeanette Kihlberg interrupts him at once. 'I said, is that clear?'

'Yes.'

Sofia understands that his defiance is because he's still used to being in charge and feels uncomfortable in the role of the accused.

'I asked how you think it feels?'

'Well, what do you think? How would you like to sit here, falsely accused of a whole lot of revolting things?'

'I'd probably think it was awful, and do anything I could to try to get things sorted out. Is that how you feel? That you want to tell us why you were arrested?'

'As I'm sure you already know, I was stopped by the police south of the city, when I was on my way home to Grisslinge. That's where we live, out in Värmdö. I'd picked up that woman who was standing at the side of the road, covered in blood. My only intention was to help her, and get her to Södermalm Hospital so she could get proper treatment. That can't be a punishable offence, surely?'

His voice, his way of pronouncing his words, the pauses and his forced calm make her feel like she's ten years old again.

'So you're saying you're innocent of causing the injuries to the plaintiff, Tatiana Achatova, as documented on the charge sheet you've already read?'

'This is utterly ridiculous!'

'Do you feel like reading what it says on the sheet?'

'Let's get this straight – I abhor violence. I never watch television except for the news, and on the rare occasions that I do watch a film or go to the cinema, I choose quality films. I simply don't wish to have anything to do with the wickedness that's so widespread in this –'

The feeling of the pine-needle-strewn path down to the lake. She had already learned as a six-year-old how to touch him so that he was nice, and she remembers the taste of Aunt Elsa's sweets. The cold water from the well, and the stiff brush on her skin.

Jeanette Kihlberg interrupts him again. 'Do you want to read it, or shall I?'

'Well, I'd rather you did. Like I said, I don't want to –'

'According to the doctor who examined Tatiana Achatova, she was admitted to Södermalm Hospital on Sunday evening at approximately 1900 hours, with the following injuries: severe ruptures in her anus, as well as . . .'

It's as if they're talking about her, and she remembers the pain.

How much it had hurt, even though he had said it was lovely.

How confused she had been when she realised what she did with him was wrong.

Sofia can't bear to hear any more and turns it off.

His terrible deeds have evidently caught up with him at last, she thinks. But he won't be punished for what he did to me. That's not fair. I'm forced to survive with my scars while he can just go on and on.

Sofia lies down on the floor and stares up at the ceiling. She just wants to sleep. But how can she?

Her name is Victoria Bergman, and he is still there.

Bengt Bergman. Her dad. He is still alive.

And no more than twenty minutes away from her.

When they hug, Sofia can tell that Jeanette has showered and smells of a different perfume to earlier. They go into the living room, and Jeanette puts a wine box on the coffee table.

'Sit yourself down. I'll get some glasses. I'm assuming you'd like some?'

'Yes, please. It's been a hell of a week.'

Get the carafe. Fill it up with wine. Fill the glass.

Sofia pours some wine.

Read the situation. Ask something personal.

Sofia notices how moist Jeanette's eyes are, and realises it's not just tiredness.

'How are you doing? You look sad.'

Eye contact. Show sympathy. Maybe a little smile.

She looks Jeanette in the eye and gives her an understanding smile.

Jeanette looks down at the table without speaking. 'Fucking Åke,' she suddenly blurts out. 'I think he's in love with that gallery owner. How stupid can you get? To be honest I don't know if I even care. I'm sick of him.' Jeanette takes a deep breath. 'What's that smell?'

Sofia thinks of the glass jars in the kitchen, of Gao behind the bookcase, and at the same time detects the acrid stench of chemicals filling the flat.

'Something to do with the drains. The neighbours are renovating their bathroom.'

Jeanette looks sceptical, but seems satisfied with the explanation.

Steer the conversation onto a different subject.

'Have you heard anything more about Lundström? Or is he still in a coma?'

'He is. But it doesn't really change anything. The prosecutor has got hung up on his medication and all that . . . Well, you know . . .'

'Have you checked out what Spider-Man told you?'

'You mean Petter Christoffersson? No, we haven't got any further with that. I don't really know what to think. If I'm honest, I think he was mainly interested in my breasts.' She laughs, and it's infectious.

Sofia feels relieved.

'Did you get much of an impression of him?'

'Just the usual, I suppose. Full of complexes, insecure, fixated on sex,'

Jeanette begins. 'Probably violent, at least when it comes to things that are important to him. And by that I mean everything that goes against his wishes or questions his ideology. He's definitely not unintelligent, but his intelligence is destructive and seems to be self-defeating.'

'You sound like a psychologist.' Sofia sips her wine. 'And I have to confess that I'm a bit curious about your diagnosis of the young man . . .'

Jeanette sits quietly for a while before going on with exaggerated seriousness. 'Suppose Petter Christoffersson is forced to interpret the meaning of an unclear situation. Let's say his girlfriend has spent the night at a male friend's. He's going to see it as a betrayal, and will always choose the interpretation he finds most negative to himself and everyone involved, specifically that she's been unfaithful –'

'Whereas she actually slept alone on her friend's sofa –' Sofia interjects.

'But,' Jeanette goes on, 'spending the night at a friend's is the same to him as fucking the friend, in every position his imagination can come up with –'

Jeanette stops herself and lets Sofia go on.

'And afterwards they'd have talked about what a moron he is, sitting at home and not suspecting a thing.'

They burst out laughing, and when Jeanette falls back on the sofa Sofia catches sight of a brownish-red spot on the pale upholstery. She quickly grabs a cushion and playfully tosses it to Jeanette, who catches it and, thankfully, puts it down beside her, hiding the spot of Samuel's blood.

'God, you sound like you could be one of my colleagues. Are you sure you've never studied psychology?'

Jeanette looks almost embarrassed.

'And what do you think about the woman he says he saw?'

'I think he saw a fair-haired, attractive woman with Samuel. He reckons he even stared at her backside. He's young and has sex on his mind all the time. Register, stare, register, stare, fantasise and then masturbate.' Jeanette laughs. 'But on the other hand, I don't think it was the same woman he delivered building materials to.'

Seem interested.

'Oh? Why not?'

'This is a guy who only sees a woman's chest or her backside. All women become one and the same.'

She drinks the last of her wine and refills her glass.

They sit in silence for a while just looking at each other. Sofia likes Jeanette's eyes. Their gaze is firm, curious. They reveal how intelligent she is. But there's something else as well. Courage, character. It's hard to put a finger on what it is.

Sofia realises she is growing more and more fascinated by her. Within the space of ten minutes all of Jeanette's feelings and characteristics have been visible in her eyes. Happiness. Self-confidence. Intelligence. Sorrow. Disappointment. Doubt. Frustration.

In another time, another place, she thinks. All she has to do is make sure that Jeanette doesn't catch sight of her darkness. She must hold it back whenever they meet, and Jeanette must never meet Victoria Bergman.

But she and Victoria are shackled to each other like Siamese twins and, as a result, also dependent on each other.

They share the same heart, and the blood flowing through their bodies is the same blood. But while Victoria despises Sofia's weakness, Sofia admires Victoria for her strength. And feels inferior to her.

She recalls how she used to shut herself away inside when anyone teased her. The way she used to eat her food up like a good girl and let him touch her.

She had adapted, which Victoria had never been able to do.

Victoria had hidden herself away deep within.

Victoria had waited and bided her time. Waiting for the moment when Sofia was forced to let her out to stop herself from sinking.

If she had just looked inside herself she would have found the strength. But instead she had tried to erase Victoria from her memory. For decades, Victoria had tried to get Sofia to realise that it was she rather than Sofia who held the key, and very occasionally Sofia had actually listened.

Like when she got the whining boy down by the river to shut up.

Like when she took care of Lasse.

Sofia can feel her headache easing, as the rubber band of her conscience stretches closer and closer to the breaking point. She feels that she'd like to tell Jeanette everything. Tell her how her father abused her. Describe the nights when she didn't dare sleep in case he would then come into her room. The schooldays when she couldn't stay awake.

She wants to tell Jeanette how it feels to wolf down food and then vomit it up. To feel the pain of a razor blade.

She wants to tell her everything.

Then suddenly Victoria's voice comes back.

'You'll have to excuse me, but the wine's had an effect and I have to go to the toilet.'

Sofia gets up and feels the alcohol rush to her head, and she giggles and steadies herself on Jeanette, who responds by putting her hand over hers.

'Sofia . . .' Jeanette looks up at her. 'I'm really glad I've met you. It's the best thing that's happened to me in . . . well, I don't know how long.'

Sofia stops, overwhelmed by the sign of affection.

'What happens to us when we don't have to meet any more? Because of work, I mean.'

Smile. Answer honestly.

Sofia smiles. 'I think we can continue seeing each other anyway.'

Jeanette goes on. 'I might like you to meet Johan some day. You'd like him.'

Sofia stiffens. Johan?

She'd completely forgotten that there are other people in Jeanette's life.

'Did you say he was thirteen?' she says.

'That's right. He's starting secondary school this autumn.'

Martin would have been thirty this year.

If his parents hadn't happened upon an advertisement for a house for rent in Dala-Floda.

If he hadn't wanted to go on the Ferris wheel.

If he hadn't changed his mind and wanted to go swimming instead.

If he hadn't thought the water was too cold.

If he hadn't fallen in the water.

Sofia thinks about how Martin disappeared after their turn on the Ferris wheel.

She looks deep into Jeanette's eyes as she hears Victoria's voice inside her head.

'How about taking Johan to the fair at Gröna Lund some weekend?'

Sofia waits for Jeanette's reaction.

'That sounds great. What a nice idea,' Jeanette says with a smile. 'You're going to love him.'

Vita Bergen – Sofia Zetterlund's Apartment

Jeanette lights a cigarette. So who is Sofia Zetterlund, really? She feels a closeness to her, but at the same time she's so out of reach. Sometimes so incredibly present, only to turn into someone else, suddenly and without warning.

Maybe that's why she's so captivated by her. Precisely because she is surprising, never predictable.

Isn't it also the case that her voice seems to change sometimes?

Once Sofia has shut the bathroom door behind her, Jeanette gets up from the armchair and goes over to the bookcase. A number of thick volumes about psychology, psychoanalytical diagnosis and the cognitive development of children. A lot of philosophy, sociology, biography and fiction. Thomas de Quincey, *The 120 Days of Sodom*, *Stiffed: The Betrayal of the American Man*, side by side with Jan Guillou's political novels and Stieg Larsson's crime trilogy.

At the far left of the shelf is a book whose title catches her interest. *A Long Way Gone: Memoirs of a Boy Soldier*. As she pulls the book from the shelf she notices a little catch sticking out of the side of the bookcase. Odd to have a lock on a bookcase, she thinks as Sofia comes into the room.

'So you like Larsson?' Sofia says.

'Which one? Stig or Stieg? The wicked one or the good one?'

Jeanette laughs and shows her the cover. Stig Larsson's *New Year*. 'The wicked one, I presume?'

'I see you've got two copies of Valerie Solanas's *SCUM Manifesto*.'

'Yes, I was young and angry back then. These days I just think it's a very entertaining book. I now laugh at what I once took dead seriously.'

Jeanette puts the book back. '*SCUM. The Society for Cutting Up Men*. I'm not that well informed, although I have read it. I must have been young at the time, a teenager, I guess. In what way do you think it's entertaining?'

'It's radical, and the entertainment value is in the radicalism. It's so unrelenting in its approach to the bad sides of men that guys end up looking so ridiculous that I can't help laughing. I was ten when I first read it, and back then I bought the whole thing. Literally. Now I can laugh at it, both the details and the book as a whole. That's much better.'

Jeanette gulps down the last of the wine. 'Did you say you were ten? I was forced to read *Lord of the Rings* by my romantically inclined dad when I was nine or ten. What sort of childhood did you have, if you were reading books like that when you were so young?'

'I picked it myself, actually.'

Sofia stands in silence, breathing deeply.

Jeanette can see that Sofia is upset and asks what's wrong.

'It's the book you were holding when I came in,' she replies. 'It had a big impact on me.'

'This one, you mean?' Jeanette pulls out the book about the child soldier and looks at the cover. A young boy carrying a rifle over his shoulder.

'Yes, that's the one. Samuel Bai was a child soldier in Sierra Leone, like Ishmael Beah. I was asked to do a fact-check for the Swedish edition, but I'm afraid I was too much of a coward to do it.'

Jeanette glances through the text on the back cover.

'Read it out loud,' Sofia says. 'The bit that's underlined on page two hundred and seventeen.'

Jeanette opens the book and reads.

> *There was a hunter who went into the bush to kill a monkey. When he was close enough and behind a tree where he could clearly see the monkey, he raised his rifle and aimed. Just when he was about to pull the trigger, the monkey spoke: 'If you shoot me, your mother will die, and if you don't, your father will die.' The monkey resumed its position, chewing its food, and every so often scratched its head or the side of its belly.*
>
> *What would you do if you were the hunter?*

Jeanette looks up at Sofia and puts the book down.

'I wouldn't,' Sofia says.

Grisslinge – a Suburb

Sofia Zetterlund takes the metro from Skanstull to Gullmarsplan, where she had parked her car the previous day. She didn't want it to be caught by the cameras that watch the roads leading in and out of central Stockholm on weekdays.

The Årsta forest colours the view from the Skanstull Bridge in shades of dark green. Down in the marina there is feverish activity, and the outdoor terrace of the Skanskvarn restaurant is already full.

After several months with little appetite, Sofia can no longer tell the difference between different types of pain. Physical nausea, which makes her throw up several times each day, has merged with her mental pain and with the torment of her tight shoes. Everything that hurts has become one, and over the course of the summer the darkness inside her has grown denser.

She has been finding it harder and harder to appreciate things she once found interesting, and things she used to like have started to get on her nerves.

No matter how often she washes she thinks she smells of sweat, and that her feet start to stink within an hour or so of showering. She carefully observes people around her to see if anyone shows any sign of detecting her bodily odours. When there is no reaction, she assumes that she is the only one bothered by them.

She's run out of paroxetine tablets, and she hasn't felt up to contacting anyone to get more.

She can't even be bothered to use the tape recorder any more.

After each session she would end up exhausted, and it would take several hours before she felt like herself again.

At the start it felt good to have someone who listened, but in the end there was nothing more to say.

She doesn't need analysis. That time has passed.

She needs action.

Sofia gets her car keys out, opens the door and sits in the driver's seat. Reluctantly she takes hold of the gearstick to put it into neutral. It goes against her every instinct, and she starts to get dizzy. The memories of the roll of toilet paper next to the gearstick, and his breath, are so clear. She had been ten years old when he turned off the motorway just before Bålsta on the way to Dala-Floda.

She feels the cold leather of the gearstick against the palm of her hand. The ridged surface tickles her lifeline and she takes a firm grasp of the knob.

She has made up her mind.

There is no hesitation left.

No doubt.

She puts the car firmly into first gear, revs hard and heads off down Hammarbyvägen towards the Värmdö road. As she passes Orminge it starts to pour with rain and the air becomes cold and damp. Every breath offers resistance.

She is having trouble breathing again.

Now the waiting is over, she thinks as she drives into the dusk.

The street lights lead her on.

The car slowly gets warmer, but she is ice-cold, deep down in her marrow, and the heat settles as no more than a sweaty skin on her. It can't get in.

Can't reach her ice-cold, clear conviction.

Nothing can soften her.

It takes her a quarter of an hour to reach Willy's discount supermarket in Gustavsberg, where she turns off and leaves the car in the customer car park. Here her memory is clear. This place didn't exist then. She's taken aback by the realisation that things can change so drastically just a couple of hundred metres from where time has stood still. Where her life has stood still.

This used to be a clump of trees where there were said to be dirty old men and alcoholics. But strangers meant well. Only those who were close to her could do her any real harm.

The forest had been a safe place.

She remembers the glade near the cottage. The one she never found again. The sunlight glittering through the leaves, the nuances of the white moss that defeated everything hard and sharp.

In the back seat she has an old workout top that's far too large for her. She looks around, then pulls the hooded top on and locks the car.

She decided earlier that she would walk the last bit. That part demands mobility. It demands reflection and reflection can give rise to compromise, but the drive has only strengthened her resolve and she isn't planning to come to her senses. She rejects all thoughts of reconciliation. He's made his choices. Now it's her turn to act.

Every paving slab is edged with memories, and everything she sees reminds her of the life she fled from.

She knows that what she is about to do is irreversible. She has reached the point at which the things he set in motion must come to an end.

As ye sow, so shall ye reap, she thinks.

She pulls the hood up and starts to walk down Skärgårdsvägen towards Grisslinge.

The clatter of the wooden shoes of her childhood follows her, echoing between the houses.

She thinks of all the times she ran up and down the streets, at a time when everything should have been play.

The child she once was wants to stop her doing what she's going to do. It wants to go on existing.

But that child must be erased.

Her parental home is a three-storey modernist-style villa. It seems smaller now than it did then, but still rises up just as threateningly towards the sky. The house looks down on her with its curtained windows and well-kept flowers creeping along the panes.

There's a white Volvo parked outside the house. They are at home.

To the left she can see the rowan tree her parents planted the day she was born. It's grown since she last saw it. When she was seven she tried to set fire to it, but it wouldn't burn.

The high fence he built to minimise the risk of neighbours seeing in gives her the perfect cover, and she creeps along the wall of the house, up onto the terrace, and peers in through the small basement window.

She had been right. Their routines are still laughably regular, and, just like every other Wednesday evening, they are in the sauna.

Inside the window she sees their clothes neatly folded on the bench.

The thought of the smell of his trousers makes her feel nauseous, the sound of the zip being pulled down, the wave of sour sweat as his trousers fall to the floor.

Carefully she opens the unlocked front door and steps into the hall. The first thing she notices is the sickly scent of peppermint tea. It reeks of sickness in here, she thinks. A sickness that has crept into the walls. She hesitates before taking off her tennis shoes, and her own smell hits her. She smells of fear and fury.

Now her shoes are next to his again.

For a moment she is overwhelmed by a feeling that everything is the way it used to be. That she has come home from a normal day at school and that she still belongs to this life.

She shakes off the feeling before it can get its teeth into her.

This world is not mine, she tells herself.

We have made our choice.

She pads into the living room and looks around. Everything is just the same. Not a single thing is standing where it hasn't always stood.

The large room is furnished with a simplicity that she always found pathetically spartan, and she remembers how she used to avoid having friends round because she was so ashamed.

On the white walls are a few paintings, mostly images from folklore, including a Carl Larsson reproduction that they were always incredibly proud of, for some reason. It's still there, in all its paltriness.

She can see straight through all their lies and delusions.

He had paid a lot for the dining-room furniture at an auction in Bodarna. It had needed serious restoration, and an upholsterer in Falun had to replace the original fabric with something very similar. Everything had looked perfect, but now the passage of time was starting to show even on the new material.

There's a faint smell of decay, of lives past their prime.

He hates change, and wants everything to stay the way he's used to. He hates it when Mum rearranges things.

It's as if he concluded at some given moment that everything was perfect, and decided to freeze time from then on.

He lived under the illusion that perfection was a permanent state that didn't require any maintenance.

He is blind to decay, she thinks, to the shabbiness of his life, to everything she sees so clearly now.

The dirt.

The stale odours.

Her diploma hangs next to the stairs leading up to the top floor. It covers the space left by the African mask that used to hang there but is now gone forever.

She goes upstairs silently, turns left and opens the door to her childhood bedroom.

She can't breathe.

The room looks like it did the day she stormed out, certain that she'd never return. There's the bed, neatly made and untouched. There's the desk and chair. A dead plant on the windowsill. Another frozen moment, she thinks.

They've preserved her memory, closing the door on what was once her life and never opening it again.

She opens the wardrobe door, and finds her clothes still inside. On a nail right at the back hangs the key she hasn't used in more than twenty years. On the floor stands the red wooden box painted with traditional patterns that she was given by Aunt Elsa the summer she first met Martin.

She runs her fingers over the pattern on the lid, steeling herself before she opens it.

She doesn't know what she's going to find in there.

Or, rather, she knows exactly what she's going to find, but doesn't know what it's going to do to her.

Inside the box are an envelope, a photograph album and a threadbare stuffed animal. On top of the envelope is the videotape she once sent to herself.

She looks over at the desktop, where she once carved loads of hearts and all sorts of different names. Her finger traces the carved letters and she tries to conjure up the faces the names represent. She can't remember any of them.

The only name that means anything is Martin's.

She had been ten and he three when they got to know each other that week out at the cottage.

The first time he had put his hand in hers he had done it without wanting anything more.

He had just wanted to touch her hand.

Sofia puts her hand over Martin's name on the desktop, and feels grief rising like sap in her chest. She had him in her hands, he used to do whatever she suggested. So full of trust.

She sees herself next to Martin's dad. The threat she thought he was. The way she had tried to play the game she knew so well. Constantly waiting for that moment, the time he would catch her and make her his. The way she had wanted to protect Martin from those adult arms, that adult body.

She giggles at her own memories and the naive assumption that all men were the same. If it hadn't been for the fact that she had seen Martin's dad touching him, everything would have been different. It was that moment that had confirmed beyond any doubt that all men knew no boundaries and were capable of anything.

But in his case she had been wrong.

Martin's dad had been a perfectly ordinary dad. He had been washing his son. That's all.

Guilt, she thinks.

Bengt and the other men made Martin's dad guilty. The ten-year-old Victoria saw the collective guilt of all men in him. In his eyes and the way he touched her.

He was a man, and that was enough. No analysis was required. Only the logical conclusion of her own thoughts.

She reads the label on the videotape in her hand.

Sigtuna 84.

A car passes at high speed down Skärgårdsvägen, and she drops the tape on the floor. To her the noise is deafening and she stands frozen, but there's nothing to suggest that they heard her down in the sauna.

It's still quiet, and it occurs to her that everything might have just stopped after she vanished from their lives.

Maybe she was the root of all the evil?

If that's true, then she has no framework to follow, no timetable to put her faith in. In spite of her uncertainty she can't resist watching the film. She has to experience everything once more.

Relief, she thinks.

She sits down on the bed, puts the tape in the video player, and turns the television on.

There's a hiss as the film starts, and she lowers the volume. The picture is sharp and shows a room lit up by a single, bare light bulb.

She sees three girls kneeling in front of a row of pig masks.

She is on the left, Victoria, smiling faintly.

The sound of the old video camera is audible.

'Tie them up!' someone hisses, then bursts out laughing.

The girls' hands are bound behind them with duct tape, and they're blindfolded. One of the masked girls brings forward a bucket of water.

'Silence. And . . . action!' the girl holding the camera says. 'Welcome to Sigtuna College for the Humanities!' she goes on, while the contents of the bucket are emptied over the three girls' heads. Hannah coughs and Jessica lets out a yelp, but Sofia sees herself sit in complete silence.

One of the girls steps forward, puts on a student cap and bends over, making a sweeping gesture towards the camera, then turns towards the girls on the floor. Sofia watches in fascination as Jessica begins to sway backwards and forwards.

'I am the representative of the student body!'

The others all burst into loud laughter, and Sofia leans forward and lowers the volume on the television a bit more, while the girl goes on with her speech.

'And to become full members you must eat the welcome gift from our school's most eminent headmistress.' The laughter gets even louder, but Sofia can tell that it's forced. As if the girls are laughing out of obligation, and not because they are genuinely amused. Goaded on by Fredrika Grünewald.

The camera zooms in to show just Jessica, Hannah and Victoria sitting on the floor.

Sofia Zetterlund sits mutely in front of the flickering television screen, feeling fury bubble up inside her. They had agreed that they would be served chocolate pudding, but Fredrika Grünewald had served them real dog shit in order to cement her hold over the younger girls.

As she sees herself in the film she feels proud. Because she had fought back, and had gained victory by being responsible for the final shock.

She had played her role to the end.

She was used to dealing with shit.

Sofia takes the tape out and put it back in the box. The water pipes are rumbling and the boiler clicks into action down in the cellar. She can hear his agitated voice from the sauna, and her mum's attempts to calm him down.

Sofia thinks it smells musty and cautiously opens the window. She looks out over the dusk-shrouded garden. Her old swing is still hanging from the tree below. She remembers it being red, but none of the paint is left. Just dry, yellow-brown flakes.

A world of facades, she thinks, as she turns and looks around the room. There's a picture of her on the wall, from when she was in year 9. Her smile is radiant and her eyes full of life. No indication of what was really going on inside her.

She had learned to play the game.

Sofia feels that she's close to tears. Not because she regrets anything, but because she suddenly comes to think about Hannah and Jessica, who got caught up in Victoria's game but never found out that it had been her idea all along.

It had turned into an experiment in guilt. A joke that became serious.

In front of Hannah and Jessica she had played the role of victim, even though she was actually the opposite.

It was a betrayal.

She spent three years sharing the shame with them.

For three years the idea of revenge held them together.

She had hated Fredrika Grünewald and all the anonymous upper-class girls from Danderyd and Stocksund, who used their parents' money to buy the nicest and most expensive brands of clothes. Who thought they were something special because of their smart names.

Four years older.

Four years more mature than her.

Who carries the greater anxiety today? Have they forgotten it, suppressed it?

Sofia sits down on the soft, pale blue carpet and leans her head back. She looks up at the ceiling and sees that the cracks in the plaster are still there. Others have appeared since she was last there.

She wonders which of them stuck to the contract they signed with their own blood.

Hannah? Jessica? She herself?

They stuck together for three years, then they lost touch.

The last time she saw them was on the train from the Gare du Nord in Paris.

She pulls out the battered photograph album and opens the first page.

She doesn't recognise herself in the pictures. It's just a child who isn't her, and when she thinks back on herself as a little girl she feels nothing.

That isn't me, nor that one who's five, nor that one who's eight. They can't be me, because I don't feel what they felt, I don't think what they thought.

They're all dead.

She remembers when the eight-year-old had just learned to tell the time, and would lie in bed pretending to be a clock.

But she never managed to trick time. Instead time had taken her under its arm and carried her away from there.

In the album in front of her she ages each time she turns a page. Seasons and birthday cakes follow on, one after another.

After the pictures from Sigtuna she had stuck in an Interrail card next to a ticket for the Roskilde Festival. On the opposite page are three blurred pictures, of Hannah, Jessica and her. She goes on looking at the pictures as she listens for sounds from the basement, but he seems to have calmed down.

They had been the Three Musketeers, even if the other two had turned their backs on her towards the end and proved themselves to be exactly the same as all the others. To start with they had shared everything and solved problems together, but when it really mattered they had let her down. When things got serious and it was time to show their character, they had burst into tears and run home to their mothers, like little girls.

She had thought they were completely stupid. Now she looks at their photographs and realises that they were just unsullied. They had believed the best of people. They had trusted her. That was all.

Sofia jumps when she hears banging and shouting from the basement. The sauna door opens, and for the first time in several years she hears his voice in person. 'Not that I imagine for a second that you're ever going to be clean, but at least this ought to get rid of the smell!'

She assumes that he's grabbed Mum by the hair and pulled her out of the sauna. Is he going to scald her or force her to stand under ice-cold water for several minutes?

Sofia shuts her eyes and thinks about what she'll do if they decide to get out of the sauna. She looks at the time. No, he's a creature of habit, so the torment will continue for at least another half-hour.

Sofia wonders what Mum usually says to her friends. How many times can you split your eyebrow open on a kitchen cupboard, how many times can you slip in the bath? Shouldn't you take more care on the stairs if you've managed to fall down them four times in the last six months? Surely people must wonder, she thinks.

On one single occasion he raised his arm to Victoria, ready to strike, but when she smashed him in the head with a saucepan he withdrew like a shark, and spent several months complaining of headaches.

Mum never hit back, just cried and came and curled up beside Victoria instead, looking for solace. Victoria always did her best, and lay awake until her mum fell asleep.

After one of their fights Mum had driven off and stayed in a hotel for several days. Dad didn't know where she'd gone and got worried, and Victoria had to comfort him as he sobbed against her chest.

On days like that she didn't go to school, and spent hours cycling around, and when the absentee notes appeared they would sign them without asking. There had been some advantages to all the arguments.

Sofia laughs at the memory. That feeling of having an advantage, a secret.

Victoria bore their weakness deep within her. They both knew that she could use it against them whenever she chose. She never did. She chose to think of them as air. She never paid them any attention, and so they never had an opportunity to defend themselves.

She sits down on the bed, picks up the little black dog made from real rabbit skin, and buries her nose in it. It smells of dust and damp. Its little yellow glass eyes stare at her, and she stares back.

When she was little she used to clutch the dog tight and look deep into its eyes. After a while a little world would open up, usually a beach, and she would explore this miniature world until she fell asleep.

But she's not going to sleep now.

This journey will free her forever.

She's going to burn all her bridges.

She hugs her dog again. It is as if she used to think no one could harm her back then as long as she held everything inside herself and played along, trying to be smarter. As if she had believed you won victories by destroying others.

That had been his logic when he suffered his attacks.

'Daddy, Daddy, Daddy,' she mutters to herself in an attempt to empty the word of all meaning.

He's sitting downstairs in the sauna, and no one has ever dared leave him. No one but Victoria. The only thing he instilled in her was the desire to escape. He never managed to teach her to want to stay.

Escape, above everything, she thinks. Self-defence mechanisms hand in hand with destructiveness.

Memories attack her from within. They sting her throat. Everything hurts. She isn't prepared for the deluge, or the images from a time she hasn't thought about for more than twenty years. She realises that she ought to have felt much more than she did, but knows that she has gone from one thing to the next, always laughing. From one humiliation to the next.

She can still hear it, that laughter. The sound gets louder until it's deafening. She rocks back and forth in her childhood bedroom. She hums quietly to herself. It's as if the voice inside her head leaks out through her clenched lips. The sound of a deflating bicycle tyre.

She covers her ears with her hands in an attempt to shut out the manic sound, a sound she once thought was happiness.

The man downstairs in the sauna had destroyed everything that could have been, partly through his sick, sadistic desires, and partly through his lachrymose self-pity.

Sofia takes the envelope from the box. It's marked with the letter M and contains a letter and a photograph.

The letter is dated 9 July 1982. Martin obviously had help writing it, but wrote his name himself, and says that it's sunny and hot and that he's been swimming almost every day. Then he drew a flower and something that looks like a small dog.

Beneath the drawing are the words SEA STACK AND SPIDER FLOWER.

On the back of the photograph she sees that it was taken in Ekeviken, on Fårö, in the summer of 1982. The picture shows Martin, five years old, under an apple tree. In his arms he's holding a white rabbit that looks like it's trying to get away. He's smiling and squinting against the sun, with his head slightly tilted.

His shoelaces are undone, and he looks happy. She strokes Martin's face gently with her finger and thinks about how he never learned to tie his shoelaces, so he was always tripping. And she thinks about the laughter that meant she could never resist hugging him.

She loses herself in the photograph, his eyes, his skin. She can still remember the way his skin smelled after a day in the sun, after his evening bath, in the morning when the folds of his pillow were still visible on his cheek. She thinks about their final hours together.

Sofia shuts her eyes, folds her arms across her chest, hugs herself.

The pipes beside the bed begin to roar. Then she hears footsteps on the stairs. Footsteps whose weight she recognises.

Her heart is beating so hard she almost can't breathe. It wasn't me, she thinks.

It was you.

She hears him clattering around in the kitchen, then turning the tap on. Then he turns it off and disappears down into the basement again.

She doesn't want to remember anything else, just wants to put an end to it all. All that remains is going down to them and doing what she came here to do.

She leaves the room and goes down the stairs, but stops at the kitchen doorway. She goes in and looks around.

There's something different.

Where there used to be an empty space under the worktop there's now a shiny new dishwasher. How many hours did she spend down there, hidden behind the little curtain, listening to the adults talking?

But something else is still there, just as she suspected.

She walks over to the fridge and looks at the cutting from *Upsala Nya Tidning*, now extremely yellow after almost thirty years.

TRAGIC ACCIDENT: 9-YEAR-OLD BOY FOUND DEAD IN FYRIS RIVER.

Sofia looks at the cutting. After reading it daily for several years, over and over again, she knows it by heart. She is taken aback by a sudden sense of unease, not what she usually felt when she read it.

The unease isn't sadness, but something else.

Just as it used to, it comforts her to read about how nine-year-old Martin had inexplicably drowned in the Fyris River. That the police didn't think there was anything suspicious about it, and were treating the incident as a tragic accident.

She feels a sense of calm spreading through her body, and the feelings of guilt gradually subside.

It had been an accident. Nothing else.

City of Uppsala, 1986

Down on the jetty she moves her hand back and forth in the water.

'It's not that cold,' she lies.

But he doesn't want to go out to her.

'Can't we go back? It smells, and I'm freezing.'

She finds his indecision annoying. First it was the Ferris wheel, then he changed his mind. Then he wanted to swim, but now he doesn't.

'Well, hold your nose if you think it smells. Look at me, you can see it isn't cold!'

She looks around to make sure there's no one around. The only people who could possibly see her would be anyone sitting in the big wheel, but she can see it isn't moving at the moment and is standing there empty.

She takes off her knitted cardigan and top and sits down on the jetty. Then she pulls off her trousers and socks, and stretches out on the jetty in just her underwear. Her skin rises in goosebumps as a cold wind sweeps her back.

'See, it isn't cold. Please, Martin, come here!'

Carefully he walks out to her and she rolls onto her side and unties his shoes.

'We've got our coats with us, so we won't freeze. Anyway, it's warmer in the water than it is on land.'

She reaches in front of her and pulls the forgotten towel from the post. 'Look, we've even got a towel to dry ourselves on. It's not wet, and you can use it first.'

Suddenly there's a shrill alarm from the Kungsängen Bridge, over by the sewage treatment plant. Martin gets scared and jumps. She laughs because she knows it's just the signal that the bridge is about to be raised to let river traffic pass. The first signal is followed by several shorter ones, and it's gloomy enough down on the jetty for the rhythmic flashing of the red light to be reflected in the trees above them. But the bridge itself isn't visible.

'Don't be scared. It's just the bridge opening to let the boats through.'

He looks lost standing there.

When she sees that he's still freezing, she pulls him closer and hugs him tight. His hair tickles her nose and she giggles.

'You don't have to go swimming if you don't dare . . .'

The bascule bridge opens, and soon a little wooden boat with its lanterns lit glides past, followed by a larger racing boat with its cab covered.

They lie entwined on the jetty as the boats pass. She thinks how empty it will be when autumn comes and he will no longer be there with her.

He lies there quietly curled up beside her.

'What are you thinking?' she asks.

He looks up at her and she can see him smiling.

'How much fun it's going to be moving to Skåne.'

She turns utterly cold.

'My cousin lives in Helsingborg and we'll be able to play nearly every day. He's got a really long car track and he's going to give me one of his cars. Maybe a Ponsack Farburg.'

She can feel her body starting to go limp, almost paralysed. Does he want to move to Skåne?

She thinks that they're going to take him away from her and she thinks about how she's going to disappear out of his life.

She looks at him. He's lying beside her gazing dreamily up at the sky.

There's a shadow over his face, like a bird's wing.

She wants to get up, but it's as if someone's got an iron grip on her arms and chest.

Where can I go? she thinks, terrified. She wants to erase everything he's said, and she wants to take him away from there.

Back to her home.

Then something happens.

Her vision blurs and she feels she's about to be sick.

And it sounds like a crow is crying directly into her ears.

She looks up in horror and right in front of her is his laughing face.

No, it's not him, it's his dad's eyes and his disgusting wet lips laughing at her scornfully. And now the crow is inside her head, and black wings are flapping over her eyes. Every muscle in her body tenses, and, terrified, she tries to protect herself.

Crow Girl grabs hold of his hair, so hard that big clumps come out.

She hits him.

In the head, in the face, on his body. Blood pours from his ears and nose and in his eyes she sees first only fear, but then something else as well.

Deep in his eyes he doesn't understand what's happening.

Crow Girl hits and hits, and when he's no longer moving her blows get weaker.

She's crying as she bends over him. He doesn't make a sound, just lies there staring at her. There's no expression in his eyes, but they're moving, and he keeps blinking. He's breathing fast and his throat is rattling.

She feels giddy, and her body is heavy.

As if in a fog she gets up, walks off the jetty and fetches a large stone from the riverbank. Her vision is spinning as she goes back to him with the stone.

When it hits his head it sounds like when you stamp on an apple.

'It isn't me,' she says. Then she lets his body sink into the water.

'Now you've got to swim . . .'

Grisslinge – Bergman House

Sofia Zetterlund takes the cutting down, carefully folds it up and puts it in her pocket.

It wasn't me, she thinks.

It was you.

She opens the fridge and sees that as usual it is full of milk. Everything is the way it always is, everything is the way it ought to be. She knows he drinks two litres each day. Milk is pure.

She remembers him tipping an entire carton over her when she didn't want to go to the cottage. The milk had poured down her head, over her body and onto the floor, but she had gone with him anyway, and then she had met Martin for the first time.

It should have been tears pouring down, she thinks, and closes the fridge door.

Suddenly she hears a buzzing sound, not from the fridge but from her pocket.

Her mobile phone.

She waits until it stops ringing.

She knows they'll soon be finished downstairs and that she'll have to hurry if she's going to have enough time, but she still goes back upstairs to her room. She has to be certain there's nothing she wants to keep. Nothing she's going to miss.

She decides to rescue the little rabbit-skin dog.

It hasn't done any harm, and actually comforted her for many years, listening to her thoughts.

No, she can't leave him.

She picks up the dog from the bed. For a moment she wonders about taking the photograph album, but no, it must be destroyed. They're Victoria's pictures, not hers. From now on she's only going to be Sofia, even if she's going to be forced to share her life with someone else forever after.

Before she pads back downstairs she takes a look in her parents' bedroom. Just like the living room, it looks the same as it always did. Even the brown floral bedspread is the same, just shabbier and paler than she remembers. On the landing she stops and listens. To judge by the murmuring from the sauna they're in the middle of the reconciliation phase. Once again she looks at the time and realises that this is one of their marathon sessions.

She goes back down into the living room and hears a noise from the basement as someone comes out of the sauna.

Every sauna session was its own performance that followed a set pattern.

Phase one used to be silence and butterflies in her stomach, and even if she knew that phase two would come, she never stopped hoping that this time would be an exception and that they would simply have a sauna the way everyone else did. When he began to fidget and run his hand over his thinning hair it was time for the next stage and a signal to Mum. Over the years she had learned to interpret and understand the signal encouraging her to make herself scarce and leave them alone.

'No, this is too hot for me,' she usually said. 'I think I'm going to go and put some water on for tea.'

But now the fat cow can't get away any more.

From what she's heard from the sauna, she understands that phase two these days is dominated by violence, in contrast to when she used to be left in there.

In her day it used to take about twenty minutes before he reached phase three, which was the worst part, with him crying and wanting to make up, and if you didn't play your cards right it could mean that you had to go through phase two all over again. Before she goes downstairs to them she looks around one last time. From now on there will only be memories left, nothing physical to return to that might be able to validate the memories.

In the living room she takes down the picture from the wall and places it on the floor. Carefully she puts her foot down on it, breaking the glass. Then she takes the print out of the broken frame and stares at the picture one last time before slowly tearing it into pieces.

The interior of a house in Dalarna.

She is standing in the foreground, naked apart from big, black riding boots that reach up to her knees. She's hiding a dirty sheet behind her back. In the background Martin is sitting on the floor, not interested in her.

Now she can only see a smiling girl and a sweet child who's playing absent-mindedly with a tin or maybe a building block. The riding boots that she was forced to wear once when he abused her are two ordinary socks, and the sheet with her blood and his bodily fluids on it is a clean nightdress.

It's like a Carl Larsson.

Only she knows that the idyll is fake.

Everyone else sees nothing but a decorative picture.

She takes a deep breath, and the stale smell of mould tickles her nose.

She hates Carl Larsson.

On the way down the stairs to the cellar she avoids the steps that she knows creak, and goes into the workshop. She picks up a plank that looks long enough, then goes into the shower room outside the sauna. She can hear them clearly now. He's the only one talking.

'Christ, you're not getting any thinner, are you? Can't you put a towel around yourself?'

She knows Mum will do as he says without protest. She stopped crying a long time ago. She's accepted that life doesn't always turn out the way you imagined.

No sadness. Just indifference.

'If I didn't feel sorry for you I'd tell you to get lost. And I don't just mean out of the sauna, but for good. But how the hell would you survive? Eh?'

Mum says nothing. Just as she always has.

For a moment she hesitates. Maybe he's the only one who should die.

But no, Mum needs to pay for her silence and her acquiescence. Without her, nothing could have happened. Silence was a precondition.

Keeping quiet means consent.

'Say something, for fuck's sake!'

They're so wrapped up in themselves that they don't even hear her pushing the plank up against the wooden handle of the sauna door and wedging it against the wall opposite.

She gets out her cigarette lighter.

Kronoberg – Police Headquarters

The phone rings, and Jeanette sees that it's Commissioner Dennis Billing.

'Hello, Jeanette,' he begins, and his ingratiating tone of voice makes her immediately suspicious.

'Hello, Dennis, my friend,' she replies sarcastically, and can't resist adding, 'To what do I owe this honour?'

'Oh, stop that,' he says, chuckling. 'It doesn't suit you!'

The false facade crumbles, and Jeanette feels instantly more comfortable.

'For over two months now I've been reading your reports without being able to understand the direction you're heading in, and suddenly I get this.' The commissioner falls silent.

'This?' Jeanette asks, feigning ignorance.

'Yes, this utterly brilliant summary of the terrible events surrounding these dead . . .' His voice trails off.

'You mean the latest report about my conclusions so far relating to the boys' murders?'

'Yes, exactly.' Dennis Billing clears his throat. 'You've done a fantastic job, and I'm glad it's over. Get a holiday request over to me, and you can be lying on a beach as early as next week.'

'I don't understand –'

'What don't you understand? Everything suggests that Karl Lundström is the culprit. He's still in a coma, and even if he does wake up it won't be possible to prosecute him. According to his doctors he's suffered extensive brain damage. He's going to be a vegetable. And as far as the victims are concerned, well, two of these unidentified . . . yes, how can I put it?' He searches for the right phrase.

'"Children", perhaps?' Jeanette suggests, feeling that she hasn't got the energy to hold back her pent-up anger.

'Perhaps not that. But if they hadn't been here illegally, then –'

'– the situation would have been different,' Jeanette finishes, before going on: 'And then we'd have put fifty detectives on the case instead of what we've got. Me and Hurtig, with a bit of help from Schwarz and Åhlund. Is that what you mean?'

'Come on, Jan, don't be like that. What are you implying?'

'I'm not implying anything, but I understand that you're calling to tell me the case is being dropped. What do we do about Samuel Bai? Even von Kwist must realise that Lundström couldn't possibly have killed him.'

Billing takes a deep breath. 'You haven't got any suspects!' he roars down the line. 'There isn't a single line of inquiry pointing in any direction at all! It might well involve organised human trafficking, and how the hell do you think we're going to tackle that?'

'I understand,' Jeanette says with a sigh. 'So you mean we have to pack up everything we've got and send it to von Kwist?'

'Exactly,' Billing replies.

Jeanette goes on. 'And von Kwist reads our files and then closes the case because there aren't any suspects.'

'That's right. See, you can do it if you try.' The commissioner laughs. 'And then you and Jens have some holiday. And everyone's happy. Is that agreed, then? The investigation and your application for leave on my desk around lunchtime tomorrow?'

'Agreed,' Jeanette replies, and hangs up.

She decides it makes sense to inform Hurtig about the new directive and goes into his office.

'I've just heard that we've got to bring our work to a close.'

Hurtig looks first surprised, then leans forward and throws his hands out. He now looks mostly disappointed. 'But that's fucking ridiculous.'

Jeanette sits down heavily and feels very tired. It seems like her body is spilling off the chair and onto the floor.

'Is it really?' she asks. She feels she hasn't got the energy to play devil's advocate, but knows it's her duty as his superior to defend their bosses' decision.

'After all, nothing much has happened so far. No decent lines of inquiry. And it's entirely possible that we're dealing with human trafficking, just as Billing says, and that's out of our jurisdiction.'

Hurtig shakes his head.

'What about Karl Lundström, then?'

'He's in a coma, for heaven's sake. He's hardly any good to us!'

'You're a poor liar, Jan! It's obvious that a paedophile –'

'That's just how it is. I can't do anything about it.'

Hurtig looks up at the ceiling. 'A murderer gets away with it and we're left sitting here with our hands tied by some bastard lawyer. All because we're dealing with boys that no one's missed! It's completely fucked up! And what about that Bergman guy? Aren't we going to bother trying to talk to his daughter? She seemed to have a lot to say, didn't she?'

'No, Jens. That's out of the question, and you know it. I think the best thing we can do right now is drop it. At least for the time being.'

She only calls him Jens when he's annoying her. But her frustration subsides when she sees how disappointed he is. After all, they have worked on this together, and he's been just as engaged in the case as she's been.

Now she's going to go home and fall asleep on the sofa.

'I'm going now,' she says. 'I've got some leave to use up.'

'Sure, whatever.' Hurtig turns away.

Gamla Enskede – Kihlberg House

Everything happens automatically. She's been through every part of it thousands of times before.

She passes the Globe. Right at the rotary by the Södermalm bakery. Enskedevägen. Everything feels routine, and as Jeanette turns into the drive in front of the garage she almost collides with Alexandra Kowalska's red sports car, for the third time in a matter of weeks. Just like the first time, the car is parked askew in front of the garage and Jeanette has to brake hard.

'Fuck!' she yells as the seat belt cuts into her shoulder. She reverses angrily, parks next to the hedge, gets out and slams the driver's door.

The summer evening in Enskede reeks of burnt meat, and she is confronted with the smell of a hundred barbecues. The sweet, heavy smells spread across the neighbourhood, into the garden, and Jeanette thinks it smells of happy families and good company. Having a barbecue presupposes company: it's not the sort of thing you do alone.

The fragile silence is broken by her neighbours' voices, laughter and excited shouts from the football pitch. She thinks about Sofia and wonders what she's doing.

Jeanette goes up the steps to the house. Just as she's about to open it the handle is pushed down from inside and she has to jump out of the way to avoid being hit by the door.

'So long, handsome.' Alexandra Kowalska is facing away from her in the doorway as she waves to Åke, who is smiling back at her from the hall.

His smile dies when he catches sight of Jeanette.

Alexandra turns round. 'Oh, hi,' she says, with a breezy smile. 'I was just leaving.'

Fucking witch, Jeanette thinks as she walks in without replying.

She shuts the door and hangs up her jacket. Handsome?

She goes into the kitchen, where Åke's standing at the window, waving. He looks at her warily as she tosses her bag on the kitchen table.

'Sit down,' she says sharply as she opens the fridge door. 'Handsome?' she goes on, then snorts. 'OK, time for an explanation. What the fuck's going on here?' Jeanette makes an effort not to raise her voice, but can feel her anger vibrating inside her.

'What do you mean? What is it you want me to explain?'

She decides to get straight to the point. She mustn't let herself be fooled by his puppy-dog eyes, which always come out at moments like this.

'Tell me why you didn't come home last night, and why you didn't even call.' She looks at him. Predictably, the puppy-dog eyes are in place.

He tries to smile but fails. 'I . . . well, I mean we. We were out. Operakällaren. There were quite a few drinks . . .'

'And?'

'Well, I spent the night in the city and Alexandra gave me a lift home.' Åke turns his head away and looks out through the window.

'Why are you looking so sheepish? Are you sleeping with her?'

He's quiet for far too long, Jeanette thinks.

Åke puts his elbows on the table, hides his face in his hands, then stares blankly ahead of himself.

'I think I'm in love with her . . .'

Here we go, Jeanette thinks with a sigh. 'Bloody hell, Åke . . .'

Without another word she gets up, grabs her bag, walks out into the hall, opens the front door and goes outside. She walks down the drive onto the road, gets in the car, takes out her mobile phone, and calls Sofia Zetterlund.

No answer.

She only gets as far the Nynäshamn road before Åke calls to say that he's taking Johan to stay with his parents for the weekend. That it might be good for them to think things over separately for a few days. That he needs to do some thinking.

Jeanette realises that's just an excuse.

Silence is a good weapon, she thinks as she pulls out onto the rotary at Gullmarsplan.

A delaying tactic.

The life she took for granted just a few months ago has been pretty much blown away, and most frighteningly, she doesn't even know if she cares.

She turns on the car radio to distract her from her thoughts.

Already she's feeling anxious about having to wake up alone in the house.

Hammarby Sjöstad – Petrol Station

On her way home from Grisslinge Sofia Zetterlund stops at the petrol station in Hammarby Sjöstad and changes clothes. In the toilet she pushes her expensive but now fire-damaged dress into the bin. She giggles to herself at the thought that it had cost over four thousand kronor. She goes out into the shop and buys a big piece of chèvre, a packet of crackers, a jar of black olives and a carton of strawberries.

As she's paying, her phone vibrates in her pocket again. This time she takes it out to see who's calling.

It stops ringing when she's being given her change. Two missed calls, she reads on the screen, as she thanks the cashier. She notes that Jeanette Kihlberg has been trying to contact her, and puts the phone back in her pocket.

Later, she thinks.

On her way out she catches sight of the display of reading glasses. Her eyes fall on a pair identical to the ones she stole on New Year's Day, seven months ago, and she stops.

She had gone to Central Station and bought a return ticket to Gothenburg. The eight o'clock train had left on time, and she had been sitting in the deserted buffet car with a cup of coffee.

Soon after they left the conductor had appeared to stamp her ticket, and as she was handing it to him she had intentionally upset the cup of hot coffee over the table with her other hand. She yelped, and the conductor rushed off to get something to wipe it up.

She smiles at the memory and takes the glasses off the rack. She puts them on and looks at herself in the little mirror.

The conductor had brought her some napkins, and she had made sure she thrust her breasts out as she leaned forward to ask if the stains on her blouse showed. With a bit of luck, he would remember her if there was any need to check her alibi later.

But she hadn't even had to show the police the stamped ticket, bought on her credit card. They had swallowed her story without question.

When the train stopped at Södertälje Syd she had darted into the toilet, pulled her hair up in a tight bun and put the stolen glasses on.

Before she got off the train she had turned her black coat inside out, so that she was suddenly wearing a pale brown one. She had sat down on a bench, lit a cigarette, and waited for the commuter train back to Stockholm and Lasse.

There was nothing that could be said, she thinks as she puts the glasses back on the rack.

No explanation would be good enough.

He had betrayed her.

Pissed all over her.

Humiliated her.

Quite simply, there was no room for him in her new life. Just leaving him and telling him to go to hell wouldn't have been satisfying enough. He would still have been out there somewhere.

She walks out of the petrol station shop and over to the car, and only now does she notice that her hair smells of smoke.

As she opens the car door she remembers how she found Lasse passed out on the sofa in the living room. An almost empty bottle of whisky told her he was probably pretty drunk. There was nothing particularly remarkable about a man who had been revealed to have lived a double life for ten years committing suicide while drunk.

It was, more than likely, expected.

She starts the engine. It purrs into life, and she puts the car into first gear and pulls away from the petrol station.

He had been snoring loudly with his mouth open, and she had to steel herself to resist the urge to wake him up and make him face the music.

She had gone silently into the bathroom and removed the belt from Lasse's burgundy dressing gown. The one he had stolen from the hotel in New York.

She drives into the city.

The 222 road, westbound. The light from the street lamps passes by above the windscreen.

Lasse had been lying on his side with his face towards the cushions, the back of his neck unprotected. It was important that the knot ended up in the right place and only left a small impression. She had tied the belt into a noose and carefully slid it over his head.

When the knot was in exactly the right place and all she had to do was pull, she had hesitated.

She had stopped to evaluate the risks, but hadn't been able to come up with anything that might implicate her.

When she was finished she would go back to Central Station to await the arrival of the afternoon train from Gothenburg, then go and pick up her car from the car park. The car would have got a ticket, but when the attendants saw her valid ticket they would have to waive the fine. And they would be able to support, if not actually prove, that she had spent the day travelling by train to and from Gothenburg.

She heads down the Hammarby hill, across the old Skanstull Bridge, and into the tunnel under the Clarion Hotel.

Discipline, she thinks. You have to stay alert and not act on impulse, because that's what can give you away.

The parking attendants, the train ticket and the conductor who had seen her in the buffet car should have been enough to remove any suspicions about her involvement. The phone books on the floor by the chair had been the final detail completing the picture.

She heads along Renstiernas gata, passes Skånegatan and Bondegatan, and turns right into Åsögatan.

She had taken a firm grip of the dressing-gown belt and pulled as hard as she could. Lasse had gasped for breath, but the drink dulled his response.

He never woke up again, and she had strung him up from the lamp hook in the ceiling. She had placed a chair beneath him, then, when she realised that his feet didn't reach it, she had filled the gap with telephone directories that she then shoved onto the floor. A clear case of suicide.

Skanstull – a Neighbourhood

Just before she reaches the Johanneshov Bridge, Jeanette Kihlberg sees from the big, round clock at Skanstull that it's twenty past nine, and decides to call Sofia again.

As she dials the number and presses her phone to her ear, she hears the siren of an emergency vehicle. In the rear-view mirror she sees three fire engines approaching at high speed.

The phone rings, but there's no answer.

Jeanette wishes she could be somewhere else, with a completely different life, and remembers a documentary she once saw about a man who had suddenly had enough.

Instead of going to work at University Hospital in Copenhagen as usual, he turned round and cycled all the way to southern France. Leaving his wife and children in Denmark and making a whole new life for himself as a blacksmith in a small mountain village. When the reporters found him, he said he didn't want anything to do with his old life. He told everyone to fuck off.

Jeanette knows she'd be capable of doing the same, leaving everything for Åke to sort out.

The only thing complicating matters was Johan, but he could always join her later. She keeps her passport in her bag, so there's actually nothing stopping her. In an odd way her anxiety seems to relent, as if the awareness that she isn't actually stuck makes it less urgent to break free.

The music on the radio is interrupted by an announcement telling people living in Grisslinge to keep their windows shut because of a serious house fire.

She drives on aimlessly.

Falling free.

Vita Bergen – Sofia Zetterlund's Apartment

Sofia Zetterlund finds the apartment deserted and empty. There's no sign of Gao, and when she goes into the room behind the bookcase she sees that he's tidied it up and cleaned it. It smells of detergent, even if there's still a faint smell of urine.

The coarse blanket has been laid neatly over the mattress.

The syringes are on the little table next to the bottle of Xylocain, and she wonders why her colleague at the clinic, Johansson the dentist, has never noticed that they're missing. Once again, fate has been her friend.

She gets irritated that Gao has shown initiative, that he has acted without her giving him orders. What's going on?

She feels an uncontrollable wave of fear rise up. The whole situation is alien to her. Suddenly things are happening that she can't influence, and something she has no control over seems to be developing.

Without actually realising how it happens, she finds herself screaming hysterically. Tears are streaming down her face, and she can't stop howling. There's so much trying to get out, all at the same time. She bangs on the walls until she loses the feeling in both arms.

The attack lasts almost half an hour, and when she's calmed down, mainly as a result of physical exhaustion, she curls up in a foetal position on the soft floor.

The smell of smoke tickles her nose.

She dreams about the scars she has on her body. Wounds that have healed, forming pale marks on her skin.

Other people's breath, making her feel nauseous, with the result that she finds it hard to kiss anyone.

Experiences are essential for memory. Things happen, are absorbed and become memories, but over time the process flattens out and forms a single whole. Several events become one. She feels that her life is a big lump, where the abuse and assaults have become one single event that in turn became an experience, that in turn became a realisation.

There is no before, nor is there any after.

What used to exist in her that is no longer there?

What was it she used to be able to see, but can't see any longer? She's tried to find new ways to develop her personality. Not as an alternative or a complement, but as an entirely new being. Unconditional acceptance.

She cuts away at the thin skin that separates her from madness. Nothing started with me, she thinks. Nothing started in me. I am dead fruit, slowly going rotten.

My life consists of a long sequence of moments, one after the other, like a collection of related facts that are all subtly different.

Suddenly she feels an outsider's perception and self-awareness.

Gamla Stan – Stockholm's Old Town

For the first time in his new country Gao Lian from Wuhan is walking through Stockholm on his own. From the apartment on Borgmästargatan he goes down the slippery stone steps on Klippgatan. He crosses Folkungagatan, then goes up the steps towards Ersta Hospital.

On Fjällgatan he sits down on a bench and looks out over Stockholm. Below him there are big passenger ferries, and out in the water small yachts bob up and down. To his left he can see Gamla stan and the palace.

The swallows crying as they dive for insects are the same birds that lived under the eaves at home in Wuhan.

The smell is the same too, even if it's cleaner here.

He crosses the bridge to Gamla stan. Curious, he listens to the strange language and thinks it sounds like the people around him are singing their words. The new language feels friendly, as if made for creating beautiful poetry, and he wonders what it sounds like when these people get angry.

He spends several hours walking through the maze of narrow streets and alleys, and after a while he begins to get his bearings and can find his way to wherever he wants to go without any problem. When dusk falls he has a clear internal map of the little city between the bridges. He will come back here, and it will be his starting point when he explores other parts of the city. He walks home up Götgatan until he reaches Skånegatan, where he turns left and continues until he reaches the apartment.

He finds the fair-haired woman inside the soft, dark room. She's lying knocked out on the floor, and he can see from her eyes that she's a long way away. He bends over and kisses her feet, then gets undressed.

Before he lies down beside her he carefully folds his outfit the way she has shown him so many times. He closes his eyes and waits for the angel to give him instructions.

Vita Bergen – Sofia Zetterlund's Apartment

Sofia Zetterlund's hair is still wet when the phone rings.

'Victoria Bergman?' an unfamiliar voice asks.

'Who wants to know?' she replies with exaggerated suspicion, even though she knows perfectly well that they would contact her sooner or later.

'I'm calling from the police in Värmdö, and I'm trying to get in touch with a Victoria Bergman. Is that you?'

'Yes, it's me. What's this about?' She tries to sound as worried as she imagines anyone would if the police were to call them late one evening.

'Are you the daughter of Bengt and Birgitta Bergman from Grisslinge in Värmdö?'

'Yes, I am . . . Has something happened? What's this about?' She's worked herself up to the point where for a few seconds she feels genuinely worried. As if she has stepped outside herself and doesn't actually know what's happened.

'My name is Göran Andersson. I've been trying to get hold of you but I haven't been able to locate an address.'

'That's funny. What's this about?'

'I'm afraid it's my sad duty to inform you that we believe your parents are dead. Their house burned down this evening, and we're assuming that the bodies we've found are theirs.'

'But . . .' she stammers.

'I'm sorry to have to break the news like this, but you're still registered at your parents' and I got your number from their lawyer –'

'What do you mean, dead?' Victoria raises her voice. 'I only spoke to them a few hours ago. Dad said they were on their way down to the sauna.'

'Yes, that's correct. We found your parents in the sauna. From what we understand at the moment, the fire started in the basement and they were unable to get out. The latch on the door might have seized, but for the time being that's just speculation. We'll know the details after a proper investigation. But it seems to have been a very tragic accident.'

Accident, she thinks. If they think it was an accident, then they can't have discovered the plank. She'd been correct in assuming that it would burn up before they managed to put the fire out.

'I appreciate that you probably need someone to talk to. I'll give you the number of a duty psychologist that you can call.'

'There's no need,' she replies. 'I'm a psychologist myself, so I've got my own contacts. But thanks for the thought.'

'Ah, I see. Well, we'll be in touch again tomorrow with more information. Have a stiff drink and call a friend. I really am very sorry to have to break the news to you like this.'

'Thank you,' Sofia Zetterlund says, and hangs up.

At last, she thinks. Her feet ache. But she feels alive.

Now there's nothing left.

She can see the end at last.

Kronoberg – Police Headquarters

As Jeanette closes the front door behind her she hears the first raindrops hit the windowsills. It's clouded over, and in the distance she thinks she can hear thunder. She gets in the car and drives away from the deserted house in Gamla Enskede while the first late-summer storm sweeps in over a grey Stockholm.

When she gets to police headquarters she clears her desk and waters the plants. Before leaving work she goes to see Jens Hurtig and wish him a good holiday.

'What are your plans?' she asks.

'The day after tomorrow I'm taking the night train to Älvsbyn, then the bus to Jokkmokk, and Mum's going to pick me up there. I'm just going to take it easy, do some fishing. Maybe give Dad a hand with the house.'

'How's he getting on after his accident with the saw?' she asks, embarrassed at not having asked sooner.

'Apparently he can still pluck the strings, even if he's not much good on the fiddle. But it feels a bit tragic that Mum has to tie his shoelaces for him.' Hurtig looks serious, then breaks into a smile. 'How about you? Peace and quiet?'

'Hardly. Gröna Lund, with Johan and Sofia. You know I'm not good with heights, but she suggested the fair, so I'll just have to grit my teeth.'

His smile turns into a broad grin. 'Try the little kids' roller coaster, or the fun house!'

Jeanette laughs and gives him a playful push in the stomach.

'See you in a couple of weeks,' she says, little suspecting that they'll see each other again in less than three days.

By which time her son will have been missing for almost twenty-four hours.

Vita Bergen – Sofia Zetterlund's Apartment

Sofia Zetterlund wakes up with Victoria Bergman and she feels whole. For two days she has lain in bed with Gao, talking to Victoria. Sofia has told her everything that has happened since they separated twenty years ago.

Victoria has mostly been silent.

Together they have listened to the tapes, over and over again, and each time Victoria has fallen asleep. The reverse of what used to happen.

Only now, forty-eight hours later, does Sofia feel ready to face reality.

She gets a cup of coffee and sits down at her computer. As soon as she was told of her parents' death she had a look at the website of Fonus, one of the big undertakers, and worked out the simplest way to get what was left of them into the ground. It's scheduled for Friday out at the Forest Cemetery.

When she checks her phone and sees that Jeanette has called several times, she feels a pang of guilt. She remembers promising to go to Gröna Lund together with Johan, and calls Jeanette straight away.

'Where the hell have you been?' Jeanette asks anxiously.

'I've been a bit under the weather, couldn't really handle answering the phone. So, what about Gröna Lund?' Sofia asks.

'Can you still make Friday?'

'Absolutely,' she replies. 'Where shall we meet?'

'At the Djurgården ferry, four o'clock?'

'I'll be there!'

The next call is to the lawyer handling the estate. His name is Viggo Dürer, an old family friend. She met him a few times when she was a child, but only has a very vague memory of him. Old Spice and Eau de Vie.

Watch out for him.

The lawyer tells her she's going to get everything, as the sole heir.

'Everything?' she says in surprise. 'But the house burned down . . .'

Viggo Dürer explains that apart from the insurance on the house, worth about four million kronor, and the plot, which is worth more than a million, her parents had savings of nine hundred thousand kronor, as well as a portfolio of shares that ought to bring in another five million if they are sold.

Sofia tells the lawyer to sell the shares as soon as possible. Viggo Dürer tries to persuade her against doing so, but she insists, and in the end he agrees to do as she wishes.

She does a few sums and realises that she will soon be worth more than eleven million kronor. She has become a wealthy woman.

Part II

Gamla Enskede – Kihlberg House

Jeanette feels happy as she puts the phone down. Sofia has just been feeling ill and hadn't felt like answering her phone. She'd been worried about nothing.

The trip to Gröna Lund means that she finally has a surprise for Johan, and at the same time she'll get to see Sofia.

Now that she's finally got some holiday, she's going to take things easy for a few days, then think about the future.

Her thoughts are interrupted by the doorbell ringing, and she goes to answer it.

Outside stands a uniformed police officer she's never seen before.

'Hello, my name's Göran,' he says, holding his hand out. 'Are you Jeanette Kihlberg?'

'Göran?' Jeanette says. 'What's this about?'

'Andersson,' he adds. 'Göran Andersson. I work out in Värmdö.'

'I see. How can I help you?'

'Well, you see . . .' He clears his throat. 'I work out in Värmdö, and a few days ago we had a serious fire out there. Two people died in what looked like an accident. They'd been having a sauna, and . . .'

'And . . . ?'

'The names of the couple who died in the fire were Bengt and Birgitta Bergman, and what looked at first to be an accident seems to be rather more complicated.'

Jeanette asks him in, apologising for not having done so before.

'Let's sit in the kitchen. Coffee?'

'No, I can't stay long.'

'So . . . why are you here?' Jeanette goes in and sits down at the kitchen table. The policeman follows her example.

'I checked them out and saw straight away that you questioned Bengt Bergman regarding an alleged rape.'

Jeanette nodded. 'Yes, that's right. But it didn't lead anywhere. He was released.'

'Yes . . . and now he's dead . . . When I called the daughter and told her what had happened, she reacted . . . How shall I put it . . . ?'

'Oddly?' Jeanette thinks of her own conversation with Victoria Bergman.

'No, more like indifferently.'

'Sorry, Göran.' Jeanette is beginning to get impatient. 'But why have you come to see me?'

Göran Andersson leans over the table and smiles.

'She doesn't exist.'

'Who doesn't exist?' Jeanette is starting to feel uneasy.

'There was something about the daughter that made me curious enough to check her out.'

'What did you find?'

'Nothing. Zilch. No records, no bank account. Nada. Victoria Bergman has left no trace of her existence for the past twenty years.'

The Chapel of the Holy Cross

A proper summer storm would have been a more suitable backdrop to the interment of Bengt and Birgitta Bergman's remains, but the sun is shining and Stockholm is looking its very best.

The trees in the park next to Hammarbyhamnen are showing off every sort of colour, from soft golden brown to dark purple, the most beautiful being the dark green maple leaves.

There are a dozen or so cars at the Forest Cemetery, but she knows none of them belongs to anyone taking part in the ceremony. She's going to be the only person present.

She switches off the engine, opens the door and gets out. It's chilly, and she takes a few deep breaths of the fresh air.

She can see the priest in the distance.

Sombre, with his head bowed.

On the ground in front of him stands an urn large enough for two people's ashes.

Dark red cherrywood. A degradable material, it had said on the undertakers' website.

A little over a thousand kronor.

Five hundred each.

They're the only ones there. She and the priest. That's what she decided.

No death notice, nothing in the papers. A quiet farewell without tears or strong emotions. No soothing talk of reconciliation, no feeble attempts to elevate the dead to something they never were.

No eulogy ascribing virtues to them that they never possessed, nothing to make them sound like angels.

No new gods are going to be created here.

She says hello, and the priest explains what's going to happen.

Since she declined any funeral service, only the obvious phrases will be spoken.

Their delivery into the hands of God the creator, and the prayer about Christ's death and resurrection being fulfilled in those created by God in His image have all been got out of the way before the cremation, without Sofia.

Dust you are, to dust you shall return.

Our Lord Jesus Christ shall awaken you at the end of days.

It will all be over in less than ten minutes.

Together they walk past a small pond and in among the trees of the cemetery.

The priest, a tall, skinny man of an indeterminate age, carries the urn. His thin frame has the slowness of an ageing man combined with eyes that suggest a young boy's curiosity.

They don't speak, and she has trouble tearing her eyes from the urn. Inside it is what remains of her parents.

After cremation the charred bones were left in a tray to cool. Anything that hadn't burned, like Bengt's hip replacement, had been removed before the bones were crushed in the mill.

Paradoxically, when her father died he also came to life for her. A door had been opened, as if a hole had been cut in the air. It's open wide in front of her, offering freedom.

Impressions, she thinks. What impressions have they left behind? She remembers something that happened a long time ago.

She was four years old, and Bengt had laid a new floor in one of the rooms in the basement. The temptation to press her hand down on the smooth, thick cement had been stronger than her fear of the anger she knew she would get. The little handprint had been there right up to the fire. It was probably still there, under the ruins of the burned-out house.

But what is left of him?

Everything physical he has left behind has been destroyed, sold or sent to auction, scattered on the wind. Soon to be anonymous objects in the possession of total strangers. Things with no known history.

The impression he has left inside her, on the other hand, will live on in shame and guilt.

A guilt she will never be able to atone for, no matter how hard she tries.

It will only go on growing and growing for her.

What did I actually know about him? she wonders.

What was hiding in the depths of his soul? What did he dream of? Long for?

He was driven by a constant lack of gratification. No matter how hot he was, he was also shaking with cold. No matter how much he ate, his stomach was always stinging with hunger.

The priest stops, puts the urn down and lowers his head in prayer. A piece of green cloth with a hole in its centre has been spread out in front of a headstone of red granite from Vånga.

Seven thousand kronor.

She tries to catch the priest's eye, and, when he finally raises his head, he looks at her and nods.

She takes a few steps forward, walks round the piece of cloth, bends over and takes hold of the cord fastened to the red urn. The first thing that strikes her is how heavy it is, and the rope digs into her hands.

Carefully she goes over to the hole, stops and slowly lowers the urn into the black hole. After a brief pause she lets go of the cord, letting it fall to land on the lid of the urn.

Her palms sting, and when she holds her hands up she sees an angry red mark on each hand.

Stigmata, she thinks.

Free Fall

The most popular attraction at the Gröna Lund fair is a renovated viewing tower, one hundred metres tall, visible from large parts of Stockholm. Passengers are pulled up to a height of eighty metres, where they hang for a moment, then fall back down at a speed of almost one hundred and twenty kilometres an hour. The fall takes two and a half seconds, and as the ride brakes, passengers are subjected to a force equivalent to three and a half Gs.

In other words, when it lands each human body weighs more than three times as much as normal.

Body weight matters on the way down.

A person travelling at a speed of a hundred kilometres an hour weighs over twelve tons.

'You know they closed Free Fall last summer?' Sofia laughs.

'Really? What for?' Jeanette squeezes Johan's arm as the queue they're standing in moves a few steps forward. The thought that Sofia and Johan will soon be hanging up there makes her dizzy.

'Someone at some fair in the States had their feet cut off by a wire. They had to close this one to do a complete safety check.'

'Christ . . . stop it! Now really isn't the time to mention that, when you're about to go up.'

Johan laughs and nudges her side.

She smiles at him. It's been a long time since she last saw him this excited.

Over the past few hours Johan and Sofia have worked their way through the Kvasten roller coaster, the Octopus, Extreme and the Catapult. They've also got photographs of themselves screaming on the Flying Carpet.

Jeanette had stayed on the ground the whole time, with a lump in her stomach.

They reach the front of the queue, and she steps aside.

Johan almost backs out, but Sofia steps up onto the platform and he follows her with an unsteady smile.

An attendant makes sure their safety harnesses are fastened properly.

Then everything happens very quickly.

The cradle starts to move upward, and Sofia and Johan wave nervously.

Just as Jeanette sees their attention being drawn to the views of the city she hears the sound of breaking glass right behind her. Agitated voices.

Jeanette turns round and sees a man about to hit another man.

It takes Jeanette five minutes to calm the situation down.

Three hundred seconds.

Popcorn, sweat and acetone.

The smells are confusing Sofia. She's having trouble working out which ones are real and which imaginary, and as she passes the radio-controlled cars the air feels stiflingly electric.

An imaginary smell of burned rubber merges with a real, sickly sweet gust from the men's toilets.

It's started to get dark, but it's a mild evening and the sky has cleared. The tarmac is still damp after the sudden downpour and the flashing coloured lights reflected in the puddles hurt her eyes. A sudden scream from the roller coaster makes her start, and she takes a step back. Someone walks into her from behind, and she hears them swear.

'What the fuck are you doing?'

She stops and closes her eyes. Tries to filter out her sensory impressions from the voice in her head.

What are you going to do now? Sit down and start crying?

What have you done with Johan?

Sofia looks around and realises she's alone.

'. . . he said he wasn't scared of heights but when the safety harness folded down it started to rain and when they were sitting tight she could tell he was shaking with fear and when the gondola started to move he said he'd changed his mind and wanted to get down . . .'

Her cheek stings, and she can feel that it's wet, salty. The hard gravel is scratching her back.

'What's wrong with her?'

'Can someone call a medic?'

'What's she talking about?'

'Does anyone know any first aid?'

'. . . and he was crying and was scared and at first she tried to comfort him when they rose up higher and higher and could see right across Uppsala and all the boats on the Fyris River and when she told him that he stopped whining and said it was Stockholm and the Djurgård ferries they could see . . .'

'I think she's saying she's from Uppsala.'

'. . . and right at the top there's thunder and lightning then everything went quiet and the people below were like little dots and if you wanted to you could squash them between your fingers like flies . . .'

'I think she's going to faint.'

'. . . and right at that moment your stomach flies into your throat and everything comes rushing towards you and it's just like you want it to be . . .'

'Let me through!'

She recognises the voice but can't quite place it.

'Get out of the way, I know her.'

A cool hand on a hot forehead. A smell she recognises.

'Sofia, what's happened? Where's Johan?'

Victoria Bergman closes her eyes.

Free Fall

The nightmare is dressed in a cobalt-blue coat, slightly darker than the evening sky over Djurgården and the Ladugårdsland inlet. It's fair-haired, blue-eyed, and has a little bag over its shoulder. Its too-small shoes are red and chafe her heels, but she's used to that and the wounds are now part of her personality. The pain makes her alert.

She knows that if she can only find it in her to forgive, they will be free, both she herself and those who are forgiven. For many years she has tried to forget, but has always failed.

She can't see it herself, but her revenge is a chain reaction.

A snowball was set in motion a quarter of a lifetime ago in a tool shed at the Sigtuna College for the Humanities, and she got caught up by it before it continued its journey towards the inevitable.

One might ask what the people who made the snowball know of its onward journey. Nothing, in all likelihood. They've probably just moved on. Forgetting the occurrence as if it were nothing more than an innocent game that both began and ended there in the shed.

She herself is trapped, frozen in the moment. For her time is immaterial, it has no healing effect.

Hate doesn't thaw. It hardens, to sharp ice crystals surrounding the whole of her being.

The evening is slightly cool, and the air damp from the scattered showers that have succeeded one another all afternoon and evening. Cries can be heard from the roller coaster. She stands up, brushes herself off and looks around. Stops, takes a deep breath and remembers why she's there.

She has a task, and she knows what she has to do.

Just below the tall, renovated lookout tower she watches the fuss a short distance away.

The fair's coloured lights cast sharp reflections on the damp tarmac.

She realises the moment when she must act has arrived, even if this wasn't how she had planned it. Fate has made it easier for her. So simple that no one will be able to understand what's happened.

She sees the boy a short distance away, alone outside the railings of the Free Fall ride.

To forgive something that can be forgiven isn't really to forgive, she thinks. Real forgiveness is forgiving something unforgivable. Something only a god can do.

The boy looks confused, and she walks slowly over to him as he turns away from her. That makes it almost laughably simple to get close, and now she's only a few metres away from him. He is still standing with his back to her.

True forgiveness is impossible, mad and unconscious, she thinks. And seeing as she expects the guilty parties to show contrition, it can never be accomplished. The memory is and will remain a wound that can never heal.

She grabs the boy hard by the arm.

He jerks and turns round as she pushes the syringe into the top of his left arm.

For a couple of seconds he looks into her eyes, confused, before his legs crumple beneath him. She catches him and puts him down gently on a bench.

No one has seen her manoeuvre.

Everything is perfectly normal.

She takes something out of her bag and carefully pulls it over his head.

The mask is made of pink plastic, shaped like a pig's snout.

Gröna Lund – Fair

Jeanette Kihlberg knows exactly where she was when she heard that Prime Minister Olof Palme had been murdered on Sveavägen.

She was sitting in a taxi, halfway to Farsta, and the man next to her was smoking menthol cigarettes. Gentle rain and feeling ill from too many beers.

But the moment when Johan vanishes will always be a black stain. Five missing minutes. Stolen from her by an overly refreshed plumber from Flen on a short visit to the capital.

A step to the side, her eyes fixed upward. Johan and Sofia hanging in the cradle on the way up, and she feels dizzy even though she's safe on the ground.

Suddenly the sound of breaking glass.

Animated shouting.

Someone crying, and Jeanette sees the cradle continue to rise.

Two men are shoving each other, and Jeanette gets ready to intervene. She glances up at Johan and Sofia. Their legs from below. Swinging.

Johan is laughing at something.

Soon at the top.

'I'm going to kill you, you bastard!'

Jeanette sees that one of the men isn't in control of his movements.

Drink has made his legs too long, his joints too stiff, his tranquillised nervous system too slow.

The man stumbles and falls helplessly to the ground.

He gets up, and his face has been scratched by the grit on the path.

Some children are crying.

'Daddy!'

A little girl, no more than six years old, with pink candyfloss in her hand.

'Can we go? I want to go home.'

The man doesn't answer, just looks around, trying to find his opponent, someone to vent his frustration on.

Jeanette's police reflexes make her act without thinking. She takes the man by the arm. 'OK,' she says gently, 'take it easy.' Her intention is to get him to think about something else. Not to sound reproachful.

The man turns round, and Jeanette sees that his eyes are glazed and bloodshot. Sad and disappointed, almost ashamed.

'Daddy . . .' the little girl says again, but the man doesn't react, just stares ahead of him without focusing.

'And who the fuck are you?' He pulls free of Jeanette's grip on his arm. 'Fuck off!'

His breath smells bitter, and his lips are covered with a thin, white film.

At that moment she hears the cradle up above being released, and the delighted cries of fear mixed with pleasure make her lose her train of thought, lose concentration.

She sees Johan, his hair all over the place, his mouth open in a roar.

She hears the little girl. 'No, Daddy! No!'

But she doesn't notice the man next to her raising his arm.

The bottle hits Jeanette on the temple, and she staggers. She feels blood running down her cheek. But she doesn't lose consciousness, almost the reverse.

With a practised movement she twists the man's arm up behind his back, drops him to the ground and is soon joined by the fair's security guards.

And now, five minutes later, she discovers that both Johan and Sofia have vanished.

Three hundred seconds.

Prince Eugen's Waldemarsudde – Island of Djurgården

Just as people who have been denied happiness all their life still manage to cling onto hope, Jeanette Kihlberg has always had a uniformly negative view in the course of her work towards the slightest hint of pessimism.

That's why she never gives up, and that's why she reacts the way she does whenever Police Constable Schwarz complains in provocatively loud terms about the weather, or how tired he is, or how little progress they're making in their search for Johan.

Jeanette Kihlberg sees red.

'For fuck's sake! Go home, you're no fucking use to us here!'

It has an impact. Schwarz flinches like a shame-faced hound, while Åhlund stands neutrally alongside. Her anger makes the wound on her head throb under the bandage.

Jeanette calms down, sighs and gestures dismissivelys towards Schwarz. 'Understood? You're relieved of duty until further notice.'

Soon Jeanette is alone. She stands hollow-eyed and frozen beside the rear deck of the Vasa Museum, waiting for Jens Hurtig, who interrupted his holiday the moment news of Johan's disappearance reached him, in order to take part in the search.

When she sees an unmarked police car approaching across the park, she knows it's Hurtig, and that he's got someone else with him. A witness who claims to have seen a young man alone down by the water the previous evening. From what Hurtig said on the radio, she knows she shouldn't harbour any great hope about the testimony. But she still tries to convince herself that she must keep hoping, however vain it might be.

She tries to gather her thoughts and reconstruct the events of the past few hours.

Johan and Sofia had vanished; suddenly they were just gone. After half an hour she had a call put out for Johan over the fair's public address system, while she waited anxiously at the information desk.

Then some security guards appeared and together they resumed her aimless search of the fair. That's when they found Sofia lying on one of the paths, surrounded by a crowd that Jeanette had to elbow her way through until she could look Sofia in the eye. But the face that until recently had been synonymous with release only turned out to underline her anxiety and uncertainty. Sofia was completely out of it. Jeanette doubted that Sofia was even capable of recognising her, let alone saying where Johan was. Jeanette hadn't stayed with her; she felt compelled to keep looking.

Another half-hour had passed before she contacted her colleagues in the police. But neither she nor the twenty officers who had dragged the water close to the fair and painstakingly searched across Djurgården had found Johan. Nor had any of the police patrols that were searching the city centre after being given his description.

After that an alert had been broadcast on local radio. Without result, until forty-five minutes ago.

Jeanette knows she's been acting correctly, but like a robot. A robot paralysed by feelings. A complete contradiction. Hard, cold and rational on the surface, but governed by chaotic impulses. The anger, irritation, fear, anguish, confusion and resignation she had felt through the night are all merging into an indistinguishable mush.

The only consistent emotion is inadequacy.

And not just towards Johan.

She has no idea how to reach Åke in Poland.

Jeanette thinks about Sofia.

How is she?

Jeanette has called her several times, but without success. If she knew anything about Johan, surely she'd have got in touch? Unless she knows something that she has to summon the courage to say?

Never mind that now, she thinks, fending off thoughts that must remain unthinkable. Focus.

The car stops, and Hurtig gets out.

'Shit,' he says. 'That doesn't look good.' He nods towards her bandaged head.

She knows it looks worse than it is. The wound was stitched on the scene, and the bandage is bloody, along with her top and jacket. 'It's OK,' she says. 'And you didn't have to cancel Kvikkjokk for my sake.'

He shrugs. 'Don't be silly. What the hell would I do up there? Make snowmen?'

For the first time in over twelve hours Jeanette smiles. Nothing more needs to be said, because she knows he realises that she's deeply grateful he's there.

She opens the door to the passenger side and helps the old lady out of the car. Hurtig has already shown the woman a picture of Johan, and Jeanette has been warned that her evidence is weak. She wasn't even able to say what colour Johan's clothes were.

'Was that where you saw him?' Jeanette points towards the stony beach by the jetty where the lightship *Finngrund* is moored.

The old woman nods and shivers in the cold. 'He was lying asleep on the stones and I shook him awake. What sort of behaviour do you call this? I asked him. Drunk, so young and already –'

'I see,' Jeanette said impatiently. 'Did he say anything?'

'No, he was just mumbling. If he did say anything, I didn't hear it.'

Hurtig pulls out the photograph of Johan and shows it to the woman again. 'And you're not sure if this was the boy you saw?'

'Well, like I said, he had the same colour hair, but the face . . . It's hard to say. As I say, he was drunk.'

Jeanette sighs and walks towards the path that runs along the shoreline. Drunk? she thinks. Johan? Rubbish.

She looks across the water towards Skeppsholmen, bathed in sickly grey mist.

How could it be so bloody cold?

She goes down towards the water and walks out onto the stones. 'Was this where he was lying? Are you sure?'

'Yes,' the woman says firmly. 'Here somewhere.'

Hurtig turns towards the woman. 'And then he walked off? Towards Junibacken?'

'No . . .' The woman pulls a handkerchief from her coat pocket and blows her nose loudly. 'He staggered away. He was so drunk he could hardly stay on his feet . . .'

Jeanette feels annoyed. 'But he went that way? Towards Junibacken?'

The old woman nods and blows her nose again.

Then an emergency vehicle passes by along Djurgårdsvägen, on its way further into the island, to judge by the noise of the siren.

'Another false alarm?' Hurtig says through clenched teeth, and Jeanette shakes her head disconsolately.

This is the third time she's heard ambulance sirens, and neither of the previous occasions was anything to do with Johan.

'I'm going to call Mikkelsen,' Jeanette says.

'National Crime?' Hurtig looks surprised.

'Yes. The way I see it, he's best suited for something like this.' She gets up and strides quickly across the stones to get back to the path.

'Crimes against children, you mean?' It looks like Hurtig immediately regrets saying this. 'Well, I mean, we don't really know what this is about yet.'

'Maybe not, but it would be a mistake not to include that as a possible hypothesis. Mikkelsen's been coordinating the search of Beckholmen, Gröna Lund and Waldemarsudde.'

Hurtig nods and gives her a sympathetic look.

When Jeanette takes her mobile phone out she sees that the battery's dead; then the police radio crackles in Hurtig's car ten metres away.

She feels a heavy weight inside her as she understands.

As if the blood in her body is sinking, trying to drag her into the ground.

They've found Johan.

Karolinska Hospital

At first the paramedics thought the boy was dead.

He was found by the old windmill at Waldemarsudde, and his breathing and heartbeat were almost non-existent.

His body temperature was dangerously low, and they could see that he had been sick several times during the unusually cold late-summer night.

There were initial concerns about his breathing, in case any of the gastric acid had ended up in his lungs.

Just after ten o'clock Jeanette Kihlberg climbed into the ambulance that was going to drive her son to the intensive care unit of Karolinska Hospital.

The room is unlit, but the weak light of the afternoon sun finds its way through the venetian blinds and the yellow strips form a pattern on Johan's bare torso. The pulsating artificial lights of the heart-lung machine play across the bed and Jeanette Kihlberg has a feeling that she is inside a dream.

She strokes the back of Johan's hand and glances at the monitor at the side of the bed.

His body temperature is approaching normal.

She knows he had large quantities of alcohol in his body. Almost three parts per thousand when he arrived at the hospital.

She hasn't slept a wink, her body feels numb, and she can't even work out if the heart pounding inside her chest matches the pulsing sensation in her forehead. Thoughts she doesn't recognise are echoing in her head, and they're frustrated, angry, frightened, lost and resigned all at the same time.

She has always been a rational person. Until now.

She looks at him lying there. It's the first time he's ever been in hospital. No, the second time. The first time was thirteen years ago, when he was born. Back then she had been completely calm. And so well prepared that she predicted she would need a Caesarean section before the doctors decided on one.

She hasn't prepared for this.

She squeezes his hand tighter. It's still cold, but he looks relaxed and is breathing calmly. And the room is quiet. Apart from the electric hum of the machines.

'Listen . . .' she whispers, aware that people who are unconscious can still hear. 'They think everything's going to be fine.'

She breaks off her attempt to instil hope in Johan.

They think? More like they don't know.

They were able to tell her about the ECGs, oxygen and drips, and explain how a probe in his throat is monitoring his temperature, and how a heart-lung machine is slowly raising his temperature again.

They were able to tell her about critical hypothermia, and how a prolonged period in the water followed by a night of heavy rain and strong winds could affect the body.

They were able to explain that alcohol expands blood vessels and accelerates a drop in temperature, and that there's a risk of brain damage as a result of the decline in the blood-sugar level.

They said they thought the worst of the danger was over and they explained that his blood gases and lung X-ray looked positive at first glance.

What does that mean?

They think. But they don't know anything.

If Johan can hear, then he's heard everything she's been told in this room. She can't lie to him. She holds her hand to his cheek. That isn't a lie.

Her thoughts are interrupted when Hurtig comes into the room.

'How's he doing?'

'He's alive, and he's going to make a full recovery. It's OK, Jens. You can go home.'

Bandhagen – a Suburb

Lightning strikes the earth one hundred times per second, which means about eight million times per day. The worst storm of the year sweeps in over Stockholm, and at twenty-two minutes past ten lightning strikes at two places simultaneously. In Bandhagen, to the south of the city, and in the vicinity of Karolinska Hospital in Solna.

Detective Sergeant Jens Hurtig is standing in the hospital car park, about to drive home, when his mobile rings. He opens the car door and gets in before answering. He sees that it's Police Commissioner Dennis Billing, and assumes he's calling to find out what's been going on.

'I heard you found Jeanette's boy. How is he?' He sounds worried.

'He's sleeping at the moment, and she's with him.' Hurtig puts the key in the ignition and starts the engine. 'It doesn't seem to be life-threatening, thank God.'

'Good, good. So she should be back in a few days, then.' The police chief smacks his lips. 'And how about you?'

'What do you mean?'

'Are you tired, or do you feel up to taking a look at something out in Bandhagen?'

'Like what?'

'They've found a woman's body, probable rape.'

'OK, I'm on my way.'

'That's the kind of thing I like. You're a good guy, Jens. And you . . .' Commissioner Dennis Billing swallows. 'Tell Jan Kihlberg I think it's perfectly in order for her to stay at home for a while to take care of her son. To be honest, I think she ought to take better care of her family. I've heard rumours that Åke's left her.'

'How do you mean?' Hurtig is starting to get tired of the commissioner's insinuations. 'Do you want me to tell her to stay at home because you don't think women should have careers and ought to look after their husbands and children instead?'

'Damn it, Jens, stop that. I thought we understood each other, and –'

'Just because we're both men,' Hurtig interrupts, 'doesn't mean we share the same opinions.'

'No, of course not.' The commissioner sighs. 'I thought that perhaps –'

'Well, I don't know. Bye for now.' Hurtig ends the call before Dennis Billing has time to say anything else clumsy or just plain stupid.

At the Solna intersection he looks out across the Pampas Marina and the rows of sailing boats.

A boat, he thinks. I'm going to get myself a boat.

The rain is pouring down on the Bandhagen High School's sports fields. Hurtig pulls up the hood of his jacket as he slams the car door. He looks around, and it all feels very familiar.

He's been here several times as a spectator when Jeanette Kihlberg has been playing in matches for the mixed police team. He remembers being surprised at how good she was, better than most of the male players, and in her role as offensive midfielder she had been the most creative of them all, the one who made the penetrative passes, saw spaces no one else saw.

In a strange way he had been able to see how her personality as a police officer was reflected in her actions on the pitch. She had influence, but without being too dominant.

He can't help wondering how she is. Although he doesn't have children of his own, nor any desire to have any, he realises that she must be having a hard time right now. Who's taking care of her now that Åke has walked out?

He knows the cases of the murdered boys have hit her hard.

And now something's happened to her own son, making Jens wish he could be something more to her than just her sergeant. A friend.

He thinks about the nameless boys. If there's a missing person, then there has to be someone who misses them.

Jens Hurtig feels dejected as he hurries over to the buildings beside the fields.

As Ivo Andrić pulls into the car park at Bandhagen High School, he catches sight of Hurtig, Schwarz and Åhlund. They're sitting in a police car and are about to leave. When Jens Hurtig raises his hand in greeting he responds before parking next to the large brick building.

Andrić stays in his car, staring out across the dark, waterlogged football pitch. At one end the little forensics tent, and at the other a forlorn, abandoned goal with a damaged net. Rain is pouring down and shows no signs of easing, and he's planning to sit in the car as long as possible. He's full of an aching tiredness, and his eyes feel gritty. He thinks about recent events and the cases of the dead boys.

For a few hot weeks of summer they had taken all his time, and Ivo Andrić is still convinced they were dealing with a single perpetrator.

Jeanette Kihlberg had done a good job, but there was one police commissioner and one prosecutor who hadn't done their jobs, and the whole business had left him feeling utterly disillusioned. His confidence in the criminal justice system had always been low, but now it had been wiped out completely.

When the prosecutor had shut down the investigation all the air had gone out of him.

Ivo Andrić pulls his jacket tighter and puts on his baseball cap. He opens the car door, gets out in the pouring rain and jogs over towards the crime scene.

Vita Bergen – Sofia Zetterlund's Apartment

Sofia Zetterlund has big gaps in her memory. Black holes that she drifts past in her dreams or on her endless walks. Sometimes the holes get bigger when she notices a smell, or when someone looks at her in a particular way. Images are recreated when she hears the sound of wooden shoes on gravel, or when she sees the back of someone in the street. On occasions like this, it's as if a whirlwind sweeps through what Sofia calls 'I'.

She knows she's experienced something that won't let itself be described.

Once upon a time there was a little girl called Victoria, and when she was three her dad built a room inside her. A deserted room where there was only pain and suffering. Over the years it became a room with sturdy walls made of sorrow, with a floor made of the desire for revenge and, lastly, a solid roof of hate.

It became a room so enclosed that Victoria hadn't been able to get out.

And she's in there now.

It wasn't me, Sofia thinks. It wasn't my fault. Her first emotion when she wakes up is guilt. All her body's systems are getting ready for flight, to defend itself.

She reaches for the box of paroxetine and uses her saliva to swallow two pills. She leans back and waits for Victoria's voice to fall silent. Not completely, it never does that, but enough for her to hear herself.

Hear Sofia's will.

What had actually happened?

A memory of smells. Popcorn, rain-wet paths. Earth.

Someone had wanted to take her to hospital, but she had refused.

Then nothing. Utterly black. She doesn't remember the stairs up to the apartment, let alone how she managed to get home from Gröna Lund.

What time is it? she wonders.

The mobile phone is on the bedside table. A Nokia, an old model,

Victoria Bergman's mobile. She's going to get rid of it. The last link to her old life.

The phone says it's 07.33, and that she's missed one call. She presses the button and reads.

She doesn't recognise the number.

Ten minutes later she's calm enough to get up. The air in the apartment is musty, and she opens the window in the living room. Borgmästargatan is quiet and wet with rain. To the left, Sofia Church rises up majestically in the middle of the late-summer greenery of Vita Bergen, and from Nytorget, slightly further away, comes the smell of freshly baked bread and exhaust fumes.

A few parked cars.

In the bicycle rack across the street one of the twelve bikes has a puncture. It wasn't like that yesterday. Details that stick, whether she wants them to or not.

And if anyone were to ask her, she could list the colours of all the bikes in the right order. From right to left, or the other way round.

She wouldn't even have to think.

She knows she's right.

But the paroxetine makes her gentler; it makes her brain calm down and makes daily life manageable.

She decides to have a shower, but at that moment the phone rings. Her work phone this time.

It's still ringing when she gets in the shower.

The water has a reviving effect, and as she dries herself she thinks that she'll soon be completely alone. Free to do whatever she likes.

It's been over three weeks since her parents died. Soon she'll have access to more than eleven million kronor. She'll have enough money not to have to worry about her finances for the rest of her life.

She can shut her practice.

Move wherever she wants. Start again. Become another person.

But not yet, she thinks. Soon, perhaps, but not yet. Right now she needs the routine that work gives her. Time when she doesn't have to think about anything, and can just function in neutral. Not having to think gives her the calm she needs to keep Victoria away.

When she's finished drying herself she gets dressed and goes into the kitchen.

She sets up the coffee machine, gets out her laptop, puts it on the kitchen table and switches it on.

On the directory enquiries website she discovers that the unfamiliar number belongs to the local police station out in Värmdö, and she gets a lump in her stomach. Have they found something? If so, what?

She stands and gets a cup of coffee as she makes up her mind to stay calm and wait. That can be a problem for the future.

She sits down at the computer, opens the folder she's named VICTORIA BERGMAN, and looks at the twenty-five files.

All numbered versions of the name CROW GIRL.

Her own memories.

She knows she's been unwell, and it's been essential to compile all her memories. For several years now she's been having conversations with herself, recording and analysing her monologues. That was how she got to know Victoria, and finally reconciled herself to the idea that they were always going to have to live together.

But now, when she knows just what Victoria is capable of, she has no intention of letting herself be manipulated.

She highlights all the files in the folder, takes a deep breath, then finally presses delete.

A dialogue box asks if she's sure she wants to delete the files.

She considers.

She's been thinking of getting rid of her conversations with herself for some time, but she's never had the courage to do it.

'No, I'm not sure,' she says out loud, and presses no.

It feels like letting out a deep breath.

Now she's worried about Gao.

She cooks a large pan of thin porridge and fills a Thermos and takes it in to him. He's lying naked on the bed in the soft, dark room, and she can see from his eyes that he's a long way away. His drawings are in a neat pile on the floor, and, even though she spent several hours cleaning, the smell of urine is still there under the smell of detergent.

What is she going to do with him? Now that he's more of a liability than an asset.

She puts the Thermos on the floor by the bed. When she walks out she slides the bookcase back into place to hide the doorway and latches it. He'll have to manage until the evening.

Tongues

lie and slander, and Gao Lian from Wuhan must be careful about what people say.

Nothing must be able to surprise him, because he has control and he is no animal. He knows that animals can't plan for deviations from the norm. Squirrels gather nuts before winter in a tree trunk, but if the hole freezes up they understand nothing. The nuts never existed because they are out of reach. The squirrel gives up and dies.

Gao Lian understands that he must be prepared for the unpredictable.

Eyes see what is forbidden, and Gao must shut his and wait for it to disappear.

Time equals waiting, and is therefore nothing.

What will happen after that is the opposite of time.

When his muscles tense, his stomach tightens and his breathing is shallow but rich in oxygen, he will be at one with everything. His pulse, previously slow, will rise to a deafening roar, and everything will happen at once.

At that moment time will no longer be ridiculous, it will be everything.

Every second will have its own life, its own story with a beginning and an end. Every hundredth of a second's doubt can have fateful consequences. It can be the difference between life and death.

Time is the best friend of the weak-willed and those incapable of action.

The woman has equipped him with pen and paper, and he can sit in the darkness for hours, drawing. He takes the subjects of his pictures from his internal bank of memories. People he's seen, things he misses, feelings he's forgotten he had.

A little bird in its nest with its young.

When he's finished he puts the sheet aside and starts again.

He never stops to look at what he's drawn.

The woman who feeds him is neither true nor false, and for Gao there is no longer any time before her. No before, and no after. Time is nothing.

All of him is turned inward, towards the mechanics of memory.

Karolinska Hospital – Bistro Amica

Jeanette leaves Johan's room and heads off to the cafeteria by the main entrance to the hospital. She's a police officer, and a female one at that, which means she can't put her work to one side, even under circumstances like this. She's aware that it would be used against her at a later date.

The lift doors open, and as she walks out into the hubbub of people on the entrance level, she looks up and sees their movements, their smiles. She fills her lungs with air that is full of life. Although she has trouble admitting it, she knows she needs a break from her bedside vigil.

Hurtig is carrying a tray holding two steaming cups of coffee and two cinnamon buns. He puts it down on the table between them before sitting down. Jeanette takes a cup. The hot coffee is warming, and she feels the urge to smoke.

Hurtig picks up his cup and looks at her closely. She doesn't like the critical look in his eyes.

'So. How's he doing?' Hurtig asks.

'It's under control. Right now the worst thing is not knowing what happened to him.'

'I can understand that, but I suppose that's something you can talk about once he's better and is allowed home. Don't you think?'

'Sure.' Jeanette sighs before she goes on. 'But sitting on my own in that silence is driving me mad.'

'Hasn't Åke been?'

Jeanette shrugs. 'Åke's got his exhibition in Poland; he wanted to come home, but when we found Johan, then . . .' She shrugs again. 'Well, there wasn't much he could do.'

Jeanette can see that Hurtig wants to say something, but cuts him off.

'And what does Billing say?'

'You mean apart from saying he thinks you should stay at home with Johan, it's your fault he ran away, and that it's your fault Åke wants a divorce?'

'He said that? Fucking snake.'

'Yep. Came right out with it, no beating about the bush.' He raises his eyebrows.

Jeanette feels exhausted and useless.

'Goddamnit,' she mutters, and looks around the room.

Hurtig sits in silence, pulls a piece off his bun and pops it in his mouth. She can see something's troubling him.

'What is it? What's on your mind?'

'You haven't let go of it, have you?' he says tentatively. 'It's pretty obvious. You're pissed off that we were taken off the case.' He brushes away some crumbs that have caught in his stubble.

'Jens, listen to me . . .' She thinks for a moment. 'I'm just as frustrated as you are about what happened, and I think it's fucking awful, but at the same time I'm smart enough to realise that it isn't economically justifiable to –'

'Refugee children. Illegal fucking refugee children . . . not economically justified. It makes me sick.' Hurtig gets to his feet, and Jeanette can see how angry he is.

'Sit down, Jens. I haven't finished.' She's surprised she can sound so firm even though she feels utterly exhausted.

Hurtig sighs and sits down again.

'This is what we do . . . I have to look after Johan, and I don't know how long that's going to take.' She pauses before going on. 'But you know as well as I do that there'll be some time for other things . . . if you understand what I mean?' She sees a flash in Hurtig's eyes, and feels something flaring up inside her as well. A feeling she'd almost forgotten. Enthusiasm.

'You mean we continue, but in the dark?'

'Exactly. This has to stay between us. If it gets out, then we're both finished.'

Hurtig smiles. 'Actually, I've already put out a few feelers that I'm hoping to get replies about this week.'

'Good, Jens,' Jeanette says, returning his smile. 'I'm with you on this, but we've got to do it properly. Who have you contacted?'

'According to Ivo Andrić, the boy from Thorildsplan had traces of penicillin in his body, as well as all the other drugs and anaesthetic.'

'Penicillin? Meaning what?'

'That the boy had been in contact with the health services. Probably with some doctor working with hidden, undocumented refugees. I know a woman who works in the Swedish Church, she's promised to help me with possible names.'

'Sounds excellent. I'm still in touch with the UNHCR in Geneva.' Jeanette can feel the future slowly coming back to her. There is one, not just a bottomless present. 'And I've got another idea.'

Hurtig looks at her expectantly.

'What do you think about getting a profile of the perpetrator?'

Hurtig looks surprised. 'But how can we get a psychologist to take part in an unofficial . . .' he begins, then the penny drops. 'Aha, you mean Sofia Zetterlund?'

Jeanette nods. 'Yes, but I haven't asked her yet. I wanted to check with you first.'

'Hell, Jeanette,' Hurtig says with a broad grin. 'You're the best boss I've ever had.'

Jeanette can see he really means it.

'Much appreciated. I'm not feeling too hot at the moment.'

She thinks about Johan, and her separation from Åke. Right now she has no idea about her personal future. Is this lonely vigil at Johan's side a taste of how things are going to be? Definitive loneliness.

Åke has moved in with his new woman.

Alexandra Kowalska. Jeanette contemplates her with some bitterness. Restorer, it had said on her business card. That sounded like the sort of person who tries to breathe fresh life into something that's dead.

Has Åke moved out for good? She doesn't know. But it might be as well if he did. He's taken the first step, and now it's up to her to give him – and perhaps herself – a bit of a push.

'Shall we go out for a cigarette?' Hurtig stands up, as if realising that he needed to interrupt Jeanette's thoughts.

'But you don't smoke?'

'Sometimes you can make an exception.' He pulls a pack from his pocket and passes it to her. 'I don't know anything about cigarettes, but I got these for you.'

Jeanette looks at the pack and laughs. 'Menthol?'

They put on their jackets and go outside the main entrance. The rain has started to ease, and over on the horizon they can just make out a bright strip of better weather. Hurtig lights a cigarette and gives it to Jeanette, then lights one for himself. He takes a deep drag, coughs, then blows the smoke out through his nose.

'Are you going to keep the house if you and Åke split up?' he asks. 'Can you afford it?'

'I don't know. But I'm going to have to try to make it work for Johan's sake. Besides, things seem to have taken off for Åke, and his pictures have started to sell.'

'Yes, I read the review in *Dagens Nyheter*. They were over the moon.'

'It feels ever so slightly bitter, subsidising his work for twenty years and then not being allowed to reap the rewards.'

She would never have believed that she and Johan meant so little that he could just turn his back on them and walk out.

Hurtig looks at her, stubs out his cigarette and holds the door open. 'Up like the sun, down like a pancake . . .'

He gives her a hug, and she realises she needs one. She reflects that signs of affection can be as hollow as dying trees. She feels that she has no ability to differentiate the dead from the living as she steels herself to return to Johan's side in the silence of the room.

Vita Bergen – Sofia Zetterlund's Apartment

Sofia Zetterlund turns off her computer and folds it shut. Now that she's decided not to delete the files about Victoria, she seems to feel lighter.

She gets up, goes over to the sink and turns on the hot tap. The hot water makes the skin on her hands tighten up and sting, and they turn red, but she keeps them there. She tests herself, forcing herself to stick it out.

The only reason she had embarked on a relationship with Mikael was that she wanted revenge on Lasse. Now it seems utterly pointless. Empty and tawdry. Lasse is dead, and his son Mikael has slowly but surely become increasingly uninteresting to her since he's been away, even if she feels tempted to reveal to him who she really is.

I'm going to end it, she thinks, finally pulling her hands out of the hot water. She switches taps and holds them under ice-cold water. At first it's nice, soothing, then the cold takes over, and once again she forces herself to stick it out. Pain must be vanquished.

The more she thinks about it, the less she misses Mikael. I'm his stepmother, she thinks, and at the same time his lover. But it's impossible to tell him the truth.

She turns the tap off and empties the sink. After a while her hands revert to their normal colour, then, when the pain has subsided completely, she sits down at the kitchen table again.

Her phone is in front of her and she knows she ought to call Jeanette. But she's reluctant. She doesn't know what to say. What she ought to say.

Anxiety hits her in the solar plexus, and she puts her hands on her stomach. She's trembling, her heart is racing, and all her energy is draining away as if someone has just cut an artery. Her head is burning and she feels that she's losing control, and has no idea what her body's about to do.

Bang her head against the wall? Throw herself out the window? Scream?

No, she needs to hear a real voice. A voice that can prove to her that she still exists, that she's tangible. That's the only thing that will silence the cacophony inside her, and she reaches for the phone. Jeanette Kihlberg answers after a dozen rings.

She can hear distortion on the line. Background noise interrupted by a bleeping sound.

'How is he?' is all Sofia can manage to say.

Jeanette Kihlberg sounds like she's in as bad a state as the line. 'We found him. He's alive, and he's lying here beside me. That's enough for the time being.'

Your child is lying beside you, she thinks. And Gao is here with me.

Her lips move. 'I can come today,' she hears herself say.

'Please do. Come in an hour or so.'

'I can come today.' Her own voice echoes between the walls of the kitchen. Did she just repeat herself? 'I can come today. I can . . .'

Johan had been missing all of one night, while Sofia was at home with Gao. They slept. Nothing else. That's right, isn't it?

'I can come today.'

Her uncertainty spreads, and suddenly she realises that she hasn't a clue about what happened after she and Johan got in the cradle to ride on Free Fall.

Distantly she hears Jeanette's voice. 'Good, see you later. I miss you.'

'I can come today.' The phone is silent, and when she looks at the screen she sees that the call lasted twenty-three seconds.

She goes out into the hall to put her shoes and jacket on. When she gets her boots down from the rack she notices that they're damp, as if they'd just been used.

She looks at them closely. A yellow leaf is stuck to the heel of the left boot, the laces of both are full of pine needles and bits of grass, and the soles are muddy.

Calm down, she thinks. There's been a lot of rain. How long does it take for a pair of leather boots to dry?

She reaches for her jacket. It too feels damp, and she takes a closer look at it.

A tear in one sleeve, about five centimetres long. She finds some small pieces of grit in the exposed padding.

There's something sticking out of one pocket.

What the hell?

A Polaroid picture.

When she sees what it's of, she doesn't know what to think.

It's a photograph of her, maybe ten years old. She's standing on a deserted beach. There's a strong wind, and her long fair hair is sticking out almost horizontally from her head. In the sand there's a row of broken-off wooden poles, and in the background she can make out a small, red-and-white-striped lighthouse. A few seagulls are outlined against the grey sky.

Her heart is pounding. The photograph means nothing to her, and the location is utterly unfamiliar.

Denmark, 1988

Sleepless, she listened for his steps and pretended to be a clock. If she could control time, he would be fooled and would leave her alone.

He's heavy, he's got a hairy back, and he's sweaty and smells of ammonia after grappling with the muck spreader for two hours. The swearing from the outhouse is audible all the way up to her room.

His bony hips chafe against her stomach as she stares up beyond his dipping shoulders.

The Danish flag draped across the ceiling is an inverted cross, its colours blood red and skeleton white.

It's easiest to do what he wants. Stroke his back and groan in his ear. It shortens the whole thing by a good five minutes.

Once the squeaking of the old bed's springs has stopped and he's gone, she gets up and goes into the bathroom. The stench of manure has to go.

He's a repairman from Holstebro, and she calls him the Holstebro pig, after the local breed, specially developed for slaughter.

She's written his name in her diary, along with the others, and at the top of the list is her pig farmer, the one she has to be grateful to for giving her somewhere to stay.

The other one is actually well educated, a lawyer or something, and works in Sweden when he's not at the farm killing pigs. She calls him the German bastard, but never when he can hear.

The German bastard is proud of using tried-and-tested, traditional working methods. His Jutland pigs are scorched rather than boiled to remove their bristles.

She turns the tap on and scrubs her hands. Her fingertips are swollen from her work with the pigs, because the pig hair catches under her nails and causes inflammation. Wearing protective gloves doesn't make any difference.

She's killed them. Numbing them with electric shocks and draining their blood, cleaning up after and rinsing the drains and taking care of the mess after the slaughter. Once he let her shoot one of them with a bolt gun, and she came close to using it on him instead. If only to see if his eyes ended up as vacant as the pigs'.

Once she's scrubbed herself reasonably clean, she dries herself and goes back to her room.

I can't bear it, she thinks. I have to get away from here.

As she gets dressed she hears the Holstebro pig's old car start up. She peeps through the curtain and looks out of the window. The car is driving away from the farm and the German bastard is walking over to the outhouse to continue repairing the muck spreader.

She makes up her mind to walk out onto Grisetå Point, and maybe over the bridge to Oddesund.

The wind is eating its way in under her clothes, and even though she's wearing both a cardigan and a jacket, she's shivering before she gets round the house.

She continues towards the railway line and follows the track out onto the headland. At regular intervals she passes the remains of pillboxes and concrete bunkers from the Second World War. The headland gets narrower, and soon she can see water on both sides, and when the railway swings off towards the bridge she can see the lighthouse a few hundred metres ahead.

She goes down to the beach and realises that she's alone. She lies down in the grass next to the little red-and-white lighthouse and looks up at the clear blue sky. She recalls how she once lay like this, and heard voices from inside the forest.

Then, as now, it had been windy, and one of them had been Martin's burbling voice.

Why had he vanished?

She doesn't know, but she believes that someone drowned him. He had disappeared down by the jetty at the same time as Crow Girl got there.

But her memories are vague. There's a black hole.

She rolls a blade of grass between her fingers and sees the rotating seed head change colour in the sun. At the top of it is a drop of dew, and beneath it sits an ant, completely still. She can see that it's missing one of its back legs.

'What are you thinking about, little ant?' she whispers, then blows on the seed head.

She lies back on her side and puts the grass straw down carefully on a stone next to her. The ant starts to move, crawling down the stem. It doesn't appear to be troubled by the fact that it's missing one leg.

'What are you doing here?'

A shadow falls across her face as she hears his voice. A flock of birds passes above his head.

She gets up and goes with him to the pillbox. It takes ten minutes, because he doesn't have much stamina.

He tells her about the war, and all the suffering the Danes had to endure during the German occupation, and how the women were raped and dishonoured.

'And all the randy little German bitches,' he sighs. 'They were whores. Fucking five thousand of the swine.'

He's told her several times about the Danish women who voluntarily embarked on relationships with German soldiers, and she has long since worked out that he himself is a German kid, a German bastard.

As they walk back she stays a few steps behind him, adjusting her dirty clothes. Her top is torn and she hopes they don't meet anyone. She aches all over, because he was more heavy-handed than usual, and the ground out here is very stony.

Denmark is hell on earth, she thinks.

Karolinska Hospital

'Bloody awful weather,' Sofia Zetterlund says as she walks into the hospital room. She has an uncertain smile on her lips, and Jeanette Kihlberg nods warily. She's pleased to see Sofia again, but there's something different about her face, something new that she can't read.

The rain is beating against the windows, and every so often the room is lit up by lightning. They stand there facing each other.

Sofia looks anxiously at Johan, and Jeanette goes over and strokes her back.

'Hello, you, good to see you,' she whispers, and Sofia reciprocates and gives Jeanette a hug.

'What's the prognosis?' she asks.

Jeanette smiles. 'If you mean the weather, pretty lousy.' Her light-hearted tone is unforced. 'But as far as Johan's concerned, things look good. He's started to come round. You can see his eyes moving under his eyelids now.' Johan's face has finally got some colour back, and she strokes his arm.

The doctors have finally dared to give an unambiguously positive assessment of his condition. And it's nice to have the company of some-one she doesn't work with. Someone she's not expected to behave like a boss towards.

Sofia relaxes and becomes herself again.

'There's no way you should blame yourself for what happened,' Jea-nette says. 'It wasn't your fault he disappeared.'

Sofia stares at her sombrely. 'No, maybe not. But I'm ashamed that I panicked. I want to be reliable, but I'm clearly not.'

Jeanette thinks back to how Sofia reacted. She had been distraught. In pieces, crying, with her face to the ground.

'I hope you can forgive me for leaving you there,' Jeanette says. 'But Johan was still missing at the time, and –'

'Goodness, yes,' Sofia interrupts. 'I can always take care of myself.'

She looks Jeanette right in the eye. 'Remember that: I can always look after myself, you never have to take responsibility for me, no matter what.'

Jeanette is almost alarmed by how serious Sofia appears and sounds.

'If I can handle blubbing company directors, I can handle myself as well.'

Jeanette is relieved to see Sofia smiling.

'Well, evidently I can't even handle a drunk,' Jeanette says. She laughs and points to the bandage on her brow.

'And what's your prognosis?' Sofia asks. Her eyes are smiling now as well.

'A bottle to the head. Four stitches that'll be taken out in a couple of weeks.'

The room is once again lit up by lightning. The window rattles and Jeanette is blinded by the bright flash.

White walls, white floor and ceiling. White sheets. Johan's pale face. Her eyes are out of focus.

'But what actually happened to you?' Jeanette hardly dares look at Sofia as she asks the question. The red lights on the heart-lung machine flash. She rubs her eyes and the colours return. Now she can see Sofia's face properly.

'Well.' She sighs, then looks up at the ceiling as though searching for words. 'It turned out that I was considerably more scared of dying than I ever thought. Simple as that.'

'You didn't think you were beforehand?' Jeanette looks at her inquisitively, and immediately feels her own fear of the inevitable clutch at her chest.

'Yes, but not like that. Not as strongly as that. It's like the idea of death doesn't really become obvious until you have children, and then I had Johan with me up there, and . . .' Sofia falls silent and puts her hand on Johan's leg. 'Life suddenly took on a different meaning, and I wasn't prepared for the fact that it could feel like that.' She turns to look at Jeanette with a smile. 'I suppose it came as a shock, suddenly realising the point of life.'

Jeanette realises for the first time that Sofia isn't just a psychologist who's easy to talk to.

She's also bearing something herself, a loss or a longing, possibly a sorrow.

And she too has experiences to work through, gaps to fill.

She feels ashamed at not having known sooner. That Sofia is a person who can't just give all the time.

'Always being strong is the same as not living,' she says, hoping Sofia realises that her words are intended as a comfort.

Suddenly Johan makes a whimpering sound, and for a fraction of a second they look at each other in surprise before realising what they've just heard. The weight inside Jeanette eases, and she leans over him.

'Darling,' she mutters, as her hands stroke his chest. 'Welcome back. Mum's here. I'm waiting for you.'

She calls a doctor, who explains that this is a natural part of coming round, but that it will be many hours before he's conscious.

'Life is slowly returning to all of us,' Sofia says when the doctor leaves them on their own.

'Yes, maybe,' Jeanette says, and makes up her mind at that moment to say what she knows. 'By the way, do you know who's lying in a coma in the next ward?' she asks.

'No idea. Anyone I know?'

'Karl Lundström,' Jeanette says. 'I went past his room earlier today. It's actually quite strange,' she goes on. 'Two corridors away Karl Lundström is lying between the same sort of sheets as Johan, and the staff care for them both with the same devotion. Life seems to be worth just the same, regardless of who you are.'

'We live in the world of men,' Sofia replies. 'Where Johan is worth no more than a paedophile. There, no one's worth more than a paedophile or a rapist. You can only be worth less.'

Jeanette laughs. 'How do you mean?'

'Well, if you're a victim, you're worth less than the paedophile himself. They'd rather protect presumed perpetrators than presumed victims. The world of men.'

Jeanette nods but isn't sure she understands. She looks at Johan lying there. A victim? She hasn't really dared think the thought. A victim of what? She thinks of Karl Lundström. No, impossible. She thinks him away.

'What sort of experiences have you had with men?' she hazards.

'I suppose I hate them,' Sofia replies. Her eyes are blank. 'As a group, I mean,' she adds, turning to look at Jeanette again. 'You?'

Jeanette isn't prepared for the question to be thrown back at her. She looks at Johan, and thinks of Åke, and her bosses and colleagues. Sure, there are pigs among them, but that doesn't apply to them all. What Sofia is giving voice to comes from a different world to hers. That's the sort of thing you just feel.

Sofia's darkness, what exactly does it consist of? Her eyes are difficult to read.

Hatred or irony, madness or wisdom? Is there really any difference? Jeanette thinks.

'I could do with a cigarette,' Sofia says. 'Do you want to come?'

At least she never bores her. Unlike Åke.

'No . . . you go. I'll sit here with Johan.'

Sofia Zetterlund picks up her coat and walks out.

Stockholm, 1987

The rowan tree was planted the same day she was born. She once tried to set fire to it, but it wouldn't burn.

The compartment is warm and smells of the people who were sitting here before her. Victoria opens the window in an attempt to air it, but it's as if the smells are ingrained in the velour seats.

The headache she's had since she woke up with the noose around her neck in the Copenhagen hotel room is starting to ease. But her mouth still feels sore and her broken front tooth hurts badly. She runs her tongue over her teeth and can feel that a piece has broken off, and thinks that she'll have to get it fixed as soon as she gets home.

The train pulls out from the station with a jolt, and it starts to pour with rain.

I can do what I like, she thinks. I can leave it all behind me and never go back to him. Will he allow that? She doesn't know. He needs her, and she needs him.

At least for the moment.

A week earlier she, Hannah and Jessica took the ferry from Corfu to Brindisi, then trains to Rome and Paris. There had been grey rain through the windows the whole way. July was more like November. Two pointless days in Paris. Hannah and Jessica had started to get homesick and they were cold and wet as they sat in their seats at the Gare du Nord.

Victoria curls up in a corner and pulls her jacket over her head. After a month interrailing through Europe, only the last stretch remains.

Throughout the entire journey Hannah and Jessica had been like rag dolls. She had grown tired of them, and when the train stopped in Lille she decided to get off. A Danish lorry driver offered her a lift, and she went with him all the way to Amsterdam. When she got to Copenhagen she cashed in her last traveller's cheques and booked into a hotel.

The voice had told her what to do. But it had been wrong.

She had survived.

As the train approaches the ferry terminal in Helsingør, she wonders if her life could have been different. Probably not. Her father stuck a knife into her childhood, and the blade is still quivering from the blow. Not that it matters now. She and the hatred belong together, like thunder and lightning. Like a clenched fist and a punch.

The journey home takes all night, and she sleeps the whole way. The conductor wakes her just before they arrive, and she feels giddy and uneasy. She has been dreaming, but can't remember of what, and all that remains of the dream is a feeling of anxiety.

It's early morning, and there's a chill in the air. She puts her rucksack on, gets off the train and walks into the large, arched concourse. As she anticipated, there's no one there to meet her, and she takes the escalator down to the metro.

The bus from Slussen out to Värmdö and Grisslinge takes half an hour, and she uses the time to make up innocent little anecdotes about the trip. She knows he's going to want to hear everything, and won't be happy if there are no details.

Victoria gets off the bus and walks slowly along the road where she once named so many things.

She sees the Climbing Tree and the Stepping Stone. The little mound she called the Mountain, and the stream that was once the River.

Even as she takes her seventeen-year-old teenage steps, part of her is only two years old.

The white Volvo is parked in the drive, and she sees them out in the garden.

He's standing with his back to her fiddling with something, while Mum is crouched beside one of the flower beds, weeding. Victoria takes off her rucksack and leaves it on the terrace.

Only then does he hear her and turn round.

She smiles and waves to him, but he looks at her expressionlessly, then turns away and continues with his work.

Mum looks up from the flower bed and nods warily at Victoria. She nods back, then picks up her rucksack again and goes into the house.

She unpacks her dirty clothes in the basement and puts them in the laundry basket. She undresses and gets in the shower.

A sudden gust of air makes the shower curtain move, and she realises he's standing outside the shower.

'Did you have a nice time?' he says. His shadow falls on the shower curtain and she feels her stomach tighten. She doesn't want to answer, but in spite of the humiliations he has subjected her to, she can't give him the sort of silent treatment that might make him reveal himself.

'Oh yes. It was good.' She tries to sound happy and relaxed, and not think about the fact that he's standing so close to her naked body.

'And you had enough money to last the whole trip?'

'Yes. I've even got a bit left. After all, I had my grant, so . . .'

'That's good, Victoria. You're . . .' His voice trails off and she hears him sniff.

Is he crying?

'I've missed you. It's been empty here without you. Well, obviously we've both missed you.'

'But I'm home now.' She tries to sound cheerful, but feels the lump in her stomach grow because she knows what he wants.

'That's good, Victoria. Finish your shower and get dressed, then your mum and I want to talk to you. Mum's making some tea.' He blows his nose in his handkerchief, then snorts.

Yes, he's crying, she thinks.

'I'm almost finished.'

She waits for him to go before turning the water off and drying herself. She knows he might be back any moment and gets dressed as quickly as she can. She doesn't even bother finding clean underwear, and puts the pair she's been wearing all the way from Denmark back on.

They're sitting quietly at the kitchen table waiting for her. The only noise is from the radio by the window. On the table is the teapot and a plate of almond biscuits. Mum pours a cup, which smells strongly of mint and honey.

'Welcome home, Victoria,' Mum says, holding out the plate of biscuits without looking her in the eye.

Victoria tries to catch her eye. Tries again and again.

She doesn't recognise me, Victoria thinks.

The plate of biscuits is the only thing that's really present.

'You've probably been looking forward to having some proper . . .' Mum loses her train of thought, puts the plate down and brushes some invisible crumbs from the table. 'After all the strange things . . .'

'It'll be nice.' Victoria lets her eyes roam around the kitchen, then looks at him.

'You had something you wanted to tell me.' She dunks the sugar-coated biscuit in the tea, and a big piece breaks off and falls into the cup. Fascinated, she watches it dissolve as the small pieces sink to the bottom, as though it had never been whole.

'Mum and I have done some thinking while you've been gone, and we've decided to move away from here for a while.'

He leans over the table and Mum nods in agreement, as if to reinforce his words.

'Move? Where to?'

'I've been asked to lead a project in Sierra Leone. To start with we'll be there for six months, then we can stay another six months if we want to.'

He slowly rubs his slender hands, and she notices how old and wrinkled they look.

So hard and eager. Burning.

She shudders at the thought of him touching her.

'But I've applied to Uppsala University and . . .' She can feel tears welling up, but doesn't want to show any weakness. That might give him an opportunity to try to comfort her. She looks down into her cup, stirs it with her spoon, making porridge with the biscuit crumbs.

'Africa's such a long way away, and I . . .'

She'll be completely at his mercy. Not knowing anyone, and with nowhere to escape to if she should need to get away.

'We've arranged for you to be able to do a correspondence course. And you'll get help a few times a week.'

He looks at her with his watery, grey-blue eyes. He's already made up his mind, so there's no point in her saying anything.

'What sort of course?' She feels a stab of pain in her tooth and rubs her chin with her hand.

They haven't even asked her about her tooth.

'It's a basic course in psychology. We thought that would suit you.'

He folds his hands in front of him and waits for her response.

Mum gets up and takes her cup over to the sink. Without a word she rinses it, dries it carefully and puts it back in the cupboard.

Victoria says nothing. She knows there's no point in protesting.

It's better to store up the anger inside her, and let it grow big. One day she'll open the floodgates and let the fire wash over the world, and when that day comes she will be merciless and unforgiving.

She smiles at him. 'I'm sure it'll be fine. After all, it's just a few months. It might be fun to see something new.'

He nods and gets up from the table, to mark that the conversation is over.

'Well, let's all get back to our own business,' he says. 'Perhaps Victoria needs to get some rest. I'm going to continue out in the garden. At six o'clock the sauna will be heated up, and we can continue our conversation then. Is that OK?' He looks expectantly first at Victoria, then at her mother.

They nod back.

That night she has trouble sleeping, and lies in bed twisting and turning.

She aches because he was so hard-handed. Her skin is stinging from the scalding water, and her crotch hurts. But she knows it will pass overnight. As long as he's content and able to sleep.

She sniffs the little dog made of real rabbit fur.

In her memory she lists the injustices, and looks forward to the day when he and everyone else will beg her for mercy.

Karolinska Hospital

Killing someone is easy. The difficulties are mainly mental, and the underlying factors for that are very different. For most people a whole range of barriers need to be bridged. Empathy, conscience and reflection usually function as hindrances against outbreaks of fatal violence.

For some people it's no harder than opening a milk carton.

It's visiting time, and there are lots of people moving about. Outside the rain is pouring down, and the storm is lashing the windows. Every so often lightning lights up the night sky, and thunder follows almost instantly.

The storm is very close.

There's a floor plan on the wall beside the lifts, and because she doesn't want to ask anyone for directions she goes over to it and checks that she isn't in the wrong place.

In one hand she is clutching a bunch of yellow tulips, and every time she passes someone she looks down to avoid eye contact. Her coat is unremarkable, as are her trousers and the white shoes with soft rubber soles. No one pays her any attention, and if anyone were to remember her, against all expectation, they wouldn't be able to remember any details of her appearance.

She could be anyone, and she is used to being ignored. Nowadays it doesn't bother her, but once upon a time the carelessness used to hurt.

A long time ago she was on her own, but she isn't any more.

At least not in the same way.

The second door on the left is his. She slips in quickly, shuts the door behind herself, then stops to listen, but can't hear anything that worries her.

Everything's quiet and, as expected, he's alone in the room.

In the window there's a small lamp, whose weak, yellow light gives the room a feverish glow and makes it seem even smaller than it actually is.

At the end of the bed is his medical chart, and she picks it up and reads.

Karl Lundström.

Beside the bed are a number of different gadgets, and two drip stands connected to his neck. There are two transparent tubes coming out of his nostrils, and another in his mouth.

He's just a lump of meat, she thinks.

One of the life-support machines is making a rhythmic, soporific bleeping sound. She knows she can't just switch them off. The alarm would go off and the staff would be there in less than a minute.

Same thing if she were to try to smother him.

She looks at him. His eyes are moving restlessly beneath his closed eyelids. Perhaps he's aware of her presence.

Perhaps he even understands why she's there, without being able to do anything about it.

She puts her bag down at the end of the bed, opens it and takes out a small syringe, then goes over to the drips.

She reads the labels: MORPHINE and NUTRITION.

No sound but the rain outside and the respirator.

She holds up the syringe, sticks it into the top of the plastic bag of nutrients and squeezes in the contents. She removes the needle, then gently shakes the bag so that the morphine blends into the sugar solution.

When she's finished, she fills a vase with water in the bathroom. Then she unwraps the tulips and puts them in the vase.

Before leaving the room she takes out her Polaroid camera.

The flash of the camera goes off at the same moment as another flash of lightning outside, the photograph comes out of the camera and the image gradually forms before her eyes.

She looks at the photograph.

The flash has completely bleached the walls and bed sheets, but Karl Lundström's body and the vase of yellow flowers are perfectly exposed.

Karl Lundström. The man who abused his daughter for years. The man who had no regrets. The man who wanted to end his worthless life in a pathetic attempt to hang himself.

The man who even managed to fail at something anyone could manage.

Opening a milk carton.

But she can help him realise his intention. She can put an end to everything.

As she carefully opens the door she can hear his breathing getting slower.

Soon it will cease altogether and liberate a number of cubic metres of fresh air for the living to breathe.

Gamla Enskede – Kihlberg House

They're sitting in silence in the car. The only sounds are the windscreen wipers and the faint crackle of the police radio. Jens Hurtig is driving, and Jeanette is sitting in the back with Johan.

Hurtig turns onto the Enskede road and glances at Johan.

'You're looking OK.' He smiles into the rear-view mirror.

Johan nods without speaking, then turns his head away and looks out of the window.

What happened to him? Jeanette wonders, and once again she's on the verge of opening her mouth to ask him how he's feeling. But this time she stops herself. She doesn't want to put any pressure on him. Nagging won't make him talk, and she knows that at this point the first move has to come from him. It will just have to run its own course. Maybe he doesn't know anything about what happened, but she has a feeling there's something he's not saying.

The silence in the car feels oppressive as Hurtig pulls into the drive outside the house.

'Mikkelsen called this morning,' he says, switching off the engine. 'Lundström died last night. I just wanted to tell you before you read it in the evening papers.'

She feels herself slump. For a moment the heavy drumming of the rain on the windscreen makes her think that the car is still moving, even though she knows it's parked in front of the garage door. Her only lead in the hunt for whoever killed the dead boys is gone.

'Would you mind waiting here, please? I'll be right back,' she says, and opens the car door. 'Come on, Johan. Let's get you inside.'

Johan walks ahead of her through the garden, up the steps and into the hall. He takes his shoes off without saying anything, hangs up his wet jacket and goes into his room.

She stops for a moment, staring after him.

When she goes back down to the drive the rain has eased to a constant shower. Hurtig is standing next to the car, smoking.

'It's become a habit, then?'

He grins and passes her a cigarette.

'So, Karl Lundström died last night,' she says.

'Yes, it looks like his kidneys just gave out.'

Two corridors away. The same night Johan regained consciousness. 'Nothing funny, then?'

'No, probably not, more likely to be the result of all the medication they were pumping into him. Mikkelsen's promised to let us have a report tomorrow, and . . . well, I just thought you should know.'

'Nothing else?' she asks.

'No, nothing much. But he had a visitor just before he died. The nurse who found him said a bunch of flowers had appeared during the course of the evening. Yellow tulips. From his wife, or his solicitor. They were the only visitors registered yesterday evening.'

'Annette Lundström? Isn't she in hospital?'

'No, not in hospital. Isolated, though. Mikkelsen said that Annette Lundström has hardly left their villa in Danderyd for several weeks now, other than to visit her husband. They went to see her this morning, to tell her what's happened . . . evidently the house smells like it hasn't been aired in weeks.'

Someone gave Karl Lundström yellow flowers, Jeanette thinks. Yellow usually symbolises betrayal.

'Am I a bad mother?' she asks.

Hurtig laughs nervously. 'No, for God's sake. Johan's a teenager now, after all. He ran off, met someone who gave him booze. He got drunk, it all went wrong and now he feels ashamed.'

Just trying to cheer me up, Jeanette thinks. But that's not right.

'Are you being sarcastic?'

But she can see that he isn't.

'No, Johan's ashamed. You can see it on him.'

He leans against the bonnet. Maybe he's right, Jeanette thinks. Hurtig drums his fingers on the car roof.

They say goodbye, and she goes back into the house. She gets a glass of water from the kitchen and takes it with her into Johan's room.

He's fallen asleep, so she puts the glass down on the bedside table and strokes his cheek.

Then she goes down into the basement, where she gathers together a load of Johan's dirty clothes for the washing machine. His sports gear and football socks. And the shirts Åke has left behind.

She pours in some detergent, shuts the door, then sits down in front of the rotating drum. Traces of an earlier life spin round before her eyes.

She thinks about Johan. Silent the whole way home. Not a word. Not a glance. He's decided that she's disqualified. And has consciously chosen to shut her out.

That hurts.

Vita Bergen – Sofia Zetterlund's Apartment

Sofia Zetterlund has done the cleaning, paid the bills and tried to take care of practical matters.

At lunchtime she calls Mikael.

'So you're still alive?' She can hear how angry he sounds.

'We need to talk . . .'

'Now isn't a good time. I'm on my way to a lunch meeting. Why don't you call this evening instead? You know what my days are like.'

'You're pretty busy in the evening as well. I've left several messages –'

'Listen, Sofia.' He sighs. 'What are we doing? Don't you think we should just call it a day?'

She's speechless, and swallows a few times. 'What do you mean?'

'Well, we clearly haven't got time to see each other. So why keep going?'

When she realises what he means, she feels a huge sense of relief. He pre-empted her by a matter of seconds. He wants to break up. Simple. No fuss.

She lets out a short laugh. 'Mikael, that's actually why I've been trying to contact you. Haven't you got five minutes so we can talk?'

After the call, Sofia sits down on the sofa.

Washing, she thinks. Cleaning and paying bills. Watering the plants. Ending a relationship. Practical matters of roughly equal significance.

She doesn't imagine she's going to miss him.

On the table is the Polaroid picture she found in her pocket.

What am I going to do with that? she thinks.

She doesn't understand. It's her in the picture, yet it isn't.

On the one hand her memories can't be trusted, Victoria Bergman's childhood is full of holes, but on the other hand the details in the photograph are so clear that they ought to stir some sort of memory in her.

She's wearing a red quilted jacket with white detailing, as well as white wellington boots and red trousers. She'd never wear that. It looks like someone's dressed her up.

The lighthouse in the background is red and white as well, which makes it look like the picture has been composed around those colours.

You can't see much of the surroundings, apart from the beach with its broken wooden poles. The landscape looks bleak, with low hillocks of tall, yellowing grass.

It could be Gotland, maybe the south coast of England, or Denmark. Skåne? North Germany?

Places she's been to, but not when she was that young.

It looks like late summer, possibly autumn, considering her clothes. It seems windy, and looks cold.

The little girl who is her has a smile on her lips, but her eyes aren't smiling. When she looks closer at the picture, she thinks her eyes look desperate.

How did this end up in my pocket? Has it been there the whole time? Did I pick it up out in Värmdö before the house burned down?

No, I didn't have that jacket on me then.

Victoria, she thinks. Tell me what it is I don't remember.

No reaction.

Not a single feeling comes to her.

Kungsgatan – Stockholm City Centre

After several years of excavations into the Brunkeberg Ridge, Kungsgatan was inaugurated in November 1911. While work was going on, they found the remains of a Viking settlement that once stood roughly where Hötorget is today.

The street, originally known as Helsingegathun, was renamed Lutternsgatan in the early eighteenth century. It was a rough area, lined with small shacks and old wooden houses.

The author Ivar Lo-Johansson wrote about the street, about the bohemians of the Klara district, and the prostitutes who lived and worked there.

During the sixties, when the city centre shifted south towards Hamngatan, the street began to decline, but after the renovations of the eighties it regained a little of its earlier status.

Prosecutor Kenneth von Kwist gets off the metro at Hötorget and, as usual, has trouble getting his bearings. There are far too many exits, and his sense of direction doesn't work underground.

A few minutes later he's standing outside the Concert House.

It's raining and he puts up his umbrella and slowly begins to walk west, up Kungsgatan.

He's in no hurry.

In fact he's rather reluctant to arrive early to his office at the Public Prosecution Authority.

He's worried. No matter how he looks at the matter, it goes wrong. No matter what he does, he's going to end up as the loser.

He crosses Drottninggatan, Målargatan and Klara Norra Kyrkogatan.

What will happen if he does nothing at all and simply hides the documents underneath everything else in the bottom drawer of his desk?

There's a chance that she'll never get to hear about them, and over time new cases will arise and the old ones will be forgotten.

But seeing as he's dealing with Jeanette Kihlberg, he doubts that she'll just move on.

Her involvement with the dead boys has been too great, and she's far too stubborn. Far too devoted to her work.

In his search for compromising facts about her, he hasn't found a thing.

Not a single complaint about her work.

She's a third-generation police officer. Both her father and her grandfather served in the Western District, and there was nothing of note in their files either.

He passes the Oscar Theatre and the Casino Cosmopol, in the former premises of the dance restaurant Bal Palais.

The whole thing's a complete mess, and right now he's the only person who can solve the problem.

Unless there's something he hasn't thought of?

An approach he's missed?

For the time being Jeanette Kihlberg is fully occupied with her son, but once he's better she'll be back at work, and sooner or later she's going to find out about the new information.

There's nothing he can do to stop that.

Is there?

Kronoberg – Police Headquarters

There's a knock on her door and Commissioner Dennis Billing steps into her office.

Jeanette notes that he looks suntanned.

'So, you're back?' he pants as he pulls up a chair and lowers his tall, heavy frame onto it. 'How are you?'

Jeanette suspects that this last question covers more than just her well-being.

'Under control. I'm waiting for Hurtig to report on his Bandhagen case.'

'So what are you doing now?' He opens the door to the corridor, where Hurtig is waiting to come in.

'Have you got anything new for us?' Jeanette leans back and stares at the broad rear view of Billing. There's a large patch of sweat just above his trousers. A clear sign that he spends too much time sitting down, she thinks.

'No, not exactly. Things are pretty calm right now, so maybe the pair of you could get back to your respective holidays.'

Jeanette and Hurtig shake their heads simultaneously, but Hurtig speaks first. 'Absolutely not. I'll take mine in the winter instead.'

'Me too,' Jeanette adds. 'Taking time off is far too much hassle.'

Billing turns and looks at her. 'Well then. Spend a few days playing solitaire until something happens. Reinstall Windows. Take it easy, basically. Bye.' Without waiting for a reply he forces his way past Hurtig and walks off.

Hurtig closes the door behind him with a grin, and pulls out the chair by the desk.

'Has the Bandhagen rapist confessed?' Jeanette leans back and stretches, then puts her hands behind her head.

'Case closed.' Hurtig sits down and goes on. 'He's going to be charged with several counts of rape against his wife, for assault on her, and, if he sticks to his story, for one case of deprivation of liberty.' Hurtig stops, and seems to be thinking. 'I think he found it a relief to have the chance to tell someone.'

Jeanette has trouble feeling any sympathy for a man like that.

Feeling rejected is no excuse, she thinks, as she sees Åke and Alexandra in her mind's eye. It's just part of life.

'Good, then we can put him to one side and get back to the case of the dead boys.'

She opens one of her desk drawers and pulls out a bright pink folder that makes Hurtig chuckle.

She smiles. 'I've learned how to make important things look uninteresting. No one would ever bother to open this.' She leafs through the documents.

'There are a few things we need to follow up on,' she says. 'Annette and Linnea Lundström. Ulrika Wendin. Kenneth von Kwist.'

'Ulrika Wendin?' Hurtig looks surprised.

'Yes, I don't think she's told us everything. We need to go with gut feeling.'

'And von Kwist?' Hurtig throws his hands up.

'There's something funny about von Kwist and the Lundström family. I don't know what it is yet, but . . .' Jeanette takes a deep breath before she goes on. 'Then there's one more name we need to check out.'

'Who?'

'Victoria Bergman.'

Hurtig seems taken aback. 'Victoria Bergman?'

'Yes. A day or two before Johan went missing I had a visit from a community officer based out in Värmdö. A Göran Andersson. I haven't had time to look into the information he gave me because of all the chaos with Johan, but he told me Victoria Bergman doesn't exist.'

'Doesn't exist? But we spoke to her!'

'Exactly, but I've checked that number again and it's no longer in use. She's alive, but using a different name. Something happened twenty years ago and she disappeared off all the registers. Something happened to make Victoria Bergman go underground.'

'Her dad? He was abusing her.'

'Yes, it's probably something to do with him. But something's telling me that the Bergman line of inquiry isn't quite dead.'

'The Bergman line of inquiry? Is there really any connection to our cases?'

'I'm going by gut feeling again. I can't help wondering why these two names should show up at virtually the same time. Fate? Coincidence? Not that it matters. There's some sort of link between our cases and the Bergman and Lundström families. Do you know they both used the same solicitor, had done for years? Viggo Dürer. That can hardly be a coincidence, so I've got Åhlund checking Dürer out.'

Jeanette can see that Hurtig appreciates the significance of what she's saying.

'Both Bengt Bergman and Karl Lundström abused their own daughters, but also other children as well. You remember Bengt Bergman and the Eritrean kids? A twelve-year-old girl and a ten-year-old boy? As usual, Birgitta Bergman gave him an alibi. Same thing with Annette Lundström, always protecting her husband, even if he himself admitted to being involved in the sex trade in children from the Third World.'

'I get it. There are threads leading somewhere. I suppose the only difference is that Karl Lundström confessed, whereas Bengt Bergman denied the allegations.'

'Yes. It's one hell of a tangle of threads, but I think they all come together somewhere. All of this fits, and it fits together with our cases. The whole thing screams cover-up. We're talking about successful men, Bergman at the Swedish International Development Cooperation Agency, and Lundström at Skanska. A lot of money. Shame in their families. And we're talking about legal cases that were handled badly, and possibly even intentionally mismanaged.'

Hurtig nods.

'And there are people around these families who don't exist,' she goes on. 'Victoria Bergman doesn't exist. And a nameless child you can buy on the Net, then castrate and dump in the bushes, a child like that doesn't exist either.'

'Are you a conspiracy theorist?'

If there was any sarcasm in Hurtig's comment, it passed her by completely.

'No, I'm not. Maybe a holist, if there's such a word.'

'Holist?'

'I believe that the whole is greater than the sum of its parts. If we don't understand the context, we can never understand the details. Don't you think?'

Hurtig looks thoughtful. 'Ulrika Wendin. Annette and Linnea Lundström. Viggo Dürer. Victoria Bergman. Where do we start?'

'I suggest we start with Ulrika Wendin. I'll call her straight away.'

Assaults on children, she thinks. From beginning to end, everything comes back to those cases. Two children with no identity, the Belarussian boy Yuri Krylov, and Samuel Bai, the former child soldier from Sierra Leone. And three women who were subjected to sexual abuse in their childhoods. Victoria Bergman, Ulrika Wendin and Linnea Lundström.

There's a knock on the door, and Åhlund comes into the room.

'That was quick,' she says, looking at him expectantly.

'Yes, it was quick because Viggo Dürer's dead.'

'Dead?'

'Yes, his body was found next to his wife's after a fire on their yacht two weeks ago. Off Simrishamn.'

'An accident?'

'Yes, a leaking gas pipe. The boat went up in a matter of seconds. They didn't stand a chance.'

Åhlund hands her a note with a phone number on it. 'Call and have a word with the officer in charge of the investigation,' he says. 'Gullberg, I think his name was.'

Jeanette dials the number. It's just as well to get it out of the way at once.

Gullberg turns out to be a talkative, amiable man with a strong Skåne accent. He tells her that the coastguard got an emergency call from Viggo Dürer's phone two weeks ago. According to Dürer, the boat was on fire and he needed help. But when they got there the boat was already fully ablaze and the two bodies pretty much charcoal.

At the small boat marina they found a car registered to Henrietta Dürer, as well as a bag of the pair's belongings, including identification documents.

'What finally confirmed that they were the Dürers was their wedding rings.' Gullberg sounds pleased with himself. 'With their names and the date engraved on them. Seeing as they didn't have any family, the bodies were cremated as soon as the coroner was satisfied.'

'And it was an accident?' Jeanette asks.

'Forensics says the fire started in the gas tank. Old boat. Dodgy pipes. We don't suspect any sort of crime, if that's what you're implying.'

'I'm not implying anything,' Jeanette says, and ends the call.

Zinkens Bar

When Ulrika Wendin walks into the little bar next to the Zinkensdamm sports complex, Jeanette notices at once that the girl has dramatically lost weight. She's wearing the same top as when they last met, only now it looks like it's several sizes too big.

Ulrika sits on the chair opposite Jeanette. 'Fucking buses,' she says, tossing her bag down. 'I've just spent half an hour with some bastard ticket inspector who wouldn't accept my ticket. It cost me twelve hundred fucking kronor because some stupid bus driver had the wrong time on his stamp.'

'What can I get you?'

The smile on the girl's thin face looks strained, her gaze is flitting about and her body language is anything but relaxed. 'I'll have whatever you're having.'

They order, and Jeanette leans back on the sofa.

'Is it OK to have a cigarette while we're waiting for the food?' Ulrika gets up before Jeanette has time to reply. Restlessness seems to be the girl's defining characteristic.

'Fine.'

They go out. Ulrika perches on the window ledge outside the bar, and Jeanette offers her a cigarette. 'Ulrika, I understand that this might be difficult, but I'd like to talk about Karl Lundström. You said before that you wanted to tell me everything. Have you done that?'

Ulrika Wendin lights the cigarette, then looks wearily at Jeanette through the smoke. 'What does it matter. He's dead now, isn't he?'

'That doesn't mean we have to stop. Have you ever talked to anyone about what happened?'

The girl takes a deep drag and sighs. 'No, they dropped the preliminary investigation. No one believed me. I don't think even my mum did. The prosecutor kept going on about how there was a social safety net for people like me, but it turned out he just thought I should get psychological help for my attention-seeking behaviour. I was just a stupid teenage whore. And as for that fucking lawyer . . .'

'What about him?'

'I read his summary. The defence statement, von Kwist said it was called.'

Jeanette nods. Occasionally a defence lawyer is brought in during the preliminary investigation, even if that's fairly unusual. 'Of course, the defence statement. Go on.'

'He wrote that I lacked all credibility, that I had nothing but problems . . . With everything, from school to alcohol. Even though he'd never met me, he made out that I was nothing. Worth absolutely nothing. I was so upset that I promised myself I'd never forget his name.'

Jeanette thinks about Viggo Dürer and Kenneth von Kwist.

Abandoned cases.

Are there more? She realises that they're going to have to check. The backgrounds of both lawyer and prosecutor would have to be thoroughly looked into.

'Viggo Dürer's dead,' Jeanette says.

'And mourned by nobody.' Ulrika stubs her cigarette out on the window ledge. 'Shall we go in?'

Their food is on the table and Jeanette starts to eat, but Ulrika doesn't so much as glance at the plate of French fries. Instead she looks out of the window, clearly thinking about something and drumming her fingers restlessly on the table.

Jeanette says nothing. Waits.

'They knew each other,' Ulrika says after a while.

Jeanette puts her knife and fork down and gives her a look of encouragement. 'What do you mean? Who did?'

Ulrika Wendin hesitates at first, then takes out her mobile phone. One of the latest models, more like a little hand-held computer.

How could she afford something like that?

Ulrika touches the screen a few times, then turns it towards Jeanette.

'I found this on Flashback. Read it.'

'Flashback?'

'Yes. Just read it. You'll see.'

On the screen is a website with a sequence of comments.

One of the posts is a list of Swedes who were said to have given financial backing to a foundation called Sihtunum i Diasporan.

The list contains twenty or so names, and once Jeanette has looked through it she sees what Ulrika Wendin means.

Apart from the two names Ulrika has mentioned, she recognises another one of them.

Vita Bergen – Sofia Zetterlund's Apartment

Sofia Zetterlund is sitting on the sofa in the living room, staring into the darkness. She hasn't bothered to switch on any lights since she got home. It's almost pitch black, except for the light from the street lamps.

Sofia feels she can no longer resist. She also knows that it isn't rational to try to resist.

They're going to have to cooperate, she and Victoria. Otherwise things will only get worse.

Sofia knows she's ill. And she knows what needs to be done.

She and Victoria make up the complicated product of a shared past, but have split into two personalities in a desperate attempt to deal with the brutalities of daily life.

They have completely different ways of defending themselves, and different strategies for healing. Sofia has held her illness at bay by clinging to routines. Her work at the practice gives her a framework that muffles the chaos within her.

Victoria is governed by hatred and rage, simple solutions and black-and-white logic, where if it proves necessary everything can be cut away.

Victoria despises Sofia's weakness, her desire to blend in and adapt. Her persistent attempts to suppress all manner of injustice and apathetically accept the role of victim.

Since Victoria returned, Sofia has been full of self-loathing and has lost the ability to see a clear path ahead of her. Everything has turned into a quagmire.

Nothing is obvious any more.

Two wildly different wills must be satisfied and distilled down to one. A hopeless equation, she thinks.

It's said that a person is shaped by their fears, and Sofia has developed her personality out of fear of being Victoria. Victoria has lain dormant within Sofia, like an opposing pole, a trampoline.

Without Victoria's characteristics, Sofia will cease to be and will become nothing but an empty shell.

Without substance.

Where did Sofia Zetterlund come from? she thinks. She can't remember.

She runs her hand over her arm.

Sofia Zetterlund, she thinks. She tastes the name, is struck by the realisation that she is someone else's creation. Her arm really belongs to someone else.

Everything started with Victoria.

I am a product of another person, Sofia thinks. Of another ego. The thought makes her dizzy, and she finds it hard to breathe.

Where can she find a point of contact? Where in Victoria is the need that Sofia fulfils? She has to find that point, but to do that she has to stop being scared of Victoria's thoughts. She has to dare to look her in the eye with an open mind. Make herself receptive to everything she has devoted her whole life to avoiding.

To start with, she has to locate the point in time when her memories are her own and not Victoria's.

She thinks about the Polaroid picture. About ten years old, on a beach wearing ugly red and white clothes. It's quite clear that she doesn't remember it. That time, that sequence, belongs to Victoria.

Sofia strokes her other arm. The pale scars are Victoria's. She used to cut her arm with a razor blade or pieces of broken glass behind Aunt Elsa's house in Dala-Floda.

When did Sofia appear? Was she there at Sigtuna? Did she go inter-railing with Hannah and Jessica? The memories are all hazy, and Sofia realises that the images in her memory only become logical and clearly structured during the time she was at university, when she was twenty.

Sofia Zetterlund was accepted at Uppsala university and spent five years living in a student apartment, then she moved to Stockholm. A psychology placement at Nacka Hospital, then a couple of years working in forensic psychiatry out in Huddinge.

After that she had met Lasse and set up her own practice.

What else? Sierra Leone, obviously.

Her life suddenly feels so depressingly short and meaningless, and she knows that's because of one single person. Her dad, Bengt Bergman, stole half her life and forced her to struggle through the other half as a prisoner of routine. Work, money, lofty ambitions, be good, make half-hearted efforts at having a love life. Hold the memories at bay by staying as busy as is humanly possible.

When she was twenty she was strong enough to take over Victoria's life, putting it behind her and embarking on her own. At university there was only one person, Sofia Zetterlund, who hid Victoria away the same way she forgot about her dad's abuse. She wiped out Victoria's existence while simultaneously losing control of her.

Sofia gets up and goes out to the hall mirror. She smiles at her reflection and sees the tooth Victoria chipped in a hotel room in Copenhagen. The neck she tied a noose around. She can feel how sinuous it is, how strong.

She unbuttons her blouse and lets her hand wander inside the fabric.

Feels a mature woman's body, remembers the way Lasse and Mikael have touched it.

Imagines how it would feel if Jeanette were to touch her. Skin against skin. Jeanette's hands would be cool and soft.

Her hand moves tentatively over her skin. She shuts her eyes and reaches inside herself. Empty. She takes her blouse off and looks at herself standing there. In the mirror she traces her own shape.

The edges of the body are so definite. Where the skin stops, the world takes over.

Everything inside is me, she thinks.

She folds her arms over her chest with her hands on her shoulders, like an embrace. Her hands move up over her cheeks, stroking her lips. She shuts her eyes again. She is taken aback by a retching sensation, and the bitter taste in her mouth.

It is simultaneously familiar and unfamiliar.

Slowly Sofia takes off her trousers and pants. She looks at herself in the hall mirror. Sofia Zetterlund. Where do you come from? When did Victoria hand herself over to you?

Sofia reads her skin like a map of her own life and Victoria's.

She feels her feet, her sore heels, whose calluses never grow thick enough to stop them breaking again.

Sofia's heels.

She runs her hands up her calves, stops at her knees. She feels the scars on them and feels the grit beneath them when Bengt took her from behind and his weight pressed and rubbed her kneecaps into the grit on the path.

Victoria's knees, she thinks.

Thighs. They feel soft under her hands. She shuts her eyes and knows how they looked afterwards. The blue marks she tried to hide. Feels how the tendons on the insides ache, like when he grabbed hold of them.

Victoria's thighs.

She keeps going, towards her back, over it. Feels irregularities she's never noticed before.

She closes her eyes, and there's the smell of warm soil, the special smell she only ever noticed from the red soil of Sierra Leone.

Sofia remembers Sierra Leone, but she doesn't remember the scars on her back, and doesn't see the connection that Victoria is trying to show her. Sometimes you have to make do with symbolism, she thinks, and remembers how she woke up in a covered pit, convinced she had been buried alive by the child soldiers who ruled through rage. She feels the heaviness in her body, the threatening darkness, the smell of mouldering cloth. And she had managed to get away.

Now she regards it as a superhuman achievement, but at the time she hadn't realised that what she was doing was actually impossible.

She had been the only member of the party to survive.

The only one who managed to bridge the chasm between reality and fantasy.

Zinkens Bar

Three names. Three men.

First Karl Lundström and Viggo Dürer. Two people whose fates seemed to be connected in an odd way. But at the same time maybe it isn't so odd, Jeanette thinks. They were members of the same foundation, and would have met at meetings and dinners. When Lundström got into trouble he had contacted a solicitor he already knew. Viggo Dürer. That was how it worked. Favours given, then favours returned.

But the list of people who financed this foundation that Jeanette had never heard of before, Sihtunum i Diasporan, also included Bengt Bergman.

Father of the missing Victoria Bergman.

Jeanette Kihlberg feels the room getting smaller.

'How did you find this?' Jeanette hands the phone back and looks at the young woman opposite her.

Ulrika Wendin smiles. 'It wasn't hard. I googled it.'

I must be a bad police officer, Jeanette thinks.

'Flashback? How reliable is that?' she asks, and Ulrika laughs.

'Well, there's a lot of shit there, but a fair bit of truth. Most of it's rumours about celebrities who've fucked up. Their names show up, then when the evening papers do the same thing they can say the information is already available on the Internet. Sometimes you can't help wondering if the journalists themselves started the muckraking.'

Jeanette reflects that she's probably right. 'What sort of organisation is it? Sihtunum i Diasporan?'

Ulrika picks up her fork and starts prodding at her fries. 'Some sort of foundation. But I couldn't find out much about it . . .'

There must be something, Jeanette thinks. I'll put Hurtig onto it.

'How did Viggo Dürer die?' Ulrika looks up from her plate.

'In a fire on a boat. An accident. The Skåne police found him off Simrishamn.'

'Did he suffer?'

'I don't know. Probably.'

'And it really did happen?'

'Yes. He and his wife have been cremated and buried.'

Jeanette looks at the girl's skinny frame. Her eyes are blank, as if they're seeing right through her plate, while her hand is making aimless patterns in the Béarnaise sauce with a fry.

She needs help.

'Ulrika . . . have you ever thought about therapy?'

Ulrika glances up at Jeanette and shrugs. 'Therapy? Not likely!'

'I've got a friend who's a psychologist, she's used to working with young people. I can see you've got a lot of things bottled up. It's pretty obvious.' Jeanette pauses before going on. 'How much do you weigh? Forty-five kilos?'

Another nonchalant shrug. 'No, forty-eight.' Ulrika gives a crooked smile, and Jeanette is filled with compassion.

'I don't know if it would suit me. I'm probably too stupid for that sort of help.'

You're wrong, Jeanette thinks. Totally damn wrong.

In spite of her fragility, Jeanette can see strength in the young woman. She's going to sort this out, if someone can just give her a helping hand.

'The psychologist's name is Sofia Zetterlund. You could see her as early as next week, if you'd like to.'

She realises that's a guess, but knows Sofia well enough to be sure she'd agree. As long as Ulrika herself wants it.

'Is it OK for me to give her your number?'

Ulrika squirms. 'Well, I suppose so . . . But no funny business, all right?'

Jeanette laughs.

'No, I promise. She's good.'

Sierra Leone, 1987

'Eat up now, Victoria.' He glares at her across the breakfast table. 'When you're finished you can put a chlorine tablet in the pool. I'm going to have a swim after my morning meeting.'

It's already more than ninety-five degrees outside, and he wipes the sweat from his brow. She nods in response and pokes at the steaming, disgusting porridge. Every spoonful expands in her mouth and she hates the sweetened cinnamon he forces her to sprinkle on top of it. His colleagues from the development agency will soon be here, and he'll leave the table. Then she can throw away the rest of her breakfast.

'How are your studies going?'

She doesn't look at him, but can feel him observing her. 'Fine,' she says flatly. 'We're reading Maslow. It's about needs and motivation.' She doesn't think he knows about Maslow, and hopes his ignorance will shut him up.

She's right. 'Motivation,' he mutters. 'Yes, well, you could do with some of that.' He looks away and goes back to his breakfast.

Needs, she thinks.

While she pretends to eat the porridge she thinks about what she's read about the hierarchy of needs, which starts with physiological needs. Needs such as food and sleep. She thinks how he is systematically denying them to her.

After that comes the need for security, then the need for love and belonging, and then the need for esteem. All things he is denying her, and will continue to deny her.

At the top of the hierarchy is the need for self-actualisation, a term she can't even understand. She doesn't know who she is or what she wants; her self-actualisation is out of reach because it's beyond her, outside her own ego. As far as her needs are concerned, he has denied her everything.

The door to the terrace opens, and a little girl, a few years younger than Victoria, stands in the doorway.

'There you are!' he says with a smile on his lips as he looks at the girl, who works as a general maid. Victoria has liked her since the very first day.

Bengt has also taken a shine to the slender, happy little girl, and has been courting her with compliments and ingratiating remarks.

At dinner on the first evening he decided that she should move out of the servants' quarters and into the main house for practical reasons. From that day Victoria has slept more soundly than she has for a long time, and even Mum seems happy with the arrangement.

You blind cow, she thinks. One day it's all going to catch up with you, and you'll have to pay the price for keeping your eyes closed.

The little girl comes into the kitchen. She looks scared at first, but calms down slightly when she catches sight of Victoria and Birgitta.

'You can clear the table when we've finished,' he says, turning towards the girl, then gets interrupted by the sound of car engines and wheels on the drive outside the open window. 'Damn, they're here already.'

He gets up, goes over to the girl and ruffles her hair. 'Did you sleep well?' Victoria can see that the girl probably hasn't slept at all. Her eyes are swollen and bloodshot, and she looks nervous as he touches her.

'Sit down and eat now.'

He winks at the girl and hands her a banknote, which she tucks away at once before sitting down beside Victoria.

'There,' he says before he goes. 'You could teach my Victoria a thing or two about appetite.' He nods towards the plate and disappears into the hall, laughing.

Victoria knows that the evening will be difficult. If he's in this good a mood in the morning, then the day usually ends with darkness.

He's behaving like some fucking colonialist, she thinks. Swedish International Development Cooperation Agency and human rights? That's just a cover for prancing about like some bastard slave owner.

She looks at the skinny little girl, who is now concentrating on her breakfast.

What has he done to her? She has some bruises on her neck, and a scratch on her earlobe.

'Well, I must say . . .' Mum sighs. 'I'm going to sort out the laundry. You two can look after yourselves, can't you?'

Victoria doesn't answer. *Well, I must say*? You never say anything. You're a silent, blind shadow without any definition.

The girl has finished eating, and Victoria pushes her plate over to her. She lights up, and Victoria can't help smiling back as the girl gets to work on the grey sludge surrounded by lukewarm milk.

'Would you like to help me with the pool? I can show you what to do.' The girl looks at her over her dish, and nods between mouthfuls.

When she's finished eating they go out into the garden and Victoria shows her where the chlorine tablets are kept.

The Swedish International Development Cooperation Agency has a number of houses on the outskirts of Freetown, and they live in one of the largest, but also the one that is most secluded. The white three-storey building is surrounded by a high wall, and the entrance is guarded by armed men in camouflage.

Victoria can hear the men's voices from inside the house. They've moved the conference here because the situation in Freetown is too unstable at the moment.

'You pull open the edge of the pack,' Victoria says. 'Then you carefully put the tablet into the water.'

She can see doubt in the girl's eyes, and remembers that the pool is strictly out of bounds for the staff.

'It's OK,' Victoria says. 'It's my pool as well, so I can say what gets done to it, and I'm saying you can.'

The girl smiles the triumphant smile of someone who for a fleeting moment is allowed to join the elite, and with an elaborate gesture she drops her hand into the pool. Her hand moves up and down before she lets go, and she watches as the tablet slowly sinks to the bottom. She pulls out her wet hand and looks at it.

'Was the water nice?' Victoria asks, and receives a nod in reply.

'Shall we have a swim before he comes?' she goes on.

The girl shakes her head and says that isn't allowed. Victoria dismisses her concerns. 'I'm telling you that you can,' she says, glancing over at the house and starting to get undressed. 'Don't worry about them, we'll hear when they've almost finished.'

She dives into the pool and swims two lengths underwater.

She floats for a while just above the bottom, and enjoys the pressure on her eardrums. The water between her and the world up above forms a dense shield.

When her air begins to run out she swims on and, as she approaches the edge of the pool, she sees that the girl has put her legs in the water.

Victoria bobs up beside her and is met by the blinding sun. The girl is sitting on the steps and smiling with the sun behind her.

'Like fish,' she says, pointing at Victoria, who laughs back.

'Come in as well. We can say I made you do it.'

It doesn't take long to persuade her, but she refuses to swim in just her pants and bra like Victoria.

'Well, you need to take your sandals off, and you can put this on.' She tosses her the thin vest she was wearing before she got in.

As the girl takes off her dress and puts on the vest, Victoria sees that she has several large bruises on her stomach and at the base of her spine. The feeling that washes over her is very odd.

The first thing she feels is rage at what he's done, then relief that it wasn't her that got beaten.

Then comes a creeping sense of shame, along with a new feeling she's never experienced before. She feels shame at being her father's daughter, but at the same time there's something that makes her lose any desire to teach the girl to swim.

She looks at the slender figure smiling as she stands at the edge of the pool in a vest that's far too big for her. Her own vest, with the crest of Sigtuna College on it.

She feels suddenly sick when she sees the girl wearing her own clothes, getting into the shallow end of the pool. Victoria tries to see what it is that he sees in the girl. She's beautiful and unspoiled, she's younger and she probably doesn't say no to him like Victoria has started to do.

Who the hell are you, thinking you can take my place? she thinks.

'Come over here.' Victoria tries to sound friendly, but she can hear that her voice makes it sound more like an order.

A memory comes into her mind. A little boy whom she loved, but who let her down and then drowned. How easy it would be, she thinks.

'Let yourself fall forward in the water, and I'll hold you from underneath.'

Victoria goes and stands next to the girl, who hesitates. 'Come on, don't be scared. I'll hold you.'

She slips gently into the water.

She feels as light as a small child in Victoria's arms.

The girl moves her arms and legs according to the instructions, but when Victoria lets go of her she stops swimming at once and starts to flail about instead. Victoria gets annoyed each time this happens, but puts up with it, slowly but surely steering the girl into deeper water.

She won't be able to reach the bottom here, Victoria thinks as she holds her head up by treading water.

She lets go.

Kronoberg – Police Headquarters

'Sihtunum i Diasporan? What does that mean?' Jens Hurtig looks inquisitively at Jeanette Kihlberg.

'It's runic Swedish for Sigtuna, and classical Greek for living in exile. So, basically, it means Sigtuna in exile, and it's a foundation made up of people who used to live in Sigtuna. The common denominator seems to be that the members all have, or had, some connection to the boarding school there.'

'The boarding school? The one Jan Guillou was at?'

'No, not that one. This one's where the king went to school. Sigtuna College for the Humanities is the largest and most prestigious boarding school in Sweden. Olof Palme went there, along with Povel Ramel and Peter and Marcus Wallenberg, if those names mean anything?' Jeanette grins, and Hurtig smiles back.

He closes the door and sits down on the other side of the desk. 'So are you saying the king supports this foundation, then?'

'No, the names of the members aren't that well known, but I'm sure you'll recognise at least three of them.'

Hurtig lets out a whistle when Jeanette shows him the list of donors.

'Dürer, Lundström and Bergman are said to have donated large sums of money to the foundation since the mid-seventies,' Jeanette goes on. 'But there's no record of the foundation in local council records, which is odd seeing as it's active in Sweden.'

'Anything else?'

'They used to own a property in Denmark, but that's been sold off. The only asset of any value was a motor yacht, the *Gilah*. The boat that Dürer and his wife were on when they died.'

'Interesting. What does it say in the description of the foundation's activities?'

Jeanette pulls out a sheet of paper and reads from it: '"The foundation's goals are to combat poverty and promote children's living conditions in all corners of the world."'

'A paedophile who helps children, then?'

'Two paedophiles, at least. The list contains twenty names, and we know for sure that two are paedophiles. Bergman and Lundström. That's ten per cent. The other names aren't known to me, apart from Dürer, who acted as the lawyer for both men. But more than two of them might be of interest. If you get my meaning?'

'I get it. Anything else?'

'Nothing we don't already know.' Jeanette leans across the desk and lowers her voice. 'Hurtig, you're better at computers than I am. Do you think it would be possible to trace whoever posted this on Flashback? Could you do that?'

Hurtig smiles but doesn't answer her question. 'Just because I'm a man doesn't mean I'm better than you at computers.'

'No, not because you're a man,' she says. 'Because you're younger than me, and you still play bloody computer games.'

Hurtig looks taken aback. 'Computer games? I wouldn't say –'

'Rubbish. Whenever we're out in the city you always linger by the windows of the game shops, and you've got calluses on your fingertips, sometimes even blisters. Once when we were having lunch you said the guy making the pizzas looked like your character in *GTA*. You're a games addict, Hurtig. No question.'

'OK, but . . .' He looks hesitant. 'Tracing the poster? Isn't that data infringement?'

'No one need know anything. If we get an IP address, we might be able to get a name. Maybe that will take us forward, maybe not. We don't need to make a big deal out of it. We're not going to harass anyone, we're not going to spy on them or keep a record of their opinion. All I want is a name.'

'OK, I'll give it a try,' Hurtig goes on. 'If it doesn't work, I might know someone who can help.'

'Great. Then there's the list of donors. Check them out while you're at it, and I'll try to get hold of Victoria Bergman.'

Once Hurtig has left the room she looks up Victoria Bergman in the police database, but, as expected, draws a blank.

There are two Victoria Bergmans on file, but neither of them is the right age to match the Victoria who was at Sigtuna.

The next step is the population database, and Jeanette logs in to the tax authority's register of all living Swedish citizens.

There are thirty-two different Victoria Bergmans.

Most of them have the more usual Swedish spelling, Viktoria, but that doesn't mean they can be automatically dismissed. Spelling is something that can change over time, and Jeanette remembers a classmate at school who swapped her Ss for Zs and at a stroke changed the mundane Susanne into the exotic Zuzanne. A few years later Zuzanne was dead from a heroin overdose.

She expands her search, and brings up the tax returns of people on the list.

Returns from all but one of them.

At number twenty-two on the list is a Victoria Bergman registered in Värmdö.

Daughter of Bengt Bergman the rapist.

Jeanette alters her search to bring up the tax return for the year before, but it's the same thing there. Victoria Bergman evidently doesn't bother declaring information about her income and possible deductions.

She goes back ten years, but there's nothing.

Not a single piece of information.

Just a name, an ID number including her date of birth and an address out in Värmdö.

Jeanette gets the bit between her teeth and searches all the registers she has access to, but no matter how hard she looks, all she finds is confirmation of what Göran Andersson from the Värmdö police told her.

Victoria Bergman had lived at the same place since she was a child, had never earned a single krona, and never had any known expenditures, no credit rating, no debts with the enforcement office and not a single hospital visit in the past twenty years.

She decides to call the tax authority herself sometime during the day to find out if there might be a mistake.

Then she remembers that she spoke to Hurtig about putting together a perpetrator profile, and comes to think of Sofia.

Maybe it's time to get that started.

What had originally been a long shot might not actually be such a bad idea. As far as she can tell, Sofia has enough experience to be able to come up with a provisional profile.

But, at the same time, it could be disastrous to rely too heavily on a description and trust a psychological evaluation entirely.

It was almost as common for an investigation to be misdirected by a poorly thought-out perpetrator profile as to be helped by a decent one. Jeanette thinks about Niklas Lindgren, the so-called Haga Man. Hadn't that investigation been hampered by the fact that the profile had been hopelessly wrong? Yes, that was the one.

Many of the country's most prominent forensic psychiatrists had declared that the perpetrator must be slightly odd, lacking close friends and intimate relationships.

When he was later arrested for eight brutal rapes and attempted murders, he turned out to be an outwardly pleasant father of two, and had been in the same job and the same relationship since he was a young man.

So she'll have to be careful and not let herself be led by Sofia Zetterlund.

Well, all or nothing. She doesn't actually have much to lose. Anyway, she needs to talk to Sofia about Ulrika Wendin. She dials the number of the practice at Mariatorget and goes over to stand by the window.

Outside, Kronoberg Park is deserted apart from one young man aimlessly walking his dog. Jeanette watches with idle interest as the dog keeps getting its lead caught around a rubbish bin, stops and looks expectantly at its master.

Ann-Britt answers, and puts Jeanette through at once.

'Hi,' Jeanette says. 'What do you know about putting together a perpetrator profile?'

'What?' Sofia replies, and Jeanette thinks she sounds calm and relaxed. 'Is that you, Jeanette?'

'Yes, who else?'

'I should have realised. Straight to the point, as usual!' Sofia falls silent, and Jeanette hears her leaning back in her chair as it creaks. 'You want to know what I know about perpetrator profiling?' she goes on. 'In purely practical terms not very much, but I presume you study the most plausible demographic, social and behavioural characteristics that the perpetrator might be thought to have. Then I'd probably start by looking at the group where he's most likely to be found, and with a bit of luck –'

'Spot on!' Jeanette interrupts, pleased that Sofia has begun speculating without any hesitation. 'These days we actually call it case analysis,' she goes on. 'That's less loaded with expectations.' She pauses before continuing. 'The point of it, like you said, is to reduce the number of possible suspects and hopefully be able to direct an investigation towards one particular person.'

'Don't you ever rest?' Sofia exclaims.

It's only been a few days since Johan was discharged from hospital, and Jeanette has already thrown herself back into her work. Is that what Sofia means? That she's emotionally cold and rational? But how else is she supposed to be?

'You know I do,' she replies, uncertain whether she should feel insulted or cared for. 'But I could really use your help with this. For various reasons there's no one else I can ask.' She realises she has to be honest. If Sofia doesn't accept the job, Jeanette has no one else to turn to.

'OK,' Sofia says after a brief hesitation. 'I presume the whole thing is based on the idea that everything we do in our lives is done in line with our personality type. So a compulsive person will usually have a tidy desk and won't usually wear a shirt that hasn't been ironed.'

'Exactly,' Jeanette says. 'And by reconstructing how a crime was committed, you can draw conclusions about the person who committed it.'

'And now you want my help?'

'We're dealing with a probable serial killer, and we've got a few names to go on. Some description and a few other details.' She leaves a dramatic pause to underline the importance of what she's about to say. 'Whoever does the case analysis has to avoid looking at any possible suspects. That would just get in the way of seeing the whole picture; it would be a filter that made it harder to see clearly.'

Sofia is silent, and Jeanette can hear her breathing get faster, but doesn't say anything.

'Could we meet at my house later this evening and talk some more?' Jeanette asks, to catch Sofia in case she's starting to have doubts. 'There's something else I'd like to ask you about.'

'Really? What?'

'We can talk about it tonight, if that works with you?'

'Sure. I'll be there,' Sofia replies in a tone of voice that is suddenly utterly devoid of enthusiasm.

They hang up, and Jeanette is struck once again by the fact that she knows nothing about Sofia.

Realising you like someone can take a matter of minutes, but getting to know them can take years.

Although Jeanette wants to get closer to Sofia, it feels like too much of a challenge. But she can't help it. She wants to give it a try, at least.

She decides to call Åke's mum and arrange for Johan to stay at his grandparents' over the weekend.

He'll be safe with them, and could probably do with a change. Someone to make a fuss over him and give him their undivided attention. Everything she herself can't offer right now.

Åke's mum is happy to help, and they agree that she'll pick him up that evening.

Then there's the phone call about Victoria Bergman.

The telephone system at the tax authority makes no allowances for who's calling, and Detective Superintendent Jeanette Kihlberg waits patiently in the line.

A metallic computerised voice informs her in a friendly but intractable way that there are thirty-seven advisers dealing with calls, and that she is number twenty-nine in the queue. The waiting time is estimated to be fourteen minutes.

Jeanette presses the button to put the call on speakerphone, then uses the time to water the plants and empty the bin while the monotonous voice slowly counts down.

You are number twenty-two in the line. Waiting time is eleven minutes.

Someone must once have recorded every possible combination of numbers, she thinks.

There's a click from the phone, followed by a crackle. 'Tax authority, how can I help?'

Jeanette introduces herself and the adviser apologises for the delay, then asks why she didn't use the direct line. Jeanette explains that she wasn't aware that there was one, and that the wait had given her time for a bit of reflection and thought.

The man laughs and asks why she's calling, and when she explains that she wants to know absolutely everything about a Victoria Bergman, born in 1970 and registered in Värmdö, he asks her to wait.

After a couple of minutes he comes back, sounding bemused.

'I presume it's Victoria Bergman, 700607, that you're interested in?'

'Maybe. I hope so.'

'In that case there's a bit of a problem.'

'Oh. What kind of problem?'

'Well, all I can find is a referral to Nacka District Court. Otherwise nothing.'

'So what exactly does it say?'

The adviser clears his throat. 'I'll read it out. "According to a decision by Nacka District Court, this individual's identity is protected. All enquiries must therefore be directed to the aforementioned authority."'

'And that's all?'

'Yes.' The adviser sighs laconically.

Jeanette thanks him, hangs up, then calls the police operator and asks to be put through to Nacka District Court. Preferably via a direct line.

The court clerk isn't quite as amenable as the adviser at the tax authority, but promises to send everything they have on Victoria Bergman as soon as possible.

Bloody bureaucrat, Jeanette thinks, before wishing the clerk a pleasant evening and hanging up.

At twenty past four she receives an email from the court.

Jeanette Kihlberg opens the attached document. To her disappointment, the information from Nacka District Court covers no more than three lines.

VICTORIA BERGMAN, 1970-XX-XX-XXXX.
CASE CLASSIFIED.
ALL INFORMATION DESTROYED.

Gamla Enskede – Kihlberg House

Jeanette hears the car arrive as it pulls into the drive and parks behind her Audi.

She has butterflies in her stomach.

Before she goes to let Sofia in she checks the mirror and adjusts her hair.

Maybe I should have put some make-up on, she thinks. But seeing as she doesn't usually, it would only feel odd and plastered on. She doesn't really know how to do it. She can manage a bit of lipstick and mascara, but after that?

She opens the door and Sofia Zetterlund comes into the hall, closing the door behind her.

'Hello, welcome!' Jeanette gives Sofia a light hug, but is worried about holding her for too long. Doesn't want to be too obvious.

Too obvious about what? she wonders as she lets go.

'Would you like a glass of wine?'

'Please.' Sofia is looking at her with a slight smile. 'I've missed you.'

Jeanette smiles back and wonders why she had felt nervous. She looks at Sofia and notices that she looks harassed.

Jeanette goes into the kitchen and Sofia follows her.

'Where's Johan?' Sofia asks.

'He's with his grandparents for the weekend,' Jeanette replies. 'Åke's mum picked him up a little while ago. He barely said goodbye before he left. Clearly it's only me he's refusing to talk to.'

'Wait him out. It'll pass, believe me.'

Sofia gazes around the kitchen, as if she's trying to avoid looking Jeanette in the eye. 'Do you know any more about what happened at Gröna Lund?'

Jeanette sighs and opens a bottle of wine. 'He says he met a girl who offered him some beer. He doesn't remember anything after that. At least that's what he's saying.'

Jeanette hands Sofia a glass.

'Do you believe him?' Sofia asks, taking it.

'I don't know. But he's clearly feeling better now, and I've made up my mind not to be the nagging mother. I won't get anything out of him that way.'

Sofia looks thoughtful. 'Would you like me to get him an appointment with Childhood and Adolescent Psychiatry?'

'God, no! He'd be livid. What I reckon he needs is normality, like a mother who's home when he gets back from school.'

'So you and Johan agree that everything's your fault?' Sofia says.

Jeanette freezes. My fault, she thinks, tasting the words. Doing the wrong thing for your child tastes bitter, it tastes of overflowing sinks and filthy floors. She fixes her gaze on Sofia and hears herself ask what she means.

Sofia puts her hand on Jeanette's with a smile. 'Just relax,' she says comfortingly. 'What happened could be a reaction to your separation, and he's pinning the blame on you because you're closest to him.'

'He thinks I've let him down, you mean?'

'Yes,' Sofia replies in the same gentle voice. 'Which is obviously irrational. Åke's the one who let him down. Maybe Johan regards you and Åke as a single entity. You're the parents who let him down. Åke's betrayal becomes your shared betrayal as parents . . .' She pauses before going on. 'Sorry, it sounds like I'm teasing you.'

'Don't worry. But how do we move on from here? How does anyone forgive a betrayal?' Jeanette takes a large sip from her glass before pushing it dejectedly away from her across the table.

The softness in Sofia's face vanishes and her voice gets harder. 'You don't forgive betrayal. But you learn to live with it.'

They sit in silence, gazing at each other.

Jeanette understands, albeit reluctantly, what she means. Life is full of betrayals, and if you don't learn to live with that, you can't really keep going.

She leans back and lets out a long breath, simultaneously letting go of the day's accumulated tension and anxiety about Johan.

A deep breath in, and her brain starts to work.

'Sofia,' Jeanette says hesitantly, 'I'd like you to meet a girl I know. Well, actually, I've said she could see you, which might have been a bit stupid, but . . .'

She stops herself to give Sofia a chance to say it's OK, and when she looks at her she gets a nod in response.

'She's pretty messed up, and I don't think she's capable of sorting things out on her own.'

'What sort of problems has she got?'

'Well, I don't really know that much, except that she encountered Karl Lundström.'

'Ah,' Sofia says. 'OK, that's good enough for me. I'll check what appointments I've got and let you know tomorrow.'

The look on Sofia's face is mysterious. Her smile seems almost shy.

'You're very lovely,' Jeanette says, relaxing in the awareness that she isn't surprised Sofia is willing to help. When it comes to offering help, she never hesitates.

'I presume Lundström is no longer suspected of being the killer, seeing as you want a profile?'

Jeanette snorts. 'Well, to start with, he's dead, but when it comes down to it, I think he was basically just the scapegoat. What do you know about sexually motivated killers?'

'You see? Straight to the point, no messing around. There are two types. Organised and chaotic. The organised ones often come from socially affluent backgrounds, at least superficially, and usually seem to be unlikely murderers. They plan their killings and leave few clues. They tie up and torture their victims before they kill them, and they seek out their victims in places where they themselves can't be traced.'

'And the other type?'

'They're the chaotic sexual killers. Often they come from difficult backgrounds and carry out their killings randomly. Sometimes they even know their victims. Do you remember the Vampire?'

'No, not off the top of my head.'

'He killed his two stepsisters and finished up by drinking their blood. I think he even ate . . .' Sofia falls silent and makes a disgusted face before going on. 'Admittedly, a lot of murderers exhibit both types of characteristic, but the evidence supports the basic division. I assume different types of killers leave different types of evidence at a crime scene.'

Once again she is struck by Sofia's speed. 'God, you're amazing! Are you sure you've never put together a perpetrator profile before?'

'Never. But I know how to read, I'm a trained psychologist, I've worked with psychopaths and so on, blah, blah, blah.'

They laugh, and Jeanette realises how much she likes Sofia and her abrupt switches between seriousness and humour. The ability to take life seriously enough that it's possible to laugh about it. About everything.

She thinks of Åke's bitter attitude, and the way he always seemed to be struggling under some physical burden that she could never understand. After all, he never took any responsibility for anything.

She lets her eyes follow the contours of Sofia's face.

Her narrow neck, her high cheekbones.

Her lips.

She looks at her hands, and the well-manicured nails that are painted a pale mother-of-pearl colour. So pure, she thinks, aware that she's thought the same thing before.

She's here now, open. What happens next only time will tell.

Gamla Enskede – Kihlberg House

Sofia is sitting on the sofa beside someone she has learned to like. She's more and more drawn to Jeanette, and she knows why. There's a physical attraction. But she also feels that Jeanette has noticed the darkness inside her. She feels safe with Jeanette even though she can't come to grips with who she is and what she's after.

Jeanette surprises her and challenges her, while at the same time genuinely seeming to respect her. And that's the foundation for her attraction.

Sofia takes a deep breath, and notices the sound of Jeanette's breathing accompanied by the rain drumming against the window ledge.

On impulse she agreed to help Jeanette with her case, but she's already starting to regret it.

In purely rational terms, Jeanette's suggestion ought to terrify her, she knows that. But at the same time there's an opportunity to exploit the situation. She'll find out all about the police investigation, and will get the chance to misdirect them.

Jeanette is calmly and factually telling her the details of the murders.

At the same time there is the awareness of who she is, who she shouldn't be. Who she doesn't *want* to be.

'They had marks on their backs, suggesting that they had been whipped.'

Deep inside her consciousness doors are being thrown open. She remembers the marks on her own back.

She wants to leave every ego behind, to be stripped down to her bare bones.

Sofia realises that she can never be integrated with Victoria as long as she doesn't accept what she's done. She has to understand, and she has to regard Victoria's actions as her own.

'And they were also mutilated. Their genitals had been cut off.'

Sofia feels an urge to escape into simplicity, to shut the door on Victoria, lock her away deep inside and hope that she'll slowly wither away.

Now she must pretend like an actress reading a script, and let her character come from within.

And that's going to take more than empathy.

It's about *becoming* the other person.

'One of the boys was completely desiccated, but another had been preserved in an almost professional way. His blood had been removed and replaced with formaldehyde.'

They sit without saying anything for a while. Sofia can feel how sweaty her hands are. She wipes them against her leg before she speaks.

The words come by themselves. The lies come automatically.

'I need to study the information you've given me, but for the time being I think we're talking about a man between thirty and forty years old. Access to anaesthetic suggests that he works in the health sector. Maybe a doctor, nurse, vet, something like that. But, like I said, I need to analyse this more closely. I'll have to get back to you.'

Jeanette gives her a look of gratitude.

Mariatorget – Sofia Zetterlund's Office

Sofia is sitting at the desk in her office eating lunch. The day's schedule is tight after Jeanette persuaded her to see Ulrika Wendin.

As she pushes the remnants of the fast food into the bin, her laptop chimes.

A new email.

The sender brings her up short.

Annette Lundström?

She opens the email and reads it.

Hello, I know you met with my husband. I'd like to talk to you about Karl and Linnea, and I'd be grateful if you could call me at the number below as soon as possible.

Interesting, she thinks, looking at the time. Five to one. Ulrika will be there soon, but she still picks up her phone and dials the number.

Ulrika sits down and crosses her legs, leans her elbows on the armrests, and clasps her hands together in her lap. Sofia does the same.

It's all about mirroring, copying physical signals such as body movement and facial expressions. Ulrika Wendin needs to recognise herself in Sofia, and feel that she's dealing with someone who's on her side. If it succeeds, Ulrika will start to mirror Sofia, and then she can use tiny, scarcely noticeable changes in her own body language to get the girl to feel more relaxed.

Right now her arms and legs are closed, and her elbows are jutting out into the room like thorns.

Her whole body radiates insecurity.

You can't be more defensive than this, Sofia thinks, lifting one leg from the other before leaning forward.

'Hello, Ulrika,' she begins. 'Thanks for coming.'

The first meeting is all about establishing trust. And Ulrika needs to feel that trust immediately. She lets Ulrika direct the conversation wherever she feels comfortable.

Sofia listens, leaning back with interest.

Ulrika explains that she hardly ever meets other people.

She might miss interaction, but whenever she ends up in a social situation she is gripped by panic. She once took an adult education course. On the first day she went along, hoping to make new friends and gain new skills, but her body stopped abruptly at the entrance to the college.

She never managed to go inside.

'I don't understand how I dared come here,' Ulrika says with a nervous giggle.

Sofia realises that the girl is giggling to hide the seriousness of what she just said. 'Do you remember what was going through your mind when you opened the door?'

Ulrika takes the question seriously and thinks about it.

'"Let's do this," I think,' she says in surprise. 'But that sounds really weird – why would I be thinking that?'

'Only you can know the answer to that,' Sofia says with a smile.

She realises that she's dealing with a girl who's made up her mind.

One who doesn't want to be a victim any more.

From what Ulrika tells her, Sofia understands that she's suffering from numerous problems. Nightmares, compulsive behaviour, panic attacks, stiffness, insomnia and feelings of disgust towards both eating and drinking.

Ulrika says the only thing she can get down without difficulty is beer.

Sofia realises that the girl needs consistent support, and a strong hand to hold.

Someone has to open her eyes and show her that another life is possible, and that it's right in front of her.

Ideally Sofia would like to see her twice a week.

If there's too long between sessions there's a risk that she'll start to question and doubt things, which would make the process much harder.

But Ulrika doesn't want to.

No matter how Sofia tries, she can't persuade Ulrika to agree to more than one session every two weeks, even when she says she won't charge.

As Ulrika leaves, she says something that worries Sofia.

'There is one thing . . .'

Sofia looks up from her notes. 'Yes?'

Ulrika looks so small. 'I don't know . . . Sometimes I have trouble . . . knowing what actually happened.'

Sofia tells her to shut the door and come and sit down again.

'Tell me more,' she says, as gently as she can.

'I . . . sometimes I think I invited them to humiliate me and rape me. Of course I know that isn't true, but some mornings when I wake up I'm convinced that I did. I'm so ashamed . . . and then I realise that it wasn't like that.'

Sofia looks hard at Ulrika. 'It's good that you're telling me this. Feelings like that are normal when you've been through the things you have. You take on some of the guilt. I appreciate that it doesn't feel any less unpleasant because I say it's normal, but you're going to have to trust me. Above all, you're going to have to trust me when I say that you didn't do anything wrong.'

Sofia waits for Ulrika's reaction, but she just sits in the chair, nodding apathetically.

'Are you sure you wouldn't like to come back next week?' Sofia tries again. 'I've got two appointments available, one on Wednesday and one on Thursday.'

Ulrika stands up. She looks forlornly down at the floor, as if she's made a fool of herself. 'No, I don't think so. I have to go now.'

Sofia resists the urge to get up and grab her arm to make her see how serious this is. It's too soon for that sort of gesture. Instead she takes a deep breath and composes herself. 'OK. Call me if you change your mind. I'll keep those appointments free just in case.'

'Bye,' Ulrika says, opening the door. 'And thanks.'

Ulrika disappears out the door, and Sofia remains behind her desk as she hears her get into the lift.

The way Ulrika thanked her lingers as a sign that she actually got through to her. From that single word Sofia deduces that Ulrika isn't used to being seen for who she really is.

Sofia makes up her mind to call Ulrika the next day to see if she's reconsidered and is ready to come back the following week. And if that doesn't work, she'll suggest that Jeanette go and see Ulrika during the week. She mustn't let go of her.

She wants to help a new life to rise from the ashes.

Sofia wraps her arms around herself and feels the irregular scars on her back.

Victoria's scars.

Sierra Leone, 1987

She grabbed hold of the boy's hair, so hard that she tore out a big clump. In her hand the roots looked like little threads.

She hit him in the head, the face and the body and she hit him for a long time. Dazed, she stood up, left the jetty and fetched a large stone down by the shore.

It isn't me, she said, letting the boy's body sink into the water. Now you must swim . . .

The girl immediately begins to thrash her arms and legs, but swallows a lot of water and sinks.

Victoria pulls away a metre or so and looks on.

Twice the girl comes up to the surface, coughing, only to sink again when she tries unsuccessfully to reach the edge. But Victoria swims calmly over to her, grabs her under the arms and pulls her up. The girl's legs won't carry her, and she collapses on the terrace beside the pool. She rolls onto her side and throws up violently. First comes the chlorinated water, then the sticky grey strings of the porridge she ate for breakfast.

After a couple of minutes the girl calms down and Victoria rocks her in her arms. 'You see,' Victoria says, 'you managed to kick me, and I was nearly knocked out.'

The girl is sobbing, and after a while she sniffs a silent apology.

'Never mind,' Victoria says, hugging her. 'But we probably shouldn't tell anyone about this.'

The girl shakes her head. 'Sorry,' she repeats, and Victoria no longer hates her.

Ten minutes later she's rinsing off the terrace with the garden hose. The girl is dressed again, and is sitting on the sunlounger under the umbrella on the veranda. Her short hair is already dry, and when she smiles at Victoria it looks like she's embarrassed. A regretful smile at having done something stupid.

Alternate between caressing and hitting, first protecting and then destroying, Victoria thinks. He's taught me that.

The voices from the living room have fallen silent, the windows are closed, and Victoria hopes that no one heard anything. The front door opens, and four men get into the big black Mercedes that's parked in the drive. Her dad stands on the steps and watches the car disappear through the gates. Then, with his head bowed and his hands in his pockets, he walks down the steps and round onto the path that leads towards the pool. Victoria can see that he's disappointed.

The girl looks away when he takes off his pants and changes into his swimming trunks. Victoria can't help giggling at the tight, flowery-patterned relics from the seventies that he refuses to replace.

Suddenly he turns and takes two steps towards her.

She can see in his eyes what's going to happen.

He tried to hit her once before, but on that occasion she grabbed a saucepan and hit him over the head with it. Since then he's never tried again. Until now.

No, not my face, Victoria thinks before everything turns red and she falls backwards against the veranda wall.

Another blow hits her forehead, then one in the stomach. Her eyes flare and she bends double.

Lying on the stones she hears the sound of the hose, then there is a burning sensation across her back and she screams out loud. He remains standing behind her and she dare not open her eyes. The heat spreads across her face and over her back.

She hears his heavy footsteps as he walks past her, down to the pool. He's always been too cowardly to dive in, and uses the steps before gliding out into the water. She knows he will swim ten lengths as usual, no more, no less. When he's done he gets out and comes back to her. 'Look at me,' he sighs, running his hand down her back.

She can feel that the nozzle of the hose has torn a large cut below her left shoulder blade.

'You look bloody awful.' He gets up and holds his hand out to her. 'Come inside and we'll get you patched up.'

When he's taken care of her wounds, she sits on the sofa wrapped in a towel, hiding her smile behind it. Hit, caress, protect, destroy, she repeats soundlessly as he explains that their negotiations have hit problems and that they'll therefore have to go back home soon.

She takes pleasure in the fact that the Freetown project has evidently turned into a fiasco.

Nothing has worked.

He explains that the agency's failed irrigation project in the north of the country has had consequences. He says the money disappears, people disappear, and the slogans about constructive nationalism and a new order are about as empty as the government's coffers.

Thirty people have died from poisoning, and there's talk of sabotage and curses. The project's been stopped, and they'll be going home four months early.

When he leaves the room she sits there and looks at his collection of fetish figures.

He's managed to get hold of twenty wooden sculptures of female figures, and they're lined up on the desk, ready to be packed away.

Colonialist, Victoria thinks. Here to collect trophies.

There's also a life-sized face mask. An ancestral mask from the Tenme tribe that reminds her of their servant girl.

As she runs her fingers over the rough wooden sculpture, she imagines that the face is alive. She strokes its eyes, nose and mouth. The surface begins to feel warm under her fingertips, and the wooden fibres become real skin under her touch.

She no longer dislikes the servant girl, because she has realised that there isn't any rivalry between them.

She realised that down by the pool.

She is more important to him, their servant girl is merely a toy, a wooden doll, a trophy.

He's going to take the mask home.

Hang it up somewhere, maybe in the living room.

Something exotic to show to dinner guests.

But for Victoria the wooden mask will be more than an ornament. With her hands she can give it a life, a soul.

If he takes the mask home with him, then she can take the girl. She has no rights, she's almost a slave. No one will miss her, because not only does she have no rights, she also has no parents.

The girl has told Victoria that her mother died in childbirth, and that her father was executed when he was found guilty of stealing a chicken. An ancient way of testing guilt known as trial by red water.

His empty stomach was filled with dry rice, then he was forced to drink half a barrel of water mixed with bark from the cola tree. Vomiting red water is a sign of innocence, but he couldn't vomit. He just swelled up with the rice and was beaten to death with a spade.

She has no one here to take care of her, Victoria thinks. She can come back to Sweden, and her name will be Solace.

That means comfort, and she can share the sickness with Solace.

She will also carry something else back to Sweden.

A seed that has been sown inside her.

Gamla Enskede – Kihlberg House

Jeanette sees that the lights aren't on in the house and realises that Johan isn't home yet. His weekend with his grandparents doesn't seem to have made much difference. He's just as reserved as before, and she's at a complete loss. She doesn't want to admit the problem to herself. Plenty of kids are troubled, but not her little boy.

He's so fragile now that she suspects that the slightest misunderstanding might break him. He probably never imagined that she and Åke would split up. After all, they'd always been there for him.

Had it been her fault? Had she, like Billing believed, worked too hard and not devoted enough time to her family?

She thinks about Åke, who had taken the first opportunity to leave a grey, uneventful life with his wife and child out in the suburbs.

No, she thinks. It isn't my fault. And we're probably better off this way, even if it's hard on Johan.

Once she's inside the house and has turned the lights on, she goes into the kitchen and warms up the remains of the pea soup from last night. The wound in her head is starting to heal, and the stitches itch terribly.

She pours herself a glass of beer and opens the paper.

The first thing she sees is a picture of Prosecutor Kenneth von Kwist, who has written an article about the lack of security in Sweden's prisons.

Fucking idiot, she thinks, closing the paper and starting to eat.

Then the sound of the door opening. Johan is home.

She puts her spoon down and goes into the hall. He's soaking wet from head to toe, and when he takes off his trainers she notices that his socks are so drenched that they squelch on the floor.

Don't make a fuss, she thinks. 'Don't worry about that. I'll deal with it. Have you eaten?' she asks.

He nods wearily in response, takes off his socks, and quickly pads past her and goes into the bathroom.

After another ten minutes in the kitchen with her soup and the newspaper, she begins to wonder what he's doing in there. No sounds from the shower, no sound at all, actually.

She knocks on the door. 'Johan?'

He eventually says something, but so quietly that she can't hear what he says.

'Johan, can't you open the door? I can't hear you.'

After a few seconds the lock clicks, but he doesn't open up.

For a couple of moments she just stands there staring at the door. A barrier between us, she thinks. As usual.

When she finally opens the door he's sitting curled up on the lid of the toilet. She can see he's freezing and pulls down a towel to wrap around him.

'What was it you said?' She sits down on the edge of the bath.

He takes a deep breath and she realises he's been crying. 'She's weird,' he says quietly.

'Weird? Who is?'

'Sofia.' Johan looks away.

'Sofia? What made you think of her?'

'Nothing particular, but she got so weird,' he goes on. 'When we were up there on Free Fall she started screaming at me, calling me Martin . . . And then when the ride was over she just walked away. I tried to follow her but I guess I was following the wrong person. That's the last thing I remember.'

She hugs him hard, then they both start to cry at the same time.

Edsviken – Lundström House

The September afternoon sun is sinking behind the large turn-of-the-century villa, tucked away down by the water. A narrow gravel drive lined with maple trees leads down to the house and Sofia Zetterlund parks her car in the turning circle, switches off the engine and looks out through the windscreen. The sky is steel grey and the rain that has been pouring down has eased slightly.

So this is where the Lundström family lives?

A short distance away she can see a boathouse through the trees. There's another building on the plot, and a swimming pool protected by a high fence. The house looks deserted, as if no one had ever moved into it. She gets out of the car, walks across the gravel towards the house, and as she walks up the broad stone steps to the front door the light in the hall goes on, the door opens and a short, slender woman wrapped in a dark blanket appears in the doorway.

'Come in and lock the door behind you,' Annette Lundström says.

Sofia shuts the door behind her and Annette Lundström sways through the hall and turns off to the left. There are stacks of big moving boxes everywhere.

Annette Lundström is forty years old, but looks closer to sixty. Her hair is a mess and she seems tired as she slumps onto a sofa covered with clothes.

'Take a seat,' she says in a low voice, gesturing towards an armchair on the other side of the coffee table.

The room is cold, and Sofia realises that the heating has been turned off already.

She considers the Lundström family's situation. Arrest for incest, paedophilia and child pornography, followed by attempted suicide. The daughter is in the custody of social services.

Sofia looks at the woman in front of her. She had probably been beautiful once, but that was before.

'Do you want coffee?' Annette reaches for the half-full carafe on the table.

'Yes, please, that would be good.'

'You can get a cup from the box on the floor.'

Sofia bends over. In a box under the table there's a jumble of badly packed crockery. She finds a chipped mug and lets Annette fill it for her.

The coffee is barely drinkable. Completely cold.

Sofia pretends it's OK, takes a few sips and puts the mug down on the table.

'Why did you want to see me?'

Annette coughs and pulls the blanket tighter around her.

'As I told you on the phone . . . I want to talk about Karl and Linnea. And I want to plead with you.'

'Plead?'

'It's like this . . .' Annette's eyes become sharper. 'I know how forensic psychiatry works. Not even death negates your oath of confidentiality. So it's no use asking you what you and Karl talked about. But there's one thing I've been wondering about. He said something to me after your meeting, that you understood him. That you understood his . . . well, his problem.'

Sofia shudders. There's a raw chill in the house.

'I've never understood his problem,' Annette goes on. 'And now he's dead, so I don't have to protect him any more. But I don't understand. I thought it only happened once. In Kristianstad, when Linnea was three. It was a mistake, and I know he told you about it. The fact that he watched those disgusting films is one thing, I might have been able to handle that. But not that he and Linnea . . . I mean, Linnea liked him. How could you understand his problem?'

Sofia feels Victoria's presence. Annette Lundström irritates her.

I know you're there, Victoria, Sofia thinks. But I'll deal with this myself.

'I've seen it before,' she eventually says. 'Plenty of times. But you're probably drawing too many conclusions from what he said. I only met him a couple of times, and he was fairly unbalanced at the time. Linnea is more important now. How is she?'

There's one big difference between Annette Lundström and Birgitta Bergman. Victoria's mother was fat, and this woman is so thin she's almost disappeared. Her skin has eaten its way into her bones, and soon there won't be anything left.

She'll just fade away and die.

But there's something familiar about her. Sofia rarely forgets a face, and is suddenly sure she's seen Annette Lundström before.

Her eyes are fixed again. 'Well . . . they've taken her away from me, she's in the Childhood and Adolescent Psychiatry unit at Danderyd. She hardly acknowledges me, and I'm not told anything. Can't you ask to see her? You must have contacts?'

'I can't just walk in and ask to speak to her,' Sofia says. 'The only way I could see her is if she wants to, and I can't honestly see how that would happen.'

'I can talk to the people in the unit,' Annette says.

Sofia sees that she's serious.

'There was something else . . .' Annette goes on. 'There's something I want to show you.' She pulls out some yellowing sheets of paper. 'I've never understood these.'

She puts three drawings on the table.

All three are drawn in crayon and signed 'Linnea' in childish writing.

Linnea five years old, Linnea nine years old and Linnea ten years old.

Sofia picks up one of the drawings.

It's by Linnea, aged five, but with the number revised, and it's a picture of a blonde girl standing in the foreground next to a large dog. Out of the dog's mouth hangs a huge tongue that Linnea had covered with dots. Taste buds, Sofia thinks. In the background there's a big house, and something that looks like a little fountain. A long chain leads away from the dog, and Sofia notes how carefully the girl has drawn the links, which get smaller and smaller until they disappear behind a tree.

Linnea had written something next to the tree, but Sofia can't read what it says.

From these characters an arrow points at the tree, behind which a man with a bent back and glasses is peering out with a smile.

In one of the windows of the house there's a figure looking out on the garden. Long hair, a happy mouth and a sweet little nose. Although the rest of the drawing is painstakingly detailed, Linnea hasn't given the figure any eyes.

Bearing in mind the picture Sofia has of the Lundström family, it isn't hard to work out that the figure in the window is Annette Lundström.

Annette Lundström, who didn't see. Who didn't want to see.

Taking that as the starting point, the scene in the garden becomes more interesting.

What was Linnea trying to show. What didn't Annette want to see?

A man with a bent back and glasses, and a dog with a large, prickly tongue?

Now she can see that it says U1660.

U1660?

Stockholm, 1988

*We cycle around the world, we play in streets and squares.
We play anything that makes a noise, even our old bike.*

Inside the villa in Värmdö Victoria Bergman stands and looks at the fetish figures on the living-room wall.

Grisslinge is a prison.

She doesn't know what to do with all the dead hours of the day. Time runs through her like an irregular river.

Some days she doesn't remember waking up. Some she doesn't remember going to sleep. Some days are just gone.

Other days she reads her psychology books, takes long walks, goes down to the water by the beach, or goes down Mormors väg to Skärgårdsvägen, main road number 222, almost perfectly straight towards the Värmdö road, where she turns at the roundabout and walks back. The walks help her think, and the cold air against her cheeks reminds her that she has a boundary.

She isn't the whole world.

She goes over and takes down the face mask, which looks like Solace in Sierra Leone, and puts it in front of her face. It smells strongly of wood, almost like perfume.

Inside the mask is a promise of another life, somewhere else, one Victoria knows she can never have. She is shackled to him.

She can hardly see through the small holes in the mask. She can hear her own breathing, feels its warmth bounce back and settle like a moist film over her cheeks. Outside in the hall she stops in front of the mirror. The mask makes her head look smaller. As if she were a seventeen-year-old with a ten-year-old's face.

'Solace,' Victoria says. 'Solace Manuti. Now we're twins, you and I.'

Then the front door opens. He's returned from work.

Victoria takes the mask off at once and runs back into the living room. She knows she's not allowed to touch his things.

'What are you doing?' He sounds cross.

'Nothing,' she replies, hanging the mask back in its place. She hears the shoe rack creak and the wooden hangers rattle against one another. Then his footsteps in the hall. She sits down on the sofa and grabs a newspaper from the table.

He comes into the room. 'Were you talking to someone?' He looks around the room before sitting down in the armchair next to the sofa.

'What are you doing?' he asks again.

Victoria folds her arms and stares at him. She knows that makes him nervous. She enjoys watching the panic grow inside him, watching him nervously pat the arms of the chair with his hands, shifting position again and again, unable to utter a word.

But when she's sat there silent for a while she feels anxiety building. She notices that his breathing is getting faster. It looks like his face is giving up. It loses colour and collapses.

'What are we going to do with you, Victoria?' he says forlornly, hiding his face in his hands. 'If the psychologist can't sort you out soon, I don't know what we're going to do.' He sighs.

She doesn't answer.

She sees Solace standing there in silence, watching them.

They resemble each other, she and Solace.

'Can you go down and turn the sauna on,' he says firmly as he gets up. 'Mum's on her way, so we'll soon be ready to eat.'

Victoria thinks that there ought to be some salvation. An arm reaching in from an unexpected direction and grabbing her, pulling her away from there. Or that her legs were strong enough to take her far away. But she's forgotten how to go about leaving, forgotten how to create a goal.

After dinner she hears Mum clattering around in the kitchen. Forever sweeping, dusting and clearing things away, all to no avail. However much she cleans and washes up, everything always looks exactly the same.

Victoria knows that it's all a sort of safe bubble that Mum can creep into in order to avoid seeing what's going on around her, and the pots and pans always make extra noise when Bengt is home.

She goes downstairs to the basement and sees that Mum has once again managed to miss cleaning the gaps between the steps where the needles from the Christmas tree are still stuck.

She goes down to the sauna, gets undressed and waits for him.

Outside the house it's February and icy cold, but in here the temperature has crept up to almost ninety degrees. That's because the sauna heater is so efficient, and he's fond of boasting of how he's connected it to the electricity network without permission.

Outside the sauna is a drainage pipe from the kitchen that runs down into the basement, and the warmth of the new heater makes the smell from the drain stronger.

The smell of onions and food waste, blood bread, beetroot and rancid cream mixes with a smell reminiscent of petrol.

Then he comes down to her. He looks sad. At the other end of the pipe Mum is washing up, while he takes off his towel.

When she opens her eyes she is standing in the living room with her towel around her body. She realises that it's happened again. She has lost time. She can feel the chafe marks in her crotch, the tenderness of her arms, and feels relieved that she didn't have to be there during the minutes or hours that have passed.

Solace is hanging in her place on the living-room wall and Victoria goes up to her room alone. She sits down on the bed, throws the towel on the floor and curls up under the covers. The sheets are cool, and she lies on her side looking at the window.

The February cold almost makes the panes crack, and she can hear the glass complain at the hard embrace of fifteen degrees below zero.

A window divided into six panes by wooden struts. Six framed pictures where the seasons have changed since they came home. In the two upper panes she can see the top of the tree outside, in the middle two the neighbours' house and the tree trunk and the chains of her old swing.

In the bottom panes she can see a white covering of snow and the red plastic swing, moving back and forth with the wind.

In the autumn there was yellow, scorched grass, the leaves falling and rotting. And since the middle of November a covering of snow that looks different every day.

Only the swing is the same. It hangs from its chains behind the six little windowpanes, like bars surrounded by ice crystals.

Glasbruksgatan – a Neighbourhood

Autumn is sweeping in from the Baltic, bathing Stockholm in a cover of heavy, cold damp.

From Glasbruksgatan, up on Katarinaberget, just below Mosebacke, the island of Skeppsholmen is barely visible through the rain. Kastellholmen, only slightly further out, is veiled in grey mist.

It's just now six o'clock.

She stops under one of the street lamps, takes the note out of her pocket and checks the address once more.

Yes, she's in the right place; now it's just a matter of waiting.

She knows he leaves at six and gets home a quarter of an hour later.

She's been waiting so long that another hour more or less doesn't make any difference.

The rain gets heavier, and she clutches her cobalt-blue coat tighter around her and stamps her feet to keep warm.

As she's going through her plan for the third time, visualising what's going to happen, she sees a black car slowly approaching. The windows are tinted, but through the windscreen she can make out a man on his own. The car stops a short distance from her and reverses into an empty parking space. Thirty seconds later the car door opens and he gets out.

She recognises Per-Ola Silfverberg at once and goes up to him.

His smile brings back memories. A big house in Copenhagen, a farm on Jutland and a pig slaughterhouse. The stench of ammonia and his firm grip on the large knife when he showed her how to cut. Up and to the right, to get to the heart.

'It's been a long time!' He walks up to her and gives her a warm hug. 'Is it just a coincidence that you're here, or have you been talking to Charlotte?'

She wonders if it matters what she says, and decides that it's completely irrelevant. There's no way he'll be able to check the veracity of whatever she says.

'Well, not entirely a coincidence,' she says, looking him in the eye. 'I was in the vicinity and remembered that Charlotte had mentioned that you'd moved here, so I thought I'd look in and see if you were home.'

'Well, I'm bloody glad you did!' He laughs, takes her under the arm and starts to cross the street. 'I'm afraid Charlotte won't be back for a couple of hours, but come in and have some coffee.'

She knows he's chairman of the board of a large investment company these days, and a man as used to being obeyed as he is unused to being questioned. There's no reason not to go inside with him.

'Well, I'm not in a hurry to get anywhere, so why not?'

His touch and the smell of his aftershave make her feel sick.

She can feel it bubbling inside her, and knows that the first thing she's going to have to do is ask to go to the toilet.

The apartment is enormous, and as he shows her around she counts seven rooms before he leads her into the living room. It's tastefully furnished with expensive but discreet furniture, all of it a pale, Scandinavian design.

There are two large windows with a view across the whole of Stockholm, and to the right is a spacious balcony with room for at least fifteen people.

'I'm so sorry, but I'm afraid I need to use the bathroom,' she says.

'No need to apologise. Out in the hall, on the right.' He points. 'Coffee? Or would you rather have something else? A glass of wine, perhaps?'

She begins to walk towards the hall. 'A glass of wine might be nice. But only if you're having one.'

She goes into the toilet, feeling her pulse pound, and in the mirror above the sink she can see a few beads of sweat on her forehead.

She sits down on the toilet and closes her eyes. Memories come back to her, and she sees Per-Ola Silfverberg's smiling face, but not the pleasant, business smile he just showed her, but the cold, empty one.

She recalls how he and the other men at the farm used to clean the pigs' innards before they were ground down into blood pudding, sausages or liver pâté. And his emotionless smile as he showed her how a pig's head became brawn.

Before she goes back into the living room she washes her hands. Hygiene is alpha and omega when it comes to slaughter, and she's memorising everything she touches. Afterwards she'll wipe off all trace of fingerprints.

Per-Ola Silfverberg is pouring out the wine, and hands her a glass. 'Now, you must tell me where you've been all these years.'

She raises the glass, lowers her nose to it and takes a deep breath. A Chardonnay, she thinks.

The man she loathes watches her as she takes a small sip of the wine, then looks him deep in the eye. She slurps audibly and lets the liquid mix with the air to bring out the flavours.

'I presume there's a reason why you've looked us up after such a long time,' says the man who hurt her.

She thinks that the wine's character is probably a blend. Spiced fruit, something like melon, peach, apricot and lemon. She detects a hint of oiliness.

Slowly and pleasurably she swallows.

'Where would you like me to start?'

Up and to the right, she thinks.

Glasbruksgatan – Crime Scene

The alarm reaches police headquarters on Kungsholmen just before ten. A woman is screaming that she's just got home and found her husband dead.

Jens Hurtig is actually on his way home when the call comes in, but seeing as he has no other plans for the evening he concludes that this would be a good opportunity to build up a bit of time in lieu.

Two weeks in some hot country will sit very nicely, and he's already decided to take his holiday when the weather is at its worst.

Even if winters in Stockholm are mostly pretty mild, and nothing like his childhood's snowy hell up in Kvikkjokk, it can be almost unbearable for a few weeks each year.

It's a neither-nor sort of weather. Not winter, but not really anything else instead.

Five degrees above freezing feels much the same as five below. It's the damp that does it. All that fucking water.

The only city in the world that might have worse winter weather than Stockholm is possibly St Petersburg, on the other side of the Baltic at the far end of the Gulf of Finland, built on a swamp. The city was first founded by Swedes, before the Russians took over. Just as masochistically inclined as the Swedes.

You're somehow supposed to enjoy the misery.

As usual, the traffic on the Central Bridge is stationary, and he switches the siren on to get through, but no matter how much people might want to let him through there's nowhere for them to move.

He zigzags between lanes until he reaches the Stadsgården exit, and turns off onto Katarinavägen. The traffic is thinner here, and he puts his foot down.

By the time he passes La Mano, the memorial to Swedes who died in the Spanish Civil War, he's going over one hundred and forty kilometres an hour.

He enjoys speed, and sees it as one of the privileges of the job.

He pulls up outside the door, where there are already two police vans parked, blue lights flashing.

In the doorway he meets a colleague on his way out. The man has taken his cap off and is clutching it tight in his hand. Hurtig sees that his face is white as chalk. White verging on green, actually, and Hurtig stands aside so he can get outside before he throws up.

Poor bastard, he thinks. The first time is never much fun. Well, not that it's ever that much bloody fun. You never get used to it. Maybe you get desensitised, which in no way means that you become a better police officer. But at least it makes it a bit easier to carry out your duties.

Police jargon can sound jokey and insensitive to outsiders. But it's also a way of distancing yourself.

When Jens Hurtig steps inside the apartment, he's pleased to have any distance. Ten minutes later he realises that he's going to have to call

Jeanette Kihlberg for assistance, and when she asks what's happened, he describes it as the most fucking awful thing out of all the fucking awful things he's seen in his whole fucking career.

Gamla Enskede – Kihlberg House

Johan is already asleep, and she's still wondering what she's going to do with him when the phone rings.

Jeanette answers it, and to her disappointment it's Hurtig. For a moment she was hoping it might be Sofia.

'What's happened now? Tell me it's important, or I'll be –'

Hurtig interrupts her. 'Yes, it's important.'

He falls silent, and in the background Jeanette can hear agitated voices. According to Hurtig, Jeanette has no option but to go back into the city.

What he's just seen isn't human.

'Some sick bastard has stabbed the man at least a hundred times, cut him into pieces, then used a roller to paint the whole apartment!'

Shit, she thinks. Not now.

'I'll be there as quick as I can. Give me twenty minutes.'

Great, so I'm letting Johan down again.

A fatal stabbing is the last thing she needs right now. She hasn't just got Johan to deal with, but also the investigation that was shut down.

And, not least, Victoria Bergman. Whose trail had gone completely dead at Nacka District Court.

The rain has started to let up, but here and there there are big puddles and she doesn't dare to drive fast for fear of aquaplaning. The air feels cold. The thermometer at Hammarby reads eleven degrees. The branches of the trees in the park below are heavy with autumn colour, and as she looks towards the city from the Johanneshov Bridge, she thinks it's incredibly beautiful.

Edsviken – Lundström House

Sofia looks at the other drawings. One shows a room containing three men, a girl lying on a bed and a figure with its head turned away. The other is more abstract and harder to interpret, but the figure occurs twice. Once in the middle of the picture, eyeless and surrounded by a blur of faces, then in the bottom left corner it's there again, on its way out of the drawing. Only half its body is visible, not its face.

She compares them with the first drawing. The same eyeless figure looking at a garden through a window. A big dog and a man behind a tree. U1660?

'What is it you don't understand about the drawings?' Sofia asks over her cup of coffee.

Annette Lundström smiles hesitantly. 'That figure without eyes. I presume it's a self-portrait, that that figure is her. But I don't understand what she's trying to say.'

How blind can you be? Sofia thinks. The woman has spent her whole life trying to keep her eyes shut. Now she thinks she can make up for that by confessing to a psychologist that she can actually see something odd in her daughter's old drawings. A lame way of trying to claim that she too can see what's going on, but that it's only just occurred to her. The guilt gets transferred to her husband and she can disclaim any involvement.

'Do you know what this means?' Sofia asks, pointing at the characters beside the tree in the first drawing. 'U1660?'

'Yes, I do understand that. Linnea couldn't write then, so she drew his name. He's the man with the bent back behind the tree.'

'And who is he?'

Annette's smile is strained. 'It doesn't say U1660. It says Viggo. That's Viggo Dürer, my friend's husband. The house Linnea drew is the one in Kristianstad. They often came to visit us down there, although they lived in Denmark at the time.'

Sofia starts. Her parents' lawyer.

Watch out for him.

Annette suddenly looks sad.

'Henrietta, one of my best friends, got married to Viggo. I think Linnea was a bit scared of Viggo, and maybe that's why she doesn't want to see him in the drawing. She was scared of the dog as well. It was a Rottweiler, and it did look rather like that.'

Sofia nods. 'But if you think that's Linnea standing in the window without any eyes, who's the girl standing next to the dog?'

Annette suddenly smiles. 'That's probably me. I'm wearing my red dress.' She puts the first picture down and picks up the second. 'And in this one I'm lying asleep in bed while the men have a party.' She lets out an embarrassed laugh at the memory.

For Sofia the meaning of Linnea's drawings is crystal clear. Annette Lundström is confusing herself with the girl in the pictures, and for her Linnea is the eyeless figure, the one turned away, or running out of the picture.

Annette Lundström can't see what's been going on around her.

But Linnea has understood everything since she was five years old.

Sofia knows she has to arrange a meeting with Linnea Lundström, with or without her mother's help.

'Is it OK if I photograph these drawings?'

'Yes, of course.'

Sofia takes out her mobile phone and takes a few pictures of Linnea's drawings, then gets up from the sofa. 'Here's what we do. You and I will go to Danderyd together. The senior psychiatric consultant there is an old acquaintance of mine. We'll explain the situation to her and maybe she'll let me see Linnea if we play our cards right.'

By the time Sofia Zetterlund pulls out onto the Norrtälje road it's almost six o'clock.

Viggo Dürer? Why can't she remember him? They sorted out her parents' estate together over the phone. The memory of his aftershave. Old Spice and Eau de Vie. That's all.

But Sofia realises that Victoria knew Viggo Dürer. She must have.

She feels restless and turns the radio on. A gentle woman's voice is talking about what it's like to live with an eating disorder. The inability to eat and drink because of a fear of swallowing, a phobia triggered by trauma. Basic bodily reflexes knocked out of line. How easy it seems to be.

Sofia thinks about Ulrika Wendin and Linnea Lundström.

Two young girls whose problems are the consequences of the actions of one man.

Ulrika Wendin won't eat, Linnea Lundström won't talk. And soon they'll be sitting opposite her with the next instalment of the man's story.

The gentle woman's voice on the radio and the sound of the traffic crawling through the drizzly darkness sends Sofia into an almost hypnotic state.

She pictures two hollow-eyed, sunken faces, and Ulrika Wendin's emaciated figure merges with Annette Lundström's.

Suddenly she realises who Annette Lundström is. Or, rather, was.

It was almost twenty-five years ago. Her face had been rounder, and she had been laughing.

The shells

of his ears listen to lies. He mustn't let any untruths in, because they'll soon reach his stomach and poison his body.

He learned not to speak a long time ago, and now he's trying to learn not to listen to words.

When he was little he used to go to the Pagoda of the Yellow Stork in Wuhan to listen to music.

Everyone said the old man was crazy. He spoke a foreign language that no one understood, and he was dirty and smelled bad, but Gao Lian liked him because his words became Gao's.

The monk gave him sounds that Gao made his own when they reached his ears.

When the fair woman makes soft sounds in beautiful melodies he thinks of the monk and his heart is filled with a lovely warmth that is his alone.

Gao draws a big, black heart with the crayons she's given him.

The stomach absorbs lies if you're not careful, but she's taught him that you can protect yourself by letting the acid in the stomach merge with bodily fluids.

Gao Lian from Wuhan sips the water, and it tastes of salt.

For a long time they sit facing each other, and Gao gives her some of his own water.

After a while no more water comes out of him. But from his neck runs blood, and it tastes red and rather sweet.

Gao looks for something that tastes sour, and then for something bitter.

When she leaves him alone he remains seated on the floor rolling a crayon between his fingers until his skin looks black.

Every day he makes new drawings and he's getting better and better at transferring his internal images onto the paper. His brain doesn't have to tell his hand what to do. He just moves the pictures from a point inside his imagination onto the paper, using his arm and hand.

He learns how to use black shadows to emphasise the white, and in the meeting of contrasts he creates new effects.

He draws a burning house.

Kronoberg – Police Headquarters

INDUSTRIALIST BRUTALLY MURDERED is the headline, and when Jeanette opens the paper she sees that they've mapped out Per-Ola Silfverberg's life and career. After leaving school he studied industrial economics, learned Chinese and was one of the first to recognise the importance of the Asian market for exporting companies. Then he moved to Copenhagen and became managing director of a company that made toys.

He and his wife moved back to Sweden, leaving behind a criminal investigation that was later dropped. He gained a reputation as a talented businessman, and over the years accumulated a growing number of boardroom responsibilities.

Jens Hurtig comes in, closely followed by Schwarz and Åhlund.

'Ivo Andrić has sent his report – I've just read it.' Hurtig hands her a sheaf of papers.

'Good, then you can tell us what he's got to say.'

Schwarz and Åhlund look expectant. Hurtig clears his throat before he begins, and Jeanette thinks he seems rather shaken. She's just relieved that the victim isn't another child, but a grown man.

'Let's see, it says, "To slaughter an animal the knife is inserted at a particular angle to reach the main blood vessels around the heart".'

'All men are animals, don't you think?' Schwarz grins. Hurtig turns towards Jeanette and waits for her to comment.

'I'm inclined to agree with Schwarz that this looks like a symbolic murder, but I doubt it's Per-Ola Silfverberg's gender that's the main reason. I'm thinking of the expression "capitalist pig", but let's not get hung up on that now.' Jeanette nods to Hurtig to continue reading from the report.

'"The autopsy on Per-Ola Silfverberg indicates another unusual type of knife injury, on the man's neck. The knife was inserted under the skin and twisted, and then the skin was sliced open from beneath."' He looks around at his audience. 'Ivo's never seen an injury like that before. The way the artery in the victim's arm was cut open is also unusual. It suggests that the perpetrator has a degree of anatomical knowledge.'

'So, not a doctor, but maybe a hunter or someone who works in a slaughterhouse?' Åhlund suggests.

Hurtig shrugs. 'Ivo also thinks there was more than one killer. That seems to be supported by the number of wounds, and the fact that some of them seem to have been made by someone right-handed, and some by a left-handed person.'

'So we might have one killer with some knowledge of anatomy, and one without?' Åhlund asks, making notes on a pad in front of him.

'Maybe,' Hurtig replies, then looks at Jeanette, who nods without saying anything. Loose threads, nothing more, she thinks.

Hurtig goes on reading: '"The body has been dismembered using a sharp instrument, such as a heavy, single-edged knife. The distribution of the wounds suggests that at least the dismemberment was conducted by two people. The broader picture suggests excessive brutality, and most of the evidence indicates that it was carried out by someone with sadistic tendencies. In this context, by sadism I mean that the individual is stimulated by imposing suffering or humiliation on others. I should add that previous forensic experience suggests that murderers of the type who took Silfverberg's life have a pronounced tendency to repeat the offence, usually in a similar way, and with a similar victim. In a case as extreme and rare as this, the relevant literature will have to be studied carefully, which will take time."'

He puts the report down, and silence descends on the room.

Two people, with different knowledge of anatomy, Jeanette thinks.

'What does his wife say?' she asks. 'Does she know if Per-Ola had received any threats?'

'We didn't manage to get any sense out of her yesterday,' Hurtig replies. 'But we're talking to her again a bit later.'

'Has she got an alibi?'

'Yes. Three friends all confirm they were with her when the murder was committed.'

'The lock was intact, so it seems likely to have been someone he knew,' Jeanette begins, but is interrupted by a knock on the door. They wait in silence for a few seconds before Ivo Andrić steps into the room.

'I happened to be passing,' Ivo says.

'So you've got something else for us?' Jeanette says.

'Yes. Hopefully a slightly clearer picture.' Ivo sighs, taking off his baseball cap and sitting down on the desk next to Jeanette. 'I'm assuming Silfverberg and the perpetrator met in the street, then went inside together. The body shows no signs of being tied up, so it was probably just an ordinary situation that got out of hand. But in spite of that, I think the murder was planned.'

'What makes you draw that conclusion?' Åhlund looks up from his notebook.

'There's no sign that the perpetrator was intoxicated, and no indication of mental illness. We found two wine glasses, but both had been carefully cleaned.'

'What can you say about the dismemberment?' Åhlund goes on.

Jeanette sits and listens. Observing her colleagues.

'The dismemberment that followed isn't the usual sort, cutting the body up so it's easier to move. It looks like it took place in the bathroom.'

Ivo Andrić describes the order in which the body was most probably dismembered, and how the perpetrator arranged the pieces in the apartment. And how the apartment had been thoroughly searched throughout the night and that morning for other evidence. The U-bends in the bathroom pipes had been examined, along with the drains and the grille in the floor.

'It's worth noting that the thighs were skilfully cut away from the hip bone with just a few cuts, and the same skill was used to cut the lower legs free from the knee ligaments.'

Ivo falls silent, and Jeanette concludes by asking two open questions, not really directing them at anyone.

'So what does the dismemberment of the body say about the killer's state of mind? And is he going to do it again?'

Jeanette looks at each of them in turn. Meets their gaze.

They sit in silence in the airless conference room, united by impotence.

Klara Sjö – Public Prosecution Authority

In spite of its name, Klara sjö is no lake, just a dirty patch of water, useless for fishing and bathing.

There's an extensive network of drains running into it, and the industry in the area and the traffic on Klarastrandsleden have led to serious pollution in the form of high levels of nitrogen, phosphorous, metals and tar. It's practically impossible to see clearly through it to any depth, just like the Public Prosecution Authority nearby.

Kenneth von Kwist leafs through the photographs of Per-Ola Silfverberg.

This is just too much, he thinks. I can't handle any more.

If it weren't for Viggo Dürer, he would be sitting here nice and quietly, counting down the days to his retirement.

First Karl Lundström, then Bengt Bergman and now P-O Silfverberg. All introduced to him by Viggo Dürer, not that the prosecutor had ever regarded them as his friends. He had merely been acquainted with them.

Was that enough for a curious journalist? Or a pedantic detective like Jeanette Kihlberg?

From personal experience he knows that the only people you can be sure of are those who are utterly selfish. They always follow a set pattern, and you know exactly what they're going to do. That's also the reason why they're the only people you can deceive successfully.

But when you run into someone like Jeanette Kihlberg, someone with an underlying sense of justice, the situation is less easy to predict.

So he can't try to shut Kihlberg up in the usual way. He'll simply have to make sure she never gets access to the material he's sitting on, and he knows that what he's about to do is criminal.

From the bottom drawer in his desk he takes out a thirteen-year-old file and switches on the document shredder. It rumbles into life, and before he begins to feed the papers into it he reads what Per-Ola Silfverberg's Danish defence lawyer had claimed:

> There are numerous allegations, the time and location of which are unspecified, which makes them particularly difficult to disprove. Fundamentally, the entire case rests on what the girl has said, and the extent to which her story is credible.

He slowly feeds the page into the shredder. There's a whirring sound, and out come tiny, illegible strips.

Next page.

> The other evidence presented in this case can neither strengthen nor weaken the credibility of what the girl has said. When questioned she has described certain acts that Per-Ola Silfverberg is claimed to have subjected her to. However, she has been unable to complete the interviews. As a result, her claims have only been able to be presented through the video recording of the police interview with the girl.

More paper, more strips.

> Regarding the video interview, the defence believes that the principal interviewer asked leading questions and steered the girl towards

specific answers. The girl also had a motive for claiming that Per-Ola Silfverberg committed these acts. If she could prove that Per-Ola Silfverberg was the cause of her mental illness, she would be allowed to leave her foster home and move back home to Sweden.

Home to Sweden, Prosecutor Kenneth von Kwist thinks, switching off the shredder.

Stockholm, 1988

There's no good reason to begin again, he had said. You've always belonged to me, and you always will. She felt as if she were two people. One who liked him, and one who hated him.

The silence feels like a vacuum.

He breathes loudly and heavily through his nose all the way to Nacka, and that sound absorbs her completely.

When they reach the hospital he switches off the engine.

'Well, then,' he says, and Victoria gets out of the car. The door shuts with a muffled thud, and she knows he's going to sit there in the silence that follows.

She also knows that he's going to stay there so there's no need for her to keep looking round to make sure that the distance between them is actually growing. Her footsteps get lighter and lighter with every metre she puts between them. Her lungs expand, and she fills them with air that's so unlike the air around him. So fresh.

Without him I wouldn't be ill, she thinks.

Without him she would be nothing, she knows, but she avoids thinking that thought to its conclusion.

The therapist she sees is past retirement age, but still working.

Sixty-six years old, as wise as her years. To begin with progress had been sluggish, but after just a few sessions Victoria had found it easier to open up.

As she steps into the clinic the eyes are the first thing Victoria sees.

They're what she longs for most. She can land safely in them.

The woman's eyes help Victoria to understand herself. They're ancient, they've seen everything and they're trustworthy. They don't panic, and they don't tell her she's crazy, but nor do they tell her she's right, or that they understand her.

The woman's eyes don't mess around.

That's why she can look into them and feel calm.

'When was the last time you felt really good?' She opens each meeting with a question that she can then use as a base for the entire session.

'The last time I ironed Dad's shirts he said they were perfect.' Victoria smiles because she knows that there wasn't a single crease on them, and that the collars were starched just enough.

Those eyes give her their complete attention, they're there just for her.

'And if you had to choose one thing that you would do for the rest of your life, would it be ironing shirts?'

'No, definitely not!' Victoria exclaims. 'Ironing shirts is really boring.' And suddenly she realises what she's said, why she said it, and how it ought to be. 'Sometimes I rearrange his desk and drawers,' she goes on, getting carried away, 'to see if he notices anything when he comes home. He hardly ever does.'

'How are your studies going?' the old woman interrupts without giving any sign of having noticed Victoria's answer.

'OK.' Victoria shrugs.

'What mark did you get for your latest assignment?'

Victoria hesitates.

She can remember what it was perfectly well, but isn't sure if she can say it.

It sounds so ridiculous.

'Excellent,' she says sarcastically. 'It said, "You have a phenomenal understanding of the neural processes, and add exciting thoughts of your own that I would like to see you develop in a longer piece of work."'

The therapist looks at her, wide-eyed, and claps her hands together. 'But that's wonderful, Victoria! Didn't you feel pleased when you got your work back with something like that on it?'

'But,' Victoria begins, 'it doesn't really matter. I mean, it's only pretend.'

'Victoria,' the psychologist says seriously. 'I know you've talked about your difficulties telling the difference between what is real and what's pretend, as you put it, or what's important to you and what isn't, as I put it . . . If you think about it, isn't this a good example of that? You claim you feel good when you iron shirts, but you don't really want to do it. And when you study, which you like doing, you do very well indeed, but' – she raises a finger and fixes her eyes on Victoria's – 'you don't allow yourself to be happy when you receive praise for something you enjoy doing.'

Those eyes, Victoria thinks. They see everything she herself has never seen, only suspected. They enlarge her when she tries to shrink herself, and they gently show her the difference between what she thinks she sees, hears and feels, and what is happening in everyone else's reality.

Victoria wishes she could see with old, wise eyes. Like the psychologist.

The lightness she feels in the psychologist's room only lasts for the twenty-eight steps down to the main entrance. Then silence in the car home.

They pass block after block, house after house, family after family. She sees a girl her own age walking arm in arm with her mother. They look so untroubled.

That girl could have been me, Victoria thinks.

She realises she could have been anyone.

But she ended up as her.

'We're going to have a talk over dinner,' he says as he opens the car door and gets out onto the street. He grabs his trousers and hoists them so far up over his stomach that she can see the outline of his testicles. Victoria looks away and walks towards the house.

The house is like a black hole that destroys everyone who enters it, and she opens the door and lets herself be swallowed up.

Mum says nothing when they come in, but she's got dinner ready. They sit around the table. Dad, Mum and Victoria. When they sit there she realises that they look like a family.

'Victoria,' he begins, folding his veiny hands and putting them on the table. Whatever he's about to say, she knows this isn't a talk. He's giving orders. 'We think you might benefit from a little change of scenery,' he says, 'and your mother and I have decided the best solution would be to combine work with pleasure.' He looks expectantly at her mother, who nods and serves him some potatoes.

'Do you remember Viggo?' He looks questioningly at Victoria.

She remembers Viggo.

A Danish man who used to come on regular visits when she was little.

Never when Mum was at home.

'Viggo has a farm in Jutland, and he needs someone to look after the farmhouse. Nothing too demanding, because of course we're aware of your current condition.'

'My current condition?' Once more she feels the pulsating fury that settles like a luminous screen over her paralysis.

'You know what I mean,' he says in a louder voice. 'You walk around talking to yourself. You have imaginary friends even though you're seventeen years old. You have tantrums and behave like a small child. We all want what's best for you, and Viggo has contacts in Aalborg who can help you. You'll be going down to his farm in the spring. And that's all there is to it.'

They sit in silence as he ends his meal with a cup of tea. He puts a lump of sugar between his lips and any moment now he'll filter the tea through it until it dissolves.

They sit in silence as he drinks. Slurping, the way he always does.

'It's for your own sake,' he concludes, then gets up and goes over to the sink, where he rinses his cup with his back to them. Mum squirms on her seat and looks away.

He turns off the tap, dries his hands and leans back against the work-top. 'You're not an adult yet,' he says. 'We're responsible for you. There's nothing to discuss.'

No, I know that, she thinks. There's nothing to discuss, and there never has been.

Kronoberg – Police Headquarters

Once Ivo Andrić, Schwarz and Åhlund have left the conference room, Hurtig leans forward across the table and speaks to Jeanette in a low voice. 'Before we go any further with Silfverberg, where are we with the old cases?'

'Not much progress. At least not from my side. How about you? Anything new?'

'Good and bad news,' he says. 'What do you want first?'

'Anything but a cliché,' Jeanette says. He loses his train of thought, and she grins at him. 'Sorry, only joking. Start with the bad news. You know that's what I prefer.'

'OK. First Dürer and von Kwist's judicial history. Apart from five or six dropped cases where they were on opposite sides, I can't see anything odd. And even that isn't particularly surprising seeing as they specialise in the same sort of crime.'

Jeanette nods. 'Go on.'

'The list of donors. Sihtunum i Diasporan is supported by a group of former students at Sigtuna College, businessmen and politicians, successful people with flawless records. There are just a few with no direct link to the school, but we can probably assume that they know a former student or have other contacts there.'

A dead end, at least for the time being, Jeanette thinks, and gestures for Hurtig to go on.

'The IP address was a bit tricky. The user who posted the list of donors only made that one comment, and I had to do some digging before I could identify the IP address. Guess where it leads?'

'A dead end?'

He throws out his hands. 'A 7-Eleven shop in Malmö. If you've got twenty-nine kronor, you can buy a ticket from a machine completely anonymously and sit down at one of the terminals for an hour.'

'And the good news?'

Jens Hurtig grins. 'Per-Ola Silfverberg is one of the donors.'

Before Jeanette Kihlberg leaves police headquarters for the day, Dennis Billing informs her of the budget for the Silfverberg case, and as she drives past Rådhuset it occurs to her that even the preliminary budget Billing has allocated is more than ten times what she was given for her work on the murdered boys.

Dead children with no papers are worth less than dead Swedes with careers and money in the bank.

If only Billing had given her enough money to get a decent perpetrator profile drawn up four months ago, when they found the first two bodies, she wouldn't have had to organise one on her own.

Now Sofia would have to do the work without payment or recognition, and Jeanette finds that embarrassing. She decides not to put any pressure on Sofia, and give her all the time she needs.

She thinks about what determines the value of a human life. Is it the number of mourners at the funeral, the financial value of the estate, or the media interest in the death? The social influence of the deceased? Their country of origin or skin colour? Or the sum of police resources allocated to a murder investigation?

She knows that the cost of investigating the death of Foreign Minister Anna Lindh had risen to fifteen million kronor by the time the Court of Appeal upheld Mijailo Mijailović's sentence for her murder, and she knows that it was widely regarded within the police as cheap in comparison to the three hundred and fifty million that Prime Minister Olof Palme's death had cost the public so far.

Vita Bergen – Sofia Zetterlund's Apartment

When Sofia Zetterlund wakes up her body feels sore, as if she's run miles in her sleep, and she gets up and goes into the bathroom.

I look terrible, she thinks when she sees her face in the mirror above the sink.

Her hair is a mess, and she forgot to remove her make-up before going to bed. The smeared mascara looks like she's got black eyes, and her lipstick is a pink smear across her chin.

What actually happened yesterday?

She wipes her face, turns and pulls the shower curtain aside. The bath is full to the brim with water. There's an empty wine bottle at the bottom, and the label floating on the surface tells her it's the expensive bottle of Rioja from the drinks cabinet.

I'm not the one who drinks, she thinks. Victoria is.

What else, apart from a few bottles of wine and a bath? Did I go out last night?

She opens the door and looks into the hall. Nothing out of the ordinary.

But when she goes into the kitchen she sees a plastic bag in front of the cupboard under the sink, and even before she bends over and unties it, she realises it doesn't contain rubbish.

All the clothes are soaking wet as she pulls them from the bag.

Her black knitted top, a black vest and her dark grey sweatpants. With a deep sigh of resignation she spreads them on the kitchen floor and examines them more closely.

They're not dirty, but they smell musty. That's probably because they've been in the bag all night, and she wrings the top out above the sink.

The water is dirty brown, and when she tastes it she can detect a hint of salt, but it's impossible to tell if the taste comes from sweat on the top itself, or from salt water outside somewhere.

She realises that she's not going to work out what she was doing last night for the time being, gathers the clothes together, and hangs them up to dry in the bathroom before pulling the plug from the bath and taking care of the wine bottle.

Then she goes back into her bedroom, opens the blinds and glances at the clock radio. Quarter to eight. No rush. Ten minutes in the shower, another ten in front of the mirror, then a taxi to the practice. First client at nine o'clock.

Linnea Lundström is coming at one o'clock, she remembers. But who is she seeing before that? She isn't sure.

She closes the window and takes a deep breath.

This can't go on. I can't carry on like this. Victoria has to go.

Half an hour later Sofia Zetterlund is sitting in a taxi, checking her face in the rear-view mirror as the car rolls down Borgmästargatan.

She's happy with what she sees. Her mask is in place, but inside she's shaking.

The difference now is that she's aware of the gaps in her memory. Before, the gaps were such a natural part of her that her brain didn't register them. They simply didn't exist. Now they're there like worrying black holes in her life.

She knows she has to learn to handle this. She has to learn to function again, and she has to get to know Victoria Bergman. The child she once was. The grown woman she later became, hidden from the world, and herself.

The memories of Victoria's life, her childhood in the Bergman family, aren't arranged like an archive of photographs where you just have to open a box, pick out a folder with a particular date or event on it, then look at the pictures. Memories of her childhood appear haphazardly, creeping up on her when she least expects it. Sometimes they pop up without external stimulus, but on other occasions an object or a conversation can throw her back in time.

In Annette Lundström's thin face Sofia had seen a girl from Victoria Bergman's first year in Sigtuna. A girl two years older than Victoria, one of the ones who whispered about her, casting sly glances at her in the school corridors.

She's sure Annette Lundström remembers what happened in the tool shed. That she had laughed at her. And she's just as sure that Annette has no idea that the woman she has just employed for therapy sessions with her daughter is the same woman she once laughed at.

She's about to do Annette a favour. Helping her daughter to get over a trauma. The same trauma she herself is going through, and one she knows can't be erased.

Yet she still clings to the hope that it might be possible, that she won't have to confront those memories and regard them as her own. Her brain has tried to spare her that by not even letting her be aware of them. But it hasn't helped. Without memories she is just a shell.

And it's not getting any better. It's just getting worse.

No matter how she looks at it, the only solution is for Victoria Bergman and Sofia Zetterlund to be integrated into a single consciousness with access to the thoughts and memories of both personalities.

She also realises that this is impossible so long as Victoria keeps pushing her away, and even loathes the part of her that is Sofia Zetterlund. And Sofia herself is resistant to the idea of reconciling herself to the violent things Victoria has done. They are two people without a common denominator.

Apart from the fact that they share a body.

Kronoberg – Police Headquarters

'You've got a visitor,' Hurtig calls to Jeanette the moment she emerges from the lift. 'Charlotte Silfverberg is sitting in your office. Do you want me to sit in?'

'No, I can handle it.' Jeanette waves him off, then continues along the corridor and finds the door to her room open.

Charlotte Silfverberg is standing with her back to the door, looking out of the window.

'Hello.' Jeanette walks in and goes over to her desk. 'I'm glad you've come. I was thinking of contacting you. How are you doing?'

Charlotte Silfverberg turns round but doesn't move from the window. She doesn't answer.

Jeanette can see that the woman looks unsettled. 'Sit down, if you'd like to.'

'That's OK, I'd rather stand. I won't be long.'

'So . . . Was there anything particular you wanted to talk about? If not, I've got a few things I'd like to ask you.'

'Go ahead.'

'Sihtunum i Diasporan,' Jeanette says. 'You husband is listed as a donor. What do you know about the foundation?'

Charlotte squirms. 'All I know is that it's a group of men who meet once or twice a year to discuss charitable projects. I think it's mainly an excuse to drink expensive wine and exchange old memories of national service. They had a tradition of going out on the *Gilah* a couple of times each year. That's their boat.'

'You never went along?'

'No. We were never asked if we wanted to go. It was a bit of a boys' thing.'

'You know that Viggo and his wife died in an accident a couple of weeks ago?'

'Yes, I read about it. A fire on board the *Gilah*.'

Jeanette thinks about Bengt and Birgitta Bergman. Also killed in a fire. In what was assumed to be an accident.

'Can you think of anyone who might have wanted to kill the Dürers? Or Viggo, in particular?'

'No idea. I hardly knew him.'

Jeanette accepts that the woman is as ignorant as she claims to be. 'So . . . what did you want to talk to me about?' she goes on.

'There's something I need to tell you.' Charlotte pauses, swallows hard and folds her arms. 'Thirteen years ago, the year before we moved here, P-O was accused of something. He was cleared and everything got sorted out, but . . .'

Accused of something, Jeanette thinks, and remembers the article she had read. So it was something compromising?

Charlotte leans back against the windowsill. 'Sometimes I feel like I'm being stalked,' she eventually says. 'There've been a couple of letters.'

'Letters?' Jeanette can't hold back any longer. 'What sort of letters?'

'Well, I don't really know. It was odd. The first one came just after the case against P-O was dropped. We assumed it was from some feminist who was annoyed that he wasn't charged.'

'What did the letter say? Have you still got it?'

'No, it was just a lot of incoherent nonsense, so we threw it away. In hindsight that was probably a silly thing to do.'

Shit, Jeanette thinks. 'What makes you think it would have come from a feminist? What was he accused of?'

Charlotte Silfverberg sounds hostile all of a sudden. 'You can look that up pretty easily, can't you? I don't want to talk about it. It's all in the past, as far as I'm concerned.'

Jeanette realises it's best not to upset the woman. 'You've got no idea who the letter was from?' Jeanette smiles ingratiatingly.

'No, like I said, it could have been someone who didn't like the fact that P-O was completely exonerated.' She stops, takes a deep breath, then continues. 'Last week another letter arrived. I've got it with me.'

Charlotte Silfverberg pulls a white envelope from her handbag and puts it on the desk.

Jeanette quickly finds and puts on a pair of latex gloves. She realises that the envelope has already been contaminated by Charlotte Silfverberg's own fingers, as well as many more in the sorting office, but she does it out of reflex.

A perfectly ordinary white envelope. The sort you can buy in packs of ten from the supermarket.

Postmarked in Stockholm, addressed to Per-Ola Silfverberg, childish writing in black ink. Jeanette frowns.

The letter is written on a white sheet of folded A4 paper. Sold everywhere in packs of five hundred sheets.

Jeanette unfolds the letter and reads. The same printed letters in black ink: YOU ALWAYS GET CAUGHT BY THE PAST.

How original, Jeanette thinks with a sigh. She looks at Charlotte Silfverberg. 'The phrasing seems odd. Most people would say, "The past always catches up with you,"' she says. 'Does that suggest anything to you?'

'It's not necessarily odd,' Charlotte replies. 'It sounds like the Danish way of saying it.'

'You appreciate that this is evidence. Why did you wait a week before bringing it in?'

'Well, I haven't exactly been myself. I've only just summoned up the strength to go back into the apartment.'

Shame, Jeanette thinks. Shame is what always gets in the way.

Whatever Per-Ola Silfverberg was accused of, it's something shameful.

Charlotte nods towards the letter. 'Last week I got two phone calls. When I answered there was just silence on the line, then whoever it was hung up.'

Jeanette shakes her head. 'Excuse me,' she says, turning towards Charlotte Silfverberg, then picks up the internal phone and dials Hurtig using the speed dial.

'Per-Ola Silfverberg,' she says when Hurtig answers. 'This morning I contacted the police in Copenhagen regarding that case against him that was dropped. Can you check if we've received a fax?'

Jeanette hangs up and leans back in her chair.

Charlotte Silfverberg's cheeks are bright red. 'I was wondering,' she begins in an unsteady voice, then clears her throat and goes on. 'Is it possible to get some sort of protection?'

Jeanette can see that this might be necessary. 'I'll see what I can do.'

'Thank you.' Charlotte Silfverberg looks relieved, quickly gathers her things together and walks towards the door, as Jeanette adds, 'I might need to talk to you again.'

Charlotte stops in the doorway. 'OK,' she says with her back to Jeanette, as Hurtig comes in with a brown folder. He drops it on Jeanette's desk and goes back to his office.

The preliminary investigation into Per-Ola Silfverberg runs to seventeen pages in total.

The first thing that strikes Jeanette is that Charlotte, besides not mentioning any details about the actual case, also neglected to mention a not entirely irrelevant fact.

Charlotte and Per-Ola Silfverberg have a daughter.

Mariatorget – Sofia Zetterlund's Office

At nine o'clock one client who was having trouble sleeping, followed at eleven by one who was dealing with anorexia.

Sofia can hardly remember their names as she sits at her desk and glances through her notes of the sessions.

Her body feels off-kilter after the previous night's lacuna. Her hands are cold and clammy and her mouth dry. Her condition isn't made any better by the fact that she knows she's about to meet Linnea Lundström. In a few minutes Sofia is going to meet herself as a fourteen-year-old. The fourteen-year-old she's turned her back on.

She arrives at the practice at one o'clock in the company of a nurse from Danderyd Hospital.

Linnea Lundström is a young woman with a body and face that look considerably older than her fourteen years. She has been forced to grow up far too early, and already carries within her body a whole lifetime's accumulated hell, which she'll have to devote the rest of her life to learning to cope with.

After quarter of an hour Sofia is starting to realise that it's not going to be easy.

She was expecting a girl full of darkness and hate, sometimes expressed through silence and sometimes through impulsive outbursts, governed by an innate destructiveness. If that had been the case, Sofia would have had something to grab hold of.

But instead she is confronted with something very different.

Linnea Lundström answers her questions shyly, her body language is defensive and her eye contact non-existent. She's sitting half turned away, fiddling with a Bratz doll on a key ring. Sofia is surprised that the senior consultant at Danderyd managed to persuade Linnea to agree to the meeting.

Just as she's about to ask Linnea what she's expecting from their session, the girl asks a question that takes Sofia by surprise.

'What did Dad actually tell you?'

Linnea's voice is surprisingly clear and strong, but her eyes are still fixed on her key ring. Sofia wasn't expecting such a direct question and hesitates. She mustn't answer in a way that will make the girl withdraw completely.

'He made a lot of confessions,' Sofia begins. 'A lot of them turned out not to be true, and others more or less true.'

She pauses to gauge Linnea's reaction. The girl hasn't moved a muscle.

'But what did he say about me?' she says a few moments later.

Sofia thinks about the three drawings Annette showed her during her visit to the villa in Danderyd. Three scenes that Linnea drew as a child, and which in all likelihood are depictions of abuse.

'Annette said that you understand . . . understood Dad. He said so to Annette. That you understand him. Do you?'

Another direct question. 'If you think you'd feel better if you understood him, maybe we can help each other out. Would you like that?'

Linnea doesn't answer immediately. She fidgets for a while, and Sofia can see her hesitating. 'Can you help me?' she finally says, putting the key ring in her pocket.

'I think so. I've got a lot of experience with men like your dad. But I need your help as well. Can you help me to help you?'

'Maybe,' the girl says. 'That depends.'

Linnea's back disappears from view as the lift doors close, and even if the girl clammed up the moment the nurse appeared, at least Sofia saw her open up. Their conversation, in spite of the reserve, exceeded her expectations, and she's optimistic about being able to get closer to the young woman – assuming that she met the real Linnea and not just a shell. From her own experience, she knows that some things can never be completely repaired.

Something will always be in the way.

Kronoberg – Police Headquarters

Jeanette Kihlberg has just had a long conversation with Dennis Billing, who after some serious persuasion has agreed to let her have two officers to protect Charlotte Silfverberg.

When they hang up she goes back to reading the Danish investigation into Per-Ola Silfverberg.

The person who reported him was Per-Ola and Charlotte's foster-daughter. She had been with the Silfverberg family since birth, living in a Copenhagen suburb. There's no indication of why she was placed in foster care.

Because the file is in the public domain, the name of the injured party has been redacted with thick black lines, but Jeanette knows she can easily find out the girl's name.

But right now she's mainly interested in discovering who Per-Ola Silfverberg is. Or was.

A pattern is starting to emerge.

Jeanette sees mistakes, things that have been neglected, not investigated, as well as manipulation. Police officers and prosecutors who didn't do their job, influential people lying and distorting the facts.

In what she's reading there's a pronounced lack of energy, an unwillingness and an inability to get to the bottom of the accusations against Per-Ola Silfverberg. The power not to investigate has been exercised with peculiar consistency.

The more she reads, the more depressed she feels about it. She works in the Violent Crime unit, but it feels as if she's completely surrounded by sex offenders.

Violence and sex, she thinks. Two things that shouldn't belong together, yet that are combined far too often.

By the time she's finished she feels drained, but knows she has to go and brief Hurtig about the new facts that have come to light. Jens Hurtig is sitting immersed in a bundle of case notes much like the one she's just been reading.

'What's that?' Jeanette points in surprise at the documents in his hand.

'The Danes sent over some more material, and I thought it might make sense for me to read it, then we can put together what we know.' Hurtig smiles at her and goes on. 'Do you want to start, or shall I?'

'I will,' Jeanette replies, and sits down. 'So, thirteen years ago Per-Ola Silfverberg was suspected of having abused his foster-daughter.'

'She'd just turned seven,' Hurtig adds.

Jeanette looks down at her notes. 'And the daughter gave detailed descriptions of, and I quote, "Per-Ola's physical methods of child rearing, using beatings and other violence against her, but she has had difficulty talking about sexual abuse."'

Hurtig shakes his head. 'Bastard . . .' He falls silent, and Jeanette continues.

'The girl keeps coming back to descriptions of P-O's physical abuse, as well as the full-on kisses he demanded from her, and his very thorough washing of her genitals.'

'Please . . .' Hurtig sounds almost pleading, but Jeanette feels that she wants to get this out of the way, and continues remorselessly.

'The girl gave specific details and described in depth her emotional reaction to the occasions when Per-Ola came into her room at night. The description the girl has given of his behaviour in her bed suggests that he has had anal and vaginal intercourse with her.' She pauses. 'That's the short version.'

Hurtig stands up. 'Do you mind if I open the window? I need some air,' he says, looking out at the park. 'Intercourse? If it's with a child, surely it has to be called rape, for fuck's sake?'

Jeanette hasn't got the energy to respond. The fresh air makes the papers flutter and the sound of children playing in the park outside merges with the background noise of clattering keyboards and the hum of the air conditioning.

'So why did they drop the case?' Hurtig turns back towards Jeanette.

She sighs and reads, '"Because it was not possible to examine the girl, it cannot be ruled out that this is not the case."'

'What? "Cannot be ruled out that this is not the case"?' Hurtig slams his hand down on the desk. 'What kind of pansy shit is that?'

Jeanette laughs. 'Yes, they simply didn't believe the girl. And when P-O's defence lawyer pointed out that the interviewer had posed what might be deemed to be leading questions to the girl during the preliminary interview with her, and might have directed her answers, well . . .' She sighs. 'Offence not proven. Case dropped.'

Hurtig opens his own file and leafs through it, looking for something. When he finds what he's looking for he pulls the document out and puts it on the desk.

'It goes on,' he says. 'After the investigation the Silfverberg family, in other words Per-Ola and Charlotte, feel that they've been vilified and no longer want anything to do with the girl. Danish social services place her with another family. Also in the Copenhagen area.'

'What happened to her after that?'

'I don't know, but hopefully she turned out OK, as they say.'

'She must be about twenty now,' Jeanette says, and Hurtig nods.

'But here's the weird bit.' He straightens up. 'The Silfverbergs move to Sweden, to Stockholm. They buy the apartment on Glasbruksgatan and everything looks rosy.'

'But?'

'For some reason the Copenhagen police wanted him to undergo a follow-up interview, and got in touch with us here in Stockholm.'

'What?'

'And we brought him in for questioning.'

Hurtig puts the document down and pushes it over to her, keeping his finger on the lines at the bottom.

Jeanette reads the part next to his finger.

Lead interviewer: Gert Berglind, Rape and Incest unit.

The children outside in the park and the keyboards in the next room are suddenly silent. No sound but the air conditioning and Hurtig's deep breathing.

Hurtig's finger. The well-manicured nail, neat cuticle.

Interviewee's legal representative: Viggo Dürer.

Jeanette reads and realises that there is another truth on the other side of a very thin veil. Another reality.

Also in attendance: Kenneth von Kwist, prosecutor.

And that reality is infinitely more unpleasant.

Denmark, 1988

She didn't like the old, decrepit people.

At the milk counter an old man got far too close with his smell of urine, dirt and cooking.

The woman at the meat counter who brought a bucket of water said it didn't matter and mopped up everything she had eaten for breakfast.

'Can you feel it?' The Swede looks at her excitedly. 'Stick your arm in a bit further! Don't be such a coward!'

The sow's screams make Victoria hesitate. Her arm is buried inside the pig, almost up to her elbow.

Another few centimetres, then she finally feels the piglet's head. Her thumb on its jaw, her fore- and middle fingers over the top of the head, behind the ears. Like Viggo has taught her. Then pull, carefully.

They think this is the last one. On the bed of straw around the mother ten yellow-stained piglets are wriggling about, fighting for her teats. Viggo has been standing alongside the whole time watching the births. The Swede took care of the first three, and the next seven came out by themselves.

The muscles of the vagina squeeze Victoria's arm tight and for a moment she thinks the sow might be cramping. But when she pulls a bit harder the muscles seem to relax, and in less than a second the piglet's halfway out. A moment later and it's lying on the bloody straw.

Its back legs twitch, then it's completely still.

Viggo bends over and strokes the piglet's back. 'Good work,' he says, giving Victoria a crooked smile.

The piglets always lie motionless for thirty seconds or so after birth. You think they're dead, then they suddenly start to move, fumbling around blindly until they find the sow's teats. But this piglet had twitched its legs. The others hadn't done that.

She counts silently in her head, and when she gets to thirty she starts to worry. Did she hold it too tightly? Pull the wrong way?

Viggo's smile fades as he examines the umbilical cord. 'Shit. It's dead . . .'

Viggo pulls his glasses down and looks at her seriously. 'It's OK. The umbilical cord is damaged. It isn't your fault.'

Yes, it's my fault. And when we leave the sow will make short work of the afterbirth, absorbing all the nutrition she can get.

She'll eat up her own offspring.

Viggo Dürer has a large farm outside Struer, and Victoria's only permanent companions besides her schoolbooks are thirty-four Danish-breed pigs, a bull, seven cows and a poorly looked-after horse. The farmhouse is a neglected half-timbered building in a flat, dull landscape with windmills, like an uglier version of Holland. A patchwork of windy, bleak fields stretches all the way to the horizon, where you can just make out a narrow stretch of blue, Venø Bay.

There are two reasons why she is here: her studies and recreation.

There are also two real reasons.

Isolation and discipline.

He calls it recreation, she thinks. But it's about isolation. Being kept away from other people and being disciplined. Learning to stay within certain boundaries. Housework and studies. Cleaning, making food and studying.

Working with the pigs. And the swine who regularly visit her room.

What matters to her are her studies. She's picked a correspondence course in psychology at the University of Aalborg, and the only contact she has with the outside world is with her adviser, who occasionally sends her unengaged written comments about her work.

Distance, she thinks. Locked away on a farm in the middle of nowhere. Distance from Dad. Distance from other people. A distance-learning psychology course, shut up in a room on her own in a house owned by a pig farmer with academic qualifications.

The lawyer Viggo Dürer had collected Victoria from Värmdö seven weeks before, and driven her almost a thousand kilometres in his old Citroën through a night-black Sweden and a newly woken Denmark.

Victoria looks out through the misted-up window at the farmyard, where the car has been parked. When it stops, it's as if it lets out a fart, groans and sinks into a submissive curtsy.

Viggo's disgusting to look at, but she knows that his interest in her is decreasing with every passing day. With each day that she gets older. He wants her to shave, but she refuses.

'Shave the pigs instead,' she tells him.

Victoria closes the blind. She just wants to sleep, even if she knows she ought to be studying. She's falling behind, not because she lacks motivation but because she thinks the course is a mess. Jumping from one thing to the next. Superficial knowledge without any deeper reflection.

She doesn't want to rush, and keeps getting stuck in the texts, then moving beyond them and into herself.

Why doesn't anyone understand how important this is? The human psyche can't be dealt with in an exam. Two hundred words on schizophrenia and delusional disorders is nowhere near adequate. Certainly not enough to wave about as proof that you've understood something.

She lies down on the bed and thinks about Solace. The girl who had made life in Värmdö bearable. Solace had become a surrogate that her dad had used for almost six months. But now she's been gone seven weeks.

Victoria starts at the sound of the front door slamming downstairs. Soon she hears voices from the kitchen and realises that it's Viggo and another man.

The Swede again? she thinks. Yes, it must be.

Carefully she sits up and gets off the bed, empties her glass of water in the flowerpot, puts it down against the floor and places her ear to it.

'Forget it!' Viggo's voice. Even though he's lived in Denmark for several years, the Swede still has trouble with the Jutland dialect, and Viggo always speaks Swedish to him.

She hates Viggo's Swedish; his accent sounds fake and he speaks more slowly, as if he were talking to an idiot.

'And why not?' The Swede sounds annoyed.

Viggo says nothing for a few seconds. 'It's too risky. Don't you get it?'

'I trust the Russian, and Berglind has vouched for him. What the hell are you so worried about?'

The Russian? Berglind? She doesn't understand what they're talking about.

The Swede goes on. 'Anyway, no one's going to miss a scruffy little brat from Russia.'

'Keep your voice down. There's a scruffy little brat upstairs who might hear what you say.'

'Yes, about that . . .' The Swede laughs, ignoring Viggo's plea and going on in a loud voice. 'How did it go in Aalborg? Is everything sorted out with the child?'

Viggo pauses before replying. 'The last documents are being dealt with this week. You can calm down, you're going to get your little girl.'

Victoria is confused. Aalborg? That must have been when . . .

She hears them moving around down there, footsteps on the kitchen floor, then the sound of the front door closing. When she peers round the curtain she sees that they're on their way to the outhouse.

She takes her diary out of the bedside cabinet, curls up on the bed again and waits. She lies there, wide awake in the darkness with her rucksack packed, as always, on the floor.

The Swede stays at the farm into the small hours. They set off at dawn, and she hears the cars leave at half past four.

She gets out of bed, puts her diary in the outside pocket, zips it up and looks at the time. Quarter to five. He won't be home until ten o'clock at the earliest, and by then she'll be long gone.

Before leaving the house she opens the cupboard in the living room.

It contains an old eighteenth-century music box that Viggo likes to show off when he's got guests, and she decides to find out if it's as valuable as he claims.

The morning sun is hot as she walks into Struer, where she manages to get a lift to Viborg.

From Viborg she catches the six thirty train to Copenhagen.

Mariatorget – Sofia Zetterlund's Office

It takes her no more than a minute in front of the computer in her office to find a picture of Viggo Dürer. Her chest is pounding as she sees his face and she realises that Victoria is trying to tell her something. It's just that the old man with the thin face and thick, round glasses doesn't mean anything to her; there's only the discomfort in her chest and a memory of aftershave.

She saves the picture on her hard drive and prints it out in high resolution.

The image shows his top half, and she studies the details of his face and clothes. He's pale, with thinning hair, possibly in his seventies, but without too many wrinkles. On the contrary, his face seems almost shiny. He has a number of large liver spots, full lips, a narrow nose and sunken cheeks. A grey suit, black tie and white shirt, and a badge on the breast pocket of his jacket bearing the logo of his legal firm.

No concrete memories at all. Victoria is giving her no images, no words, just vibrations.

She puts the printout in the document basket on her desk, sighs disconsolately and looks at the time. Ulrika Wendin is late.

The thin young woman returns Sofia's greeting with a weak smile. Her eyes look hollow.

Several days of hard drinking, Sofia thinks. 'How are you?'

Ulrika gives a wry smile and looks bashful, but doesn't hesitate to tell her. 'I was in a bar on Saturday, met a guy who seemed OK, so I took him home. We shared a bottle of Rosita and then we went to bed.'

Sofia doesn't see where the story is going, so nods in encouragement and waits.

Ulrika laughs. 'I don't know if I really did it. I mean, if I took him home. It feels a bit like someone else did that, but I suppose I was pretty hammered.'

Ulrika pauses briefly and takes a packet of chewing gum from her pocket. Several 500-krona notes come with it.

Ulrika quickly pushes them back into her pocket without comment.

Sofia knows that Ulrika is unemployed and hardly has access to that sort of money. Where's all that come from? she wonders.

'I was able to relax,' Ulrika goes on, without looking at her. 'Because I wasn't the one sleeping with him. I have vestibulitis. Embarrassing, huh? I can't just choose to let anyone inside, but it was OK with him because it wasn't me lying there.'

Vestibulitis? Not her lying there? Sofia considers the rape that Karl Lundström subjected Ulrika to. She's aware that one of the causes of vestibulitis is believed to be excessive washing of the genitals. The mucus membranes dry out and become fragile, the nerves and muscles are both weakened, and there's constant pain.

Memories of scrubbing for hours in a steaming shower, the coarse sponge and the smell of soap, but never being able to wash away the stench of him.

Forced to become someone else to dare to feel longing, closeness. To be able to be normal. Ruined forever because of what a man had done. Sofia can feel her blood boiling.

'Ulrika . . .' Sofia leans over the desk to underline her question. 'Can you tell me what pleasure is?'

The girl sits quietly for a while before she answers. 'Sleep.'

'How is your sleep?' Sofia asks. 'Can you tell me about it?'

Ulrika breathes in with a deep sigh. 'Empty. It's nothing.'

'So pleasure for you is not feeling?' Sofia thinks of her chafed heels, the pain she needs in order to feel calm. 'Pleasure is nothing?'

Ulrika doesn't answer the question, but straightens her back and says angrily instead, 'After those bastards raped me in that hotel I drank every day for four years.' Her eyes are black. 'Then I tried to pull myself together, but I can't see what the fucking point is. I always end up back in the shit.'

'What sort of shit do you end up in?'

Ulrika slumps in her chair.

'It's like my body isn't mine, or that it sends out signals that make people think they can do whatever the fuck they like with me. People can hit me, they can fuck me, no matter what I say or do. I tell them it fucking hurts, but that doesn't make any difference.'

The vestibulitis, Sofia thinks. Unwanted intercourse and dry membranes. This is a girl who doesn't know how it feels to desire anything, who has simply learned to dream about avoidance. And being inside the void of sleep is obviously a release.

Perhaps Ulrika's behaviour in the bar contained one important element. A situation where she could make the decisions, where she was in control. Ulrika was so unused to acting on her own desires that she simply didn't recognise herself.

It would be easy to think this was a case of dissociation. But dissociation doesn't develop in teenagers, it's a child's defence mechanism.

This is more like confrontational behaviour, Sofia thinks, in the absence of a better description. A sort of cognitive self-therapy.

Sofia is aware that the girl was drugged in the hotel room, with something that paralysed her lower body and led to her becoming incontinent.

She realises that Ulrika's condition, including possibly anorexia, self-loathing, relatively low-level alcoholism and a background of abusive and exploitative boyfriends, probably goes back to this one event seven years ago.

Everything is Karl Lundström's fault.

Ulrika suddenly turns even paler. 'What's that?'

Sofia doesn't understand what she means. The girl's gaze is fixed on something on the desk.

Five seconds' silence. Then Ulrika gets up from her chair and picks up the printout from the document basket. The picture of Viggo Dürer.

Sofia doesn't know how to react. Shit, she thinks. How could I be so thoughtless? 'That's Karl Lundström's lawyer' is all she manages to say. 'Have you met him?'

Ulrika looks, stares at the picture for a few seconds, then puts it down on the desk. 'Oh, forget it. Never seen him before. I thought it was someone else.' The girl tries to smile, but Sofia doesn't find the result very convincing.

Ulrika Wendin has met Viggo Dürer.

Gamla Enskede – Kihlberg House

'So, what do we do about the daughter?' Hurtig looks at Jeanette.

'Obviously she's of great interest to us. Find out as much as you can about her. Name, address and so on. Well, you know the sort of thing.'

Hurtig nods. 'Shall I put out an alert for her?'

Jeanette considers. 'No, not yet. Let's hold off and see what we can find out about her.' She gets up to go back to her office. 'I'll call von Kwist and suggest a meeting tomorrow, so we can find out what the hell happened.'

After a short call to the prosecutor to set up a meeting about the dropped investigation into P-O Silfverberg, Jeanette gets in her car to drive home.

Stockholm strikes her as greyer and wetter than ever. A city in black and white. On the horizon the clouds are breaking up, and between their shining edges she can see glimpses of blue sky. When she gets out of the car there's a smell of earthworms and wet grass.

Johan is sitting in front of the television when Jeanette gets home just after five, and from what she can see in the kitchen it looks like he's already eaten. She goes over to the sofa and kisses the top of his head.

'Hello, darling. Had a good day?'

He shrugs his shoulders and doesn't answer.

'We've had a card from Grandma and Grandad. I left it on the kitchen table.' He turns the volume up.

Jeanette goes back into the kitchen, picks up the postcard and looks at the picture. The Great Wall of China, tall mountains and a rolling green landscape. She reads the back. They're fine, but missing home. The usual.

She clears the draining board and fills the dishwasher before going upstairs to have a shower.

When she comes back down, Johan has vanished into his room, and she can hear him playing one of his computer games.

She and Åke had talked about stopping Johan playing the most violent games, but soon realised there was no point. All his friends have them, so a ban would have no effect at all. Have I been overprotective? she wonders, then suddenly gets an idea.

Which game has he been going on about recently? The one everyone apart from him has got? She goes into the kitchen and calls Hurtig.

'Hi. Can I have your help with something?'

He sounds out of breath. 'Sure. What with? Anything I need to look up?'

'You could answer this in your sleep. What's the most popular computer game right now?'

'*Assassin's Creed*,' he replies instantly.

'No.'

'*Counter-Strike*?'

Jeanette recognises the name. 'No, unless I've got this wrong, I don't think it's an action game.'

Hurtig is breathing hard down the line, then there's the sound of a door closing. 'You must be thinking of *Spore*?' he eventually suggests.

'Yep, that was it. Is it violent?'

'That depends on how you choose to play, but there's an evolutionary element where you have to develop your character from a tiny cell to master of the universe, and a bit of violence can come in handy now and then.'

The computer noises from Johan's room go quiet, he opens the door, goes into the hall and starts putting his shoes on. Jeanette asks Hurtig to wait a moment while she asks Johan where he's going, but the only answer she gets is the front door closing.

When he's gone she smiles forlornly and picks up the phone. 'I came home early today because I was worried Johan might have shut himself away in his room or disappeared to a friend's. And since I got home he's managed to do both.'

'I understand,' Hurtig says. 'And now you want to surprise him?'

'Yep. Forgive my ignorance, but if you lend me the game, could I copy it onto Johan's computer and then give it back to you?'

Hurtig doesn't answer straight away, and she imagines she can hear him chuckling.

'OK,' he finally says. 'Let's do it this way . . . I'll come over now and install the game for Johan, so he gets a surprise this evening.'

'You're a good guy. If you haven't eaten yet, I can offer you pizza?'

'Thanks, that'd be great.'

'What kind do you want?'

He laughs. 'You could probably answer that in your sleep. What's the most popular pizza these days?'

She gets the hint. 'Provençale?'

'No.'

'Four Seasons?'

'No, not that either,' Hurtig says. 'Nothing fancy.'

'In that case, you probably mean Vesuvio?'

'That's the one! Vesuvius.'

A noise wakes Jeanette. She gets up from the sofa and sees the two empty pizza boxes on the table. Of course, she thinks. Hurtig came, we ate pizza, and I fell asleep while he was installing the game.

She can see a light from the doorway to Johan's room, pads over and pushes the door open.

Hurtig and Johan are sitting at the computer with their backs to her, deeply absorbed in some sort of blue insect floating around on the screen.

They're so immersed in the game that they don't notice her.

'Get it! Get it!' Hurtig whispers with quiet insistence, slapping Johan on the back when the insect swallows up what looks like a hairy red spiral.

Jeanette's first instinct is to ask what the hell they think they're doing at four o'clock in the morning and send them to bed, but just as she opens her mouth she stops herself.

Forget it. Let them play.

She curls up on the sofa again, pulls the blanket over her and tries to get back to sleep.

She rolls over onto her stomach to the sound of muffled laughter from Johan's room. She's quietly grateful to Hurtig, but at the same time it surprises her that he's so irresponsible that he doesn't seem to understand that a teenager needs his sleep if he's to cope with school.

His training later on tomorrow is probably ruined now. Hurtig might manage to work, but Johan's going to be like a zombie.

She soon realises it's pointless trying to sleep. She rolls onto her back and stares at the ceiling.

She can still make out the three letters Åke once wrote on the ceiling in green paint when he was drunk. The fact that he'd painted over them the following day hadn't helped, and like so many other things he had promised to sort out, nothing more ever happened. An H, an F and a C stand out through the otherwise white ceiling: Hammarby Football Club.

If we end up selling the house, he'd better help me, she thinks.

There'll be loads of paperwork and estate agents going on about home staging. But no, Åke will just piss off to Poland, drinking champagne and selling old paintings he'd have destroyed years ago if I hadn't stopped him.

She imagines what it would be like if they signed the divorce papers.

The legally prescribed six-month period between marriage and divorce suddenly feels like limbo to Jeanette. And after that comes the nightmare of dividing their assets. But she can't help smiling at the thought that she actually has a legal right to half of their shared assets, and wonders if she ought to scare Åke by pretending to demand her share, just to see how he reacts. The more paintings he sells before the divorce goes through, the more money she could get.

More laughter from Johan's room, and although Jeanette's happy on his behalf, she feels lonely.

Please, Sofia, come to me soon, she thinks, lying on her side as she huddles up beneath the blanket.

She longs to feel Sofia pressed against her.

Vita Bergen – Sofia Zetterlund's Apartment

Sofia gets the tape recorder, sits by the window and looks down into the street. It's stopped raining. A woman walking a black-and-white Border collie passes by on the opposite pavement. The dog makes her think of Hannah, who was so badly bitten by a similar dog shortly after they got home from interrailing that she had to have a finger amputated. Yet she remained devoted to dogs.

Sofia switches on the machine and starts talking.

What's wrong with me?

Why can't I feel the same tenderness and love for animals as everyone else?

I certainly tried plenty of times when I was a child.

First it was stick insects, because they were easier than fish, and were more suitable because he was so bloody allergic to Esmeralda, who had to go and live with someone else who liked cats. Then there was the attempt to get something for the summer, a baby rabbit that died in the car because it didn't occur to anyone that even bog-standard rabbits need water, then the goat we borrowed that spent all summer having a phantom pregnancy, and all anyone remembers are the sticky black pellets of shit that got everywhere and kept getting stuck to your feet. Then there were the hens that nobody liked, then the neighbour's horse for a while, before the rabbit that was faithful and happy and obedient and warm, looked after come rain or shine, fed before school, but the rabbit got bitten by the neighbour's German shepherd, which probably wasn't evil to start with, but anyone who's been beaten probably ends up getting seriously pissed off and attacking anything weaker . . .

This time she doesn't get tired of her voice. She knows who she is.

She sits there by the window, peering down through the venetian blind at everything going on outside, and letting her brain work.

The rabbit couldn't get away, because there was snow blocking everywhere it could have taken cover and the dog bit it on the scruff of the neck the same way it had bitten the three-year-old who had been feeding it ice cream. Because the dog hated everything, it hated ice cream too and bit the kid's face and no one really cared, they just sewed up the wounds as best they could. And they all hoped for the best, and then there was the horse again, and riding lessons and ponies and love hearts in diaries that were actually for some older guy you wanted to like you or at least look at you as you stood there in the corridor with your new breasts and tightest trousers. When you could smoke properly without coughing or being sick like you did when you'd taken Valium and drunk too much and been stupid enough to go home and fall over in the hall and Mum had to take care of you and you just wanted to sit in her lap and be as young as you actually were and feel her hugs and the smell of sneaky cigarettes seeing as Mum was scared of him as well and kept her smoking a secret . . .

She switches off the tape recorder, goes into the kitchen and sits down at the table.

She rewinds, then takes the tape out. She now has a sizeable collection of memories lined up neatly on the shelf in the study.

Gao's light, almost soundless steps, then the creaking sound of the door behind the bookcase in the living room.

She gets up and goes in to him, in their secret, soft and safe room.

He's sitting on the floor drawing, and she sits down on the bed and puts a fresh cassette in the tape recorder.

The room is a den, a place of refuge where she can be herself.

Klara Sjö – Public Prosecution Authority

Words are streaming out of Kenneth von Kwist's mouth as he explains his role in the follow-up interview with P-O Silfverberg, and Jeanette notices that he's doing so without checking a single fact. Von Kwist has all the details in his head, and she has a growing feeling that he's reciting a story he's learned by heart. The prosecutor peers at her as if he's trying to work out what she's after.

'As I remember it, the Copenhagen police called in the morning,' he says. 'They wanted me, in my capacity as a prosecutor, to sit in on the interview with Silfverberg. The session was conducted by former police commissioner Gert Berglind, and Per-Ola Silfverberg had his own lawyer, Viggo Dürer, present.'

'So there were just the four of you?'

Von Kwist nods, then takes a deep breath.

'Yes, we talked for a couple of hours, and he denied all the allegations. He claimed that his foster-daughter had always had a vivid imagination. I recall him saying that she had been abandoned by her biological mother soon after birth and had been placed in foster care with the Silfverberg family. I clearly remember that he was very sad and deeply affronted about having such allegations made against him.'

When Jeanette asks him how he can remember something that happened so long ago in such detail, he replies that he has an excellent memory and a quick mind.

'Was there good reason to believe him?' Jeanette attempts. 'I mean, Per-Ola and his wife left Denmark as soon as he was released, and to my mind at least, that seems to suggest that he had something to hide.'

The prosecutor lets out a deep sigh. 'We were confident that he was telling the truth.'

Jeanette shakes her head in bewilderment. 'Even though his daughter claimed he'd done all manner of things to her? It seems quite incredible to me that he should be exonerated so easily.'

'Not to me.' The prosecutor's eyes narrow behind his glasses. A faint smile plays on his lips. 'I've been doing this so long that I know that mistakes and miscalculations are always happening.'

Jeanette realises she's not going to get any further and changes the subject.

'What can you tell me about the Ulrika Wendin case?'

'What do you want to know?' He takes a deep gulp of water. 'That was seven years ago now,' he goes on.

'Yes, but with your excellent memory I'm sure you remember that it was the same Gert Berglind who was in charge of the investigation into Karl Lundström, which was also dropped. You didn't see any connection?'

'No, it never occurred to me that there might be one.'

'When Annette Lundström gave Karl an alibi for the night that Ulrika Wendin was raped, you dropped the case. You didn't even check if her information was correct. Have I got that right?'

Jeanette can feel herself getting angry, and tries to control herself. She knows she mustn't explode. That she must stay calm no matter what she might think of the prosecutor's actions.

'I made a choice,' he says calmly. 'A decision based on the information I had available to me. My interview was concerned with whether or not Lundström had been present. And my interview with him showed that he hadn't been. It was as simple as that. I had no suspicions that he might have been lying.'

'You don't think now that you should have followed the whole thing up rather more rigorously?'

'Annette Lundström's account was just one part of the information I had, but obviously it could have been followed up better. Everything could have been followed up better.'

'And you told Gert Berglind and the investigating team that they should continue?'

'Of course.'

'Yet that didn't happen?'

'That would have been a decision they made based on all the facts at their disposal.'

Jeanette sees von Kwist's smile. His voice is that of a snake.

Jutas Backe – Stockholm City Centre

The Mental Health Care Reform that came into force on 1 January, 1995, intended to integrate the mentally ill into society, was poorly thought out. The fact that it had a very personal impact on the chairman of the committee behind the reform, the minister of social affairs, Bo Holmberg, is a bitter irony. His wife, Foreign Minister Anna Lindh, was murdered by a man whom the Court of Appeal decreed was mentally ill, and who ought therefore to have been in secure accommodation. A large number of hospitals may have been closed in the 1970s, but it's impossible not to wonder what might have happened if the Mental Health Inquiry had reached a different conclusion.

There are approximately two thousand beds in homeless shelters in Stockholm, and five thousand homeless people, most of them with alcohol and drug problems, which means that there's a constant battle for them to get a roof over their heads.

Because something like half of them also suffer from some form of mental illness, fighting often breaks out over the available beds, and many of them therefore choose to sleep elsewhere.

In the large caverns beneath St Johannes Church whole colonies of people have developed, all sharing the fact that they have fallen outside the protection of ordinary society.

In the damp, cathedral-like spaces they have found something resembling security.

Small shelters made of plastic or tarpaulin stand alongside some pieces of cardboard and a sleeping bag.

The quality of these shelters varies hugely, and some could almost be regarded as rather elegant.

At the top of Jutas backe she turns onto Johannesgatan and walks along the churchyard railing.

Every step carries her closer to something new, a place where she might be able to stay, and be happy. Change her name, change her clothes, and get rid of the past. A place where her life can take a new direction.

She pulls her woolly hat from her coat pocket and takes care to hide her blonde hair as she puts it on.

The familiar tingle in her stomach is back, and, just like last time, she wonders what to do if she needs to go to the toilet.

It had all resolved itself in the end, seeing as the victim had let her in, had even invited her in. Per-Ola Silfverberg had been naive, far too trusting for his own good.

He had been standing with his back to her when she drew the large knife and cut the artery on his lower right arm. He had slumped to his knees, turned round and looked at her, then at the pool of blood on the pale parquet floor. His breathing was laboured, but he still tried to get up, and she had let him, knowing he didn't stand a chance. When she took out her Polaroid camera he had looked surprised.

It had taken her almost two weeks to track the woman down to the caves beneath the church. In spite of her background, Fredrika Grünewald had ended up on the streets, and had over the past ten years become known as the Duchess. She knows that the Grünewald family, as a result of Fredrika's poor judgement and risky investments, has lost the whole of its fortune.

For a while she wasn't sure about following through with her plan to exact revenge on Fredrika Grünewald, since everything's already gone to hell for her, but you have to finish what you've started.

There's no space for sympathy.

Memories of Fredrika Grünewald come back to her once more. She sees a filthy floor and hears their breathing. The stench of sweat, damp earth and machine oil.

No matter whether Fredrika Grünewald was the instigator or just someone carrying out her role, she was guilty. Choosing not to act can also confer guilt.

She turns into Kammakargatan, then left again down into Döbelnsgatan. She's now on the opposite side of the church, where the entrance is supposed to be. She slows and looks hard for the door the beggar told her about. Some fifty metres ahead of her she sees a dark figure standing under a tree. Beside him is a grey metal door, ajar, and from inside comes the faint sound of voices.

She's found the caverns.

'And who the fuck are you?'

The man steps out from the darkness under the tree.

He's drunk, which is good, because his memory of her will be vague, possibly even non-existent.

'Do you know the Duchess?' She looks him in the eye, but because he's badly cross-eyed she finds it hard to know which one to focus on.

He stares back. 'Why?'

'I'm a friend of hers, and I need to see her.'

The man chuckles to himself. 'Oh, so the old bag's got friends? I'd never have guessed.' He pulls out a crumpled cigarette packet and lights a butt. 'What's in it for me? I mean, if I show you where she is.'

She's no longer sure he's drunk. There's a sudden clarity in his gaze that scares her. What if he remembers her?

'You can have three hundred if you show me where she is. All right?'

She gets out her purse and gives him three hundred-krona notes that he looks at with a satisfied grin before holding the door open for her and gesturing to her to go in.

A cloying, suffocating stench hits her, and she pulls a handkerchief from her pocket. She holds it over her nose and mouth to stop herself from throwing up, as the man chuckles at her reaction.

The staircase is long, and when her eyes have got used to the darkness she can see a faint light at the bottom.

When she steps out into the large cavern she can't believe her eyes. It's the size of a football pitch and the roof must be ten metres high. All around there's a clutter of tents, boxes and shelters around small open fires and a mass of people lying or sitting around the fires.

But the most noticeable thing is the silence.

The only sounds are low whispering and snoring.

There's something respectful about the place. As if those who live here have come to a tacit agreement not to disturb one another, to let each of them be in peace with their own worries.

The man walks past her, and she follows him into the shadows. No one seems to have noticed her.

'This is where the old bag hangs out.' He points to a den made of black bin bags, large enough for at least four people. The entrance is covered with a blue blanket. 'I'm off now. If she asks who showed you the way, just say it was Börje.'

When she squats down she can see someone moving inside. Slowly she removes the handkerchief from her mouth and takes a cautious breath. The air is thick and stuffy, and she makes an effort to breathe through her mouth. She takes out the piano wire and hides it in her hand.

'Fredrika?' she whispers. 'Are you there? I need to talk to you.'

She moves near to the entrance, takes the Polaroid camera from her bag and carefully pushes the blanket aside.

If shame has a smell, then that's what hits her nose.

Mariatorget – Sofia Zetterlund's Office

Ann-Britt informs her that Linnea Lundström has arrived, and Sofia Zetterlund goes out into the waiting room to meet her.

Just as with Ulrika Wendin, Sofia intends to use a three-stage process in her treatment of Linnea.

The first part of the treatment is exclusively about stabilisation and trust. Support and structure are the keywords, and Sofia hopes medication won't be needed, for either Ulrika or Linnea. But it can't be ruled out yet. The second part is about remembering, discussing, reliving and working on the sexual trauma. Finally, in the last phase, the traumatic experiences have to be separated from sexual experiences now and in the future.

Sofia had been surprised by Ulrika's story of picking up a stranger from the bar, a purely sexual act that had clearly made Ulrika feel better.

Then she remembers Ulrika's reaction when she caught sight of the picture of Viggo Dürer. Dürer had a central role in Linnea's childhood.

What role might he have played in Ulrika's life?

Linnea Lundström sits down opposite Sofia. 'Feels like I was only just here,' she says. 'Am I so ill I've got to come here every day?'

Sofia is relieved that Linnea is relaxed enough to be making jokes.

'No, it's not about that. But it's good to have frequent sessions at the start, so we can get to know each other quickly.'

Very gradually, Sofia leads the conversation towards the subject that is the real reason for her meetings with Linnea: the girl's relationship with her father.

Sofia would rather Linnea bring the subject up herself, as she had done during their meeting the previous day, and soon enough her hopes are fulfilled.

'Do you think I'd understand myself better if I understood him better?'

Sofia pauses before answering. 'Maybe . . . But first I want to be completely sure that you think I'm the right person to talk to.'

Linnea looks surprised. 'Well, who else is there? My friends, or what? I'd die of shame . . .'

Sofia smiles. 'No, not necessarily any of your friends. But there are other therapists.'

'You talked to him. You're the most suitable, at least according to Annette.'

Sofia looks at Linnea and decides that the best word to describe her is 'stubborn'. I can't lose her now, Sofia thinks. 'I understand . . . So, back to your father. If you want to talk about him, where would you like us to begin?'

Linnea digs a crumpled piece of paper out of her pocket and puts it on the desk. It looks like she's embarrassed. 'I kept something from you yesterday.' Linnea hesitates, then pushes the piece of paper towards Sofia. 'This is a letter Dad wrote to me this spring. Read it.'

The handwriting is beautiful, but difficult to decipher. The letter was written during a flight just a few weeks before Karl Lundström was arrested.

The first part is just the usual phrases. Then it gets increasingly fragmentary and incoherent.

> Talent is patience, and fear of defeat. You have both qualities, Linnea, so you have all the prerequisites for success even if it doesn't feel like it now.
>
> But for me all is past. There are wounds in life that quietly devour the soul like leprosy.
>
> No, I need to seek out shadow! Healthy and alive try to get near, follow them in awe and keep them dear, I shall seek a home in the home of shadows.

Sofia recognises the phrase. Karl Lundström had talked about the home of shadows during their first meeting in Huddinge. He had said it was a metaphor for a secret, forbidden place.

> Everything is in the book I have with me. It's about me and about you.
>
> It says that I only desire what thousands, perhaps millions, have done before me and that means my actions are sanctioned by history.

The impulses to the desires are not in my conscience, but in the collective interaction established by others. By others' desires.

I am only doing what the others have done, and my conscience should feel clear. Yet my conscience still says something is wrong! I don't understand!

Of course I could ask the Oracle of Delphi, Pythia, the woman who never lies.

Thanks to her, Socrates realised that a wise man knows he knows nothing. The ignorant man believes he knows something he doesn't know, and is therefore doubly ignorant because he doesn't understand that he doesn't know! But I realise that I don't know!

Does that mean I'm wise?

This is followed by several lines that are illegible, then a large, dark red stain that Sofia presumes is red wine. She looks up at Linnea again and raises a questioning eyebrow.

'I know,' the girl says. 'It's a bit weird – he was probably drunk.'

Just like Socrates, I'm a criminal accused of corrupting youth. But of course he was a pederast, and perhaps his accusers were right? The state praises its gods and the rest of us are accused of worshipping demons.

Socrates was just like me! Are we wrong? Everything is in this book! By the way, do you know what happened in Kristianstad when you were little? Viggo and Henrietta? It's in this book!

Viggo and Henrietta Dürer, Sofia thinks. Annette Lundström mentioned the Dürers, and Viggo was in Linnea's drawings.

Sofia recognises Karl Lundström's ambivalent attitude to right and wrong from her conversation with him in Huddinge, and the pieces of the puzzle begin to fall into place. She continues reading, although the letter unsettles her.

The great sleep. And blindness. Annette is blind and Henrietta was blind, as befits girls from Sigtuna College.

She realises that Henrietta Dürer had been in the same class as Annette Lundström. She too had worn a pig's mask, grunting and laughing. She had been called something different then, something common, Andersson, Johansson? But she had been one of them, masked and blind.

And she had married Viggo Dürer.

This is too much. Sofia feels her stomach clench.

Linnea interrupts her thoughts. 'Dad said you understood him. I think he's talking about someone like you in the letter, a Pythia, as he puts it . . . Mind you, he does sound very odd.'

'What's the book he's referring to?'

Linnea sighs again. 'I don't know . . . He read so much. But he often talked about a book called *Pythia's Instructions*.'

'*Pythia's Instructions*?'

'Yes, although he never showed it to me.'

In less than a week she's met two young women whose lives have been ruined by one and the same man. Even if Karl Lundström is dead, she's going to see that his victims get justice.

What is weakness? Being a victim? A woman? Exploited?

No, weakness is not turning that to your advantage.

'I can help you remember,' she says.

Linnea looks at her. 'Do you think so?'

'I know so.'

Sofia opens her desk drawer and takes out the pictures that Linnea drew when she was five, nine and ten years old.

St Johannes Cavern – Crime Scene

The Swedish Order of St Johannes has been active since the twelfth century, under the motto 'In aid of the poor and the sick'. It is therefore providential that the caverns beneath St Johannes Church on Norrmalm in Stockholm should be used as a place of refuge for the impoverished and outcast.

The banner of the Order of St Johannes is depicted on the entrance to the cavern, an inverted knight's coat of arms in the form of a white cross on a red background, put there by someone wanting to declare that anyone might feel safe here, no matter who they are. It is, however, not a logical act of providence but, rather, a mocking inversion of it when the message of safety occasionally doesn't ring true, and in this instance a cry for help echoes between the walls down in the crypts.

Jeanette Kihlberg is woken by her phone at half past six in the morning, and Police Commissioner Dennis Billing orders her to get into the city as soon as possible, because a woman has been found murdered in the caverns below St Johannes Church.

She quickly scribbles a note to Johan and leaves it on the kitchen table along with a hundred-krona note, before quietly slipping out and getting in the car.

She calls Jens Hurtig. He's already had a call from central command and should be there in fifteen minutes, traffic permitting. According to what Hurtig has heard, the atmosphere down in the caverns resembles a lynch mob, so they arrange to meet outside.

A lorry with a flat tyre in the Söderleden Tunnel means that the traffic is at a standstill. She realises she's going to be late and calls Hurtig to tell him to go in before she gets there.

On the Central Bridge the traffic starts to move again.

There are three police vans, blue lights flashing, and a dozen officers are busy trying to secure the entrance to the caverns.

As Jeanette goes over towards Åhlund, she catches sight of Schwarz a bit further away in front of a heavy metal door. 'How's it going?' She has to shout to make herself heard.

'Total chaos.' Åhlund throws his arms out. 'We've emptied the whole place of people, almost fifty of them in total. As you can see . . .' He gestures with his hand. 'What the hell, they've got nowhere else to go, have they?'

'Have you called the City Mission?' Jeanette steps aside to let through an officer on his way to deal with one of the most aggressive protesters.

'Of course, but they're full and can't help us right now.'

Åhlund waits for her to speak, and Jeanette thinks for a moment before going on.

'OK. Order a local transport bus to come over here as soon as possible. They can warm up in there and we'll be able to talk to any of them who've got anything to say. But I'm assuming most of them aren't feeling too cooperative. They usually aren't.'

Åhlund nods and pulls out his radio.

'I'll go down and see what's happened. Hopefully it won't be too long before they can go back inside.'

Jeanette goes over to the metal door, where Schwarz stops her and gives her a white breathing mask.

'I think you'll want this.'

He wrinkles his nose.

The stench really is unbearable, and Jeanette pulls the rubber bands behind her ears and checks that the mask is sitting tightly over her nose before she goes down into the darkness.

The large cavern is bathed in the sharp glow of floodlights, and there's a rumble from the generator powering them.

Jeanette stops and looks out across the bizarre underground society.

A shanty town, like something out of the slums of Rio de Janeiro. Homes made out of rubbish and things found in the street. Some had been constructed with a fair degree of skill and an eye for aesthetics. Others were just childish dens. In spite of the muddle, there is a sense of order about the whole thing.

An underlying desire for structure.

Hurtig is standing some twenty metres away and waves her over. She makes her way carefully through the heaps of sleeping bags, bin bags, boxes and clothes. Beside one of the tents is a small shelf full of books. A paper sign says that the books are free to be borrowed, as long as they are brought back.

She knows that the prejudice about homeless people not being intellectual or interested in culture is unfounded. The step that leads down here is probably no greater than a bit of bad luck, some unpaid bills or a bout of depression.

Hurtig is standing by a tent made of large plastic bags. In front of the entrance hangs a shabby blue blanket, and she can see that there's someone lying inside.

'OK, what's happened?' Jeanette crouches down and tries to see into the tent.

'The woman inside is named Fredrika Grünewald, known as the Duchess, seeing as she's supposed to come from some noble family. We're already checking that out.'

'Good. What else?'

'A few witnesses say a man called Börje came down here yesterday afternoon in the company of an unknown woman.'

'Have we got hold of this Börje?'

'No, not yet, but he's something of a celebrity down here so it shouldn't be difficult. We've put an alert out.'

'Good, good.' Jeanette moves closer to the opening of the tent.

'She's in a really terrible state. Her head has pretty much been severed from her neck.'

'Knife?' She stands up and straightens her back.

'Don't think so. We found this.' Hurtig holds up a plastic bag containing a long steel wire. 'This was probably the murder weapon.'

Jeanette nods. 'And no one down here did it?'

'I don't think so. If she'd just been, well, beaten to death and then robbed, then maybe . . .' Hurtig looks thoughtful. 'But this is something different.'

'So nothing was stolen from her?'

'No. Her purse is still here, containing almost two thousand kronor and a valid monthly travel card.'

'OK. So what do you think?'

Hurtig shrugs. 'Revenge, maybe. After killing her, the murderer smeared her with excrement. Mostly around the mouth.'

'Oh, Jesus.'

'Ivo's going to check if it's her own shit, but if we're lucky it'll be the murderer's.' Hurtig gestures towards the tent, where Ivo Andrić and a couple of his colleagues are busy putting the body inside a grey mortuary bag for transport to Solna.

The forensics team lift off the plastic acting as a tent, and now Jeanette can see the whole of the tragic little home. A small camping stove, a few tins, and a pile of clothes. Carefully she picks up a dress and notes that it's Chanel. Hardly used.

She reads the labels on the unopened tins of food and sees that several of them have been imported. Mussels and goose liver pâté. Not the sort of thing you find in the Co-op.

What was Fredrika Grünewald doing down here? she thinks. She doesn't seem to have been short of money. There has to be another reason. But what?

Jeanette looks around at her belongings. Something's missing. She closes her eyes tightly, trying to clear her mind, then see the whole picture without any preconceptions.

What is it I'm not seeing? she thinks.

'Jeanette.' Ivo Andrić taps her on the shoulder. 'One thing, before I go. It's not human excrement on her face. It's dog shit.'

And that's when she sees it.

It isn't something missing.

It's something that shouldn't be there.

Denmark, 1988

Dare you today, then, you weak fucker? Dare you? Dare you? No, you don't dare! You don't! You're too weak! You're pathetic! It's hardly surprising no one cares about you!

The shabby houses on Istedgade, the hotels, bars and sex shops lining the pavements, and she turns into a calmer side street, Viktoriagade. It's hardly been a year since she was last here, and she remembers that the hotel is very close, right next door to a record shop.

A year ago she had chosen the hotel with great care. In Berlin she had lived on Bergmannstrasse in Kreuzberg, and the circle was closed when she arrived here. Viktoriagade had been a logical place to die.

As she opens the old wooden door to the reception area, she notes that the neon sign with the hotel's name on it is still broken. Behind the desk sits the same bored man as last time. He gives her the keys and she pays with some crumpled notes she found in a biscuit tin in Viggo's kitchen.

Altogether she has almost two thousand Danish kronor and over nine hundred Swedish. That's enough for a few days. Maybe the music box she stole from Viggo will be worth a few hundred more.

Room number 7, where she tried to hang herself a year ago, is on the second floor.

As she goes up the creaking wooden stairs she wonders if the crack in the porcelain sink has been repaired yet. Before she made up her mind to hang herself she had thrown a bottle of perfume against the edge, and the porcelain had cracked all the way to the drain.

But after that everything was very undramatic.

The hook in the ceiling came loose and she woke up on the bathroom floor with the belt around her neck, a thick lip and part of her front tooth missing. She had wiped up the blood with a T-shirt.

Afterwards it was as if nothing had happened. The bathroom looked exactly the same, apart from the crack in the sink and the hole in the ceiling left by the hook. It had been an almost invisible, meaningless act.

She unlocks the door and goes into the room. Just as before, a narrow bed stands by the right-hand wall, there's a wardrobe on the left and the window onto Viktoriagade is just as filthy as it was before. The room smells of smoke and mould and the door to the little bathroom is open.

She kicks off her shoes, tosses her rucksack on the bed and opens the window to air the room.

From outside she can hear the rumble of traffic and the barking of stray dogs.

Then she goes into the bathroom. The hole in the ceiling has been filled and the crack in the sink has been repaired with silicone and has become a dirty grey streak.

She shuts the bathroom door and lies down on the bed.

I don't exist, she thinks, then laughs.

She gets her diary and a pen out of her bag and starts to write.

Copenhagen, 23 May 1988

Denmark is a shit country. Pigs and farmers, German girls and German boys.

I am holes and cracks and meaningless acts. In Viktoriagade and in Bergmannstrasse. Then raped by Germans on Danish soil. At the Roskilde Festival, three little German boys.

Now humiliated by a Danish German bastard in a bunker built in Denmark by the Germans. Denmark and Germany. Viggo is German Danish. A German whore's bastard Danish son.

She laughs out loud. 'Solace Manuti. Comfort me, I am crazy.'

Crazy. How the hell can anyone be called that?

Then she puts the diary down. She isn't crazy. Everyone else is.

She thinks about Viggo Dürer. The German bastard.

He deserves to be strangled and dumped in a bomb shelter out on Oddesund.

Born out of a German cunt, and dead in a German shithole. Then the pigs could eat him up.

She picks up her diary again.

She stops and leafs back through it. Two months, four months, six months.

She reads:

Värmdö, 13 December 1987

Solace won't wake up after what he did in the sauna. I'm scared she might be dying. She's breathing and her eyes are open, but she's completely gone. He was hard with her. Her head hit the wall while he was at it and she looked like a game of pickup sticks afterwards. Spilled out across the bench in the sauna.

I've bathed her face with a damp cloth, but she won't wake up.

Is she dead?

I hate him. Goodness and forgiveness are just another form of oppression and provocation. Hate is purer.

Victoria leafs forward a few pages in the diary.

Solace wasn't dead. She woke up, but she didn't say anything, she just had a stomach ache and cramped like she was going to give birth. Then he came to us, into our room.

When he saw us he looked very unhappy at first. Then he blew snot all over us. He put his finger against one nostril and blew snot out of the other!

Couldn't he just have spat on us?!

She hardly recognises her own handwriting.

24 January 1988

Solace refuses to take off the mask. I'm starting to get tired of her wooden face. She just lies there whining. She squeaks. The mask must have grown into her face, like the wooden fibres have eaten into her.

She is a wooden doll. Silent and dead, she just lies there and her wooden face squeaks because it's so damn damp in the sauna.

Wooden dolls don't have children. They just swell in damp and heat.

I hate her!

Victoria closes the diary. Outside the window she hears someone laugh.

That night she dreams of a house where all the windows are open. It's her task to close them, but as soon as she closes the last one, one she's already closed opens again. The strange thing is that she's the one who decides that all the windows can't be closed at the same time, seeing as her task is far too easy. Closing, opening, closing, opening, on and on until she gets fed up and sits down on the floor and pees.

When she wakes up the bed is wet and it's run through the mattress and onto the floor.

It's no more than four o'clock in the morning, but she decides to get up. She washes herself, gathers her things together, leaves the room, taking the sheet with her and dumping it in a bin out in the corridor, and then goes down to reception.

She sits down in the little cafe and lights a cigarette.

This is the fourth or fifth time in less than a month that she's woken up after wetting the bed. It's happened before, but never so frequently, and never in connection with such vivid dreams.

She gets some books out of her rucksack.

Her university psychology course book and several books by R. J. Stoller. She likes the fact that someone with a name so close to the Swedish word for crazy can write about psychology, and finds it just as amusing, if not ridiculous, that the paperback of Freud's *Theory of Sexuality* that she's also brought with her is so thin.

Her copy of *The Interpretation of Dreams* is so dog-eared now that it's almost falling apart, but in contrast to what she expected before she began reading, she found herself in complete opposition to Freud's theories.

Why should dreams be an expression of subconscious lust and hidden, internal conflict?

And where's the sense in hiding your own intentions from yourself? That would be like her being one person when she was dreaming, and someone else when she woke up, and what would be the logic in that?

Her dreams simply reflect her thoughts and fantasies. They might include symbolism, but she doesn't believe she could get to know herself better by thinking too much about their meaning.

It seems idiotic to try to solve life's problems by interpreting your own dreams. She thinks it might actually be dangerous.

What if you were to read something into them that wasn't there?

It's more interesting that her dreams are so clear and lucid; she realised this after reading an article on the subject. She's aware that she's dreaming while she's asleep, and she can influence what happens in her dreams.

She giggles to herself as she concludes that each time she's wet herself in her sleep, it's been an active choice.

It gets even funnier when you consider that people who have lucid dreams are, according to psychological research, supposed to have unusually high brain capacity. In other words, she wets herself because she has a brain that is considerably more refined and better developed than other people's.

She stubs out the cigarette and pulls out another book. An academic overview of attachment theory. How an infant's relationship with its mother affects the future life of the child.

Even though the book isn't on the reading list for her course, and also makes her feel depressed, she can't help dipping into it every so often. Page after page, chapter after chapter about something she had been denied by others, but had also abdicated from herself. Relationships with other people.

Everything was wrecked by her mother as soon as she was born, and the ruins of her ability to form relationships have been carefully managed by her father, who denied anyone else access to her.

She no longer smiles.

Does she miss relationships? Does she actually long for anyone else at all?

She certainly doesn't have any friends to miss, nor any friends who might miss her.

Hannah and Jessica are long since forgotten. Have they forgotten her as well? And the promise they made to one another? Eternal friendship and all that?

But there is one person she has missed since she arrived in Denmark. And it isn't Solace. Down here she's been able to manage without her.

She misses the old psychologist at Nacka Hospital.

If she had been here now, she would have realised that Victoria visited this hotel for a specific reason: to relive her own death.

But Victoria has realised what needs to be done.

If you can't manage to die then you can become someone else instead, and she knows how to go about that.

First she's going to take the ferry to Malmö, then the train to Stockholm, then the bus out to Tyresö, where the old woman lives.

And this time she's going to tell her everything, precisely everything she knows about herself.

She has to.

If Victoria Bergman is to be able to die properly.

Mariatorget – Sofia Zetterlund's Office

Linnea Lundström is sitting in the chair on the other side of the desk, and Sofia is surprised how quickly she has managed to gain the girl's trust.

'This is you, isn't it?' Sofia asks, pointing at the three drawings. 'And this is Annette?'

Linnea looks surprised, but says nothing.

'And perhaps this is a friend of the family?' Sofia points at Viggo Dürer. 'From Skåne. Kristianstad.'

Sofia gets the impression that the girl relaxes slightly. 'Yes,' she sighs, 'but he didn't look like that then. He was thinner.'

'What was his name?'

Linnea hesitates, and when she eventually answers she does so in a whisper. 'That's Viggo Dürer, Dad's lawyer.'

'Do you want to tell me about him?'

The girl's breathing becomes shallow and less regular, as if she's struggling for air. 'You're the first person who's ever understood my drawings,' she says.

Sofia thinks about Annette Lundström, who had pretty much misunderstood every single detail of Linnea's pictures.

Linnea's response comes quickly, and is surprisingly blunt, even if she doesn't address the actual content of the drawings. 'He was . . . I liked him when I was little.'

'Viggo Dürer?'

She looks down at the floor. 'Yes . . . He was nice to start with. Then, once I was about five, he could be really strange.'

Linnea herself has taken the initiative to talk about Viggo Dürer, and Sofia realises that the second stage of her treatment has started. Remembering, and dealing with the memories.

Sofia considers the drawing of Viggo Dürer and his dog in the Lundström family's garden in Kristianstad. Karl Lundström had himself mentioned the event in the letter Linnea had with her. Linnea despises her father, but is frightened of Viggo. She did what Viggo said, and Annette and Henrietta were simply blind. Shutting their eyes to what was going on around them.

As usual, Sofia thinks.

And Karl Lundström had also written that Viggo was doubly ignorant, and from the rest of Lundström's letter she could deduce that by this he meant that Viggo was both wrong and unaware that he was wrong.

There's only one question remaining, Sofia thinks. What is Viggo doubly ignorant about?

She's quite sure that she knows what Karl Lundström meant, and leans across the desk to look Linnea in the eye. 'Do you want to tell me what happened in Kristianstad?'

Klara Sjö – Public Prosecution Authority

Prosecutor von Kwist isn't actually from a noble family, he just decided to add a 'von' to his name when he was at school to make himself seem special. He is still incredibly vain, and very careful about both his reputation and his appearance.

Kenneth von Kwist has a problem, and is extremely worried. In fact he's so worried about a conversation he's just had with Annette Lundström that it feels as if his dormant gastric catarrh is starting to turn into a full-blown ulcer.

Benzodiazepines, he thinks. So addictive that any witness statement from someone taking them is highly questionable. Yes, that must be it. Heavy medication had made Karl Lundström imagine absolutely everything.

Kenneth von Kwist stares at the pile of papers on the desk in front of him.

Five milligrams of Stesolid, he reads. One milligram of Xanor and, finally, .75 milligrams of Halcion. Daily. Completely damn incredible.

The withdrawal symptoms must have been so severe that Lundström would have confessed to anything just to get a new dose, he thinks as he reads the transcript of the interview.

It's a considerable text, almost five hundred printed pages.

But still Prosecutor von Kwist has his doubts.

There are far too many people involved. People he knows personally, or at least thought he knew.

Had he himself simply been a useful idiot all along, helping a group of paedophiles and rapists to go free?

Had Per-Ola Silfverberg's foster-daughter been right when she accused him of abusing her?

And had Ulrika Wendin really been drugged by Karl Lundström and taken to a hotel where she was raped?

The truth is staring Prosecutor von Kwist straight in the face. He has allowed himself to be used, it's as simple as that. But how can he wash his hands of all this without simultaneously letting down his so-called friends?

He notes recurrent references to conversations that had taken place out at forensic psychology in Huddinge. Karl Lundström had evidently had a couple of meetings with a psychologist, Sofia Zetterlund.

Is it possible to hush all of this up?

Kenneth von Kwist gets himself an indigestion tablet, calls his secretary and asks her to get hold of a number for Sofia Zetterlund.

Mariatorget – Sofia Zetterlund's Office

When Linnea Lundström has left the practice Sofia spends a long time writing up their conversation.

She's got into the habit of using two ballpoint pens, one red, one blue, to differentiate between what her client says and her own thoughts.

As she turns the seventh sheet of A4 to start on the eighth, she is suddenly seized by a paralysing weariness. It feels like she's been asleep.

She looks back a couple of pages to refresh her memory about what she's written, and starts reading at random from the page she's marked with a 5.

The text is Linnea's story, written in blue ballpoint.

> Viggo's Rottweiler is always tied up somewhere. To a tree, or the railings by the steps to the house, or to a rumbling radiator. The dog tries to jump at Linnea and she skirts around it. Viggo comes into her room at night, the dog stands guard outside on the landing, and Linnea remembers the reflections in the dog's eyes in the darkness. Viggo shows Linnea an album of photographs of naked children, the same age as her, and she remembers the flash of the camera in the darkness, and she's wearing a big black hat and a red dress that Viggo has given her. Linnea's dad comes into the room, Viggo gets angry, they argue, and Linnea's dad walks out and leaves them alone.

Sofia had been surprised at the torrent of words pouring out of Linnea. As if her story had been lying dormant inside her, formulated long ago, and could finally flow freely as soon as she had someone to share her experiences with.

> Linnea is very frightened of being alone with Viggo. He's nice during the day, and nasty at night, and sometimes the things he

does to her mean she can't walk without help. I ask what Viggo did to her, and Linnea replies that she 'thinks it was his hand and his sweetie, and then he took pictures and told me not to say anything to Dad and Mum'.

Linnea repeats 'his hands, his sweetie, and then flashes from his camera', then she says that Viggo wants to play cops and robbers, where she's the robber and has to wear handcuffs. The handcuffs and his rough sweetie chafe all morning even though Linnea is asleep, yet not quite asleep because the flashes from the camera are red on the inside of her eyelids when she closes her eyes. And everything is outside and not inside, like a buzzing gnat in her head . . .

Sofia is breathing harder and harder. She doesn't recognise the phrases.

She sees that the rest of the text has been written with the red pen.

. . . a buzzing gnat that can get out if she hits her head against the wall. Then the gnat can fly through the window which can also let out the rancid smell of a German bastard's hands that smell of pigs and his clothes that smell of ammonia no matter how much he washes them, and his sweetie that tastes of horsehair and ought to be cut off and fed to the pigs . . .

Ann-Britt comes into the office, waving to let her know it's urgent. 'You've got a call waiting. Prosecutor Kenneth von Kwist wants you to get in touch as soon as you have a moment.'

Sofia remembers a house surrounded by fields.

She used to sit by the dirty window upstairs, watching the seabirds' movements against the sky. The sea hadn't been far away.

'OK. Let me have his number and I'll call him straight back.'

And she remembers the cold metal against her hand as she squeezed the bolt gun. She could have killed Viggo Dürer.

If she had, then Linnea's story would have been different.

The memories fade, like an ice cube melting faster the harder you hold it.

She looks at the notes again. The last three pages are Victoria's words. Victoria Bergman, telling the story of Viggo Dürer and Linnea Lundström.

> . . . the bumps of his vertebrae are visible through his clothes even when he wears a suit. He forces Linnea to undress and play his games with his toys in her room where the door is always locked except once when Annette, unless it was Henrietta, interrupted them. She felt ashamed because she was half naked on the floor on all fours while he was fully clothed and said that the little girl wanted to show him she could do the splits and then they wanted her to do it again, and when she did the splits and then a backbend the pair of them clapped, even though it was actually really sick because she was twelve years old and had breasts almost like a grown-up . . .

Sofia recognises some of what Linnea had said, but the words are mixed up with Victoria's memories. Even so, the text doesn't wake up any new memories.

The lined page is covered with incoherent writing.

She dials the prosecutor's number.

Prosecutor von Kwist briefly explains why he wanted to talk to her, about Karl Lundström's medication with benzodiazepines, and wonders what her opinion is.

'It doesn't make much difference. Even if Karl Lundström said what he did under the influence of heavy medication, his story is ultimately corroborated by his daughter. She's the important one now.'

'Heavy medication.' The prosecutor snorts. 'Do you know what Xanor is?' Sofia can hear the familiar masculine arrogance and feels herself starting to get angry.

She makes an effort to speak softly and slowly, and tries to sound pedagogical, as though she were talking to a child. 'It's generally accepted that patients who are prescribed Xanor for any length of time develop a dependency. Withdrawal is difficult, and however good someone feels when they take Xanor is matched by how bad they feel when it wears off. One of my clients described Xanor as a very quick ricochet between heaven and hell. That's why it's classified as a narcotic. Unfortunately, not all doctors choose to avail themselves of that knowledge.'

She hears the prosecutor take a deep breath. 'Good, good. I can hear you've done your homework.' He laughs and tries to smooth things over. 'Well, I still can't help thinking that what he said he did to his daughter isn't right –' He interrupts himself mid-sentence.

'I don't just believe that you're wrong. I know you are.' Sofia thinks about everything Linnea has said.

'What do you mean? Have you got any evidence, apart from his daughter's account?'

'I've got a name. Linnea has mentioned a man called Viggo Dürer several times.'

As soon as Sofia mentions the lawyer's name, she regrets having said it.

Glasbruksgatan – Silfverberg House

What caught Jeanette's attention in Fredrika Grünewald's tent was a bouquet of yellow tulips, and it wasn't just the colour that made her react, but the card attached to one of the stems.

The clock in Katarina Church strikes six muffled chimes, and Jeanette suffers a pang of guilt once more because she's still at work and not at home with Johan.

But after her discovery in Fredrika Grünewald's tent it's vital to keep up the momentum. That's why she and Hurtig are now standing outside the Silfverberg family's exclusive apartment. They've called to arrange a meeting.

Charlotte Silfverberg shows them into the living room. Jeanette goes over to the large picture window and gasps at the view. Straight ahead are the National Museum and the Grand Hôtel. To the right is the sailing ship now used as a youth hostel, the *af Chapman*. She can't imagine that there's a more beautiful view of Stockholm from anywhere. Jeanette turns round and sees that Hurtig has already sat down in one of the armchairs.

'I suspect this is going to be quick.' Charlotte Silfverberg is standing next to the other armchair, with both hands on the back as if to keep her balance.

Jeanette sits down on the sofa. 'To start with, I'd like to know why you didn't tell me about your daughter.' She says it as if in passing, then leans over to get her notepad. 'Or, rather, your foster-daughter.'

Charlotte Silfverberg answers without hesitation. 'Because she's a closed chapter to me. She messed up once too often and is no longer welcome in this house.'

'What do you mean?'

'I'll give you the short version.' Charlotte Silfverberg takes a deep breath before going on. 'Madeleine came to us as a baby. Her mother was very young and also suffered from severe mental illness, so wasn't able to look after the child. So she came to us, and we loved her like she was our own. Yes, we carried on loving her even though she was so difficult throughout her childhood. She was often sick, whining all the time. I don't know how many nights I sat up with her while she just screamed and screamed. She was simply inconsolable.'

'And you never found out what was wrong with her?' Hurtig leans forward and puts his hands on the coffee table.

'What was there to find out? The girl was . . . well, how can I put it – damaged goods.' Charlotte Silfverberg purses her lips, and Jeanette feels like punching the woman in the face.

Damaged goods.

Is that what it's called these days when you treat a child so badly that it resorts to the only defence it's got? Screaming.

Jeanette keeps her eyes fixed on the woman and is slightly scared by what she sees. Charlotte Silfverberg isn't just a woman in mourning. She's also a cruel person.

'Well, she got older and started school. Daddy's little girl. She and Per-Ola spent all the time they could together, and that's what went wrong. A girl shouldn't have such a close relationship to her father. She developed such a hero complex towards him that P-O felt it was time to set firm boundaries for her. I suppose she felt hurt, and started to make up all sorts of unkind things about him to get her own back.'

'Unkind things?' Jeanette can no longer restrain her anger. 'For God's sake, the girl said Per-Ola forced himself upon her.'

'I'd prefer it if you could watch your language when you talk to me.' Charlotte Silfverberg holds up both hands as if to fend her off. 'I don't wish to talk about this any further. End of discussion.'

'I'm afraid we're not quite finished yet.' Jeanette puts her notebook down. 'You have to realise that she is under suspicion for the murder of your husband.'

Only now does Charlotte Silfverberg seem to understand the seriousness of the situation, and nods mutely.

'Do you know where she is today?' Jeanette goes on. 'And can you describe Madeleine? Does she have any distinguishing features?'

The woman shakes her head. 'I presume she's still in Denmark. When we went our separate ways she was taken into care by social services and placed in a children's psychiatric clinic.'

Charlotte Silfverberg suddenly looks very tired, and Jeanette can't help wondering if she's about to cry. But she collects herself and goes on. 'She has blue eyes, and fair hair. Unless she's dyed it, of course. She was very pretty as a child, and she might well have become a beautiful young woman. But of course I don't know . . .'

'No distinguishing features?'

The woman looks up. 'She was ambidextrous.'

Hurtig lets out a laugh. 'So am I.'

'Jimi Hendrix was the same, so is Shigeru Miyamoto.'

'Shigeru Miyamoto?'

'Video game genius at Nintendo,' Hurtig explains. 'The man behind *Donkey Kong*, among others.'

Jeanette brushes aside these irrelevant details. 'So Madeleine could use both hands equally well?'

'Of course,' Charlotte Silfverberg replies. 'She would often sit and draw with her left hand while she was writing with her right.'

Jeanette thinks about what Ivo Andrić had said about Per-Ola Silfverberg's stabbing. That the distribution of the blows suggested it had been carried out by two people.

One right-handed, the other left-handed. Two people, each with their own knowledge of anatomy.

Hurtig looks at Jeanette and she knows him well enough to see that he's wondering if it's time to show Charlotte the card. Jeanette nods discreetly and he puts his hand in his pocket and pulls out a small plastic evidence bag.

'Does this mean anything to you?' He pushes the bag over towards Charlotte Silfverberg, who looks uncomprehendingly at the little card inside it. On the front is a picture of three little pigs, and beneath them the words 'CONGRATULATIONS ON YOUR BIG DAY!'

'What's this?' She picks up the bag, turns the card over and looks at the back. First she seems surprised, then she laughs. 'Where did you get hold of this?'

She puts the card back on the table, and all three of them stare at the photograph attached to the back of it.

Jeanette points to the photo. 'What's this photograph of?'

'That's me – when I graduated from school. Everyone leaving had pictures of themselves, and we swapped them with each other.' Charlotte Silfverberg smiles in recognition at the picture of herself, and Jeanette thinks she looks nostalgic.

'Can you tell us something about the school you attended – I mean, your high school?'

'Sigtuna?' she says. 'What do you mean? What could Sigtuna have to do with P-O's murder? And where did you get that card from?' She frowns and looks first at Jeanette, then at Hurtig. 'That is why you're here, isn't it?'

'Yes, of course, but for a number of reasons we'd like to hear about your time in Sigtuna.' Jeanette tries to make eye contact with the woman, but she's still facing Hurtig.

'I'm not deaf!' Charlotte Silfverberg raises her voice, and now turns towards Jeanette and looks her deep in the eye. 'And I'm not an idiot either! So if you want me to tell you anything about my schooldays, you're going to have to clarify to me *what* you want to hear, and *why* you want to hear it.'

'Sorry, I'll explain.' Jeanette glances at Hurtig for help, but he just stares up at the ceiling with a look of scorn. Jeanette knows what he's thinking. Fucking bitch.

Jeanette takes a deep breath. 'It's just a way for us to find out a number of things we're wondering about.' She pauses. 'We're investigating another murder, this time a woman who I'm afraid has turned out to have a connection to you. That's why we need to know a bit about your time at Sigtuna. She's a former classmate of yours. Fredrika Grünewald. Do you remember her?'

'Fredrika's dead?' Charlotte Silfverberg looks genuinely shaken.

'Yes, and there are certain indications that suggest we may be dealing with the same murderer. That card was next to her body.'

Charlotte Silfverberg sighs deeply and adjusts the tablecloth. 'One shouldn't speak ill of the dead, but she wasn't a nice person, Fredrika. You could see that even then.'

'How do you mean?' Hurtig leans forward again and puts his hands on his knees. 'Why wasn't she a nice person?'

Charlotte Silfverberg shakes her head. 'Fredrika is without doubt the most repulsive person I've ever encountered, and I honestly can't say that I'm going to mourn her death. Rather the opposite, if anything.'

Charlotte Silfverberg falls silent as her words echo between the freshly painted walls.

What sort of person is she? Jeanette thinks. Why is she so full of hate?

The three of them sit in silence, and Jeanette looks around the spacious living room. Silfverberg's blood is hidden by a millimetre-thick layer of the shade of paint known as 'Stockholm white'.

Hurtig clears his throat. 'Tell us about it.'

Charlotte Silfverberg talks about her time at Sigtuna College, and both Jeanette and Hurtig let her speak without interruption.

She strikes Jeanette as genuine. She doesn't hide the fact that she was one of Fredrika's underlings. Helping to bully students and teachers alike.

They listen to Charlotte Silfverberg for more than half an hour, and at the end Jeanette leans forward and reads from her notes. 'If I were to summarise what you've just said, you remember Fredrika as a devious person. She got the rest of you to do things you didn't really want to do. You and Henrietta Nordlund were her closest friends. Is that right?'

Charlotte Silfverberg nods.

'And on one occasion you subjected three girls to a highly degrading initiation ritual. On Fredrika's orders?'

'Yes.'

Jeanette looks at Charlotte Silfverberg and sees something that could be called shame. The woman is ashamed. 'Do you remember the girls' names?'

'Two of them left the school, so I never got to know them.'

'What about the third one? The one who stayed?'

'Yes, I remember her fairly well. She acted as if nothing had happened. She was cold as ice, and if you went past her in the corridor she almost looked a bit proud. After what happened, no one ever did anything to her. We left her alone.' Charlotte Silfverberg falls silent.

'What was the girl's name?' Jeanette closes her notepad and gets ready to go home at last.

'Victoria Bergman,' Charlotte Silfverberg says.

Hurtig groans as if he's just been thumped in the stomach, and Jeanette feels like her heart has skipped a beat. She drops her notepad on the floor.

Sista Styverns Trappor – a Neighbourhood

Chance is a negligible factor when it comes to serious crimes. A fact with which Jeanette Kihlberg is well acquainted after years of complex murder cases.

When Charlotte Silfverberg said that she had been at school with Victoria, the daughter of the rapist Bengt Bergman, Jeanette realised it couldn't be a coincidence.

Hurtig says goodbye outside the home of the Silfverberg family and starts walking towards Sista Styverns trappor, to go down the steps back to the city centre. She gets into the car, and before she starts the engine she sends Johan a text saying that she'll be home in fifteen minutes.

In the car on the way home Jeanette thinks about the strange conversation she had with Victoria Bergman a few weeks ago. She had called Victoria in the hope that she might be able to help with the investigation into the dead boys, seeing as her father had featured in a number of other cases involving the rape and sexual exploitation of children. But Victoria had been dismissive, and said she hadn't had any contact with her parents for twenty years.

Jeanette remembers that Victoria had left a strong impression of bitterness and said that her father had abused her as well. One thing is very clear. They need to get hold of her.

The rain has set in, visibility is poor, and as she passes Blåsut there are three cars by the side of the road. One is badly buckled, and Jeanette assumes they've run into one another. The emergency services are already there, along with a police car with its warning lights flashing. A colleague from the traffic unit is directing the traffic, which slows as it funnels into just one lane, and she realises she's going to be at least twenty minutes late.

What am I going to do with Johan? she thinks. Maybe it's time to contact the psychiatry unit after all?

And why hasn't Åke been in touch? Maybe he could take some of the responsibility for a while? But as usual, he's busy living his dreams and has no time for anyone but himself.

Never being good enough, she thinks, as the traffic grinds to a complete halt, fifty metres from the intersection for Gamla Enskede.

They don't have divorce papers yet, but maybe they should take the plunge? They would still have six months before they had to decide for good.

They can always change their minds.

If their separation leads to divorce, as everything seems to suggest, how are they going to be there for Johan?

Perhaps the lunch queue in the cafeteria of police headquarters isn't the best place to raise the matter, but since Jeanette knows how hard it is to get hold of Police Commissioner Dennis Billing she seizes the opportunity.

'What's your impression of your predecessor, Gert Berglind?'

'Practical Pig,' he says after a pause, turning his back on her and piling a ladleful of mashed potatoes onto his plate. She waits for him to go on, but when nothing more comes she taps him on the shoulder.

'Practical Pig? What do you mean by that?'

Dennis Billing continues compiling his lunch. Meatballs, cream sauce, salt gherkin and, finally, a spoonful of lingonberry jam. 'More of an academic than a police officer,' he goes on. 'Between the two of us, he was a bad boss who was rarely there when you needed him. Committees here, there and everywhere, and all those lectures.'

'Lectures?'

He clears his throat. 'Precisely. Shall we sit down?'

He chooses a table at the far end of the room, and Jeanette realises that for some reason the commissioner would rather talk in private.

'He was active in the Rotary Club and a whole load of foundations,' he says between mouthfuls. 'He was a Good Templar, religious, not to say exaggeratedly pious. He lectured all over the country on ethical questions. I heard him talk a couple of times, and I have to admit that he was engaging, even if what he said was mostly clichés. But maybe that's how it works? People just want confirmation of what they already know.' He grins, and even if Jeanette finds his cynical tone off-putting she feels inclined to agree with him.

'You mentioned foundations? Do you remember which ones?'

Billing shakes his head as he rolls a meatball back and forth between the sauce and the jam. 'Something religious, I seem to recall. His kindly manner was legendary, but between us I can say that he probably wasn't as pious as he liked to make out.'

Jeanette pricks up her ears. 'OK. I'm listening.'

Dennis Billing puts his knife and fork down and takes a sip of his low-alcohol beer. 'I'm telling you this in confidence, and I don't want you blowing it out of proportion, even though I have a feeling you're going to since you haven't let go of Karl Lundström yet. That's fine, as long as your work doesn't suffer, but I'll have to put my foot down pretty hard if I discover that you're up to something behind my back.'

Jeanette smiles. 'Don't worry about it. I've got more than enough on my hands right now. But what does Berglind have to do with Lundström?'

'He knew him,' Billing says. 'They had dealings with each other through one of Berglind's foundations, and I know they saw each other several times a year at meetings down in Denmark.'

Jeanette feels her pulse quicken. If they're talking about the foundation she's got in mind, maybe they're on to something.

'In hindsight,' Billing goes on, 'now that we know what sort of things Lundström was into, I think that perhaps the rumours that circulated about Berglind had a grain of truth in them.'

'Rumours?' Jeanette is trying to keep her questions as brief as possible, because she's worried that her voice might betray her excitement.

Billing nods. 'It was whispered that he hired prostitutes, and several female colleagues complained of sexual advances, harassment, basically. But nothing ever came of it, and then he suddenly died. Heart attack, fancy funeral, and all of a sudden he was a hero. He got the credit for coming to grips with racism and sexism within the force, although you and I both know perfectly well that's rubbish.'

Jeanette nods back. She finds herself liking Billing. They've never spoken this openly to each other before. 'Did they socialise privately as well? Berglind and Lundström, I mean.'

'I was coming to that . . . Berglind had a photograph on the bulletin board in his office that vanished a few days before Lundström was questioned about the rape in that hotel. What was the girl's name? Wedin?'

'Wendin. Ulrika Wendin.'

'That was it. It was a snapshot of Berglind and Lundström, each holding up a massive fish. When I pointed out that it was inappropriate for him to question the girl, he claimed he had only a passing acquaintance with Lundström. He was biased, and he knew it, but he did all he could to hide it. The holiday photo went up in smoke, and all of a sudden Lundström was just a passing acquaintance.'

The foundation, she thinks. It had to be the same foundation that Lundström, Dürer and Bergman financed. Sihtunum i Diasporan.

Kronoberg – Police Headquarters

Fredrika Grünewald was killed by someone she knew, Jeanette Kihlberg thinks. At least that's the hypothesis we need to work from.

The woman's body hadn't shown any indication at all that she had tried to defend herself, and her meagre home had been as tidy as could be expected. The murder hadn't been preceded by a fight, and Fredrika Grünewald must therefore have let her murderer in, and then been overpowered. Grünewald was also in poor physical shape. Even if she had only been forty years old, the last ten years on the streets had left their mark.

According to Ivo Andrić, her liver was in such a poor condition that she probably had no more than two years left to live, so the killer had gone to a lot of trouble for nothing.

But if Hurtig was right, and the act was motivated by revenge, then the primary aim hadn't been to murder her, but to humiliate and torment her. And in that respect the perpetrator had been one hundred per cent successful.

The preliminary results suggested that she had taken between thirty and sixty minutes to die. In the end the piano wire had cut so deeply into her throat that her head was only connected to her body by her vertebrae and a few sinews.

They had also found traces of glue around her mouth, and Ivo Andrić guessed they were from ordinary duct tape. That would explain why no one heard any screaming or shouting.

The pathologist had also made a number of interesting observations concerning the procedure. Ivo Andrić believed there was an anomaly in the way the murder had been carried out.

Jeanette pulls out the post-mortem report and reads:

> If there was one murderer, they were physically strong or acting under the influence of adrenalin, and they are also skilled enough to be able to use both hands simultaneously.

Madeleine Silfverberg, Jeanette thinks, but was she strong enough, and why would she attack Fredrika Grünewald?

> The woman was probably suffocated by having dog excrement pushed down her throat.
>
> Her mouth and the airways in her nose, as well as between her throat and ears, contain not only excrement, but also traces of vomited shrimp and white wine.
>
> There might have been two perpetrators, which perhaps seems more likely. One strangles the victim and the other holds her head still and feeds her excrement.

Two people?

Jeanette Kihlberg leafs through the witness statements she's been sent. The interviews with the people in the cavern beneath St Johannes Church hadn't been particularly easy to conduct. There weren't many who wanted to talk, and – out of those who were willing – most had to be regarded as less than credible because of drug and alcohol abuse or mental illness.

The only thing Jeanette thinks is worth following up is the fact that several witnesses claimed to have seen a man named Börje come down into the cavern with an unknown woman. There was an alert out for Börje, but there were no results yet.

As far as the woman was concerned, the witnesses were very vague. One said she was wearing some sort of covering over her head, while others mentioned both fair and dark hair. According to the combined statements, her age was somewhere between twenty and forty-five, and the same variation applied to height and build.

A woman? Jeanette thinks. That seems unlikely. She's never come across a woman who carried out this sort of premeditated, brutal murder before.

Two killers? A woman with a man helping her?

Jeanette regards that as a much better explanation. But she's convinced that this Börje wasn't involved. He has been a well-known resident of the crypt for several years, and isn't a violent man, according to the witnesses.

As Jeanette walks along the corridor to Hurtig's office she asks herself a rhetorical question.

Are we dealing with the same murderer as in the case of the dismembered financier, Silfverberg?

Not impossible, she concludes, and goes in without knocking.

Hurtig is standing by the window, looking thoughtful. He turns round, walks behind the desk and sits down heavily in his chair.

'I forgot to say thanks for your help with that game,' she says, smiling at him. 'Johan's delighted.'

They look at each other in silence.

'What did Denmark have to say?' she finally asks. 'About Madeleine Silfverberg, I mean.'

'My Danish isn't great.' He smiles. 'I spoke to a doctor at the treatment home she was placed in, and throughout all the years she was being treated she maintained that P-O Silfverberg had sexually assaulted her. She also claimed there were other men involved, and that it all happened with her mother Charlotte's blessing.'

'But no one believed her?'

'No, she was thought to be psychotic and severely delusional, and was under heavy medication.'

'Is she still there?'

'No, she was discharged two years ago and, according to their records, moved to France.' He looks through his papers. 'To a place called Blaron. I've put Schwarz and Åhlund on it, but I think we can forget her.'

'Maybe, but I still think we ought to check her out.'

'Especially if she's ambidextrous.'

'Yes, what was all that about? Why haven't you ever mentioned it before?'

Hurtig grins. 'I was born left-handed, and I was the only one in the school. The other kids teased me and said I was handicapped. So I learned to use my right hand instead, and as a result I can use both.'

Jeanette thinks about all the unguarded things she's ever said, unaware of what consequences they may have had. She nods. 'But, to go back to Madeleine Silfverberg, did you ask the doctor if he thought she could be violent?'

'Of course, but he said the only person she ever harmed at the hospital was herself.'

'Yes, they usually do that.' Jeanette sighs, thinking of Ulrika Wendin and Linnea Lundström.

'God, I'm starting to get sick of all the fucking shit we have to dig through.'

They look at each other across the desk, and Jeanette recognises Hurtig's sudden helplessness all too well.

'We can't give up, Jens,' she says, trying to sound consoling, but hearing how trite it sounds.

He straightens and attempts a smile.

'Let's sum up what we've got,' Jeanette says. 'Two people have been killed. P-O Silfverberg and Fredrika Grünewald. Their murders are unusually brutal. Charlotte Silfverberg was in the same class as Grünewald, and the world is small enough for us to assume that we're dealing with a double murderer. Possibly in both senses.'

Hurtig looks doubtful. 'You say "possibly". How confident are you that we're dealing with two killers? Do you mean we should assume that?'

'No, but we should bear it in mind as we work. You remember what Charlotte Silfverberg said about the humiliation ritual at boarding school?'

He looks out the window, and a subdued smile spreads over his face as he realises what Jeanette means. 'I get it. The two other girls who went through that, the ones who disappeared. Silfverberg couldn't remember their names.'

'I want you to contact the school in Sigtuna and ask them to send their registers. Ideally their school yearbooks as well, if that's possible. We've got a number of names that might be of interest. Fredrika Grünewald and Charlotte Silfverberg. Their friend, Henrietta Nordlund. But I'm still most curious about our missing Victoria Bergman. What does she look like? Haven't you wondered that as well?'

'Yep,' he says, but Jeanette can see that he hasn't.

'There's another factor we ought to consider before we continue, but that's not something we'll be dealing with in today's meeting, if you get my meaning?' Hurtig looks interested again and he gestures for her to go on. 'We've got Bengt Bergman, Viggo Dürer and Karl Lundström. Considering that the three of them, and Per-Ola Silfverberg as well, were all involved in the foundation Sihtunum i Diasporan, maybe that's got something to do with all this. And Billing told me something interesting over lunch. Our former commissioner, Gert Berglind, knew Karl Lundström.'

Hurtig perks up properly now. 'What do you mean? They saw each other socially?'

'Yes, and not just that. They knew each other through a foundation. Any idiot can work out which foundation that might be. Quite a can of worms, this, wouldn't you say?'

'Yes. Bloody hell!' The committed Hurtig is back, and Jeanette smiles in welcome.

'OK,' she says, 'I've noticed you've had something on your mind, and I don't think it's just work worrying you. Has anything happened?'

'It's Dad again. Looks like he's going to have even more trouble with his carving and fiddle playing from now on.'

Oh no, Jeanette thinks.

'I'll keep it short, since we've got a lot to do. But to start with he was given the wrong medication after the accident with the saw. The good news is that the hospital's accepted liability, so he's going to get compensation, but the bad news is that he got gangrene and his fingers have to be amputated. And he also managed to get hit in the head by a Ferrari GF.'

Jeanette is just gaping.

'I can see you don't know what a Ferrari GF is. It's Dad's ride-on mower, pretty big.'

If it hadn't been for the smile on Hurtig's face, Jeanette would have imagined something terrible.

'What happened?'

'Well . . . He was trying to free some branches that had caught in the blades, jacked the machine up on a wooden stake, crawled underneath to get a better look, then of course the stake snapped. Their old neighbour had to sew his head up after Mum had shaved his hair off. Fifteen stitches, right on top of his head.'

Jeanette can't speak, all she can think of are two names, Jacques Tati and Carl Gunnar Papphammar.

'He's always OK.' Hurtig waves his hand dismissively. 'What do you think I should do after I've spoken to Sigtuna College? There are a few hours to go before the case meeting.'

'Fredrika Grünewald. Check out her story. Start with why she ended up on the street and then try to work backwards. Preferably with as many names as possible. We're working on revenge as the motive, and we need to track down people she knew. People she managed to upset, or might otherwise be thought to have a few bones unpicked with her.'

'I dare say people like her probably have enemies scattered around all over the place. Upper class, crooked deals, deception, sham companies. Walking over dead bodies and selling their friends to get a good deal.'

'You're so prejudiced, Jens. Anyway, I know you're a socialist.' She laughs loudly and gets up to leave.

'Communist,' Hurtig says.

'What?'

'I mean, I'm a communist. There's a hell of a difference.'

The impure parts

can be touched and you have to watch out for strangers' hands, or hands that offer money to be allowed to touch. The only hands that are allowed to touch Gao Lian are the fair woman's.

She combs his hair, which has grown long. He thinks it's also got lighter, and maybe that's because he's spent so much time in the dark. As if the memory of light has been stored in his head and coloured his hair like rays of sunlight.

Right now it's completely white in the room, and his eyes are having trouble seeing. She's left the door open and brought in a bowl of water to wash him, and he's enjoying her touch.

As she's drying him there's a ringing sound from the hall.

Hands plunder if you're not on your guard, and she's taught him to have complete control over them. Everything they do must have a meaning.

He trains his hands by drawing.

If he can capture the world and take it inside him and then let it out again through his hands, he need never fear anything again. Then he will have the power to change the world.

Feet go to forbidden places. He knows that, because he left her once to look around the city outside the room. That had been wrong, and he realises that now. There is nothing out there that is good. The world outside his room is evil, and that's why she protects him from it.

The city had seemed so clean and beautiful, but now he knows that beneath the ground and the water there are the remains of millennia of human cadavers, and that inside the buildings and inside the living there is only death.

If the heart gets sick the whole body gets sick and you die.

Gao Lian from Wuhan thinks about the blackness in people's hearts. He knows that evil manifests itself there as a black stain, and that there are seven ways into the heart.

First two ways, then two more ways and finally three ways.

Two, two, three. The same year the city he was born in, Wuhan, was founded. The year 223.

The first way to the black stain is from the tongue, which lies and slanders, and the second is through the eyes, which see what is forbidden.

The third way is through the ears, which listen to lies, and the fourth is through the stomach, which digests the lies.

The fifth is through the impure parts, which let themselves be touched, the sixth through the hands, which plunder, and the seventh through the feet, which go to forbidden places.

It is said that at the moment of death a person sees all that is in their heart, and Gao wonders what he will see.

Birds, perhaps.

A hand offering comfort.

He draws and writes. Piling paper on top of paper. The work makes him calm, and he forgets his fear of the black stain.

The ringing sound echoes again.

Gamla Enskede – Kihlberg House

Everything is connected somehow, Jeanette Kihlberg thinks as she takes the lift down to the garage beneath police headquarters to get in the car and drive home. Even if her day's work is over, she can't stop thinking about all the peculiarities and strange coincidences.

Two girls, Madeleine Silfverberg and Linnea Lundström. Their fathers, Per-Ola Silfverberg and Karl Lundström. Both suspected paedophiles. Lundström also suspected of the rape of Ulrika Wendin. And the paedophile's wife, Charlotte Silfverberg, and the murdered Fredrika Grünewald went to school together in Sigtuna.

She drives towards the exit and waves at the guard. He waves back and raises the barrier. The strong sunlight dazzles her and for a moment she can't see anything.

The same lawyer, Viggo Dürer, who also had Bengt Bergman as a client. And Bergman's missing daughter, Victoria, had been at Sigtuna.

Then there was the deceased police commissioner, Gert Berglind, who had conducted interviews with both Silfverberg and Lundström. All of them involved in the same foundation. Prosecutor von Kwist? No, Jeanette thinks, he isn't involved. He's just a useful idiot.

Per-Ola Silfverberg and Fredrika Grünewald murdered. Possibly by the same person.

Karl Lundström dying in the hospital. Bengt Bergman dying in a fire with his wife, just like Viggo.

Accidents? Yes, according to the police investigations.

But Jeanette has her doubts. Someone means these people ill, and it's got something to do with that foundation.

As she pulls up outside the house and gets out, Jeanette realises that she needs help. She feels a pressing need to talk to someone she trusts, someone she can be open and personal with. Sofia is the only person who meets those criteria.

A breeze is blowing the leaves of the large birch tree and sweeping along the wall of the house. It's an unreliable, damp wind, and Jeanette takes a deep breath. Please, no more rain, she thinks, looking at the red, exhaust-fume evening sky over to the west.

The house is deserted and empty. On the kitchen table is a note from Johan telling her that he'll be spending the night at David's because they're planning to have a LAN party.

A LAN party? she thinks, fairly sure that he's explained what that means to her at some point. Is she such a bad mother that she doesn't even keep up to date with her son's leisure interests? Presumably it's something to do with computers.

She gets the phone and dials Sofia Zetterlund's number. It rings almost ten times before Sofia answers. Her voice sounds hoarse and strained.

'Have you got time for a chat?'

Sofia doesn't answer immediately. Then she clears her throat. 'I don't know. Is it important?'

Jeanette isn't sure she's picked the right time to call, but decides to adopt a gentle tone in an effort to soften her up. 'Hard to say how important it is.' She laughs. 'Åke and Johan, as usual. Just stuff. I could do with someone to talk to, that's all . . . It was good to see you last time, by the way. How are you getting on with you-know-what?'

'I-know-what? What do you mean?'

It sounds like Sofia is giggling, but Jeanette thinks she must have heard wrong. 'You know, what we talked about at my house last time. The perpetrator profile.'

No response. Jeanette thinks it sounds like Sofia is dragging a chair across the floor. Then the sound of a glass being put down on a table.

'Hello?' she says tentatively. 'Are you still there?'

A few more seconds of silence follow before Sofia answers. Her voice is much closer now and Jeanette can hear her breathing.

Sofia is talking faster.

'In less than a minute you've asked four questions,' she begins. 'Have you got time for a chat? How are you getting on with you-know-what?

Hello? Are you still there?' Sofia sighs, then goes on. 'Here come the answers: I don't know. I haven't started yet. Hello yourself. I'm still here, where else would I be?'

She's just teasing me, Jeanette thinks. 'Do you want to meet up?'

'Yes, I want to. I just need to sort this out. How about tomorrow evening?'

'Yes, that would be great.'

Once they've hung up Jeanette goes into the kitchen and gets a beer from the fridge. She goes into the living room and sits down on the sofa and opens the bottle with her cigarette lighter.

She already knew that Sofia was a complicated person, but this is something else. Once again, Jeanette is forced to admit that she has an unhealthy fascination with Sofia Zetterlund.

It's going to take time to get to know you, Sofia, Jeanette thinks, taking a deep swig of beer.

But I'm damn well going to give it a try.

Gamla Enskede – Kihlberg House

Jeanette meets Johan in the doorway the next evening. He's going to be spending the night at a friend's again, to play video games and watch films. She tells him not to stay up too late.

He takes his bike and walks down the gravel path. When he disappears round the corner she goes inside, and from the living room window she sees him jump on the bicycle and head off down the road.

Jeanette breathes a deep sigh of relief. Finally alone.

She feels happy, and when she thinks about the fact that Sofia is coming over, she feels expectant.

She goes into the kitchen and pours herself a small whisky. She lets the yellow liquid wash over her tongue and burn her gullet. Feels the warming sensation in her chest.

After a shower she wraps herself in a big towel and looks at herself in the mirror. She opens the bathroom cabinet and takes out her make-up bag, which is covered by a thin layer of dust.

Cautiously she highlights her eyebrows. The lipstick is trickier. A smudge of bright scarlet ends up too high and she wipes it off with her towel and starts again. When she's done she presses her lips together on a sheet of toilet paper. She carefully smooths out her skirt and strokes her hips. This is her evening.

Sofia looks shocked, and then bursts out laughing. 'Are you serious?'

They're sitting on opposite sides of the kitchen table and Jeanette has just opened a bottle of wine. She can still taste the sweet whisky on her tongue.

'Martin? I called him Martin?' Sofia looks amused at first, but her smile soon dies. 'A panic attack,' she says. 'The same thing that happened to Johan, I imagine. He had a panic attack when he saw you get hit on the head with a bottle down below.'

'A trauma, you mean? But how would that explain the gap in his memory?'

'Traumas give people memory lapses. And the lapse usually includes the moments before the trauma occurred.'

Jeanette understands. A panic attack, a teenage boy full of hormones. Obviously everything has a chemical explanation.

'So, these new cases?' Sofia looks curious. 'Brief me about where you are. What have you got?'

Jeanette spends twenty minutes telling Sofia about the two latest cases. Sofia listens intently, and nods with interest.

'The first thing that strikes me about Fredrika Grünewald,' Sofia says when Jeanette has finished, 'is that faecal matter is involved. Shit, basically.'

'And . . .'

'That seems symbolic. Almost ritualistic. As if the perpetrator is trying to say something.'

Jeanette recalls the flowers found inside the tent, next to the dead woman.

Karl Lundström had received yellow flowers as well, but that could be coincidence.

'Have you identified a suspect?' Sofia asks.

'Nothing definite yet,' Jeanette begins. 'But we've got a link to a foundation called Sihtunum i Diasporan. Both Lundström and Silfverberg were involved with it. And there's a lawyer, Viggo Dürer, who's mixed up in it as well. But he's dead too, so we can forget him.'

'Dead?'

'Yes, a few weeks ago. He died in a fire on his boat.'

Sofia looks taken aback, and Jeanette thinks she can see something in her eyes. Eventually she says, 'I had a strange phone call the other day,' and Jeanette can see she isn't sure if she should go on.

'In what way was it strange?'

'Prosecutor Kenneth von Kwist called me and implied that Karl Lundström had been lying. That he had made everything up under the influence of his medication. I couldn't work out what he was getting at.'

'That's not too difficult. He wants to save his own skin. He ought to have ascertained that Lundström wasn't on any medication before the interview. If he missed that, he's screwed.'

'I think I made a mistake.'

'How do you mean?'

'I mentioned one of the men Linnea says assaulted her, and I got a feeling he recognised the name. He went very quiet.'

'Can I ask who it was?'

'You just mentioned him. Viggo Dürer.'

Jeanette realises at once why Kenneth von Kwist had sounded odd. She doesn't know if she should indulge in schadenfreude, because Dürer seems to have been a nasty piece of work, or just feel sad, because of the revelation that he had evidently assaulted a little girl. 'I'll bet my right hand that von Kwist is going to try to hush this up. It's no exaggeration to think he'd be seriously damaged if it got out that he was involved with paedophiles and rapists.'

She reaches for the wine bottle.

'Who is this von Kwist, anyway?' Sofia holds out her empty glass and lets Jeanette refill it.

'He's worked at the Public Prosecution Authority for over twenty years, and the Ulrika Wendin case isn't the only one that got tossed out at the preliminary investigation stage. And just because he works for us doesn't mean he was the smartest law graduate of his year.' She laughs, and when she sees the puzzled look on Sofia's face, she explains: 'It's no secret that it's the least talented of the successful graduates who end up working for us in the police, or for the enforcement agency or the national insurance office.'

'How come?'

'Simple. They're not smart enough to become business lawyers for some big export company, or to run their own firms for much higher salaries. Von Kwist probably dreams of becoming a hotshot criminal lawyer, but he's far too stupid.'

Jeanette thinks of her ultimate superior, the county police commissioner for Stockholm, one of the most high-profile police officers in the country. Who never takes part in serious debates on criminality, but is happy to appear in gossip magazines and go to gala premieres in expensive outfits.

'If you want to put the squeeze on von Kwist, I can help you with evidence,' Sofia says, tapping her glass with her fingernail. 'Linnea showed me a letter in which Karl Lundström implies that Dürer had abused her. And Annette Lundström let me take photographs of some drawings Linnea did when she was little. Pictures describing the abuse. I've got it all with me, if you'd like to see it?'

Jeanette nods mutely as Sofia gets out her handbag and shows her Linnea's drawings and a photocopy of the letter from Karl Lundström.

'Thanks,' she says. 'This will definitely come in useful. But I'm afraid it's more circumstantial than definite evidence.'

'I understand,' Sofia says.

They sit without saying anything for a while before Sofia goes on. 'Apart from von Kwist and Dürer . . . Are there any more names?'

'Yes, there's one more that keeps cropping up. Bengt Bergman.'

Sofia starts. 'Bengt Bergman?'

'He was reported for the sexual abuse of two children. A boy and girl from Eritrea. Children without papers who don't officially exist. Case dropped. Signed off on by Kenneth von Kwist. Bergman's lawyer was Viggo Dürer. Do you see the connection?'

Jeanette leans back and drinks a large gulp of wine. 'There's another Bergman. Her name was Victoria, and she was Bengt Bergman's daughter.'

'Was?'

'Yes. About twenty years ago she ceased to exist. There's nothing after November 1988. But I've spoken to her on the phone, and she wasn't exactly reticent about her relationship with her father. I think he abused her sexually and that's why she disappeared. And Bengt and Birgitta Bergman no longer exist either. They died recently in a fire. Poof, and then they were gone as well.'

Sofia's smile is hesitant. 'You'll have to excuse me, but I don't understand.'

'Lack of existence,' Jeanette says. 'The common denominator for the Bergman and Lundström families is their lack of existence. Their histories are blacked out. And I think both Dürer and von Kwist participated in that.'

'And Ulrika Wendin?'

'Yes, you know her, of course. Raped by a number of men, including Karl Lundström, in a hotel room seven years ago. They injected her with an anaesthetic. Case dropped by Kenneth von Kwist. Yet another case blacked out.'

'Anaesthetic? Like those dead boys?'

'We don't know if it was the same anaesthetic. There was no medical examination conducted.'

Sofia looks irritated. 'Why not?'

'Because Ulrika waited more than two weeks before going to the police.'

Sofia appears thoughtful, and Jeanette waits, realising that she's weighing something up.

'I think Viggo Dürer tried to bribe her,' she says after a while.

'Why do you think that?'

'When she was with me she had a new computer and a whole lot of money. She managed to drop a few 500 krona notes on the floor. And she caught sight of a picture of Viggo Dürer that I'd printed out and left on my desk. When she saw it she flinched, and when I asked if she knew him she denied it, but I'm fairly certain she was lying.'

Gamla Enskede – Kihlberg House

The residential area of Gamla Enskede was laid out in the early years of the last century, so that ordinary people could have their own house with two bedrooms, a kitchen, a cellar and a garden, all for the same price as a two-room apartment in the city.

It's early evening and the clouds are building. A grey darkness settles over the suburb and the big green maple turns black. The mist over the lawn is steely grey.

She knows who you are.

No. Stop it. She can't know. That's impossible.

She doesn't want to admit it to herself, but somewhere Sofia suspects that Jeanette Kihlberg has a hidden agenda, and is drawing her into a trap.

Sofia Zetterlund swallows. Her throat feels like someone's rammed a dry apple into it.

Jeanette Kihlberg swirls the last of her wine around the glass before drinking it. 'I think Victoria Bergman is the key,' she says. 'If we can find her, we solve the case.'

Take it easy. Breathe.

Sofia Zetterlund takes a deep breath. 'Why do you think that?'

'Just a feeling,' Jeanette says, scratching her head. 'Bengt Bergman used to work for the Swedish International Development Cooperation Agency, in Sierra Leone among other places. The Bergman family lived there for a while during the late eighties, which feels like yet another coincidence.'

'I'm not with you.'

Jeanette laughs. 'Well, Victoria Bergman was in Sierra Leone and Samuel Bai was from Sierra Leone. And it's struck me that there's you as well, you've been there too. You see, it really is a small world.'

What does she mean? Is she implying something?

'Maybe,' Sofia says thoughtfully, while her insides are churning with anxiety.

'One or more of the people we're looking into knows the murderer. Karl Lundström, Viggo Dürer, Silfverberg. Someone in the Bergman or Lundström families. The murderer might just as easily be someone inside that constellation as outside it. Either way. I still think Victoria Bergman knows who the murderer is.'

'And what are you basing that hypothesis on?'

Jeanette laughs again. 'Instinct.'

'Instinct?'

'Yes, I've got three generations of police blood in my veins. My instinct's hardly ever wrong, and in this case I get a strong feeling whenever I think about Victoria Bergman. Call it my cop's blood, if you like.'

'I've had a first go at putting together a psychological profile of the perpetrator. Do you want to see it?' She reaches for her bag, but Jeanette stops her.

'I'd love to, but first I want to hear what you've got to say about Linnea Lundström.'

'I saw her recently. For therapy. And I think she was exploited by more than just her dad.'

Jeanette looks at her intently. 'And you believe her?'

'Absolutely.' Sofia considers the situation. And feels that the moment has arrived when she could open up and reveal parts of herself that she has kept hidden up to now. 'I had therapy myself when I was younger, and I know how liberating it can be to get the chance to talk about everything. Being able to talk about what you've been through without any inhibitions and interruption, and to have someone who really listens. Someone who may have been through the same thing but has devoted a lot of time and money to educating themselves to understand the human psyche and who takes your story seriously and is there for you and helps to analyse things, even if it's just a drawing or a letter, and who can draw conclusions and isn't just wondering what drugs it might be suitable to prescribe, and who isn't necessarily trying to find fault, find a scapegoat, even if -'

'Hey,' Jeanette interrupts her. 'What's going on, Sofia?'

'What?' Sofia opens her eyes and sees Jeanette in front of her.

'You disappeared for a moment.' Jeanette leans across the table and takes Sofia's hands. Strokes them gently. 'Is it difficult to talk about?'

Sofia feels her eyes pricking as tears well up, and she wants to give in. But the moment has passed and she shakes her head.

'No. What I was trying to say is that I think Viggo Dürer was involved.'

'Yes, well, that would explain a whole lot.' She pauses, and seems to be choosing her words.

Wait, let her go on.

'Go on.' Sofia hears her own voice as if she were standing alongside. She knows what Jeanette's about to say.

'P-O Silfverberg lived in Denmark. Viggo Dürer too. Dürer defends Silfverberg when he's accused of abusing his foster-daughter. He defends Lundström when he is accused of raping Ulrika Wendin.'

'Foster-daughter?' Sofia is having trouble breathing, and reaches for her wine glass to hide her agitation. She raises it to her lips, and sees that her hand is trembling.

Her name is Madeleine, she's got fair hair and she likes it when you tickle her tummy.

Screaming and crying when she was welcomed into the world with a blood test.

The little hand clutching a forefinger.

Stockholm, 1988

She didn't have to make an effort, because the stories seemed to come by themselves, and sometimes it was like she predicted the truth. She would come up with a lie, and then it happened. She liked having such a strange power.

As if she could steer the world around her with her will, just by lying and having her lies come true.

The money lasts all the way home from Copenhagen to Stockholm, and she gives the eighteenth-century music box that she stole from the farmhouse in Struer to a drunk outside Central Station. At a quarter past eight in the morning Victoria gets on the bus from Gullmarsplan to Tyresö, sits down right at the back and opens her diary.

The road is in a poor state because of all the construction, and the driver is going far too fast. That makes it hard to write. The letters get very shaky.

Instead she sinks into the notes of her sessions with the old psychologist. Everything is recorded in her diary, every single one of their meetings. She puts her pen back in her bag and starts to read.

3 March

Her eyes understand me, and that feels safe. We talk about incubation. That means waiting for something, and maybe my incubation period will soon be over?

Am I waiting to get ill?

Her eyes ask me about Solace and I tell her that she's moved out of the wardrobe. We share the bed now. The stench from the sauna has accompanied us to bed. Am I already ill? I tell her that the incubation period started in Sierra Leone. I was carrying the illness in me when we left, but I didn't get rid of it when we got home.

The infection remained inside me and made me mad.

His infection.

Victoria prefers not to call the psychologist by her name. She likes thinking about the old woman's eyes; they make her feel safe. The therapist *is* those eyes. And in them Victoria can also be herself.

The bus stops, and the driver gets out and opens a hatch on the side. There seems to be something wrong. She seizes the opportunity, grabs her pen and starts to write.

25 May

Germany and Denmark belong together. North Friesland, Schleswig-Holstein. Raped by German boys at the Roskilde Festival, then by a Danish German bastard. Two countries in red and white and black. Eagles fly over the flat fields, shitting on the grey patchwork and landing on Helgoland, a North Friesian island where the rats fled when Dracula carried the plague to Bremen. The island looks like the Danish flag, the cliffs are rust red, the sea foams white.

The bus starts again. 'Sorry for the delay. We're now on our way to Tyresö.'

During the remaining twenty minutes of the journey Victoria reads her diary from cover to cover, and when she gets off she sits down on a wooden bench at the bus stop and continues writing.

Children are born in BB, the maternity ward, and BB is Bengt Bergman, and if you put the letter B against a mirror you get the number eight.

Eight is Hitler's number, because H is the eighth letter of the alphabet.

And now it's 1988. 88.

Heil Hitler!

Heil Helgoland!
Heil Bergman!

She packs her things and walks towards the Eyes' house.

The living room of the villa in Tyresö is light and the sun is shining through the white lace curtains in front of the open terrace door. She's lying on her back on a sun-warmed sofa and the old woman is sitting opposite her.

She is going to tell everything, and it's as if there's no end to what needs to be said.

Victoria Bergman is going to die.

First she talks about interrailing a year before. About a nameless man in Paris in a room with cockroaches on the ceiling and leaking pipes. About a four-star hotel on the beach promenade in Nice. About the man in bed beside her, who was an estate agent and smelled of sweat. About Zurich, but she remembers nothing of the city, just snow and nightclubs and the fact that she jerked a man off in a park.

She tells the Eyes that she's convinced external pain can wipe out internal pain. The old woman doesn't interrupt her, just lets her talk freely. The curtains sway in the breeze, and she offers Victoria coffee and cake. It's the first time she's eaten anything since she left Copenhagen.

Victoria talks about a man called Nikos whom she met when they got to Greece. She remembers his expensive Rolex on the wrong wrist, and the fact that he smelled of garlic and aftershave, but not his face, and not his voice.

She tries to be honest in what she says. But when she talks about what happened in Greece it's hard to stick to the facts. She can hear how crazy it all sounds.

She had woken up in Nikos's home and went into the kitchen to get a glass of water.

'And Hannah and Jessica are sitting at the kitchen table, and shout at me that I need to pull myself together. That I smell bad, that I've bitten my nails so much they must hurt, and that I have rolls of fat and varicose veins. And that I've been mean to Nikos.' The old woman smiles at her like she usually does, but her eyes aren't smiling, they look worried.

'Did they really say that?'

Victoria nods. 'Hannah and Jessica aren't really two people,' she says, and it's like she suddenly understands herself. 'There are three of them.'

The therapist looks at her with interest.

'Three people,' Victoria goes on. 'One who works, is dutiful, and . . . well, obedient and moral. And one who is analytical, wise and understands what I have to do to feel better. Then there's one who tells me off, a real moaning minnie. She gives me a guilty conscience.'

'A Worker, an Analyst and a Moaning Minnie. Do you mean that Hannah and Jessica are two people who have different characteristics?'

'Not really,' Victoria replies. 'They're two people who are three people.' She laughs uncertainly. 'Does that sound muddled?'

'No, I think I understand.'

She's silent for a moment, then she asks Victoria if she'd like to describe Solace.

Victoria thinks about this, but isn't sure that she has a good answer. 'I needed her,' she eventually says.

'And Nikos? Do you want to talk about him?'

Victoria laughs. 'He wanted to marry me. Can you imagine? Ridiculous!'

The woman says nothing, changes position in the armchair and leans back. It looks like she's thinking about what to say next.

Victoria suddenly feels sleepy and bored. It's no longer so easy to talk, but she feels that she wants to. The words seem sluggish and she has to make an effort not to lie. She feels ashamed in front of the Eyes.

'I wanted to torment him,' she says after a while, and as she does so she feels a great calm.

Victoria can't help grinning, but when she sees that the old woman doesn't seem at all amused she puts her hand over her mouth to hide her smile. She feels ashamed again and has to make an effort to find her way back to the voice that's helping her talk.

When the psychologist leaves the room shortly afterwards to go to the toilet, Victoria can't resist looking to see what she's written, and she opens the notepad as soon as she's alone.

Transitional object.

African fetish mask, symbol for Solace.

Cloth dog, Tramp, symbol for security in childhood.

Who? Not father or mother. Possibly relative of childhood friend. Most likely adult. Aunt Elsa?

Memory lapses. Reminiscent of DID/MPD.

She doesn't understand, and is soon interrupted by footsteps in the hall.

'What's a transitional object?' Victoria feels let down, because the therapist has been writing things they haven't talked about.

The old woman sits down again. 'A transitional object,' she says, 'is an object that represents someone or something that you have problems being separated from.'

'Such as?' Victoria fires back.

'Well, a stuffed toy or a blanket can comfort a child because the object represents its mother. When she's not there, the object is there in her place, and helps the child move from dependency on its mother to independence.'

Victoria still doesn't understand. After all, she isn't a child, she's an adult. A grown-up.

Does she miss Solace? Was the wooden mask a transitional object?

She doesn't know where Tramp, the little dog made out of real rabbit fur, came from.

'What are DID and MPD?'

The old woman smiles. Victoria thinks she looks sad. 'I can tell you've read my notes. But they aren't absolute truths.' She nods towards the notepad on the desk. 'They're just my reflections on our conversations.'

'But what do DID and MPD mean?'

'They're a way of describing someone who has several autonomous personalities inside them. It isn't –' She stops herself, and looks very serious. 'It isn't a diagnosis,' she continues. 'I want you to understand that. It's more like a personality trait.'

'What do you mean?'

'DID stands for dissociative identity disorder. It's a logical self-defence mechanism, the brain's way of handling difficult things. A person develops different personalities that act independently, separate from each other, in order to deal with different situations in the best possible way.'

What does that mean? Victoria thinks. Autonomous, dissociative, separate and independent? Is she separate and independent from herself through other people who are inside her?

It sounds ridiculous.

'Sorry,' Victoria says. 'Can we continue later? I think I need to get some rest.'

She falls asleep on the sofa. When she wakes up it's still light outside, but the curtains are still, the light is paler and it's quiet. The old woman is sitting in her armchair, knitting.

Victoria asks the therapist about Solace. Is she real? The old woman says she might be an adoption, but what does she mean by that?

Hannah and Jessica definitely exist, they were in her class in Sigtuna, but they are also inside her as the Worker, the Analyst and Moaning Minnie.

Solace is also real, but she's a girl who lives in Freetown in Sierra Leone, and her real name is something different. But Solace Manuti is inside Victoria, and she's the Helper.

She herself is the Reptile, who only does what it wants, and the Sleepwalker, who watches life pass by without doing anything about it. The Reptile eats and sleeps, and the Sleepwalker stands outside and watches what the other parts of Victoria are doing, without intervening. The Sleepwalker is the one she likes least, but simultaneously she knows that it's the one with the greatest chance of survival, and it's this part that she must cultivate. The others need to be removed.

Then there's Crow Girl, and Victoria knows it isn't possible to remove that part of herself.

Crow Girl can't be controlled.

On Monday they go into Nacka. The therapist has arranged for a medical examination to ascertain whether Victoria was subjected to sexual abuse as a child. She has no desire to report her father, but the therapist says it's likely that the doctor will file a report with the police.

She'll probably also be referred to the forensic medicine unit in Solna for a more thorough examination.

Victoria has explained to the woman why she doesn't want to report anything to the police. She regards Bengt Bergman as dead, and she wouldn't be able to face seeing him during a trial. Her desire to have her injuries documented has other motivations.

She wants to start again, get a new identity, a new name and a new life.

The therapist says she can have a new identity if the justifications are sufficiently strong. That's why they have to go to the hospital.

As they pull into the car park of Nacka Hospital, Victoria has already begun to plan her new future.

The previous future never existed, because Bengt Bergman took it from her.

But now she is going to get a chance to begin again. She's going to get a new name and a confidential ID number. She's going to be good, get an education and find a job in a different city.

She's going to earn money and take care of herself, maybe get married and have children.

Be normal, like everyone else.

Gamla Enskede – Kihlberg House

Gamla Enskede is dark, and almost silent, just a few youngsters out on the road. Through the thin, leafless, fairly tragic honeysuckle hedge a blue-grey light shines in from the neighbours' living-room window, indicating that they, like most other people at this time, are watching television.

Jeanette gets up, goes over to the window and lowers the blinds, turns round and sits down next to Sofia.

She sits quietly and waits. It's up to Sofia to decide if they're going to continue talking about work or move on to more private matters.

Sofia reminds Jeanette about the perpetrator profile. 'Shall we take a look at it?' she asks. Sofia leans over the edge of the sofa and takes a notepad out of her bag.

'OK,' Jeanette replies, disappointed that Sofia has chosen to go on talking about work.

But it's not that late, she thinks. And Johan's spending the night somewhere else. We've got plenty of time.

'There's a lot to suggest that we're dealing with a person who fulfils the requirements for borderline diagnosis.' Sofia leafs through her pad. 'This is someone who thinks in terms of either/or, where he's divided the whole world into black and white. Good and evil. Friends and enemies.'

'You mean people who aren't his friends automatically become his enemies? A bit like George W. Bush said before he invaded Iraq?' Jeanette smiles.

'Something like that,' Sofia replies, smiling back.

'Can you say anything about the fact that the murders were so brutal?'

'It's a matter of seeing the act, well, the murder, as a language of its own. An expression of something.'

'Oh?' Jeanette thinks about what she's seen.

'So, the perpetrator is staging his own internal drama outside of himself, and we have to work out what this person is trying to say. To start with, I think the murders were planned.'

'I'm convinced of that as well.'

'But at the same time, the excessive violence suggests that the murders were committed in a temporary outburst of fury.'

'So what might this be about, then? Power?'

'Absolutely. A strong need to dominate and have total control over another person. The victims have been carefully selected, yet seem simultaneously random. Young boys with no identities.'

'It seems so sadistic. What can you say about that?'

'That the murderer enjoys seeing the victim's impotence and helplessness. Maybe it's even an erotic feeling for him. A genuine sadist can't experience sexual pleasure any other way. Sometimes their victim is held captive and the abuse goes on for a long time. It's not unusual for such abuse to end in murder. These acts are usually carefully planned, and not the result of a fit of rage that's come out of nowhere.'

'But why so much violence?'

'As I said, some perpetrators take satisfaction from inflicting pain. It may be a necessary form of foreplay leading to other types of sexual expression.'

'And the embalming of the boy we found at Danvikstull?'

'I think that was an experiment. A whim, almost.'

'But what could have made someone turn out like that?'

'There are as many different answers to that question as there are perpetrators, and psychologists, too, for that matter. And now I'm talking in general terms, rather than specifically about the immigrant boys.'

'What do you think?'

'I think this sort of behaviour arises from early disturbances during the development of the personality, as a result of physical and mental abuse.'

'So the victim becomes a perpetrator?'

'Yes. Usually the perpetrator has grown up under extremely authoritarian circumstances with elements of violence, where the mother has been passive and submissive. As a child he might have lived under the constant threat of divorce and felt responsible for that. He learned to lie at an early age to avoid beatings, has had to intervene to protect one parent, or has had to take care of one parent in degrading situations. He had to be that parent's comforter instead of himself being comforted. He might have witnessed dramatic attempts at suicide. He probably started fighting, drinking and stealing at an early age, without this getting any reaction from adults. In short, he has always felt unwanted and basically like a problem.'

'So you think the perpetrator had a terrible childhood?'

'I think what Alice Miller thinks.'

'Who?'

'She was a psychologist who said it was utterly impossible for someone who grew up in an environment of honesty, respect and warmth to ever want to torment anyone weaker and harm them for life.'

'There's something in that. But I'm not entirely convinced.'

'No, sometimes I doubt it. There's a proven link between excess production of male sex hormones and an inclination to commit sexual assaults. You can also regard physical and sexual violence against women and children as a way for a man to construct his masculinity. Through violence the man acquires the power and control that society's traditional gender and power structures suggest are his right.'

'I see.'

'And there's a connection between social norms and degrees of perversion that, in basic terms, suggests that the more double standards there are in a society, the more likely this sort of boundary transgression is.'

Jeanette feels like she's talking to an encyclopedia.

Cold facts and crystal-clear explanations piled on top of one another.

'OK, while we're talking generally about this sort of perpetrator, can we go back to Karl and Linnea Lundström?' Jeanette says. 'Can someone who has been subjected to sexual abuse in childhood have no memory of it at all?'

Sofia takes time to consider this. 'Yes. Both clinical practice and memory research support the idea that very traumatic events during childhood can be stored but are not accessible. Problems arise if those types of memories lead to police investigations, because it has to be proved that the alleged assaults actually took place. We can't ignore the possibility that an innocent man might be accused and possibly convicted for an act of this sort.'

Jeanette is starting to pick up the pace, and already has her next question formulated. 'And can a child in an interview situation be steered to talk about sexual abuse that never actually happened?'

Sofia gives her a serious look. 'Sometimes children have trouble with the concept of time, such as when or how often something occurred. They often think that grown-ups already know everything they might have to say, and are more inclined to omit sexual details than place particular stress on them. Our memories are intimately connected to our perceptions. In other words, what we see, hear and feel.'

'Can you give me an example?'

'One clinical example is a teenage girl who smells her boyfriend's semen and realises that this isn't the first time she's encountered that smell. And that instigates a process through which she comes to remember her father's abuse of her.'

'So how do you explain why Karl Lundström became a paedophile?'

'For some individuals, other people have no emotional reality. They know about the concept of empathy, but it has no qualitative meaning. And people who function that way can be capable of doing terrible things.'

'But how could he have hidden it?'

'In an incestuous family, the boundaries between adults and children are unclear and hazy. All needs are satisfied within the family. The daughter often switches roles with the mother, and might replace her in the kitchen, for instance, but also in bed. The family does everything together, and from the outside looks like the ideal family. But the internal dynamics are severely disturbed and the child has to satisfy its parents' needs. The child often takes more responsibility for its parents than the other way round. The family exists in isolation, even though it might have a superficial social life. To escape scrutiny the family will move to another place every so often. Karl Lundström was probably a victim himself. And, as Miller says, it's tragic if you hit your own children to avoid having to think about what your own parents did.'

'What do you think's going to happen to Linnea?'

'More than fifty per cent of women who suffer incest try to commit suicide, often in their teens.'

'That reminds me of the quote "There are many ways to cry: noisily, quietly, or not at all".'

'Who said that?'

'I don't remember . . .'

A welcome silence follows.

Jeanette can feel the heavy subject matter becoming too much for her. She could do with a good laugh, a really good laugh that would chase out the images of raped and abused children.

She refills their glasses and takes the initiative to change the subject. 'How do *you* cry? Quietly, noisily or not at all?'

Sofia smiles gently. 'It depends on the situation. Sometimes noisily, and sometimes not at all.'

'And how do you laugh?'

'Pretty much the same way, I suppose.'

Jeanette isn't sure how to continue. 'Do you . . .' she begins, but doesn't get any further.

Why am I hesitating? she thinks. After all, I know just what I need right now.

Human warmth.

'Hold me,' she says eventually.

Without Jeanette noticing, Sofia has put her arm around her, and as Sofia leans over and kisses her it feels like a natural extension of the embrace.

It isn't a long kiss.

But it makes Jeanette giddy. As if all the wine they've drunk during the evening has gone to her head in the space of five seconds.

She wants more. She wants to experience the whole of Sofia.

But something tells her they ought to wait.

Their lips separate, and she strokes Sofia's cheek.

That's enough.

For the moment, at least.

Kronoberg – Police Headquarters

Stockholm's implacable winter is hostile and windy; the cold creeps in everywhere and is almost impossible to defend against.

During the six months of winter it's dark when the citizens wake up and go to work, and it's dark in the evening when they head home again. For months people live their lives in a dense, suffocating shortage of natural light while they wait for the release of spring. They shut themselves off, withdrawing into their own private worlds, avoiding unnecessary eye contact with their fellows and shutting out the world around them with the help of iPods, MP3 players and mobile phones. Down in the metro there's a scary silence, and every disruptive noise or loud conversation is met with hostile glares or stern comments. For outsiders, Stockholm is a place where not even the sun has enough energy to penetrate the steel-grey sky and, if only for an hour or so, shine down on the godforsaken inhabitants.

On the other hand, Stockholm in its autumn finery can be incredibly beautiful. The houseboats lining Söder Mälarstrand, bobbing in the waves and lurching stoically in the wake of vulgar motorboats, jet skis, Skeppsholmen's sophisticated motor yachts, and the white ferries on their way to Drottningholm and the Viking town on Björkö. The clear, pure water embraces the steep grey and rust-red cliffs of the islands at the heart of the city, and the trees spill out in colourful patterns of yellow, red and green.

As Jeanette Kihlberg drives in to work the sky is high and clear blue for the first time in weeks, and she takes a long detour via the quaysides that line Lake Mälaren's shores.

She feels intoxicated.

A single kiss. Five seconds that struck her right in the heart.

When Jeanette walks into Jens Hurtig's office, he's sitting cleaning his service pistol. A Sig Sauer, nine millimetre. He doesn't look happy.

'Weapons maintenance?' Jeanette grins. 'You can do mine as well.' She goes off to her office and gets her pistol out of the desk drawer.

'So what do we know about Fredrika Grünewald?' Jeanette asks as she hands him the gun.

'She was born here in Stockholm,' he says nonchalantly, undoing the holster and removing the pistol. 'Her parents live out in Stocksund, and haven't had any contact with her for the past nine years. Apparently she lost most of the family fortune on bad investments.'

'How?'

'Without her parents' knowledge, she pumped everything they had, almost forty million, into a number of new businesses. Do you remember Wardrobe.com?'

Jeanette thinks. 'Only vaguely. Wasn't that one of those dot-com companies that was supposed to be invaluable, then crashed on the stock market?'

Hurtig nods as he puts a bit of gun grease on a cloth and begins to polish the pistol. 'Exactly. The idea was to sell clothes online, but it collapsed with hundreds of millions in debt. The Grünewald family were among the worst affected.'

'And it was all Fredrika's fault?'

'According to her parents, but I don't know. They don't seem to be going short of anything. They still live in their villa, and the cars parked in the drive must be worth about a million each.'

'Did they have any reason to want to be rid of Fredrika?'

'Don't think so. After the dot-com crash she dropped all contact with her parents. They think it was because she felt ashamed.'

'What did she live on? I mean, even if she was homeless, she seemed to have money.'

'Her dad said that he felt sorry for her, in spite of everything, and every month he used to pay fifteen thousand into her account. Which probably explains things.'

'Nothing funny there, then.'

'No, not as far as I can see. Secure childhood. Good grades in junior school, then boarding school.'

'No husband or children?'

'No children,' he goes on. 'And according to her parents she wasn't in a relationship. None that they knew about, anyway.' He puts the last parts of the pistol back in place, then puts it down on the desk.

'Maybe I'm just being conservative, but that seems a bit odd to me. I mean, there ought to have been a man of some sort over the years.'

Jeanette studies Hurtig, and catches a fleeting glimpse of the roguish look he gets when he's got an ace up his sleeve.

'Guess who was in the same class as Fredrika Grünewald?'

'I have my suspicions. Who?'

He hands her some sheets of paper. 'These are the class registers for everyone who attended Sigtuna College at the same time as Fredrika.'

'OK, so who is it, then?' She takes the lists and begins to leaf through them.

'Annette Lundström.'

'Annette Lundström?' Jeanette Kihlberg looks at Hurtig, who smiles at her surprise.

It's as if someone has opened a window and let in some new, fresh air.

The sun is shining outside Jeanette's window as she settles down to read the material Hurtig has given her.

Class registers from Sigtuna College covering the years that Charlotte Silfverberg, Annette Lundström, Henrietta Nordlund, Fredrika Grünewald and Victoria Bergman were there. So, Annette and Fredrika had been in the same class.

Annette has fair hair, and several of the people in the cavern under St Johannes Church had said they saw a fair-haired woman in the vicinity of Fredrika's tent.

But Börje, the man who had shown the woman the way and who could hopefully identify her, is still missing.

Should she bring Annette Lundström in for questioning? Check her alibi and maybe even arrange a line-up? But that would reveal her suspicions to Annette, and make the ongoing inquiry harder. Any lawyer would get her released in the time it took to say the word 'homeless'.

No, better to hold off and leave Annette in ignorance, at least until

Börje shows up. But she could call Annette in for a meeting on the grounds that it's about Linnea's abuse.

She could lie, and say that Lars Mikkelsen had asked her to. That might work.

That's what I'll do, she thinks, unaware that her enthusiasm is going to delay the resolution of the case rather than speed it up, and will indirectly cause a number of people unnecessary suffering.

Klara Sjö – Public Prosecution Authority

Kenneth von Kwist runs his hands over his face. A small problem has become a big one. Possibly even insoluble.

At last he has realised that he was an idiot for helping P-O Silfverberg and Karl Lundström. He has also been an idiot for being so focused on his career all these years, doing the bidding of others. What had he got for it?

Fate caught up with Dürer, the lawyer, but what if Karl Lundström and P-O Silfverberg were actually guilty? He's starting to suspect that they might have been.

Under the leadership of the previous police commissioner, Gert Berglind, everything had been so simple. Everybody knew everyone else and you just had to socialise with the right people to climb the hierarchical ladder.

Lundström and Silfverberg had been close friends of both Gert Berglind's and Viggo Dürer's.

Since Dennis Billing had taken over, collaboration with the police hadn't been quite so smooth.

Where Kihlberg is concerned, at least he has a well-formulated plan for how their relationship could be improved, while simultaneously drawing her attention in a different direction, at least temporarily, thus giving him time to sort out the problem of the Lundström family.

Two birds with one stone, he thinks. Time to start putting things right.

It's no longer a secret in police headquarters that Jeanette Kihlberg, trailing her sergeant Jens Hurtig behind her, is conducting a private investigation into the dropped cases of the murdered immigrant boys, and the rumour has also reached Prosecutor Kenneth von Kwist.

He also knows that an unofficial search is under way for Bengt Bergman's daughter, that all documents relating to Victoria Bergman have been declared confidential, and that Kihlberg drew a blank from Nacka District Court.

He dials the number of a colleague at the court in Nacka.

His plan is as devious as it is simple, and is based on the idea that legal exceptions are always possible, so long as all parties agree to keep quiet about it. In other words, that the colleague in Nacka stays silent and that Jeanette Kihlberg will be willing to kiss his feet in gratitude.

Five minutes later Kenneth von Kwist leans back contentedly in his chair, folds his hands behind his head and puts his feet up on his desk. That was that, he thinks. Now there's just Ulrika Wendin and Linnea Lundström left.

What have they told the police and that psychologist?

He has to admit that he has no idea, at least not as far as Ulrika Wendin is concerned. Linnea Lundström has obviously said something compromising about Viggo Dürer, but he doesn't know what it is yet, even if he fears the worst.

'Fucking kid,' the prosecutor mutters, thinking about Ulrika Wendin. He knows that the girl has met both Jeanette Kihlberg and Sofia Zetterlund, and has therefore breached their informal contract. The fifty thousand kronor that were supposed to keep her quiet evidently hadn't been enough.

He must confront Ulrika Wendin and get her to realise what she's dealing with. He takes his feet off the desk, adjusts his suit and sits up straight in his chair.

One way or another, he needs to silence both Ulrika Wendin and Linnea Lundström.

Greta Garbos Torg, Södermalm

Former small businessman Ralf Börje Persson, founder of Persson's Building and Construction Ltd, has been homeless for four years. It all started well, the business was successful, lots of good contracts, new house, new car and even more work. But when competition for jobs got tougher and criminal gangs entered the building trade with cheap, illegal workers from Poland and the Baltic States, it started to go downhill. The pile of unpaid bills kept growing, until the point where it was no longer possible to hold on to the car and the house.

The phone that had once been so busy went silent, and his so-called friends vanished or didn't want anything to do with him.

One evening, four years ago, Börje went out to the shops and never returned. What was supposed to be a turn around the block had become a walk that still hasn't ended.

Börje is standing outside the state-run off-licence on Folkungagatan. It's a few minutes past ten o'clock and in his hand he's holding a lilac plastic bag containing six export-strength lagers. Norrlands Guld, seven per cent alcohol content. He opens the first can, tells himself this is the last liquid breakfast he's going to have, and that he'll get a handle on his life as soon as he gets rid of the shakes. He just needs one can to restore his equilibrium. And he believes that he's earned a beer. Now that he's going to start afresh.

The promise is redeemed the moment it is made.

The first thing he's going to do once he's finished his beer and life has got a bit simpler is take the metro to police headquarters at Kronoberg and tell them what happened down in the cavern under St Johannes Church.

He hasn't been able to miss the flyers about the Duchess's murder, and it's pretty obvious to him that he was the one who showed the murderer where to go. But could it really have been that pale woman, not much older than his own daughter, who had executed his sister in misfortune in such a bestial way?

The beer is warm, but it does its job, and he drains the can in one long, deep swig.

He walks slowly east, turns into Södermannagatan and continues until he reaches Greta Garbos torg, close to Katarina Södra School. The school that the reclusive actress attended as a child.

There's a paved circle in the middle of the square, with hornbeams and horse chestnuts planted around the edge of the circle. Ralf Börje Persson finds a bench in the shade, sits down and thinks about what he's going to say to the police.

No matter how he looks at it, he can't escape the conclusion that he was the only person to see Fredrika Grünewald's murderer.

He can describe the coat the woman was wearing. And her dark voice. And the unusual dialect. And the blue eyes that looked so much older.

After reading what the papers have written about the murder, he knows that a Jeanette Kihlberg is leading the investigation, and she's the one he needs to ask for at reception in the police station. But he's reluctant. His time on the street has led him to develop severe police paranoia.

Maybe it would be better if he wrote a letter and sent it to the police instead?

He takes out his pocket diary, tears out a blank page and holds it down on the leather cover. He takes a pen out of his coat pocket and thinks about what to write. How should he phrase it, and what are the important facts?

The woman had offered him money as thanks for him showing her the way down into the cavern. When she took out her purse he had seen something that caught his interest, and if he had been a police officer investigating a murder, that particular observation would have been extremely important, for the simple reason that the number of suspects would decrease dramatically.

He writes, explicitly enough so that his meaning won't be misinterpreted.

Ralf Börje Persson bends over to get another beer out, feels his belt strain against his stomach, reaches out and finally grabs one corner of the plastic bag just as he feels a stabbing pain in his chest.

His eyes flare. He falls from the bench and ends up on his back, with the note still in his hand.

The cold from the ground makes its way to his head, where it meets the warmth of intoxication. He shivers, and then everything explodes. It's as if a train has driven straight into his head.

Kronoberg – Police Headquarters

Annette Lundström doesn't see through the deception and comes in the following day.

'Hasn't the case been closed now that Karl's dead? And why isn't Mikkelsen –'

'I'll explain,' Jeanette interrupts. 'But there's also something else I want to talk to you about. How do you know Fredrika Grünewald?' she asks, and watches Annette's reaction.

Annette Lundström frowns and shakes her head.

'Fredrika?' she says, and Jeanette gets the impression that her surprise is genuine. 'What about her? What's she got to do with Karl and Linnea?'

Jeanette waits for Annette to go on of her own accord.

'Well, what can I say? We were in the same class for three years, but we haven't seen each other since then.'

'What can you tell me about her?'

'How do you mean? What she was like at school? But that's twenty-five years ago.'

'Try anyway,' Jeanette prompts.

'We didn't really have much to do with each other. We were in different gangs, and Fredrika hung out with the popular girls. The tough crowd, if you know what I mean?'

Jeanette nods to say she understands, and gestures for her to go on.

'The way I remember it, Fredrika was top dog in a gang of wannabes.' Annette falls silent and looks thoughtful as Jeanette takes out a notepad.

'You want to know what I thought about Fredrika Grünewald?'

Annette suddenly snarls. 'Fredrika was a bitch who always got her way. She had a court of faithful lackeys who always stuck up for her.' She looks aggressive all of a sudden.

'Do you remember their names, these lackeys?'

'They came and went, but the most faithful were probably Henrietta and Charlotte.'

Still looking down at the pad, Jeanette asks, as if in passing, 'You mentioned that Fredrika was a bitch. What do you mean by that?'

Annette doesn't move a muscle. 'I can't think of anything specific, but they were horrible, everyone was terrified of ending up the butt of their pranks.'

'Pranks? That doesn't sound terribly serious to me.'

'No, most of the time it probably wasn't. There was really only one time when they badly crossed the line.'

'What happened?'

'There were two or three new girls who were going to be initiated, but it got out of hand.' Annette Lundström falls silent, looks out of the window and adjusts her hair. 'Why are you asking all these questions about Fredrika?'

'Because she's dead, murdered, and we need to build up a picture of her life.'

Annette Lundström looks thoroughly bewildered. 'Murdered? But that's awful! Who'd do something like that?' she says, as simultaneously a note of hesitancy creeps into her eyes.

Jeanette gets a definite impression that Annette knows more than she's letting on.

'You said it once got out of hand . . . What exactly happened?'

'It was terrible, and it should never have been hushed up. But as I understand it, Fredrika's father was a good friend of the headmistress, as well as one of the largest donors to the school. I presume that was why.' Annette Lundström sighs. 'But of course you know that already?'

'Of course,' Jeanette lies. 'But I'd still be grateful if you could tell me what happened. If you feel up to it, I mean.' Jeanette leans across her desk and switches on the tape recorder.

Annette's story is a tale of humiliation. Of young girls goading one another to do things they would never have done otherwise. During the first week of the new school year Fredrika Grünewald and her acolytes had identified three girls who would have to undergo a particularly disgusting initiation ceremony. Dressed up in dark capes and wearing home-made pig masks, they had taken the three girls down to a tool shed and poured ice-cold water over them.

'What happened after that was entirely Fredrika Grünewald's idea.'

'And what did happen after that?'

Annette Lundström's voice is trembling. 'They were forced to eat dog shit.'

Jeanette feels completely empty.

That single word. She feels her brain crash and then reboot.

Dog shit.

Charlotte Silfverberg hadn't said a word about that. But perhaps that wasn't so strange.

'Tell me more. I'm listening.'

'Well, there isn't really much more. Two of the girls fainted, but the third apparently ate it and threw up.'

Annette Lundström goes on, and Jeanette listens with distaste.

Victoria Bergman, she thinks. And two as-yet-unidentified girls.

'Fredrika Grünewald, Henrietta Nordlund and Charlotte Hansson were the ones who got blamed for it all.' She lets out a deep sigh. 'But there were more girls involved.'

'Did you say that Charlotte's surname was Hansson?'

'Yes. But she's not called that now. She got married fifteen, twenty years ago . . .' The woman's voice trails off.

'Yes?'

'She got married to Silfverberg, that man who was found murdered. That was so terrible –'

'And Henrietta?' Jeanette interrupts, to stop having to go into a specific case.

The answer comes quickly, as if in passing. 'She married a man named Viggo Dürer,' Annette Lundström says.

Two pieces of news for the price of one, Jeanette thinks.

Dürer again. So Henrietta was his wife. And now the Dürers are both dead.

Possibly murdered, even if the forensic examination of their burned-out boat suggested it was an accident.

The pieces are starting to fall into place as the image clears.

Jeanette is certain that Per-Ola Silfverberg's and Fredrika Grünewald's murderer is somewhere in the constellation of people that has now been expanded by another two names, and she looks down at her notepad.

Charlotte Hansson, now Charlotte Silfverberg. Married/widow of Per-Ola Silfverberg.
Henrietta Nordlund, later Dürer. Married Viggo Dürer. Dead.

'Do you remember the names of the girls who were the victims?'
'No, sorry . . . It's all so long ago.'
'OK . . . Well, I think we're done here,' Jeanette says. 'Unless there's anything you'd like to add?'
The woman shakes her head and stands up.
'Get in touch if you remember anything else about the two girls.'
Annette Lundström leaves with a worried look on her face. Jeanette once again feels that she knows more than she's letting on.
Jeanette is switching off the tape recorder when the door opens and Hurtig pops his head in. 'Am I disturbing you?' He looks serious.
'Not at all.' Jeanette turns her chair to face him.
'How important is the last witness in a murder investigation?' he asks rhetorically.
'What do you mean?'
'Börje Persson, the man who was seen down in the cavern before Fredrika Grünewald was murdered, is dead.'
'What?'
'Heart attack this morning. We got a call from Södermalm Hospital when they realised there was an alert out for him. Apparently he had a note in his hand, so I sent Åhlund and Schwarz to fetch it. They've just got back.'
Hurtig puts a page torn from a pocket diary in front of her.
The handwriting is neat.

To Jeanette Kihlberg, Stockholm Police.
I think I know who killed Fredrika Grünewald, also known as the Duchess, beneath Saint Johannes Church.
I claim the right to anonymity, because I prefer not to get involved with the authorities.
The person you are looking for is a woman with long, fair hair

who was wearing a blue coat at the time of the murder. She is of average height, has blue eyes and a slim build.

Beyond that it's probably pointless saying anything more about her appearance, seeing as such a description would be based on personal opinion rather than fact.

But there was one distinguishing feature that might interest you. She is missing her right ring finger.

Vita Bergen – Sofia Zetterlund's Apartment

To forgive is a big thing, she thinks. But to understand without forgiving is so much bigger.

When you don't just see why, but can also understand the whole sequence of events that leads up to a final sick act, it makes you feel giddy. Some call it inherited sin, others predestination, but really it's just ice-cold, unsentimental causality.

An avalanche after a shout, or the rings on water after a tossed stone. A taut piece of wire across the darkest part of a cycle path, or a hasty word and a punch in the heat of the moment.

Sometimes it's a considered and conscious act, where the consequences are merely one consideration and satisfaction of desire another.

In the emotionless state where empathy is just a word, seven letters with no content, you start to approach evil.

You abdicate from all humanity and become a wild animal. Your tone of voice darkens, the way you move changes and the look in your eyes becomes dead.

She goes into the bathroom and gets the box of sedatives from the cabinet, takes two paroxetine and swallows them down with a quick jerk of her head. It'll soon be over. Viggo Dürer is dead and Jeanette Kihlberg knows that Victoria Bergman is a murderer.

'No, she doesn't know that,' she says in a loud voice. 'And Victoria Bergman doesn't exist.' But there's no point pretending. The voice is there, and it's stronger than ever.

She goes back into the living room, then the kitchen. Her vision is shimmering, like at the start of a migraine.

The red lamp is glowing, to indicate that the little machine is recording.

She holds the recorder in front of her, hands trembling; she's wet with sweat it's as if she's outside of her body, looking at herself sitting at the table.

Sofia feels she's in two places at the same time.

She's standing beside the table, and she's inside the girl's head. The voice is dark and monotonous and it echoes inside her and simultaneously bounces off the walls of the kitchen.

When she was trying to understand Victoria Bergman, the recorded monologues had functioned as catalysts, but now the reverse is true.

Her memories include explanations and answers. They are a manual, a guide to life.

Sofia is interrupted by a loud noise from the street, and the voice vanishes. She feels like she's just woken up, switches off the recorder and looks around.

There's an empty blister pack of paroxetine crumpled up on the table and the floor is filthy, covered with muddy footprints. She gets up and goes out into the hall, where she finds her shoes damp and dirty with soil and grass.

So she's been out again.

Back in the kitchen she sees that someone, presumably her, has laid the table for five people, and notices that she's also put names by their places.

She leans over the table and reads the cards. To her left Solace will be sitting next to Hannah, and on the other side Sofia and Jessica will be sitting next to each other. She has put Victoria at the head of the table.

Hannah and Jessica? she thinks. What are they doing here? Hannah and Jessica, whom she hasn't seen since she left them on the train from Paris more than twenty years ago.

Sofia sinks down onto the floor and discovers that she's holding a black marker in her hand. She puts it aside and looks up at the white ceiling. Vaguely she hears the phone ring out in the hall, but she's not going to answer and shuts her eyes.

The final thing she does before the roaring in her head drowns out all other sounds is to switch the tape recorder on again.

Then darkness and silence. The roaring stops, and she's calm and can rest while the pills start to work.

She sinks deeper into sleep, and Victoria's memories come back to her in rolling waves, first as sounds and smells, then as images.

The last thing she sees before her consciousness finally goes out is a girl in a red jacket standing on a beach in Denmark, and only now does she realise who the girl is.

Kronoberg – Police Headquarters

'The murderer's missing her right ring finger,' Jeanette repeats, sending a silent, posthumous call of thanks to the man named Ralf Börje Persson.

'Not entirely insignificant.' Hurtig grins.

'It's just tragic that one of our best leads comes from a witness we can't talk to,' Jeanette says. 'Billing's given me a gang from the police academy who are going through the class registers from Sigtuna, from all years. They've already started calling former pupils and staff, and there are three names that I'm particularly keen to see pop up over the course of the evening.'

'I get it – you mean the victims of that initiation ritual. Victoria Bergman and the other two who disappeared?'

'Exactly. And there's one other phone call that needs to be made. The most important one, so I'm leaving that to you, Hurtig.' She hands him the phone. 'The person you need to call used to be the school's headmistress. She's retired these days and lives in Uppsala. She was evidently aware of what happened, and was actively involved in hushing it up. She'll be able to give us the names, at least, and if she can't remember them she can help us find their records. Make the call, I'm wiped out and my blood sugar's crashed, so I'm going down to the cafeteria for coffee and something sweet. Do you want anything?'

'No thanks.' Hurtig laughs. 'You never let up. I'll call the head, you go and get some coffee.'

She gets back to her office just as Hurtig hangs up.

'Well? How did it go? What did she say?'

'The girls' names were Hannah Östlund and Jessica Friberg. We'll be getting their personal details sometime this evening.'

'Good work, Hurtig. Do you think any of them's missing a ring finger?'

'Friberg, Östlund or Bergman? Why not Madeleine Silfverberg?'

Jeanette looks at him with amusement. 'She may have a motive for her foster-father, but I can't see any direct connection to Fredrika Grünewald.'

'OK. But that's not enough. Anything else?'

'Henrietta Nordlund married the lawyer, Viggo Dürer.'

Hurtig says nothing, just nods thoughtfully.

'And, last but not least . . . During the initiation ritual in Sigtuna, Hannah Östlund, Jessica Friberg and Victoria Bergman were served dog shit by Fredrika Grünewald. Need I say more?'

He breathes out and looks suddenly very tired. 'No thanks, that's enough for now.'

It doesn't matter how exhausted he is, she thinks. He's never going to give up.

'How's your dad getting on?'

'Dad?' Hurtig rubs his eyes and looks amused. 'They've amputated several fingers from his right hand, and now he's being treated with leeches.'

'Leeches?'

'Yes, they stop the blood coagulating after amputations. And they actually managed to save one of his fingers. Can you guess which one?'

Hurtig grins and yawns at the same time, before pre-empting her and answering his own question.

'His right ring finger.'

Gamla Enskede – Kihlberg House

When Jeanette Kihlberg gets home she's so wiped out that she doesn't even notice the smell of cooking from the kitchen at first.

Hannah and Jessica, she thinks. Two shy girls that nobody remembers terribly well.

Tomorrow, if the school yearbooks arrive as promised, at least she'll be able to put a face to Victoria Bergman. The girl with the highest marks in every subject but behaviour.

She hangs up her jacket, goes into the kitchen and finds that the worktop she left beautifully clean that morning now looks like a bomb has hit it. There's a faint haze in the living room, evidence of something burning, and there's an open pack of fish fingers on the kitchen table, next to the remains of a head of lettuce.

'Johan? Are you there?' She looks out into the hall and sees light from his room.

She's worried about him again.

According to his teacher he's missed several lessons this week, and when he has been there he's been distant and uninterested. Gloomy and introverted.

He's also got into fights with classmates on several occasions, something that has never happened before.

'Knock-knock,' she says, opening the door to his room. He's lying on his bed with his back to her. 'How are you, darling?'

'I made dinner for you,' he mutters. 'It's in the living room.'

She strokes his back, then turns and can see through the doorway that he's laid the table. She kisses him on the forehead, then goes to look.

On the table is a plate containing some cremated fish fingers, instant macaroni and some lettuce, neatly arranged with a hefty dollop of ketchup. The cutlery is on a napkin beside the plate, and there's a glass of wine, half filled, and a lit candle.

He's made her dinner. That's never happened before. And he's gone to a lot of trouble over it.

Damn the mess in the kitchen, she thinks. He's done this to cheer me up.

'Johan?'

No response.

'You've no idea how happy this makes me. Aren't you going to have any?'

'I've already eaten,' he calls irritably from his room.

She feels suddenly dizzy and incredibly tired. She doesn't get it. If he wants to cheer her up, why reject her like that? 'Johan?' she repeats.

More silence. She goes and sits on his bed, until she realises he's fallen asleep. She turns out the light, carefully closes the door and goes back to the living room. When she sees the table Johan's laid for her again, she almost bursts into tears.

She sighs as she remembers how she and Åke would spend evenings in front of the television, eating chips and laughing at some bad film, but the way she feels now that's hardly a period of her life that she misses. It had been a sterile wait for something better, an emotionally stunted existence that had relentlessly swallowed evening after evening, going on for months, years.

Life is too precious to be wasted waiting for something to happen. Something that can help you move on.

She can't remember what she had hoped for, what she had been dreaming of.

Åke, on the other hand, had fantasised about how his coming success would give them the opportunity to realise their shared dreams. He had said she'd be able to leave the police, and got angry when she had said it was her life and that all the money in the world wouldn't change that. As for her idea that dreams had to remain dreams if they weren't to disappear, Åke had dismissed that as nothing but pseudo-intellectual rubbish picked up from trashy magazines.

After that argument they hadn't spoken for several days, and even if that occasion hadn't been decisive, it had been the beginning of the end.

Vita Bergen – Sofia Zetterlund's Apartment

Sofia wakes up on the living-room floor. It's dark outside and she notices that it's just past seven o'clock, but she has no idea if it's morning or evening.

When she gets up and goes out into the hall, she sees that someone has written on the mirror with the marker. In childish handwriting it says 'UNA KAM O!' and Sofia recognises Solace's jagged scrawl at once. The African serving girl had never learned to write properly.

UNA KAM O, Sofia thinks. It's Krio, and she understands the words. Solace is asking for help.

As she wipes the writing off with her sleeve she sees that there's something else further down the mirror, written with the same pen, but in tiny, almost unhealthily neat handwriting.

Silfverberg Family, Duntzfelts Allé, Hellerup, Copenhagen.

She goes into the kitchen and sees that there are five used plates and the same number of glasses on the table.

There are two full bags of rubbish in front of the sink, and she pokes through them to get an idea of what was eaten. Three bags of crisps, five bars of chocolate, two packets of pork chops, three large bottles of fizzy drink, one roast chicken and four cartons of ice cream.

She can taste vomit in her mouth and can't be bothered to look in the other bag, seeing as she knows what it contains.

Her diaphragm is aching and cramping, and her giddiness is slowly subsiding. She decides to tidy up and suppress whatever's happened. The fact that she lost control and gorged on food and sweets.

She picks up a half-full bottle of wine and goes over to the fridge. She stops when she sees the notes, newspaper cuttings, ads and her own drawings, all stuck to the fridge door. Hundreds of them, layer upon layer, held up by magnets and tape.

A lengthy article about Natascha Kampusch, the girl who was held prisoner in a cellar outside Vienna in Austria. A detailed plan of the secret room Wolfgang Priklopil built for her.

On the right a shopping list in her own handwriting: Polystyrene. Carpet glue. Duct tape. Tarpaulin. Rubber wheels. Latch. Electric cable. Nails. Screws.

On the left a picture of a taser.

Several of the drawings are signed 'Unsocial mate'.

Antisocial friend.

She sinks slowly down onto the floor.

Kronoberg – Police Headquarters

When Jeanette drives Johan to school he appears to be in a good mood, and it seems silly to keep going on about the events of the night before. At the breakfast table she had thanked him again for dinner, and he had actually given her a little smile. That would have to do.

The first thing she sees when she opens the door to her office is a package sitting on her desk.

Three yearbooks from Sigtuna College for the Humanities.

After a couple of minutes she finds her.

Victoria Bergman.

She reads the caption below the photograph. Runs her fingers along the rows of young students in identical uniforms, and concludes that Victoria Bergman is standing in the middle row, second from the right, is slightly shorter than average, and looks rather more childlike than the others.

The girl is thin, fair-haired and probably blue-eyed, and the first differences Jeanette notices are her serious expression and the fact that she doesn't have breasts, unlike the other girls.

Jeanette thinks that there's something familiar about this serious little girl.

She's also struck by how ordinary she looks, which for some reason isn't at all what she was expecting. The fact that she isn't wearing make-up makes her look almost grey alongside the other young girls, all of whom seem to have made an effort to look as good as possible. She's also the only one who isn't smiling.

Jeanette opens the next book and finds Victoria Bergman's name in the list of pupils not present. The same thing happens in the last year, and Jeanette has a feeling that Victoria Bergman was good at hiding even then, as she pulls out the first yearbook and looks at the picture again.

It had been taken almost twenty-five years ago, and she assumes it's useless for identification purposes today.

Or is it?

There's something about the look in those eyes that she recognises. A fleeting impression.

Jeanette Kihlberg is so deeply immersed in the photograph that she jumps when the phone rings.

Kenneth von Kwist says his name in his most ingratiating voice, and Jeanette feels annoyed at once. 'Oh, it's you. Why are you calling?'

He clears his throat. 'Don't be so abrupt. I've got something for you that you're going to like. Make sure you're on your own in the office in ten minutes' time and look out for a fax.'

'A fax?' She doesn't know what he's up to, but is immediately suspicious.

'You're about to receive some information that is for your eyes only,' he goes on. 'The fax you'll be getting consists of documents from Nacka District Court, dated autumn 1988, and you're the first person apart from me to read them since then. I presume you know what this is about?'

Jeanette is speechless. 'I understand,' she finally manages to say. 'You can trust me.'

'Good. Well, don't forget, and good luck. I have every confidence in you and I'm relying on this remaining confidential.'

Wait, she thinks. This is a trap.

'Listen, don't hang up. Why exactly are you doing this?'

'Let's just say . . .' He thinks for a moment before clearing his throat again. 'This is my way of apologising for having put a wrench in the works before. I want to make up for that, and, as I'm sure you're aware, I have my contacts.'

Jeanette still doesn't know what to believe. His words are apologetic, but his tone of voice is just as self-satisfied as always.

When they hang up she leans back in her chair and picks up the yearbook again. Victoria Bergman looks just as evasive as before. Jeanette is still having trouble working out if this is all a cunning joke.

There's a knock on the door and Hurtig comes in. His hair is wet and his jacket is soaked.

'Sorry I'm late. Fucking awful weather.'

The fax machine seems to be churning out paper forever, and Jeanette has her hands full moving the sheets from the floor to her desk. When the machine falls silent she gathers all the sheets together and puts them in a heap in front of her.

In September 1988 the National Board of Forensic Medicine reported that Victoria Bergman had been subjected to serious sexual abuse before her body reached full maturity, and Nacka District Court had therefore agreed to grant confidentiality for her personal details.

Jeanette is disgusted by the cold language. Full maturity – what does that mean?

She reads on and finds the explanation further down. The girl, Victoria Bergman, had, according to the board, been subjected to extensive sexual violence between the ages of zero and fourteen. A gynaecologist and a forensic medical officer had conducted a thorough examination of Victoria Bergman's body and had found that the girl was severely damaged.

Yes, that was actually what it said. Severely damaged.

Finally she reads that it hadn't been possible to determine who had carried out the assaults.

Jeanette is astonished. That thin, fair-haired, serious little girl with the evasive look in her eyes had evidently chosen not to press charges against her father.

She thinks about the reports filed with the police against Bengt Bergman that she herself had been involved with previously. The two

Eritrean refugee children, subjected to whipping and sexual assault, and the prostitute who had been badly beaten, whipped with a belt and anally raped with an object of some sort.

The second report, from the Stockholm County Police Authority, confirmed that in interviews it had emerged that the plaintiff, Victoria Bergman, had been subjected to sexual abuse at least since the age of five or six.

Well, surely it isn't possible to remember much further back than that? Jeanette thinks.

It's certainly difficult to evaluate the credibility of such a witness. But if the abuse had begun when she was very young, it could be presumed that she was already being exploited sexually even then.

Hell, she'd have to show these documents to Sofia Zetterlund, regardless of her promise to von Kwist. Sofia would be able to explain how a little girl who had been subjected to so much would be affected mentally.

The last thing in the report says that the police officer responsible for the investigation believed that the threat against the plaintiff was sufficiently serious that she should be granted a protected identity.

Here, once again, it had not been able to ascertain the identity of the abuser.

Jeanette realises that she's going to have to contact the people responsible for these investigations as soon as possible. It may have been twenty years ago, but with a bit of luck they might still be in the same jobs.

Jeanette goes over to the small side window, which is slightly open. She taps out a cigarette, lights it and takes a deep drag.

If anyone comes in and complains about the smell of smoke, she'll force them to read what she's just read. Then she'll hand them the packet of cigarettes and direct them to the open window.

Back at her desk she reads the report from the psychiatric department of Nacka Hospital. The contents are fundamentally the same as the other documents. The plaintiff should be granted a protected identity in light of what had emerged during some fifty therapy sessions, which had dealt partly with sexual abuse between the ages of five and fifteen, and partly with sexual abuse after the age of fifteen.

Fucking bastard, Jeanette thinks. It's a shame you're dead.

Hurtig comes in with coffee, and they each pour a cup. Jeanette tells him to read through the court files from the beginning, while she tackles the final recommendation of the court.

She gathers together the thick bundle of paper and glances at the last page, to satisfy her curiosity over which police officer had investigated the case.

When she sees who had signed the report and recommended that the court grant confidentiality to Victoria Bergman, she almost chokes on her coffee.

Hans Sjöquist, authorised medical officer
Lars Mikkelsen, detective superintendent
Sofia Zetterlund, accredited psychologist

Vita Bergen – Sofia Zetterlund's Apartment

It could have been different.

The linoleum floor is cold and sticks to Sofia Zetterlund's naked shoulder. It's dark outside.

The lights of cars passing by in the street play across the ceiling, to the sound of nervous rustling from the trees' dry autumn leaves.

She's lying on the kitchen floor next to a couple of bin bags containing vomited food, staring up at the fridge. The open ventilation window in the kitchen combined with the window open in the living room is making the pieces of paper on the fridge door flutter in the cross breeze. If she screws up her eyes they look like flies' wings, buzzing against a mosquito net.

Beside her is a table laid for a party, with dirty plates and unwashed cutlery.

Nature morte.

Once bright candles, now remnants of wax.

Sofia knows that she won't remember anything tomorrow.

Like when she once found that glade down by the lake, in Dala-

Floda, where time stood still and which she spent weeks trying to find again. She has lived with gaps in her memory since she was a small child.

She thinks about Gröna Lund and what happened the night Johan went missing. Images try to take hold within her.

Sofia shuts her eyes and turns her gaze inward.

Johan had been sitting beside her in the Free Fall cradle, and Jeanette had been standing outside the railing watching them. Slowly they had risen, metre by metre.

Halfway to the top she got scared, and when they passed the fifty-metre mark vertigo was welling up. Her irrational response had come out of nowhere.

She hadn't dared to move. And hardly dared to breathe. But Johan had laughed and swung his legs. She had asked him to stop, but he had just grinned at her and carried on.

Sofia remembers thinking that the bolts holding the cradle were being put under unnaturally great pressure, and would eventually come loose. And they'd crash to the ground.

The cradle had been swaying and she had begged him to stop, but he hadn't listened. Arrogant and smug, he had just swung his legs harder.

And suddenly Victoria had been there.

Her fear had vanished, her thoughts cleared, and she was calm again.

And then it all went black once more.

She had been lying on her side. The grit on the tarmac chafing her hip, through her coat and top. Eating its way through.

A smell she had recognised. A cool hand against a hot brow.

She had screwed up her eyes and through the wall of legs and shoes she had seen a bench, and beside the bench she had seen herself from behind.

Yes, that was it. She had seen Victoria Bergman.

Had she been hallucinating?

But she hadn't been delirious. She had seen herself. Her fair hair, her coat, her bag.

It was her. It was Victoria.

She had been lying down, and had seen herself twenty metres away.

Victoria had gone up to Johan and taken him by the arm.

She had tried to call to Johan, to tell him to look out, but when she opened her mouth no sound came out.

Her chest feels tight, as if she's going to suffocate. A panic attack, she thinks, and tries to breathe more slowly.

Sofia Zetterlund remembers seeing herself pull a pink mask over Johan's face.

She's lying on her kitchen floor in Borgmästargatan and knows that in twelve hours she won't have any recollection of having lain on the kitchen floor in Borgmästargatan thinking that in twelve hours she would have to get up and go to work.

But right now Sofia Zetterlund knows that she has a daughter in Denmark.

A daughter named Madeleine.

And right now she remembers that she once went to find Madeleine.

But she doesn't know if she's going to remember that tomorrow.

Denmark, 1988

It could have been good.

Could have been fine.

Victoria doesn't know if she's in the right place; she feels confused and decides to take a walk round the block to collect her thoughts.

She's got a surname to go on, and now she knows that the family lives in Hellerup, one of Copenhagen's smarter suburbs, full of detached villas. The man is managing director of a company that makes toys, and lives in Duntzfelts allé with his wife.

Victoria takes out her Walkman and switches the tape on. A recently released Joy Division compilation. As she walks along the avenues 'Incubation' plays, and the music rattles monotonously in her earphones.

Incubation. Brooding, hatching. Baby birds, snatched away.

She has been an egg-laying machine.

All she knows is that she wants to see her daughter. Then what?

Who cares if it all goes to hell? she thinks as she turns onto the next road, yet another tree-lined avenue.

She sits down on a junction box next to a dustbin, lights a cigarette and decides to sit there until the tape stops.

'She's Lost Control', 'Dead Souls', 'Love Will Tear Us Apart'. The cassette changes side automatically: 'No Love Lost', 'Failures'. People walk past, and she wonders what they're staring at.

When Victoria walks up to the family's villa she sees that there's a brass sign on the stone wall beside the gate, and she knows she's found the right place.

Mr and Mrs Silfverberg and their daughter, Madeleine. She smiles. How ridiculous. Victoria and Madeleine, like the Swedish princesses.

She looks around to make sure no one's watching, then climbs over the wall and drops down the other side. There are lights on downstairs, but the upper two floors are dark. She sees that the balcony door on the first floor is open.

A drainpipe makes a useful ladder, and soon she's opening the door wider.

A study, full of bookcases, and on the floor is a big rug.

She takes off her shoes and pads carefully out onto a large landing. There are two doors on her right, and three on her left, one of which is open. At the far end of the landing is a staircase leading to the other floors. From downstairs comes the sound of a football match on television.

She looks in through the open door. Another study, with a desk and two shelves full of toys. She doesn't bother with the other rooms, since she assumes no one would leave a baby behind a closed door.

Instead she creeps over to the stairs and starts to go down. The staircase is shaped like a U, and she pauses halfway to look down at a large room with a stone floor and a door at the far end, presumably the front door.

An enormous chandelier is hanging from the ceiling, and against the left-hand wall there's a pram with its hood up.

She acts instinctively. There are no consequences, nothing but the here and now.

Victoria goes down the flight of stairs and places her shoes on the bottom step. She's no longer worried about creeping around. The noise from the television is so loud she can hear what the commentators are saying.

Semi-final, Italy against the Soviet Union, nil–nil, Neckar Stadium, Stuttgart.

A glazed double door stands open next to the pram. Through the doors she can see Mr and Mrs Silfverberg watching television, and in the pram is her baby.

Incubation. Egg-laying machine.

She's not the bird of prey here, she's only taking back what's hers.

Victoria goes to the pram and bends over the child. The baby's face is quite calm, but she doesn't recognise it. At the hospital in Aalborg the child had looked different. Her hair had been darker, her face thinner and her lips less full. Now she looks like a cherub.

The baby is sleeping, and it's still nil–nil in the Neckar Stadium in Stuttgart.

Victoria pulls the thin blanket back. Her child is wearing a blue onesie; her arms are bent and her hands are clenched, resting on her shoulders.

Victoria picks her up. The noise from the television gets louder, which makes her feel safer. The little girl is still asleep, warm against her shoulder.

The noise gets even louder, and she hears someone swear inside the room.

One–nil. The Soviet Union takes the lead at Neckar Stadium in Stuttgart.

She holds the baby up in front of her. The girl is smoother now, and paler. Her head looks almost like an egg.

Suddenly Per-Ola Silfverberg is standing in front of her, and for a few silent seconds she stares at him.

She can't believe it.

The Swede.

Glasses and cropped fair hair. The sort of yuppie shirt that bankers usually wear. She's only seen him in filthy work clothes, and never in glasses.

She can see her own reflection in them. Her child is resting against her shoulders in the Swede's glasses.

He looks like an idiot, his face is completely white, slack and expressionless.

'Come on, Soviet Union,' she says as she rocks the baby in her arms.

Then the colour returns to his face. 'Christ! What the hell are you doing here?'

She backs away when he takes a step closer to her, reaching out for the child.

Incubation. The time between the moment of infection and the outbreak of illness. But also the brooding period. Waiting for an egg to hatch. How can the same word describe waiting to have a baby and waiting for illness to break out? Are they the same thing?

The Swede lunging at her makes her lose her hold of the baby.

Its head is heavier than the rest of the body and she sees the baby turn half a revolution in its fall towards the stone floor.

The head is an egg that cracks.

The yuppie shirt flaps back and forth. It is joined by a black dress and a portable phone. His wife starts to panic, and Victoria can't help laughing, seeing as no one is bothered about her any more.

Litovchenko, one–nil, the television reminds them.

'Come on, Soviet Union,' she repeats as she slumps down by the wall.

The baby is a stranger, and she makes up her mind not to care about it.

From now on it's just an egg in a blue onesie.

Kronoberg – Police Headquarters

What the hell, Jeanette Kihlberg thinks, as an uncomfortable feeling spreads through her body.

The fact that Lars Mikkelsen had been involved in the investigation into Victoria Bergman isn't really so strange, but it's striking that he concluded that her identity needed to be protected, seeing as there was no court conviction behind the case.

What's more remarkable is that a psychologist named Sofia Zetterlund had conducted the psychological analysis. It couldn't be her Sofia, because she wouldn't have been twenty at the time of the investigation.

Hurtig looks amused. 'That's one hell of a coincidence. Call her at once.'

Almost too odd, Jeanette thinks. 'I'll call Sofia, and you call Mikkelsen. Ask him to come over to see us, preferably today.'

As soon as Hurtig leaves the room she dials Sofia's number. No answer on her home number, and when she calls the practice the secretary tells her Sofia's ill.

Sofia Zetterlund, she thinks. What are the odds that Victoria Bergman's psychologist in the eighties would have the same name as the Sofia she knows, who also happens to be a psychologist?

A search on the computer tells her that there are fifteen Sofia Zetterlunds in the whole of Sweden. Two of them are psychologists, and they both live in Stockholm. Her Sofia is one of them, and the other has been retired for years and is registered as living in a nursing home in Midsommarkransen.

That must be her, Jeanette thinks.

The whole thing seems almost planned. As if someone were making fun of her and had plotted out the entire sequence of events. Jeanette doesn't believe in coincidence – she believes in logic, and logic is telling her that there's a connection. It's just that she can't see it yet.

Holism again, she thinks. The details seem incredible, incomprehensible. But there's always a natural explanation. A logical context.

Hurtig is standing in the doorway.

'Mikkelsen's in the building. He's waiting for you by the coffee machine. And what are we going to do with Hannah Östlund and Jessica Friberg? Åhlund says they're both unmarried and registered in the same swanky suburb to the west of the city. They're both local government lawyers.'

'Two women who've evidently stuck together all their lives,' Jeanette says. 'Keep looking. Check if the other calls have come up with anything, and put Schwarz onto checking databases and local papers. We'll hold off on paying them a visit for the time being. I don't want us to mess things up, and we need much more to go on. Right now Victoria Bergman is of greater interest.'

'And Madeleine Silfverberg?'

'The authorities in France didn't have much to offer. All we've got is an address in Provence, and we've hardly got the resources to head off down there the way things are these days, but obviously that's a step we might have to take if everything else gets bogged down.'

Hurtig agrees, and they leave the room. Jeanette finds Lars Mikkelsen by the coffee machine. He's holding two cups in his hands and smiles at her.

Jeanette takes one of the cups. 'It's good that you could come. Shall we go into my office?'

Lars Mikkelsen stays almost an hour and explains that he was fairly inexperienced when he was given the Victoria Bergman case.

Finding out about what had happened to Victoria had undeniably been draining, but it also convinced him that he had made the right choice of career.

'Every year we receive about nine hundred reports of sexual assaults.' Mikkelsen sighs and crumples up his empty coffee cup. 'In over eighty per cent of the cases we're dealing with male offenders, and often they're someone the child knows.'

'But how common is it really?'

'In the nineties there was a big study of seventeen-year-olds that found that one in eight girls had been abused.'

Jeanette does some quick calculations. 'So in a normal school class you can assume that there's at least one girl with a dark secret. Maybe two.' She thinks of the girls in Johan's class, and about the fact that he probably knows someone who's been sexually exploited.

'Yes, that's more or less how it is. Among boys the figure is estimated to be one in twenty-five.'

They sit silently for a moment, thinking about the dark statistics.

Jeanette is the first to speak. 'So you handled Victoria's case?'

'Yes, I was contacted by a psychologist at Nacka Hospital who had a patient she was concerned about. But I don't remember the psychologist's name.'

'Sofia Zetterlund,' Jeanette interjects.

'Yes, that sounds familiar. That was probably it.'

'The psychologist who was involved in the Karl Lundström case with you has the same name.'

'Yes, now you come to mention it.' Mikkelsen rubs his chin. 'Strange . . . But I only spoke to her over the phone a couple of times, and I'm not good at remembering names.'

'That's only one of many coincidences in this case.' Jeanette gestures towards all the folders and bundles of documents on her desk. 'If only you knew how tangled this is starting to get. But I know it's all connected somehow. And Victoria Bergman's name keeps cropping up everywhere. What exactly happened?'

He thinks. 'Well, I was contacted by Sofia Zetterlund because she'd had a lot of conversations with the girl and had come to the conclusion that her situation needed to be dramatically changed. That drastic measures were called for.'

'Such as protecting her identity? But who was she being protected from?'

'Her dad.' Mikkelsen takes a deep breath and goes on. 'Remember that the abuse started when she was small, in the mid-seventies, and the legislation was very different then. In those days it was called sexual indecency with a descendant, and the law wasn't changed until 1984.'

'There's nothing about a conviction in any of my documents. Why didn't she report her dad?'

'She refused to, simple as that. I had plenty of conversations with the psychologist about it, but it didn't help. Victoria said she'd deny everything if we filed charges. All we had was the documentation of her injuries. Everything else was circumstantial, and in those days that wasn't good enough. Today he would have got between four and five years. And would have had to pay damages, somewhere in the region of half a million.'

'It needs to be pricey.' It might sound a bit crass, but Jeanette can't be bothered to explain. She presumes Mikkelsen understands what she means. 'So what did you do?'

'The psychologist, Sofia Zetterberg –'

'Zetterlund,' Jeanette corrects him, appreciating that Mikkelsen wasn't exaggerating when he said he had trouble with names.

'Yes, that's right. She believed it was vital that Victoria be separated from her father and get the chance to begin again, under a new name.'

'So you arranged that?'

'Yes, with the help of a medical officer, Hasse Sjöquist.'

'I saw that in my files. What was Victoria like to talk to?'

'We got fairly close, and as time went by I think she started to trust me.'

Jeanette looks at Mikkelsen and can see why Victoria would have felt safe with him. Like a big brother coming to the rescue when the other children are being mean. Sometimes she feels something similar herself. A desire to make life a bit better, if only in her little corner of the world.

'So you arranged for Victoria Bergman to get a new identity?'

'Yes, Nacka District Court agreed with our recommendation and decided to make the whole thing confidential. That's the way it works, so I've got absolutely no idea what she's called these days, or where she lives, but I hope she's OK. Even if I have to say that I have my doubts.' Mikkelsen looks sombre.

'That's going to cause me problems, because I have a feeling that Victoria Bergman is the person I'm looking for.'

Mikkelsen stares at Jeanette uncomprehendingly.

She gives him a brief summary of what she and Hurtig have found out, emphasising how vital it is that they find Victoria. If for no other reason than to rule her out of the investigation.

Jeanette notices that it's almost five o'clock, and concludes that Sofia Zetterlund the elder will have to wait till tomorrow. First she wants to talk to her own Sofia.

She gets her bag and goes down to the car to drive home. She dials the number, then holds the phone against her shoulder as she reverses out of her parking space.

The call goes through, but there's no answer.

Victoria Bergman, Vita Bergen

It could have been different. It could have been good.
Could have been fine.
If only he'd been different. If only he'd been good.

Sofia is sitting on the kitchen floor.

She's muttering to herself, rocking back and forth.

'I am the way, I am the truth and I am the life. No one comes to the father except through me.'

When she looks up at the fridge door and sees the mass of notes, scraps of paper and newspaper cuttings she bursts out laughing, spraying saliva everywhere.

She's familiar with the psychological phenomenon *l'homme du petit papier*. The man with scraps of paper.

The obsessive need to make constant notes everywhere about your observations.

Filling your pockets with tiny dog-eared notes and interesting newspaper articles.

Always having a pen and paper handy.

Antisocial friend.

Unsocial mate.

Solace Manuti.

In Sierra Leone she acquired a new friend. An antisocial friend she gave the name Solace Manuti.

An anagram of unsocial mate.

It had been a play on words, but a desperately serious one. One survival strategy was to create fantasy characters who could take over when Dad's demands on Victoria got too much to bear.

She had emptied her guilt into her personalities.

Every glance, every whistle, every pointed gesture – she has interpreted everything as proof of her unworthiness.

She has always been dirty.

'If we confess our sins, he is faithful and just. Cleanse us from all unrighteousness.'

Lost in her own internal labyrinth, she spills some wine on the table.

'For I have satiated the weary soul, and I have replenished every sorrowful soul.'

She pours a second glass of wine and drains it before going into the bathroom.

'Ye who prepare a table for Gad, and fill up mixed wine unto Meni, I will even assign you to the sword, and ye shall all bow down in the slaughter.'

The hunger fire, she thinks.

If the hunger fire goes out, you die.

She listens to the roaring inside her, and to the blood burning in her veins.

Eventually the fire will die down and then her heart will be charred and end up as a large black stain.

She pours more wine, rinses her face, drinks and retches, but forces herself to finish the glass, sits down on the toilet, wipes herself with a towel, gets up – and puts her make-up on.

When she's finished she looks at herself. She looks good. Good enough for her purpose.

She knows that when she stands at the bar and appears bored, she never has to wait long.

She's done it so many times before.

Almost every night.

For several years.

The feelings of guilt have been a comfort, because she feels secure in guilt. She has anaesthetised herself and sought acknowledgement among men who only see themselves and therefore can't acknowledge her. Shame becomes a liberation.

But she doesn't want them to see anything but the surface. Never to look inside her.

That's why her clothes are sometimes dirty and torn. Stained with grass from lying on her back in a park. She knows that the present is a moment that will be a gap in her memory tomorrow.

They'll compete to see who can buy her the most expensive drink. Like flies on a sugar cube. The winner gets the back of his hand stroked and, after the third drink, her thigh against his groin. She is genuine, and her smile is always real.

She knows what she wants them to do to her, and she's always very clear about saying so.

But if she's going to be able to smile she needs wine, she thinks, and takes a swig from the bottle.

She can feel herself crying, but it's only wetness on her cheek and she carefully wipes it away with the ball of her thumb. Mustn't damage the surface.

Suddenly the phone rings from her jacket pocket, and she weaves out into the hall.

She sees it's Jeanette, presses reject and then switches the phone off. She goes into the living room and sits down heavily on the sofa. She starts reading a magazine she finds on the table, and leafs through to the centrefold.

So much time has passed, and still the same life, the same necessity.

A colourful picture of an octagonal tower.

She squints through the drink, focuses her gaze and sees that it's a pagoda next to a Buddhist temple. The article is about a guided tour to Wuhan, provincial capital of Hubei, on the eastern side of the Yangtze River.

Wuhan.

Alongside is an article about Gao Xingjian, Nobel Prize winner, and a big picture of his novel *One Man's Bible.*

Gao.

She puts the magazine down and goes over to the bookcase. Carefully she pulls out a book with a worn leather binding.

Eight Treatises on the Nurturing of Life, from 1591, by Gao Lian.

She sees the catch holding the bookcase in place.

Gao Lian.

Gao Lian from Wuhan.

First she hesitates, then slowly lifts the catch, and with a tiny, scarcely audible creak the door slides open.

Bella Vita, Victoria Bergman
Vita Bergen – Sofia Zetterlund's Apartment

Bella vita. Good life.

It could have been different. It could have been fine.

Could have been good.

If only he'd been different. If only he'd been good.

Just been good.

Drawings everywhere. Hundreds, maybe thousands of childish, naive drawings scattered across the floor or stuck to the walls.

All of them very detailed, but done by a child.

She sees the house in Grisslinge, before and after the fire, and there's the cottage in Dala-Floda.

A bird in a nest with its chicks, before and after Victoria attacked it with a stick.

A little girl by a lighthouse. Madeleine, her little girl, taken from her.

She remembers the afternoon she told Bengt she was pregnant.

Bengt had flown up from his armchair, with a look of terror. He had rushed over to her and screamed, 'Get up!'

He had grabbed her arms and dragged her from the sofa.

'Jump, for God's sake!'

They had stood facing each other, with him panting in her face. The smell of garlic.

'Jump!' he had repeated. She recalls shaking her head. Never, she had thought. You can't make me.

She remembers him crying after he sat down in his armchair again and turned his back on her.

She looks around the room she has used as a place of refuge. Among all the drawings and scraps of paper on the walls she sees a newspaper article about Chinese refugee children arriving at Arlanda with fake passports, a mobile phone and fifty American dollars. And how they then go missing. Hundreds of them, every year.

A sidebar of facts about the *hukou* system.

In one corner the exercise bike she's been using. Cycling for hours, then anointing herself with fragrant oils.

She remembers how Bengt had grabbed her hand and squeezed it. 'Up onto the table!' he had sobbed, without looking at her. 'Up onto the table, for God's sake!'

It had felt like she was inside a different body as she finally climbed onto the table and turned to face him.

'Jump . . .'

She had jumped. Climbed up onto the table and jumped again. And again. And again.

She had carried on jumping until the African girl had come down the stairs. She was wearing the mask. Her face was cold and expressionless. Empty, black eye sockets with nothing behind them.

It didn't die, Sofia thinks.

Madeleine is alive.

Sunflower Nursing Home

The next morning Jeanette drives straight to Midsommarkransen to visit the older Sofia Zetterlund. She eventually finds a free parking space close to the metro station and switches off the engine of her old Audi.

The nursing home that is Sofia Zetterlund's registered address is located in one of the yellow modernist blocks near Svandammsparken.

Jeanette has always liked the districts of Aspudden and Midsommarkransen, built in the 1930s as small towns within the city. Not a bad place to spend your final years, she thinks.

But she also knows that there are cracks below the idyllic surface. Until just a few years ago the Bandidos motorcycle gang was based just a few blocks away.

She smokes a cigarette before she goes in, thinking about Sofia Zetterlund the younger.

Is it because of Sofia that she's started smoking so much? She's now up to something like a pack a day, and has caught herself trying to conceal the fact from Johan on several occasions, like a naughty teenager. But the nicotine makes her think better. Freer, faster. And now she's thinking about Sofia Zetterlund, the Sofia she might be falling in love with.

Or is it just a temporary feeling, no more than a childish infatuation after a kiss? A passing fancy?

Anyway, what does being in love really mean?

She once discussed the subject with Sofia, and was confronted with an entirely new way of looking at it. For Sofia, being in love wasn't something mysterious or pleasant. She said it was the same as being psychotic. The object of love is just an idealised image that doesn't match reality, and the person in love is merely infatuated with the feeling of being in love. Sofia had compared it to the way a child might ascribe feelings to a pet that it couldn't really have.

She stubs out the cigarette and rings the bell of the Sunflower Nursing Home.

Now for Sofia the elder.

After a short conversation with the manager she is shown to the dayroom.

At the far end of the room, by the balcony door, sits a woman in a wheelchair, staring out through the window.

She's very thin, and dressed in a long blue dress that reaches all the way to the tips of her toes. Her hair is completely white, and reaches to her waist. She's wearing garish make-up, blue eyeshadow and bright red lipstick.

'Sofia?' The manager goes over to the woman in the wheelchair and puts a hand on her shoulder. 'You've got a visitor. It's a Jeanette Kihlberg from the Stockholm police, and she'd like to talk to you about one of your old patients.'

'They're clients.' The old woman's reply is rapid, and not without a hint of contempt.

Jeanette pulls up a chair and sits down beside Sofia Zetterlund.

She introduces herself and explains why she's come, but the old woman doesn't deign to look at her.

'Well, as you know, I'm here to ask a few questions about one of your old clients,' Jeanette says. 'A young woman you saw twenty years ago.'

No response.

The old woman is still staring at something outside. Her eyes look clouded. Cataracts, Jeanette thinks. Could she be blind?

'The girl was seventeen years old when you treated her,' Jeanette goes on. 'Her name is Victoria Bergman. Does that name mean anything to you?'

The woman finally turns her head, and Jeanette can see a trace of a smile on the old face. It seems to soften.

'Victoria,' Sofia the elder says. 'Of course I remember her.'

Jeanette breathes out. She decides to get straight to the point and moves her chair a bit closer. 'I've got a picture of Victoria with me. I don't know how good your eyesight is, but do you think you might be able to identify her?'

Sofia smiles broadly. 'Oh, no. I've been blind for the past two years. But I can describe what she looked like back then. Blonde hair, blue eyes. She had a wry smile and the look in her eyes was always intense, focused.'

Jeanette studies the picture of the serious young girl in the school yearbook. Her appearance matches the old woman's description. 'What happened to her after you stopped treating her?'

Sofia laughs again. 'Who?' she asks.

Jeanette starts to get suspicious. 'Victoria Bergman.'

The distant look in Sofia's face returns, and after a couple of seconds Jeanette repeats her question.

Sofia's face breaks into a smile again. 'Victoria? Yes, I remember her.' Then the smile fades, and the woman rubs her cheek with her hand. 'Does my lipstick look all right? Is it messy?'

'No, it looks fine,' Jeanette replies. She's starting to worry that Sofia Zetterlund has problems with her short-term memory. Alzheimer's, probably.

'Victoria Bergman,' Sofia repeats. 'A peculiar story. By the way, you smell of smoke . . . Are you offering?'

Jeanette finds the abrupt twists in the conversation bewildering. It's clear that Sofia Zetterlund has problems keeping hold of the threads in conversation, but that doesn't necessarily mean that her long-term memory is damaged.

'Smoking isn't allowed in here, I'm afraid,' Jeanette says.

Sofia's response is probably less than entirely truthful. 'I know that, but it is in my room. Push me back in there and we can have a smoke.'

Jeanette pushes her own chair back, gets up and carefully turns Sofia's wheelchair. 'OK, let's go and sit in your room instead. Where is it?'

'Last door on the right at the end of the corridor.'

Jeanette gestures to the manager that they're leaving the day room for a while.

Once they're in her room, Sofia insists on sitting in the armchair and Jeanette helps the old woman to get comfortable. Then she sits down at the little table by the window.

'Now, let's have a smoke.'

Jeanette hands her the lighter and cigarettes, and Sofia lights up. 'There's an ashtray on the chest of drawers, next to Freud.'

Freud? Jeanette turns round.

Sure enough, there's an ashtray behind her, a large one made of crystal, and next to it is a snow globe.

Usually the image inside the globe is children playing, or snowmen, or some other winter scene. But Sofia's snow globe contains an image of a very sombre-looking Sigmund Freud.

Jeanette stands up to reach the ashtray. Once she's there she can't resist shaking the globe.

Freud's snowed in, she thinks. At least Sofia Zetterlund has a sense of humour. Then she repeats her question. 'Did you ever meet Victoria Bergman again after she was granted a protected identity?'

The old woman seems more alert now that she's got a cigarette in her hand. 'No, never. There was a new law about secret personal details, so no one knows what her name is now.'

Nothing new so far, although at least Jeanette has confirmation that there's nothing wrong with the old woman's long-term memory.

'Did she have any distinguishing features? You seem to remember her appearance very well.'

'She was a very intelligent girl. She was probably too intelligent for her own good, if you know what I mean.'

'No. What do you mean?'

Sofia's reply has little to do with Jeanette's question. 'I haven't seen her since the autumn of 1988. But ten years later I got a letter from her.'

'Do you remember what she wrote?'

'Yes, but not word for word, obviously. It was mainly about her daughter.'

'Her daughter?' Jeanette's curiosity is aroused.

'Yes. She was pregnant, and put her child up for adoption. She didn't say much about it, but I know she went off to look for the child in the early summer of 1988. She was living with me at the time. For almost two months.'

'She lived with you?'

The old woman suddenly looks very serious. It's as if her skin tenses up and the wrinkles become smoother. 'Yes. She was having suicidal thoughts and it was my duty to look after her. I would never have let Victoria go if I hadn't realised that it was absolutely vital for her to see the child again.'

'Where did she go?'

Sofia Zetterlund shakes her head. 'She refused to say. But when she came back she was stronger.'

'Stronger?'

'Yes. As if she'd put something very difficult behind her. But what they did to her in Copenhagen was wrong. You shouldn't do that to anyone.'

Stockholm, 1988

Just been good.

'You're dead to me!' Victoria writes at the bottom of the postcard, then posts it at Central Station in Stockholm. The picture on the front shows King Gustav XIV Adolf sitting in a gilded chair with the queen standing beside him, smiling and showing that she's proud of her husband and that she's the subordinate partner, ever obedient.

Just like Mum, she thinks as she walks down into the metro.

Victoria thinks Queen Sylvia's smile looks like the Joker's huge red ear-to-ear lips, and she recalls hearing that someone had said that the king was a real pig in private, and that when he wasn't confusing people from Arboga with those from Örebro, he would flick matchsticks at the queen just to humiliate her.

It's Midsummer's Eve, and therefore a Friday. Victoria wonders how a holiday that was originally a celebration of the summer solstice could now always take place on the third Friday in June, regardless of where the sun is.

You're slaves, she thinks, looking derisively at the drunk people getting into the cool metro carriages with their bags full of food. Obedient lackeys. Sleepwalkers. She doesn't think she's got anything to celebrate, and is just heading back to Sofia's house in Tyresö.

It was good that she returned to Copenhagen, because now she knows that she doesn't care.

The child might as well have died, it wouldn't have made any difference.

But it didn't die when she dropped it on the floor.

She doesn't remember much of what happened after the ambulance came, but the baby didn't die, she knows that much.

The egg was cracked but not ruined, and nothing was ever reported to the police.

They let her go.

And she knows why.

As the train passes Gamla stan and crosses the bridge over the waters of Riddarfjärden she can see the Djurgård ferries and, a bit further away, the roller coaster at Gröna Lund, and realises that she hasn't been to a fair for three years. Not since the day Martin went missing. She doesn't know exactly what happened to him, but she thinks he fell in the water.

As she walks in through the gate she can see Sofia sitting in a garden chair in front of the little red house with its white gables. She's sitting in the shade of a large cherry tree, and as Victoria gets closer she sees that the old woman is asleep. Her fair, almost white hair is draped over her shoulders like a shawl, and she's wearing make-up. Her lips are red and she's wearing blue eyeshadow.

It's chilly, and Victoria picks up the blanket Sofia has put over her feet and wraps it around her.

She goes into the house and, after a search, finds Sofia's handbag. In the outside pocket is a worn, brown leather purse. She finds three hundred-krona notes inside and decides to leave one. She folds the other two and puts them in the back pocket of her jeans.

She puts the purse back and goes into Sofia's study. She finds the notepad in one of the desk drawers.

Victoria sits down at the desk, opens the pad and starts reading.

She sees that Sofia has written down everything Victoria has said, sometimes verbatim, and Victoria is astonished that Sofia has also managed to describe Victoria's movements, or her tone of voice.

Victoria presumes that Sofia must know shorthand, and writes her notes up afterwards. She reads slowly and considers everything she reads.

After all, they have had more than fifty sessions.

She picks up a pen and changes the names so that they're right. If it says that Victoria had done something when it was actually Solace who was the guilty party, she corrects it. Things need to be right, and she doesn't want the blame for something Solace has done.

Victoria works hard and doesn't notice time passing. As she reads she pretends to be Sofia. She frowns and tries to diagnose her client.

On the edge of the pages she writes down her own reflections and analysis.

When Sofia hasn't understood what Solace was talking about, Victoria explains in the margin in tiny, clear writing.

She really doesn't understand how Sofia could have got so much wrong.

Victoria is so absorbed in her work that she doesn't put the pad down until she hears Sofia moving around in the kitchen.

She looks out through the window. On the other side of the road, down by the lake, a group of people are sitting and eating. They've taken over the jetty and have laid out a spread for their Midsummer celebrations.

There's a smell of dill from the kitchen.

'Welcome back, Victoria!' Sofia calls from the kitchen. 'How was your trip?'

She replies that it had gone well.

The baby is just an egg in a blue babygrow. Nothing more. And she's put all that behind her.

The bright evening turns into a night that's almost as bright, and when Sofia says she's going to bed, Victoria stays on the stone steps listening to the birds. A nightingale is calling plaintively from a tree in the next garden and she can hear the sounds from the party down on the jetty. It makes her think of Midsummer celebrations in Dalarna.

They would start with a trip to the Dala River to watch the church boats, before it was time for dancing around the midsummer pole, erected by the men with a lot of huffing and puffing. Women with wreaths of flowers in their hair laughed more than they had in ages, but not for too long because once the vodka started to flow and all the other men's women looked so much better than their own, there was a good chance of getting a slap on the cheek from a hand telling you how fucking fat you were. And how everyone else had it easy, with a woman who was horny and happy and grateful, not just miserable and grey. And that it was just as well to curl up next to her and fiddle and poke even though you said you had a stomach-ache and he said that you'd eaten too many sweets even though you'd hardly had the money for a fizzy drink and spent the time wandering about instead, watching all the other kids with great clouds of candyfloss buy raffle tickets . . . Victoria looks around. It's quiet down by the lake and the sun is just visible over the horizon. It will only be gone for an hour or so before rising again. It never gets dark.

She stands up, a little stiff from the hard steps. She doesn't feel tired, even though it's almost morning.

The sharp gravel hurts her bare feet and she walks along the edge of the lawn instead. By the gate a flowering lilac is wilting, but even though the flowers look withered they still smell.

The road is deserted, and she goes down to the jetty. Some seagulls are feasting on the remains of the evening's festivities, spread out around an overflowing bin. They take off reluctantly and fly out across the lake, shrieking. The water's black and cold and a few fish are up and about, snapping at the insects flying just above the surface. She lies on her stomach and stares down into the darkness.

The ripples on the water made her reflection hazy, but she likes seeing herself like that. It makes her look prettier.

The licking of lips and his tongue stuck in your mouth, which probably tastes of vomit because two bottles of cherry wine come back up easier than they slip down. There could be fifteen guys, all goading one another on, and the hut wasn't exactly big. They used to play cards to see who got to go in the other room with you. If they were outside then maybe it was the slope behind the school, which you could roll down and end up in a heap just a couple of metres from the path, and people looking the other way when you looked up at them from below and you only yelled at the kid that he'd just said he wanted to go swimming after the Ferris wheel. And now you're standing there shivering, so you might as well jump in instead of going on about the new nanny who's supposed to be so lovely . . .

In the water Victoria sees Martin slowly sink and disappear.

On Monday morning she is woken by Sofia, who tells her it's eleven o'clock and that they'll be driving into the city soon.

When Victoria gets out of bed she sees that her feet are dirty, her knees are scratched and her hair is still wet, but she can't remember what she was doing during the night.

Sofia has got breakfast ready out in the garden, and as they eat she explains that Victoria will be seeing a doctor named Hans who's going to examine her and document what he finds. Then, if they have time, they're going to meet a policeman named Lars.

'Hasse and Lasse?' Victoria giggles. 'I hate cops,' she snarls, pushing her cup away demonstrably. 'I haven't done anything.'

'Apart from taking two hundred kronor from my purse, so you can pay for the petrol when I fill up.'

Victoria doesn't know what she feels, but it's like she's sorry for Sofia.

It's a new experience.

Hasse is a doctor at the National Board of Forensic Medicine in Solna, and he examines Victoria. This is the second examination, after the one at Nacka Hospital a week ago.

When he touches her, spreading her legs and looking inside her, she wishes she was back at Nacka Hospital instead, where the doctor had been a woman.

Anita or Annika.

She doesn't remember.

Hasse explains to her that the examination might feel a bit uncomfortable, but that he's there to help her. Wasn't that just what she'd always been told?

That it might feel funny, but that it's for her own good.

Hasse looks all over her body, and he makes notes about what he sees using a little tape recorder.

He looks inside her mouth with a pocket torch, and his voice is factual and monotonous. 'Mouth. Damage to the mucous glands,' it says.

And the rest of her body.

'Crotch. Inner and outer genitals, scarring from forced dilation at a premature age. Anus, scarring, premature, healed injuries, forced dilation, swollen blood vessels, fissures in the sphincter, anal fistula . . .

Scarring from sharp objects on the torso, chest, thighs and arms, approximately one-third of them premature. Evidence of bleeding . . .'

She shuts her eyes and thinks that she is doing this so she can start again, become someone else and forget.

At four o'clock the same day she meets Lars, the policeman she needs to talk to.

He seems observant, like when he realises that she doesn't want to shake his hand when they first meet, and he doesn't touch her.

The first conversation with Lars Mikkelsen takes place in his office, and she tells him what she's already told Sofia Zetterlund.

He looks sad when she answers his questions, but he doesn't lose sight of what he's doing and Victoria feels surprisingly relaxed. After a while she starts to feel curious about who Lars Mikkelsen really is, and she asks him why he does this sort of work.

He looks thoughtful and takes his time answering.

'I think this sort of crime is the most disgusting of all. Far too few victims get justice, and far too few offenders get put away,' he says after a while, and Victoria feels the remark is aimed at her.

'You know I'm not going to help put anyone away?'

He looks at her seriously. 'Yes, I know, and I'm sorry about that, even if it isn't unusual.'

'Why do you think that is?'

He smiles warily and doesn't seem bothered by her easy tone. 'You seem to be questioning me now,' he says. 'But, to answer your question, I think that basically we're still living in the Dark Ages.'

'The Dark Ages?'

'Yes. Have you ever heard of bride kidnapping?'

Victoria shakes her head.

'In the Dark Ages men could force a marriage by kidnapping and sexually assaulting a woman. Because she'd been sexually exploited, she was forced to marry the man and at the same time he got the right of ownership to all her property.'

'So?'

'It's about property and dependence,' he says. 'Originally, rape wasn't regarded as a crime against the woman who was the victim, but as a property crime. The rape laws came about to protect a man's rights to valuable sexual property, either through marrying the woman off or keeping her for his own use. The woman had no say in the matter. She was merely a piece of property whose fate was decided by men. There are still traces of that medieval view of women in attitudes towards rape. She could have said no, or she did say no, but she meant yes. She was dressed so provocatively. She just wants to get revenge on the man.'

His speech surprises Victoria. She had never imagined a man could think like that.

'And in the same way the medieval attitude towards children is still with us,' Lars Mikkelsen concludes. 'To this day, adults regard children as their own property. They punish them and raise them according to their own laws.'

He looks at Victoria. 'Are you satisfied with my answer?'

He seems genuine, and passionate about his work. She really does hate cops, but he doesn't behave like a cop.

It's night, and Sofia's asleep. Victoria creeps into the study and closes the door carefully behind her. Sofia hasn't said anything about Victoria writing in her notes, and probably hasn't discovered it yet.

She gets the book out and continues from where she was interrupted. She likes Sofia's handwriting:

> Victoria has a tendency to forget what she herself said ten minutes ago, or a week ago. Are these 'lapses' ordinary gaps in her memory or a sign of DID?
>
> I've noticed that most of these lapses occur when she's talking about subjects she isn't usually capable of discussing. Her childhood, and her earliest memories.
>
> Victoria's story is associative, one memory leads to another. Is one specific personality talking, or does Victoria behave more childishly because it's easier to talk about memories if she adopts the behaviour she had as a twelve- or thirteen-year-old? Are the memories real, or are they mixed up with Victoria's current thinking about those events? And who is this Crow Girl to whom she refers so often?

Victoria sighs and adds:

> Crow Girl is a mixture of all the rest of us, apart from the Sleepwalker, who hasn't worked out that Crow Girl exists.

Victoria works through the night, and at six o'clock she starts to worry that Sofia will wake up soon. Before putting the book back in the desk drawer, she leafs through it at random, mostly because she has trouble putting it down. Then she discovers that Sofia has seen her annotations after all.

Victoria reads the original text on the very first page of the notebook.

> My first impression of Victoria is that she's highly intelligent. She has good background knowledge of my work and of what therapy entails. When I pointed this out at the end of the session, something unexpected happened, which showed that as well as being intelligent she also has a very hot temper. She snapped at me. Told me I 'didn't know shit'. and that I 'was a total zero'. It's been a long time since I saw someone so angry, and this undisguised anger in her troubles me.

A couple of days ago Victoria had commented on this.

> I wasn't at all angry with you. It must be a misunderstanding. I said I was the one who didn't know shit. That I was a total zero. ME, not you!

And evidently Sofia had read what Victoria had written, and had left her own response.

> Victoria, sorry if I misunderstood. But you were so angry that I could hardly make out what you were saying, and you gave the impression that it was me you were angry at.
>
> It was your fury that troubled me.
>
> I've read everything you've written in this notebook, and I think you have a lot of interesting things to say. Without any exaggeration, I can say that your analysis is in many instances so pertinent that it's better than mine.
>
> You've got the makings of a psychologist. Go to university!

There's no more space in the margin after that, and Sofia has drawn an arrow pointing over the page. There she has added:

But I'd appreciate it if you asked for permission before borrowing my notebook. Perhaps you and I could have a talk about what you've written, when you feel ready?

Hugs from Sofia.

Sunflower Nursing Home

'What did they do to Victoria in Copenhagen?' Jeanette asks. 'And do you remember what the letter said?'

'Give me another cigarette, and maybe I'll remember.'

Jeanette hands Sofia Zetterlund the pack.

'So, what was it we were talking about?' she asks after taking a couple of deep drags on the cigarette.

Jeanette is starting to lose patience. 'Copenhagen and the letter you got from Victoria ten years ago. Do you remember what she wrote?'

To Jeanette's surprise Sofia laughs out loud. 'Would you mind passing me Freud . . . ?'

'Freud?'

'Yes, I heard you messing about with him when you got the ashtray. I may be blind, but I'm not deaf yet.'

Jeanette gets the little snow globe containing Freud's bust from the chest of drawers while the old woman lights another cigarette.

'Victoria Bergman was very special,' Sofia begins, slowly turning the snow globe in her hands. The smoke from the cigarette curls around her blue dress and the snow inside the globe swirls about. 'You've read my final recommendation, and the court's judgement about protecting Victoria's identity, and you're aware of the reasons behind that. Victoria was subjected to extreme sexual abuse by her father and probably other men as well.'

Sofia pauses, and Jeanette finds herself astonished at how the old woman keeps switching between intellectual clarity and dementia-like confusion.

'But what you probably don't know is that Victoria also suffers from multiple personality disorder, or dissociative identity disorder, if those mean anything to you?'

Now Sofia Zetterlund is the one directing the conversation.

Jeanette is vaguely aware of the concepts. Sofia the younger had once explained that Samuel Bai had had a personality disorder of that sort.

'Even if it's extremely rare, it's not really that complicated,' Sofia the elder goes on. 'Victoria was forced to invent different versions of herself in order to survive and cope with the memories of her experiences. When we gave her a new identity, she had documentation that one of her split personalities really existed. That was the conscientious part of her, the one that could get an education, work, basically live a normal life.'

Sofia smiles again, winks at Jeanette with one cataract-blurred eye and shakes the snow globe.

'Freud wrote about moral masochism,' Sofia adds. 'The masochism of a dissociative individual can lead them to relive their own abuse by allowing one of their alternative personalities to do the same thing to others. I detected a trace of this in Victoria, and if she hasn't received help dealing with her problems as an adult, there's a great risk that this personality is still inside her. It will be acting like her father to torment itself, to punish itself.'

Sofia puts her cigarette out in the pot plant on the table, then leans back in her armchair. Jeanette sees the distant look on her face return.

She leaves the Sunflower Nursing Home ten minutes and one reprimand later. She and Sofia each smoked five cigarettes during their conversation, and were caught red-handed by the manager and a nurse who came to give Sofia her medication.

She gets in behind the wheel and turns the key in the ignition. The engine splutters, but refuses to start. 'Fuck!' she swears.

She walks down to the Midsommarkransen shopping centre, and the Tre Vänner bar, opposite the metro station. The bar's half full and she finds an empty table by the window facing the park, orders a coffee and calls Hurtig's number.

Mariatorget – Sofia Zetterlund's Office

Can't it be said that feeling full to overflowing is one symptom of dissatisfaction? Sofia Zetterlund is walking down Hornsgatan, absorbed in herself. And isn't dissatisfaction the source of all change?

She knows that sooner or later she's going to have to tell Jeanette who she really is. Explain that she used to be ill, but is now well. Is it as easy as that? Will just telling her be enough? And how will Jeanette react?

When she tried to help Jeanette put together the perpetrator profile, she was really just talking about herself, unsentimentally and without emotion. She hadn't needed to read the descriptions of the crime scenes because she knew what they looked like. Or what they should have looked like.

When she walks into reception Ann-Britt calls to her.

Sofia Zetterlund is first surprised and then annoyed when Ann-Britt tells her that she had received calls from both Ulrika Wendin and Annette Lundström.

All future sessions with Ulrika and Linnea have been cancelled.

'All of them? Did they say why?' Sofia leans over the reception desk.

'Well, Linnea's mum said she was feeling better now, and that Linnea was back at home.' Ann-Britt folds the newspaper she had been reading before going on. 'Apparently she's got custody of her daughter again. The decision to take her into care was only temporary, and now that everything's fine she didn't think Linnea needed to see you any more.'

'What an idiot!' Sofia can feel her anger building. 'So now she suddenly imagines she's competent to decide what sort of treatment the girl needs?'

Ann-Britt gets up and goes over to the water cooler beside the kitchen. 'Maybe she didn't quite put it like that, but that was pretty much what she said.'

'And what was Ulrika's reason?'

Ann-Britt pours a glass of water. 'She didn't say much, just that she didn't want to come again.'

Sofia turns and walks to the lift and goes back down, then out onto the street, heading east along St Paulsgatan. At Bellmansgatan she turns left, past the Maria Magdalena churchyard.

Fifty metres ahead she catches sight of a woman from behind, and there's something about the broad, rolling hips and the way the feet point outwards that she recognises.

The woman's head is bowed, as though weighed down by some internal burden. Her hair is grey, pulled up into a bun.

Sofia's stomach tightens and she feels cold and sweaty. She stops, and watches the woman turn the corner into Hornsgatan.

Memories, difficult to reconstruct. Fragmentary.

For more than twenty years the memories of her other selves have lain buried like sharp splinters deep inside her – shattered pieces of another time and another place.

She starts walking, speeds up and jogs to the corner, but the woman has vanished.

Kronoberg – Police Headquarters

It's late in the afternoon in October and Jeanette is sitting in her office with a sheet of A3 in front of her containing a diagram of all the names that have cropped up during the investigation.

She's put the names in groups and marked the relationships between them, and as she picks up her pen to draw a line from one name to another, Hurtig comes rushing into her office, just as the phone rings.

Jeanette can see the call is from Åke and gestures to Hurtig to wait.

He looks frustrated. 'Don't answer that,' he says. 'We have to leave.'

Jeanette stares at Hurtig and holds two fingers up in the air. 'Åke, I can't talk right now.'

He sighs. 'That doesn't matter. We need to talk –'

'Not now!' she snaps. 'I've got to go, I'll be home in an hour or so.'

Hurtig shakes his head. 'No, no, no,' he says in a low voice. 'You won't be home that soon.'

'Åke, hang on a moment.' She turns to Hurtig. 'What did you say?'

'Annette Lundström has called. We've got to –'

'Just a moment.' She picks up the phone again. 'Like I said. I can't talk now.'

'As usual, then.' Åke sighs. The line goes quiet. He's hung up, and Jeanette feels her cheeks burn as tears well up.

Hurtig is holding out Jeanette's jacket. 'Sorry, I didn't mean to.'

'Don't worry.' She pulls her jacket on as she herds Hurtig out, turns off the light and closes the door.

While they jog down the stairs to the garage Hurtig tells Jeanette what's happened.

Annette Lundström has contacted them. Someone's put a photograph through her letter box.

A Polaroid of someone she recognises.

She didn't want to say more over the phone.

Hurtig drives fast. First the Essinge motorway, then Norrtull and Sveaplan. He weaves between lanes, blowing his horn angrily at cars that block the way in spite of the blue lights and siren.

'Why did she call you?' Jeanette asks.

Hurtig brakes hard for a bus pulling up at a bus stop. 'I don't know.'

After the roundabout at Roslagstull the traffic thins and they turn onto the E18.

'Is Åke fucking with you?'

The outside lane is free of cars, and Hurtig speeds up. Jeanette sees that they're going more than one hundred and fifty kilometres an hour now.

'No, I can't really say that. It's probably something to do with Johan, and . . .' She can feel herself getting close to tears again, this time not out of anger, but of a crushing feeling of not being good enough.

'He's OK. Johan, I mean.'

Jeanette realises that Hurtig is glancing at her, and that he's trying to be discreet. Jens Hurtig can be abrupt and taciturn, but Jeanette knows that he's quite sensitive under the surface, and realises that he cares about how she's feeling.

'But he's at a difficult age,' Hurtig goes on. 'Hormones and all that crap. And with Åke moving out as well –' He stops himself, as if he's aware of how clumsy the comment was. 'There's something funny about it, though.'

'About what?'

'About that age. Considering what happened in Sigtuna. Hannah Östlund, Jessica Friberg and Victoria Bergman. I mean, at that age everything seems to get blown out of proportion. Like the first time you fall in love.' Hurtig smiles, and seems almost embarrassed.

What Jeanette experiences at that moment must be one of the human intellect's great mysteries. An igniting spark. A flash of genius.

She already knows who is in the photograph Annette Lundström has received.

But she says nothing.

They drive the last few kilometres in silence.

Now that everything has fallen into place, Jeanette wants to get her suspicions confirmed as quickly as possible.

As they turn into the drive they see Annette Lundström standing on the steps in front of the large house. Jeanette thinks she looks tired and shrunken.

While they're getting out of the car a man approaches from the neighbouring house. He introduces himself and says he saw a woman he didn't recognise put something through the Lundströms' letter box earlier that day.

'She came walking from down there.' He points along the street. 'And because we look out for one another round here, well . . .' He falls silent, and Jeanette understands what he means.

The Swedish suspicion of strangers, she thinks.

'And you didn't recognise her?' Hurtig asks.

'No. Never saw her before. Fair-haired. Nothing special about her clothes. Nothing remarkable at all, really. She went up to the letter box and put something through it. I didn't see what.'

Jeanette looks at Hurtig, who merely nods back. The man seems credible.

'OK, well, thanks for your help,' Jeanette says, then turns towards Annette Lundström while the man goes back home.

They go into the hall together, then into a bare living room.

A quantity of moving boxes, empty curtain rails, lots of dust.

Annette Lundström sits down on one of the boxes while Jeanette stops just inside the door and looks around.

There are pale patches on the walls where paintings once hung. Holes and marks from dirty hands.

There's a bottle of cognac on the windowsill, next to an overflowing ashtray. The air in the room is suffocating.

What had been a warm and welcoming room just a few days before is now just a dirty, empty space. A nothing, between one place and another.

A home that has been abandoned for another.

'It's all my fault. I should have said something earlier.' Annette's voice is monotonous, and Jeanette can't help thinking that it might not be just the alcohol making her seem listless. She's probably on tranquillizers.

Jeanette leans against the door frame. 'What should you have said?'

She looks at the woman's eyes, red from crying. They seem distant, and it takes her a long time before she answers.

'I should have been honest the last time we met. I think it's all about the past. Fredrika wasn't a good person, and she's got a lot of enemies . . . She is . . . or was . . .' Annette falls silent. It looks like she's having trouble breathing and Jeanette hopes she isn't about to start hyperventilating and get hysterical.

'It's her in the photograph,' Annette says, picking up an unstamped envelope and holding it out to Jeanette.

The lack of a stamp confirms the neighbour's statement that it had been delivered by hand.

Jeanette takes the envelope, puts it on the windowsill and pulls on a pair of latex gloves before opening it.

'It's her!' Annette says.

Jeanette stares at the photograph, a Polaroid of the dead Fredrika Grünewald.

A lifeless face, its mouth wide open, its blank eyes contorted in the anguished moment of death.

Blood is running down Fredrika's pale blouse, and the piano wire has cut deep into her rigid neck.

Taken just seconds before she died.

But that isn't the important thing. What matters is that the hand holding the piano wire is missing its ring finger.

Jeanette thinks about the posthumous letter she received from Ralf

Börje Persson. He had ended by saying that the perpetrator was missing a ring finger.

In spite of the tragedy of the situation, Jeanette feels something like relief.

She has had all the facts in front of her all along, but sometimes you can't see the wood for the trees. Not exactly a dereliction of duty, but possibly poor police work, she thinks, and finally the moment arrives when everything falls into place. Unimagined connections become clear, dissonance turns into harmony and nonsense takes on a new, coherent pattern.

'It's Hannah Östlund,' Annette Lundström says.

Kronoberg – Police Headquarters

The photograph has confirmed Jeanette's suspicions, and all the loose threads are coming together to form a whole. She'll soon know how solid that whole is.

Her gut feeling is real, but she also knows it can be treacherous. In police work the right feeling is important, but it mustn't get the upper hand and cloud your vision. Recently she's been so scared of appearing to be driven by her emotions that she hasn't listened to them, and has just been staring blindly at facts.

Jeanette thinks about the life-drawing class she took during her first years with Åke. The teacher had explained how the brain is constantly deceiving the eye, which in turn deceives the hand holding the charcoal. You see what you think you ought to see, and ignore the way things look in reality.

A picture with two subjects, depending on what you focus on. An optical illusion.

Hurtig's innocent remark had brought her up short, made her drop her guard and just see what was there to be seen.

Understand what was there to be understood, and ignore how it ought to be.

If she's right, she's a good police officer who's done her job and therefore deserves her salary. No more than that.

But if she's wrong she'll be criticised and her competence will be called into question. The idea that she made a mistake because she's a woman and by definition no good as a lead investigator will never be said out loud, but will be there between the lines.

During the morning she shuts herself away in her office, tells Hurtig she doesn't want to be disturbed, and starts sending out requests for fingerprints and DNA.

She should get replies during the course of the day.

Right now it's important that she find Victoria Bergman, and while she waits for the answers to her requests, she reads through the notes she made during her conversation with the old psychologist, and is once again astonished at the young Victoria's fate.

Raped and sexually assaulted by her dad throughout the whole of her childhood.

Her new, secret identity has made it possible for her to start a new life, somewhere else, far away from her parents.

But where has she moved to? What's become of her? And what did the old psychologist mean when she said that what they did to Victoria in Copenhagen was wrong? What had they done?

Is she mixed up in the murders of Silfverberg and Grünewald?

She doesn't think so. All she knows for sure so far is that Hannah Östlund killed Fredrika Grünewald. The idea occurs to her that Jessica Friberg was possibly holding the camera, but that's still supposition. After all, the picture could in theory have been taken using a timer.

What was it Sofia had said about the perpetrator? That they were dealing with someone with a split self-image? With the diagnosis of borderline, and who therefore experiences an indistinct boundary between themselves and others. Whether or not that's correct will be proved by future questioning, and for the time being is of less importance.

If it hadn't been for the murder of Charlotte's husband, P-O Silfverberg, she would have understood everything much sooner.

Really it was Charlotte who should have been murdered. After all, she had received a threatening letter. Why it ended up being her husband could only be a matter of speculation, but it was undeniably a gruesome way of exacting revenge.

It's all so obvious, Jeanette thinks. It's one of the laws of human nature that everything that has been hidden away in the nooks and crannies of the soul will struggle to find its way up to the surface.

She should have concentrated on Fredrika Grünewald and her classmates at Sigtuna, and on the incident that everyone had mentioned.

There's a knock on the door, and Hurtig comes in.

'How are you getting on?' He leans against the wall just to the left of the door, as if he's not going to stay for long.

'Fine. I'm waiting for information I should be getting today. Any time now, I hope. And once I've got that we can put out a nationwide alert.'

'Is it them, do you think?' Hurtig walks over to the visitor's chair and sits down.

'Probably.' Jeanette looks up from her notepad, pushes her chair back from the desk and puts her hands behind her head.

'Have you had a chance to talk to Åke? Since you had to hang up when we headed off to Edsviken?' Hurtig looks worried.

'Yes, I spoke to him after we got back. Apparently Johan's having trouble accepting Alexandra. He called her a whore, and then all hell broke loose.'

Hurtig laughs.

'He's got guts, that boy.'

Swedenborgsgatan, Södermalm

Sofia Zetterlund is getting ready to go home. She feels completely wiped out.

Outside the Indian summer is colouring the light in the street a fiery yellow, and the wind that had been rattling the windows earlier seems to have died away.

As Sofia leaves the practice she can sense winter in the air. In Mariatorget a flock of jackdaws has gathered to prepare for the journey south. By the Södra station she sees the woman again.

She recognises the gait, the broad, swaying hips, the feet pointing outward, the bowed head and the tight grey bun.

The woman disappears into the station, and Sofia hurries after her. The two heavy doors swing back on her, and when she finally makes it into the hall of the station the woman has vanished again.

Sofia jogs over to the turnstile.

The woman isn't there, but she couldn't possibly have had time to get in, go through the turnstile and down the escalator.

Sofia turns and walks back. She checks in the restaurant and the tobacconist's.

There's no sign of the woman anywhere.

The setting sun is casting golden reflections on the windows and the facades of the buildings outside.

Fire, she thinks. Charred remnants of people's lives, bodies and thoughts.

Kronoberg – Police Headquarters

The sun is peeping through the breaking clouds, and Jeanette gets up from her desk. She looks out through the window, gazing across the rooftops of Kungsholmen, and takes a deep breath. She fills her lungs and then lets the air out in a deep, liberating sigh.

Hannah Östlund and Jessica Friberg, she thinks. Schoolmates of Charlotte Silfverberg, Fredrika Grünewald, Henrietta Dürer, Annette Lundström and Victoria Bergman at Sigtuna College for the Humanities.

You always get caught by the past.

As she had guessed they would be, Hannah Östlund and Jessica Friberg are both missing, and after she presented her evidence to Prosecutor von Kwist, he agreed to issue a warrant for their arrests. Suspected on reasonable grounds of the murder of Fredrika Grünewald. As far as the murder of P-O Silfverberg is concerned, the evidence is less compelling. Suspected on good grounds.

It is now a matter of waiting, watching events develop and biding her time.

The big question is still the motive. Why? Is it really something so simple as revenge?

Jeanette has her theory about cause and effect ready, but the problem is that when she tries to formulate how it all fits together, the whole thing seems completely unlikely.

Could they have murdered the Bergmans and the Dürers as well? Caused those fires?

What about Karl Lundström?

But if so, why would they want those deaths to look like accidents?

She's interrupted by the internal phone ringing, and she turns round, leans across the desk and presses the button to answer.

'Yes?'

'It's me,' Jens Hurtig says. 'Come to my office if you want to see something interesting.'

Hurtig's door is open, and when she goes in she sees that both Åhlund and Schwarz are there as well. They look at her, and Schwarz grins and shakes his head.

'Listen to this,' Åhlund says, pointing at Hurtig.

Jeanette forces her way between them, pulls up a chair and sits down. 'Let's hear it.'

'Polcirkeln,' he begins. 'Nattavaara parish registry. Annette Lundström, née Lundström, and Karl Lundström. They're cousins.'

'Cousins?' Jeanette doesn't quite understand.

'Yes, cousins,' he repeats. 'Born three hundred metres apart. Karl and Annette's fathers are brothers. Two houses in a village in Lapland named after the Arctic Circle. Exciting, isn't it?'

Jeanette isn't sure that 'exciting' is the right word. 'Unexpected, perhaps,' she replies.

'It gets better.'

It looks to Jeanette as though Hurtig's about to laugh.

'The lawyer, Viggo Dürer, used to live in Voullerim. That's just thirty or forty kilometres from Polcirkeln. That's no distance up there. Thirty kilometres and you're practically neighbours. And I can tell you something about the village of Polcirkeln.'

'And this bit's really funny,' Schwarz interjects.

Hurtig gestures to him to keep quiet. 'In the eighties a story got into the papers. About a sect, with branches all over northern Lapland and

Norrbotten, with its headquarters in Polcirkeln. A bunch of Laestadians who'd lost it big time. You might have heard of the Korpela movement?'

'No, I can't say that I have, but I presume you have.'

'From the thirties,' Hurtig says. 'A doomsday cult in eastern Norrbotten. Prophecies of the end of the world and a ship of silver that would collect the faithful. They spent their time having orgies that, according to biblical quotations, meant they were affirming the child inside them, they played leapfrog on the roads, went around naked and so on. One hundred and eighteen people were interrogated and forty-five were fined, and some were charged with sexual activity with minors.'

'And what happened in Polcirkeln?'

'Something similar. It started with a report to the police about a movement calling themselves the Psalms of the Lamb. The complaint was about the sexual abuse of children, but the problem was that it was anonymous. Annette and Karl Lundström were named, as well as their parents, but nothing could be proved. The police investigation was dropped.'

'Jesus,' Jeanette says.

'I know. Annette Lundström was only thirteen years old. Karl was nineteen. Their parents were in their fifties.'

'What happened after that?'

'Nothing, really. The story about the sect faded away. Karl and Annette moved south and got married a few years later. Karl took over his dad's construction company, bought a share of a larger construction syndicate, and then became managing director of a company in Umeå. After that the family moved around the country, wherever Karl was sent for work. When Linnea was born they were living in Skåne, but of course you already know that.'

'And Viggo Dürer?'

'His name appears in one of the articles. He was working in a sawmill and spoke to the paper. I quote: "The Lundström family is innocent. The Psalms of the Lamb never existed, it's just something you journalists made up."'

'Why was he interviewed? Was he one of the people named in the police complaint?'

'No. But I imagine he wanted to get in the papers as much as he could. He was probably already ambitious, even then.'

Jeanette thinks about Annette Lundström.

Born in an isolated village up in Norrland. Possibly involved as a child in a sect in which sexual abuse of children took place. Married to her cousin Karl. The sexual abuse continues, spreading like poison through the generations. Families fracture. Implode. They wipe themselves out.

'Are you ready for more?'

'Sure.'

'I've checked Annette Lundström's bank account, and . . .' Hurtig pauses for a moment before going on. 'You always say you should act on gut feeling, so I did, and it turns out that someone recently paid half a million kronor into her account.'

Shit, Jeanette thinks. Someone really wants to hush up what happened to Linnea.

Judas money.

Johan Printz Väg – a Suburb

Ulrika Wendin switches her mobile off and heads down into the metro at Skanstull. She feels relieved that the secretary rather than Sofia Zetterlund herself had answered when she called to say she wasn't going to come any more.

Ulrika Wendin is ashamed that she has allowed herself to be silenced.

Fifty thousand isn't a lot of money, but she's been able to pay the rent for the next six months, and buy herself a new laptop.

At the barrier to the metro she sticks her foot far enough under the metal bar to activate the sensor so she can pull the turnstile towards her and slip through.

Von Kwist had sounded upset that she had been to see Sofia. Probably worried that the conversational therapy would reveal what Viggo Dürer and Karl Lundström had done to her.

Ulrika Wendin thinks about Jeanette Kihlberg, who had seemed OK despite being a cop.

Should she have told her everything?

No. She doesn't feel up to going through it all again, and besides, she doubts anyone would believe her. Much better to keep quiet, because if you stick your chin out you're likely to get punched.

Nine minutes later she gets out of the train at Hammarbyhöjden and walks through the barrier with no problem. No ticket inspector either on the train or by the exit.

Finn Malmgrens väg, past the school and through the little patch of woodland between the houses. Johan Printz väg. In through the front door, up the stairs, unlock the door and in.

A heap of post. Advertising flyers and free papers.

She shuts and locks the door, and puts the safety chain on.

As she sinks down onto the hall floor she starts to cry. The pile of paper is soft against her back and she lies on her side.

In all the years she has lived with boyfriends who hit her, she has never cried.

When she came home from school and found her mum completely out of it on the sofa she didn't cry.

Her grandmother had described her as a well-brought-up child. A quiet child who never cried.

But now she does, and as she does so she hears someone in the kitchen.

Ulrika Wendin gets to her feet and walks towards the kitchen door.

There's a stranger standing in the kitchen, and before she has time to react he punches her on the nose.

She hears it crack.

Edsviken – Lundström House

Linnea Lundström flushes the charred remnants of the burned letter from her father down the toilet and goes back to her room.

Everything is in order.

She thinks about her psychologist, Sofia Zetterlund, who told her how Charles Darwin got the idea for his book *The Origin of Species*. How it appeared in his mind in the space of a second, and how he spent the rest of his life gathering evidence for his thesis.

Sofia also told her how Einstein's theory of relativity appeared in his mind in less time than it takes to clap your hands.

Linnea Lundström understands how they felt, because she is now looking at life with exactly the same clarity.

Life, which had once been a mystery, is now a dull reality, and she herself is just a shell.

Unlike Darwin, she doesn't have to search for evidence, and unlike Einstein, she needs no theory. Some of the evidence is inside her, like pink scars on her soul. More is visible on her body, in the form of injuries and damage to her genitals.

In absolute terms, the evidence is there when she wakes in the morning and the bed is soaked with urine, or when she gets nervous and can't hold it in.

Her father formulated the thesis long ago. At a time when she herself could say just a few words. In a paddling pool in the garden in Kristianstad he had put his thesis into practice, and since then the thesis had gone on to become a lifelong truth.

She remembers his soothing words on the edge of the bed.

His hands on her body.

Their shared bedtime prayer.

'I long to touch you and satisfy your desires. Seeing your pleasure makes me happy.'

Linnea Lundström pulls the chair away from the desk and puts it under the hook in the ceiling. She knows the lines by heart.

'I want to make love to you and give you all the love that you deserve. I want to caress you tenderly inside and out, the way only I can.'

She takes her belt from her jeans. Black leather. Rivets.

'I take pleasure from looking at you, everything about you gives me desire and pleasure.'

A noose. A step up onto the chair and the buckle of the belt around the hook in the ceiling.

'You will experience a much higher level of satisfaction and pleasure.'

The belt around her neck. The sound of the television down in the living room.

Annette with a box of chocolates and a glass of wine and *Swedish Idol.*

Maths test tomorrow. She's been studying all week and knows that she'd get a good mark.

A step out into thin air. The audience applauds loudly when the studio manager holds up a sign.

A little step, and the chair topples over to the right.

'It is truthfully an expression of the divine.'

Hammarbyhöjden – a Suburb

Ulrika Wendin doesn't know how it's happened, but she's still on her feet. Her face is numb and she's staring straight into the stranger's eyes. For a moment she thinks she can see something like sympathy. A flicker of pity.

Then she comes back to reality and takes a couple of stumbling steps backwards, out into the hall, while the man watches her in silence.

Then everything happens very fast, but to Ulrika it seems to last an eternity.

She throws herself to the side, and slips on the pile of post, but manages to keep her balance before she grabs at the door handle.

Fuck, she thinks as she hears rapid footsteps behind her.

Both the lock and the security chain.

Her hands are familiar with the movements, yet it still feels like she's fiddling with the chain for several minutes. As she throws herself out through the door she feels a hand on her back.

Her neck feels constricted. She can hear him panting right behind her and realises that he's caught hold of the hood of her jacket.

She doesn't think. Doesn't even have time to feel frightened. She's running solely on adrenalin. She twists free of his grasp, turns and kicks out as hard as she can, hoping for the best.

She hits him between the legs.

Run, run, for fuck's sake, she thinks, but her legs won't obey her.

She stands and watches the thickset man sink onto the stone landing out in the stairwell.

Only when she sees the man's contorted face looking up at her does she realise that her whole body is shaking.

He snarls something inaudible and tries to get up.

And then she runs.

Down the stairs. Out of the front door and straight ahead. Past the bike shed. Around the tree by the cycle path and in among the shadows of the trees. Not looking back. Just running.

There's no one in sight. She dare not run back, and in front of her is a little hill covered in bushes, and on the far side the lights of the apartment blocks.

Dusk. Tall pine trees, the ground stony and uneven, and why the hell did she run into the woods?

Then she sees him.

Ten metres away. He grins at her, and she thinks he's got a knife in his hand. His arm is outstretched, as if he's holding something, but she can't see the blade. He walks towards her quite calmly, and she quickly realises why. Her only way out is the hill behind her, covered in tangled bushes.

She takes a chance. Turns and runs straight into the darkness among the twigs and thorns.

She screams. As loud as she can, and she does not look back.

Clambering upward, the branches scratching her face and arms.

She thinks she can hear his breathing, but it might just be her own.

She screams again. But it just sounds tight and rattling, and makes her breathless. Then she's through the bushes. A few stunted pines, and the hill slopes downward and she runs.

The back of a building. Some cellar steps. She feels her stomach lurch when she sees that the door is open and the light is on inside.

If the light's on, it means there's someone there. Someone who can help her.

She pushes the last branches aside and throws herself down the steps, into the basement. 'Help,' she croaks. A corridor with storage compartment doors. 'Help me,' she repeats.

The door. Close the door.

She turns round. Hears his panting breath outside, approaching the steps. With a final burst of effort she rushes for the door and slams it shut.

Two seconds. She has time to notice that there are some removal boxes in the corridor, big cardboard boxes and on top of them are some rag rugs. One of the doors has been wedged open.

'Is anyone there?'

No answer. Her forehead is wet with sweat, and she's breathing heavily. Her heart is pounding so hard she thinks it's going to burst through her skin. There's no one here.

The door handle. He's tugging at it. Then she hears a rattle from the lock.

Keys?

But how did he get into her flat, anyway? Has he got keys?

Never mind.

She turns round to continue along the corridor, but at that moment the light in the ceiling goes out. The door is still rattling, and beside it the light switch is glowing like a red dot in the darkness. But she moves away. Doesn't dare go closer to the door.

She feels her way further in. Sticking close to the wall, and only now does she notice the smell.

A cloying, sickly smell. Sewage? Excrement? She doesn't know.

The corridor continues to the left and she goes round the corner. No light switch, and she hurries onward, deeper into the darkness. The storage compartments are made of chicken wire. She knows exactly what they look like, even though she can't see anything and can only feel the metal netting with her hands.

Then she sees another red light switch just a couple of metres away.

She hears the outside door open, and he switches the light on.

Right in front of her, five metres away, a closed door. No latch. Just a keyhole.

On the left there's a niche in the wall containing a large metal container and a load of pipes.

Enough space to hide behind.

She quickly creeps over, tucks herself in among the pipes and presses against the wall.

This is where the smell is coming from.

Sulphur, she thinks. The big metal container is a fat separator, and she has a vague recollection that there's a pizza restaurant in the building.

She hears him come closer. The footsteps stop, very close by.

He moves again. She shuts her eyes. Hopes he can't hear her breathing and the pounding of her heart.

As long as she doesn't start sniffing. The blow to her nose was pretty severe. She can't breathe through it and she's bleeding. Her top lip feels warm.

She realises that it's hopeless.

Completely hopeless.

She can see his boots in the gap between the fat separator and one of the thick pipes. He's just standing there, less than a metre away from her. Not saying anything.

She stays where she is, squeezed between the metal container and the wall. The seconds go by and she thinks a good minute must have passed before he starts hitting the pipe with something.

A ringing sound, then another, and another. Light blows, and she knows it's the handle of the knife.

There's a sour taste in her mouth, and it catches at the back of her throat.

He starts to pace up and down. His boots creak and the banging against the metal pipe gets louder, as if he's losing patience.

Then she sees what's in the corner, less than an arm's length from her. Some narrow copper pipes, sawn off at the top. The spikes could do some damage if they struck the right spot.

She reaches out for them, but stops.

Her open hand is shaking, and she realises that it's pointless.

She hasn't got the energy. Hasn't got the energy to do a bloody thing.

Just kill me, she thinks. Kill me.

Tantoberget – Island of Södermalm

She sees the car approaching and takes shelter behind some bushes. Behind her, far below, is the greenery of Tantolunden, and the sun is just visible as a thin fringe above the rooftops. The narrow spire of Essinge Church is a thin spike in front of Smedslätten and Ålsten.

Down on Tantolunden's large area of grass a few people are still defying the cold. Two of them are throwing a Frisbee, even though it's almost dark. Over towards the shore she can see someone taking an evening swim.

The car stops, the engine cuts out and silence descends.

During all those years in Danish institutions she has tried to forget, but always failed. Now she is going to finish what she once made up her mind to do, long, long ago.

The women in the car will make it possible for her to return home.

Hannah Östlund and Jessica Friberg must be sacrificed.

Apart from the boy at Gröna Lund, she has been dealing with sick people. Taking the boy had been a mistake, and when she realised that she let him live.

When she injected him with pure alcohol he had passed out and she had put the pig mask on him. They had spent the whole night out at Waldemarsudde, and when she finally realised that he wasn't her half-brother she had regretted what she'd done.

The boy was innocent, but the women waiting for her in the car aren't.

To her disappointment she doesn't feel any joy, not even relief.

The visit to Värmdö had also been a disappointment. Grandma and Grandad's house was a burned-out shell and they were both dead.

She had been looking forward to seeing the expression on their faces when she stepped through the door and confronted them.

His expression when she told him who her father was.

Daddy and Grandad, Bengt Bergman the bastard.

Foster-father P-O, on the other hand, had understood. He had even begged for forgiveness and offered her money. As if his fortune were large enough to compensate for his deeds.

There isn't that much money in the world, she thinks.

At first the pathetic Fredrika Grünewald hadn't recognised her. Which wasn't really so strange, because it had been ten years since they last met at Viggo Dürer's farm in Struer.

That was when Fredrika had told her about Sigtuna.

How Fredrika had stood by and enjoyed the show.

Sometimes lives had to be sacrificed. And through death those lives took on meaning.

She remembers their blank eyes, the sweat and the collective excitement in the room.

She pulls her cobalt-blue coat tighter around her and makes up her mind to go over to the car and the two women she knows all about.

When she puts her hands in her pockets to make sure she hasn't forgotten the Polaroid pictures her right hand stings.

She didn't regard it as much of a sacrifice to cut off her ring finger.

You always get caught by the past, she thinks.

Part III

Denmark, 1994

You mustn't think that summer will come, unless someone starts it off
And makes everything summery, then the flowers will soon be here.
I make it so that the flowers bloom, I make the pasture green,
And now summer is here, because I've just removed the snow.

The beach was deserted, apart from them and the seagulls.

She was used to the cries of the birds and the noise of the waves, but the rustling of the big windbreak made of thin blue plastic annoyed Madeleine. It made it hard to sleep.

She was lying on her stomach and the sun was baking her body. She had folded the big beach towel so it covered her head, but had left a little gap so she could see what was going on if she had her head facing the side.

Nine Lego figures.

And Karl and Annette's little girl, playing happily by the water's edge.

Everyone was naked except for the pig farmer, because he said he had eczema and couldn't stand the sun. He was down by the water, keeping an eye on the girl. His dog was there too, a big Rottweiler that she had never learned to trust.

She sucked her tooth. It never seemed to want to stop bleeding, but it wouldn't come out.

Closest to her, as usual, sat her foster-father. Every now and then he ran his hand down her back or rubbed some sunscreen on her. He had asked her twice to turn over and lie on her back, but she pretended to be asleep and unable to hear him.

She turned her head under the beach towel and looked in the other direction. There the beach was completely empty, nothing but sand all the way to the bridge and the red-and-white lighthouse in the distance.

But there were more seagulls in that direction, possibly because some visitor hadn't tidied up properly when they left.

'Turn onto your back now.' His voice was mild. 'You might burn.'

She obeyed without a word, and shut her eyes as she heard him shake the bottle of sunscreen. His hands were warm, and she didn't know what she ought to feel. It was nice and nasty at the same time, just like her tooth. It itched in a tingly sort of way, and when she ran her tongue around its root its wobbliness made her shudder, in the same way that she shuddered at the touch of his hands.

She knew that her body was more developed than many girls the same age. She was much taller than they were, and had even started to get breasts. At least she thought she had, because they felt swollen and itched as if they were growing. And that was why her tooth itched, because it would soon fall out. There was a new tooth that was going to grow from beneath the old one, an adult tooth.

He stopped touching her, sooner than she was expecting.

A subdued female voice asked him to lie down, and she heard her elbows press into the sand.

She cautiously turned her head. Through the gap in the towel she saw it was the fat woman, Fredrika, and she sat down beside him with a smile.

She thought about the Lego figures. Tiny plastic people that you could do whatever you liked with, and they carried on smiling even when you melted them in the oven.

She couldn't stop watching as the woman leaned over towards his waist and opened her mouth.

Through the gap in the towel her head was soon moving slowly up and down. She had just been for a swim, and her hair was stuck to her cheeks and it all looked very wet. Red and wet.

She thought about when they were up at Skagen and her foster-father hit her for the first time. It had been on a beach with a lot of people, and they were all wearing swimming costumes. She had gone over to a man sitting alone on his blanket, drinking a cup of coffee and smoking. She had pulled down her swimming costume in front of him because she had thought the man wanted to see her naked.

He had just looked at her with a wry smile as he blew out the smoke, but they had been furious and Daddy P-O had dragged her away by the hair. 'Not here,' they had said.

Now everyone was just curious, and the shadows of their bodies were starting to block the light.

Her tooth itched, and she could feel how cold the air was when the sun disappeared.

They looked on and she looked on. There was nothing to be ashamed of.

One of the new, fair-haired women took out a camera. It was the type that froze the pictures and spat them out at once. A polar camera, that was it. They made the molecules stand still.

The windbreak rustled, and she shut her eyes again when the camera clicked.

Then suddenly her tooth came loose.

The hole in her gum ached and felt cold, and she rolled the tooth around her mouth as she watched.

It itched, and tasted of blood.

Södermalm

The beginning of the end is a burning blue car at the highest point of Tantoberget.

A burning hill in the middle of Södermalm isn't the sort of thing that Jeanette ever expected to be the missing piece that would help her see the whole picture. As she and Jens Hurtig pass Hornstull at high speed and catch sight of Tantoberget, it looks like a volcano.

Before the patch of land between became a park, Tantoberget was pretty much a dump, a cemetery for human refuse, and now, once more, it has become a site for scrap and waste.

The fire at the highest point of the park is visible from most of Stockholm, and the flames leaping up from the burning car have set fire to an autumn-dry birch. It's sparking and crackling, and the fire is threatening to spread to the little allotment cottages a dozen metres away.

Hannah Östlund and her classmate from Sigtuna College for the Humanities, Jessica Friberg, are wanted by the police on suspicion of two murders. The car that is being devoured by the flames up on the mountain is registered to Hannah Östlund, and that's why Jeanette has been called in.

As she opens her car door to get out, she can smell the hot, poisonous, black smoke.

It stinks of oil and rubber and melting plastic.

In the front seats of the car, through the fatally hot flames, she can see the silhouettes of two lifeless bodies.

Barnängen – Södermalm

The evening sky is bathed in the yellow glow of light pollution from the centre of Stockholm, and only the Pole Star is visible to the naked eye. The artificial lights in the form of street lamps, neon tubes and light bulbs make the open site below the Skanstull Bridge gloomier than if the city had been blacked out and the starry sky the only source of light.

The few nocturnal pedestrians crossing the older Skans Bridge alongside and glancing up towards Norra Hammarbyhamnen see nothing but light and shadows, in an alternately dazzling and blinding display of light pollution.

They don't see the crouched figure walking along the old, abandoned railway track; they don't see that the figure is carrying a black plastic bag and turns off the track to stand on the quayside, where it's swallowed up by the shadows of the bridge.

And no one sees the bag being swallowed by the black water.

The figure opens a car door and gets into the driver's seat, puts the light on and pulls a bundle of papers from the glove compartment. After a couple of minutes the light goes out and the car starts.

The woman in the car recognises the sky's sick yellow light from other places.

She sees what other people don't.

Down on the quay by the old goods line she had seen small trucks rattle past, fully laden with dead bodies. Out in the water she saw a frigate flying the Soviet flag and knew that the crew was sick with scurvy after months on duty in the Black Sea. The sky over Sevastopol on the Crimean peninsula had been the same mustard yellow as here, and in the shadows of the bridge lay the ruins of bombed-out houses and the slagheaps of waste from the rocket factories.

She had found the boy in the bag at the closest metro station to the Babi Yar ravine outside Kiev over a year ago. The station has the same name as the concentration camp the Nazis constructed on the site, where so many people she had known were killed during the war.

Syrets.

She can still taste the boy in her mouth. It's a yellow, fleeting taste a bit like rapeseed oil; like light-polluted skies and fields of grain.

Syrets. The very word seems to drip with the yellow taste.

The world is split in two, and only she knows it. The two worlds are as different as an X-ray picture is from a human body.

The boy in the plastic bag is in both worlds right now. When they find him they will see how he looked when he was nine years old. His body is preserved like a photograph of the past, embalmed like an ancient boy king. A boy forever.

The woman in the car keeps driving north, through the city. She looks at the people she passes.

Her senses are highly refined, and she knows that no one can have any idea of what she's like inside. No one knows what goes on inside her. She sees the anguish that is permanently present around people. She sees their evil thoughts painted in the atmosphere surrounding them.

She herself can't be seen. She has a capacity to be invisible in a room full of people, her image doesn't register on their retinas. But she is always present in the moment, observing her surroundings and understanding them. And she never forgets a face.

A short while ago she saw a woman on her own go down to the quayside of Norra Hammarbyhamnen. The woman had been unusually scantily clad for the time of year, and she had sat by the water for almost half an hour. When she eventually stood up to leave, a street lamp had lit up her face and she had recognised her.

Victoria Bergman.

It's been more than twenty years since she last saw her, and then the girl's eyes had been burning, almost invincible. They had contained an immense strength.

Now she had seen a dullness in them, a sort of tiredness that had spread through her whole being, and her experience of people's faces tells her that Victoria Bergman is already dead.

Gilah

To eat your own children is a barbarian act!
– Soviet proclamation, Ukrainian SSR, 1933

Father had eaten pigeon, and was telling stories to little Gilah, his daughter.

'Darling *tokhter*.'

She was hungry, had only had grass to eat, but it was probably worse for the boy in the other house. His body was so weak that he fell over when he tried to walk.

'Story. About boat and witch.'

Father kissed her on the forehead, and she noticed the bad smell from his mouth. 'Once upon a time there was a father and a mother, and they had a little girl whose name was Gilah Berkowitz. She was so small, but she grew very fast. Just like you . . .'

He smiled, poked her tummy, and it tickled, but she didn't laugh.

'One day little Gilah said to her father: I want a boat of gold with oars of silver, so I can fetch food for you and my brothers. Please, make me a boat like that, Father.'

'Please, Father,' she whispered.

'Little Gilah got her boat of gold and silver, and every day she went down to the river and fished, and came home with food for her father, mother and brothers. And every evening her mother went down to the river and called: Come back to shore now, little Gilah.'

Mother is sick, she thought. Her mouth all black, and her face completely white.

Father looked at her. 'What did little Gilah say then? When Mother was calling for her?'

'Boat of gold, let Gilah drift to the shore,' she said, and heard her mother coughing in her bed.

Father's hands were cold and his face was shiny. Maybe it was fever. A girl who lived at the end of the street had died of fever and been eaten by her mother. The girl's mother was an ugly, mean witch. Not like her own mother, who had been so pure and lovely before she got sick.

'Yes, that's what happened. Every day for many, many years. Little Gilah grew and got bigger and bigger, and Mother came to the shore each evening and called, but then one evening . . .' He fell silent as Mother coughed in her bed again.

But Gilah didn't want to listen to Mother's cough. 'Tell me more,' she cried instead, and laughed as Father lifted her up. 'Into the oven with the witch!'

He held her high in the air. Now he was tickling her tummy again, and this time it was properly funny.

But soon Mother coughed even louder and Father no longer looked happy. He turned silent and serious and put Gilah down on the floor and ran his hand through her hair.

She could see he was sad, but she wanted to hear the end of the story, when the witch went up in flames.

'I can't tell you more. I have to look after your mother. She needs water.'

There isn't any water, Gilah thought. It's hot and dry and Mother has said that everything out in the fields that Stalin hasn't taken has died. Mother has also said that she's going to die soon, that she'll cough herself to death. Drying out, just like the crops.

'There's no point getting water,' Gilah said.

Father looked at her sternly. 'What do you mean?'

He probably knew, because he had always said Mother was an oracle, someone who knew everything that was happening out in the world, and who was always right.

'Mother says she's going to die.'

His eyes were wet and he didn't reply, but he took Gilah's hand. Then he stood up, went over to the closet, and took out his hat and coat, even though it was so hot outside. He shivered, and then he left.

Gilah stood by the window and watched her father go down the street. She knew it was dangerous out there, and only Father was allowed to go out, not Mother, not her brothers, and not her. There were dead bodies lying out there, and they had to be eaten because there was hardly anything else to eat, except for grass, leaves, bark, tree roots, worms and insects. Eaten up. Because they weren't doing any good otherwise, those dead bodies.

Gilah Berkowitz had never eaten chicken before.

Father says he stole it, but she didn't believe him.

Now it was on her plate. Her brothers didn't want any, and when she tasted it she couldn't understand why. It was the best thing she'd ever eaten.

A pity Mother was dead and couldn't taste it.

She ate the moist meat greedily, and felt her strength returning. But she wasn't happy because she was thinking of Mother the whole time.

The way she had looked when she died. Her skin yellow, and her mouth black. Gnarled, and sort of shiny.

She had spent her last days screaming before she gave up.

Since then the house had been quiet.

Gilah missed her the way she was before the sickness. When she used to let Gilah sit in her lap and drink warm milk from a glass bottle. When she thought up funny games. When she and Father would kiss and cuddle and were happy. When she tucked Gilah in and read from the Torah.

The last bit of chicken tasted best of all, and Gilah realised that was because there was no more to eat. Never again would she taste a chicken as good as Father's.

> Under the Nacht und Nebel directive, civilians who jeopardise the security of the Third Reich will be sentenced to death. Anyone breaking the Nacht und Nebel regulations or withholding information about enemy activities will be arrested.
>
> – *German proclamation, Second World War*

Twelve years later Gilah Berkowitz is travelling through a disintegrating Germany. She can still taste the yellow flavour of her father's chicken.

The white bus with red crosses painted on its sides was no guarantee of free passage, because there were no longer any international rules. A red cross on the white roof of a van was an easy target for British aircraft, who had complete control of the skies. But there were no problems at German roadblocks, because the convoy was being escorted by the Gestapo.

Gilah was stronger than most of her fellow prisoners, and one of the few that were still conscious.

When they left Dachau there had been forty-four men, forty-five in total including her. At least four were dead and several more were well on the way. They were all suffering from boils, infected wounds and chronic diarrhoea, and many more would die unless the store of essential supplies was replenished soon.

She too was in a very bad way. Four large carbuncles on her neck, her stomach a terrible mess, and the infection she had had in her crotch for the past couple of weeks was worrying her. She had ruptured veins on the inside of her thighs, as if she had blood poisoning, but she couldn't get treatment here on the bus because her genitals weren't the same as everyone else's.

No one must know, and the only person who did know probably wouldn't survive the war.

The reason her secret had remained intact during her time in the camp was that one of the guard commanders had taken a liking to her from the start. Or a liking to him, depending on how you looked at it. The fat guard commander had a taste for hermaphrodites, or *Ohrwürmer*, earwigs, as he called them, and he had leaped at the chance to acquire his very own earwig in exchange for a bit of protection and some food every now and then.

It was the fat man who had given her those injuries in her crotch, but in spite of her shame she had never tried to escape from the camp. Now, though, when people were saying she was going to be free, she was prepared to make an attempt to escape. Freedom wasn't something you were given, it was something you chose for yourself.

Something you took.

In her pocket Gilah Berkowitz had a document that confirmed she was a Danish citizen and had the right to receive care at the Neuengamme Camp near Hamburg, and then transportation to a quarantine centre in Denmark. But for her the truth had been a relative concept for so long that she no longer believed in anything. Nothing was falser than the truth.

In her pocket she also had the thumbscrew, a small wooden vice that she had been given by the guard commander to help distract her from pain. It had helped against headaches and stomach cramps, and now it helped her with the churning feeling in her crotch. She put the vice on her thumb and tightened it. One turn, then another, as she looked around inside the bus.

The stench and angst were the same as in Dachau.

Gilah closed her eyes and tried to think of freedom, but it was as if it had never existed, and would never exist. There was no before or after Dachau. The memories were there, but they didn't feel like her own.

She had arrived at Lemberg in western Ukraine two years ago, thirteen years old, but with the body of a twenty-year-old man. She had stolen a suitcase from a German military bus, been captured by the Gestapo, and became one of the thousands of Nacht und Nebel detainees who were taken to the extermination camps.

The Germans hadn't examined her when she arrived, just threw her a card and some work clothes. There was no need for a medical examination, she was healthy and strong.

She had liked the forced labour, whether it was digging ditches or putting together machine parts. To begin with her body had got stronger and she had enjoyed watching her fellow prisoners give way, one after the other. She had been tougher than all the adult men in the camp.

It became harder towards the end, but she had endured until the white buses arrived.

Only Scandinavian citizens were being collected, and when the last of the Danish names had been called out Gilah had raised her hand in the air.

They had dressed her in a grey coat and marked it with a white cross to indicate that she was a free person.

Vita Bergen – Sofia Zetterlund's Apartment

Sofia Zetterlund is walking along Renstiernas gata and looks up at the rock face to her right. Located in a cavern blasted out of the rock, thirty metres below Sofia Church, is the biggest server farm in Sweden. The steam lies like a white cloud across the street, and the autumn evening's chilly gusts of wind keep blowing it against the jagged rocks.

Excess heat. As if things are boiling away down there.

She knows that the underground transformers and generators are designed to ensure that all the digitised information belonging to Swedish authorities would survive a disaster. And among them are the confidential files about her. About Victoria Bergman.

She passes through the thick, damp cloud, and for a brief moment she can't see anything.

Soon she's standing outside the front door of her building. She takes a quick look at the time. Quarter past ten, which means that her walk has lasted about four and a half hours.

She doesn't remember which streets and places she's been to; she can hardly remember what she was thinking about during the walk. It's like trying to remember a dream.

I'm walking in my sleep, she thinks as she taps in the door code.

She climbs the stairs, and the sharp echo from the heels of her boots wakes her up. She shakes the rain from her coat, adjusts her damp blouse, and when she finally puts the key in the lock she has no recollection of the long walk at all.

Sofia Zetterlund remembers that she had been sitting in her office, and had imagined Södermalm as a labyrinth, with the door to her practice on St Paulsgatan as its entrance, and the door to her apartment in Vita bergen as the exit.

She doesn't remember saying goodbye to the receptionist, Ann-Britt, and leaving the practice quarter of an hour later.

Nor does she remember the man she met in the bar of the Clarion Hotel at Skanstull, whose room she went back to; nor the fact that he was surprised that she didn't want payment. She doesn't remember stumbling out of the hotel lobby, eastward along Ringvägen, then down Katarina Bangata to Norra Hammarbyhamnen to stare at the water, the barges and warehouses lining the quay opposite, or walking back up to Ringvägen where it curves north and becomes Renstiernas gata and passes below the steep rock faces of Vita bergen.

And she doesn't remember finding her way home, to the exit from the labyrinth.

The labyrinth isn't Södermalm, it's the brain of a sleepwalker, with its canals, its system of nerves and signals, its innumerable bends and intersections and dead ends. A walk through streets at dusk, in a sleepwalker's dream.

The key clicks in the lock; she turns it twice to the right and opens the door.

She's found her way out of the labyrinth.

Sofia looks at the time, and all she wants to do now is sleep.

She takes off her outdoor clothes and goes into the living room. On the table are piles of papers, files and books. The accumulated evidence of her efforts to help Jeanette compile a perpetrator profile for the murders of the immigrant boys.

A silly idea, she thinks, idly picking up a few of the documents. It hadn't led anywhere. They had ended up with a kiss, and Jeanette hadn't mentioned it since that night out in Gamla Enskede. Perhaps it had just been an excuse to meet?

She feels dissatisfied because the work is unfinished, and Victoria isn't helping, not showing her any memories. Nothing.

She knows she killed Martin.

But the others? The boys without names, and the boy from Belarus?

No memories. No nagging sense of guilt.

She goes over to the bookcase concealing the soundproofed room. As she lifts the catch to slide the bookcase aside, she knows the room will be empty. The only things left in there are the remnants of herself and the smell of her own sweat.

Gao Lian has never sat on the exercise bike, but his sweat has run through her hair, down her back and over her arms. She has cycled round the world several times, without moving a centimetre. She has been pedalling in place.

Gao Lian from Wuhan is all over the room, even though he doesn't exist. In drawings, in newspaper cuttings, on pages of notes, and on a pharmacy receipt on which she circled the initial letters of her purchases, spelling out the name GAO.

Gao Lian came to her because she needed someone who could channel her guilt. Pay the bill she owed humanity.

She has believed that all the articles, all the newspaper cuttings about the dead children, have been about her. As well as keeping up with what has been going on, she has been looking for explanations, and has found them inside herself.

She understands why she invented him. As well as being a substitute for her own feelings of guilt, he has been a surrogate for the child she wasn't allowed to keep.

But somewhere along the way she lost control of Gao.

He didn't turn into the person she had wanted him to be, so in the end he ceased to exist, and she no longer believes in him.

Gao Lian from Wuhan never existed.

Sofia goes into the hidden room, pulls out the rolled-up evening papers, unfurls them and lays them out on the floor. MUMMY FOUND IN BUSHES and MACABRE FIND IN CENTRAL STOCKHOLM.

She reads about the murder of Yuri Krylov, the orphan boy from Molodechno in Belarus, who was found dead out in Svartsjölandet in the spring, and she's particularly interested in what she's underlined in the article. Details, names, places.

Did I do that? she wonders.

She turns the mattress. The draught makes more pieces of paper and little notes fly up around her. The dust from the paper tickles her nose.

Pages torn from a German edition of Zbarsky's study of Russian methods of embalming. Printouts from the Internet. A detailed description of the embalmment of Lenin, written by a Professor Vorobyov of the Institute of Anatomy in Kharkov, Ukraine.

Sofia puts the articles down when her phone rings, and she sees that it's Jeanette. She gets up to answer and looks around the room.

The floor is covered with a thick layer of papers, and there's hardly an empty surface anywhere. But the meaning, the explanation, the big Why?

The answer's here somewhere, she thinks as she picks up the receiver.

A person's thoughts shredded into little pieces of paper.

A psyche on display.

Klara Sjö – Public Prosecution Authority

The lies are white as snow and don't affect the innocent.

Prosecutor Kenneth von Kwist is pleased with his arrangements and convinces himself that he has solved the problems that have arisen in an exemplary fashion. Everyone is happy.

Jeanette Kihlberg has her hands full with Victoria Bergman, and he himself has arranged secret deals with Ulrika Wendin and the Lundström family.

Prosecutor Kenneth von Kwist tries to convince himself that all the problems are solved, at least temporarily. It's just that he's worried another one may have appeared.

He thinks about the report that he destroyed in the document shredder. Papers that would have helped Ulrika Wendin, but would obviously have damaged the lawyer Viggo Dürer, former police commissioner Gert Berglind and, by extension, himself as well.

Have I done the right thing? the prosecutor thinks.

Kenneth von Kwist has no answers to his own questions, which is why his unease has now spread to his gullet in the form of heartburn and indigestion.

The prosecutor's stomach ulcer prods his conscience.

Gamla Enskede – Kihlberg House

The pleasures of a quiet life, Jeanette Kihlberg thinks as she parks outside her house in Gamla Enskede. Right now she misses simplicity and routine. Feeling content at the end of a long, hard day at work, and then being able to put work behind her.

Johan is spending the night in the city with Åke and Alexandra, and as soon as she steps into the hall she feels the emptiness of the house. The absence of a family.

Since Åke moved out it also smells different. Reluctantly she realises that she actually misses the smell of oil paint, linseed oil and turpentine. Had she been too intolerant? Too weak to give him a last push in the right direction when he had doubted his talent? Maybe, but it doesn't matter now. Perhaps the marriage is over, and nothing he does is dependant on her any more.

The women in the car were in all likelihood Hannah Östlund and Jessica Friberg. Ivo Andrić is currently hard at work trying to confirm their suspicions.

She'll have the answers tomorrow, and if she's right it will mean that the case can be sent to the prosecutor's office and declared closed.

But first they need to search the women's homes. Find evidence of their culpability, then it will be up to her and Hurtig to put everything together and hand it over to von Kwist. Not that she thinks she's done a particularly good job. Just followed a winding path and, with the help of a bit of luck and experience, reached a conclusion.

Fredrika Grünewald and Per-Ola Silfverberg had been murdered by two vengeful women.

Folie à deux. Symbiotic psychosis, as it's also known, occurs almost exclusively within families. For instance, a mother and a daughter living apart but sharing a mental illness. Although Hannah Östlund and Jessica Friberg aren't actually related, they did grow up together, attended the same schools and then chose to live close to each other.

Someone had left yellow tulips beside Grünewald. And the night Karl Lundström died he also received yellow tulips. Could they have killed him as well? An overdose of morphine? Well, why not? Karl Lundström and Per-Ola Silfverberg were both paedophiles who had abused their own daughters. That must be the connection. Yellow tulips and Sigtuna College are the common factors.

Revenge, she thinks. But how the hell could it have such extreme consequences?

Jeanette gets the loaf out of the freezer, breaks off a couple of slices and puts them in the toaster.

She realises she can't expect to find answers to everything.

Jeanette, she thinks, you have to learn that if there's one thing you can't expect as a police officer, it's peace of mind. You can't understand everything.

The toaster rattles, and the phone rings. Åke, of course.

He clears his throat. 'Yes, I want to take Johan to London this weekend. A football match. Just him and me. Just be a dad, I suppose . . .'

Dad? So you want to do that now, do you? she thinks. 'OK. Is he up for it?'

Åke laughs quietly. 'Oh yes, not much doubt about that. London derby, you know.'

Åke falls silent, and Jeanette thinks about their life together, which seems so far away now.

'Erm . . .' he finally says, 'do you fancy having lunch before Johan and I set off?'

She hesitates. 'Lunch? Have you got time for that?'

'Yes, that's why I'm asking,' he says, sounding annoyed. 'How about tomorrow?'

'The day after would be better. But I'm waiting to get the go-ahead to search a couple of houses, so we might have to keep it provisional.'

He sighs. 'OK. Let me know when you can make it, then.' And he hangs up.

She mirrors his sigh down the dead line, gets up from the table and takes the toast from the toaster. Not good, she thinks as she gets the butter. This isn't good for Johan. Not a hint of stability. She remembers the comment Hurtig made. 'At that age everything seems to get blown out of proportion,' he had said, and in the case of Östlund and Friberg that couldn't have been more true.

But what about Johan? Her own teenager? First the separation, then what happened at Gröna Lund, and now all this bloody shuttling between her, who hardly has any time for him, and Åke and Alexandra, who are behaving like teenagers themselves and hardly know what they're going to be doing in two days' time.

She forces herself to eat the last piece of dry, cold toast, then goes back to the phone. She needs someone to talk to, and the only person who qualifies is Sofia Zetterlund.

The autumn evening is full of stars and glitteringly beautiful, and just as Jeanette is wondering what it is about people that makes everything go so completely fucking wrong, Sofia answers.

'I miss you,' she says.

'Me too.' Jeanette feels warmth returning. 'It's lonely out here.'

Sofia's breathing feels very close. 'Here too. I want to see you again soon.'

Jeanette shuts her eyes and imagines that Sofia really is there with her, that she's lying against her shoulder and whispering in her ear, right beside her.

'I dozed off a little while ago,' Sofia says. 'I dreamed about you.'

Jeanette still has her eyes closed as she leans back in her chair and smiles. 'What did you dream?'

Sofia laughs quietly, almost shyly.

'I was drowning, and you rescued me.'

Vita Bergen – Sofia Zetterlund's Apartment

Sofia Zetterlund puts the phone down and sinks onto the floor. She's just been speaking to Jeanette, but doesn't know what they were talking about.

A vague idea of mutual signs of affection. An indistinct longing for warmth.

Why is it so complicated to say what you really think? she wonders. And why do I have so much trouble not lying?

She feels that she needs to pee so she gets up and goes into the bathroom, and as she pulls down her pants and sits down she realises that she must have been to the Clarion Hotel earlier. The man she must have met has left traces on the inside of her thighs.

A thin crust of dried semen is stuck to her pubic hair, and she washes herself at the sink. Afterwards she dries herself carefully using the guest towel and then goes back into the room behind the bookcase. The room that had once been Gao's, but which is now a museum to Victoria's erratic path through life. Odysseus, she thinks. The answers are in here.

In here is the key that fits the lock on the past.

She leafs through Victoria Bergman's papers, trying to organise the sketches, notes and torn-out newspaper articles. She knows what she's looking at, yet still doubts it.

She sees a life that was once hers, and that, when reconstructed, becomes, if not her own, then at least a life. Victoria's life. Victoria Bergman's life.

It's a tale of decay.

One name keeps recurring in many of the notes, and it rouses strong feelings in her.

Madeleine.

Her daughter and sister.

The child she once had with her own father.

The girl she was forced to give up for adoption.

Among the notes about Madeleine there is also a photograph, a Polaroid picture of a girl aged about ten standing on a beach, dressed in red and white.

Sofia inspects the picture carefully and is convinced that it's her daughter. She recognises some of her own features in the way the girl looks. Her face looks troubled and the photograph makes Sofia feel very unsettled. What sort of an adult has Madeleine become?

On another sheet she reads about Martin. The boy who vanished during a trip to the fair, and who was later found drowned in the Fyris River. The boy she hit on the head with a stone and dumped in the water. The police wrote his death off as an accident, but ever since she has been living with the guilt that her actions inexorably brought with them.

Sofia remembers the visit to Gröna Lund when Johan Kihlberg disappeared. There are similarities with Martin's disappearance, but she's sure she would never have harmed Johan. He probably vanished of his own accord, or was taken by someone else. Someone who later thought better of it, seeing as Johan was found unharmed.

Sofia Zetterlund goes on looking through the scribbled memories. Puts one sheet aside and picks up another. Reads and remembers what she felt at the moment she wrote the note. She had been living in a cloud of medication and alcohol, suppressing all the unpleasant memories. Hiding parts of herself away deep beneath her skin.

It had worked for years.

At its thinnest points, the skin is a fifth of a millimetre thick, yet still forms an impenetrable line of defence between inside and outside. Between rational reality and irrational chaos. At this precise moment her memory is no longer hazy and unclear, but beautifully crystal clear. But she doesn't know how long the moment will last.

Sofia reads Victoria's diary entries from her time at boarding school in Sigtuna. Two years of torment, bullying and mental torture. Words that recur in the diary are 'revenge' and 'retribution', and she remembers dreaming of going back one day and blowing up the whole school. Now two of the people referred to in the entries are dead.

She knows Victoria had nothing to do with their deaths.

But even if she's innocent of those murders, she knows what she has done.

She's killed her parents. She set fire to her childhood home, the house in Grisslinge, out in Värmdö, and since then she has sat in her soundproofed room and drawn the burning house in crayon on picture after picture.

Sofia thinks about Lasse, her former partner and most meaningful relationship. But she can't feel the same hatred for him as she does for her parents. Boundless disappointment would be a better description, and for a brief second she is seized by doubt. Did she really kill him as well?

The memories of having done so are emotionally very strong, but she can't see the actual sequence of events inside her that would confirm that she really did it.

But she knows that the fact that she has actually murdered others is something she will have to come to terms with for the rest of her life. It's something she must learn to accept.

Judar Forest – Nature Reserve

Squeezed in between Ängby and Åkeshov in the west of Stockholm is the city's first nature reserve.

Ice and rock formed the landscape, which consists of forest and open fields, as well as a small lake. The passage of glaciers is visible in the form of large blocks of rock and stony moraine ridges. First the ice pressed the ground down one thousand metres, then ripped it apart and scattered it with boulders torn from the ground rock.

Here and there in the forest there are the remains of a wall that wasn't raised by the ice, but by human hands. According to tradition, the stones were piled up by Russian prisoners of war.

The lake in the centre of the forest is called Judar Lake. The name is derived from the Swedish word *ljuda*, 'to make a sound', but etymologically it has nothing to do with the cries of the emaciated labour force, nor with the scream that is currently echoing through the forest.

A young, fair-haired woman in a cobalt-blue coat is staring up at the starry sky above the trees.

Thousands and thousands of burning points.

After emptying her lungs of rage once more, Madeleine Silfverberg walks back to the car, which is parked by a cluster of trees close to the lake.

The third scream echoes inside the car, five minutes later, at almost ninety kilometres an hour.

The world is a windscreen with the road at its centre and blurred trees at the edge of her field of vision. She shuts her eyes and counts to five as she listens to the sounds of the engine and the friction of the tyres on the road surface. When she opens her eyes again she feels calm.

Everything has gone as planned.

Soon the police will pay a visit to the house in Fagerstrand.

Beside the large bunch of yellow tulips on the kitchen table they'll also find a couple of neatly arranged Polaroid pictures that document the murders.

Karl Lundström lying in his bed in Karolinska Hospital.

Per-Ola Silfverberg, slaughtered like a pig in his elegant apartment.

The police already have the third picture, because she left it in the Lundströms' mailbox. It shows Fredrika Grünewald in her tent in the crypt beneath St Johannes Church with her fat, greasy face contorted in a dead grimace.

When the police go down into the cellar they'll find the reason why the house stinks.

The forest suddenly stops, there are more buildings and she lowers her speed. Soon she has to stop completely at the intersection of Gubbkärrsvägen and Drottningholmsvägen, and as she waits for a few cars to pass she drums restlessly on the steering wheel with nine fingers.

Hannah Östlund had lost her finger after being bitten by a dog.

She had used a bolt cutter.

As Madeleine pulls out onto Drottningholmsvägen she thinks about those who will soon die, and about those who have already died, but also about those she wishes she had had the pleasure of killing.

Bengt Bergman. Her dad and grandad. Daddygrandad.

The fire took him before she got there. But no one can take her own fire. It's going to take others.

First it's going to take the woman who once called herself her mother.

Then it's going to take Victoria, her real mother.

As she heads along Drottningholmsvägen back into the city, she reaches for the drink she got from McDonald's, pulls the lid off and sticks her hand in among the ice cubes. She puts a handful in her mouth and chews them greedily before swallowing.

There's nothing purer than water that has frozen. The isotopes are cleansed of earthly dirt and become receptive to cosmic signals. If she eats enough of the frozen water, it will spread through her body and change its properties. Make her brain sharper.

Denmark, 1994

I bring plenty of water to flow in the stream, so that it skips and rushes.
I bring lots of swallows that fly, and midges for the swallows.
I bring new leaves for the trees, and little birds' nests here and there.
I make the evening sky beautiful, because I make it so rosy.

She wiggled the loose tooth up to the left. It was getting close to coming out, not now, but maybe this evening.

She closed her mouth. It tasted of blood and stung like ice.

The tooth fairy had given her five hundred kronor. One hundred for every tooth she put under her pillow. She'd saved the money in her secret box, the one under the bed that now contained six hundred and twenty-seven kronor, what with the money she had taken from the pig farmer.

She had spent the whole summer with him, and this was the third time her foster-parents had come to visit. She never called them Mum and Dad, because they weren't her real parents. Calling them Per-Ola and Charlotte were also out of the question, because they might get the idea that she respected them. Instead she called them 'you' and 'you'.

This time they had their friends from Sweden with them.

And those two new fair-haired ones. Lawyers or something.

They looked like angels, but she thought they were really weird. It was almost as if they were on her side, because they were clearly hesitant when everything started in the evenings. But they weren't locked up the whole time like her, they were free to come and go as they liked, and that was why they were weird. Because they always came back.

And one of them had had a finger bitten off by her dog. But she still spent the whole time spoiling it, and that was weird too.

The room she lived in was the smallest in the house, and it smelled musty. It contained a creaking bed, an old wardrobe that smelled of mothballs and a small window facing the yard. All she had to play with were some crayons, yellow typewriter paper and a box of Lego.

Reluctantly she had built a house on the big, green Lego base. It was on the floor, and she began to stick the little figures to the base. All in all there were nine plastic people, the same number of people staying on the farm at the moment, apart from herself and the little girl the Swedes had brought with them.

She arranged the figures so they were standing in a long line in front of the Lego house. She had to pretend that five of them were women, because there were only male figures available, and soon they were all standing there with their plastic smiles.

The pig farmer and the two lawyer women.

The man they called Berglind, who was a policeman even though he didn't act like one. That was the only one of the plastic figures that looked the way it should. Not only because it was in a police uniform, but because it also had a moustache, just like him.

Next to him stood Fredrika, who was much fatter than her Lego version. And then the couple who were the little girl's parents. Karl and Annette.

At the right-hand end of the line stood her foster-parents.

She stared at them while her tongue played with the loose tooth. She was lost in her thoughts when she heard someone unlocking the door.

'It's time to go. Have you packed? You haven't forgotten your beach towel this time?'

Two questions in one that demanded both a yes and a no, meaning that she couldn't keep quiet.

She couldn't just nod or shake her head, and it was one of his tricks to get her to talk to him.

'I've packed everything,' she mumbled.

He shut the door, and it reminded her of when she had lost her first tooth.

He had told her what happened when children left their teeth for the tooth fairy.

If you left them in a glass of water or under your pillow when you went to bed, a little fairy would come flying in at night and give you something in return. She collected children's teeth, far away somewhere she had a big castle that was built of teeth, and she paid one hundred kronor per tooth.

He had helped her get rid of the first one, so that she would soon be rich.

That was when they came to visit at the start of the summer. She had been sitting where she is now, but on a little stool, and he had tied some strong cotton thread around her tooth. Then he had tied the other end to the door handle, and told her he was just going to get something. But he was lying, and instead slammed the door shut with a loud bang.

Her tooth had flown out onto the floor as the door slammed shut, and that had given her the first hundred kronor.

But the tooth fairy hadn't flown into her room that night. It was him, creeping into her room when he thought she was asleep, lifting her pillow and leaving the money.

After that she had to show she deserved the money, and she had realised that the tooth fairy wasn't a magical creature, but only a man who bought baby teeth.

Kronoberg – Police Headquarters

Jeanette turns on the desk lamp and spreads the pictures out in front of her.

Hannah Östlund's burned, sunken face. A woman in her forties, in what should be the prime of life. A complete stranger to Jeanette just a short while ago, but now one of the principal suspects for a series of murders. Nothing in life is what it seems, she thinks. So much of it is something else entirely.

Hannah's right hand is missing its ring finger, and Jeanette's suspicions are confirmed.

The identities of the bodies need to be definitively confirmed from DNA samples as soon as possible; then the amount of carbon dioxide in their blood has to be measured. That could give them a cause of death.

A vacuum cleaner hose had carried the poisonous gases from the exhaust pipe into the car, and, because the two women had their seat belts on, Jeanette assumes that they had committed suicide together.

Next picture, Jessica Friberg, Hannah's friend. Similarly burned beyond recognition.

The characteristic fire-related haematomas that aren't the result of mechanical injury.

The woman died in the fire.

Her skull became severely overheated; her blood would have started to boil between her skull and the protective layers within.

Folie à deux. Two people sharing the same misconceptions, the same persecution complex, the same hallucinations and insanity.

Usually there's one person who's sick and another who's governed by the first, a more dominant and disturbed individual.

Which of the women was the driving force? she wonders. Does that even really matter? She's a police officer, and it's her job to collect the facts, not sit and speculate about cause and effect. Right now the two women are echoes of the past that will soon have faded away and vanished, leaving just their bodies behind.

Fire, she thinks. Hannah and Jessica in a burning car.

Then Dürer and the boat.

The Bergman couple and their burned-out house.

It can't be a coincidence. She makes a mental note to take it up with Billing at the earliest possible opportunity. If he agrees with her, those cases can be looked at again.

Jeanette picks up the phone and dials the prosecutor's number. As usual, Kenneth von Kwist is taking his time issuing a search warrant, even though in this instance it's no more complicated than signing a piece of paper.

She has trouble concealing her contempt for the prosecutor's incompetence, and perhaps he notices, because his replies to her questions run to two syllables at most, and he sounds disengaged.

But he does promise her that she can have the warrant within an hour, and as they hang up Jeanette wonders where von Kwist finds the motivation to go to work each morning.

Before going to Hurtig's office to update him in advance of their visit to the homes of the two dead women, she heads towards Åhlund's office.

She has a job for him and Schwarz to work on for the rest of the day.

The lawyer, Viggo Dürer, she thinks. Even if he's dead, we need to know more about him. There may be evidence hidden away in his past that might lead us to the murderer.

Jeanette is aware that someone has paid half a million kronor into Annette Lundström's bank account, and she suspects it could well be a bribe, even if they haven't been able to trace where the money came from. Sofia had also told her that Ulrika Wendin had plenty of cash, and implied that Dürer might be behind it. And in the letter Karl Lundström wrote to his daughter, Linnea, the lawyer is mentioned as a potential paedophile, something also suggested by the pictures Linnea drew as a child.

Klara Sjö – Public Prosecution Authority

Prosecutor Kenneth von Kwist isn't feeling well.

His stomach ulcer is one thing; his anxiety that everything is about to go to hell another.

The secret to quickly regaining your self-control is Diazepam Desitin.

The discomfort of having to take the medicine rectally is outweighed by the strong sense of calm that spreads soon afterwards, and he says a silent prayer of gratitude to his private doctor who at short notice had provided him with a generous prescription of the drug. And he's also been told to take a glass of whisky three times a day to enhance its calming effects.

The anxiety he feels has nothing to do with Hannah Östlund or Jessica Friberg.

It has its foundations in the feeling that everything is starting to slip utterly beyond his control. He leans back in his chair to think things through one more time.

He knows that Viggo Dürer organised bribes for Annette Lundström and Ulrika Wendin, although he's perfectly aware that it had originally been his idea.

Obviously that isn't good, and under no circumstances must it become known.

One possibility might be to try to butter up Jeanette Kihlberg a bit more, to portray himself in a better light. It's just that at the moment he has no more information to give her, apart from the things that absolutely mustn't come to her attention.

If he were to reveal what he knows about Viggo Dürer, Karl Lundström, Bengt Bergman and former police commissioner Gert Berglind, he would inevitably be dragged down as well.

He would quite literally be crushed. Humiliated and thrown out of his profession. Unemployed and exposed.

Whenever he had done favours for Dürer, Berglind or Lundström, the rewards came quickly, usually in the form of money, but occasionally in other ways. On the most recent occasion that he got rid of some compromising documents for Dürer, he was advised to rearrange his investment portfolio, and just a few days later the banking crisis hit and his old shares would have been worthless. Then there were all the racing tips he'd received over the years. He begins to count on his fingers before he gives up and realises that he has been part of a system of reward that is more comprehensive, and probably stretches further up the corridors of power, than he could have imagined.

The Diazepam Desitin tranquilliser he's taken makes Kenneth von Kwist calm, and he can think more rationally, but it gives him no ideas about how to solve his dilemma. So he decides to procrastinate for a bit longer, waiting to see what happens, and using the time to stay on good terms with everyone involved, particularly Jeanette Kihlberg.

It's a passive, compliant position, but it's unsustainable. It isn't possible to sit on two chairs at the same time.

Nowhere

When Ulrika Wendin wakes up at first she can't feel anything, then a wave of pain breaks over her. Her face is throbbing, her nose aches and she has the taste of blood in her mouth.

It's pitch black, and she has no idea where she is.

The last thing she remembers is the stench of the fat separator in the cellar. The man who chased her through the woods must have knocked her out somehow.

She curses herself for having taken the money. She's blown the fifty thousand in less than a week.

Maybe someone thought she was still talking, in spite of the money. But going to the police hadn't led anywhere. No one had believed her.

Why the hell am I lying here? she thinks.

Her face feels stiff and her mouth tight. She's lying on her back, naked, and she can't move because her hands have been taped together behind her back.

On both sides of her there are coarse wooden walls, and when she tries to get up she is blocked by a pair of iron bars running above her knees and chest.

What she had initially thought was dried, stiffened blood on her face turns out to be a piece of tape fastened across her mouth. She's lying in something damp, and assumes she must have wet herself.

I've been buried alive, she thinks. The air is dry and stiflingly warm, and it smells like a root cellar.

Panic hits her, and she starts to hyperventilate. She doesn't know where her scream comes from, but she knows it's there even if she doesn't hear it.

Breathe through your nose. Calm down. You can handle this, she thinks. You've taken care of yourself almost your whole life without ever needing anyone's help.

Five years ago, when she had just turned sixteen, she had found her mother's lifeless body on the kitchen floor, and since then she's been alone. She's never turned to social services when she's been short of money – she'd rather steal food – and she's kept up with the rent thanks to Mum's meagre life insurance. She's never been a burden to anyone.

She doesn't know who her dad is; her mum took that secret with her to heaven. If that's where you end up if you've used alcohol and pills to slowly but deliberately drink yourself into an early grave before you've even reached forty.

Her mum hadn't been mean, just unhappy, and Ulrika knows that unhappy people are capable of doing things that might seem mean.

Real evil is something else entirely.

Grandma won't start to worry for a week or so, she thinks. They aren't usually in touch more often than that.

Her breathing is getting slower and her thoughts more rational.

Maybe that psychologist, Sofia Zetterlund, will miss her? Ulrika regrets calling to cancel all her appointments.

What about Jeanette Kihlberg? Maybe, but probably not.

Her heartbeat returns to normal and, even if it's still hard to breathe, she's regained command of her senses. Temporarily, at least.

Her eyes have got used to the darkness, and she knows she isn't blind. The shadows around her are different shades of grey, and above her she can make out the shape of what looks like a boiler, connected to a mass of pipes.

The wall rumbles at regular intervals. There's a metallic screech, a bang, and then it's quiet for a few seconds before the rumbling starts up again.

Her first idea is that it's the sound of a lift.

A boiler and pipes . . . a lift?

So where is she?

She turns her head, trying to find any source of light.

Only when she forces her head backwards, so far that it feels like her arteries and throat are going to burst through her neck, does she catch a glimpse of something.

Behind her she can see a narrow strip of light reflected faintly off a wall.

Sjöfartshotellet – Södermalm

Revenge tastes of bile, and it doesn't matter how many times you brush your teeth, you won't get rid of the taste. It eats its way into your enamel and gums.

Madeleine Silfverberg has checked into the Sjöfarts Hotel in Södermalm, and is in the bathroom tidying herself up. In a few hours she's going to meet the woman who once called herself her mother, and she wants to look as beautiful as possible. She pulls an eyeliner from her bag and applies some light make-up.

Just like hatred, revenge forms tiny, threadlike wrinkles in an otherwise beautiful face, but whereas bitterness gives you deep lines around your mouth, revenge settles around the eyes and forehead instead. The marked groove between her eyes, just above her nose, has been getting deeper. Her worries have made her frown for far too long, and she has grimaced too many times because of the sour taste in her mouth.

There has never been time to forget, and between the person she once was and the person she is today lies a whole universe of events and circumstances. She imagines that other versions of herself exist in parallel worlds.

But this world is hers, and it's here that she's killed five people.

She closes the make-up bag and goes out into the little hotel room, and sits down on the bed where thousands of people have already sat, slept, made love and probably felt hate.

The suitcase lying at the foot of the bed is so new that she has no feelings for it yet, but it contains all she needs. She has called Charlotte Silfverberg and said she wants to meet. That they need to talk and that she'll leave her in peace after that.

In a few hours' time she'll be sitting opposite the woman who once called herself her mother. And they'll talk about the pig farm outside Struer and everything that happened there.

Together they will remember that time in Denmark, and talk about events in the pig shed the way other, normal people talk about nice holiday memories. But instead of beautiful sunsets, fine-grained sand and lovely restaurants, they'll be talking about boys who were drugged and forced to fight each other, about men sweating on top of young girls, and about women who called themselves mothers looking on excitedly.

They will talk for as long as necessary, and she will illustrate her story with Polaroid pictures that reveal what her foster-parents had done.

She'll show her the documents from Copenhagen University Hospital that show that she was a breech birth, and that she was taken from her biological mother along with the placenta. It also says that she was thirty-nine centimetres long, weighed almost two kilos, and was placed in an incubator with suspected jaundice. At the postnatal clinic she was judged to be a month younger than the documents said.

In her suitcase there are more documents, and she knows them all by heart. One of them is from the Childhood and Adolescent Psychiatry unit in Copenhagen.

The seventh line: 'The girl shows signs of depression.' Two lines below: 'She has an ingrained habit of self-harm, and can be violent.' Next page: 'Has repeatedly accused her father of sexual abuse, but has not been regarded as credible.'

Then a note in the margin written in pencil that has become almost illegible over the years, but she knows what it says: 'Based largely upon the mother's claims that the girl has always had a vivid imagination, which is corroborated by the fact that she often talks incoherently about a farm in Jutland. Recurrent delusions.'

Another document has a social service stamp at the bottom, and is an official authorisation for her 'placement in a family home.'

Family home, she thinks. A nice phrase.

She shuts the suitcase and wonders what's going to happen next, afterwards, when she's finished talking and her foster-mother has understood the nature of the choices facing her.

Revenge is much the same as a cake: you can't have it and eat it too. Once revenge has been carried out you have to go on in the blunt awareness that you need to find new meaning in an otherwise meaningless life.

But she knows what she's going to do. She's going to return to the house in Saint-Julien-du-Verdon in Provence. To the cats, to her little studio, and to the calm isolation of the fragrant lavender fields.

When it's all over she's going to stop hating and learn to love. It will be a time for forgiveness, and after twenty years in the dark she needs to learn to see the beauty in life.

But first the woman who once called herself her mother must die.

Fagerstrand – a Suburb

'Who are we doing first?' Hurtig asks as he drives out along Drottningholmsvägen. 'Hannah Östlund or Jessica Friberg?'

'They practically live next door to each other,' she says. 'We'll do the closest one first, Hannah Östlund.'

After the roundabout at Brommaplan they head west along Bergslagsvägen, and the rest of the journey passes in silence, which suits Hurtig.

One characteristic he appreciates in his boss is her ability to make silence feel comfortable, and as they pass the Judar Forest nature reserve he gives her a little smile.

They turn off into the residential area, down towards Fagerstrand.

'OK, pull up along here,' Jeanette says. 'It must be that house over there.'

He brakes and steers past the long hedge surrounding the house, then heads up the drive and parks in front of the garage.

The large house is partially lit up, even though its owner obviously can't be at home. The lights are on in the hall and kitchen, and in one of the rooms on the first floor.

As they walk up to the house he catches a glimpse of something through the kitchen window that they've seen before.

A vase of yellow flowers.

Jeanette folds up the warrant bearing von Kwist's signature and puts it in her inside pocket as Hurtig opens the unlocked door.

A heavy, sweet smell hits them, and Hurtig instinctively takes a step back.

'Shit,' he exclaims with a look of disgust.

The house is silent apart from the sound of flies trying desperately to get out through the closed windows. 'Wait here,' Jeanette says, and closes the door again.

She goes back to the car, opens the boot, and gets out a couple of white breathing masks, four blue polythene shoe covers and two pairs of latex gloves. Since their visit to the cavern below St Johannes Church she has made sure always to have some breathing masks handy. Just in case.

She goes back, gives Hurtig the protective gear and sits down on the step. She stretches her legs and can feel the tiredness in her body. The stench from inside the house is lingering in the air.

'Thanks.' Hurtig sits down beside her and begins to pull the plastic covers over his black leather shoes. Jeanette notes that they look expensive.

'Are those new?' She points at them and smiles at him.

'I don't know,' he says with a laugh. 'Probably, seeing as the guy they came from has a fairly immaculate fashion sense.'

Jeanette thinks he looks embarrassed, as if he were ashamed. But before she has time to ask him about it, he gets up, adjusts his trousers, and makes a move to go inside the house.

Jeanette pulls on the rubber gloves and follows him.

They don't see anything odd in the hall. Some hooks holding a few coats in muted colours. An umbrella leaning against a dresser, on top of which are a phone book and a calendar. The walls are white, and the floor is grey. Everything looks normal, but the penetrating smell tells them that they're going to find something disgusting.

Hurtig goes first, and they take care not to touch anything unnecessarily. Jeanette does her best to put her feet down where Hurtig's have been. Forensics can be fussy, and she doesn't want to get told off for not being careful.

After the hall they reach the kitchen, and when Jeanette sees what's on the table she knows that they've come to the right place, even if it doesn't explain the revolting smell.

On the table

in Hannah Östlund's kitchen there are two Polaroid pictures. Jeanette walks over and picks up one of them. Hurtig looks at the picture over her shoulder.

'Silfverberg,' she says, then puts it down and picks up the other one. 'Look at this.'

He stares at the picture for a few seconds. 'Karl Lundström,' he says. 'So they killed him as well? It wasn't what the doctor said, that Lundström died when his kidneys packed up after too much morphine.'

'That's what it looked like, but they could have messed with his drip. There wasn't a proper investigation because his death seemed natural, but the thought had actually already occurred to me.'

She looks at the arrangement of pictures on the kitchen table.

Something's nagging at her, but she can't put her finger on what it is, and her thoughts are interrupted by the sound of a car pulling up outside.

Jeanette goes out onto the front step to greet Ivo Andrić and the forensics team. She pulls off her mask and takes a deep breath of the fresh air. Whatever it is inside the house, it's best to let forensics go first.

Ivo gets out. When he catches sight of Jeanette his face breaks into a smile. 'So . . .' He screws his eyes up. 'What have we got today?'

'We don't know anything apart from the fact that something in there stinks.'

'You mean it smells of death?' His smile fades.

'Something like that, yes.'

'You and Hurtig can wait outside for the time being.' Ivo gestures to the forensics team. 'We'll go in and check it out.'

Hurtig sits down on the step again, and Jeanette takes out her phone. 'I'll give Åhlund a call. I put him and Schwarz onto looking into Dürer.'

Hurtig nods. 'I'll yell if anything happens here.'

Jeanette walks over to the car. She's just getting into the passenger seat when Åhlund answers.

'How are you getting on? Anything interesting about Dürer?'

Åhlund sighs. 'The Danes aren't being a massive help, but we've done our best.'

'OK. Tell me.'

'Dürer arrived in Denmark on the white buses when he was five. He'd been in the camp at Dachau.'

The Second World War? she thinks. A concentration camp, in other words. She quickly calculates Dürer's age. He was seventy-eight when he died.

'There were a number of Danes in Dachau, including Dürer's parents, but they didn't survive.'

'What happened to him?'

'According to the Danish tax office, for a long time he declared an income from pig farming. But it doesn't look like the business went very well. Some years he doesn't appear to have had any income at all. The farm was in Jutland, a place called Struer, and it was sold ten years ago.'

'How did he end up in Sweden?'

'Towards the end of the sixties he pops up in Vuollerim. And got a job as an accountant at a sawmill.'

'Not as a lawyer?'

'No, and that's what's a bit strange. I can't find any evidence of him having any formal qualifications. No exams, no degree.'

'And in all the years that he worked as a lawyer, no one ever thought to check him out and verify his professional credentials?'

'No, not from what I can see. But he was being treated for cancer, and –'

Jeanette sees Ivo Andrić come out of the house and say something to Hurtig.

'I've got to go now, we'll continue later. Good work, Åhlund.'

She puts the phone back in her jacket and walks over to the waiting men.

'Two dead dogs in the cellar. That's where the smell's coming from.'

Jeanette breathes out. It looks as if the pathologist is smiling, and she presumes that, just like her, he's relieved that it's not a human body this time.

'The animals look like they've been slaughtered,' he goes on. 'But we haven't found anything interesting to report about the rest of Hannah Östlund's home, at least not at first glance.'

'OK, get back to me when you've taken a closer look at Jessica Friberg's house,' Jeanette says to Ivo as Hurtig nods to him and starts walking towards the car.

Swedenborgsgatan – Södermalm

Sofia Zetterlund is sitting in the window of the little bar opposite the eastern exit from the Mariatorget metro station. She hasn't yet recovered from her breakdown the previous day, and stares out at the bald horse-chestnut trees over an untouched plate of hash. In summer this is one of the leafiest streets in the city, but now all she can see are the gloomy skeletons of the trees. The branches stand out against the grey sky like the veins in a lung.

Soon the snow will be here, she thinks.

Instead of eating she leafs through a gossip magazine someone has left on the table. One article catches her eye, because it's about a young woman she coached for a while. The pseudo-celebrity, nude model and now porn actress Carolina Glanz.

The article makes her lose her appetite even more. Miss Glanz, according to the magazine's well-placed sources, has managed in the little more than a month to have her second breast enhancement, marry and then divorce a rich American, perform in a dozen films for a major porn producer, and write a book about it all. An autobiography. Twenty-two years old.

Sofia tosses the magazine aside and sits there for another ten minutes without touching her food. Tiredness and oversensitivity after several nights of disturbed sleep – or, rather, troubled wakefulness – are having a paralysing effect on her, and in the end she begins to pick at the plate in a feeble attempt to summon up some enthusiasm.

Although she asked for the egg to be raw, they've fried it. Raw egg, not fried. But they still got the order wrong.

She pushes the plate away, gets up and leaves the bar.

Pull yourself together now, she thinks as she checks that she remembered to pick up her purse. You've got a job to do.

As she crosses the street she catches sight of someone she recognises. Huddled up and wearing a dark coat and a red woolly hat.

'Annette?'

The dark figure doesn't seem to have heard her and just walks past.

'Annette?' Sofia repeats in a louder voice, and this time the woman stops and turns round.

Sofia takes a few wary steps towards her. Annette Lundström flinches as if she is frightened.

Annette just stands there with a vacant expression while the wind whistles around them. Her face is droopy and grey beneath the red hat.

'Where are you heading?' Sofia tries.

She can see that Annette is only wearing slippers, and has no tights on. She's moving her lips slightly, but Sofia can't make out what she's saying. She realises that something has happened to Annette. It's her, yet somehow it isn't.

'Annette . . . How are you?'

Then she looks at Sofia. 'I'm going to move . . .' she says quietly in a weak voice. 'Back to Polcirkeln.'

She takes Annette's hand, which is ice-cold. She must be freezing.

'You're very lightly dressed,' Sofia says. 'Wouldn't you like to come with me and I'll get you some coffee?'

Reluctantly Annette Lundström allows herself to be led to St Paulsgatan and up to Sofia's office.

'Sit yourself down here for a bit,' Sofia says to Annette, pulling a chair over for her. As she sits down, one sleeve rides up, and Sofia catches sight of a plastic bracelet around her wrist. A white patient's bracelet, marked PSYCHIATRY, SOUTH STOCKHOLM.

Of course, Sofia thinks.

She asks Annette to wait a moment, and goes to see Ann-Britt. In a low voice she asks her to get some coffee and mineral water. 'Annette Lundström is a patient at one of South Stockholm's psychiatric units. Can you call around and check?'

Five minutes later Annette Lundström starts to thaw out. Her face has regained a bit of colour, but is still slack and expressionless. She lifts the coffee cup to her lips with trembling hands and Sofia notices that Annette's fingertips are covered in cuts.

'What am I doing here?' The woman's eyes are darting about and she looks confused.

She puts her cup down, raises her hand to her mouth and starts biting at a cut on her index finger.

Sofia leans across the desk. 'We're just warming up for a bit. But you said you were on your way to Polcirkeln. What are you going to do there?'

The answer is confident. 'Go to see Karl and Viggo and the others.'

She pulls off a scrap of skin and rolls it between her fingers before popping it in her mouth.

Karl and Viggo? Sofia thinks. 'What about Linnea?'

Annette shuts her eyes, and a faint smile appears at one corner of her mouth. 'Linnea is back home with God.'

Sofia starts to feel worried, even if it's possible to interpret Annette's words in many different ways, considering the state she's in. 'How do you mean, "Linnea is back home with God"?'

Annette opens her eyes and smiles broadly. The look in her eyes is distant and, together with her smile, forms an image that Sofia recognises.

Psychosis. A portrait of a person who isn't the person she used to be.

'First I have to go to Polcirkeln . . .' Annette mutters. 'To Karl and Viggo, then I'm going home as well, to God and Linnea . . . Viggo gave me money, and said Linnea didn't need to see any more psychologists. So she could go home to God.'

Sofia tries to gather her thoughts. 'Viggo Dürer gave you money?'

'Yes . . . Wasn't that nice of him?' Annette looks at her with glassy eyes. 'I can use the money to go to Polcirkeln and build a temple where we can prepare for the glory that will soon be here.'

They're interrupted by the phone. Sofia apologises and picks up the receiver.

'She's a patient at Rosenlund,' Ann-Britt says. 'They'll be here to pick her up in fifteen minutes.'

Sofia hangs up and regrets not waiting longer before asking Ann-Britt to call the psychiatric clinics. Rosenlund is pretty much just round the corner, less than a kilometre away, and Sofia would have liked longer to talk to Annette.

Now she's only got fifteen minutes, and will have to be extremely efficient.

'Sigtuna and Denmark,' Annette Lundström says, out of nowhere, evidently immersed in herself. 'Everyone from Sihtunum is welcome to live in Polcirkeln. That's one of the ground rules.'

'Polcirkeln, Sihtunum and Denmark, you say? And what are these ground rules?'

Annette Lundström smiles as she looks at her bleeding fingers with her head bowed.

'The Original Order,' she says. 'Pythia's instructions.'

Village of Polcirkeln, 1981

And I make wild strawberries for the children, because I think they deserve them,
And other nice little things that are right when children are little.
And I make such lovely places, where the children can run around,
Where the children can be full of summer, and their legs full of life.

Pariah.

She has found the word in the dictionary, and she knows the definition by heart.

An outcast, a despised person.

The entire Lundström family are pariahs up here, and no one in the village talks to them.

It's the games that others don't like. But that's only because they don't understand them. They can't sing the Psalms of the Lamb, and they've never heard of the Original Order.

The fact that she has been engaged to Karl for almost a year, since she turned twelve, is something else that the others find ugly. Karl is almost nineteen, and he's her cousin.

She loves him, and they're going to have a child of love as soon as she's old enough.

The others don't understand that either.

And now things have gone so far that they've got to move away from here. Fortunately Viggo has been able to help them sort everything out, and she's going to start school in Sigtuna in the autumn. There will be friends there, people who are like them and understand.

She knows that if it weren't for Viggo, they would be nothing.

He's the one who has shown them the way, and helped them to understand how the world really is. And he's the one who's going to help them now, when everyone else, every single neighbour, has turned against them.

Viggo looks focused and nods silently when he sees her. He has a large paper bag with him, and she knows it contains presents for her. He's been travelling, as far away as the Soviet Union.

He smiles at her, and she goes into her room.

If only they could stop talking soon, he can come in and give her the presents, and after that they can continue with the preparations for her impending marriage to Karl.

She's going to be a good mother to her child, and a good wife to her husband, and for that to happen, she needs to practise.

Mariatorget – Sofia Zetterlund's Office

'Every morning when I wake up, I think everything's normal,' Annette Lundström says. 'Then I remember that Linnea isn't here any more. I wish I could make the most of that short moment when everything feels normal.'

Linnea is dead? Sofia thinks.

There are brief periods of lucidity even in psychosis. Sofia realises that this is one of them, and quickly formulates another question to stay in contact with Annette Lundström.

'What's happened, Annette?'

The woman smiles. 'My beloved daughter is with God. It was predetermined.'

Sofia realises she won't get any further with that question now. 'What was Linnea's relationship with Viggo Dürer?' she asks instead.

Annette's rigid smile fills Sofia with disquiet. 'Relationship? Oh, I don't know . . . Linnea liked him. They played together a lot when she was little.'

'She told me that Viggo Dürer abused her.'

Annette's face darkens, and she goes back to gnawing at her fingers. 'Impossible,' she says defiantly. 'Viggo's so prudish, so concerned about not upsetting anyone.'

Annette lets out a deep sigh and lowers her head. She starts to talk in a quiet voice, and Sofia realises she's quoting something.

'Outside the Home of Shadows you shall behave with modesty in body and spirit,' she says. 'There are people who do not understand you and wish you harm, slandering you and then imprisoning you.'

Sofia understands where the words come from.

She glances at the clock. The orderlies from the psychiatric clinic will be here any moment. 'You're talking about the Home of Shadows,' she begins. 'Karl did that as well. He described it as a sort of sanctuary.'

Silence. Annette Lundström needs questions rather than suppositions.

'What is the Home of Shadows?' Sofia asks instead.

She's right. Annette looks up at her.

'The Home of Shadows is the original country,' she says, 'where mankind can be close to God. It's the land of children. But it also belongs to adults who understand how ancient man lived. Men, women and children, hand in hand. We are all children inside.'

Sofia shudders. A country for children, created by adults for their own desires.

She is beginning to suspect that Annette Lundström's psychosis not only contains an element of truth, but might even be some sort of confession. What she is saying sounds logical if you are aware of what she's talking about. Her psychosis is prompting her to confess.

'Do you meant a physical place, or is it a state of mind?'

'The Home of Shadows exists where the faithful are; it only exists in the presence of the chosen children of men. On sacred ground in beautiful Jutland, and in the forests up in Polcirkeln.'

Sofia pauses to think. Denmark and Polcirkeln again.

She forces herself to smile. 'Who was it who led the faithful?' she goes on in a breezy tone of voice, as if to make light of everything.

It works, and Annette lights up. 'Karl and Viggo,' she begins. 'And P-O, of course. He and Viggo took care of all the practical matters. They made sure the children were happy, that they had everything they could have wanted.'

'And what was your role? And the children's?'

'I . . . we women probably weren't that important. But the children were obviously among the initiated. Linnea, Madeleine, and the adopted children, of course.'

'Madeleine? The adopted children?'

It's as if everything Annette says demands a follow-up question.

But her answers are unforced, and Sofia can only assume that what the woman is telling her is true.

'Yes. We called them Viggo's adopted children. He helped them come to Sweden from terrible conditions abroad, and they lived on the farm until he found new families for them. Sometimes they only stayed a matter of days, and sometimes a few months. We raised them in accordance with the word of Pythia –'

Annette jumps at the sound of the internal phone, and Sofia realises that the orderlies from Rosenlund have arrived.

One last question.

'Who else was at the farm? You said there were several women?'

Annette Lundström's smile is still in place. Sofia thinks it looks dead, empty and hollow.

'Everyone from Sigtuna,' she says happily. 'And of course there were others who came and went. Other men as well. And their Swedish children.'

Sofia knows that this is something she's going to have to tell Jeanette, and makes a mental note to call her as soon as possible.

The handover takes place without drama, and five minutes later Sofia is sitting alone in her office, tapping a pen against the edge of her desk.

Psychosis, she thinks. Psychosis as a form of truth serum.

Highly unusual, not to mention improbable.

She's just found out from the Rosenlund staff that Linnea Lundström hanged herself in her home while Annette was watching television in the living room.

It feels as if Linnea was there very recently. Sofia can see her in her mind's eye, sitting in the chair on the other side of the desk. A young girl who wanted to talk, wanted to feel better. They had been making progress in their sessions, and she feels deep sorrow about what has happened.

She looks out of the window. The two orderlies who came to collect Annette Lundström are leading her towards a car park on the other side of the street. The woman's thin, hunched figure looks so frail, as if the wind and rain out there could tear her apart.

A slender, grey silhouette dissolving into air.

A life torn to shreds.

Glasbruksgatan – Silfverberg House

Hurtig gets in the driver's seat and pulls out his mobile while he waits for Jeanette to finish talking to Ivo Andrić. Before Jeanette has time to open the car door he manages to type a quick message. 'Talk tonight? Are you sending the pictures?'

He starts the car and winds down the window to let some fresh air in as Jeanette jumps into the passenger seat and smiles at him.

Ivo Andrić's good mood seems to have been infectious, and she pats Hurtig cheerily on the thigh.

'So what do we do now?' he says.

'We should probably go and see Charlotte Silfverberg and tell her what we know. Her husband was murdered, and it looks like these two women did it, and she's got a right to know before she reads about it in the papers.'

Hurtig drives through the cordon, out of the open gate and onto the street.

They sit in silence all the way past Södra Ängby and Brommaplan, and as they're passing Alvik and can see the boats down at Sjöpaviljongen he turns to Jeanette. 'Do you like boats?'

'Not much,' she says. 'I'm probably the type that prefers a summer cottage.'

'You mean you prefer simplicity?' he says.

'Yes, something like that.' Jeanette sighs. 'Simplicity. God, that sounds dull.'

He can see that she's contemplating saying something. 'Billing and von Kwist will probably be pleased that these cases are solved,' she says eventually. 'But I'm not, and you know why?'

Her question surprises him. 'No, I can't say that I do.'

'I don't prefer simplicity at all,' she says emphatically. 'Think about it . . . Everything about this case feels too simple, too neat. It was already nagging at me in Östlund's kitchen, but I couldn't put my finger on what it was. And in Hannah Östlund's home we find the photographs. But they only show the murder victims. If you want to show that you've carried out a series of murders, why not make it as obvious as possible? Why isn't there a picture of Hannah or Jessica painting Silfverberg's apartment with his blood, something like that?'

He doesn't quite understand what Jeanette's getting at. 'But Annette Lundström identified Hannah Östlund from the picture at the caverns.'

'Yes, I know.' Jeanette sounds irritated. 'Annette said it was Hannah because she was missing her ring finger, but that was the only reason. Why doesn't Hannah show her face? And there's something else that's bothering me. Why did they kill their dogs in such a revolting way?'

Jeanette's got a point, Hurtig thinks. But he's not entirely convinced. 'So you mean it could be someone else? Someone who arranged the whole thing? The photographs and so on?'

She shakes her head. 'I don't know . . .' Jeanette gives him a serious look. 'This might sound like a long shot, but I think we should take another look at Madeleine Silfverberg. I'll ask Åhlund to check the hotels in the city. After all, Madeleine had a good motive for killing her father.'

This is going too quickly for him. 'Madeleine? That seems a bit far-fetched.'

'Maybe it is.'

Jeanette gets out her phone as Hurtig passes beneath the Essinge motorway and heads towards Lindhagensplan. She asks Åhlund to get lists of people staying at the main hotels, then she pauses, takes out a pen and writes something down before ending the call. The conversation is over in less than a minute.

'Åhlund says Dürer owned three properties in Stockholm. An apartment on Ölandsgatan that has already been sold. Another one on Biblioteksgatan, and a villa out in Norra Djurgården. I think we should check them out once we've spoken to Charlotte Silfverberg.' She looks down at her notes. 'Hundudden – do you know where that is?'

Always boats, he thinks. 'Yes, there's a small marina out there. Fairly exclusive, I believe . . . Hang on, did you say Ölandsgatan? That's the Monument block, isn't it, where Samuel Bai was found dead?'

'Not much we can do about that one. After Dürer's death the apartment was renovated and then sold. We'll have to check out Biblioteksgatan and Hundudden.'

Just as they're getting out of the car, the door to the building opens and Charlotte Silfverberg emerges with a small suitcase in her hand.

The woman's body language and the look on her face scream hostility.

'Are you going somewhere?' Jeanette gestures towards the case.

'Just a cruise to Åland, nothing special,' Charlotte Silfverberg says with forced laughter. 'I need to get away and think about something else. It's a cultural trip, you have some wine and listen to an expert talk about their work. This evening it's Lasse Hallström. He's one of my favourite directors.'

Still smug and arrogant, Hurtig thinks. Not even the murder of her husband has changed her. How do people like that even exist?

'This is about P-O,' Jeanette says. 'Perhaps we shouldn't do this out in the street. Shall we go back up to the flat?' Jeanette gestures towards the door.

'Here on the street will do fine.' Charlotte Silfverberg purses her lips and puts her suitcase down on the pavement. 'What do you want?'

Jeanette tells her what they found out at Hannah Östlund's home.

The woman listens intently in silence, doesn't ask a single question, and, when Jeanette has finished, her response is immediate. 'OK, great, so now we know who did it.'

Hurtig is taken aback by the emotionless statement, and sees Jeanette react as well.

'Not that I know anything about police work,' Charlotte goes on, fixing her eyes on Hurtig and holding his gaze a fraction too long before turning towards Jeanette. 'But it seems to me as if you've been almost incredibly lucky to be able to solve this so quickly. Or am I wrong?'

Hurtig can see that Jeanette is bubbling with rage and knows that she's counting to ten.

The woman smiles maliciously. 'And lucky for me that Hannah and Jessica killed themselves,' she says. 'Otherwise they'd probably have tried to kill me as well. Maybe it was me they were really after, not P-O?'

Now he can feel his own temperature rising. 'That might be your opinion,' he says. 'But I must say I really can't understand it. What could they possibly have against such a charming, sensitive person as you?'

Jeanette stares at him, and he understands he's crossed the line.

The woman's eyes flash. 'Sarcasm really doesn't suit you. Hannah and Jessica were crazy, even as teenagers. When they chose to shut themselves away, I suppose their madness had the space to blossom.'

He realises that there's nothing else to say. Seeing as the perpetrators are dead, the case will be closed. Even though Jeanette still seems to have her doubts, he thinks.

'Well, thank you,' Jeanette says.

Charlotte Silfverberg nods and picks up her suitcase. 'Here's my taxi, so perhaps we can put an end to our little chat now.' She waves at the car as it drives up and pulls over to the kerb.

Hurtig opens the back door, and, as the woman gets in, he can't resist.

'Say hi to Lasse,' he says, before closing the door.

That's the last time they see Charlotte Silfverberg. Twelve hours later she'll be fighting for her life in the chill waters of the Åland Sea.

Skanstull – a Neighborhood

Sofia Zetterlund is about to set off into her labyrinth again.

She picks up the receiver to call Jeanette, but changes her mind and puts it down again. Linnea is dead, she thinks. A feeling of despair washes over her. She needs to take the rest of the day off.

She changes into a little black dress, a long grey coat and the high-heeled shoes that are far too small for her and chafe her heels. She finishes putting on her make-up, nods a silent goodbye to the receptionist and heads out into Swedenborgsgatan.

She's sleepwalking as she turns onto Ringvägen, heading towards the Clarion Hotel down at Skanstull. 'You bastards,' she mutters as the sound of her heels on the pavement is muffled by the haze of the dream and gets softer and softer.

Soon the Sleepwalker doesn't hear the cars passing her, doesn't see the people.

She nods to the doorman at the entrance to the hotel and goes inside.

The bar is at the far end of the building, and she sits down at a table and waits.

Go home, she thinks. Sofia Zetterlund has gone home. No, she's gone to the supermarket on Folkungagatan to buy groceries, then she's going to go home and make dinner.

Go home and eat alone.

When the waiter notices her she orders a glass of red wine. One of their finest.

Victoria Bergman raises the glass to her lips.

Go home.

The Sleepwalker is gone and she looks around.

One of the men at the bar turns round to stare out of the large glass window overlooking the Skanstull Bridge. She looks at him. He has a bloated, vacant expression.

She makes eye contact almost immediately. But it's too soon to act. She must have patience, make them wait. That enhances the experience. She wants to make them explode. See them lying on their backs, exhausted and defenceless.

But he mustn't be too drunk, and the man at the bar is anything but sober, his face wet with sweat in the glow of the lights on the shelves behind the bar, and he's unbuttoned his shirt and loosened his tie because the alcohol has made his throat swell.

He's of no interest, and she looks away.

Five minutes later her glass is empty and she discreetly signals for a refill. As the waiter serves her the room gets noisier. A group of men in suits sit down on the sofas to her left. A total of thirteen men in expensive suits, and a woman in a Versace dress.

She shuts her eyes and listens to their loud conversation.

After a few minutes she knows that twelve of the suits are Germans, probably from the north of Germany, maybe Hamburg. The dress is their Swedish hostess, and her poor, broken German comes from Gothenburg. The last of the suits hasn't said a word yet, and when she opens her eyes she's curious about him.

He's sitting on the armchair closest to her, and is the youngest member of the group. He looks shy when he smiles and is probably the one whom his colleagues give an encouraging slap on the back to if he ever disappears to his room with female company. Between twenty-five and thirty, and not too handsome. The handsome ones aren't as good in bed, because they generally assume their looks mean they don't have to try. But it really doesn't matter how good they are, because it isn't the act itself that she enjoys.

It takes her less than five minutes to entice him to her table, order fresh drinks and get him to relax.

He orders a dark beer, and she has a third glass of wine.

'*Ich bezahle die nächste Runde*,' she says. She'll get the next round, because she's not an escort girl.

His shyness soon vanishes and his smile is relaxed as he talks about his work and the conference in Stockholm, how important it is to network in his business, and obviously there's a hint at how much he earns. The human male has no glorious display of feathers to act as bait. He uses money instead.

His money is visible in his suit, his shirt and tie; it's there in his aftershave and it shines from his shoes and tiepin. Yet he still has to imply that he has an expensive car in the garage and a well-stocked investment portfolio. The only thing he doesn't mention is that he has a wife and children at home in the villa outside Hamburg, but that's not too hard to work out, seeing as he's wearing a wedding ring and accidentally revealed a photograph of two little girls when he opened his wallet.

He'll do, she thinks.

She does it to get close to them. For a brief period she can be their wives, daughters and lovers. All at the same time. Then they disappear out of her life.

It's the emptiness afterwards that's nicest.

Victoria Bergman puts her hand on the man's thigh and whispers something in his ear. He nods, and looks simultaneously uncertain and expectant. She's just about to tell him that there's nothing to worry about when she feels a hand on her shoulder.

'Sofia?'

She starts and her body becomes inexplicably heavy, but she doesn't turn round.

Her eyes are still focused on the young man's face, but it looks blurred all of a sudden.

His features are merging together, her head is spinning, and for a moment it feels like the world is rotating an extra turn.

She wakes very quickly, and when she looks up there's a stranger in a suit sitting beside her. She realises that she's got her hand on his thigh and quickly jerks it away.

'Sorry, I –'

'Sofia Zetterlund?' the voice repeats behind her.

She recognises it, but is still surprised to find that it belongs to one of her former clients.

Hundudden – Island of Djurgården

From the windows in the stairwell of the building opposite they have a good view into the apartment. Hurtig and Jeanette quickly realise that the five-room apartment on Biblioteksgatan registered to Viggo Dürer's company has been completely cleaned out.

On the way to Dürer's property in Norra Djurgården Jeanette has a feeling that they're going to find the same thing there – nothing. The forest gets thicker and the buildings sparser.

Shadows are soon descending around them, it's starting to feel chilly and Jeanette asks Hurtig to turn the heating up. It feels like they're driving through a tunnel of black pine trees, and Jeanette is surprised that there are places like this so close to the city. She is being lulled into a meditative calm that's abruptly interrupted when her mobile rings. It's Åhlund.

'I've checked hotels in and around Stockholm,' he says.

'And?'

'There are seven guests with the first name Madeleine, but no Madeleine Silfverberg. I checked them out anyway, just in case. If she's using a false identity, she might have chosen to keep her first name. That's fairly common. And she might be married, of course. We don't really know anything about her.'

Jeanette agrees. 'Good thinking. Have you found anything interesting?'

'I don't know. We can definitely write off six of them – I've managed to get hold of them – but the seventh is missing. Her name's Madeleine Duchamp, and she booked in using a French driving licence.'

Jeanette perks up. A French driving licence?

'She checked out of Sjöfartshotellet, down near Slussen, earlier today.'

'OK.' She calms down slightly. Even if Madeleine has lived in the south of France for the past few years, according to their information she's still a Danish citizen. 'I want you to go to the hotel and talk to the staff. Find out anything you can, but try to get a description, above everything else.'

They end the call, and Hurtig looks at her inquisitively. 'Is it still worth a try, do you think?'

'I don't know,' she says. 'But I don't want to miss anything.'

Hurtig nods and slows down as the road curves once more. 'Here it is,' he says, turning off onto a narrow gravel track.

The forest is dense and seems to surround the property.

They get out of the car and find themselves standing in front of a metal gate more than two and a half metres tall. 'Can you climb?' Hurtig sighs. 'Or shall we try to find a way through the undergrowth?'

'We could always try the doorbell,' she says, pointing at the entry-phone beside the gate.

Hurtig rings three times without getting an answer, then turns towards Jeanette. She thinks he looks a bit deflated.

'We climb over,' she decides, and puts her torch in her mouth so she has both hands free. She scrambles up nimbly, swings over the spiked iron railings at the top and lands softly on the gravel drive on the other side.

Hurtig has a harder time, but is soon standing beside her with a smile on his face and a long tear in his jacket. 'Damn, I didn't know you could climb like that.' He seems to have livened up, and she smiles back at him.

The drive leads up to a large, grey, two-storey stone house, probably built at the turn of the last century and renovated relatively recently. Next to two tall, dark pine trees to the left of the house there's an outbuilding, a garage, also built of grey stone but about a hundred years later.

Jeanette switches on her torch and notes that the grass in the large plot is tall, and that in spite of the renovations everything looks unkempt, an impression reinforced by the fact that the fruit has been left to rot on a number of apple trees, bathing the garden in a sweet, musty smell.

The house is dark, and they realise at once that there's no one home.

Through the window in the front door they can see a little blue flashing light, a sign that the burglar alarm is switched on.

Jeanette crouches down in front of the garage. 'Wheel tracks,' she says. 'Relatively fresh.' The grit in front of the garage is almost dry, protected by the branches of the trees above. The drive is covered with pine needles and the tyre tracks are clearly visible.

Hurtig puts his hands in his jacket pockets and shivers. 'Come on, let's take a look inside the house.'

They walk around the villa, but it looks just as abandoned as Dürer's apartment in the city. Jeanette peers in through a window. At least there's furniture here, she thinks, as she sees a couple of sofas, a table and a piano. All covered by a thick layer of dust.

Camouflaged by the darkness and the trees behind the garage is a car, covered by a tarpaulin. A Citroën, dark blue, showing signs of rust.

'Hang on . . .' She stops and sweeps the beam of her torch along the bushes in front of the house. 'Do you see? What's that?'

The torch is aimed at part of the foundation, between two of the windows.

'There's a cellar. Or there used to be. The windows have been covered up.'

She nods. 'Just what I was thinking.'

One of the big blocks of granite looks very different than the others. It's roughly the size of a cellar window, while the other bricks used in the foundation are smaller.

They do another circuit of the house and count a total of eight cellar windows that have been covered by new stones. The garage doesn't appear to have a cellar.

'Does it mean anything,' Hurtig wonders, 'or do you think it's just an unusual way of insulating the place?'

'I don't know . . .' Jeanette shines the torch at one of the blocks again. 'It must have been a hell of a job getting them in. I've got a feeling someone wanted to hide the fact that there is a cellar, rather than . . .'

Hurtig scratches his chin and looks thoughtful. 'I don't know. But we'll find out if we can get a search warrant. Do you think we should put a watch on the house in case someone shows up?'

'No, not yet. But I think we should take a closer look at the garage before we go.'

It's big enough for two cars, the doors are locked, and there's only one little window high up in the stone wall at the back. The outbuilding reminds Jeanette of a small bunker, and she gives Hurtig a wry smile. 'Have you got any tools with you?'

Hurtig smiles back. 'There's a toolbox in the boot. Are we going to break in?'

'No, just take a look at what's in there. And I want to take a sample of the paint on that car, just in case.'

'Agreed. Off you go, then, you're clearly better at climbing than I am.'

Two minutes later Jeanette is back with a penknife and a heavy wrench. She scrapes off a few flakes of paint from the car and puts them in a small plastic evidence bag, then hands the wrench to Hurtig. She can't reach the window herself.

He stands on tiptoe, and, as he pulls his arm back to strike at the window, he looks at her over his shoulder. 'What do we do if an alarm starts shrieking?'

'What all vandals do. Run like hell.' She grins. 'Just hit it . . .'

Three heavy blows on the window, and the sound of breaking glass seems deafening to her.

Then complete silence. They wait for ten seconds before Jeanette speaks.

'Give me a leg up, then,' she says, pointing at the broken window.

Hurtig cups his hands, and she climbs up.

There's just room for her to stick her head and the torch through the window. The beam plays across a sturdy workbench below the window, then across a concrete floor towards some heavy-duty shelving against the wall nearest the house. She points the beam around the room, then returns to the shelving.

Completely deserted. Not a single thing inside, as far as she can see. The workbench and shelving are quite empty.

That's all. A perfectly ordinary garage, albeit very spacious and tidy, which doesn't seem to have been used for anything but parking cars.

Skanstull – a Neighborhood

People say it's dangerous to wake a sleepwalker.

Sofia Zetterlund's awakening in the Clarion Hotel perhaps doesn't entirely support that thesis, but her physical reaction is so strong that she's having trouble breathing, and her pulse rate goes so high that she can't get up from her seat.

'Sofia, are you OK?'

In front of her stands Carolina Glanz.

She sees a face stiff from cosmetic surgery. It's a miracle of the human physiognomy that it can still express concern.

'Geht es Ihnen gut?' she hears distantly from the man beside her.

She's no longer bothered about him. *'Ja,'* she replies in a tone of derision, and finally manages to stand up. 'I have to go,' she then says to the young woman, and pushes past her roughly, without meeting her anxious gaze.

She doesn't look back once as she walks away from the bar, through the lobby and out into the street.

Go home . . . I have to go home.

She goes over the pedestrian crossing towards the Ringen shopping centre, ignoring the red light, which leads to angry horn blowing and sudden braking. When she reaches the other side her legs feel like they can no longer carry her, and she sits down on one of the benches outside the shopping centre and hides her face in her hands.

Her head is still spinning, and she doesn't notice her tears, or the driving rain.

Or the fact that someone sits down beside her.

'You shouldn't go there any more,' Carolina Glanz says after a while.

Sofia calms down slightly, and the young woman puts her hand on her back. What the hell am I doing? she wonders. This is beneath me.

She straightens up and takes a deep breath before looking irritably at the girl and snapping, 'What do you mean by that? And why are you following me?'

Close up, her face looks even worse. It might seem OK in front of a camera, but in the flat, grey afternoon light her doll-like, unnatural features look grotesque. She appears at least fifteen years older than she actually is.

'I hang out at the Clarion a lot, and I've seen you there a few times,' Carolina says. 'I know a few people who work there, and they think you're on the game. I actually had to stop them from throwing you out.' She attempts a smile through her make-up and surgery.

A few times? Shouldn't go there anymore? Sofia finally realises.

Victoria.

Sofia softens slightly as she looks at Carolina Glanz.

Maybe she's not a lost cause after all?

'I haven't been sleeping well recently,' Sofia says. 'And I've split up with someone and maybe I'm not quite myself.'

'Let's go and get some coffee,' Carolina suggests, nodding towards the entrance to the shopping centre. Sofia presumes she means the cafe in the middle of Ringen.

'Sure,' she says. 'We can't sit here, can we, it's pouring.'

As they walk into the shopping centre Carolina Glanz tells her that she's got a contract with a major publisher, and that for the first time in her life she feels like she's doing something she can be proud of. They get coffee and sit down at one of the tables.

'The book's going to be a sensation,' Carolina says dramatically, and Sofia marvels at the young woman's ability to just shake herself and move on. From one thing to the next, with just one goal. To make a living from celebrity.

Selling herself in any way she can.

She can't help agreeing with those who say it shows entrepreneurial spirit.

She thinks about herself, and her efforts to do the exact opposite. To keep her identity secret from everyone, and never reveal who she is at all costs, even to herself.

Today everything has come close to disaster.

Her thoughts are interrupted when the young woman's mobile phone rings. After a short conversation she looks apologetically at Sofia and explains that her publisher wants to see her, so she's got to go.

And, just as suddenly as she appeared, Carolina Glanz is gone.

Her appearance makes men and women alike stop and look round, and as she disappears she leaves a furrow of curious faces behind her, from the cafe to the exit of the shopping centre.

Sofia realises that that's precisely what Carolina wants. Here I am. Look at me. Give me your attention, and I'll give you all my secrets.

She decides to sit there for a while, at least until her hair has dried, and the more she thinks about Carolina Glanz, the more certain she gets.

She's envious of the young woman.

Her cosmetic surgery acts like a costume. Hidden behind all the putty and silicon, Carolina Glanz dares to reveal everything about herself. Her costume gives her the courage to play every note on the emotional scale, from foolish vulgarity to sharp intelligence. Because Sofia doesn't doubt that Glanz is actually an extremely intelligent, determined young woman. There's a logic to Carolina Glanz's behaviour, an instinctive logic that also seems to come from her heart. She knows how to show who she is.

Unlike me, Sofia thinks.

She knows that inside her there's a permanent fancy-dress party going on, where the participants' characteristics are so varied and diametrically opposed to one another that they can't actually make up an entire person. No matter how odd it might sound, Carolina Glanz with her constructed exterior is more authentic and coherent than Sofia will ever be.

There isn't even a me, she thinks.

Then the rushing sound in her head is back. A never-ending stream of voices and faces. Simultaneously inside and outside her.

She stares at the people going towards the exit, and after a while she sees their bodies moving through the shopping centre, vague, elongated streaks in different colours, like cars moving past on a motorway. But sometimes she can freeze the image and look at their faces, one after the other.

Two blonde girls are walking towards the exit of the shopping centre, each one with a dog on a lead.

They bear a striking resemblance to Hannah and Jessica.

Two people who are three people, she thinks. Or rather three fragments of one personality.

The Worker, the Analyst and the Moaning Minnie have their models in her old classmates Hannah Östlund and Jessica Friberg. Two girls who were very similar, almost like mirror images of each other. Like a single, apathetic shadow of a person.

Victoria used those personality fragments to avoid having to do anything dull, but they were also substitutes for feelings in herself that she doesn't like.

Thinking she knows best, or pessimism, or pettiness. Also unquestioning obedience, subservience, obsequiousness and fawning. Being just one of a flock of clever blondes. The very qualities that Victoria had seen in Hannah and Jessica.

The Worker, the Analyst and the Moaning Minnie mean nothing to her any more. She can take care of all the banal emotions and qualities that they represented, it's all just a matter of being more mature and either abandoning or accepting the trivial parts of her nature.

Even a dog ought to be able to learn to do that.

Go home, she thinks. I have to go home.

Nowhere

Ulrika Wendin doesn't know how long she's been tied up in the dry, warm room. The darkness knocked out her awareness of time a while back.

The silence is as oppressive as the darkness, and all she can hear are sounds inside her. Sometimes she wakes up because she can no longer feel her body, and the lack of sensory information makes her feel like she's in a vacuum, drifting weightlessly without a sense of complete darkness and silence.

She realises that she's got to find a way to free her arms, which are taped together behind her back, before they become useless. With a great effort she occasionally manages to raise her body enough to be able to move them and regain some degree of feeling. But the intervals are getting longer, and her room for manoeuvre is limited by the metal bars just centimetres above her chest and knees.

She leans her head back again and looks up. The strip of light is still there. It occurs to her that the light is the Milky Way, and that the galaxy contains as many stars as there are cells in a human brain. Perhaps everything in there will blur together and turn uniformly grey in the end? Is it all just an optical illusion?

Is she seeing things from inside her own mind?

Her throat stings with thirst the whole time, and she's probably dehydrating faster because of the heat and her fits of crying.

The only way to keep her mouth producing saliva is to lick the tape covering her mouth. The bitter taste of the glue makes her feel sick, but she still licks the inside of her lips and along the edges of the tape at regular intervals.

If only she could produce enough saliva, it might come free altogether. But the worst thing that could happen would be to throw up, because then she would suffocate.

Even though she's seriously dehydrated, she feels as if she needs to empty her bladder. But she can't do it. Her body won't obey her, and no matter how hard she tries, she can't squeeze out a single drop. It only works if she gives up and stops trying. Then the warmth spreads over her crotch and thighs.

It's a hot, itchy feeling.

She soon notices the cloying smell. She doesn't know if she's imagining it, but it feels like her urine makes the air a bit more moist, and she takes long, deep breaths through her nose.

She knows it's possible to survive for quite a long time without food. Several months, she seems to recall. But how long can you survive without water?

Her chances of survival ought to be better if she moves as little as possible, lying still and not burning up so many fluids. Minimising her physical exertions. And not crying.

Ulrika Wendin's eyes are dry as they look at the shades of grey-black above her, and her tongue sticks to the roof of her mouth as she slips into unconsciousness again.

In her dream she's drifting in space and looking down on herself.

In the distance she imagines she can hear a sound of something breaking, and she realises that it must be the centre of the galaxy exploding.

Baltic Sea – MS *Cinderella*

One day you find out that your life has been the blink of an eye, Madeleine thinks, as she looks in the mirror in the tiny bathroom of her cabin. Life is an almost imperceptible yawn, and then it ends so abruptly that you've hardly had time to notice it's started.

The ship rolls, and she holds on to the door frame and sits down on the bunk. On the table is a glass of ice cubes next to an open bottle of champagne, and she pours a second glassful into the toothbrush mug.

One day you're standing there with a stupid smile on your lips, reading in your mental diary about all the hopes and dreams you once had, she thinks, raising the mug to her lips and taking a sip of champagne. The bubbles tickle the roof of her mouth. It tastes of mature fruit, with hints of minerals, herbs and roasted coffee.

Her internal diary is full of uneventful pages that are largely empty. Days that have passed without making any memorable impression. Aeons of existence that have been nothing but waiting. Yes, she's waited so long that time and waiting have become the same thing.

Then there are other days. The terrible moments that made her who she is. The years she spent growing up in Denmark are like a pair of red knickers in a machine full of white wash.

Madeleine puts her headphones on and plugs them into her phone. She lies back on the bunk and listens.

Joy Division. First the drums, then a pumping bass, a simple hook, and finally Ian Curtis's monotonous voice.

The ship's irregular rolling and swaying relaxes her and the drunk people making a noise outside her door feel comforting in their unpredictability. The unexpected doesn't scare her. It's security that makes her feel anxious.

The rain is lashing the cabin window, and it feels like Ian Curtis is singing just for her in his slurred voice.

Confusion in her eyes that says it all. She's lost control.

The singer, just twenty-four years old and suffering from epilepsy, committed suicide by hanging himself. But she's not going to commit suicide. That would mean losing, and letting them win.

And she gave away the secrets of her past, and said I've lost control again.

She thinks about the fact that the woman who once called herself her mother sometimes used to say she'd rather be called by her first name, seeing as she wasn't actually Madeleine's real mother. On other occasions it most definitely had to not get out that Madeleine was the family's foster-daughter. It was just as arbitrary as it was humiliating.

But that's not why she has to die.

If you stand in silence and look on while grown men abuse a young girl, you very quickly lose any claim to mercy for yourself. And if you take pleasure in watching naked, drugged young boys fighting in a pig-pen, and don't care when one of the boys dies, you deserve no forgiveness. Everyone who was involved has realised that, one way or another, she thinks, seeing their dead bodies in front of her.

Fury is growing inside her, and she rubs her temples hard. She knows it's crazy of her to compare herself to Nemesis, the goddess of revenge, but that's the self-image she has nurtured her whole life. A girl who arrives at school one day together with her tame lion. Someone to be frightened of, and someone you have to respect.

A few hours later, and halfway to Mariehamn, in the Åland Islands, she goes down the corridor towards the nightclub at the front of the ship. She mustn't be too late, or too early.

Everything will soon be over, and she can move on and shape her own future without having the voices of the past screaming in her ear.

The bar is full of people, and Madeleine has to push her way through the tables. The music is loud, and on a small stage two women are performing in front of a karaoke machine. They're singing badly out of tune, but the audience likes their provocative dancing and there's a lot of whistling and clapping.

You're like tame livestock, she thinks.

Charlotte is sitting alone at one of the tables by the big panoramic window.

The woman she never called her mother is dressed primly in a dark jacket, a black skirt and a pair of grey tights, and Madeleine thinks it looks like she's dressed for a funeral.

Charlotte stares straight at her, and their eyes meet for the first time in a very long while.

'So . . . We meet again after all these years,' Charlotte says, screwing her eyes up. Studying her.

I hate you, I hate you, I hate you . . .

'I was foolish enough to think that we were finished with each other,' she goes on. 'But when I found P-O I had a feeling that you might be back.'

Madeleine sits down opposite Charlotte and looks directly into the woman's eyes without saying anything. She feels that she'd like to smile, but can't get her lips to obey. She wants to reply, but doesn't know what to say, and although she has spent years formulating her accusation speech, she is suddenly struck dumb.

Like a machine that's run down.

'The police asked about you, but I didn't say anything.' Charlotte chews each syllable several times, as if the words taste bitter and she wants to get rid of them as quickly as possible. Sometimes her mouth moves but nothing comes out, and it looks like she's spasming. She's squirming uncomfortably, picking at imaginary crumbs on the table, then takes a deep breath and lets out a heavy sigh. 'What do you really want?' she asks wearily, and Madeleine can see more than just cruelty in the soon-to-be-dead woman's eyes. Behind Charlotte's green irises she can detect a hint of genuine bemusement.

Does she not understand? Madeleine wonders.

No, that can't be possible. She was there, after all. She stood by and watched.

On the other hand, ignorance and innocence are just other names for evil, she thinks.

I hate, hate, hate . . .

She shakes her head. 'Yes, I'm back, and I think you know why.'

Charlotte's eyes flicker. 'I don't understand what you –'

'You understand well enough,' Madeleine interrupts. 'But before you do what you have to do, I want the answers to three questions.'

'What three questions?'

'First I want to know, what was I doing with you two?' Madeleine asks, but assumes she's seeking the impossible. Like asking for the meaning of life, the point of everything, or how much sorrow a human being can bear.

'That's easy,' Charlotte replies, as if she hasn't understood the true meaning of the question. 'Your grandfather, Bengt Bergman, knew P-O through their work for a foundation, and together they decided that we should look after you when your mum went a bit crazy.'

She's only scratching the surface, Madeleine thinks.

'But you were always so obstinate, and we were forced to treat you harshly,' Charlotte goes on.

Madeleine thinks about the men who came to her room at night. Remembers the pain and shame. Everything that formed a hard little ball inside her that gradually became a stone and that has since become part of her body.

She can't answer, because she doesn't understand the question, Madeleine thinks. But nor have any of the others she's killed. When she asked them, they just stared at her stupidly, as if she were talking another language.

'Who made the decision about my operation?' Madeleine asks without commenting on what Charlotte has just said.

Charlotte looks at her coldly. 'P-O and I did,' she says. 'Obviously after consulting doctors and psychologists. You used to fight and bite, and the other children were scared of you, so in the end we gave up. There really wasn't any other option.'

Madeleine remembers how they got the voice in her head to shut up in Copenhagen, but since then she hasn't been able to feel anything. Nothing at all.

After Copenhagen only ice cubes have any taste, and Madeleine realises that here too she's reached a dead end. She's never going to know why.

She has been searching for answers, and has killed those who couldn't bring themselves to share the truth that then, now and forever after is conspicuous in its utter absence.

Just one question remains.

'Did you know my real mum?'

Charlotte Silfverberg starts digging through her handbag and holds out a photograph. 'This is your crazy mother,' she snarls.

They go out on deck together. The rain has stopped and the sky is still. The Baltic night is blue with damp, and the dark sea is unsettled.

The rolling waves strike threateningly at the stern of the MS *Cinderella* with a powerful hiss, and the breaking seawater hits the hull with full force and throws up a thin cloud of mist that falls on the foredeck like gentle rain.

Charlotte is staring blankly ahead of her, and Madeleine knows that she has decided. She has made her choice.

There's nothing more to say. Words are finished, and only action remains.

She sees Charlotte go over to the railing. The woman she has never called mother bends over and takes off her boots.

She climbs up onto the railing and throws herself into the darkness without a sound.

The MS *Cinderella* forges relentlessly ahead. Doesn't even slow down.

What am I doing? Madeleine thinks, feeling pointlessness penetrate the wall of determination. Am I going to be free when they're all gone at last?

No, she realises, and her clarity is a white page being turned in a dark room.

Kronoberg – Police Headquarters

It's already late morning and Jeanette is sitting at her desk with her eyes firmly fixed on a vent in the ceiling, but she's not aware of what she's looking at because her mind is busy thinking about Sofia Zetterlund.

After the trip to Hundudden, Jeanette had gone straight home, utterly wiped out. She had called Sofia just before midnight, but hadn't got an answer, nor had Sofia replied to the two or three texts she'd sent after that.

As usual, she thinks, feeling very alone. It's time for Sofia to take the initiative. Jeanette doesn't want to be clingy, there's nothing less attractive than that, and she's not about to call again. Besides, Åke has phoned to remind her about lunch. They've agreed to meet at a restaurant down on Bergsgatan, even if she can't honestly say that she's looking forward to it.

Jeanette starts to play with a ballpoint pen as she glances at the piles of papers relating to the two dead women, Hannah Östlund and Jessica Friberg.

Her hopes of reopening the cases involving the fires at the Bergmans' house and Dürer's boat were dashed the moment Billing snorted at her and said she was a conspiracy theorist. Besides, according to him those cases had already been thoroughly investigated.

There's a knock at the door, and Åhlund looks in. 'Sorry,' he says breathlessly. 'I didn't have time to get to the hotel yesterday, so I looked in this morning instead. Which turned out to be rather fortuitous.'

'Come in.' Jeanette bites the end of the pen. 'What do you mean, fortuitous?'

He sits down opposite her. 'I spoke to the receptionist who saw Madeleine Duchamp when she checked in and out.' He laughs. 'If I'd gone yesterday evening I wouldn't have seen him. But he was on duty today.'

'And what did he say about Duchamp?'

Åhlund clears his throat. 'A woman between twenty and thirty. Travelling alone, spoke poor English. Evidently they don't keep copies of the personal details of EU citizens, but the receptionist remembered that the woman had dark hair in the picture on her driving licence.'

Dark hair, Jeanette thinks. 'So he described her hair on her driving licence. I'm more interested in what she looked like in reality.'

Åhlund clears his throat again. 'He said she was pretty, but seemed extremely shy. Wouldn't look him in the eye, just stared down at the floor, and had her face hidden under a big woolly hat.'

Great, Jeanette thinks. Not much of a description. 'Anything else? Tall, short?'

'Average height, ordinary build. Considering that he's a receptionist, I have to say he was very bad at remembering a face. But there was one thing that struck him.'

'What's that?'

'He said the woman came down several times that evening to ask for ice cubes.'

'Ice cubes?'

'Yes, he thought it was a bit odd, and I'm inclined to agree with him.'

Jeanette smiles. 'Me too. Well, our receptionist doesn't sound like he could give much information to a police artist. What do you think?'

'No, I'm afraid not. Seems like he saw too little of her. Which might be interesting in itself. I mean, she seems to have been careful to hide her appearance.'

Jeanette sighs. 'Yes, it sounds like it. I wonder why. Well, that'll have to do for now. Thanks.'

Åhlund disappears through the door again, and Jeanette decides to call Prosecutor Kenneth von Kwist.

The prosecutor sounds tired when Jeanette shares her suspicions that Viggo Dürer organised bribes for Annette Lundström and probably Ulrika Wendin. To Jeanette's surprise, he isn't as intractable as she had expected.

She sits and stares at the phone in bemusement. What's happened to von Kwist? When the phone rings her mind is somewhere else altogether. She answers absent-mindedly, and the receptionist tells her that a Kristina Wendin wants to talk to her.

Wendin? she thinks, and perks up.

The woman introduces herself as Ulrika's grandmother, and says she's worried because her granddaughter hasn't been in touch for several weeks.

'Perhaps she's gone away?' Jeanette suggests. 'Who knows, she might have saved up a bit of money and simply gone on holiday?'

The woman coughs drily. 'Ulrika hasn't got a job. Where would she get the money to go on holiday?'

'Most people who go missing usually turn up within a few days. But that's not to say we won't take this seriously. Do you have keys to Ulrika's home?'

'Yes, I do,' Kristina Wendin says.

'OK, this is what we do,' Jeanette concludes. 'I'll head out to Ulrika's apartment this afternoon with one of my colleagues. Can you meet us there with the keys?'

Should I be worried? she thinks. No, not yet. Stay rational.

Worrying at such an early stage is just a waste of energy, seeing as she knows what usually happens. At best they might find something that could give them a clue as to where Ulrika is, and at worst they'll find something to indicate that she disappeared against her will. But usually the result is somewhere in between. In other words, nothing. When the phone rings again she feels a tingle in her stomach and lets it ring a few times because she doesn't want to seem too eager.

'Jeanette Kihlberg, Stockholm police,' she says with a smile on her lips, briefly forgetting Ulrika Wendin.

'Good morning,' Sofia Zetterlund says. 'Have you got a moment?'

A moment? she thinks. I've got all the time in the world for you.

'Good morning? It's almost lunchtime.' Jeanette laughs. 'It's lovely to hear from you, but I'm snowed under with work.'

She isn't really lying. She looks at the mess on her desk. All the information they have on Hannah Östlund and Jessica Friberg is squeezed into about three hundred pages of A4 paper, a series of Polaroid pictures, a bouquet of yellow tulips and the forensics officer's photographs of the two dead dogs in the basement.

'OK, I haven't got much time myself,' Sofia says. 'Just let me speak, and you can listen while you get on with your work. After all, everyone knows that women have two brains.'

'OK. Fire away . . .'

Jeanette opens the folder marked J. FRIBERG, and can hear Sofia drawing breath, as if she is filling her lungs with air for a lengthy monologue.

'Annette Lundström was admitted into the hospital three days ago,' she says. 'Acute psychosis, brought on by her daughter Linnea's suicide. Annette found her hanged in her room in their home in Edsviken. Her nurses told me –'

'Stop,' Jeanette says, closing the file instantly. 'Tell me that again.'

'Linnea's dead. Suicide.' Sofia breathes out.

The Lundström family, wiped out by itself. Jeanette thinks of the last time she saw Annette. A piece of human wreckage. A ghost. And Linnea . . .

'Are you still there?'

Jeanette closes her eyes. Linnea's dead, she thinks. That didn't have to happen. So fucking unnecessary.

'I'm listening. Go on.'

'Annette Lundström managed to get out of Rosenlund Hospital yesterday. When I was on my way back from lunch I found her out in the street, realised she wasn't too well and took her back to my office. She told me that Viggo Dürer had paid a large sum of money to silence both her and her daughter. That's why Linnea stopped her sessions with me.'

'I was afraid of that. Well, at least we've got it confirmed.'

'It looks like an unofficial settlement,' Sofia goes on. 'I'd bet that if you were to check Annette Lundström's bank account, you'd find a few irregularities.'

'Already done,' Jeanette says. 'But we can't trace the account that the money was transferred from. I'm not surprised by what you're saying, but I'm genuinely sorry to hear about Linnea.'

And Ulrika, she thinks. What's happened to her?

Ulrika made a double impression on Jeanette, strong and brittle at the same time. For a moment she wonders if the girl is capable of killing herself. Like Linnea.

'So . . .' Jeanette goes on. 'We've already got what Linnea said in her sessions with you, and her drawings, Karl Lundström's letter and now what Annette has told you. How is she? Could she be a witness in a trial?'

Sofia snorts. 'Annette Lundström? God, no. Hardly. Not in her current state. But if the fever subsides, then . . .'

Jeanette thinks Sofia's tone sounds rather too playful considering what she's just said. 'Fever? What do you mean by that?'

'Well, psychosis is a fever of the central nervous system. It's an illness that can break out if there's a sudden change in a person's life, and in this instance both Annette's husband and daughter have died within a short space of time. It's not unusual for treatment to take ten years.'

'I see. Did she say anything else?'

'She said she wanted to go to Karl and Viggo in Polcirkeln, and build a temple. From the look in her eyes, she's already there. Far off in eternity, if you know what I mean?'

'Maybe. But that business about Polcirkeln isn't actually too far from reality.'

'No?'

'No. I'll tell you something you might not know. Polcirkeln is a real place in Lapland. Annette grew up there, and Karl was her cousin. They both belonged to a breakaway sect of Laestadians who called themselves the Psalms of the Lamb. The police received reports of sexual abuse involving the sect. And their lawyer, Viggo Dürer, lived in Vuollerim for a while as well, not far from Polcirkeln.'

'OK, now it's my turn to stop you,' Sofia says. 'Cousins? Karl and Annette were cousins?'

'Yes.'

'The Psalms of the Lamb? Sexual abuse? Was Viggo Dürer involved?'

'We don't know. It never went to court. The sect dissolved and everything was forgotten.'

Sofia falls silent, and Jeanette presses the phone closer to her ear. She can hear heavy breathing, close and distant at the same time.

'It sounds like Annette Lundström wants to return to the past,' Sofia says, in a darker voice. She laughs.

That voice again, Jeanette thinks. A shift in tone, often followed by a change in Sofia's personality.

'How's the investigation going, anyway?' Sofia asks.

Jeanette is reminded of how little they've spoken to each other recently, and how hectic the past few days have been for her.

'I probably shouldn't say any more over the phone.' It would be better to tell her everything when they meet face-to-face. 'Listen . . .' Jeanette tries. 'Maybe we could –'

'I know what you're about to say. You want to see me, and I want to see you as well. But not today. Could you come and pick me up from the practice tomorrow afternoon?'

Jeanette smiles. That was a long time coming, she thinks. 'That suits me fine. I couldn't do tonight anyway, because I want to see Johan before he goes off to London with Åke. I –'

'Look, I've got to go now,' Sofia interrupts. 'I've got a client in five minutes, and you said you were pretty busy. We can deal with the rest tomorrow. OK?'

'OK. But –' The line goes dead.

Jeanette feels empty, as if all the energy has drained out of her. If only Sofia weren't so difficult, so unpredictable, she thinks.

She feels dizzy all of a sudden, her pulse is racing, and she has to rest her hands on the top of her desk.

Take it easy now. Breathe . . . Go home. You're stressed out. Pack it in for the day.

No. First lunch with Åke, then out to Johan Printz väg in Hammarby to find out what's happened to Ulrika Wendin.

She sits down again and looks at the mess on her desk as she takes deep, slow breaths. The evidence against Hannah Östlund and Jessica Friberg. The photographs that confirm the women's guilt. Case closed and Billing happy.

But there's definitely something not quite right.

Vita Bergen – Sofia Zetterlund's Apartment

Sofia feels exhausted after her conversation with Jeanette. She's sitting at the kitchen table with a glass of white wine, even though she knows she ought to be at the practice to see a client.

Getting to know yourself isn't that different from getting to know other people, she reflects. It takes time, and there's always something you don't understand, something that slips through your fingers. Something contradictory.

It's been that way with Victoria for a long time.

But Sofia feels that she's made a lot of progress in recent days. While she still has trouble controlling Victoria, they've started to get closer to each other.

It had been Sofia who had called Jeanette, but Victoria who ended the call, and she can remember every word that was spoken. That isn't usually the case.

Victoria had lied to Jeanette, saying she was at the practice waiting for a client, and Sofia was one hundred per cent aware of the lie, and even encouraged it.

It had been their shared lie, not just Victoria's.

In fact she also remembers parts of the previous day's events at the Clarion Hotel, for the hour or so when Victoria had taken over. Obviously she remembers Carolina Glanz turning up, and what happened afterwards, but she can also remember fragments of the conversation Victoria had with the German businessman, and has a reasonably clear image of what he looked like, how he moved.

This is a positive development, and it helps her understand what might have happened with her memory lapses recently. When she wakes up in bed in the morning with muddy boots and has no idea what she's been doing during the night.

She's starting to get an idea of why Victoria has spent countless evenings and nights getting drunk and picking up men in bars. She thinks it's got something to do with liberation.

In spite of everything, she, Sofia Zetterlund, has been the leading personality for almost twenty years now, and she has a feeling that Victoria is trying to make her presence known through her misbehaviour. Trying to shake Sofia up a bit and remind her that she exists, and that her will and her feelings are just as important as Sofia's.

She drinks the last of the wine, gets up and moves her chair closer to the stove before turning on the exhaust fan and lighting a cigarette. Victoria wouldn't have done that, she thinks. She'd have smoked at the table and drunk three glasses of wine instead of one. Red, rather than white.

I am someone Victoria invented, she thinks. In other words, nothing started with me, I'm just a means of survival, a way of being normal, like everyone else. A way of suppressing the memories of abuse. But it didn't last.

When she's been at her worst, she has imagined the kitchen as an autopsy lab, and that all the bottles and jars contained formalin, glycerine and potassium acetate, substances used for embalming. Where she's previously seen surgical instruments used for dissection she now sees a perfectly ordinary toolbox half open in the cleaning cupboard, with a hacksaw blade sticking up next to the shaft of a small hammer.

The smoke swirls up towards the filter and she can make out the blades of the fan behind it. She looks up under the extractor hood and sees a faintly vibrating shimmer of shadows from the spinning fan blades. Like the prelude to an epileptic migraine.

Struer, she thinks.

There were big fans in the cellar under Viggo Dürer's house in Jutland, equipment meant to dry out pig meat, and sometimes the dull rumble down there had kept her awake all night and given her a headache. The door to the cellar had always been kept shut.

That's how it should be, she thinks. The memories should come naturally, when I'm not making an effort.

It's like holding on to a slippery bar of soap. It works if you're relaxed, but if you squeeze too tight you lose it.

Relax, she thinks. Don't try to remember, just let it happen.

Johan Printz Väg – Ulrika Wendin's Apartment

Hurtig picks Jeanette up outside the Västermalm shopping centre. She opens the door and jumps into the passenger seat.

Hurtig turns into St Eriksgatan. 'So it was Ulrika Wendin's grandmother who called you?'

'Yes. She's been trying to get hold of Ulrika, without any luck,' Jeanette says. 'She'll be waiting for us outside the apartment with the keys.'

Something's happened to the girl, she thinks. Take it easy. Don't assume the worst until we know more. Ulrika might simply have met a guy, fallen in love and spent a few days in bed with him.

'How did lunch go?' Hurtig asks.

To start with, Åke had wanted to talk about Johan and how he was living now.

He had looked thinner than she remembered, he'd let his cropped hair grow out, and she reluctantly had to admit to herself that she missed him. Maybe you became blind to each other over time? Start to see only the problems rather than the things you once liked?

But then Åke went on to boast about his success and how much having Alexandra Kowalska as his agent had meant for him.

After that he took out the divorce forms.

Already signed, the same signature he used on his paintings, and she reacted with a short but intense feeling of disappointment.

Not because this great step was on the verge of being taken, but because he was the one taking the initiative. Because he got there first.

She was quite relieved when lunch was over and they went their separate ways.

When she'd left Åke she had called Johan and they'd agreed to have an evening in front of the television watching films and football at home in Enskede. A match on television could hardly compete with seeing a

Premier League derby live, but Johan had actually sounded happy when she made the suggestion. She glances at her watch. She really mustn't make him wait for her this time.

'You seem a bit distracted,' Hurtig says. 'I asked how lunch was.'

Jeanette is woken from her thoughts. 'Oh, we mainly talked about practical matters. About the divorce and so on.'

They're driving past the Thorildsplan station and Jeanette spares a thought for the first dead boy. That feels so long ago. As if years have passed since the mummified corpse was found in the bushes just twenty metres away from them.

'By the way . . .' Jeanette says as they pull out onto the Essinge motorway, heading south. 'I've got some sad news for you. Linnea Lundström is dead. Suicide. She hanged herself at home.'

They say nothing more during the drive, and as they pull into the car park outside Ulrika Wendin's apartment Hurtig breaks the silence. 'My sister hanged herself as well. Ten years ago. She was only nineteen.'

Jeanette doesn't know what to say. What is there to say?

'I . . .' She's reminded once again of how little she knows about her colleague.

'It's OK,' he says, and his forced smile is gone now. 'It's shit, but you learn to live with it. We did what we could. It's been worse for Mum and Dad.'

'I . . . I'm really sorry. I had no idea. Do you want to talk about it?'

He shakes his head. 'To be honest . . . no.'

She nods. 'OK. But just say if you do. I'm here.'

A short, slim woman is standing smoking beside the door, looking around as if she's waiting for someone.

They walk up to the waiting woman, who, quite rightly, turns out to be Ulrika Wendin's grandmother. She's got bleached blonde hair and introduces herself as Kickan.

They go through the front door and up the stairs. Outside the door to the apartment the woman pulls out a key ring and Jeanette remembers the last time she was here.

She had talked to Ulrika about the rape Karl Lundström subjected her to, and the memory fills her with sadness. If there's any kind of poetic justice, things will turn out OK for the girl in the end. But Jeanette has her doubts.

Kickan Wendin puts the key in the lock, turns it twice to the left and opens the door.

In Hannah Östlund's home in Fagerstrand the stench had come from two dead dogs.

The smell here is, if possible, even worse.

'What's happened?' Kickan Wendin looks anxiously at Hurtig, then Jeanette, and makes a move to step inside the hall, but Jeanette stops her.

'It's probably best if we wait outside,' she says as she gestures to Hurtig to go in and take a look around.

The woman looks shaken. 'But what's that terrible smell?'

'We don't know yet,' Jeanette says as she watches Hurtig go through the apartment. A minute later he comes back out to them.

'Empty,' he says, holding out his hands. 'Ulrika isn't here, and the smell is just rubbish. Old prawn shells.'

Jeanette breathes out. Only prawn shells, she thinks, then puts her arm on the woman's shoulder and turns her round. 'Let's go outside for a chat. Follow me.'

'I'll take another look around,' Hurtig says, and Jeanette nods in response.

Once they're outside Jeanette suggests going to sit in the car. 'There's a Thermos of coffee, if you'd like some.'

Kickan shakes her head. 'My break's almost over, and I have to get back to work.'

They sit down on a bench and Jeanette asks her about Ulrika, but it turns out that the woman doesn't have any real insight into her granddaughter's life. She doesn't actually know anything of significance, and from the little she does say Jeanette concludes that she doesn't even know that Ulrika was raped.

As Kickan Wendin turns and starts to walk away, Jeanette gets into the driver's seat, lights a cigarette and waits for Hurtig to come out.

'Traces of blood in the hall.' Hurtig hits the roof of the car with his hand and Jeanette jumps.

'Blood?'

'Yes, so I thought it best to call Ivo.'

'Did you check that it was really blood? Was there much?'

'Just a few spots. Dried stains on the floor just inside the door, but it's definitely blood.'

Klara Sjö – Public Prosecution Authority

'Von Kwist,' the prosecutor says warily when Jeanette Kihlberg calls him for a second time in just a few hours. The pressure at the top of his stomach gets worse as she tells him that Ulrika Wendin is believed to have gone missing, and when he hangs up he feels sick.

Fucking hell, he thinks, getting up from his desk and going over to the drinks cabinet.

While the ice machine is rattling he gets out a bottle of smoky malt whisky and pours himself a large glass.

If Prosecutor Kenneth von Kwist had been a creative person, his swearing would have been more varied than bloody, fucking and hell. But he isn't that sort of person. 'Fucking hell,' he repeats, therefore, and downs the whisky in one gulp.

The whisky is hardly going to help his stomach ulcer, but down it goes, and he feels the alcohol hit the acid reflux somewhere around chest height.

When Detective Superintendent Jeanette Kihlberg called him that morning, in the heat of the moment he thought it best to do as she asked. Now, after the second conversation, he realises that in a worst-case scenario, Ulrika Wendin's life might be in danger, and he quietly admits to himself that even though he can hardly be accused of being a particularly conscientious person, he does have his limits.

Goddamn kid, he thinks. You should have taken the money and run. And kept quiet.

Now things might come to a very bad conclusion.

The prosecutor shudders and remembers something that happened about fifteen years before, when he was invited to visit the former police commissioner Gert Berglind's summer cottage out in the archipelago, on Möja.

Viggo Dürer had been there with another man, a Ukrainian who had some sort of murky connection to the lawyer, and who couldn't speak a word of Swedish.

They had sat in the kitchen, and Dürer and Berglind had fallen out about something. Berglind had become noisy and upset, while Dürer sat there without speaking for a long time, before turning to the Ukrainian and saying something quietly in Russian. While Berglind had carried on ranting angrily, the Ukrainian had left the kitchen and gone to the hutch where the police chief kept his prizewinning rabbits.

Through the open kitchen window they had heard two whimpering squeaks, and a few minutes later the Ukrainian had come in with two freshly skinned breeding rabbits worth about ten thousand kronor each. The commissioner had turned white as a sheet and quietly asked them to leave.

At the time, Kenneth von Kwist had assumed that Berglind was upset at the prize money he'd miss out on, or possibly that he was sad about the rabbits, but now he realises that the police chief had been terrified, and well aware of what sort of person Viggo Dürer was.

He shuts his eyes and prays that he hasn't realised it too late.

The smoky whisky makes him think of Viggo Dürer's smell. As soon as he came into a room you noticed it. Was it fried garlic that he smelled of?

No, the prosecutor thinks. More like gunpowder or sulphur. That seems like a contradiction, because he knows that Dürer also had the ability to blend in, to disappear into a crowd somehow.

If one were inclined to show any respect to Kenneth von Kwist, it would be tempting to say that contradictions weren't his strong point. If one were inclined to be rather less generous, and thus closer to the truth, one might say that his view of contradictions was that they simply didn't exist. There is just right or wrong, and nothing in between, which is a very bad quality in a prosecutor.

Yet now he admits that Viggo Dürer was a contradictory person.

Capable of being extremely dangerous, but also a weakling who moaned about heart problems, like he had the last time they met, shortly before he died. And now he's left this bloody mess behind, von Kwist thinks, and it's landed right in my lap.

'Lawyer and pig farmer,' he mutters into his whisky glass. 'That doesn't make any sense.'

Vita Bergen – Sofia Zetterlund's Apartment

The Helper, Solace Manuti, had borne Victoria's daughter, Madeleine, in her round, swollen belly, and it was Solace who suffered the cramps, sickness, swollen legs and aching back. That had been her final task before Victoria forgot her.

Sofia looks at the drawings she has spread out on the table in the living room. They all show a naked child with a fetish mask covering her face. The same girl, the same skinny legs and round stomach. The same Helper. On the table next to the drawings is a photograph of a child holding a Kalashnikov. Unsocial mate. A child soldier.

Sofia thinks of the ritual circumcisions that have left so many boys in Sierra Leone sterile. Out in the countryside the boys would wear the dried scraps of skin on necklaces to prove that they belonged to God, and to protect against evil spirits, but in the hospitals in the cities the foreskins were discarded with the rest of the hospital's rubbish, among plastic pipettes and disposable syringes, and taken out to the dumps in the suburbs. A lot of boys ended up sterile after being circumcised, but in the cities there was less chance of infection.

Lasse's sterilisation had been as free from risk as it was voluntary. Vasectomy isn't a ritual, even though it ought to be, nor is there anything ritualistic about an abortion or, as she herself once did, handing your baby over to strangers. Her thoughts move on to Madeleine. Does she hate me? Was she the one who killed Fredrika and P-O? And, if she was, am I next?

No, she thinks. According to Jeanette, it wasn't just one person. She had mentioned 'the people' who were the murderers, not 'the person'.

She puts the drawings of Solace aside and realises that she's soon going to have to burn all her notes and newspaper cuttings, rip out the walls of the concealed room and get rid of everything inside it.

She has to become clean, free from her background. The way it looks at the moment, she can hardly move at home without being reminded of the lies that have helped her stay alive.

She needs to learn to remember properly. Not look for answers in static documents.

Let Victoria act, she thinks. But try not to disappear.

If you squeeze the bar of soap too tight you lose it.

Don't try to remember, just let it happen.

Victoria gets a notepad from her study and a bottle of wine out of the glass-fronted cabinet, a French Merlot, but can't find the corkscrew and has to push the cork in with her thumb. Tomorrow Sofia is going to see Jeanette, and she needs to be properly rested. So she has to drink, and red wine is better for sleep than white.

Tonight Victoria is going to concentrate on her daughter, writing down all her thoughts and trying to get to know her. Tomorrow Sofia will get to work on the perpetrator profile again.

But first, Madeleine.

'Grew up with Charlotte and P-O Silfverberg,' she writes. 'With all that that entailed.' Victoria thinks for a while before adding: 'Probably abused. They were the same sort of people as Bengt.' She takes a sip of wine. Its taste warms her and the acidity makes her tongue prickle.

'Madeleine had a special relationship with Viggo Dürer,' she goes on to write, without really knowing why. But when she thinks about it she realises what she meant. Viggo was the sort of person who laid claim to people, and patterns like that always recur.

He did it with both Annette and Linnea Lundström, Victoria thinks, and he tried to do it with me.

'The worst thing about Viggo is his hands,' she writes. 'Not his genitals.'

In fact she can't actually remember ever seeing Viggo naked, and he was only violent occasionally, and then only with his hands. He didn't hit, but scratched and squeezed. He rarely cut his nails and she can still recall the pain of them digging into her arms.

His assaults were like dry masturbation.

'Madeleine hated Viggo,' she goes on, and now she no longer needs to think, the associations come unforced, and her pen scratches quickly across the paper. 'No matter what sort of adult Madeleine has become, she hates her foster-father, and she hates Viggo. As a child she had no name for her feelings, but she has always hated. As far back as she can remember.'

Victoria is using her own thoughts as a starting point, and transferring them to her daughter. She doesn't change the text even when she suspects that she's getting ahead of herself; she can make changes later.

'There are several possible versions of Madeleine as an adult. Perhaps she is quiet and cowed and lives a reclusive life. Maybe she's married to one of her father's friends in the sect, maybe she silently puts up with continued abuse. Or possibly another Madeleine has got help from someone on the outside and has made a break from her family and fled abroad. If she's strong she may have moved on, but it's likely that her whole life will be tainted by the abuse and it will be hard for her to have a normal relationship with a partner. Yet another Madeleine could be driven by forces like hate and revenge, and she has spent her whole life trying to find different ways to either suppress or find an outlet for these feelings. This Madeleine lives a reclusive life at times, but can never forget what she suffered. She is a proactive person, who lacks –'

She stops. This is Sofia writing, not her, and she's writing about Victoria. She doesn't usually express herself this clearly. She's even forgotten the wine; it looks like she's hardly touched it.

'She is a proactive person who lacks any driving forces in life apart from hate and revenge,' Sofia concludes. 'Her only chance to move on is to free herself from these driving forces. And there are no easy solutions to that problem.'

Sofia puts the pen and notepad down on the table.

She realises that Madeleine is going to come and see her, sooner or later.

She also realises what's starting to happen between her and Victoria.

Sofia won't resist any longer.

Vasastan – Hurtig's Apartment

The building Jens Hurtig lives in was built in the late 1800s, and belongs to the part of Norrmalm still known unofficially as Siberia, a name that comes from the fact that it used to be regarded as distant, and that moving from central Stockholm to its small workers' housing was regarded as a form of exile. Now it is part of the city centre, and the small two-room apartment Jens Hurtig has been renting for the past two months isn't exactly a gulag, even if the lack of a lift leaves something to be desired. Particularly when he has something to carry. Like now, a clinking bag of bottles in each hand.

He unlocks the door and is confronted by the usual mountain of advertising leaflets and free papers, even though he's put a sign up over the letter box, politely asking not to receive them. But he can't help feeling for the poor bastards who trudge around these buildings with heavy bundles of leaflets from the supermarkets, and on the sixth floor they are rejected by signs on every door.

He puts the bags down in the hall, and five minutes later he's sitting in front of the television in the living room with a beer in his hand.

TV3 is showing old repeats of *The Simpsons*. He's seen this episode so many times that he knows the lines by heart, and reluctantly admits to himself that the programme usually makes him feel safe. He still laughs in the same places as before, but today his laughter feels flat. It has no firm foundation.

When Jeanette told him about Linnea Lindström's suicide, all the old feelings washed over him again – his memories of his sister still haven't left him. They never will.

It was the image of a young girl lying on a slab in the mortuary that sent him straight off to buy beer after work, and it's the same image that is now making him lose interest in watching the antics of yellow cartoon characters on television.

The last time he saw his sister she had been lying on her back with her hands clasped over her stomach. She had looked determined, her lips had been almost black, and one side of her face and neck was bruised blue from the noose. Her skin had felt dry and cool, and her body had given the impression of being very heavy, even though she was so small and thin.

He reaches for the remote and switches the television off. Now the screen is showing only his own reflection, legs crossed in the armchair, a bottle of beer in his hand.

He feels lonely.

How lonely must she have felt?

No one had understood her. Not him, not their parents and not the psychiatrists, whose efforts had largely consisted of group therapy and trial medication. What was going on inside her remained out of reach to all of them, the hole she had fallen into had been too deep, too dark, and in the end she hadn't been able to bear the loneliness, of being shut up inside herself.

At the time there hadn't been any scapegoats, no one to blame except the depression itself. Today he knows that that isn't true.

Society itself was and is responsible. The world outside was too hard for her. It promised her everything, but without actually offering her anything at all. Nor was it able to help her when she became ill. Then, as now, it had been politically dysfunctional. The strong survive, and the weak have to manage on their own. She had persuaded herself that she was weak, and she had gone under.

If he had understood that then, perhaps he could have helped her.

If she had had cancer, all the resources of the health service would have been thrown at her, but instead she had been subjected to a patchwork of treatment in which each of the various therapists hadn't known what the others were doing. He's convinced that her medication only exacerbated her illness.

But that wasn't the real problem.

Hurtig knows that his sister's great dream had been to be a musician or a singer, and she had had the support of her family. But the signals sent out by society were that that wasn't a valid career choice. Nothing worth setting your sights on.

Instead of standing on a stage somewhere she had studied economics, the sort of thing you were supposed to study if you were clever, and it had ended with her hanging herself in her student room.

Simply because all the rest of us made her believe that her dreams weren't worth following, he thinks.

Gamla Enskede – Kihlberg House

It's quarter to nine when the football match kicks off, and they haven't had time to watch the film she's rented. Who cares if it's a late night? she thinks. The evening has been such a success that she doesn't want to spoil it by nagging at Johan about bedtime.

She glances at him, scarcely visible where he's lying on the sofa behind the crisp packets, soft drinks and the takeaway cartons from one of the countless Thai restaurants on Södermalm. The amount he can eat is quite incredible, she thinks, particularly when you consider that he never used to like Thai food. But on the other hand he's growing so fast you can almost hear it, and his tastes and preferences are changing so quickly she's having trouble keeping up.

As far as his taste in music is concerned, it started with hip hop, then slid unnoticed into Swedish punk, and for a while came dangerously close to hardcore skinhead on the fringes of the far right, before one day back in the spring she discovered him listening to David Bowie.

She smiles at the memory. The strains of 'Space Oddity' had confronted her when she got home from work, and at first she had trouble coming to terms with the fact that her son liked the same music she had listened to when she was his age.

But this evening is all about football, and his preferences in that are nowhere near as changeable.

He's always supported the Spanish team, which is busy making its opponents look like temporary visitors at the top table. He has a favourite team in each of the top leagues, and they've always stayed the same, even if they could obviously never compete with his beloved Hammarby. Those stripes never wash out, she thinks with a smile.

The first goal in the televised match doesn't take long. Johan's team is celebrating, and he's not slow to join in with the players, jumping up from the sofa. 'Yes! Did you see that?' His face is one big smile, and he leans towards her with his hand raised for a high five, which she returns, somewhat surprised. 'God, that was good!'

'That was seriously good,' she agrees. 'I hardly had time to see it!'

After a short discussion of the goal and the passing play that preceded it, they fall into a silence that Jeanette feels is similar to what she and Hurtig often share, a silence that makes her feel relaxed. While she's trying to find a way that doesn't sound too stupid and motherly to say how nice she thinks the evening has been, he pre-empts her.

'Shit, Mum. Nice that we don't have to talk the whole time.'

She feels warm all over. She's not even bothered about him swearing, but then she's never particularly aware of her own language. Åke was often quick to point that out.

'It's more fun watching football with you than Dad,' he goes on. 'He always has to talk the whole time, and he moans at the referees even when they're right.'

She can't help laughing. 'Yep, I have to agree with you there. Sometimes I can't help wondering if he thinks the matches are all about him.'

Maybe that was a bit mean towards Åke, she thinks. True, though. But she takes deep satisfaction from what Johan has just said, and she knows why. She wonders if he's noticed that she and Åke seem to have slipped into a sort of competition. A parental contest to see who deserves Johan's loyalty most. She presumes that she's leading at the moment by a goal or two, maybe.

'Poor Dad,' Johan says after a while. 'Alex isn't very nice to him.'

Three–nil, Jeanette thinks in an attack of schadenfreude that's immediately replaced by a lump in her stomach.

'Oh? How do you mean?'

He squirms. 'Oh, I don't know . . . She talks about money all the time and he doesn't understand, just nods and signs everything without reading it. She acts like he works for her rather than the other way round, which is how it's supposed to be, isn't it?'

'Do you like spending time with them?' Jeanette regrets the question as soon as she asks it. She doesn't want to fall back into the role of prying mother, but Johan doesn't seem bothered.

'With Dad. Not with Alex.'

At half-time in the match he clears the table and pours what's left of the crisps into a bowl. She's noticed that he's started to leave the lid down on the toilet these days. Little gestures that show he wants to make a good impression. Be a good son.

Little things, she thinks. God, how I love you, little Johan, even if you're not that little any more.

'Er, I . . .' He's just sat down again and has a shy smile on his face.

'Yes?'

He fumbles in his pocket and pulls out his little black leather wallet with the team logo on it and looks through the note compartment until he finds what he's looking for.

A small photograph, passport size. He takes a quick look at it, then pushes it across to her.

It's a picture of a pretty girl with dark, messy hair, trying her best to look hard.

Jeanette gives Johan a quizzical look, and when she sees the twinkle in his eyes she realises that the girl in the photograph has a similar picture of him.

Observatory Hill

Sofia Zetterlund walks into the large, bright rotunda of the Stockholm City Library, slows down and listens to the silence. It's early in the morning, and the library is almost empty. Just a few people walking, heads tilted, along the shelves that line the circular walls of the three-storey central hall.

The collection houses almost seven hundred thousand books, and in here she won't be distracted by anyone. Everyone is immersed in their own business. All you can hear is slow footsteps, the rustle of paper and, every now and then, the sound of a book being quietly closed. Sofia looks up and begins to count shelves, sections, books with brown spines, red, green, grey and black. She glances down at the floor, shaking off the compulsive thoughts, and tries to focus on the reason she's here.

The biographies are what interest her most. And an older work on sadism and sexuality. She goes over to one of the catalogue terminals to see if the books are available, discovers that they are, and walks up to an information desk.

The librarian is a middle-aged woman with her hair and shoulders covered by a hijab, and her dark complexion makes Sofia assume she's from the Middle East.

The woman looks familiar.

'How can I help you?' Her voice is cool and soft, and Sofia can only detect a faint trace of an accent that sounds like a Norrland dialect. Persian, perhaps, or Arabic?

'I was wondering if you could help me find Richard Lourie's book about Andrei Chikatilo, and *Psychopathia Sexualis* by Krafft-Ebing?'

When the woman begins typing the titles without a word, Sofia notices that one of her eyes is brown while the other is pale green. She's probably partially blind. Possibly pigment damage after an accident. A violent past. Someone might have beaten her.

'Your parking permit has expired,' the woman says.

Sofia jerks. The woman is talking, but her lips aren't moving, her head is still bowed, and those strange eyes are still concentrating on the screen, not her.

It's time to get it renewed. And you ought to park in the garage instead. The car won't like standing out of doors this long.

Parking permit? She can't remember when she last used her car, or even thought about it, still less where it's actually parked.

'Sorry, are you OK?' The woman is looking up at her. The pupil of her injured, pale green eye is much smaller than the healthy one. Sofia doesn't know which eye to focus on.

'I . . . It's just a headache.'

All of a sudden she's certain she's never seen the woman before.

The librarian's smile looks worried. 'Would you like to sit down? I could get you a glass of water and an aspirin . . .'

Sofia takes a deep breath. 'Nothing to worry about. Have you found the books?'

The woman nods and stands up. 'Come with me, I'll show you where they are.'

As she follows in the librarian's quiet footsteps she thinks about her own healing process. Is this how it works? Piece by piece, the ghosts in her brain are being revealed.

Everything becomes a game of identities, which includes strangers as well. Her own ego is so narcissistic that she thinks she knows every single person, and that they know her. She herself is at the centre of the world, and her ego is still that of a child.

This is how Victoria Bergman's ego feels, and it's a significant insight.

She now realises that the woman with her hair in a tight bun, the one she's seen walking down the street several times, was just a projection of her own ego.

She was seeing her own mother, Birgitta Bergman. Obviously one of her suppressed mental ghosts.

Once she's found the books she sits down at one of the desks and takes out the notebook she had been writing in the previous evening. Twenty pages of thoughts about her daughter, and she makes up her mind to spend an hour or two in the library carrying on the work of getting to know Madeleine before she makes a start on Lourie and Krafft-Ebing.

She's feeling brittle, and she knows she has to make the most of that state.

Central Station

Jeanette has pushed the start of her day back a couple of hours so she can drive Johan to school, and is going to be even later because her old Audi, for the umpteenth time, decides to break down at Gullmarsplan. She pulls over to the side of the road and can't even be bothered to get angry before calling for a tow truck. She makes up her mind that the Audi, despite Åhlund's best efforts, will have to go to its final resting place at the scrapyard out in Huddinge.

She knows she needs a car, and that the state of her finances won't let her buy a new one. But she's too proud to ask Åke for money.

As she heads down into the metro she thinks about Johan. Saying goodbye to him hadn't been as difficult as she had expected. For the first time in ages they separated without her being left with a sense that there was a lot of unfinished business between them.

Just as she gets on the train, her mobile rings. She can see it's Hurtig and suddenly remembers what he told her about his sister the previous day. So fucking tragic. That's pretty much all there is to say.

She settles into a window seat at the end of the carriage before answering.

'I've got two things to tell you,' he begins. 'They're both pretty alarming.'

She can hear how wound up he sounds. 'Go on.'

'At roughly the same time we were out at Dürer's at Hundudden, Charlotte Silfverberg committed suicide.'

Jeanette feels as if she's just gone deaf. 'What did you say?'

'The Finland ferry, MS *Cinderella*, the night before last. According to a number of witnesses, Charlotte Silfverberg was alone on deck. She climbed up onto the railing and jumped. The witnesses didn't have time to intervene, but they alerted the coastguard.'

As the speakers in the carriage announce that the next stop is T-Centralen, Jeanette tries to absorb the news. No, she thinks. Not another suicide. 'A number of witnesses, did you say?'

'Yes. No doubt at all. The coastguard found the body this morning.'

A clear case of suicide, then? First Linnea Lundström, and now this. Another family intent on wiping itself out.

Yet she can't help feeling dubious.

'Get someone to call the shipping company to ask for the passenger list,' she says as the train stops and she stands up.

'Passenger list?' Hurtig sounds surprised. 'What for? Like I said –'

'Suicide, I know. But do you think Charlotte Silfverberg seemed the type to take her own life?' She gets out onto the platform and continues towards the stairs down to the Blue Line. 'When we last saw her she wanted to get away for a while, have a few glasses of red wine, and see her hero, Lasse Hallström. What if something happened on the ferry that made Charlotte Silfverberg make that fatal choice?'

'I don't know,' Hurtig says wearily. 'But there are more than ten witnesses on the ship who all confirm what happened.'

She stops on the first step and leans against the handrail. 'Sorry, maybe I didn't express myself very clearly.' OK, she thinks, stay calm. Maybe I'm getting carried away. 'You're probably right. We'll hold back on the shipping company. You said you had another piece of news?'

She listens to what Hurtig has to say, and soon she's jogging down the steps through the crowd.

What he's just told her means they're going to have to put everything else to one side.

An Iwan Lowynsky from the Ukrainian security police in Kiev, from their department for international crime, is trying to get hold of her regarding the case of a missing person.

The dossier about the dead immigrant boys that Jeanette sent to Interpol six months ago has finally done some good. A DNA match.

Mariaberget – Södermalm

Sofia Zetterlund has decided to walk all the way to work, and at Slussen she opts for the longer route, up to the top of Mariaberget and past the old lift.

Her bag of books is heavy and rubs against her hip as she walks across the cobblestones of Tavastgatan, and at the junction with Bellmansgatan she decides to stop off in the Bishop's Arms and study the books over a late lunch.

She orders that day's special, and finds a seat in a corner. While she waits for the food she starts looking through the book about the Russian serial killer Andrei Chikatilo, but is distracted by the erroneous title of the Swedish edition, *The Mass Murderer*. 'Mass murderer' means Stalin or Hitler. They killed people not because of some primitive instinct, but for ideological reasons, and developed means of extermination on an industrial scale. Chikatilo murdered one person at a time, in a long, bestial series.

She discovers that every other chapter is about the policeman who eventually solved the case, which ran to more than fifty murders, and decides to skip those. She wants to know how Chikatilo functioned, not read about police work. To her disappointment she soon finds that the book mostly contains descriptions of the murders, and fantastical speculation about what the murderer might have been thinking. Any more profound analysis of his psyche is entirely absent.

Even so, she finds a number of the ideas interesting, but resists the temptation to tear the pages out, and instead turns down the corners of pages she's thinking of using when she puts her ideas together. The person who couldn't control her impulses and had no qualms about defacing books was Victoria. Sofia is sensible and controlled, she reflects, as she feels how much her shoes are chafing. Everything has its price.

When the waiter brings her food she orders a beer. She eats a few mouthfuls but realises she isn't hungry just as a group of Germans comes into the pub. They sit down at the next table, and one of the women turns to Sofia. '*Sie müssen sehr stolz auf ihn sein?*'

'*Ja, sehr stolz*,' Sofia replies, without having any idea what the woman means.

She pushes her plate away and goes back to the book about Andrei Chikatilo. After reading for a while she begins to discern a pattern that she'd like to discuss with Jeanette. She makes a few notes in the margin and gets her mobile out. Jeanette answers almost instantly.

There isn't really anything new to say, Sofia just wants reassurance that their meeting is still on, and as soon as Sofia hears Jeanette's voice she's reminded of the fact that she misses her.

Jeanette hasn't forgotten that they're going to meet, but seems stressed. Sofia assumes Jeanette's got a lot of work to do and keeps it brief. 'Well, see you at my office,' she says. 'Then we can go to my favourite bar and have a couple of beers and talk shop for an hour or so. Then when we're done with that we can get a taxi back to your place. OK?'

Jeanette laughs. 'And talk about anything apart from work. Sounds good. Big hug.'

Not back to my place, Sofia thinks. The apartment is still festooned with all of Victoria's notes, newspaper articles and scraps of paper.

She needs to take care of that soon. Burn the whole lot.

She puts the biography of Chikatilo aside and gets out the old overview of sadism and sexuality. It's in surprisingly good condition, which is probably due to the fact that it doesn't get taken out very often, and she soon realises why. *Psychopathia Sexualis* is written in old-fashioned, long-winded English that's very difficult to understand. After half an hour's reading she decides that the book is entirely useless in most respects, not just because she can't understand it all, but because its conclusions are obsolete. She herself saw through Freud at the age of seventeen, and ever since then has been sceptical about seeing things in symbolic terms, and about cast-iron theories. She has dismissed all writing about women's feelings and desires because it has, without exception, been carried out by men. A position that she has never had any reason to reconsider.

On the other hand, she thinks that Freud's opinions about libido, life instinct and sexual desire are still relevant and interesting. That the libido, alongside aggression, is the strongest urge of humankind.

Attraction, longing, desire and lust, in combination with violence.

Sofia closes the book, gets up and goes over to the bar to pay. She hands the bartender a couple of notes. 'Who are they?' she asks, nodding towards the group of Germans.

'The Germans?' The bartender laughs. 'They're on a pilgrimage, walking in the Great Man's footsteps. They're crazy for anecdotes about him.'

'The Great Man?'

'Yes. Stieg Larsson, you know?' The bartender smiles and hands over her change.

As she leaves the Bishop's Arms she takes out her notepad again. She thinks about Madeleine, and writes a few lines as she walks over the cobbles.

Her writing is almost illegible.

'Madeleine is her mother's sister, and her father is also her grandfather, and she has the right to hate them more than anyone. If I didn't know that I set fire to the house in Värmdö myself, I'd be inclined to believe that it was Madeleine.'

Kronoberg – Police Headquarters

Jens Hurtig is sitting in a chair on the other side of Jeanette's desk, following her conversation with the Ukrainian police officer Iwan Lowynsky on speakerphone with growing interest.

Schwarz and Åhlund are listening from the doorway.

'Where did he disappear?' Jeanette repeats the question because she didn't catch the name of the metro station in Kiev where the boy used to hang out, and the place where he was last seen.

'Syrets. Syrets station. Near Babi Yar. Never mind. I send you details.'

'Funny.' Schwarz grins. 'Went missing from a metro station in one part of the world, found at another. In a slightly worse condition, of course.'

Jeanette's glare makes Schwarz shut up instantly, and he realises it's time to retreat.

Hurtig wonders how the hell Schwarz ever got his badge.

'You said there were two people missing from the Syrets station. Two boys, both child prostitutes. Brothers. Itkul and Karakul Zumbayev. Is that correct?'

'Correct,' Lowynsky replies.

A long silence. Hurtig guesses that Jeanette is waiting for a more explicit answer.

'Karakul is still missing?' she tries instead.

'Yes,' Lowynsky says in reply.

'And their connections to . . . Sorry, I didn't get this down right, Kyso –'

'Kyzylorda Oblast. Parents are gypsies from region in south Kazakhstan. Brothers born in Romanky outside Kiev. Get it?'

'Yes . . .' Hurtig sees Jeanette frowning as she makes notes.

'So,' Lowynsky says, and Hurtig thinks it sounds like he's yawning. 'Duty calls. Keep in contact?'

'Of course. Thank you.'

'You will have our identikit in two hours. Thank you, Miss Killberg.'

There's a crackle on the speakerphone as Iwan Lowynsky hangs up.

'Killberg.' Hurtig smiles. 'If he thinks that's how your name is pronounced, he must think it pretty funny considering what your job is.'

Jeanette doesn't seem to notice the joke, or else her mind is busy elsewhere. When she's this focused it can be hard to reach her, he thinks, and looks at the clock. Long past lunchtime. 'What do you say? Shall we go out and get some food?'

She shakes her head. 'No, I can't eat now. But I'd like a walk.'

Five minutes later they're walking down Bergsgatan towards Kungsholmen Church. Hurtig is shivering, and as he rubs his hands together to get the circulation going he feels old. His body has started to feel the cold in a way it's never done before, and he knows that the only thing that helps is a really hot shower. But that will have to wait.

Beside the door of the kebab shop stands an old man playing well-known tunes on an untuned violin, and Hurtig is fascinated by how he can manage to keep his fingers warm in the cold. It doesn't sound any good, but he puts a twenty-krona note in the little paper cup by the man's feet.

Hurtig goes in and orders a large lamb kebab. 'Seeing as I can't think on an empty stomach, unlike you, you can tell me how you believe we ought to proceed.' He opens the bag, pulls out the foil-wrapped bundle and starts to bite into the pitta bread.

'There's one thing that struck me,' Jeanette begins. 'And it was actually Schwarz's moronic comment that made me realise it.'

'OK, I'm being slow.'

'The boy vanished from and was found at metro stations. Coincidence, do you think?'

'To be honest, I don't know.'

'How about this?' she goes on. 'The same person who seized the boy in Kiev also dumped him in Stockholm. And I think that person is a seasoned traveller in Eastern Europe, or maybe comes from there. Knows the area. Knows what he's doing.'

'How can you be so sure that –'

'I'm not. I just said I think, not that I know.'

Hurtig bites into the meat. 'Lowynsky said two gypsy brothers went missing at the same time,' he says between mouthfuls. 'One is our boy, and the other is still missing. What do you think about that, then?'

'I think the other boy is dead too, and is lying somewhere in Stockholm waiting to be found.'

'You're probably right,' he concedes. 'What about the identikit? Do you think we can expect anything from that?'

She shrugs her shoulders. 'Probably not too much, considering that it was put together from the evidence of one single witness who may have seen the person who abducted the boys. And that witness is an eight-year-old girl who's blind in one eye and couldn't say how old the man might be. You remember what Lowynsky said? In one interview the girl said he was forty, in another that he was really old, but of course we both know you can hardly ever rely on a child's estimate of someone's age.'

He drops the remainder of the kebab in a rubbish bin before they go back inside police headquarters, and opens the bag of chips as they enter the lift. Jeanette's mobile rings, and her face breaks into a smile.

'Hi. How are you getting on?'

Hurtig guesses that it's Sofia Zetterlund. He looks at Jeanette's face as she talks. Yep, she's definitely in love, he thinks.

She presses the lift button repeatedly, as if that might make it skip a few floors and get up quicker.

'Of course. That's sounds great. My car's broken down, so I'll get the metro and pick you up, then we'll take it as it comes.'

Hurtig assumes they're going out for a meal, then back to Jeanette's in Gamla Enskede, where they can have the whole house to themselves now that Johan is with Åke.

And it's Friday night as well, so they can have a drink or two.

'And talk about anything apart from work,' Jeanette says, laughing. 'Sounds good. Big hug.'

Hurtig wolfs down the chips as the lift pings and the doors slide open. Jeanette puts her phone back in her jacket pocket and looks at him thoughtfully. 'I think I might be in a relationship with Sofia,' she says, to his surprise.

Mariatorget – Sofia Zetterlund's Office

Sofia has been sitting at her desk for more than two hours, adding to her reading about Andrei Chikatilo with research both on the Internet and in the books she's got in her office. She's starting to compile a fair bit of material that might be of interest to Jeanette.

Over a period of some ten years Chikatilo killed more than fifty people in an area around the eastern Black Sea, in southern Ukraine and Russia. He killed boys and girls, and usually castrated the boys, almost without exception. On several occasions he ate part of his victims.

She looks down at her notes.

EXTREME PREDATORY BEHAVIOUR, CANNIBALISM, CASTRATION, NEED TO BE SEEN.

Why didn't he conceal his victims better? she wonders, thinking about both Chikatilo and the murderer in Stockholm. That's actually a question that has never been answered.

Sofia believes that the murderer wants to talk about his shame. It might sound contradictory, but someone driven by such peculiar sexual urges probably became aware very early in life that he was different, a perverse individual. Revealing his shame in public isn't just a show of regret, it's a way of seeking contact. She also has an idea about the castrations that she hopes to be able to explain to Jeanette.

She looks at the clock on the computer screen. In just under an hour, she thinks. She's aware that it might be difficult to persuade Jeanette that her conclusions fit, because they feel far too morbid to accept.

When Chikatilo killed women, he ate their wombs. In the cases of the immigrant boys, the police hadn't found any evidence of cannibalism, but the bodies had been missing their genitals. Her theory isn't fully formulated yet, and she needs to think it through a couple more times before embarking on a discussion with Jeanette that could spoil the whole evening.

What she's read about Chikatilo has disgusted her, and she's going to have to ration the details.

Cannibalism, she thinks, looking at the empty chair on the other side of the desk.

She remembers sitting here on a couple of occasions and discussing the phenomenon with Samuel Bai when he had come to her for therapy back in the spring. Samuel had said that the rebel army used cannibalism as a way of violating and humiliating their victims, but that there had also been a ritualistic aspect to it.

Eating a heart had been a way of appropriating the enemy's strength.

What else had he said?

Suddenly she can feel her headache coming back, the same throbbing ache as earlier in the day. Flashing in front of her eyes, a jagged stripe making her vision lose all focus. An epileptic migraine. But the attack is over in thirty seconds or so.

Sofia gets up and goes to the filing cabinet where she keeps her records. She unlocks it and quickly finds Samuel's file and takes it back to the desk with her.

When she opens it she finds that it only contains one sheet of paper, and when she reads what she wrote it becomes clear that it's just the notes of the first exploratory session, as well as a few lines from the two following meetings. Nothing from their other sessions.

Sofia takes out the diary where she records all her appointments.

They met nine times in May. In June, July and August he had come to see her twice a week, always punctual, never missing a session. From her diary it is abundantly clear that Samuel came to see her a total of forty-five times. She knows that's right, and doesn't need to count again. Her records also show that they met fifteen times on a Monday, ten times on Tuesdays, seven times on Wednesdays, and eight times on Thursdays. They only met on a Friday five times.

Sofia closes the diary and goes out to see Ann-Britt.

'Would you mind checking how many times Samuel Bai came to see me, please?' she says. 'I think I may have forgotten to invoice social services in Hässelby.'

Ann-Britt frowns and looks surprised.

'No, you haven't,' she says. 'It's been paid.'

'OK, but how many times did he come?'

'It was only three times,' Ann-Britt says. 'You decided not to see him again after he attacked you. Surely you remember that?'

Just as her headache strikes with renewed force, from the corner of her eye Sofia sees Jeanette come through the door.

Mariatorget – Sofia Zetterlund's Office

'Sorry I'm a bit late,' Jeanette says, giving her a hug. 'It's been a hell of a day.'

Sofia is standing stock-still, frozen by Ann-Britt's words echoing in her head.

It was only three times. You decided not to see him again after he attacked you. Surely you remember that?

No, Sofia doesn't remember. She has no idea what's going on. Everything is falling apart, while at the same time coming together.

She can see Samuel Bai in her mind's eye. He spent session after session sitting opposite her, telling her about growing up in Sierra Leone and the abuses he had committed. In order to summon up one of his many personalities, she had once handed him a model motorcycle that she'd borrowed from Johansson, the dentist whose surgery was next door.

A model of a red-lacquered Harley-Davidson from 1959.

When he saw the motorcycle he was like a different person. He had punched her and . . .

Only now does the full memory return.

. . . picked her up with both hands tightly clasped around her neck, as if she were a doll.

Sofia realises that she's been mixing up her memories and creating a new memory out of a number of different events. Squeezing millions of water molecules together to form a single snowball.

Sofia can feel Jeanette's arms around her and the warmth of her cheek. Skin against skin, the proximity of another person.

Sticky chocolate cake, she thinks, hearing her mother's voice.

Two eggs, two hundred and fifty grams of sugar, four tablespoons of cocoa, two teaspoons of vanilla sugar, one hundred grams of butter, one hundred and fifty grams of flour and half a teaspoon of salt.

'Sorry I'm a bit late, it's been a hell of a day.'

'That's OK,' she says, pulling away from the embrace.

Reality comes back, her field of vision expands and her hearing returns to normal, while at the same time her pulse rate drops. Sofia looks at the receptionist. 'I'm going now. See you tomorrow,' she says, leading Jeanette towards the door. They go out to the lobby and into the lift.

As the door closes and the lift begins to move downward Jeanette takes a step towards her, cups her face in both hands and kisses her.

At first Sofia stiffens, taken aback, but gradually feels a sense of calm spreading out as her body softens, and she shuts her eyes and returns the kiss. For a moment everything stops. Sofia's head is completely silent, and the way she feels as the lift finally comes to a stop and their lips part might best be described as happiness.

What's happening? she thinks.

Everything is going so fast.

First she was sitting at her desk, then she went through Samuel Bai's records, and after that Ann-Britt said he only came to see her three times. And then Jeanette arrived, and kissed her.

She looks at the time. An hour?

She thinks back and quickly realises that there's a gap in her memory. The past hour feels like it's been on fast-forward, and Jeanette's kiss seems to have acted like the stop button. Sofia is breathing calmly again now.

Three times? she thinks, but knows that that's right.

She has clear memories of three sessions with Samuel Bai.

No more.

The other memories are false, and are mixed up with the time she spent working for UNICEF in Sierra Leone. Everything is becoming clearer, and she gives Jeanette a smile. 'I'm glad you've come.'

Their walk to the other side of Södermalm resembles the Sleepwalker's route. A semicircular detour, Swedenborgsgatan to Södra station, then down to Ringvägen, past the Clarion Hotel, turning north into Renstiernas gata towards the hills of Vita bergen.

Jeanette's voice whispering in her ear, her arm around her waist and a light kiss on her neck. The warmth of her breath.

'Things are starting to move at work,' she goes on. 'The boy we found at Thorildsplan has been identified. His name is Itkul, and he's one of two brothers who've been missing for some time.'

The calmness Sofia feels is very pleasant. She's fragile, open to everything being said to her, prepared for the possibility that Victoria might react, but she feels calm at the prospect.

It's time to lower her guard and just let everything happen.

'And the other brother?' Sofia asks, even though she's sure the boy is dead.

'His name is Karakul, still missing.'

'Sounds like human trafficking,' she says.

'The brothers were working as prostitutes.' Jeanette sighs and falls silent, but Sofia has no problem realising what she means. She can see the chain of events as clearly as if it had been spelled out to her.

The arm around her waist again, and the warmth of Jeanette's breath once more. 'We've got an identikit,' she says. 'But I'm not expecting much. The witness is an eight-year-old girl who's blind in one eye, and as far as the face in the picture is concerned, it's – how can I put it – neutral? I can't even see it in my mind's eye now, even though I've spent half the afternoon staring at it.'

Sofia nods. She's never had a face in mind while she's been working on the perpetrator profile. But a blank slate. This type of murderer is faceless until they get caught, and then they look like anyone at all, like an ordinary man in the street.

'And then there's Karl Lundström and Per-Ola Silfverberg,' Jeanette goes on. 'We know who killed them. Their names were Hannah Östlund and Jessica Friberg. They were also responsible for killing the homeless woman in the cavern. They've committed suicide, you'll probably see it in the papers soon. Almost everyone involved was at boarding school in Sigtuna.'

Sofia replies to Jeanette, but doesn't hear what she says. Possibly something along the lines of not being surprised. But she is.

Hannah and Jessica? Sofia thinks. She knows she ought to be reacting more strongly than she is, but she feels nothing but emptiness, and that's because it can't be right. Victoria knows Hannah and Jessica, and they're not murderers. They're apathetic little girls who like dogs, and Jeanette's got it all wrong, but she can't tell her that, not yet.

'How can you be so sure it was those two?'

Sofia imagines she can see a hint of doubt in Jeanette's eyes. 'Several reasons. Among other things we've got a picture of Hannah Östlund killing Fredrika Grünewald. She's got a very specific distinguishing feature. She's missing her right ring finger.'

Sofia knows that's true. Hannah was bitten by a dog and had to have her finger amputated.

Nonetheless . . . Jeanette's explanation sounds a bit too rehearsed.

Now Sofia takes the initiative for a kiss. They stop in a doorway on Bondegatan and Jeanette's arms slip under Sofia's coat.

They stay in the doorway for a while, wrapped up in the warmth of their embrace.

Physical closeness can be so liberating. Five minutes in which thoughts drift apart, only to collect themselves into a new, clearer structure afterwards.

'Come on,' Jeanette eventually says. 'I'm hungry, I didn't have any lunch.'

Jeanette gives Sofia a serious look as she opens the door to the bar. 'Charlotte Silfverberg has committed suicide,' she says. 'Several people saw her jump from a Finland ferry late in the evening of the day before yesterday. It feels like everyone involved in this story ends up dead before their time. There's only Annette Lundström left, and we both know what sort of state she's in.'

As they step inside the glazed porch, Sofia isn't thinking about Annette or Charlotte.

She's thinking about Madeleine.

Jeanette interrupts her thoughts. 'What's annoying me most about all this,' she says as she takes her jacket off, 'is that I never got to meet Victoria Bergman.'

Sofia can feel her skin tighten and shrink.

'Although I did talk to her once, funnily enough.'

Hello, my name's Jeanette Kihlberg, I'm calling from the Stockholm police. I've actually been given this phone number by your father's lawyer, who's wondering if you'd be able to act as a character witness for your father in a forthcoming trial.

'What's funny about that?' Sofia says.

'She was given a protected identity and disappeared off all official registers. But at least I got the chance to meet her former psychologist.'

Sofia already knows what Jeanette's going to say.

'We haven't actually seen each other since then, and it's so strange that I didn't even consider talking to you about it over the phone. Victoria's psychologist has got exactly the same name as you. She lives in a nursing home out in Midsommarkransen.'

Stockholm, 1988

Walk in silence, don't walk away in silence.
See the danger, always danger.
Endless talking, life rebuilding.
Don't walk away.

The last time. The farewell, their last meeting.

If she had her way, she would go on seeing her, but the decision she had made meant she had to go against her own will completely.

Victoria Bergman could never see Sofia Zetterlund again.

She knocked but didn't wait for an answer. Sofia was sitting in the living room with her knitting, and looked up at her as she entered the room. Her eyes seemed tired, and perhaps like she hadn't slept that night either, and perhaps she had also been thinking about their impending separation.

Sofia's smile was as tired as her eyes. She put her knitting down and gestured to Victoria to sit on the sofa. 'Would you like some coffee?'

'No, thanks. How long can I stay?'

Sofia looked at her warily. 'One hour, like we agreed. You were the one who suggested that, and you made me promise not to make any attempt to persuade you otherwise.'

'I know.' She sat down on the sofa, as far away from Sofia as possible. It's the right decision, she thought. This is the last time, it has to be.

But she was reluctant. Soon she would have the decision of the Nacka District Court in her hand, and then Victoria Bergman would no longer exist. Part of her felt that she wasn't yet finished with herself, that Victoria wasn't just going to disappear simply because she had arranged for it to happen in legal terms. Another part of her knew that this was absolutely the right decision, her only possibility to heal.

Become someone else, Victoria thought. Become like you. She cast a quick glance at the psychologist.

'There's one thing we have never really finished talking about,' Sofia said. 'And because this is our last session, I'd like to –'

'I know what you mean. What happened in Copenhagen. And Aalborg.'

Sofia nodded. 'Do you want to tell me?'

She didn't know where to start. 'You know I had a baby last summer,' she attempted, as Sofia looked at her encouragingly. 'In a hospital in Aalborg . . .'

It had been the Reptile who gave birth for her. The Reptile who had stored up the pain and hardly made a noise during the birth. The Reptile who had squeezed out an egg and then crept away to lick its wounds.

'A little bundle of jaundice that they put in an incubator,' she went on. 'She's probably got learning difficulties as well, considering that he's the father and I'm the mother.'

Why was Sofia staying so bloody quiet? Only the Eyes, looking at her, prompting her. Carry on talking, they seemed to say. But she couldn't do more than just think about what she ought to say, the words wouldn't come out.

'Why is it that you don't want to tell me?' Sofia eventually asked.

It had survived when she dropped it on the floor, anyway.

But forget her now. Forget Madeleine. She's just an egg in a blue onesie.

'What is there to say?' She could feel a welcome anger bubbling inside her. Better that than anxiety, than shame. 'Those bastards stole my baby. They drugged me and dragged me to some quack at University Hospital in Copenhagen and forced me to sign a load of papers. Viggo had arranged everything. Papers saying I had been declared legally incompetent in Sweden, papers saying Bengt had power of attorney, papers saying the baby was born four weeks earlier than it really was, because I would have been of age then. They covered their backs the whole way with masses of papers. If I was to claim that I was of age when the baby was born, they had papers saying I had been declared incompetent. If I dared to suggest that the baby was born on a particular date, they could produce another piece of paper saying that it had been born four weeks earlier, before I came of age. All those fucking papers, important names that couldn't be contradicted. I'm of age now, but I wasn't then, when the baby was born. Back then I was mentally ill and incompetent. And, on their papers, seventeen years old rather than eighteen, just to make sure.'

'What are you saying? That they forced you to give up your baby?'

I don't know, Victoria thought.

She had been passive, and probably had to take a share of the blame herself. But her resistance had been almost entirely broken down by then.

'Pretty much,' she said after a pause. 'But it doesn't matter now. Nothing can be done, not a bloody thing. They've got the law on their side and I just want to forget it all. Forget that bloody child.'

All she had wanted was to be allowed to see the baby once more. But they wouldn't let her, and when she did it anyway, tracking the child down and finding the foster-family, the Swede's lovely family in their lovely house in Copenhagen, that's when she dropped it on the floor.

Obviously she wasn't mature enough to have a baby.

She couldn't even manage to keep hold of it, and maybe she had actually dropped it on purpose.

Stop it now, stop thinking. But that didn't work.

The child was all out of proportion, so it leaned to one side when you picked it up and the head was far too big and she was fucking lucky the skull didn't crack like an egg when it hit the lovely marble floor and didn't even bleed. Now she had finally proved that she wasn't capable of taking responsibility for herself and her actions, so of course it was just as well that she'd signed all those papers . . .

'Victoria?' Sofia's voice sounded distant. 'Victoria?' it repeated. 'How are you feeling?'

She could feel that she was shaking and her cheeks felt hot. At first the whole room seemed very distant, then suddenly very close, as if her eyes were a camera shifting focus from telephoto to wide-screen in no more than a second.

Shit, she thought as she realised she was sitting there crying like a baby, incompetent and inadequate.

I hope you can come to terms with your memories had been the last thing Sofia said to her, and Victoria didn't look back as she walked along the path towards the bus stop, with autumn slowly creeping across the trees around her.

Come to terms with my memories? How the hell am I supposed to come to terms with them?

They have to go, and you, Sofia Zetterlund, are going to help me with that. But at the same time I have to forget you, however that's supposed to happen.

If you only knew what I've done.

I've stolen your name.

When Victoria filled in the forms applying for a protected identity, she had expected someone else to have responsibility for choosing a new name, that it would somehow be allocated to her along with her new ID number. But on the bottom line of one of the forms there had been three empty boxes where she had to suggest a first name, a surname and a middle name if she wanted one.

Without really thinking about it she had written 'Sofia' in the first box, skipped the second because she didn't know what Sofia's middle name was, and in the third box she had written 'Zetterlund'.

Before the clerk had even collected the documents she had started practicing her signature.

Victoria sat down on the bench at the bus stop and waited for the bus that was going to take her into the city, to her new life.

Harvest Home Restaurant

She remembers everything now. The meetings with Sofia and the medical examination at Nacka Hospital.

Her cleansing, her healing process, has moved into yet another phase. She's starting to get used to her new memories, and no longer reacts to them as strongly.

To the left of the bar's entrance they find a free table by the window, and as they are about to sit down Jeanette points to a little brass sign on the wall above the table. 'Maj's Corner?'

'Maj Sjöwall,' Sofia says absent-mindedly. She knows that the author visits the bar almost every day.

The Dutchman who owns the bar with his Swedish wife comes over to the table, welcomes them and hands them the menu.

'This is your place, so you can decide,' Jeanette says, smiling.

'In that case, two pints of Guinness and two Västerbotten cheese pies.'

The owner compliments them on their choice, and while they wait Jeanette tells Sofia that Johan has got himself a girlfriend.

Sofia asks questions, and soon realises that although she's the one handling the conversation, Victoria is doing the thinking. She doesn't even need to take part in the conversation, it's taking care of itself, and it's a very peculiar, synchronous experience. Like having two brains.

Sofia is talking to Jeanette, and Victoria is thinking about her daughter.

This synchronous state stops abruptly. Sofia is completely focused on Jeanette again, and feels ready to talk about the perpetrator profile. But she makes up her mind to hold back on her theory about castration and cannibalism while they're eating, and decides to start by talking about shame and the murderer's desire to be seen.

She looks around. The tables closest to them are empty, and there's no one who might overhear their conversation. 'I think I've come up with something about the immigrant boys' murderer,' she says, as Jeanette starts to eat. 'I might be wrong, but I think we might have missed a number of important things about the perpetrator's psyche.'

Jeanette looks at her with interest. 'OK?'

'I think that the combination of castration and embalming is actually entirely in line with the perpetrator's logic. Through mummification, the young boy's childhood is permanently preserved for posterity. The murderer sees himself as an artist, and the corpses are his self-portraits. A series of artworks where the motif is his shame about his own sexuality. He wants to show who he is, and the lack of genitals is one way of marking this.'

Sofia considers what she's just said, and realises that she might have been too categorical.

Him? she thinks. It could also be a her. But it's easier to talk about a him.

Jeanette puts her knife and fork down, wipes her mouth and looks intently at Sofia. 'Maybe the murderer wanted the bodies to be found? After all, he hasn't made much of an effort to hide them. And artists always want attention and appreciation, don't they? I mean, I used to be married to one.'

She understands me, Sofia thinks, and nods. 'He wants to put on a show, be seen. And I don't think he's finished yet. He won't stop until he gets caught –'

'Because that's what he's after,' Jeanette concludes. 'Subconsciously. He's got something to tell the world, and in the end he won't be able to bear doing it in silence.'

'Something like that,' Sofia says. 'And I also think the murderer is documenting what he does.' She thinks about her own bizarre exhibition space at home in the apartment. 'Photographs, notes, a compulsive collection. Are you familiar with the concept of *l'homme du petit papier*?'

Jeanette eats some more of the pie while she thinks.

'Yes, actually,' she finally says. 'While I was training I read a Belgian police investigation into a man who murdered his brother. The newspapers called him "*L'homme du petit papier*", the man with scraps of paper. When the police searched his home they found piles of paper that reached all the way to the ceiling in places.'

Sofia's mouth feels dry, and she pushes her pie aside, not even half finished. 'Then you understand what I mean. He's collecting himself, if I can put it like that.'

'Yes, something along those lines. Every word, every sentence, every single piece of paper was important to him. I remember that the amount of evidence was so extensive that they could hardly put together a coherent case. Even though everything they needed to convict him was in his little flat, right in front of their eyes.'

Sofia takes a sip of the dark, bitter beer. 'According to one theory, an unhealthy or stunted libido will express itself through various forms of deviant behaviour. Such as unusual sexual fantasies. If the libido is directed inward, towards the individual himself, it leads to narcissism and –'

'Stop!' Jeanette interrupts. 'I know what libido is, but can you explain in a bit more detail?'

Sofia can feel herself becoming cold and distant. If only Jeanette could understand how hard this is for her. How much it's taking out of her to talk about someone who enjoys tormenting others, and who can only feel contentment from other people's mortal terror. What she's saying isn't just about other people, it's also about herself.

About the person she thought she was. About what she herself has suffered.

'Libido is motivation, what you long for, lust after, what you want. Without it humanity wouldn't exist. If we didn't want anything in life we'd just lie down and die.'

Sofia glances at her half-eaten pie. If she'd had a hint of an appetite earlier, it's completely vanished now. 'One common belief,' she goes on mechanically, 'is that the libido can be disrupted by destructive relationships, particularly with your mother and father during childhood. Just think of all the irrational compulsive disorders, like a fear of germs or manic handwashing. In those cases the most important thing in life, its dream and desire, has become cleanliness.'

Sofia falls silent. Everyone wants to be clean, she thinks. And Victoria has struggled for that all her life.

'So how do people handle it?' Jeanette asks, putting a big piece of

Västerbotten pie in her mouth. 'I mean, not everyone becomes a serial killer because they didn't get along with their parents.'

Victoria smiles at Jeanette's appetite and likes what she sees: a person with an appetite for more than just food. For knowledge and experiences. An intact person with an undisturbed libido. Someone to be envied.

'I don't like Freud, but I agree with what he says about sublimation.' Victoria notices the quizzical look on Jeanette's face and explains: 'That's a defence mechanism where repressed needs find expression through creativity and artistic activity and . . .'

She loses her train of thought when Jeanette bursts out laughing, turns round, and points at the brass sign above her seat. 'So you, or Freud, mean that someone who's written a book about inhuman murders could have become a serial killer instead?'

Victoria joins in with her laughter, and they look into each other's eyes. They stay like that, in the depths of recognition, while their laughter slowly fades away and is replaced by wonder. 'Go on,' Jeanette says once they've calmed down and the moment is over.

'It's probably easiest if I read from my notes,' Sofia says. 'And you can just ask if you want me to elaborate on anything.' Jeanette nods, still with a smile on her lips.

'The perpetrator is in many respects still a child,' Sofia begins. 'His gender identity may be uncertain, and he is probably impotent, in the clinical sense. Impotent literally means "without power", and this individual has thought of himself as powerless since he was a child. He may have been the butt of jokes, someone other people laughed at, an outsider. In his isolation he has constructed an image of himself as a genius, and it is this that other people can't handle. He believes he is meant to become something big. He is driven by a desire for revenge, but when that day never comes he begins to feel physically sick at the sight of the world around him living and loving. He finds this incomprehensible. Because of course he is the genius. And his frustration spills over into anger. Sooner or later he discovers that violence turns him on, and he gets sexually excited by seeing another person's powerlessness. The same powerlessness that he himself feels, which may in turn lead to him killing.' Sofia puts her notepad down. 'So, boss, any questions?'

Jeanette says nothing, and is just staring blankly ahead of her. 'You've done your homework,' she eventually says. 'The boss is happy. Very happy.'

Wollmar Yxkullsgatan – Södermalm

Jeanette is feeling slightly drunk. After the food they had another two beers, and it was her idea for them to continue their walk before catching a taxi home.

'Ugh, I woke up here once when I was fourteen. The old Maria Centre.'

Jeanette points at the entrance to the Maria Treatment Centre, and remembers how she had been picked up from there one sunny summer's morning by her father, who had been anything but pleased to find his beloved daughter a complete wreck and covered in vomit. The night before, she and some friends had been celebrating the start of the summer holidays by drinking a whole bottle of Kir, with predictably disastrous consequences.

'And there I was thinking you were a good little girl,' Sofia says, stroking her cheek teasingly.

Her touch makes Jeanette feel warm, and she wants to get home as soon as possible. 'I was, as well. Until I met you. Shall we give up and get a taxi?'

Sofia nods, and Jeanette notices that she seems serious and thoughtful again.

'There's one thing I've been wondering about,' Sofia says while Jeanette looks around for a taxi. 'After you found Samuel Bai, you came to my practice to ask some questions about him, didn't you?'

Jeanette can see a free taxi further down the street. 'Of course, you'd met him a few times, hadn't you? Three sessions, I think you said.' Jeanette turns round, and sees Sofia start. 'Is anything wrong?'

'Can you remember if you told me how you found Samuel? I mean, if you revealed any details that I couldn't have found out otherwise?'

'I told you everything. Such as the fact that someone had struck him in the eye. If memory serves, it was his right eye.' She steps out into the road to wave down the taxi, which pulls up at the kerb.

When she turns back towards Sofia she sees that she's gone completely pale. Jeanette opens the taxi door and leans in.

'Just a moment, please,' she says to the driver. 'We're heading out to Gamla Enskede. Can you give us a couple of minutes? Please, start the metre running.'

She takes Sofia under the arm and leads her a few steps away from the car. She can feel that Sofia is shaking, as if she were freezing. 'What is it?'

'It's OK,' Sofia says quickly. 'But I'd like you to repeat everything you told me about Samuel.'

Jeanette can see that for some reason this is extremely important. It had been the second time she'd met Sofia, and she had been attracted to her even then. Her memory of what she said is crystal clear.

'I told you that someone had hanged him and then thrown hydrochloric acid at him. We assumed there were at least two perpetrators because Samuel was too heavy for one person. I know I told you the rope was too short. It takes a certain length of rope for the person hanging themselves to be able to reach up to the noose from whatever they're standing on.'

Sofia's face is ashen. 'Are you sure you told me all that?' she says, almost in a whisper.

Jeanette is getting worried, and puts her arm around Sofia. 'I felt I could tell you. We talked for quite a long time, because you told me you had treated a woman who was suspected of having murdered her husband the same way. Probably the same woman that Rydén, the medical officer, mentioned.'

Sofia's breathing is fast and shallow. What's going on? Jeanette wonders.

'Thanks,' Sofia says. 'Let's go back to your place.'

Jeanette strokes her hair. 'Are you sure? We can skip the taxi and walk for a bit longer, if you'd rather?'

'No, I'm fine. Let's go.'

As Sofia makes a move to go back to the taxi she suddenly bends over and throws up over her shoes. Three pints of Guinness and four bites of Västerbotten cheese pie.

Stockholm, 2007

You gotta stand up straight unless you're gonna fall,
then you're gone to die.
And the straightest dude I ever knew,
was standing right for me all the time.

She was on her way to the Forensic Psychiatry Department in Huddinge to meet a woman who was suspected of murdering her husband. She was having trouble concentrating, and felt tired and overworked. She was looking forward to having a holiday, a few days off in New York. She turned up the volume of the stereo and began to sing along.

Oh, my Coney Island baby, now. I'm a Coney Island baby, now.

She thought about the man who had just been to see her in the practice. His wife was going to leave him if he didn't do something about his sex addiction. He himself thought that his desire for sexual stimulation was all to do with how potent he was, and boasted about how sly he was when it came to deceiving his wife. How good he was at coming up with alibis. On several occasions he had said he was working outside the city and would be home late. At Central Station he would buy a train ticket with cash. With his ticket firmly in his hand he would board the train and find the conductor before getting off at the next station. When he got home that night he would leave the stamped ticket in a dish in the kitchen, well aware that his wife would check to see if his story was true.

Sofia parked outside Huddinge Hospital. She got out of the car and walked in through the main entrance. After a routine security check she was allowed through to the visiting room. The woman suspected of murder was already seated on a chair at the table.

'This whole thing's a miscarriage of justice,' the woman began. 'I had nothing to do with my husband's death. He committed suicide, and then they arrest me. Is that really how it works?'

'Yes,' Sofia replied. 'I'm afraid it is. But I'm not here to look at the question of guilt, but to see how you are. Do you know why you're under suspicion?'

'Yes and no. I'd been working in Gothenburg for a few days, and on the way home we had a bit of wine in the dining car. I took a taxi home, and when I got back to the apartment he was hanging there. I tried to lift him down, but he was too heavy, so I called for the police and an ambulance. While I was waiting I started tidying up, and of course in hindsight I can see that that was a stupid thing to do.'

'Why was it stupid?'

'When I found him the phone books were on the floor under the chair he'd been standing on. I don't know why, but I picked them up and put them back in their place.' The woman started to cry. 'The police said the rope was too short and that it was impossible for him to have hanged himself without help.'

Sofia listened to the woman's story with mounting resignation. It seemed clear that her husband had discovered that the rope was too short, and had put the phone books on top of the chair before he climbed up. But instead of trying to comfort her, the police had cuffed her and taken her off to prison, under suspicion of murder.

Gamla Enskede – Kihlberg House

They walk up the drive from the taxi towards Jeanette's house. She's ashamed that the garden looks such a mess, the grass hasn't been cut and there are fallen leaves everywhere.

Jeanette smiles at Sofia, and as they go in a text message reaches her phone. 'They've made it to the hotel,' she says with relief once she's read the short message from Johan.

'I said there was no need to worry. Do you think Åke's taken Johan with him because he feels guilty about something?' Sofia says.

Jeanette looks at her. The colour has returned to her face and she looks much more alert.

She hangs up her jacket, then takes Sofia's. 'Who isn't feeling guilty?'

'Well, the man you're trying to find, for instance,' Sofia shoots back instantly, evidently keen to return to the conversation they had had in the pub. 'But if someone's capable of abusing and murdering children, then they'd probably have to have a rather more relaxed conscience than usual.'

'Yes, that would have to be true.' Jeanette goes into the kitchen and opens the pantry.

'If the person in question is also living a normal life at the same time, then –'

'Could he, though? Live a normal life?' She gets out a bottle of red wine and puts it on the table as Sofia sits down.

'Yes,' Sofia says. 'But it takes a huge amount of effort to keep the different personalities apart.'

'So you mean a serial killer could have a wife and children, be conscientious in his job and see his friends, without revealing his double life?'

'Absolutely. A loner is much easier to find than someone who seems completely normal from the outside. At the same time, that normality itself might be what triggered the sick behaviour.'

Jeanette pulls the cork out of the bottle and pours two glasses. 'You mean all the demands of everyday life need some kind of vent?'

Sofia doesn't answer, just nods as she takes a sip of wine.

Jeanette does the same before going on. 'But someone like that would surely have to stand out somehow?'

Sofia looks thoughtful. 'Yes, some obvious signs would be, for instance, that his eyes might flit about nervously, and he might prefer not to make eye contact, which in turn would make those around him regard him as slippery and difficult to get close to.' Sofia puts her glass down. 'I've recently read a book about a Russian serial killer, Andrei Chikatilo, and his former workmates said they had only very hazy memories of him, even though they had worked together for several years.'

'Chikatilo?' Jeanette doesn't remember the name.

'Yes. The cannibal from Rostov.'

Suddenly Jeanette recalls with revulsion a documentary she saw on television a few years ago.

She had changed channels somewhere in the middle.

'Please, can't we change the subject . . . ?'

Sofia gives her a strained smile. 'OK, but not entirely,' she says. 'I've got an idea about the perpetrator that I'd like your opinion about. We won't say any more about cannibalism, but I'd still like you to bear it in mind while I tell you what I think might be going on. OK?'

'OK.' Jeanette drinks some more wine. Red as blood, she thinks, and seems to detect a hint of iron somewhere behind the taste of grapes.

'Something happened to the perpetrator in his childhood,' Sofia says. 'Something that influenced him for the rest of his life, and I think it's got something to do with his gender identity.'

Jeanette nods. 'Why do you think that?'

'I'll start with an example. There's a genuine case of a fifty-year-old man who abused his three daughters, and wore women's clothes while he did so. He claimed he had been forced to dress as a girl when he was a child.'

'Like Jan Myrdal,' Jeanette interjects with a laugh. She can't help it, and she knows why. Laughter as a defence against unpalatable subjects. If she's supposed to sit here and keep the thought of cannibalism at the back of her mind, then she can permit herself a laugh or two.

Sofia loses her thread. 'Jan Myrdal?'

'Yes, experimental child rearing. It got quite common again in the seventies, if you remember? Sorry, we're getting off the subject. I interrupted you . . .'

The joke seems to have fallen flat. Sofia frowns before going on.

'It's an interesting element in a certain type of offender mentality. The perpetrator returns to childhood, to the time when he first became aware of his own sexuality. The fifty-year-old claimed that his real gender identity was female, a young girl's, and he was convinced that the games he introduced his daughters to were entirely normal in a relationship between child and parent. Through those games he could both relive and sustain his own childhood. And what he perceived to be his true sexual identity.'

Jeanette raises the glass to her mouth again. 'I get it. I think I can see what you're getting at. The castration of the boys is a ritual, and it's about reliving something.'

Sofia looks at her sharply. 'Yes, but not just anything. It's a symbol for the loss of sexuality. Now that I think about it, I wouldn't be surprised if the perpetrator in this case is someone who at an early age went through a change of sexual identity, either voluntary or involuntary.'

Jeanette puts her glass down on the table. 'You mean a sex change?'

'Maybe – if not physically, then definitely mentally. The murders are so extreme that I think you ought to be looking for an equally extreme offender. Castration symbolises a loss of sexual identity, and embalming is the technique used to preserve what the perpetrator regards as his work of art. Instead of painting with oils, the artist uses formalin and embalming fluid. Just as I said earlier, it's a self-portrait, but not just of shame. The central motif is a loss of sexual belonging.'

Interesting, Jeanette thinks. It sounds logical, but she's still dubious. She still doesn't understand why Sofia began the conversation by talking about cannibalism.

'Wasn't it the case that the dead boys were missing their genitals?' Sofia says.

Then she understands, and suddenly feels nauseous again.

Icebar, Stockholm

If Sweden appears to outsiders to consist of equal parts of freedom, state-run off-licences and high income tax, then Stockholm appears to city planners to consist of one-third water, one-third parks and one-third buildings.

In the same way, a sociologist can divide Stockholm's inhabitants into poor, rich and very rich. In this last group, however, the division is rather different.

The properly rich do everything they can not to flaunt their wealth, while those living in the suburbs compete to look and behave like multimillionaires. In no other city the size of Stockholm do you see so few Jaguars and so many Lexuses.

In the bar where Prosecutor Kenneth von Kwist is well on his way to getting seriously drunk on rum, cognac and whisky, the clientele consists of the rich and the very rich. The only thing spoiling the socio-economic structure is a group of Japanese men who look like they're on a field trip to an exotic zoo. Which, in a way, they are.

The delegation is here at the invitation of the Stockholm judicial system, and is from the office of public prosecutions in Kobe. The conference is taking place in the first hotel in the world to have a bar where it's always winter.

The glass in von Kwist's hand is made entirely of ice, and is currently full to the brim with whisky from the distillery in Mackmyra, a drink that seems to appeal greatly to their Japanese guests.

What a bunch of fucking puppets, he thinks, looking around hazily. And I'm one of them.

Their party consists of twelve young Japanese lawyers, and with him and his colleagues from the Public Prosecution Authority, there are fifteen of them in total, all wearing thick silver outfits with hoods and heavy gloves that make the below-freezing temperature inside the bar bearable long enough for them to empty their wallets. The cold blue lighting from the blocks of ice that make up the interior of the bar gives a surreal impression, and it feels like he's in a cartoon series about futuristic Michelin men.

The visit to the ice bar is the culmination of the ten-hour-long conference programme, and, if the prosecutor has learned anything during the day, it's that it isn't possible to learn anything on days like this.

'Another one,' he mutters to the bartender, putting his glass down hard on the bar.

The prosecutor sips his fourth or fifth whisky of the evening, feels his mood getting steadily worse, and knows he needs a break from this.

He decides to have a cigar before taking his leave. He needs to think, even if somewhere behind the fog of alcohol he realises that no matter what he might think in his current state, he won't remember it tomorrow. But he still excuses himself, pushes his way through the almost-full bar, hands over his gloves and the bulky silver jacket, and goes out onto the street to be alone for a while.

But he gets no further than lighting the cigar before he is interrupted by a tap on the shoulder.

He turns round and is about to say something cutting when he is hit in the face by a clenched fist. His cheek burns from the lit end of the cigar, which crumbles and falls to the ground while he himself stumbles from the blow and loses his balance.

Someone's holding him in a tight grip, and puts their knee on his back. The prosecutor is lying helpless with his face against the pavement.

Von Kwist's body immediately activates the defence mechanism that is managed by its fastest and most durable muscles. The ones in charge of his eyes.

He shuts them tight and begs for his life.

The grip soon relaxes. Ten seconds later he dares to open his eyes and gets to his knees.

What the hell just happened?

Långholmen Island

Långholmen is an island in the centre of Stockholm, and forms a distinct part of the city. It is about a kilometre long, and not quite five hundred metres across, and for many years it was Stockholm's prison island. One of Långholmen's inmates was Hanna Hansdotter. The last woman in Sweden to be sentenced to death for witchcraft.

Madeleine drives onto the island across the Pålsund Bridge, and parks behind Sjömansskolan. She knows the way because she's been here before.

She's spent several nights staying at the camping site beneath the Western Bridge. There are too many people, and she doesn't want to have to answer any questions from curious tourists. But it's better than Sjöfartshotellet, where she felt watched the whole time.

Since she got back from Mariehamn she's spent all her time in the car. A restless day with no other goal but tracking down her real mother. She's got the photograph Charlotte gave her in her pocket.

She's done what she set out to do, and now she wants to wipe out the body she was born from. It's turned out to be harder than she expected. Viggo had once said he'd seen Victoria Bergman down by the water in Norra Hammarbyhamnen, and Madeleine has been there several times, but hasn't found her.

And time will soon be running out. Her deal with Viggo needs to be completed.

Madeleine gets out of the car and walks over to the quayside. The water here is as black as it was out in the Åland Sea.

She puts her headphones on, turns on the radio and tunes it in between two frequencies. A faint wordless hiss that usually makes her feel calm, but now she only feels frustrated, and she digs out Clint Mansell's film score to *Requiem for a Dream* instead. With the opening notes of 'Lux Aeterna' thundering in her head, she starts walking up towards the former prison building.

When she reaches the old stone wall she stops and looks at it with a degree of reverence. She thinks about all the people who have passed through here. Understands all the anger that was stifled by the work of cutting the rectangular blocks from lumps of granite, and can feel in her own chest the hatred that would have pounded beneath the rough prison uniforms of the prisoners who were forced to build their own wall.

And she thinks about the moment when she finally decided not to be a victim any more.

France, 2007

Don't take my hate away. It's the only thing I've got.

The sun was high above the mountain ridge, the snaking road was eating its way along the sides, and five hundred metres below the Verdon River looked like a thin turquoise line. The safety barriers are low and death no further away than a few seconds' hesitation or a wrong reflex decision when you encountered another vehicle. Above her were another two hundred metres of mountain that ended in bright blue sky, and there were regular warnings of landslides. Every time she passed one of the signs she let out a loud yell, because the thought of being buried under an avalanche of cold rock appealed to her.

If I'm going to manage to live, Madeleine thought, then they can't be allowed to.

She didn't believe in a longing for revenge as a way for a victim to cling to life. No, it was hate that kept her breathing, that had kept her alive since her time in Denmark.

Will the hate stop when they're dead? she thought. Will I have peace?

She realised at once that the questions were irrelevant. She was free to choose, and her choice would be the simple, original path.

In many primitive cultures revenge was a duty, a fundamental right that gave the victim the opportunity to regain respect. Retribution marked the end of a conflict, and the right to vengeance was unquestioned; the act in itself was the actual resolution of the conflict, and there was never any need for analysis.

She remembered what she had had to learn when she was very small. When she was still unspoiled and could acquire proper knowledge.

She had learned that all people live their lives in two different worlds. One is a prosaic life and the other poetic, but only certain people have the ability to move between the worlds and experience them as separate from each other, or as synchronous, symbiotic.

One world was like an X-ray picture, the prosaic world, while the other was a naked, living, poetic human body. The one that she had now chosen to enter.

The road sloped down steeply, and after a bend she shut her eyes and took her hands off the wheel.

The next few seconds, containing the possibility that she was heading straight for a low, poorly maintained road barrier and on into the deep ravine, were transformed into a liberating confluence.

Life and death at the same time.

When she opened her eyes again she was still in the middle of the road, with the drop a safe distance away on the other side of the roadway. She had survived with several metres to spare.

Her heart was pounding hard and her whole body shivering. This was happiness. Exaltation at not being afraid of dying, yet simultaneously a sense of lightness.

She knew that a person wasn't dead once their heart stopped beating. When the brain was disconnected from the heart it entered a new state where there was no time. Time and space lost their meaning and consciousness went on existing forever.

It was all about how you regarded your own existence, and how you saw death. If you knew that death was just another state of consciousness, then you didn't need to hesitate before killing. You weren't sentencing someone to a lack of existence, you were just sentencing them to enter a new state, beyond time and space.

She was approaching another bend, and this time she slowed down, but moved into the other lane before sweeping round the edge of the rock face. Then she shut her eyes after the bend, when she was back on the straight. No oncoming cars.

No death this time either. But life and death in a short period of symbiosis.

Gamla Enskede – Kihlberg House

They've finished the red wine and have moved into the living room, leaving the discussion of paedophilia and cannibalism in the kitchen.

Those thoughts can lurk in a dark corner until tomorrow.

And they've switched to white wine. It feels lighter, cleaner, and Jeanette starts to feel better as the conversation slips onto more private subjects.

She talks about her evening together with Johan, when they watched football, and Sofia agrees that that's the right way to handle him.

'Johan will be fine,' Sofia says. 'He'll survive the divorce, believe me. Have you and Åke signed the papers yet?'

'Yes, when we met yesterday at lunchtime. Before they left for London. It feels very definite, somehow.'

If Jeanette has ever hesitated up to now because of some sense that she had to be faithful to Åke, that feeling is gone. Maybe because of something as simple as signing divorce papers.

Sofia's reaction is a cautious smile. She puts her wine glass down and looks at Jeanette.

'You mean a lot to me,' Jeanette says. 'You've made me realise that . . .'

She tails off. Can't quite express how she feels.

'Realise what?' Sofia prompts. Her smile is no longer shy.

It's expectant.

Jeanette tries to find the right words, but isn't confident that she'll ever be able to find them.

'That I'm not as uncomplicated as I thought,' she tries.

'You mean sexually?'

'Yes.'

Jeanette suddenly finds it much easier to breathe.

That a single word can make so much difference . . .

Yes.

She's just said yes to Sofia.

It just happens.

One kiss, then they leave the living room.

Up the stairs.

A kiss is a start. As the night outside is mother of the day.

For the first time in she doesn't know how long, Jeanette wants to go to bed.

Blood is pumping through her body in an entirely new way, yet it still feels so familiar.

A pure, original feeling of liberation, of released longing.

Sofia rolls over on the bed and puts her hands under the pillow. The contours of her naked hips distract Jeanette.

What's going on? she thinks. It's as if her movements are happening automatically, as if she can't control them.

Everything just happens.

She explores Sofia with her eyes closed. Letting her hands, lips and skin see for her. Sofia's neck is warm and vibrates against her mouth. Her breasts are soft and taste of salt. It's a strong body, a powerful body that she wants to make her own. Her stomach slowly moves up and down, and Jeanette's fingertips detect soft little hairs that get more numerous and coarser below her navel.

Her tongue is soon inside her and her own arousal flares.

She feels dizzy. As if everything is fluid and her brain is finally giving way to her body and not the other way. The room around them no longer exists.

Their movements are soft and unquestioned and she loses herself in the warmth down there. Hardly notices when Sofia rolls onto her side and lies the other way up.

Come closer, she thinks.

Sofia understands. Every muscle in Sofia's body understands.

Everything is fluid and they merge together to form a single beating heart, a single simmering being.

She thinks she might be crying.

Her tears are of release and gratitude, and time no longer exists. Later she would come to think of this night as simultaneously as long as an eternity and as short as a moment.

Afterwards the bed is warm and damp and Jeanette pushes the covers aside. Sofia's hand strokes her stomach in soft, slow movements.

She glances down at her naked body. It looks better when she's lying down than standing up. Her stomach is flatter and the scar from the Caesarean section seems smoother.

If she squints, she looks pretty good. If she examines carefully, all she sees are liver spots, veins and cellulite.

Sofia's body is purer, like a teenager's, and right now it's moist with sweat. On her arms and back Jeanette can see little white lines, almost like scars.

Gamla Enskede – Kihlberg House

They're lying in the warmth of the bed, and Sofia has no idea how many hours have passed since they got in.

'You're wonderful,' Jeanette says.

I'm not, Sofia thinks. Her cleansing process is exhausting, and she had been too hasty in thinking that she was no longer shocked by her memories. What she now knows about herself turns everything upside down. If most of her memories are constructed out of things other people have told her, then what's left of her past?

How can memories like that arise?

How can they be so strong that she could seriously believe that she had murdered several children, and Lasse too? What else is false apart from her memories, and how will she ever be able to trust herself again?

Maybe it's best not to remember after all?

As soon as she is alone again she can at least do a search for Lars Magnus Pettersson, that would be a concrete act, and if he's dead she'll be able to find out about it. But with Samuel she can't do much more than wait for her memories to return.

She feels wiped out, but Jeanette seems unaffected by the hours they've spent in bed, apart from the fact that she's glowing with sweat and her face is slightly flushed.

'What are you thinking? You seem a bit distant.' Jeanette strokes her cheek.

'Oh, it's nothing. I'm just trying to catch my breath.' Sofia smiles.

Jeanette's body is so strong, so powerful. As for her, she'd rather be a bit rounder, more feminine, but knows that's a vain hope that will never be realised. No matter how much she eats.

There's one thing that she ought to have told Jeanette already. When she spoke to her on the phone the day after her meeting with Annette Lundström.

The adopted children.

'When I met Annette she was incoherent, and I had trouble working out how much of what she said was in her imagination or not. But there's one detail I've been thinking about since then, and I think you ought to ask her about it when you see her.'

Jeanette's eyes narrow. 'What's that?'

'She mentioned adopted children. Said Viggo Dürer helped children from difficult backgrounds abroad come to Sweden, and that they used to live with him until he found new families for them. Sometimes they only stayed a few days, sometimes several months.'

'Jesus . . .' Jeanette runs a hand through her hair, which is wet with their combined sweat, and Sofia gently strokes her arm with the back of her hand.

'An adoption agency? As well as being a pig farmer, a lawyer and an accountant at a sawmill. Multitasking, to put it mildly. He's supposed to have been in a concentration camp as well.'

Sofia is brought up short. 'A concentration camp?'

'I can't put together a picture of the man,' Jeanette says. 'He just doesn't seem to make sense.'

A memory comes back to Sofia. Flaring up like a dazzling spark before fading and leaving a blind spot on her retina.

All the randy little Danish bitches. They were whores for the Germans. Five fucking thousand of the swine.

A memory of a beach in Denmark and Viggo assaulting her. Or had he? All she remembers is that he had played one of his 'games' with her, groaning and rubbing himself against her, sticking his fingers in her and then getting up and walking away. She had been left lying there, her body sore from the stony ground, and her top had been torn. She wants to tell Jeanette, but can't.

Not yet. It's the shame that's stopping her, it's always shame that gets in the way.

'Come here,' Jeanette whispers. 'Move closer to me.'

Sofia curls up with her back to Jeanette. She huddles like a child, shuts her eyes, and enjoys the closeness, warmth and the calm deep breathing from the body behind her.

They lie there in silence, and soon she realises that Jeanette has fallen asleep. She lies awake for a while, but when sleep finally comes it's more of an unsettled doze. A state she has experienced many times before, neither sleep nor wakefulness, nor a dream.

She leaves her body, glides up the wall and lies down on the ceiling.

The feeling is soothing and pleasant, like drifting around in water. But when she tries to turn her head and look at herself and Jeanette down below under the sheets, every muscle in her body seems to be locked and the pleasant feeling is instantly replaced by panic.

Suddenly she's lying back in bed again and she can't move, as if her body has been paralysed by some sort of poison. She realises that someone is sitting on her, an indescribable weight that's numbing her body and making it impossible to breathe.

The unknown body leaves her, and even if she can't turn her head and look around, she senses that the body has got off her and is getting out of bed behind her before leaving the room like a fleeing shadow.

Then the feeling of paralysis vanishes as quickly as it arrived. She can breathe again and starts moving her fingers, then her arms and legs. She realises that she's wide awake when she hears the sound of deep breathing beside her, and calms down. She knows she's going to need Jeanette's help if she's to stand any chance of becoming whole.

When did everything really begin? When did she invent her first alternative personality? When she was very young, of course, since dissociation is the defence of a child.

She glances at the time. Just after four thirty. She won't be able to sleep now.

She can take Gao, Solace, the Worker, the Analyst and the Moaning

Minnie off the list, because she understands them. They've all played out their roles.

That leaves the Reptile, the Sleepwalker and Crow Girl. They're more difficult, because they're closer to her, and weren't created from people around her. They *are* her.

The Reptile is probably the next in line to disappear. That personality's behaviour follows a simple logic with its roots in the primitive, she's worked that much out, and it's that idea she needs to bear in mind when she isolates, deconstructs and analyses that particular personality.

Simultaneously destroying it and incorporating it.

Sofia Zetterlund, she thinks. I have to meet her. She'll be able to help me remember how I used these personalities as a child and teenager. But can I really go and see her?

If I do, will it be as Sofia or as Victoria?

Or like today, both of us, simultaneously?

She lies there for a bit longer before carefully getting up and starting to put her clothes on.

She needs to move ahead, needs to heal, and she can't do that here, alone in the darkness.

She needs to go home.

She leaves a note for Jeanette on the bedside table, shuts the bedroom door and calls for a taxi.

Libido, she thinks as she sits at the kitchen table waiting for the taxi. The life instinct. When does it stop? What does her own libido consist of?

She watches a fly crawling up the kitchen window. If she was starving and there was nothing to eat except that fly, would she eat it?

Barnängen

The first thing the woman sees is the corner of a black plastic bag. Then she realises that she ought to call the police. She's on her way home from a bar and it's after four o'clock. Late, sure, but nothing for her to worry about, seeing as she got fired from her job as a housekeeper two years ago and no longer has to worry about such banal concerns as regular sleep and normal responsibilities.

The evening hadn't ended the way she had hoped, and she's standing half drunk and disappointed on the quayside at Norra Hammarbyhamnen, not far from Skanstull and a stone's throw from the ferry to Sickla, watching the black bag bob in the water.

At first she's inclined not to care, but then she remembers all the detective shows she's seen on television, where a member of the public finds the body. So she gets down on her knees at the edge of the quayside and pulls at the bag. And for the same trite reason she carefully opens the bag, and to her surprise realises that her suspicions were correct.

In the bag is a withered arm. A leg and a hand.

But what she hasn't counted on is how her own body would react when she saw a dead body for the first time.

The woman's first thought is that it must be a doll that's rotted in the water. When she sees that it isn't a doll, and that the small child's eyes are missing, its tongue appears to have been bitten off and its face is covered with bite marks, she throws up.

Then she calls the police.

At first no one believes her, and it takes her more than seven minutes to persuade the male officer in charge of the emergency call centre that she's actually telling the truth.

When she hangs up she notices that her phone is shiny with vomit.

She sits down on the quayside, with a firm grip on the plastic bag to make sure it doesn't disappear, and then she waits.

She knows what she's holding, but pretends it's something else. Tries to forget what she just saw. A child's face shredded by another person's teeth.

Human teeth really aren't meant to cause damage.

Vita Bergen – Sofia Zetterlund's Apartment

It's early morning, and she's sitting at the computer in her study and staring at the screen.

Lasse's alive, she thinks.

The address is the same, Pålnäsvägen in Saltsjöbaden, and she's also managed to find out that he travels a lot for his work. She's found his name on a list of participants at a conference in Düsseldorf that took place just three weeks ago.

She finds herself laughing. Admittedly, he had betrayed her, but she hadn't killed him as a result.

Now that she's got confirmation of that everything feels so trivial. She hasn't just invented alternative lives for herself, but for other people, too, dragging them down with her in her own internal collapse. Lasse is alive, and maybe he is living a double life as well, just like before, but with some other woman. His life has moved on outside her own enclosed world. And she's actually pleased about that.

The process has escalated.

She still has a lot to do before she can allow herself a few hours of sleep. She's on something of a roll, and she has to make the most of it. She feels focused, and the buzzing in her head is soothing.

She gets up and goes into the kitchen.

Behind the kitchen door there are two bin bags full of paper. She's started clearing out the concealed room, and will soon be able to get rid of everything. But she isn't quite finished yet.

During the night she had one question ringing in her head: What is the serial killer's libido, and might she be able to find her own by studying that of others? The most extreme, deviant examples?

There are piles of paper on the kitchen table along with the biography of Andrei Chikatilo, and she tears out the pages she marked earlier with folded corners.

She reads that it takes time for the enzymes in the brain to break down experiences and create a second ego. That the second ego isn't scared of gutting a stomach of its contents, or cooking and eating a womb, while the first ego trembles with horror at the very thought.

Andrei Chikatilo was as divided as one cell from another.

Eggs and cells, she thinks. Dividing.

Primitive life. The life of a Reptile.

Sticky chocolate cake. Two eggs, two hundred and fifty grams of sugar, four tablespoons of cocoa, two teaspoons of vanilla sugar, one hundred grams of butter, one hundred and fifty grams of flour and half a teaspoon of salt.

There's another article on the kitchen table. About Ed Gein, born 1906 in La Crosse, Wisconsin, died 1984 at the Mendota Mental Health Institute in Madison.

The article is about what the police found in Gein's home, and she's stapled it to a picture of a snake swallowing an ostrich egg, the largest single cell in the world.

Gein's home had looked like an exhibition space.

There were four noses, a large quantity of intact human bones and fragments of bones, one head in a paper bag, another in a canvas bag, and nine labia in a shoebox. Gein had fashioned bowls and bed frames out of human skulls, seats and face masks out of human skin, a belt of women's nipples and a lampshade with the skin of a face. They also found ten women's heads with their scalps sawn off, as well as a pair of lips as the toggle on a roller blind.

Gender and bestiality belong together, which is why she's stapled the photograph of the snake swallowing the egg to the article about Ed Gein.

Another part of the picture is being despised by other people. But what comes first? Loathing yourself, others, or your own sexuality?

As far as Andrei Chikatilo is concerned, people disliked him because of what they saw as the offensively feminine way he moved, his sloping shoulders, his whole appearance, actually, and they were disgusted by his habit of constantly touching his genitals. He murdered and ate parts of his victims because he couldn't get sexually aroused any other way. He followed his reptilian, primitive urges. One central part of Ed Gein's complex case was his desire to have a sex change and transform himself into his own mother. He tried to make a costume from the skin of women's corpses that he dug up, so he could wear it and become a woman.

The article refers to an interrogation where the ritual was described as transsexual, and in the margin Victoria had noted with a red pen:

THE REPTILE CHANGES ITS SKIN.
MAN BECOMES WOMAN, WOMAN BECOMES MAN.
BLURRED GENDER IDENTITY/SEXUAL BELONGING.
EAT – SLEEP – FUCK.

Needs, she thinks, remembering what she read during her studies about Abraham Maslow's hierarchy of needs. She also recalls where she was when she read about it. In Sierra Leone, more specifically in the kitchen of the house they were renting outside Freetown, just before Solace came into the room. Victoria had been eating her father's disgusting porridge, with far too much sweetened cinnamon.

While she pretends to eat the porridge she thinks about what she's read about the hierarchy of needs, which starts with physiological needs. Needs such as food and sleep. She thinks how he is systematically denying them to her. After that comes the need for security, then the need for love and belonging, and then the need for esteem. All things he has denied her, and is continuing to deny her. At the top of the hierarchy is the need for self-actualisation, a term she can't even understand. As far as her needs are concerned, he has denied her everything.

Now she knows.

She created the Reptile in order to be able to eat and sleep.

Later in life she also used the Reptile to be able to make love. When she and Lasse slept together, it was the Reptile that allowed him inside, because that was the only way for her to enjoy a man's body. And the Reptile had group sex with Lasse in a nightclub in Toronto. But when she slept with Jeanette the Reptile wasn't present, she's quite sure of that, and the realisation fills her with a joy so intense it makes her eyes water.

But what else has the Reptile done? Has it killed?

She thinks about Samuel Bai.

She had met him outside a McDonald's at Medborgarplatsen, and had taken him home and drugged him. Then she had showered and, when he woke up again and was still groggy, she had revealed her body to him, luring him to her and finally killing him by smashing a hammer into his right eye.

The bestiality of the Reptile. The bestiality of the murderer. She had enjoyed it.

Or had she?

She gets up from the kitchen table, so quickly that the chair topples over onto the floor, and hurries into the living room. The sofa, she thinks, the bloodstain on the sofa that Jeanette once came close to seeing. Samuel's blood.

She literally turns the sofa upside down, examining the cushions and upholstery down to the smallest detail, but the stain isn't there. It isn't there because it had never been there.

The Reptile isn't her hunger fire. It's a fake, imaginary libido.

She laughs again and sits down on the sofa.

Everything that happened from when she met Samuel at Medborgarplatsen to when she was sitting here fresh from the shower is true. But she never attacked him with a hammer.

All she had done was throw him out when he started pawing at her.

Simple as that.

The last time she saw Samuel was when she threw him out. She's sure of that now.

He had enemies, and had been beaten up several times. A fight that got out of hand? It's up to the police to find that out. Not her.

She goes back into the kitchen and opens the fridge. A dirty beetroot and a few eggs. She gets two out and rolls them in her hand. Two unfertilised female sex cells, cold against her palm.

She shuts the fridge, gets an aluminium bowl out of the cupboard above the sink, and cracks the eggs. Then two hundred and fifty grams of sugar, four tablespoons of cocoa, two teaspoons of vanilla sugar, one hundred grams of butter, one hundred and fifty grams of flour and half a teaspoon of salt.

She stirs the mixture with a fork before she starts to eat it.

The Reptile is cold-blooded and enjoys being a living creature. It suns itself on the beach or on a warm rock in a summer meadow. She remembers how, as a little reptile, she had burrowed her head into her father's armpit; the smell of his sweat was security, and in there she could feel what it was like to be an animal, without any self-assumed responsibility for feelings and deeds.

That's the only memory she has of ever feeling secure with her father. No matter what else he went on to do, that memory is priceless.

At the same time she knows she never had a chance to satisfy her own daughter's needs. Madeleine has no memories of her, no memories of her mum.

No security at all.

Madeleine must hate me, she thinks.

Institute of Pathology

Jeanette feels a pang of disappointment. When she woke up and found the bed empty she had hoped Sofia was in the shower or downstairs in the kitchen making breakfast for them. She hadn't said anything to suggest she was in a hurry to get home. But Jeanette still has a smile on her face as she lets the duvet slip down to her feet and rolls onto her back, stretching her arms and legs out and looking at her naked body.

The night was wonderful, and she can still detect Sofia's scent, as if she were still close by.

Almost electric, Jeanette thinks.

As if Sofia's touch had charged her with electricity. An intense, sparking red pulse.

They had talked and made love until four o'clock, when Jeanette, sweaty and breathless, had said she felt like a teenager in love, but that they really did have to bear in mind that there was a new day ahead.

Jeanette had fallen asleep, feeling as safe as a child.

After a quick shower she goes down to the kitchen, which is bathed in the glow of the weak autumn sun. The thermometer outside the kitchen window says it's fifteen degrees, even though it's only half past eight in the morning. It looks like it's going to be another beautiful day.

It isn't. But it will be incredibly long.

It's just after nine o'clock when Jeanette gets out of the taxi at the pathology lab in Solna.

Ivo Andrić is waiting for her with two double espressos.

He's an angel, she thinks, as her late night meant she'd had to do without her morning coffee.

'Have you spoken to Hurtig? Maybe he'd like to be here as well?'

Of course; she hadn't got round to that. But, on the other hand, she hadn't even been awake forty-five minutes yet. She shakes her head as she calls his number.

The mummified body of a boy, estimated to be between ten and twelve years old, has been found in a black plastic bag in Norra Hammarbyhamnen. The body bears a striking resemblance to the boy found dead at Thorildsplan.

Karakul, she thinks as the call goes through.

Good timing. She's not superstitious, but she can't help thinking that the call from Iwan Lowynsky was oddly well timed.

Hurtig answers, and Jeanette updates him about what's happened, and tells him what she's found out about Annette Lundström since yesterday. She asks him to try to have a talk with her.

'Don't forget to ask if Annette can tell us more about Viggo's adopted children, and try to organise a regular interview at headquarters as early as possible without causing any friction. And by that I mean free of bureaucratic interference.'

Ivo Andrić unlocks the door and they go inside. On the metal table is a cloth-covered bundle, and on the workbench over by the wall is a mass of photographs. She can see that the pictures are of their first victim, Itkul Zumbayev, the mummified boy found at Thorildsplan.

'So, what do you know?' she asks as he uncovers the body. She feels an instinctive revulsion at what she sees. The mouth is open, the skin has been loosened by the water, and her first impression is that his life came to an end mid-movement, and that the body is now decomposing.

'The injuries are almost identical to those of the Thorildsplan victim. Signs of whipping and violence from a blunt instrument. Randomly distributed needle marks. Castrated.'

The boy is lying on his back, his arms are raised, bent in front of his face, which is turned to one side. She thinks it looks like a frozen image of the moment of death, as if the last thing the boy did was try to defend himself.

'I suspect that the body is going to contain traces of Xylocain adrenalin,' Ivo Andrić goes on, and Jeanette is suddenly transported back in time several months. 'The samples have been sent to the forensic chemistry lab. As you can see, his feet are tied together with duct tape. That was used last time as well.'

She's having trouble breathing, and her heart is beating harder. Organised fights, she thinks. That thought had struck her back in the spring, and Ivo had actually also mentioned it.

'There are a few striking differences from the boy at Thorildsplan,' Ivo says. 'Can you see what they are?'

The pathologist gently touches one of the boy's arms. One hand is missing. The right hand.

Now she can also see what else is different from the body at Thorildsplan. Although she's having trouble keeping her eyes on the boy's face, Ivo's emphasis on the similarity of the injuries had made her miss the other, most obvious difference.

He gestures across the body. 'Bite marks. On large parts of the body, but particularly the face. Do you see?'

She nods weakly. It's more like someone's actually bitten chunks out of him than just left marks. 'There's something I'm wondering. This body has a different . . . How shall I put it? Colour? The boy at Thorildsplan was more yellowy brown. This one's almost greenish black. Why is that?'

How the hell could Sofia have been so right? she thinks. Less than twelve hours ago they had been sitting in the kitchen discussing cannibalism. She starts to feel sick again.

Ivo frowns. 'Too early to say yet, but this boy has been in the water for at least two or three days, and has probably been subjected to a different, more thorough type of mummification.'

'How long has he been dead?' she gulps. Her nausea is making it hard even to talk.

'Same thing there. Difficult to say, but I think we're talking about a longer time than the boy at Thorildsplan. Possibly six months longer, which as I'm sure you can see might mean a number of things.'

'Yes, pretty much anything. The boys died at roughly the same time, or one died before the other, or the other way round.' Jeanette sighs, and Ivo gives her an almost hurt look. 'Sorry, this is getting to me, that's all,' she explains. 'Anything else I should know?' She feels incredibly tired. The boy on the slab is guaranteed to give her nightmares, and she's trying not to look at him, but she can see his body from the corner of her eye the whole time, and it now feels as if it's reaching out to her.

'Yes, a couple more things.'

She can see that Ivo Andrić is thinking hard, and realises that he's trying to find the right words. His scrupulousness sometimes makes what he says sound like a prepared statement, and can mean that he loses sight of the big picture because of all the details he wants to convey. But he is very thorough.

'The body at Thorildsplan was missing its teeth,' he finally says. 'This boy isn't, so I've taken an imprint of them.' He goes over to the workbench and picks up the little mould. 'Super Hydro, very good, easy to work with, no bubbles in the imprint.'

'An imprint of his teeth?' Jeanette's heart begins to race again, but she makes an effort to stay calm. 'That's vital for identification.'

'Of course . . . We've got a good imprint, and that usually gives us a clear answer.'

The pathologist seems almost nervous, something she's never seen in him before. He turns round quickly and puts the mould back on the workbench before picking up a picture of Itkul Zumbayev, the body at Thorildsplan. Jeanette's pulse is racing.

'I'm not entirely sure yet, but you might be able to see from this picture that the boy's jaw is slightly crooked?' He taps the picture with his finger. 'The boy on the table also has a crooked jaw. My guess is that they're brothers.'

Jeanette breathes out. Ivo Andrić doesn't need to be sure, because she is.

Itkul and Karakul. Of course. It's logical. She can't get a word out, and Ivo looks questioningly at her. 'Even if the victim at Thorildsplan had no teeth,' he says, 'it's possible to estimate roughly how his teeth would have looked, particularly if there are any abnormalities. I didn't really pay much attention to his crooked jaw at the time, but right now it's of great interest.'

'Yes, you can say that again.' She can hear that she almost sounds like Hurtig, and she can hardly wait to tell him about this. 'You've obviously been kept up to date about what happened yesterday? That the boy at Thorildsplan has been identified?'

Ivo looks surprised. 'What are you saying?'

Jeanette feels herself getting angry. How incompetent could a person be and still get to call themselves a boss? Dennis Billing had promised to contact Ivo yesterday.

'We've got a name for the boy at Thorildsplan, and we might have a name for this boy as well. He might very well be called Karakul Zumbayev, and his brother, in all likelihood, is called Itkul.'

Ivo Andrić throws up his hands. 'OK, if I'd known that then obviously this would all have been a bit quicker. But let's just be pleased. The picture is starting to get clearer.'

'You're right.' Jeanette gives him a pat on the shoulder. 'You've done a terrific job.'

'One more thing,' Ivo says, pulling at the duct tape around the boy's feet. 'I've found fingerprints, but there's something odd.'

Jeanette stiffens.

'Odd? What's odd about that? Surely it's –'

For the first time ever Ivo Andrić interrupts her. 'It's odd,' he says, 'because the fingerprints on the tape have no papillary ridge pattern.'

Jeanette considers this. 'So you're saying that the fingerprints had no fingerprints?'

'Pretty much, yes.'

The perpetrator has been careful up to now, she thinks. No fingerprints at Thorildsplan, Danvikstull or out in Svartsjölandet. So why get careless now? Although, on the other hand . . . If you don't have any fingerprints, why not leave some?

'Could you elaborate, please? Whoever bound his ankles was wearing gloves?'

'No, definitely not. But this individual's fingertips don't leave any prints.'

'And why would that be?'

He looks bewildered. 'It's peculiar. I don't know yet. I've read of cases where perpetrators have rubbed silicon on their fingertips. But that's not what's happened here. From the tape I managed to get a print of part of a palm, and it's definitely bare skin I can see there, but at the end of the fingers it's just, let's say . . .' He leaves a long pause.

'Yes?'

'Blank,' Ivo Andrić suggests.

Nowhere

Ulrika Wendin understands that whoever is keeping her captive isn't going to let her live. At the same time she also knows that her chances of getting out of here by herself are getting smaller and smaller with each passing hour. Her body is deteriorating rapidly and she's worried that lack of nutrition is making her sluggish and apathetic. Her only chance is to hold out as long as she can and hope that someone finds her.

Can weakness of the body be countered by the brain working better? She's heard of people who voluntarily choose to live an isolated life, hermits, wise men, and monks who live shut up in monasteries, meditating and learning to be at one with themselves. Some are even said to have learned to levitate, floating above the ground.

Now that she can hardly feel her own body any more, she's starting to understand how they do it. Sometimes it almost feels like she's floating in the dark space surrounding her, for long periods she doesn't even think about where she is, and she's also started travelling in her mind.

She spends a long time reciting multiplication tables. Then she moves on to listing all the countries she can think of in alphabetical order, and after that capital cities. The effect is that other, new thoughts come to her as she trawls through old knowledge she thought she'd forgotten.

When she recites the names of American states there are only four missing.

She realises that she knows much more than other people have had her believe. In her mind she builds up a mental map of Europe's coastline, from the White Sea to the Black Sea. Then Asia and Africa and the rest of the world.

In the end she looks down at the world from above, as if she were a satellite, and she knows that what she sees matches reality.

She doesn't need a map to know what the world looks like.

She doesn't know if it happens in a dream or reality, but she feels someone removing the tape and coughs as two hands take hold of her face and push something into her mouth. A porridgy sludge that tastes dry and very bitter.

Then she is left alone, gliding back out into space and the stars.

Gradually Ulrika Wendin lets go of her body and disappears into the twinkling darkness.

It tastes like walnuts.

Rosenlund Hospital

Annette Lundström has seen darkness. That's the first thing that occurs to Hurtig when he enters the room. Her face is sunken and grey, and her body so thin that it feels like he might break her hand when he introduces himself.

He doesn't, but her hand is ice-cold, which makes her even more like a ghost.

'I don't want to be here,' she says in a low, broken voice. 'I want to be with Linnea and Karl and Viggo. I want to be where everything's the way it used to be.'

He suspects that this isn't going to be an easy task. 'I understand, but you'll have to wait a little while for that. First we're going to have a little talk, you and I.'

He feels unsettled, and he knows why.

The room reminds him of the one where his sister spent much of the last six months of her life.

But now he's here in his capacity as a police officer, and he takes a deep breath and makes a concerted effort to suppress his memories.

'Can you help me get out of here?' Annette Lundström's voice is pleading, almost hopeful. 'I'm going back to Polcirkeln, it's been so long since anyone checked the house up there. The plants need watering and all the apples . . . It is autumn now, isn't it?'

'Oh yes,' he says. 'I come from Kvikkjokk myself, and that's not so very far from Polcirkeln. But it's winter up there now.'

His attempt at adopting a familiar tone seems to work. Annette Lundström brightens up a little and looks him in the eye. Her gaze is unnerving, and there's a distance in her eyes that he has no words for.

Madness, he thinks. No, more the eyes of someone who's left this world and is in another. A psychologist would probably call it psychosis, which is exactly what the doctor he just spoke to said. But he has a feeling that the woman's physical and mental fragility are portents of something, and that this is what he can see in her eyes.

She's going to die soon. Die of grief.

'Kvikkjokk,' the thin voice says. 'I went there once. It was so beautiful. It was snowing as well. Is it snowing outside now?'

'Not here. But up there it's snowing. Are there more people you're thinking of seeing when you go to Polcirkeln, apart from Karl, Viggo and Linnea?'

'Gert, of course, and P-O and Charlotte, and their daughter. Hannah and Jessica probably won't come.'

Hurtig is hurriedly making notes. 'Who's Gert?'

She laughs. A dry, rasping sound that makes him flinch. 'Gert? Doesn't everyone know who he is? He's so clever, one of the best policemen in Sweden. You ought to know that, as a policeman.'

Clever policeman, he thinks. Like hell. Practical Pig, Gert Berglind. 'I've only got a few questions, and I'd be really happy if you could try to answer them.'

'I forgot to mention Fredrika as well,' Annette says.

'Good,' Hurtig says appreciatively, writing down the names. The whole Sigtuna gang, all murdered, apart from the murderers themselves, Hannah Östlund and Jessica Friberg. No, all except one, he realises once he's written down the last name.

'Victoria Bergman? Will she be there too?'

Annette Lundström looks surprised. 'Victoria Bergman? No. Why would she?'

Kronoberg – Police Headquarters

'Schwarz, Åhlund and Hurtig's reports are all done, I'm just waiting for yours now,' Commissioner Dennis Billing says when Jeanette bumps into him on her way to her office. 'But perhaps you've got more important things to do than put an end to this?'

Jeanette is only half listening, because she's still thinking about what she saw in the pathology lab. 'No, no, not at all,' she replies. 'You'll have it later today, so you can send it to von Kwist tomorrow morning at the latest.'

'Sorry if I sound a bit brusque,' Billing says. 'I think you've done a good job, solving this so quickly. It wouldn't have looked good in the papers if it had dragged on. But von Kwist is off sick at the moment, so someone else will be dealing with this until he gets back. Anyway, there's no rush, since the perpetrators are beyond our reach, so to speak.' The commissioner smiles.

'What's wrong with von Kwist?' Jeanette asks. The last time she saw the prosecutor he had looked the same as usual, and hadn't complained of being unwell.

'Something to do with his stomach. Suspected ulcer, I think he said when he called, and that's not surprising when you consider how hard he works. Good man, that Kenneth.'

'The best we've got,' Jeanette says, continuing towards her office. Perfectly aware that the irony will go over Billing's head.

'Hell, he's the best,' he echoes, sure enough. 'Well, better get back to the mines.'

'What do you mean?'

'I mean that now that another murdered boy has appeared, we're opening the case again. You can keep Hurtig. Åhlund and Schwarz are at your disposal as long as nothing more important crops up.'

More important? Jeanette thinks. My case is only being reopened because it would look bad otherwise. 'We're cosmetic, you mean?' she says, opening the door to her room.

'No, no, not at all.' The police chief falls silent. 'Well, maybe you could put it like that. Cosmetic. Oh, Jan, you're pretty smart sometimes. I'll remember that one. Cosmetic.'

Jeanette goes into her office and glances at the identikit picture pinned to the bulletin board by her desk. The drawing says nothing to her. It could be anyone at all.

It could actually be a woman just as easily as a man, she thinks.

Now that she comes to think about it, the face does seem peculiarly vague. Surely there ought to be some kind of distinguishing features? But at least the artist managed to include a couple of birthmarks, one on the chin and one on the forehead. Is that the sort of thing that children notice?

While she's looking at the picture she calls Ivo Andrić to ask for a more thorough examination of Ulrika Wendin's flat. As the phone rings Jeanette considers what Ulrika told her about the rape in the hotel room, and about Lundström filming the assault.

She also recalls that Lundström had said in his interview that he had been present when other recordings of child pornography were made, even if he hadn't mentioned the one involving Ulrika.

Ivo Andrić picks up, and promises to go back to Ulrika Wendin's apartment with a forensics team. When she ends the call Jeanette is left sitting there with the receiver in her hand and a lump in her stomach.

Lundström's films, she thinks. It's actually possible that they might contain something that could help in the search for Ulrika Wendin.

She dials Lars Mikkelsen's number on the internal phone.

What if the recording from the hotel room is in Lundström's collection? And why hasn't she asked herself that before now? If what Ulrika said was accurate, and she's never doubted that, then the film ought to be of vital importance. The fact that Karl Lundström is dead doesn't mean that the other perpetrators couldn't be charged.

She sighs to herself. This investigation really has been low priority. If only she'd been given more resources, they could have been more thorough.

When Mikkelsen finally answers she explains why she's calling and asks if he has anyone who could go through the material they seized.

'Well, not really,' Mikkelsen replies evasively. 'We've already got more than enough going on.'

'I understand,' Jeanette says. 'How about if I come over and pick the films up, and go through them myself? That would work, wouldn't it?'

Do I really want to do this? Jeanette wonders when she realises what she's just suggested.

'Well, there's no official reason why not. But you'll have to sign a load of documents agreeing not to divulge their contents and so on, and of course the films mustn't leave the building. A lot of Lundström's films were still on VHS and haven't been digitised yet, which means you'll have to go through the stuff we seized yourself.'

Jeanette thinks he sounds irritable, but presumes it has nothing to do with her.

'Great, I'll come over at once,' she concludes, and hangs up before Mikkelsen has time to answer.

OK, she thinks. No going back now.

Mikkelsen isn't there when she arrives, but he's asked a colleague to look after her. He's a young man with a thin beard and a ring in his nose, and he comes to get her outside Mikkelsen's office. 'Hi, you must be Jeanette Kihlberg,' he says. 'Lasse told me to let you into the storeroom and get you to sign for anything you need.' He gestures for her to follow him. 'This way, then.'

Once again she wonders what could make a grown man voluntarily spend his days watching children being abused by other grown men, in slow motion, frame by frame. Members of the same species. Friends and colleagues. It could be their childhood friends, old classmates, at worst their dad or brother.

'Here it is,' Mikkelsen's colleague says, unlocking a perfectly ordinary office door. 'Come and find me when you're done. My office is down there.' He points along the corridor.

She looks at the door in surprise, but doesn't really know what she was expecting.

Surely there ought to be some sort of warning sign, she thinks. 'Enter at your own risk' or, even better, 'No entry'.

'If you need any help, just yell.' The young police officer turns away and walks back to his office.

Jeanette Kihlberg takes a deep breath, opens the door to National Crime's collection of child pornography and steps inside.

She knows that from now on she's never going to look at the world with the same eyes again.

This is where it starts, she thinks. Zero hour.

Sunflower Nursing Home

Her little car is parked in Klippgatan, and Sofia Zetterlund realises that her resident's parking permit has quite rightly expired. Apart from a generous quantity of wet fallen leaves, the car has also been covered with a mass of parking tickets. Considering how long it's been parked here illegally, it's a wonder it hasn't been towed away.

She thinks about the previous day's visit to the library, and how her encounter with the librarian with the veil and the pigment-damaged eye had made her think about her car and the parking permit.

That was when her cleansing process had seriously begun.

The memory had appeared so suddenly that she had imagined the librarian was talking to her.

Your parking permit has expired.

She unlocks the car door and gets a small brush out of the glove compartment. Deviations, she thinks as she brushes the rotting leaves from the windscreen wipers and roof.

Deviations from the norm make her remember, they wake her from sleepwalking, without necessarily having anything to do with the memories that spark into life.

No memory is unimportant for the brain, she thinks. On the contrary, it's often the most trivial memories that are dominant, whereas you suppress the things you ought to remember. The brain doesn't trust itself, doesn't trust its ability to handle difficult things, so it would rather remember where you parked the car than the fact that you were raped by your dad.

Logical, touching and tragic, she thinks. All at the same time.

She puts the brush and the parking tickets in the glove compartment and gets in behind the wheel. She's slept for barely three hours, but still feels rested.

Before she starts the car to drive out to the Sunflower Nursing Home, she takes her notepad from her bag and turns to an empty page. 'Deviations', she writes, then puts the pad back in her bag.

She pulls out into Bondegatan and isn't yet sure if she's going to get out of the car at the home as Victoria Bergman or Sofia Zetterlund. Nor does she know that another deviation from normality will have a decisive impact on what happens.

When she pulls up at the Sunflower Nursing Home twenty minutes later, she catches sight of a woman standing outside smoking, leaning on a walking frame. The light from the lamp above the doors means that her face is partly in shadow and partly clouded by the smoke from the cigarette, but Sofia knows that the woman is Sofia Zetterlund.

She recognises everything. Her movements, posture, clothes. She recognises everything, and approaches the woman with her heart pounding.

But no memories come to her, everything just feels empty.

Her old psychologist exhales the last of the smoke, then turns her head in such a way that the light falls across her face.

The red-painted lips and blue eyeshadow are the same as before, the wrinkles in her forehead and cheeks are somewhat deeper, yet still the same, and wake no memories.

Only when she sees the deviation do her memories wash over her in an absolute torrent.

Her eyes.

They're no longer her old psychologist's eyes, and what's missing, the deviation from the norm, makes her remember everything.

Her therapy sessions in Sofia's home in Tyresö and at Nacka Hospital. Summer butterflies in the garden, a red kite against a blue sky, the sound of Victoria Bergman's footsteps on the hospital floor, steps that got lighter and lighter as they approached the door of Sofia Zetterlund's office.

As she steps into the clinic the eyes are the first thing Victoria sees. They're what she longs for most. She can land safely in them.

The woman's eyes help Victoria to understand herself. They're ancient, they've seen everything and they're trustworthy. They don't panic, and they don't tell her she's crazy, but nor do they tell her she's all right, or that they understand her.

The woman's eyes don't mess around. That's why she can look into them and feel calm.

They see everything she herself has never seen, only suspected. They enlarge her when she tries to shrink herself, and they gently show her the difference between what she thinks she sees, hears and feels, and what is happening in everyone else's reality.

Victoria wishes she could see with old, wise eyes.

Now cataracts have made the Eyes blind and empty.

Victoria Bergman goes up to the woman and puts a hand on her arm. Her voice is choked. 'Hello, Sofia. It's me . . . Victoria.'

A smile spreads across Sofia Zetterlund's face.

Johan Printz Väg – Ulrika Wendin's Apartment

Ivo Andrić stops the car outside Ulrika Wendin's apartment and gestures to the forensics officers in the other car to follow him. Two young women and a young man. Ambitious and thorough.

He unlocks the door, and they go inside.

Right, he thinks. A fresh look. Fresh thinking.

'We'll start with the kitchen,' he tells the forensics team. 'You've seen the pictures of the blood. Look for details. I was only here for an hour, and didn't have time to go through everything with a fine-tooth comb.'

Fine-tooth comb, he thinks. A new term he's learned. From the receptionist at the pathology lab, a nice girl from Gothenburg who talks oddly.

Once work in the apartment is under way he thinks about his morning's examination of the mummified boy. So depressing, the whole thing, yet still progress. They've got an impression of his teeth, and the DNA samples will be checked against the Ukrainian information about the Zumbayev brothers.

Kazakhs, he thinks as he looks at one of the bloodstains on the floor. When he lived in Prozor there had been a couple of families of Kazakh extraction. He had become good friends with the father of one of the families. His name was Kuandyk, and on one occasion he had explained how important traditional names were to Kazakhs. His own name meant something like 'happy', and as the pathologist thinks about Kuandyk's cheerful demeanour and loud laugh, it strikes him that it had been a good name for him.

Kuandyk had also told him that the choice of name often reflected the expectations people had of the newborn child. One boy in the village in southern Kazakhstan that Kuandyk came from ended up being called Tursyn. His parents had had several children who had died within days of being born. Tursyn literally meant 'let it stop', and his parents' prayers had actually been answered.

Andrić hears the two female forensics officers exchange a couple of words. The fridge door opens and the compressor rumbles.

Itkul and Karakul, he thinks. The fact that the dead boys were of Kazakh origin had made him think about his old friend from Prozor, and during the morning he had found out what their names meant. It saddens him to consider what their parents must have thought about their sons' futures. Itkul means 'dog's slave', and Karakul 'black slave'.

'Ivo?' One of the female forensics officers interrupts his thoughts. 'Can you come here for a moment?'

He turns round. The young woman is pointing at the fridge door, which is half open. Ulrika Wendin doesn't seem to have been a big eater. The fridge had been completely empty the last time he was here, and obviously still is this time.

'Do you see?' The officer indicates an area just inside the fridge door, right next to the edge, where she's just dusted some of the ash-grey powder to gather fingerprints. He squats down and looks.

An impression of three fingers, and the scenario begins to take shape for him.

He knows that one person assaulted another person in this kitchen, and then cleaned up after them. While they were cleaning, someone wiped the blood from the fridge door with their left hand and held the door open with the right, at the point he's staring at.

He doesn't even need a magnifying glass to see that the prints match something he's seen before, in fact as recently as that morning.

Sunflower Nursing Home

Sofia's room in the Sunflower Nursing Home is like a doll's house version of the house on Solbergavägen in Tyresö.

There's the same worn armchair and bookcase from the old living room, and they're sitting facing each other across the same little kitchen table. The glass globe with the snowed-in Freud is in its place on the chest of drawers, and Victoria can even detect the smell of Tyresö from twenty years ago.

It's not just a torrent of memories that washes over her, but questions too.

She wants to know everything, and she wants confirmation of what she already knows.

In spite of her age there doesn't seem to be anything wrong with Sofia's memory.

'I've missed you,' Victoria says. 'Now that I'm sitting here with you, I'm ashamed at the way I behaved.'

Sofia smiles gently. 'I've missed you too, Victoria. I've thought about you a lot, and have often wondered how you were. You shouldn't feel ashamed of anything. On the contrary, I remember you as a strong young woman. I believed in you. I thought you'd be able to take care of yourself. And you have, haven't you?'

Victoria doesn't really know how to reply. 'I have . . .' She changes position. 'I have problems with my memory. It's got a bit better recently, but . . .'

The old psychologist looks at her with interest. 'Go on. I'm listening.'

'As recently as last night,' she begins, 'I realised that I didn't murder my former partner. For almost a year I believed that I had, but it turns out that he's alive and I'd imagined the whole thing.'

Sofia looks concerned. 'I see. Why do you think that might be?'

'I hated him,' Victoria says. 'I hated him so much I thought I had killed him. It was some kind of revenge. Just for myself, in my imagination. It's almost pathetic.'

She can hear that her voice is starting to sound like the young Victoria's.

'Hate and revenge,' Victoria goes on. 'Why are they such strong driving forces?'

Sofia's answer comes quickly. 'They're primitive emotions,' she says. 'But they're also emotions that are unique to human beings. An animal doesn't hate, and it doesn't seek revenge. I think this is really a philosophical question.'

Philosophical? Yes, maybe, Victoria thinks. Her revenge on Lasse had probably been just that.

Sofia leans across the table. 'I'll give you an example. A woman is out driving her car and when she stops at a red light a gang of youngsters comes over to the car and one of the young men breaks the window with a long metal chain. Terrified, the woman drives away, and when she gets home she discovers that the chain had got caught in the bumper and that the young man's hand had been ripped off.'

'I get it,' Victoria says.

The blank cataract eyes stare emptily at her. 'Have *you* had your revenge? Have you stopped hating? Are you no longer scared? There are so many questions to consider.'

Victoria thinks for a while. 'No, I don't hate him any more,' she eventually says. 'Now, in hindsight, I can actually say that the false memory helped me get over him. Sometimes the feelings of guilt were unbearable, but today, sitting here, I feel completely cleansed as far as Lasse's concerned.'

Damn it, she thinks. I ought to have felt much worse. But maybe somewhere deep inside I always doubted that he was actually dead.

She doesn't know. It's all very hazy.

Sofia folds her old, veiny hands. Raised, mauve blood vessels, and Victoria recognises her ring. She remembers Sofia telling her she had once been married, but that her husband died young and she had chosen to live alone after that. Like a swan, Victoria thinks.

'You talk about cleanliness,' the old woman says. 'That's interesting. The psychological meaning of revenge implies some sort of resolution, which in turn means both a physical confrontation with an enemy and an internal, psychological process with implications of cleansing, and reaching self-awareness.'

This is exactly how it should be, Victoria thinks. Just like it used to be.

But can revenge really be a cleansing process? Her thoughts turn to Madeleine and the notepad in her bag. In contains at least fifteen pages of suppositions, many of them probably wrong and presumptuous, but she had taken as her starting point the fact that Madeleine was driven by the same feelings that she had felt. Hatred and revenge.

Perhaps hatred can also be cleansing?

Victoria takes a deep breath before daring to say one of the things she came here for.

'Do you remember that I gave birth to a baby, a daughter?'

The old woman sighs. 'Yes, of course I do. I also know that her name is Madeleine.'

Victoria feels her muscles tense up. 'What else do you know about her?'

She feels deep regret at not having fought harder to keep the child, at not having protected the little girl, holding her tight and making sure she slept soundly at night.

She could have fought, should have fought, but she had been too weak to do it.

Far too broken and full of hate towards everything.

Back then, hatred had only been destructive.

'I know she had a difficult time,' Sofia says. Her face looks powerless, and the wrinkles seem to deepen further as she turns towards the window. 'And I also know that nothing the girl said was deemed sufficient to bring charges,' she goes on after a short pause.

'How do you know she had a difficult time?'

Another sigh from the old woman. She pulls out a cigarette and opens the window slightly, but makes no move to light the cigarette, just rolls it distractedly between her fingers. 'I've followed Madeleine's progress through a contact at University Hospital in Copenhagen. What happened was truly awful . . .'

She imagines she can see a spark ignite in Sofia Zetterlund's misty gaze. 'Give me a light, would you? I don't know what I've done with my lighter. Nicotine makes me think better.'

Victoria takes out her own lighter and helps herself to a cigarette from the old woman's pack.

'Have you ever met Madeleine?'

'No, but like I said, I know what happened to her, and I've seen pictures of her. My colleague in Copenhagen sent me another photograph a couple of years ago, just after my sight went. I haven't been able to look at it myself, but I've got it here if you'd like to see it. It's in one of the books in the bookcase. The same shelf as Freud, third book from the left, a reference book with French binding. Take a look at it while I tell you about capsulotomy and sensory deprivation.'

Victoria jerks. Capsulotomy? Isn't that . . . ? 'Have they lobotomised Madeleine?'

The old woman smiles faintly. 'That's a matter of definition. Let me explain.'

Victoria feels angry, confused and expectant as she walks over to the bookcase. Tragic, she thinks as she pulls out the book. I haven't seen my daughter in twenty years, and when I finally find her it's in the appendix to an encyclopedia from the fifties.

The photograph shows a girl wrapped in a blanket in a hospital bed. The resemblance between Madeleine and Victoria herself is striking. An oppressive feeling creeps through her stomach.

'Can I keep it?'

Sofia nods, Victoria sits down again and the old woman lights another cigarette as she starts to explain. Gradually Victoria slips back to her time in Tyresö, and she shuts her eyes and imagines that she's there again, that it's summer and they're sitting in Sofia's bright kitchen.

'Madeleine was operated on a few years ago,' the old psychologist begins.

Denmark, 2002

When little 'un came to earth, it was in May when the cuckoo called,
Mama said all was aglow, bright spring green and sunlight.
The lake shone like silver, and the cherry tree was in bloom,
And the swallow, quick and cheery, arrived along with spring.

The room was as white as it was black, and she stared helplessly up at the ceiling, unable to move because her arms were fastened to the bed.

She knew what awaited her, and she remembered the voice on the crackling radio two months before, just after they made the decision.

Professor of Psychiatry Per Mindus was one of Sweden's leading authorities on anxiety disorders and compulsive behaviour syndrome. During his time at the Karolinska Institute he was introduced to neurosurgery and the surgical technique known as capsulotomy. In layman's terms, the technique involved going into the part of the brain known as the capsula interna and cutting the nerves that were believed to contribute to mental illness.

The thick leather straps chafed against her wrists, and she had given up trying to pull free. The medication meant she could feel a secure, warm apathy spreading through her blood.

The technique, which was used for fifty years, was increasingly questioned in the 1990s, because in half of all cases it led to a deterioration in both abstract thinking and the ability to learn from mistakes.

'Is the girl ready for the operation?'

She heard the voice that she had learned to dislike over the course of the past few weeks.

'I'm very busy and would like to get it done as soon as possible.'

Why's he in such a rush? she thought. A round of golf, or a visit to his mistress?

Someone turned on a tap. Washed their hands. Then the smell of surgical fluid.

The warmth in her body was making her tired, and she felt she was about to fall asleep. If I do, she thought, then I'll wake up as a completely different person.

She could feel the draught of a doctor's coat and realised someone was standing beside the bed. His mouth was covered by a paper mask, but the eyes were the same. She sneered at him.

'You'll see, it'll all be fine,' he said.

'Drop dead, you Swedish bastard!' she replied, then sank into the warm half-doze.

She could hear the crackle from the radio again, barely tuned in.

Criticism of Per Mindus's use of capsulotomy increased when it emerged that he had been lying about having been given authorisation for his experiments. One of the leading experts on compulsive disorders claimed that the technique had severe side effects. It was also claimed that when a follow-up report was published, it had been written by someone who was responsible for deciding which patients should be capsulotomised, and who alone evaluated the effectiveness of the treatment.

She was still tied down when they rolled her into the operating room. Still drowsy from all the medication, but alert enough to understand what was about to happen.

Kronoberg – Police Headquarters

The room is as white as it is black. Shelf after shelf of old VHS cassettes, CDs, hard drives and boxes of photographs. All carefully marked with the name of their previous owner, and a time, place and date.

Nothing in Jeanette Kihlberg's twenty-year career in the police force has prepared her for this, and when she realises the extent of the accumulated documentation of abuse she feels dizzy. Is it that we want to be blind? she wonders. That we don't want to see?

Evidently it's more important that interest rates stay low, house prices rise, or your flat-screen TV is plasma or LCD. You fry your gammon steak and wash it down with a three-litre wine box. You'd rather read a badly written thriller about the horror of it than deal with it in real life.

George Orwell and Aldous Huxley had no idea how right they were, she thinks, while at the same time being perfectly aware that she's no better herself.

She wanders aimlessly around the room, not quite sure where to start looking for Karl Lundström's films.

On one of the shelves she sees a name she recognises. A fifty-four-year-old inspector with the Stockholm police who bought child porn on the Internet over a period of years. Jeanette remembers reading about the case. When Mikkelsen and his colleagues caught him, the officer had over thirty-five thousand illegal images and films in his home.

Jeanette reads the titles, and a lot of the films speak for themselves. 'Photo Lolita', 'Little Virgins', 'Young Beautiful Teens', and 'That's My Daughter'. One of the films has a Post-it note stuck to it, and Jeanette sees that it says the film shows a girl tied down and assaulted by an animal.

She works out fairly quickly how the archive is categorised. In most cases by the date when the assaults occurred and, when that isn't known, by the time of seizure. The locations of the seizures remind her of the lists of places in her old school atlas. Obviously the big cities, Stockholm, Gothenburg and Malmö. If the number of sick individuals is constant, then there should be more of them there. Smaller towns such as Linköping, Falun and Gävle, mixed up with villages she's never heard of. From north to south, east to west. No community seems too small, too remote or too well-to-do not to contain people with paedophile tendencies.

The names are all male. Shelf after shelf of men's names. Common surnames like Svensson and Persson, but also a few that sound more aristocratic. Jeanette is struck by the low proportion of foreign names. It may be more common for migrants to beat their children, but they evidently don't like abusing them sexually, Jeanette thinks, just as she finds a cardboard box labelled KARL LUNDSTRÖM.

Almost holding her breath, she lifts the box down onto a table and opens it. Inside she finds about ten films. She reads their labels and sees that several were filmed in Brazil in the eighties, and remembers that Mikkelsen had called them cult films in paedophile circles, but no matter how cult they are, they hold no interest to her and she puts them back.

She tucks the others under her arm and makes her way to the young police officer's office.

He's sitting with his back to her. On his screen Jeanette can see a photograph of a bare-chested man standing beside a bed on which lies a naked Asian boy. The man's face is distorted, and Jeanette thinks it looks like someone's tried to conceal his identity.

'Already finished, ready to throw up, or in need of a strong cup of coffee?' He turns round and gazes at her with a serious expression.

'All three,' Jeanette says, looking him in the eye.

'Kevin, by the way,' he goes on, holding out his hand. 'And if you're wondering, it's because Mum was crazy about *Dances with Wolves*. Well, I'm a bit older than that, but she liked Kevin Costner's earlier films and wanted to give me an original name.' He pauses, then his face breaks into a broad smile. 'Mind you, at nursery school there were three Kevins and two Tonys. The one with the most unusual name was Björn.'

'Really?' Jeanette realises that the young man is trying to keep the tone light for her sake, presumably to keep her spirits up. But she doesn't feel up to smiling back.

He clears his throat. 'I'll get us some coffee before you go into the viewing suite and suffer a couple of hours of really unpleasant close contact with the worst of humanity. OK?' He gets up, still smiling, and goes over to a coffee machine in one corner of the room.

'Thanks, I could do with some,' Jeanette says.

Kevin hands Jeanette a cup, then sits down again. 'Did you find what you were looking for?' he asks.

'I don't know. We'll see,' she replies, tasting the coffee and discovering that it's as strong as she was hoping for. 'Maybe.'

They sit in silence, drink their coffee and look at each other for what feels like several minutes before Jeanette breaks the silence.

She points at the image of the half-naked man on the screen. 'Do you know who that is?'

'Yes, we found it on the Net and we think he's Swedish.'

'What makes you think that?'

He leans closer to the screen. 'Can you see what that is?' he says, putting his finger on an object on the bedside table, next to the naked boy.

'No. What?'

'If you zoom in and make the picture a bit sharper, you can see it's a box of Swedish headache pills. According to the price tag it was bought sometime in April from a chemist in Ängelholm. At the moment I'm checking debit card records that might match, and it looks like a certain preschool teacher is going to be getting a visit from us soon.'

'As easy as that?' Jeanette asks.

'As easy as that,' Kevin confirms, then goes on. 'Whoever put these pictures online used Photoshop to hide the man's identity, so now we're trying to get his face back, but it's difficult, and takes a lot of computer capacity. The FBI is doing the same, and I dare say they'll get there first. They've got slightly more resources than we do.'

'I saw that one of our colleagues is among the seizures,' Jeanette says, putting her cup down.

'Yes, that was Operation Sleipner.' Kevin leans back. 'We picked up about a hundred people, and apart from the one you're referring to we got another couple of police officers in Stockholm.'

'I'm not great at maths, but you said you picked up a hundred people, and three of them were police officers. In other words, three per cent were in the police. There are twenty thousand of us in the whole of Sweden, so we make up, what, .2 per cent of the population? That means that possession of child porn is over ten times more common among police officers than it is among other people.'

Kevin nods. 'Well, I'd better get on. A seized computer has just arrived and I need to go through it – apparently it's urgent.' Kevin gets up from his chair. 'And if you're thinking that only men are interested in child porn, I can tell you that this computer comes from a woman.' He opens the door and walks out. 'I'll show you where you can watch your films.'

Jeanette picks up the video cassettes and follows him out of the room.

'A woman, you say?'

'Just came in. A seizure out in Hässelby,' he explains as he heads off along the corridor. 'In Fagerstrand, if I remember rightly.'

'Fagerstrand?'

'Yes. Her name's Hannah Östlund. Or was. She's dead now.'

Sunflower Nursing Home

Victoria listens, trying not to interrupt Sofia. She has to make an effort to keep her anger in check, and chooses to concentrate on the internal illusion that she's back in the house on Solbergavägen.

'If you were to speak to a neurosurgeon, he or she probably wouldn't agree that capsulotomy is the same as lobotomy. Perhaps it could be described as an upgraded version of lobotomy, I don't know, but just like lobotomy it was intended to check deviant behaviour . . .'

Deviant, Victoria thinks. It's always about deviations. A person is only deviant if there's a predetermined scale. And psychiatry is subsidised by the state. So, in practice, politicians decide what is sick and what isn't. But surely things ought to be different within psychology? There are no clear boundaries there, and if there's one thing that she knows for sure, it's that everyone is deviant and non-deviant at the same time.

'In Sweden, and of course even in Denmark, where the procedure was carried out, we have a long history of dubious interventions with people who have been regarded as having learning difficulties, or are otherwise aberrant. I remember one case where a fourteen-year-old boy was given electric shock treatment for six weeks because his devoutly Christian parents found him masturbating. In their world, that was deviant behaviour.'

Victoria finds herself wondering how people like that even have the right to vote.

'Being religious ought to be regarded as deviant,' she says.

Sofia smiles briefly, then sits in silence for a while, and Victoria listens to the sound of the old woman breathing. It's quick and shallow, just like it was twenty years ago, and when she finally speaks again, her voice is more serious. 'To get back to the point,' she says quietly, but in a sharp tone. 'As you know, frontal lobotomy was an operation on the frontal lobe of the brains of people demonstrating deviant behaviour. The connection between the lower part of the brain and the frontal lobe was severed, and approximately one in every six patients died. The Medical Council knew the risks but never intervened. I started my professional career in the early 1950s, and I've seen a lot of terrible things over the years. The majority of lobotomy patients in Sweden were women. They were described as dissolute, aggressive or hysterical. And they were made to pay a very high price.'

Taliban politics, Victoria thinks. She's listening attentively to Sofia, still with her eyes closed, and she realises that this is the first time she's ever heard even a hint of anger in the old woman's voice. It feels good. Alleviates her own fury.

'Unlike lobotomy, capsulotomy isn't a fatal intervention, as far as we know, and that's why they decided to use the procedure on Madeleine. They cut through the nerves in her capsula interna, the inner capsule of the brain, in the hope that her mental health problems – compulsive disorder and disruptive behaviour – would abate. But it was a complete failure, and actually had the opposite effect.'

Victoria can no longer keep her eyes shut or stay quiet. 'What happened to her?'

Sofia looks angry. 'Her lack of inhibitions got worse, her impulse control vanished more or less entirely, while at the same time her intellectual ability actually seemed to get sharper, oddly enough.'

Victoria doesn't understand. 'That sounds like a contradiction.'

'Yes, maybe . . .' Sofia blows out a large smoke ring that sails above the table and breaks against the glass of the window. 'The brain is fascinating. Not just each separate part and function in itself, but also the interplay between them. In this instance you might compare the procedure to building a dam across a river to block the flow. But the result was that the river found new ways around the dam, and grew in strength.'

Victoria picks up the bag containing her notepad.

Denmark, 2002

And that's why, Mama says, I'm nearly always happy and gay.
I think the whole of life is like a sunshiny day.

The hospital environment didn't scare her, because she'd spent large parts of her childhood being treated for one thing or another. If it wasn't stomach aches, which it almost always was, it was feeling sick or dizzy, or bad headaches.

The worst thing was when she was alone with P-O in the big house with all the toys.

P-O, the man she had never called her father, who had taken pity on her but then discarded her when she was no longer good enough to be his daughter.

Everything around her had had a name, but was always something else. Daddy wasn't Daddy and Mummy wasn't Mummy. Home was actually somewhere else, and being ill was like being well. When someone said yes it meant no, and she could remember how confused she had been.

The brain is the only organ in the human body that has no feeling, and can therefore be operated on even while the patient is conscious.

And goodness, how cross they were when she went to the police and told them what P-O and his so-called friends got up to in the shed that was meant for pigs, not young boys who were angry with each other. Screaming and crying and punches left and right, before they sent her away to a new place that they told her she should call home from now on. But there it was just dark and silent and her arms were strapped down, just like they were now.

The doctor had said that if they just did a bit of cutting inside her head, she would no longer think everything was so complicated. She wouldn't have violent outbursts, and the hope was that she would be able to take care of herself. If only they could snip through a few unhelpful connections in her head, everything would be fine.

Daddy would mean Daddy in the same way that Mummy would mean Mummy.

She was woken from her thoughts by someone lifting her up in bed. But she kept her eyes shut because she didn't want to see the knife that was going to cut her.

Admittedly, they had actually said that they didn't use knives any more, because times had changed and they had more refined methods now. Something to do with electricity that she didn't quite understand, but she had nodded when they asked if she did, because she hadn't wanted to cause any more trouble than she already had.

Trouble, trouble, trouble, that's all you are. That's what Charlotte, the woman she had never called Mother, had always said whenever anything broke or fell on the floor. And it often did. If it wasn't wobbly glasses full of milk, it was slippery plates, or windows that were so thin that you couldn't see them until they were lying in pieces on the floor.

Someone took hold of her head and she felt the cold steel of a razor blade.

First the scraping sound as they shaved off the hair at the back of her head, then the pain, and finally the sound of the electric knife.

The future of the procedure was decided when Christian Rück, a psychiatrist at the Karolinska Institute, demonstrated that a combination of the negative side effects of treatment, as well as difficulties with its practical implementation, meant that it should not be used for anything other than strictly controlled experiments.

It's going to be fine, she thought. Now I'm going to be well, just like everyone else.

Rosenlund Hospital

Not Victoria Bergman, Hurtig thinks. Why not?

All the other names from Sigtuna are written on the notepad in front of him.

'But you did know Victoria?'

'Only from school,' Annette says. 'She wasn't part of our group.'

'Your group?'

The woman squirms. For the first time in their conversation a flicker of awareness appears in her eyes. 'I don't know if they'd want me to say,' she eventually says.

Hurtig has to make an effort to keep his voice sounding calm and friendly. 'Who wouldn't want you to?'

'Karl and Viggo. And P-O and Gert.'

The men, in other words, he thinks. 'But Karl, P-O, Viggo and Gert are all dead.'

Shit, why did I say that? he thinks the moment he says it.

Annette Lundström looks utterly confused. 'Stop it. Why are you teasing me? I don't think this conversation is fun any more. You can go now.'

'Sorry,' he says. 'I was wrong. I'll go very shortly, but there's one thing I've been wondering about. Of course Viggo was –' He breaks off. Think before you speak. Play it her way. 'Of course Viggo is a good person, and I've heard that he helps poor children to have a better life in Sweden, that he finds adoptive families for them. Is that right?'

The woman frowns. 'Well, of course it is. Haven't I already said that? I told that other police officer, that Sofia what's-her-name. Viggo was so kind to those children.'

A lot of information, Hurtig thinks. He makes notes as she talks, and a bizarre world is starting to take shape on his pad. He doesn't yet know if what he's looking at is real or just the world view of someone suffering from psychosis, but he's going to have plenty to talk to Jeanette about, because he can see patterns in what Annette Lundström is saying, even if she's confusing basics concepts like time and space.

She's talking about Sihtunum i Diasporan, the foundation that Viggo Dürer, Karl Lundström and Bengt Bergman were all involved in. It all sounds so nice, the way Annette describes it. The adopted children got along so well in Sweden, and the project abroad helped so many poor people.

'Do you know Victoria's father, Bengt Bergman?'

'No,' she replies. 'He helped Karl, P-O, Gert and Viggo to fund the foundation, but I've never met him.'

Another direct answer, and a correct one at that. OK, he thinks. Just one more question.

'Pythia's instructions. What does that mean?'

Once again the woman looks uncomprehending. 'Don't you know? Your colleague asked about that as well, that Sofia I spoke to a few days ago.'

'No, I don't actually know. But I've heard that it's a book. Have you read it?'

She looks bemused again. 'No, of course I haven't.'

'Why not?'

The emptiness returns to the woman's eyes.

'I've never seen a book with that title. Pythia's instructions are the original words, they're ancient and must never be questioned.'

She falls silent and looks down at the floor.

As Hurtig leaves Rosenlund Hospital behind him and pulls out onto Ringvägen, his thoughts slowly begin to settle into a pattern that makes sense.

Pythia's instructions, he thinks. Something exclusively for the men. Rules and truths that they invented for their own purposes. The term that best seems to describe it is 'brainwashing'.

He's sure that Jeanette will have something to say about all this, and as he stops at a traffic light he wonders how she's getting on. When she called to say that she was going to take a look at Lundström's films, he had wished he could have been there to support her. He knows she's tough, but how tough do you have to be not to end up a complete wreck?

Twenty minutes later, when he opens the door of the room in National Crime where Jeanette is sitting, the answer to his question is etched on her face.

Sunflower Nursing Home

Victoria Bergman is writing frenetically. Line after line about her daughter, Madeleine, while Sofia Zetterlund sits beside her and listens to the rasp of the pen.

Her cataract-stricken eyes can't see, but they're staring at Victoria.

'I understand that you're not finished with yourself yet,' the old woman says.

Victoria isn't listening to her, but after a while she stops writing, looks at the notepad, and circles a few key sentences before she puts her pen down.

CAPSULOTOMY HAD OPPOSITE EFFECT.
SUICIDAL BEHAVIOUR – COMPLETE LACK OF IMPULSE CONTROL.
MANIC IDEAS TAINTED BY RITUAL.

Then she looks up at Sofia, who holds out a trembling, wrinkled hand. She takes it, and soon feels a sense of calm return.

'I'm worried about you,' Sofia says quietly. 'They haven't gone yet, have they?'

'What do you mean?'

'Crow Girl and the others.'

Victoria swallows. 'No . . . Not Crow Girl, and maybe not the Sleepwalker. But all the others have gone. She helped me with that.'

'She?'

'Yes . . . I've been seeing a psychotherapist for a while. She's been helping me with my problems.'

I've helped myself, Victoria thinks. The Sleepwalker has helped me.

'Really? A psychologist?'

'Hmm . . . She's a lot like you, actually. But obviously she doesn't have your long experience.'

Sofia Zetterlund smiles enigmatically, squeezes Victoria's hand a bit tighter before letting go of it, then picks up the pack of cigarettes again. 'Let's have another one each. After that I daren't have any more. The manager is a hard woman, even if she must have a good heart somewhere.'

A good heart? Who has a good heart?

'Victoria, you wrote to me a few years ago and told me you were working as a psychologist. Are you still doing that?'

No one has a good heart. The ground in all human hearts is more or less stony.

'Sort of.'

Sofia seems happy with the answer, lights her cigarette and hands one to Victoria. 'Well, then,' she says. 'You've made an old woman very happy, but rather tired, and I don't think I can do anything more at the moment. I lose my focus and start to forget, and then I get sleepy. But the new pills they've put me on are better, and I'm much brighter than I was when that police officer came to ask about you.'

Victoria says nothing.

'I was more muddled then,' Sofia goes on. 'But to be honest, not as muddled as that policewoman probably thought. Sometimes it's useful being this old, you can pull out a bit of dementia whenever you need to. Except when I'm muddled for real, of course. Obviously it's hard to pretend when you don't need to.'

'What were they doing here?' Victoria asks.

Sofia blows another smoke ring over the table. 'They were looking for you, of course. The one who was here was named Jeanette Kihlberg. I promised I'd ask you to contact her if I heard from you.'

'OK, I'll do that.'

'Good . . .' Sofia smiles weakly and sinks into her chair.

Nowhere

Her body is just a few centimetres from the ceiling, and she's looking down on herself, at the girl who's tied up, thirsty and starving in a coffin under the ground.

She has a narrow tube in her mouth and they're feeding her the bitter, dry sludge she was given before. Food that just makes her weaker, an anti-food. Nuts and seeds, and something that tastes like resin, but she doesn't know what it is.

But she no longer cares. She feels light and happy.

Her mouth tastes of glue and she feels euphoric, as if she had the answers to all the mysteries of the universe.

She tries twisting her body, but it's stuck tight. She can't do it, no matter how hard she tries.

Not long ago she could drift, free as an astronaut in space, but now her body is tied down.

She starts to feel cold, an indescribable chill that makes her body shake inside.

Yet she still isn't frightened.

It's just the water inside her turning to ice.

The cold spreads out to her skin, and it feels like the ice inside is swelling and is going to burst out of her body, splitting her skin. Like when you put a glass bottle full of water in the freezer, and it breaks when the liquid expands into ice.

She smiles at the analogy.

Before she bursts and explodes into a thousand tiny fragments of glass she sees the man standing over her.

It's Viggo Dürer.

Kronoberg – Police Headquarters

The room that Kevin, the young police officer, shows her into is claustrophobically small and in no way merits its name.

'This is the viewing suite,' he says sarcastically, gesturing for her to sit down.

She looks around. A desk, a computer screen and various different video players, so that you can look at most films regardless of format. In the middle of the desk is a mixer board that makes it possible to stop the film and move forwards or backwards frame by frame. There's a switch to zoom in, and another to make the image sharper. Then other buttons and controls that she hasn't got a clue about. And a muddle of cables and leads.

'As soon as I find anything on Hannah Östlund's computer I'll bring it in to you,' he goes on. 'Well, just call me if you need anything.'

Once Kevin has shut the door behind him the room falls completely silent, and not even the air conditioning is audible any more. She looks at the stack of video cassettes, hesitates, then grabs one of them and puts it in the machine.

There's a crackle, and the screen in front of her begins to flicker. Jeanette takes a deep breath and leans back in the chair, at the same time putting her hand firmly on the wheel that will let her stop the film if it gets to be too much. She thinks of the deadman's handle that makes a train stop if the driver has a heart attack.

The first film contains exactly what Karl Lundström had said it did, and Jeanette can't bear to watch more than a minute before turning it off. But since she knows she has to look through the whole tape, she focuses her eyes alongside the screen and fast-forwards.

From the corner of her eye she can see the film blurrily, without any details, but clearly enough to see if the scene changes. After twenty minutes the machine stops with a loud click, then begins rewinding the film automatically.

Jeanette knows what she's just seen, but doesn't want to believe it's true.

She feels unable to absorb the fact that there are people who take pleasure in this. Who pay a lot of money to get hold of this sort of film, and risk their whole lives by collecting them. Why isn't it enough to fantasise about the perverse and forbidden? Why do they have to turn their sick fantasies into reality?

The second film is, if anything, even more unpleasant.

During the thirty minutes or so while she spools through the film, keeping her eyes focused beside the screen doesn't help, and instead she stares one metre above it.

On the wall is a photocopy of a cartoon. It shows a fat man, grinning and running towards the viewer with an iron bar in his hands. He's wearing a striped hat, and his teeth would give a dentist nightmares.

The little girl in the film is crying as the three men take turns penetrating the Thai woman.

The man in the cartoon is wearing a pair of dark trousers, his chest is bare, and he's got heavy boots on his feet. The look in his eyes is intense, almost crazy.

One of the men puts the girl on his lap. He strokes her hair and says something that Jeanette thinks is 'Daddy's little girl has been naughty'.

Jeanette notices the corner of her mouth getting wet, and when she licks her lips she can taste salt. Usually crying feels like a relief, but now it only enhances the feeling of disgust and impotence, and she finds herself thinking about the death penalty and people getting shut away and forgotten about. Doors to be locked and keys thrown away. She even sees scalpels performing castrations in anything but a chemical way, and for the first time in a very long time she feels hatred. An unreasonable, unforgiving hatred, and for a moment she understands why some people choose to publicise the names and pictures of convicted sex offenders without thinking of the consequences for their families.

At that moment she realises that she is a human being, even if she is a very bad police officer. A police officer and a human being. An impossible combination? Maybe.

The man in the cartoon is saying what she's feeling, and she understands what it's doing there.

That it has to be there so that the people working here don't forget that they're human beings as well as police officers.

Jeanette removes the film, puts it back in its box and inserts the third film.

Like the previous two, it starts with flickering noise. Then a shaky camera that seems to be looking for something, stops, zooms in, and the picture comes into focus. Jeanette thinks it looks like a hotel room, and gets a strong sense that this could be the film she's searching for.

She hopes she might be wrong, but her gut feeling is telling her it's the right one.

Whoever is holding the camera seems to realise that it's far too close, zooms out again and adjusts the focus once more. A young girl is lying splayed out on a large bed, and beside the bed are three half-dressed men.

The girl is Ulrika Wendin, and one of the men is Bengt Bergman, Victoria Bergman's father. The man Jeanette questioned when he was under suspicion for rape, and who was later released when his wife gave him an alibi.

Just as the door behind her opens and Jens Hurtig walks in, Jeanette looks up once more at the photocopied cartoon a metre above the ongoing rape.

The man in the cartoon is yelling, 'With a decent iron bar you can take the whole world by surprise!'

Hurtig stops behind her, takes a firm grip of the back of the chair and looks at the screen showing the rape scene. 'Is that Ulrika?' he asks quietly, and Jeanette nods in confirmation.

'Yes, I'm afraid it looks like it.'

'Who are they?' Jeanette feels Hurtig's hands tighten on the chair. 'Anyone we recognise?'

'So far only Bengt Bergman,' she replies. 'But that one' – she points at the screen – 'he's been in other films. I recognise his birthmark.'

'Only Bengt Bergman,' Hurtig mutters, and sits down as the camera sweeps around the room. A window with a view of a poorly lit car park, with the men's grunting in the background, then back to the bed.

'Stop!' Hurtig says. 'What's that in the corner?'

Jeanette turns the wheel to the left. The image stops and she rewinds, frame by frame.

'There,' he says, pointing at the screen as the camera passes one corner of the room. 'What's that?'

Jeanette pauses the film, increases the contrast of the picture, and can see what he means. In the dark corner someone is sitting on a chair watching the scene unfolding on the bed.

Jeanette zooms in, but can only make out the outline of the figure. No clear facial features.

Hurtig's suggestion of trying to see what's in the background gives Jeanette an idea. 'Wait here,' she says, and gets up. Hurtig looks at her in surprise as she opens the door and calls for Kevin.

The young police officer comes out into the corridor.

'Could you come in here for a minute, please?'

'Just a moment.'

Kevin goes back into his room and comes out again holding a CD in his hand. 'Here,' he says, handing it to Jeanette and then saying hello to Hurtig. 'That's what I've found so far on Hannah Östlund's computer, and I have to say I've never seen anything like it.' He gulps before going on. 'This is something else entirely. This has . . .'

'This has what?' Jeanette asks, looking at the clearly shocked young officer.

'I don't know how to put it, it's like it's got a philosophy or something . . .'

She looks at him intently, wondering what he means, but doesn't want to ask. She'll soon be seeing it herself. But before that she needs his help.

She takes hold of the wheel and moves slowly forward, frame by frame. As the camera sweeps across the window and the parking lot she stops. Outside there are a number of cars parked.

'Can you make the picture sharp enough to see the registration numbers?' she asks, turning to Kevin.

'I get you,' he says, leaning over the mixing desk and zooming in on the cars, then making the image crystal clear by quickly pressing a few buttons.

'And now you'd like me to find out who owns the cars?' he says.

'Have you got time?' Jeanette asks, smiling at him.

'Only because you're a friend of Mikkelsen's,' he says. 'Just don't let it become a habit.'

He winks at her, writes down the registration numbers and goes back to his room.

From the corner of her eye she sees Hurtig looking at her from one side.

'Impressed?' she asks as she removes the video cassette and inserts the CD.

'Very,' he replies. 'So what are we watching next?'

'Films from Hannah Östlund's computer.' She leans back and steels herself for what's about to come. 'Let's see if it is even worse, as he implied.'

'Is that even possible?' Hurtig mutters as a small room appears on the screen. The soundtrack of the film is full of tinny hissing.

Jeanette thinks it looks like a shed. In the background are a wheelbarrow and some buckets, rakes and other garden equipment.

'This looks like it was filmed from a television,' Hurtig says. 'You can tell by the flickering and the sound quality. The original was probably an old VHS.'

The picture lurches for a few moments as whoever's holding the camera seems to lose their balance.

Then a face appears, hidden behind a home-made mask that's supposed to be a pig. The snout is made out of what looks like a plastic mug. The camera pulls back to reveal more people. They're all wearing capes and similar pig masks. Now three girls are visible as well, on their knees behind a large plate with something unidentifiable on it.

'That must be Hannah and Jessica,' Hurtig says, pointing at the screen.

Jeanette nods, recognising the girls from the photograph in the school yearbook.

She realises that this must be what Annette Lundström had talked about. The initiation ritual that got out of hand and led to Hannah and Jessica leaving the school.

'And the one next to them must be Victoria Bergman,' Jeanette says, looking at the thin, fair-haired girl with bright blue eyes. It seems to her that Victoria is smiling. But it isn't an amused smile, more mocking. It's almost as if she's in on it, Jeanette thinks. That Victoria knows what's going to happen. There's also something vaguely familiar about her that she can't put her finger on, but she soon has other things to think about.

One of the masked girls takes a step forward and starts speaking.

'Welcome to Sigtuna College for the Humanities,' she says, as someone empties a bucket over Hannah, Jessica and Victoria. The soaked girls spit, cough and hiss.

Hurtig shakes his head. 'Bloody upper-class brats,' he mutters.

They watch the rest of the film in shared silence.

The final sequence shows Victoria leaning forward and starting to eat the contents of the plate in front of them. When one of the girls in the background takes off her mask and throws up, Jeanette recognises her as well. The young woman puts her mask on again, but the few seconds were enough.

'Annette Lundström,' Jeanette declares.

'Shit, yes . . .'

'How did your meeting with her go?' Jeanette asks.

'Kind of OK,' he says, and clears his throat. 'Some useful information, I think. But we can deal with that later.'

As they start to watch the next film she soon understands what Kevin meant about Hannah Östlund's films having some sort of philosophy.

The scene they're watching appears to be taking place in a pigpen at a farm. There's hay on the ground, which is dark with mud, or possibly something else. Shit, Jeanette thinks with disgust, pig shit. A row of people walk into the shot; they're all fully dressed and they sit down in a row around the pigpen, and she recognises all of them.

From the left, Per-Ola Silfverberg, then his wife, Charlotte, holding a small child, and Jeanette presumes that must be their foster-daughter, Madeleine. Then Hannah Östlund, Jessica Friberg and lastly Fredrika Grünewald. And at the edge of the picture is a man's profile.

It feels like all Jeanette has seen in the past few hours are images from her own nightmares about the cases she's been investigating recently. All the key players are there, pretty much everyone who's involved, and for a moment she is seized by a sense of unreality, as if she were actually in a nightmare, and she feels compelled to sneak a look at Hurtig.

OK, she thinks. He's in the nightmare as well, and is just as dumbstruck as I am.

When two naked boys step into the picture – or, rather, are shoved in by someone hidden behind the camera – the nightmare is complete.

Itkul and Karakul, she thinks, even though she knows they can't be the brothers from Kazakhstan because they hadn't been born when this film was recorded. Besides, these boys are clearly of East Asian origins.

They start to fight, first feebly and warily, then more intensely, and when one of them manages to get hold of the other one's hair, the second boy is furious and flails around wildly. But it doesn't help. A powerful blow to the head floors him.

Then the other boy sits on top of him and starts punching him.

Jeanette is feeling sick and freezes the picture. Organised dogfights, she thinks. Had Ivo been right from the very start?

'Christ,' she says to Hurtig with a sigh. 'Is he beating the other boy to death?'

Hurtig looks at her intently, but says nothing.

She fast-forwards instead, which makes is slightly easier to bear the abuse that follows.

After a couple of minutes she punches the stop button and returns to normal speed again. To her relief she sees that the boy on the ground is still alive; his chest is moving up and down as he breathes. The other boy gets up and stands in the middle of the filthy floor of the pen. Then he walks towards the camera, and just before he disappears out of view he gives it a quick smile. She quickly rewinds a few frames, and freezes the image once more, in the middle of the boy's smile.

'Do you see that?' she says.

'I see it,' Hurtig replies quietly. 'He's proud.'

She lets the film run again, but nothing more happens apart from the child in Charlotte Silfverberg's lap starting to wriggle, and just as she starts to comfort the child the film stops.

Philosophy, Jeanette thinks. Just as with the film from Sigtuna College, the sexual elements are incomprehensible to her, and she wonders if this is really all about sexuality.

Who could get turned on by this?

'Can you manage any more?' she asks Hurtig.

'To be honest . . . I don't know.' He looks tired and demoralised.

They're interrupted by a quick knock at the door, and Kevin comes in with some sheets of paper in his hand. 'How are you getting on?' he asks. 'Have you seen the film on the farm?'

'Yes,' Jeanette replies, then falls silent because she doesn't know what she can say about what she's just watched.

'The rest of the material on Östlund's computer is more obvious child pornography,' Kevin says, and Jeanette decides instantly that those films will have to wait. That's a case for National Crime. She's got what she needed. Evidence of the sect's existence, and that Ulrika Wendin's story was true. Maybe she'll also be able to find out who was sitting in the corner during the rape.

'Would you be able to help me compare this profile with the man in the hotel room?' she asks, rewinding the film to the part where the man in profile is visible.

'Sure.' With a few quick movements Kevin brings up the two sequences alongside each other on the screen. There's no doubt that it's the same man.

'How did you do with the registration numbers?' She can hear how agitated her voice sounds.

He nods. 'Printouts from the vehicle registry from the time when the recording was made.'

Jeanette looks at the list of names to whom the cars were registered. She's aware that it might contain innocent people who just happened to be staying the night at the hotel where the recording was made. But when she sees the names beside the various registration numbers, she realises that she's looking at a list of the men who raped Ulrika Wendin. A list of names as guilty as the row of spectators in the film they just watched of the pigpen at the farm.

The names on the list are all followed by dates of birth and ID numbers:

BENGT BERGMAN
KARL LUNDSTRÖM
ANDERS WIKSTRÖM
CARSTEN MÖLLER
VIGGO DÜRER

Just as Jeanette opens her mouth to read the list out to Hurtig, her mobile phone starts to vibrate in her inside pocket.

Kronoberg – Police Headquarters

Jens Hurtig can tell from Jeanette's terse responses and facial expression that Ivo Andrić had something very important to say.

'The same person that dumped the boy in Norra Hammarbyhamnen was in Ulrika Wendin's flat,' Jeanette says, putting her mobile back in her inside pocket. 'The fingerprints from the tape match some that Ivo found on Ulrika's fridge. And it's probably someone who's been treated for cancer.'

'Cancer?' Hurtig says. 'How does that work?'

'Chemotherapeutic drugs, cell poisons, can have side effects in the form of anaemia, hair loss or depleted bone marrow, for instance, but certain drugs can also lead to inflammation of the soles of the feet and palms of the hands, as well as the toes and fingers. The side effects can lead to bleeding and the loss of skin from the fingers, and that's what Ivo thinks happened in this case.'

'OK. So he suspects that the person who tied the bag over the boy has been treated for cancer. How sure is he?'

'Ivo's compared pictures of the side effects with our prints, and he says he's ninety per cent sure, maybe ninety-five.'

'That's a lot to take in all at once,' Hurtig says. 'National alert for Ulrika Wendin, then?'

Jeanette nods. The look on her washed-out face gives Hurtig a lump in his stomach, because he can see that she likes the girl.

He turns his head to study the printout in Jeanette's hand. 'So, those are the men who were at the hotel when Ulrika Wendin was raped,' he says. 'Bengt Bergman, Karl Lundström, and . . .' He leans closer to get a better look. 'Viggo Dürer?'

'That bastard keeps popping up. He's been at the edge of the picture the whole time, and now literally in those depraved films.'

'And he's dead, along with Bergman and Lundström. What about the other names, then? Anyone we know? Anders Wikström and Carsten Möller?'

'Don't you remember? Karl Lundström mentioned an Anders Wikström who had a cottage in Ånge. When he was first questioned, the bastard said that one of the films he had on his computer had been filmed there.'

Hurtig remembers now. Someone named Anders Wikström had cropped up early on in the investigation into Karl Lundström. But the only Wikström they had found in Ånge had been a senile old man who had been written off immediately.

'But that line of inquiry was dismissed by Mikkelsen,' he points out.

'Yes, it was.' Jeanette looks thoughtful. 'But Anders Wikström exists, and now we've got his ID number.'

'And Carsten Möller?'

'No idea.' She gets her mobile out again, taps in a number and puts the phone to her ear. 'Åhlund? Put out a national alert for Ulrika Wendin at once, then I'd like you to check something for me. No, two things, actually . . .' Hurtig hears her repeat the names and ID numbers of Anders Wikström and Carsten Möller.

Jeanette is as terse with Åhlund as she had been with Ivo Andrić. Hurtig watches as she quickly makes notes on the printout containing the names of the men who raped Ulrika Wendin and the registration numbers of their cars. A few minutes pass with Jeanette issuing curt orders, and Hurtig realises that Åhlund is working hard at the other end of the line.

Jeanette looks completely exhausted as she ends the call. But Hurtig reflects that this is nothing to worry about, seeing as she works best when they're under pressure. 'What did Åhlund say?' He glances at the printout and sees that Jeanette has written the word 'surgeon'.

'Carsten Möller used to be a paediatric doctor before he moved to Cambodia. The trail ends there. And Anders Wikström doesn't own a cottage in Ånge. But on the other hand he was reported missing in Thailand six months ago.'

'So at least there is an Anders Wikström,' Hurtig says. 'Lundström was a bit confused, wasn't he? Maybe he got them muddled up? Anders Wikström was in the film, whereas someone else might own a cottage in Ånge. That could be it . . .'

Jeanette agrees, and Hurtig looks around the room. I hate them, he thinks, all the bastards who do things that mean a room like this has to exist.

'So,' Jeanette says, 'how did your talk with Annette Lundström go?'

He thinks about the film of the girls at Sigtuna College. It hadn't looked like Annette Lundström was enjoying her role as a bully. She had been sick.

'Annette's deep in psychosis,' he says. 'But she did confirm most of what Sofia Zetterlund told you, and I think there's a pattern in what she said, even though she isn't well. She wants to go to Polcirkeln, and she reeled off a list of the people who would be there . . .' He pauses to get his notepad out. 'P-O, Charlotte and Madeleine Silfverberg, Karl and Linnea Lundström, Gert Berglind, Fredrika Grünewald and Viggo Dürer.'

Jeanette looks at him. 'God, I'm so sick of all those names.'

She stands and begins to gather up the films. 'I just want to get out of here.'

Hurtig adds that Annette Lundström had repeated what she had previously said about Dürer being involved in adoptions.

'He had foreign children at the farm in Struer and up in Polcirkeln.'

'Shit.' Jeanette sighs. 'Polcirkeln . . .'

'I know the geography up there pretty well,' Hurtig says, 'and it won't take long for our colleagues in the Norrbotten force to go door-to-door in Polcirkeln. I mean, it's just a few houses.'

On the way down to the car Jeanette's phone rings again. She looks at the screen. 'Forensics,' she says as she answers.

The conversation is over in less than thirty seconds.

'Any news?'

Jeanette takes a deep breath. 'The samples of paint we took from the car at Dürer's villa are identical to the traces found out in Svartsjölandet. So the lawyer could have been the person who dumped the boy out there by the jetty back in the spring, and –' She breaks off and slaps her forehead. 'Fuck!' she exclaims. 'Åhlund told me Dürer had been treated for cancer –'

'So those could be Dürer's fingerprints that were found –'

'In Ulrika's flat.'

'Which means that Dürer might still be alive . . .'

Hundudden – Island of Djurgården

'So who was found dead on the boat if it wasn't Viggo?'

Jeanette has her suspicions, and gets her phone out again.

Detective Superintendent Gullberg of the Skåne police answers after seven long rings, and she explains the situation.

He immediately adopts a defensive attitude and does what a lot of people do when they feel threatened. He goes on the attack. 'Are you questioning the autopsy?' he says irritably. 'Our medical officers are good.'

'Have you got their report to hand?'

'Yes,' he mutters grouchily. 'Give me a moment.' She hears him rustling some papers before he returns. 'What do you want to know?'

'Does it say anything about the man having cancer?'

'No . . . Why should it?'

'Because he had been treated for cancer.'

Gullberg falls silent. 'Oh shit . . . It says here that he was in excellent health for his age. The physique of a fifty-year-old, apart from being slightly overweight –'

'He was almost eighty.'

Gullberg clears his throat, and she realises that he has worked out that they might have made a mistake. 'Autopsies are performed quickly after accidents,' he says. 'The lab in Malmö does what they're told, but they aren't infallible. And we had no reason to –'

'Don't worry. You don't have to explain. Does it say anything else in their report?'

'Now I come to look at it more closely, it mentions that some of the fillings in the dead man's teeth were done in South-East Asia.'

Thailand, Jeanette thinks. Anders Wikström.

The police van with tinted windows pulls up behind them and the head of the response unit jumps out from the passenger seat. He slaps the side of the van hard and walks over to Jeanette as the back doors open and nine masked police officers get out in total silence. They divide themselves into three groups. Eight of them are armed with sub-machine guns, and the ninth has a bolt-action rifle.

The officer in charge is unmasked, and as he walks up he introduces himself and says they're ready to go in. As a result of the evidence from the paint samples, Dennis Billing has agreed to authorise a search of Viggo Dürer's villa at Hundudden. The new information they have received from Skåne and the fact that they've found what could be Dürer's fingerprints in Ulrika Wendin's apartment helped to convince him.

'Is that really necessary?' Jeanette asks, nodding towards the man with the rifle.

'PSG-90. In case the operation demands a sniper,' the officer in charge replies officiously.

'Let's just hope it doesn't,' Hurtig mutters.

'OK, let's go in.' Jeanette turns and glances at Hurtig.

'Just one question.' The head of the unit clears his throat. 'Well, this has all been a bit quick, so our advance information is somewhat sketchy. What's the primary target, and what sort of resistance can we expect?'

Before Jeanette has time to answer, Hurtig steps forward. 'We believe that objective number one, a young woman, could be in the building,' he says. 'The objective's name is Ulrika Wendin, and we suspect that objective number two, the homeowner, has kidnapped objective number one and is holding her captive. Objective number two is an approximately eighty-year-old lawyer, and as far as resistance is concerned, we haven't got a fucking clue.'

Jeanette gives Hurtig a shove. 'Stop it,' she hisses, then turns to the head of the unit. 'I apologise for my colleague. He can be rather trying at times. But most of what he said is correct. We suspect that the owner of the house, a lawyer named Viggo Dürer, is holding Ulrika Wendin captive in there. Obviously he could be armed, but we don't know.'

'Good,' the man says with a stiff smile. 'Let's do it,' he says, and jogs back to his subordinates.

'You need to lose that attitude.' Jeanette goes and stands by the car and waits for the heavily armed officers to enter the house ahead of them. The officer in charge raises his right arm to get his men's attention, then gives his orders. 'Alpha to the front and the main entrance. Bravo will go in through the rear, and Charlie will secure the garage to the side of the house. Any questions?'

The masked officers don't say a word.

'OK, let's go!' he concludes, lowering his arm.

Jeanette hears Hurtig mutter '*Jawohl, mein Führer*' to himself, but can't be bothered to comment.

Everything happens very fast after that. The first group of three men force the gate with a heavy bolt cutter and move quickly up to the main entrance, where they take positions on either side of the door. The second group disappears out of sight round the left-hand side of the house, and the third heads towards the garage. Jeanette hears the sound of breaking glass and a cry telling anyone inside the house that it's the police, and that they should lie down on the floor.

'Ground floor secured!' they hear from inside the house, and Hurtig comes to stand beside her. 'Sorry,' he says. 'It was a stupid thing to say.

I actually like these guys, but sometimes I think they get a bit carried away with the militarism.'

'I know what you mean,' she says, touching his arm lightly. 'The difference between them and the thugs can sometimes be hard to see.'

Hurtig nods.

'First floor secured!'

'Garage secured!'

Jeanette watches as the head of the unit emerges from the house and gives the signal that it's OK for them to approach.

'The house is empty, but it was alarmed,' he says when Jeanette and Hurtig reach the steps. 'One of the old sort, not connected to a security company, just designed to make a hell of a racket. Effective once upon a time, but not these days.'

'Is everything under control otherwise?'

'Yes. No girl on either the ground or first floors. The basement's empty, but we're checking for concealed spaces.'

The six masked men who had been inside the house come out onto the steps.

'Nothing,' one of them says. 'You can go in now.'

First came nothing, then came nothing, and then came nothing, she thinks, remembering the lyrics to an old song by Kent as she goes through the door with Hurtig and the other police officers gather on the lawn.

They walk through the sparsely furnished hall into the living room. The house smells musty, and there's a thin layer of dust like a dull skin covering all the furniture and ornaments. The walls are covered with paintings and old posters. Most of them have a medical theme. On one of the bookcases there's a skull next to a stuffed bird, and the room looks to Jeanette like some sort of museum.

She goes over to the shelves and pulls out one of the books. *Forensic Medicine Textbook*, she reads. Published in 1994 by the Institute of Forensic Medicine at Uppsala University.

The kitchen isn't quite as musty, and Jeanette detects the sharp smell of cleaning fluid.

'Bleach,' Hurtig says, sniffing the air.

Jeanette can't see anything of immediate interest in the kitchen. She goes out into the hall and up the stairs to the first floor. In the background she can hear Hurtig going through the kitchen cupboards.

The bedroom is empty apart from a wardrobe and a large bed with no sheets or blankets. Just a bare, stained mattress. As Jeanette opens the wardrobe door Hurtig calls to her from downstairs, but before she goes down she looks at the neatly hung dresses, blouses and suits. A strange feeling washes over her as she sees the old-fashioned women's underwear. Corsets and suspender belts made of nylon and other synthetic materials, and white underpants made of coarse linen.

In the kitchen Hurtig is searching through one of the drawers. He's laid a number of different objects on the worktop beside him.

'He has damn strange things in his cutlery drawer,' he says, pointing at the row of tools.

Jeanette looks closer and sees a number of pairs of pliers, a small saw and several different sizes of tweezers. 'What's this?' she says, holding up a wooden stick with a small hook at the end.

'Weird, but so far not illegal,' he says. 'Come on, let's take a look at the basement.'

The cellar smells of mould, and down there they find nothing but a box of half-rotten apples, two fishing rods and a pallet with eight bags of easy-mix concrete on it. Otherwise the four damp rooms are completely empty, and she can't help wondering why it took six police officers almost ten minutes to work out that there were no hidden rooms.

It's a disappointed Jeanette and an equally frustrated Hurtig who emerge onto the steps in front of the response unit and their commanding officer.

'OK, just the garage left before we can go home,' she says, and starts walking dejectedly towards the building next to the house.

One of the masked police officers comes up beside her and pulls his balaclava up to free his mouth. 'The only thing we noticed once we'd forced the door was that the window was broken. Looks like someone broke it with the wrench we found on the ground outside.'

Rather shame-faced, Hurtig goes over to the officer who's holding a sealed plastic bag containing the wrench. He says something, looks uncomfortable, then climbs up onto the concrete drain cover immediately behind him. Jeanette notes that the concrete looks new, and presumes that this was why those bags of cement were in the cellar.

She looks into the garage, but doesn't even bother going inside. She already knows that the only things in there are a workbench and some empty shelves. Nothing else.

They walk back to the car. Jeanette is disappointed that they found nothing useful at all and have made no progress. But at the same time she's relieved that they didn't find Ulrika Wendin dead inside the house.

Hurtig gets in the driver's seat, starts the car and pulls out onto the main road leading back to the city.

They drive the first few kilometres without speaking. Then Jeanette breaks the silence.

'Did you say it was you who broke the window because you didn't have a key? Or did you confess that you don't know how to pick a lock?'

Hurtig grins. 'No, I didn't have to confess that I'm useless at picking locks. He said they got into the garage using a sledgehammer. It was impossible to get the door open because it had been bolted from the inside.'

'Stop the car, for God's sake!' Her yell makes Hurtig slam on the brakes automatically, and the police van behind them blows its horn angrily, but stops as well.

'Drive back, fast as you fucking can!'

Hurtig gives her a quizzical look, then turns the car round and puts his foot down, making the tyres smoke. Jeanette winds down the window and sticks out her arm, and the van does a quick U-turn when she gestures for it to follow them.

'Fuck, fuck, fuck,' she mutters through clenched teeth.

Nowhere

During her internal journeys, when she's in a sort of hibernation, she feels neither pain nor fear, and hopes to be able to take some of her new-found spiritual strength back to earth with her.

She makes another attempt at the states of America. To begin with she could do all but four of them, then she learned them all, but now she's lost four or five again.

Columbia, she tries. Warner, Columbia and NLC.

No sound, even though she's screaming inside. Her brain is going to wither as well, just like her body.

Warner isn't a state, nor is it a Canadian province. She's thinking of American film companies. Columbia Pictures, Warner Brothers and New Line Cinema.

She tries tensing her muscles, but can't feel anything at all. She has no body, yet it still hurts, and she thinks she must be moving because she imagines she can hear the sound of skin scraping against wood. A dry, rasping squeak. She can't move her tongue either, and suspects she must be getting close to the end, that her body is on its way to dissolving into nothingness.

Warner Brothers, New Line Cinema.

She can see images from the film *Seven*, distributed by New Line Cinema.

She's got it on her computer, and has seen it several times.

She remembers the seven deadly sins in the order that the murders occur, beginning with gluttony, where the killer forces a fat man to eat himself to death.

Then greed, where a businessman is drained of blood.

And then sloth . . .

She can't get any further, because she suddenly realises what they're going to do to her.

The man in the film who was punished for his sloth had been tied to a bed in a dark room, and she feels sick when she thinks of the way he looked.

His grey-brown skin had almost split away from his skull, his veins and bones seemed to have eaten their way half out of him, and he had looked like one of those bodies that have been found in peat or whatever it is.

A thousand years old, but with the expressions on their faces almost intact.

Is that what she looks like now?

Then she hears a scratching sound, followed by a metallic bang, so loud that it makes her ears pop.

The police are here, she thinks. They're unlocking the door to let me out.

The light that falls into the room where Ulrika Wendin is tied down is so bright that it feels like the corneas of her eyes are catching fire.

Hundudden – Island of Djurgården

The door of Viggo Dürer's garage had been locked with a solid metal bolt from the inside. The garage was empty. There were no other doors, and just one small window that even a child couldn't have got through.

It's like a classic crime mystery. The locked room.

When Hurtig had started saying how hard it had been to break the door open, it had struck Jeanette that there had to be another way into Dürer's garage. She and Hurtig are now standing inside it together with the unit commander, and once she's explained her reasoning the three of them turn round and look at the solid wooden shelving. The hidden door must be behind there.

The unit commander gives the order to fetch a crowbar, and two of the masked officers disappear off towards the van at the gate.

Jeanette carefully inspects the way the shelves are constructed. The sides are sturdy and on the inside of them there are large rivets on steel rails that appear to be attached to the back of the sides, as well as the roof and floor of the shelving, like a large metal rectangle. It's suddenly apparent that the shelving is fastened from the other side, since there are several thick screws sticking out of the metal rails. She shouldn't have just accepted that the garage was empty, she sighs to herself. Now they may have lost valuable time.

The two officers return with a crowbar each, and begin to prise off the metal rails. Behind them are grooves in the concrete that must be the outline of the door, and a third officer begins to pull at one of the screws. There's a loud noise and the door opens a few centimetres. Another few tugs and the gap grows to ten centimetres.

Ulrika, Jeanette thinks. For a brief moment she has time to paint a terrifying mental picture of what might be behind the shelving. Ulrika Wendin's body, bricked into the wall. But the illusion vanishes the moment the door flies open.

Inside is a cramped niche in the wall, perhaps half a metre deep, and a very narrow flight of steps leads down into the darkness to the left. In the ceiling of the niche a broken catch is swinging from a loop. She can feel the tension rising in every vein and muscle.

Then the response unit takes over again.

Their commander takes two of his most experienced officers with him, and after what feels like at least ten minutes a voice calls from the hole in the ground. 'Cellar secure!'

Jeanette and Hurtig hurry down the narrow staircase and are hit by a dry, rancid smell. Nothing, Jeanette convinces herself. They haven't found anything down here.

She remembers Ulrika Wendin. Her face, her voice, the way she moved. If they had found her down here, dead or alive, they wouldn't have declared the cellar secure.

The staircase leads to an almost square room, perhaps five by five metres, with a closed door in the far wall. A lit bulb hangs from a chain in the ceiling, and on the floor there are two large dog cages. The walls are covered with maps, photographs, newspaper cuttings and layer upon layer of pieces of paper, all different sizes.

'What the hell . . . ?' Hurtig groans at the sight of the dog cages, and Jeanette can see that he's thinking the same thing she is.

There are toys hanging from the ceiling on pieces of string. Jeanette counts twenty or so, including a little wooden dog with wheels and a bunch of broken Bratz dolls. But the main impression is one of paper and more paper. *L'homme du petit papier*, she thinks.

Viggo Dürer is the man with scraps of paper. How could Sofia have got it so right?

The room also contains a small shelf holding a row of bottles and jars, and a low, open cupboard with more stacks of papers and documents. On top of the cupboard are two miniature toy monkeys, one with a pair of cymbals and the other with a drum.

She takes a closer look at the bottles on the shelf. Some are marked with chemical symbols, others with Cyrillic writing, but she has a pretty good idea what they contain. Even though they are all sealed, there is a faintly acrid smell.

'Embalming fluids,' she mutters, turning towards Hurtig, who looks even paler now.

The door at the far end of the room opens. 'We've found the other entrance, and another room,' the unit head says, and she thinks his voice sounds unsteady. 'It seems to be . . .' He breaks off and pulls off his balaclava. 'A drying room or something . . .' His face is white as chalk.

A drying room? Jeanette thinks.

He shows them into a narrow corridor, barely a metre wide and between six and seven metres long. It's made entirely from concrete and comes to an abrupt end at a ladder leading up to a hole in the ceiling. A strip of light is shining on the metal of the ladder.

Halfway along the left-hand wall is a steel door.

'The drying room?' Jeanette indicates the door, and the unit head nods.

'The ladder leads up to the garden behind the house,' he goes on, as if to take their attention away from the closed door. 'You might have noticed –'

'The drain cover?' Hurtig interrupts him. 'I was standing on top of it less than half an hour ago.'

'True,' the unit head replies, 'but if we'd opened the cover from the outside we'd only have seen mesh over a dark hole.'

She turns to Hurtig and the unit head, who are standing listlessly outside the steel door. 'I'm going to open it,' she says. 'Why is it closed, anyway?'

The head of the response unit just shakes his head and takes a deep breath. 'What the hell are we dealing with here?' he says slowly. 'What kind of sick bastard are we after?'

'We know his name is Viggo Dürer,' Hurtig replies. 'And we have a rough idea of what he looks like, but we have no idea of what sort of person he is –'

'Whoever did this isn't a person,' the unit head interrupts. 'This is something else altogether.'

They look at one another but say nothing. The only sounds are the wind hitting the garage roof and the other police officers moving around up in the garden.

Something has scared these men so much that they're not sure about showing us what they've found, Jeanette thinks, and feels suddenly hesitant. She thinks of her hellish experience at National Crime that afternoon.

Hurtig gives the door a light nudge.

'There's a light switch to the right of the door,' the unit head says.

'There's fluorescent lighting in there, unfortunately.' Then he turns away, and the steel door slowly slides open.

In the belief that hesitation and reflection are just a waste of time, Jeanette switches the light on at once and takes a step inside. In a fraction of a second her brain makes a long sequence of instinctive decisions that lead her to take an entirely rational view of what's inside the room.

First she registers everything she sees, and once she's done that she's going to shut the door and leave the rest to Ivo Andrić.

Time stops for her.

She registers that Ulrika Wendin isn't in the room, and that no other living person is either. She also registers that there are two large extractor fans mounted on each of the end walls, and that there are four thin steel cables running across the room.

She registers what's hanging from the cables, and what's standing on the floor in the middle of the room.

Then she shuts the door.

Hurtig has backed away a few steps and is now leaning against the concrete wall with his hands in his pockets, staring down at the floor. Jeanette can see his jaw moving, as if he were chewing on something, and she feels sorry for him. The head of the response unit turns round again as he hears the door close. He breathes out and rubs his forehead, but says nothing.

When Ivo Andrić arrives with the forensics unit, Jeanette and Hurtig look at their young, untroubled faces with melancholy sympathy. Even if the assistants will only be dealing with the anteroom of Dürer's museum, the room with the newspaper cuttings, old toys and scraps of paper, they'll still have to see the unnameable horrors in the drying room.

Now wearing plastic gloves, Jeanette and Hurtig take a first look at the vast quantity of documents, and after a while it's as if they've come to a tacit agreement not to discuss what they saw in the other room. They know what's in there, and in the fullness of time Ivo Andrić will give them answers. That's enough.

Sofia had been right again, Jeanette thinks. A retrospective exhibition of castrations, or a loss of sexual belonging. Well, why not?

She's experiencing the same heavy tiredness she felt after sitting in front of the screen in National Crime, and forces herself to look for signs of light. One is that there's still hope that Ulrika Wendin is alive, and that hope gives Jeanette strength.

They're photographing the material and making a rough catalogue of what it contains. The more thorough examination will be done later, and not by them, so it's important not to forget their first impressions, when their awareness of what they're seeing is still relatively uncontaminated.

At first glance, the main categories appear to be cuttings from newspapers and magazines, photographs, handwritten documents, everything from small notes to long letters, as well as artefacts, primarily toys. There's another category for copies of articles and extracts from books. How much of it is personal memories or documentation of criminal activity is in most cases impossible to determine. Among the photographs are Polaroids of Samuel Bai, whom she can easily recognise by the RUF scars on his chest.

The bottles and jars on the shelf in the room will obviously be examined by the forensics team, and Jeanette wastes no time on them. She has a rough idea of what they contain. Formalin, formaldehyde and similar substances and chemicals used for embalming.

Nor do she and Hurtig touch the dog cages and the small drain in the middle of the room, even if they can't help glancing in that direction occasionally.

The work proceeds quickly and with a degree of detachment towards what they're seeing. That's why Hurtig barely reacts when he finds an illustrated description of the tools used for embalming, and recognises the implements he found in the kitchen drawer up in the house. Pliers, a saw, tweezers, and lastly a wooden stick with a hook at the end.

They find several newspaper clippings about the three boys at Thorildsplan, Danvikstull and Svartsjölandet, but there don't appear to be any clippings about the boy who was found a few days ago down in Norra Hammarbyhamnen.

What's striking is that the majority of the clips are from Soviet or Ukrainian newspapers. It's hard to work out what the articles are about because neither Jeanette nor Hurtig can read Cyrillic, and because almost all of them lack illustrations. They're marked with dates, in a range running from the early 1960s to fairly recently, the summer of 2008. The articles will have to be scanned and sent to Iwan Lowynsky at the Ukrainian security police.

Jeanette soon decides to break off her work with the material, and agrees with Hurtig that they've got enough for the time being, and that the overall picture will become clear later.

Just one more thing, she thinks.

She's standing in front of the low cupboard with the toy monkeys, looking at a photograph attached to the middle of the wall with a drawing pin. There's something about the picture that she recognises. It conjures up memories of the films at National Crime, and the person she saw in them looks very similar to the one in the photograph. The man in the picture is sitting on the veranda in front of a house. Probably Viggo Dürer, but there's also something familiar about the house.

She takes the picture down from the wall, and sits on the floor with it still in her hand as she looks at Hurtig with eyes that she presumes must look bloodshot and tired.

'Do you want to go back to the office?' she asks.

'Not really.'

'Me neither. But I can't go home, because I don't feel like being alone tonight, and I don't even want to see Sofia, if I'm honest. The only person I think I can bear being with at the moment is, actually, you.'

Hurtig looks almost embarrassed. 'Me?'

'Yes, you.'

He smiles. 'I don't feel like being on my own tonight either. First those films, and now this . . .'

All of a sudden she feels a new sort of closeness to him. They really have been through the day from hell together.

'We can sleep at work tonight,' she finds herself saying. 'How about it? Get some beers and just relax? Forget about all this, we won't even mention it. Just forget everything for one single bloody evening?'

He laughs quietly. 'OK. Why not?'

'Great. But before we knock off I have to call von Kwist. He's damn well going to have to drag himself to work, sick or not. We need to upgrade the hunt for Dürer to a national search. Besides, I want to check out this picture.' She shows Hurtig the photograph she's just taken down from the wall.

Klippgatan, First Flight of Steps – Södermalm

When she leaves the Sunflower Nursing Home, Sofia drives to Norra Hammarbyhamnen. The Sleepwalker will never come here again, and she wants to see the place one last time.

She sits on the quayside for a while. Tries to work out why she has kept coming back here, time after time. A short distance away there's a police cordon and some forensics officers. She wonders what's happened. Maybe someone has jumped from the bridge. That sort of thing happens. After ten minutes she walks back to the car and drives home.

Unaware that she's being followed.

She parks down by the London Viaduct and walks up Folkungagatan, and just as she's passing Erstagatan she hears a sudden loud noise.

A man is standing beside his car a few metres away from her. He's just slammed the boot shut, and looks at her in surprise as he locks it.

Calm down, Sofia, she thinks. It's over now.

But it isn't. Not really.

Just as she's about to turn into Klippgatan she hears another noise that seems unnaturally loud to her.

It's the bell on the door of the little corner shop. The owner emerges in the company of a small, bent old woman.

'Take care now, Birgitta,' he says. 'Those steps up to the church can be slippery.'

The woman has her grey hair in a bun, and mutters something before she turns away, putting a couple of weekly magazines in her bag.

Sofia stares. It isn't possible, she thinks.

The woman's face is lowered and shadowed by the lighting of the shop sign, but Sofia recognises her chubby neck and stares at the little dimples in her cheeks.

She remembers putting her finger on them, laughing and asking why they were called dingles.

Victoria's legs are shaking as the woman turns into Klippgatan and starts walking towards Sofia Church. That familiar rear view, the rounded hips, the tight bun and the rolling gait.

She takes a few steps in the same direction, but her legs can hardly bear her.

The magazines sticking out of the woman's bag are *All Year Round* and *Saxon's Weekly*, and Victoria knows that they will spend a few days on the coffee table until they've been read. Then they'll be demoted to the toilet, where they'll stay until the crosswords are finished.

You don't exist, she thinks. You're a product of my imagination. Get lost.

She can still feel the heat of the fire on her face, hear the beams crunch and crackle before they finally crash down into the basement. Bengt and Birgitta Bergman are buried in the Woodland Cemetery in a casket of dark red cherrywood. At least they ought to be.

At the bottom of the first flight of steps the woman stops beside a rubbish bin, hunts through the contents and pulls out a beer can, which she triumphantly puts in her bag to reclaim the deposit on. As Victoria gets closer she can see that the woman's brown wool suit is dirty and worn, and that her shoes are filthy and scuffed.

Then the old woman laboriously begins to climb the steps on Klippgatan, leaning against the handrail. Just like the stairs at home. The ones she cleaned and cleaned, without it ever making any difference.

Victoria follows her. Grabs onto the cold handrail and is transported back in time. 'We have to talk,' she says. 'You can't just go without explaining what's going on. You're dead. Don't you get it?'

The woman turns round.

It isn't her. Of course it isn't.

The woman looks at her warily for a moment, then turns back and continues up the steps to the path through the little park at the top.

Victoria is left there alone, but just a few metres away, at the bottom of the steps, is someone who's as alone as she is.

Kronoberg – Police Headquarters

A phone call from hell reaches Prosecutor Kenneth von Kwist as he's standing with a glass of champagne in his hand outside the restaurant of police headquarters talking to the female national police chief about the importance of cutting back your geraniums at exactly the right time.

The prosecutor knows nothing about plants, but over the years he's learned that the art of conversation is to ask questions first and then transform the information received into general and uncontroversial statements of fact. Some people would call it empty chatter, but von Kwist believes it to be a social gift.

When his phone rings he excuses himself, puts his glass down and moves away. Before he answers he has already decided that when he gets back to the police chief he is going to say that February is a good month to prune your houseplants, but that he'll say this with a degree of caution.

He sees on the screen that it's Jeanette Kihlberg, and a lump appears in his stomach. He doesn't like getting calls from her. Whenever she calls it means trouble.

'Yes?' he says, hoping it won't take long.

'We need to put out a national alert for Viggo Dürer,' Jeanette says without any introductory pleasantries, which annoys him. Surely it's only good manners to say who you are before getting to the point? The prosecutor also realises that his hopes of getting back to the party quickly and picking up the interesting conversation about plants are about to be dashed.

'We believe that Dürer's alive, and I want to issue a warrant for his arrest,' she goes on. 'Top priority. Airports, ferries, border posts –'

'Stop, stop, hold your horses,' he interrupts, playing dumb. 'Who is this? I don't recognise the number.'

Damn, he thinks. Viggo Dürer's alive.

That could explain the attack outside the ice bar. The prosecutor touches his still-aching jaw.

'It's me, Kihlberg. I've just left Dürer's house on Djurgården, I'm on my way back into the city.'

'So whose body was found in the boat?'

'That hasn't been ascertained yet, but I think it might be Anders Wikström.'

'And who the hell might that be?'

'You ought to know that. His name cropped up in the Karl Lundström case.'

Jeanette Kihlberg pauses, and he sees an opportunity to put the brakes on the conversation. 'So . . .' he says, as slowly as he can. 'On what grounds, Detective Superintendent, do you wish to take such a drastic measure as invoking paragraph seven of chapter twenty-four of the Judicial Procedure Act? The second clause? There isn't a possibility that you're being overhasty once again?'

He can hear her drawing breath, and he's amused by the certainty that she's about to explode. He continues, even more slowly, as he sees Dennis Billing get out of a taxi and walk in through the main entrance. 'I mean, over the years you and I have had a number of dealings with each other, and, if we're being completely frank, Detective Superintendent, there's been more than one occasion when you've lacked sufficient evidence for your assertions and have had to take a couple of trips to Canossa.' He's on the point of saying 'my dear', but stops himself. To his surprise, he hears Jeanette laugh.

'Very funny, Kenneth,' she says, and he feels disappointed that she hasn't flown into a rage and let rip with the torrent of feminist drivel he was expecting.

Before he manages to think of a suitable riposte, Jeanette goes on without any audible sign of excitement. 'Beneath Dürer's garage we've discovered things that would make your favourite murderer Thomas Quick green with envy. But unlike that case, we're on firm ground, if you understand what I mean? I'm talking body parts, torture instruments and equipment for a hell of a lot of medical experiments. And from what I could see, Dürer isn't just guilty of one or two murders. You're more likely to have to count them by the dozen, then round the total up. There's no doubt at all in my mind that we've got the right man. He's documented everything. The whole lot.'

His head is spinning. 'Can you repeat that?'

Prosecutor Kenneth von Kwist takes a deep breath and tries to think of relevant questions, suitable legal objections, significant contradictions in her analysis of the situation, whatever the hell might justify his desire to postpone issuing a warrant for Dürer's arrest.

But his head is empty.

It's as if someone has built a firewall between his brain and his larynx. He knows what he wants to say, but his mouth won't move. His entire army of brain cells has mutinied and is refusing to obey orders, and with the phone pressed to his ear all he can do is listen to the pious, conceited Jeanette Kihlberg in silence. She's like a spot on your arse, he thinks. And what the hell has Dürer been up to?

Body parts? he wonders.

The prosecutor's chain of associations is as short as it is logical, but his new medication, together with the alcohol, makes it easier for him to suppress that particular thought. His intoxication is helping him not to lose his mind completely, but he's starting to feel distinctly nauseous.

'Ivo Andrić is still out there with forensics. I've cordoned off the immediate vicinity and given orders for radio silence. All communication is to be conducted via personal phones rather than an open line. I've also imposed a complete ban on talking about what we've found to anyone not directly involved, because I don't want the papers there at such a sensitive time. There aren't any close neighbours, but anyone living nearby is probably wondering why there's so much traffic. But there's nothing we can do about that.'

She pauses, and von Kwist clenches his fist in his pocket and prays that she's finished at last, that everything's going to be nice and quiet and he can get back to others at the party. After all, he only wants to be happy, drink some free wine and eat canapés with his colleagues.

Please, let it end soon, he begs of the God he turned his back on at fifteen after a heated argument with his confirmation priest and to whom he has never returned. But whoever he is praying to is either holding a grudge, deaf or simply not there, because Jeanette Kihlberg continues. The prosecutor's legs are now feeling so weak that he doubts they can hold him much longer, so he grabs the nearest chair and sits down.

'Look, I'm convinced that putting out a national alarm for Viggo Dürer is an absolute necessity,' Jeanette goes on. 'I want your consent, but because I can hear that you're at a party and presumably can't get away easily, we'll have to leave the paperwork till later. You've either got to trust me, or explain to my boss tomorrow morning why the national alarm was delayed so long. It's your choice, basically.'

Finally she stops, and he hears the sound of a car braking hard, then her colleague Jens Hurtig swearing.

'And there's no doubt at all that it's Dürer?' The prosecutor has regained the power of speech after a short rest on the chair, and he still wants to believe in the possibility that someone else might be responsible, but her answer is immediate and is, even for anyone doubtful, difficult to misinterpret.

'No,' she says, and Prosecutor von Kwist realises that he is about to embark on his very own walk to Canossa.

'In that case you have my consent to take whatever measures you think necessary.' He falls silent and tries to think of a remark that will restore his authority and suppress his fear that he's going to end up in the most terrible mess. 'Even if you want to, can you at least wait a while before getting Dürer added to the FBI's most wanted list?' That's the best he can come up with on the spur of the moment, but he's not happy with it. He realises that it didn't hit home the way he hoped it would.

Dennis Billing is coming towards him with two glasses of sparkling wine, and the prosecutor gets ready to end this dreadful conversation.

But he doesn't know what to say. It feels like he's caught in a trap. The more he struggles to get free, the more stuck he gets.

'I'll leave the FBI till tomorrow,' Jeanette Kihlberg says. 'He'll probably end up on their list anyway, whether you like it or not.' He hears her draw breath and sigh theatrically. 'And as far as Henry IV's walk to Canossa is concerned,' she says, in a tone of voice matching his earlier overemphatic and slow delivery, 'I believe that recent research has shown it to be a masterstroke on Henry's part, and that he came out of it better than the corrupt Pope Gregory. Correct me if I'm wrong. After all, you're the historian, and I'm just a silly woman.'

He hears the phone click. When Jeanette's boss, Dennis Billing, slaps him on the back and hands him a glass of wine, he's bubbling with suppressed rage.

Who the hell is she suggesting is corrupt?

Klippgatan – Second Flight of Steps

The myth of Oedipus is one of the oldest stories of revenge. When Oedipus came to Pythia as a child, she foresaw that he would kill his father, the king of Thebes, and then marry his mother. To escape this fate the boy's parents decided to have him killed. But the man who was charged with carrying out the murder took pity on the child and chose instead to raise him as his own son. Unaware of the prophecy, Oedipus went on to kill his father and marry his mother, the dowager queen.

Murder. Betrayal. Revenge.

Everything is cyclical.

The Bergman family is a snake swallowing its own tail, and Madeleine doesn't want to be part of this vicious circle any more.

At Gröna Lund, Madeleine had found Victoria Bergman by chance, and because she believed that the boy holding her mother's hand was her half-brother, she had acted on impulse, too hastily.

This time she has found her by the Skanstull Bridge, where Viggo had seen her before, but couldn't bring herself to go up to her.

Now Madeleine is standing at the Klippgatan stairs, having followed the little blue car deeper into Södermalm.

She looks at the woman who is her mother on the other side of the street.

Victoria Bergman.

She's huddled up, and looks like she's freezing.

Madeleine gets out of the car, hurries across the road, and is just ten metres behind her when she reaches the pavement. She feels inside her jacket pocket. The revolver is cold, metallic.

Loaded with six bullets. Implacable and merciless, with one crystal-clear purpose.

The key to her freedom.

A man closes the boot of his car and Victoria Bergman jumps, clearly frightened by the noise. Then the door of the shop on the corner opens. An old woman comes out and stops outside the door, fumbles with her bag, then sets off towards the steps leading up to the church.

The woman who is her mother follows the old woman.

Tragicomic.

Everyone is following everyone else, and Madeleine realises that she herself has always walked behind someone, been a few steps after them, living each moment too late. She has always found herself staring at someone else's back, but when she catches up with them and kills them she still hasn't been able to leave them behind. They are never behind her, they are always in front of her, or on the periphery, like hazy, disturbing faces without meaning.

Madeleine can see that Victoria Bergman is suffering from chafed heels, just like her.

She's limping as if she were walking on glass, and Madeleine gets a glimpse of how she herself is going to look in twenty years. Her body thin and brittle. Never relaxed. Restless, aimless wandering through life.

What if they hadn't taken me away from you? Madeleine thinks. What would have happened then?

No P-O. No Charlotte.

Would she have had a better life?

The woman who is her mother says something to the old woman, who is now halfway up the flight of steps. But Madeleine can't hear any words, just her own memories.

Charlotte lying to the psychiatrist at University Hospital in Copenhagen, and then shouting at her in the hospital car park.

Charlotte snapping that she's a horrible, unwanted child and that Charlotte's life was ruined the day she came to them.

Charlotte catching Madeleine by surprise when she's watching the video her foster-parents have hidden.

Three girls, one eating excrement.

Around them people in pig masks.

Just like in the pigpen at Viggo's farm.

As a punishment for watching the film she is grounded and P-O visits her every night.

What would her memories of childhood have looked like if she had grown up with her real mother?

Madeleine isn't prepared for the emotions flooding over her. She hasn't got words for them. Her emotions have long been dormant. So long that only the memory of them is stored in her body, not linked to any particular event.

These emotions manifest themselves in a tear running down her cheek.

A solitary, heavy tear of longing for something that never existed.

The old woman walks up the second flight of steps and disappears into the darkness.

Victoria Bergman stays where she is, leaning against the railing. Behind her the silhouette of Sofia Church looks like a vast beacon raised against the sky.

Madeleine approaches. Stops at the bottom of the steps and looks at the bowed back from behind.

Then she sees it slowly straighten up. Victoria raises her head, and her pale hand takes a firm grip of the handrail.

Death is rich in comparison to life, Madeleine thinks, putting her hand in her pocket and taking hold of the revolver.

Life is monotonous, and fairly easy to learn. A journey from scream to scream where your hopes are limited and words of explanation vanishingly few.

Victoria turns round, and for a brief moment they look at each other.

Memories she's never possessed come to her, growing like a wave about to hit a stony beach.

A single tear for a stolen past, and she feels cold and tired as she realises that she has reached the bottom and only the journey back remains. She wants to get away from the cold, to thaw out.

Her head fills with images.

Memories she wishes she had had wash over snapshots of her past. A swell forcing its way with a gentle hiss between algae-covered rocks, only to subside and slowly withdraw to the sea.

A mother with her daughter in her arms. The comforting warmth of a soft breast. A hand caressing her chin and stroking her hair.

A daughter doing a drawing for her mother. A smiling sun in a blue sky, and a girl playing with a dog in a green field.

A mother carefully removing a splinter from her daughter's finger. She gets a plaster, although there's really no need. And hot chocolate and cheese sandwiches.

A daughter coming home from school with an apron she's sewn for her mother. Blue, with red hearts on it. The seams are a little crooked, but it doesn't matter. The mother is proud of her daughter.

The tear stiffens on Madeleine's cheek. A single tear of longing, absorbed by her skin and leaving a pale, almost invisible trace of salt.

They could have loved each other.

Could have.

But were denied the chance.

Victoria's gaze is distant, hidden behind a veil of madness. She can't see me, Madeleine thinks. I'm invisible.

She loosens her grip on the revolver.

Mum, she thinks. I feel sorry for you, and it's enough of a punishment to let you live. You're like me. No past, and no future. Like the first empty page in an unwritten book.

Victoria Bergman starts to climb upward. Slowly at first, but soon with quicker, more determined steps. She reaches the top of the first flight, then the second.

Then she too is gone.

Madeleine realises that she's done the right thing.

There's nothing more to do and her body slumps, in a fraction of a second of relief.

From now on you're all dead to me, she thinks. I'm putting my burden down here. I'm too tired, someone else will have carry it now.

There's just one thing she has to do. Babi Yar. After that she'll never come back, and she's decided to leave her mother tongue behind her as well. Never again will she utter a word of either Swedish or Danish. Never again, not after the final word she says now.

'Sorry,' she says, without a single person to hear her.

Gilah

On Monday 29 September 1941, all Jews living in Kiev and its suburbs must show up at 08:00 at the corner of Melnikova and Dokterieva Streets (near the graveyard). Documents, money and valuables must be taken. Also take warm clothes, underwear, etc. Those who disobey and are found in/at another place will be shot.

Father was silent during the meal, and apart from the hand moving the spoon between the dish and his mouth, back and forth, he sat completely still. She counted twenty-eight spoonfuls of soup before he put the spoon down in the empty dish, picked up his napkin and wiped his mouth. Then he leaned back, put his hands behind his head and looked at her brothers. 'You two, go to your room and gather up the last of your things.'

Her heart was beating hard as she reluctantly swallowed another spoonful of soup and tore off a piece of bread. She missed her mother's soup; this just tasted of soil.

Her brothers picked up their dishes, stood and put them in the washing-up bowl by the wood stove.

'Do your dishes first,' he said, and she recognised the irritable tone. 'It's good porcelain, and they might let us keep it. Better that than leave it here and be sure of losing it. Put the silver cutlery in the wooden tray by the door.' She could see him shifting position from the corner of his eye, and perhaps he was irritated by her as well? Sometimes he got cross when she didn't eat up.

But not this time. When her brothers began clattering their dishes he smiled, stretched across the table and ruffled her hair.

'You look worried,' he said. 'There's nothing to be scared of, is there?'

No, she thought. Not for me, but for you.

She avoided meeting his gaze. She knew he was staring at her.

'Beloved *tokhter*,' he said, stroking her cheek. 'We're only being deported. They'll put us on a train and take us somewhere. East, maybe. Or north, to Poland. There's not much we can do about it. We'll just have to start again, wherever it is.'

She tried to smile, but it didn't really work because she was starting to have doubts about whether she was doing the right thing.

She had seen the notice on a wall down by the Monastery of the Caves, where the Orthodox fools locked themselves away. Voluntarily living their whole lives on bread and water in small caves without windows, to get closer to God. They were fools.

On the sign the Germans had put up, it said that all the Jews in the city had to go to the Jewish cemetery.

Why didn't they ask the Orthodox to go to their cemetery?

Just three days ago no one in the street had known about their roots. After all, they didn't live in the Jewish quarter, and weren't particularly religious. But the day after she had sent the letter with their names and address to the Germans, everybody knew about it, and some of the neighbours who had been their friends up till then had spat at her when she went to the market.

You *shmegegge*, she thought, glancing quickly at her father as her brothers went into the bedroom to pack the last of their things.

She knew she wasn't his child.

She used to think she was, because before Mother died no one spoke about it, but now everyone but him knew about it. Even her brothers knew, and that was why they hit her when they got fed up with hitting each other. That was also why they were able to use her body as they liked.

Mamzer.

For several years she had thought that the way people looked at her and whispered was because of something else, that she was ugly or was wearing shabby clothes, but it was because they knew she was illegitimate. She had got confirmation when she was at the greengrocer's and bumped into one of the girls in the neighbourhood who maliciously told her that Mother had spent ten years living with the handsome painter who lived two blocks away. Her brothers had called her *mamzer* several times, and she hadn't known what the word meant. But when she met the girl in the greengrocer's she had worked out that it meant she wasn't part of the family.

She looked at her father again. The soup was cold, and she couldn't get another spoonful down.

'Just leave that,' he said. 'But eat the bread up before we leave.' He passed her the last scrap of dry bread. 'After all, we don't know when we're next going to get any food.'

Maybe never, she thought, putting the bread in her mouth.

She sneaked out when her father went to get the wheelbarrow that their belongings would be taken away on. Apart from a thick sweater, trousers, socks and a pair of shoes that she had taken from one of her brothers' suitcases and was now carrying under her arm, she had nothing else with her except her father's shaving knife.

She ran down the streets with her dress flapping around her legs, and it felt as if everyone were staring at her.

Mamzer.

Even though it was barely light there were a lot of people on the streets. The sky was dirty grey and covered with clouds, but on the horizon there was a streak of morning red that made her anxious. She avoided groups of uniforms, German and Ukrainian alike. They seemed to be working together.

Where was she going to go? She hadn't even thought about that. Everything had happened so quickly.

Out of breath, she stopped at a street corner where there was a little cafe. She looked around. She had run a long way and didn't know where she was. There were no street signs at the intersection and she quickly made up her mind not to worry about where she was and to go into the cafe toilet and use the shaving knife. As she opened the door she noticed that her bare shins were muddy.

Soon she was standing in front of the cracked mirror in the toilet, hoping that no one would disturb her since there was no lock on the door. She began by rinsing the mud from her legs under the flush on the toilet, which was really just a hole in the ground. There was no paper or towel in there, and no sink either. The water was almost dark brown.

She got changed, but because she didn't want to be caught naked she first put her brother's trousers on under her dress, then pulled the dress off and pushed it down into the bin with her underwear. Then she got down on her knees, held her head over the hole and pulled the flush again. It smelled awful and she held her breath to stop herself being sick.

She had to pull the chain three times to get her hair wet enough. Then she got up and stood in front of the cracked mirror. The shaving knife was cold in her hand.

She started by getting rid of the long, dark hair at the back of her head, then the sides. Suddenly she heard male voices outside the door and froze.

She shut her eyes. If they opened the door then that was it, she'd never be able to hold it shut.

But the voices quickly disappeared, and a few minutes later her hair was almost completely shaved off and she smiled at her reflection.

Now she was someone who could be of use, someone who could work. Not a *mamzer*.

I'm going to be strong, she thought. Stronger than Father.

Hundudden – Island of Djurgården

'This is it,' Jeanette says, opening the steel door in the cellar beneath Viggo Dürer's garage and pointing with her arm before immediately going back to her work in the outer room.

The pathologist looks in through the doorway with a strong sense of reluctance. He realises immediately that this is going to take all night.

The grief he had suffered over many years is nothing compared to the collective despair contained in this room. The room itself is an installation, a calculated staging of sorrow, death and perversion.

Only three hours later can he begin to see an end to his work.

One by one his colleagues have excused themselves, and he sympathises with them. Now he's left alone with just one forensics expert. A young man who, despite the look of revulsion on his face when he entered the room, has gone on working almost mechanically without complaint. Ivo can't help wondering if his young colleague is forcing himself to put up with it because he feels the new recruit's pressure to put his best foot forward, no matter what the cost.

'You've done a good job,' the pathologist says, switching off the tape recorder he's holding in front of his mouth. 'There's no need for you to stay any longer. We're almost done, and I can finish up myself.'

The young man glances at him. 'No, thanks. I can manage.' He smiles a wan, almost watery smile, and Ivo looks at him curiously.

He switches on the recorder again. Everything has to be documented.

In front of him are the four steel cables, and from the corner of his eye he can see the object on the floor. He's trying not to look at it, and begins with what's hanging from the cables, attached to small hooks.

'In summary: the genitals of forty-four boys, the organs preserved using a technique that's a combination of taxidermy and embalmment. The material used as stuffing is ordinary clay.' He begins to walk along the cables with his eyes attached to the ceiling. 'The type of clay varies, but in most cases it appears to be a type of fuller's earth not found in Sweden,' he adds dully, and clears his throat.

He turns round and glances at the object on the floor.

He wouldn't like to call it a sculpture, but recognises that it's a description that comes fairly close to the truth.

A sculpture of a human insect. A sick fantasy.

Then he returns to the steel cables again. 'Forty-four photographs, one of each boy; the pictures were taken after embalmment, with dates added by hand, running from October 1963 to November 2007.'

He curses the fact that there are no names or locations, then walks further along the cable and stops at the other end, next to the wall, beside the large extractor fan.

'At the end of each of the four steel cables there are completely dried hands, all of them amputated above the wrist. Eight in total. To judge by the size of the hands, they also appear to have come from children . . .'

And now for the very worst thing of all, he thinks, and walks towards the middle of the room as he looks at the young forensics officer, who is taking down the photographs with his back to him. 'In the middle of the floor . . .' Ivo Andrić begins, but then speech fails him.

He shuts his eyes and tries to find the right words. What he's looking at can scarcely be described verbally. 'In the middle of the floor,' he tries again, 'is a construction consisting of body parts that have been sewn together.' He walks around the hideous sculpture. 'Here once again the technique is taxidermy using clay, as well as traditional embalming.' He stops and stares at the head, or, rather, the heads.

An insect from hell, he thinks.

He wants to look away, but one detail remains.

'The body parts are joined together with coarse thread, probably a sturdy sort of fishing line. As far as the limbs are concerned, arms as well as legs, they all appear to belong to children, and have been joined in a manner that resembles –'

He breaks off suddenly, because he usually refrains from personal observations of the objects he's documenting. But this time he can't help it.

'Resembles an insect,' he says. 'A spider or a centipede.'

He breathes out and switches off the recorder as he turns towards the young man. 'Have you got the photographs I picked out?'

A short nod in response, and Ivo shuts his eyes for a moment of silent contemplation.

The Zumbayev brothers, he thinks. And Yuri Krylov and the as yet unidentified body, the boy from Danvikstull. He recognised all four of them from their photographs. He has examined their desiccated bodies so thoroughly that there's no doubt whatsoever that it really is them, and in some way it feels like a relief. 'And the fingerprints,' he says, opening his eyes again. 'Can I see the pictures once more?'

A hundred digital images of the same, blank, cancer-eaten fingertips that they had previously found on the fridge in Ulrika Wendin's flat.

The fingerprints are all over the place in here, and Ivo Andrić realises that the end is close.

Kronoberg – Police Headquarters

Since Jeanette and Hurtig got back to police headquarters they've avoided talking about what they found in Dürer's cellar, but they're united in the tacit realisation that the investigation that has gone on all spring and summer is finally heading towards a conclusion.

Now we just have to find Ulrika, Jeanette thinks.

'Where do you think that is?' Hurtig asks thoughtfully as he looks at the photograph they found under Dürer's garage.

'Could be anywhere.'

The police up in Norrbotten have just told them that the Lundström family's old house in Polcirkeln has been demolished, and that the same thing applies to the property Dürer owned in Vuollerim.

'Looks like Norrland,' Hurtig goes on, 'but I've seen houses down in Småland that look the same. A run-of-the-mill forester's house. There are thousands of them, all around the country.' He puts the photograph down and tips his chair back with one foot on the floor.

'Give it here,' Jeanette says, and Hurtig passes her the photograph.

Viggo Dürer is sitting on the veranda in front of a small cottage, looking into the camera. He's smiling.

To his right is a small window with the curtains drawn, and in the background the edge of a forest. It looks to Jeanette like a perfectly ordinary holiday snap. But there's something about it that she recognises.

She lights a cigarette and blows the smoke out through the gap in the small side window, nervously tapping the cigarette with one finger even though there's no ash to knock off.

'I think I saw it on one of Lundström's videos,' she says.

They're interrupted when the door opens and Schwarz comes flying in, closely followed by Åhlund. They're both drenched. The water from Schwarz's cropped head forms a small pool on the floor.

'Christ, it's coming down,' Åhlund says, tossing his wet coat over an empty chair and squatting down while Schwarz leans against the wall and looks around the room.

'So what have you got?' Jeanette asks.

Åhlund tells them that among Hannah Östlund's possessions was a deed of gift declaring that Hannah was assuming ownership of a house in the village of Ånge, south of Arjeplog in Lapland.

'And that's not all,' Åhlund goes on. 'Hannah Östlund in turn donated the house to Sihtunum i Diasporan. For the foundation "to use as necessary," I think it said.'

'Why didn't we see it when we went through the foundation's assets?' Hurtig asks.

'Probably because it was never legally ratified. According to the land registry it's still in Hannah Östlund's name.'

'So who gave the house to Hannah in the first place?' Jeanette asks eagerly, getting the feeling that things were really moving now.

'His name was Anders Wikström,' Schwarz says.

Jeanette walks round the desk and goes to stand by the window. 'The same Wikström who took part in raping Ulrika,' she says, lighting another cigarette.

What was wrong with all those men? she wonders, aware that she'll probably never get an answer to that.

'So what's the connection between Anders Wikström and Karl Lundström?' Schwarz asks.

Hurtig explains how it all fits together. 'Lundström said they recorded one of the films in Wikström's cottage in Ånge, outside Sundsvall, because that's where Wikström lived. But there's evidently another Ånge, in Lapland.'

Only now does Jeanette realise what it was that she recognised. The curtains, she thinks, picking up the photograph they found at Dürer's home once more.

'Do you see?' she says, pointing animatedly at the picture. 'In the window behind Dürer?'

'Red curtains with white flowers,' Åhlund says.

Jeanette gets her phone out and dials the prosecutor's number. 'I'll call von Kwist and arrange transport to Lapland. I just hope we aren't too late.' Her thoughts go to Ulrika, and she prays that she's still alive.

Arlanda Airport

There are still two hours to go before the plane takes off when Madeleine completes her electronic check-in and heads towards the security control. She's travelling light and the only things the customs officers have to check are her handbag and cobalt-blue coat. She's forced to abandon her cup of ice before she gets to the desk.

Frozen water can be explosive, she thinks as she tips out the last pieces of ice. In some ways that's true.

She closes her eyes as she passes through the metal detector. For some reason the magnetic field always affects her and the scar at the back of her head tingles. Sometimes it even gives her a headache.

She gets her bag and coat off the conveyor belt and goes into the departure hall. Large groups of people unsettle her. Too many faces, too many possible life stories, and the people are all so tragically unaware of their own vulnerability. She speeds up and heads directly to passport control.

As she waits in the queue her headache arrives. The magnetic field has done its thing and she reaches for a pill from her bag and swallows it as she runs her fingers over the scar beneath her hair.

The border police officer examines her papers, a French passport in the name of Duchamp and a one-way ticket to Kiev, Ukraine. He scarcely looks at her before handing the documents back. She notes the time and checks the screens. The departure looks like it's going to be on time, in ninety minutes, and she settles down to wait in a corner at the back of the lounge.

After Kiev and her appointment at Babi Yar she's going to leave everything behind her. Her agreement with Viggo is the conclusion to it all. Now that Victoria Bergman has gone for good, there's nothing left to do.

She's tired, terribly tired, and the sound of all the voices is horribly irritating. An unholy mix of banal conversations and noisy arguments that only make her headache worse.

She tries to listen to the noise without hearing individual words and sentences. But it doesn't work, there are always voices that take over.

She gets her mobile out of her bag, puts on the headphones and selects the radio option. She tunes into a frequency with nothing but static. A low, soothing hiss, and now she can hear herself think.

I'm down at the beach at Venø Bay, collecting stones, she thinks.

The sound of the sea and the wind is mine alone. I'm ten years old and I'm wearing a red jacket, red trousers and white wellington boots.

The hissing in her headphones is the sea, and her thoughts drift off. The Åland Sea a few days ago.

The woman who called herself my mother couldn't bear the shame, she thinks. I showed her pictures of her just standing by and watching without doing anything.

Pictures of children screaming in pain, pictures of children who don't understand what's happening, pictures of me, ten years old, naked on a blanket on the beach.

She couldn't bear it, and took her shame with her down into the depths.

There's a sudden change in the static and Madeleine remembers the faint sound of a motorway somewhere in the background. A smell of shampoo and fresh sheets. She shuts her eyes and lets the images come. The room is white and she is small, just a few days old, lying in someone's arms. Women in neatly pressed white uniforms, some with masks over their mouths. She's warm, full, content. She feels safe and doesn't want to be anywhere but there, with her ear against a chest that rises and falls in time with her own breathing.

Two hearts beating the same pulse.

A hand stroking her belly, it tickles, and when she opens her eyes she sees a mouth in which one of the front teeth is chipped.

Martin

The water was lapping under the jetty and he curled up close to Victoria. He didn't understand how she could be so warm even though she was only wearing underpants.

'You're my little boy,' she said in a quiet voice. 'What are you thinking?'

The boats sailed past slowly, and Victoria waved at the men steering them. He liked motorboats, and would have liked to have one, but he was too little. Maybe he'd have one in a few years, when he was as big as she was. He imagined what the boat would look like and soon he remembered what his cousin had promised him.

'How much fun it's going to be moving to Skåne. My cousin lives in Helsingborg and we'll be able to play nearly every day. He's got a really long car track and he's going to give me one of his cars. Maybe a Ponsack Farburg.'

She didn't answer, but he thought her breathing was a bit funny. Jerky and fast.

'Next summer we're going abroad. The new au pair's going to come too.'

Martin was thinking about boats, cars and planes, and knew he wanted them all as soon as he got a bit bigger. He'd have lots of land and more than one garage and maybe his own pilots, chauffeurs and boat captains. Because he didn't think he'd be able to drive them himself. After all, he couldn't even tie his own shoelaces, and sometimes the other children said he was stupid. Although really he was just a bit slow developing, like his mum always said.

Suddenly there was a strange noise from the bushes on the slope behind them. A squeak, like a little mouse, then a sound like his mum's pinking shears sometimes made, the ones he wasn't allowed to cut paper with. Victoria turned round and he shivered when she got up and the warmth from her body disappeared.

She put on her top and pointed towards the bushes. 'Do you see, Martin . . . ?'

There was more rustling. A bird came hopping out on one leg, and it didn't look very well. It appeared all messed up and its other leg was missing. 'She can't fly,' Victoria said, creeping towards it. 'Her wings are broken.'

He thought the bird looked mean. It was staring at him, and its head was lowered, and if you looked like that then you had to be horrid.

'Make it go away, please.' He tried to hide under the towel, but it didn't help. The bird was still there. 'Make it go away, Victoria . . .'

'All right . . .' He heard her sigh, and then he peeped round the edge of the towel and saw her stretching out her hand towards the bird, slowly, and it was sitting completely still now, as if it wanted to be caught.

Finally she grabbed it and picked it up off the ground. He couldn't understand how she could be so brave. 'Take it away, a long way away,' he said, feeling safer.

She laughed at him. 'What? Are you scared of it? But it's only a bird!'

'Take the horrid bird away,' he said loudly. 'Put it in a bin so it dies!'

Victoria patted the bird's head and it pecked gently at her fingers, but she didn't seem to mind. Martin hoped it would bite her so she realised how dangerous it was.

'OK,' she said. 'Stay there and don't fall in the water.'

'I promise,' he replied. 'Hurry back.'

He lay down on his stomach, crept to the edge of the jetty and watched the boats again. There was one with an old lady rowing, then two motorboats. He waved at the drivers, but neither of them saw him.

Then he heard the sound of voices and bicycle tyres on the path and looked up.

There were three of them coming along the path, one on a bike and two walking. He recognised all three from school and he didn't like them. They were much bigger and stronger than he was, and they knew it. They caught sight of him and came down towards the jetty and stopped.

Now he was properly scared. The bird was better than this, and he hoped Victoria would soon be back.

'Little Martin!' This from the biggest one, and he was grinning. 'What are you doing down here all on your own? The river monster might get you.'

He didn't know what to say, so he just stood and looked at them.

'Can't you speak, or what?' One of the others this time. They looked very similar and Martin thought they might be twins. They were in year 5, anyway, and the biggest one was in year 6.

'I . . .' He didn't want to seem cowardly, so he decided to say he'd done something that he hadn't actually dared to do. 'I've been for a swim,' he said.

'You've been for a swim?' This was the biggest one again, and he tilted his head and frowned. 'Well, we don't believe you. Do we?' He turned to the others, and they joined in when he started laughing. 'Go swimming again, and we'll believe you. Jump in!' He walked out onto the jetty and it started to sway, making the wood creak.

'Stop it . . .' Martin backed away a few steps.

'Maybe we should help you get in?' the biggest one said.

'Maybe,' one of the others said.

'Definitely,' the third one joined in.

Please, Victoria, he thought. Come back.

Why was she taking so long? Why did she have to go so far?

Sometimes when Martin got really scared his body went all stiff. It was like it decided to stand as still as it could, like a statue, and that would help him avoid whatever the horrid thing was.

Martin's body was completely stiff and hard when they picked him up, holding him between them, then swung him back and forth like a hammock between two trees.

He looked up at the sky as they swung him, and just as the three boys let go a little star twinkled.

Nowhere

The light from the bulb in the empty room is hurting her eyes. She's lying naked on a cold, grey concrete floor, and her hands are still tied behind her back, and there's still tape over her mouth. Her legs are tied at the ankles as well.

A large ventilation unit rumbles intermittently. Otherwise the room is just grey concrete, apart from the door, which is made of shiny metal.

She's curled up in a foetal position with her head to one side, and about a metre away stands a man with a hammer drill in his hand.

Heavy black boots, worn jeans and a naked, sweaty upper body with a swollen stomach that bulges over the waist of his trousers.

She can't take her eyes off the hammer drill. It's huge, and the drill bit is very thick.

She can't bear to look into the man's empty eyes, and continues staring at the drill. She sees that the cord is attached to the end of an extension lead just inside the door. The muscles in the man's coarse fist tense, and the drill bit starts to spin.

The sound of the machine gets louder, then he eases up and the machine goes quiet. She shuts her eyes, hears his heavy footsteps leaving the room, and doesn't open them again until she hears him come back.

He's put a wooden stool down on the concrete floor and has climbed up onto it. Next to the stool is an almost empty bottle of vodka.

The drill starts up again, and the air is filled with dry concrete dust.

She has no idea what he's doing, and just wants to scream, but the tape over her mouth is stopping her and all she can manage instead is a little groan, a bubble of air from her stomach, and she starts to worry that she might be sick.

The concrete dust tickles her nose, and she feels like she's going to sneeze.

She looks on in silence as he reaches for the bottle of vodka and takes a deep swig. Close up, she can see that his eyes are bloodshot, and she realises that the dead look on his face is because he's drunk.

His fat, naked torso is dirty and on his shoulders and arms there are a number of tattoos. There's a snake coiled around his right arm, and on the other barbed wire loops around women's heads. '*Eto konets, devotchka*,' he says, stroking her cheek.

She shuts her eyes and feels his thick fingers fumble over her face before they pull the tape from her mouth with a sharp tug. It hurts badly, but she swallows her scream.

She can feel a hot trickle of blood running over her lips, and realises that the strong tape has torn her skin.

'*Devotchka* . . .' he mutters quietly while she coughs, and she feels him stroke her hair. She can hardly speak a word of Russian, but she knows that word. *Devotchka* means 'little girl', she learned that from watching *A Clockwork Orange*, when she wanted to know what the young women who were raped in the film were being called.

'You drink,' he says, and she hears the glass bottle scraping on the floor.

Is he going to rape her? And what's he going to do with that drill apart from make a hole in the ceiling?

She slowly shakes her head, but his fingers grab hold of her chin and force her to open her mouth. His hands smell of machine oil.

When she feels the bottle hit her teeth she looks up, and as the alcohol stings the wounds around her mouth she can see that he's attached a hook to the ceiling. And he seems to be holding something that looks like a thin nylon rope in the same hand as the bottle of vodka.

A noose, she thinks. He's going to hang me.

'Drink, *devotchka* . . . Drink!' His voice is soft, almost friendly.

Like hell I will. Drink your fucking vodka yourself.

She peeps through her eyelashes and watches as he drinks more from the bottle, then shakes his head. He lifts her head and puts the noose around her neck. Then he lets out a short laugh and pats her lightly on the cheek. 'Hey, me Rodya . . .' He grins and points at himself. 'And you?'

'Rodya . . . Go fuck yourself,' she says. The first words she's spoken since they locked her up.

'No,' he says. 'I fuck you.'

He begins to tighten the noose around her neck. He pulls it so tight that it forces her larynx down. She groans and the urge to vomit returns.

He grabs hold of her body and rolls her over onto her side. He takes something out of his pocket, and when he grabs her wrists and the pressure on them eases she realises that it's a knife, and that he's freed her hands.

'I fuck you dead. *Eto konets, devotchka.*'

He pulls her up by the rope, which tightens even more, and her vision starts to flicker as he leans her back against the concrete wall.

Soon she'll be dead, and she doesn't want that.

She wants to live.

If she's allowed to live, she'll never go back to the life she lived before. She'll realise her dreams. Not hide away or be scared of failure, and she'll show everyone that she deserves to be taken seriously.

But now she's going to die.

She thinks about everything she didn't know she knew. The coastline of Europe and the fifty states of America. She knows all their names now, they come to her all at once, and the four she had trouble remembering were Rhode Island, Connecticut, Maryland and New Jersey, and that's because they're so small on her world map. She feels her arm fall slack to the floor as the cord burns into her neck.

Kronoberg – Police Headquarters

The Swedish police have access to six helicopters, model EC135, manufactured by Messerschmitt, best known for supplying the Luftwaffe with fighter planes during World War II.

Jeanette Kihlberg and Jens Hurtig are standing on the roof of police headquarters waiting to be picked up. Jeanette demanded that the prosecutor organise a helicopter so that they can get to the north of Norrland as fast as possible – and that they should have backup from the response unit. Prosecutor von Kwist had agreed to her demands.

Jeanette goes over to the edge of the roof and looks out across the Stockholm night.

Hurtig comes and stands next to her, and they look at the view together in silence.

'The world is a fine place and worth fighting for,' Hurtig suddenly proclaims solemnly.

'How do you mean?' Jeanette asks, looking at her colleague.

'Hemingway,' he explains. 'From *For Whom the Bell Tolls*. I've always liked that line.'

'It's nice,' she says back, smiling.

'After everything I've seen today, I can only agree with the second part,' he says, then turns and walks away.

Jeanette watches him go, and wonders what he's thinking about. Probably the same thing she is, Viggo Dürer's subterranean chamber of horrors.

How sick can a person get? she wonders. And what made him like that?

God, it's big, Jeanette thinks as the helicopter approaches. It looks like a small passenger plane, with two engines on the roof, and she realises that it won't be able to land just anywhere, as she had imagined. Even though it's more than fifteen metres away from them, they crouch down instinctively when the helicopter lands on the roof. They hurry over, under the shrieking rotor blades, and are met at the door by the first pilot and the head of the response unit.

'Jump in!' the unit head shouts. 'We can do the safety procedures once we're in the air.'

In total there are eleven people sitting on long benches running along the sides of the helicopter. Full combat gear, and an almost devout atmosphere if you didn't count Hurtig's persistent questions. 'Seven hundred and fifty kilometres, as the crow flies,' he says. 'How long's that going to take? Three hours?'

'No, longer than that,' the unit head says. 'We haven't got the weather or the wind in our favour. Say four hours. We'll be there sometime around half past four, so you should probably try to get some sleep.'

Kiev

He's travelled under a false name many times before. But this time it's different.

This time the name on his travel documents is a woman's. His real name.

Gilah Berkowitz.

There hadn't been any problems at the Swedish or Latvian border controls, and the Ukrainian customs officers aren't usually interested when a Swedish passport is presented. Real or fake, it doesn't matter, all they see are the stars of the EU logo.

Before she goes out to the waiting car she buys a pack of cigarettes from a tobacco seller with wrinkled hands whose dark blue veins stand out from the skin.

Her chest feels tight, a painful throbbing. Then the cough again. A dry, sharp cough that tastes of dust. '*Konets*,' she mutters. It will soon be over. The cancer has spread and she knows that there's nothing more that can be done.

The thickset man in the driver's seat starts the car and pulls out of the car park. To the driver and the estate agent, Gilah Berkowitz is just an upper-class Swedish-Ukrainian lady interested in icons. She's paying seventy euros a day for a five-room apartment on Michailovska, close to Maidan Square, and the price includes the use of a four-wheel-drive SUV, the sort of vehicle that never gets stopped by the local police. Not even if you drive the wrong way down a one-way street right in front of their eyes.

She knows how things work here. Everything works. As long as you've got money.

People will do anything to make a living, and the situation is particularly favourable right now, since the country has been hit hard by the financial crisis. The problems in Western Europe are nothing in comparison. Here you can find your salary cut by thirty per cent from one day to the next.

As the car leaves the airport she thinks about what she's seen over the years on the streets of this country. A hotbed of economic creativity that never ceases to amaze her. Almost ten years ago she tested the hypothesis that a person in dire straits would do whatever they were told and not question their orders, as long as the reward was big enough.

The subject of the experiment was a young, single woman who already had two jobs but still had trouble making ends meet. She had contacted the woman and offered her barely two euros an hour to stand at a particular street crossing every morning and count the number of children who went past without an adult accompanying them.

The first week she had gone to check that the woman was actually there at the allotted time, which she was, without fail. Then she did spot checks, and the woman was always there with her black notebook, even if there was heavy rain or snow.

After testing the hypothesis that hopelessness was for sale, she had applied it to people whose consciences were blacker and whose desperation was greater. It had worked satisfactorily every time.

She looked thoughtfully out of the car window. Her contact in Kiev is no exception. His name is Nikolai Tymoschuk. Kolya. A desperate person who knows that money is the only language that doesn't lie.

As they head towards the city, she gets her mobile phone from her bag and calls Kolya's number. The trust between them is based on their mutual conviction that the financial rewards balance the risks. Or, as she prefers to put it: the rewards are so generous that the risks are always of subordinate interest.

The conversation lasts barely ten seconds, because Kolya knows exactly what preparations he needs to make for the following day. He doesn't have any questions.

When the car pulls up outside the apartment she tells the driver that she won't need him again. A couple of crumpled notes are exchanged, and they shake hands.

She unlocks the door to the apartment, and exhaustion finally catches up with her. She's anticipating another attack of dizziness and puts her hand to her heart before the pain starts.

Her face contorts against the cramps, her eyes flare, and she feels several of her false nails break as she clutches her chest.

A minute later the attack passes and she goes into the living room and puts her case down on the sofa. It smells musty, like inside a person, and as she unpacks she lights one of the strong Woodbines she bought at the airport from the woman with the veiny hands. She smokes out the stuffy smell of whoever was staying there before her.

Five minutes later she's standing by the open living-room window looking down on the narrow, potholed and winding Michailovska three floors below.

She pulls the curtain aside and peers up between the rooftops. The cloud-free night sky is high and cold. Autumns are short here, and the smell of winter is already in the air.

So this is the end, she thinks. Back where it all started.

She can hardly remember the names of the places here, but she remembers Thorildsplan, Danvikstull and Svartsjölandet. She can still recall the taste of the last boy. The slippery taste of rapeseed oil.

And before them the children who haven't been found yet. Möja, Ingarö, the Norrtälje channel, the forests of Tyresta.

There were girls as well. Buried in the woods on Färingsö, at the bottom of Malmsjön, in a reedbed at Dyviksudd. All in all, more than fifty children.

Most of them from Ukraine, but some from Belarus and Moldova.

She had learned to be a man. A dead Danish soldier and some male hormones had assisted the transformation that had begun when she left her father and brothers.

And in the end she had been stronger than her father.

She is deep in thought and the phone on the coffee table rings several times before she hears it. But she knows what the call is about, and does not hurry to answer it or finish her cigarette.

The man at the other end says exactly what is expected of him. One single word.

'*Konets* . . .' says a dark, rasping voice before the line goes dead, and Gilah Berkowitz knows that Rodya has done his job with the Wendin girl.

The only thing she regrets is that she was forced to break off her experiment on the girl's body.

She goes over to the window again and opens it, letting the cold into the room as her thoughts turn to the next day.

Konets . . . she thinks, and coughs drily. The end is getting close for me too.

The conclusion to everything.

Kolya will make sure there's no one in the vicinity of the Babi Yar monument between one and three o'clock the following night.

After almost seventy years, the promise she made will be fulfilled. It's taken her twenty years to raise the person who's going to help her.

Nowhere

Her head is banging against the wall, the nylon cord is pressing into her throat, and something large inside her mouth presses against her soft palate.

But she can't hear or sense anything. She just drifts away and doesn't even notice her hand suddenly feeling its way over the concrete floor and grabbing hold of something warm.

She watches everything from where she's resting in the air, just beneath the ceiling, and sees herself close her hand around the handle of the hammer drill, which hasn't yet cooled down after the thickset man made the hole in the ceiling.

The drill starts with a howl that gets muffled slightly as the drill bit eats its way into the man's stomach, and that's when she realises that her strength really does come from below, from the earth itself.

Ulrika Wendin shuts her eyes, and when she opens them again she can move at last. It takes several more seconds for her to remember that her feet are bound with duct tape, that she's sitting on a concrete floor in a cellar, nowhere.

She's surrounded by a cloying, stifling smell. It reminds her of whey cheese, the same smell from biology classes when the teachers forced the children to dissect cow eyes with small scalpels. She twists her head. Beside her, leaning against the same wall, a man is sitting and staring at her with a broad smile on his lips. Her other hand is trapped beneath his vast bulk. He has a hole in his stomach, and that's where the smell is coming from.

'*Eto konets, devotchka*,' he mutters, still smiling. The expression on his face is no longer blank, and it strikes her that he looks almost happy.

As for her, she's experiencing a calmness that she's never felt before. A calmness so great that it leaves no room for hatred or forgiveness.

He coughs, and now even his eyes are smiling. 'You are strong, *devotchka*,' he says in a whisper as a trickle of blood escapes his mouth.

She has no idea what he means. She tries to swallow, but it hurts badly, and she realises that her larynx is damaged.

She looks on in fascination as he makes a great effort to reach into the pocket of his filthy jeans. The hole in his stomach keeps throbbing.

The knife, she thinks. He's looking for his knife.

But it isn't a knife. It's a mobile phone. So small that it almost vanishes into his huge hand.

A bleep. Then another one before he puts the phone to his ear.

It feels to her like an eternity before she hears the ringing tone get interrupted by a voice at the other end, and the man is still staring happily at her.

While his eyes slowly fill with blood he utters one single word.

'*Konets*,' he says, and as the phone slips from his hand the light in his eyes has already gone out.

She doesn't know how long she sits there with the drill in her hand, and she hardly notices when she puts it down, removes the tape from her ankles and stands up.

She has to get out of there, but first she needs to find something to wear, and she walks on unsteady legs into the next room, where she finds a pair of thin, white protective overalls.

It's snowing, it's cold, and she isn't dressed for it, but she has no choice.

The snow reaches almost to her knees as she stumbles down the slope towards the edge of the forest.

Lapland – Northern Sweden

Jeanette and Hurtig are the last to get out of the helicopter, and as the engines fall silent she can hear nothing but the wind in the branches of the spindly pine trees, covered with a thick layer of snow. Winter comes early in the mountains, a thousand kilometres north of Stockholm. It's cold, and the snow crunches under their boots. The only light is from the lamps on the response unit's helmets.

'We'll split into groups of three, and approach the cottage from all four sides.'

The head of the unit indicates the directions on a map, then points at Jeanette and Hurtig. 'You two come with me, we'll take the shortest route straight to the cottage. We'll go slowly, so the others have time to get round without being spotted. OK?'

Jeanette nods, and the other police officers give the thumbs up.

The forest is thin, but every now and then she still manages to brush against a branch, covering her with snow that seeps under her collar. The heat of her body meets the cold snow and she shivers as it melts and runs down her back. Hurtig is marching ahead of her with long, determined strides, and she can see that he's on home territory. He probably spent his entire childhood in Kvikkjokk walking through similar forests in similar conditions.

The unit head slows down and holds a hand up. 'We're here,' he says quietly.

Through the trees Jeanette can see the cottage, and recognises it at once from the photograph. There's a faint glow in one of the windows, and she can see the veranda where Viggo Dürer sat and smiled at the camera, but she can't see any sign of life inside the house.

At that moment the forest bursts into life and the specially trained police officers rush towards the cottage with their weapons drawn.

As Jeanette follows Hurtig towards the house with her eyes firmly on the ground, she sees footprints leading in the opposite direction.

There's a trail of bare footprints leading through the snow, from the house into the forest.

Vita Bergen – Sofia Zetterlund's Apartment

The hall is full of black bin bags and Victoria is going to make sure it all disappears.

Everything must go, every last scrap of paper.

The answers to her questions aren't there, they're inside her, and the healing process has progressed far enough for her to feel she'll soon have full access to her memories. The notes and newspaper clippings helped her to take the first steps, but she no longer needs them. She knows which way she needs to go.

Gao's room is empty now, the exercise bike is in the living room, she's taken the mattresses up to her storage compartment in the attic, and all that remains is to rip out the insulation.

She ties the last bag and puts it in the hall. She needs to get rid of the bags herself, but she doesn't yet know how that's going to work. In total there are twelve bags, 125 litre capacity each, and she's going to have to hire a trailer or a van to move everything in one trip.

The simplest solution would obviously be to take it all to a recycling centre, but that doesn't feel right. She's going to need a ritual farewell. A symbolic act of closure, like a book burning.

She goes over to the bookcase in the living room and closes the door to Gao's room.

As she lifts the hook to slot it into the catch she stops, takes the hook out, lets it hang against the side of the bookcase, and then repeats the action. Once more, then again, and then once again.

There's a memory in that action.

Viggo Dürer's cellar at the farm in Struer, and the room within.

A shudder runs through her body. She doesn't want to return to that memory.

Lapland

The world is white and cold and she's been running through the loose snow for what feels like an eternity.

Despite her dehydration and lack of sleep in the last twenty-four hours, she's wide awake. As if her body is forcing itself on, even though it has no reserves left.

The weather is also helping, and the cold drives her forward. Sharp snowflakes sting her face.

A few times she's found herself running into her own footsteps and realises that she's been going in circles. She can hardly feel her feet any more, and is having trouble walking. When she stops to try to warm them up she listens for the sound of anyone in pursuit. But everything is completely silent.

The world is so white that not even the darkness of night can hide its clarity, which strikes her in the form of cotton-wool cold as she makes her way through the sparse forest, and she knows she's not going to live to be much older than this.

An hour more or less, depending on how long it takes to freeze to death, and she curses her stupidity in not searching the house for some better clothes to wear.

It's below freezing, and she's barefoot and wearing just a thin pair of protective overalls.

An hour, ordinarily such a negligible period of time, now feels like the most precious thing there is, and that's why she's running to meet her fate with an open heart. With the freezing air stinging at her throat she stumbles on, as if salvation existed, and the branches lashing her face create the illusion that she's on her way towards something. Towards a place that is beyond such concepts as onward, ahead and later.

Ulrika Wendin takes a deep breath and runs as though hope did exist in a world of rock, snow and cold.

She runs and thinks, thinks and runs. She remembers what has been, without regretting her choices, and allows herself to dream about things that haven't yet happened. Things she's done, things she's going to do.

But the cold is relentless, and is making her breathing irregular.

Above the white treetops she can see a thin, reddish-yellow strip, and knows that dawn is coming, but holds out no hope that the rising sun will be able to warm her sufficiently. The Swedish winter sun is a worthless sun, no good for anything. Even if it's the same sun that burns African farmers' fields to dust, up here in the north it's ice-cold.

Life, she thinks once more, and the thought repeats as she hears the sound of a helicopter approaching. Ulrika stops and listens. The helicopter is getting closer and closer, and when it's something like a kilometre away she hears it slowly sink; then the sound of the engines dies away and finally stops altogether. They're close, she thinks. Maybe even at the house she was held captive in, and she knows she has to hurry if she's going to find her way back.

She tries to retrace her steps, but the wind has already covered her tracks.

Her legs are moving forward, and the numb soles of her feet aren't bothered by the stones and branches bruising and cutting her. Pain means life, she tells herself, realising that the helicopter might mean that someone has come to rescue her. Once more she is filled with hope that there might be a future.

Her tracks in the snow are getting fainter and fainter, until eventually the wind has had long enough to erase them completely. Now the cold is hurting so much that it's anaesthetising her, and her nerves do what they can to deceive her. Her whole body is screaming with cold, but her brain is telling her that she's sweating. As she stumbles on, it feels like her clothes are scalding her.

The last thing Ulrika Wendin does in life is tear the oversized overalls off. Then she lies down naked in the cold, white snow and understands that it's over. Life goes on, she thinks. It always does.

And at least she's warm now.

Vita Bergen – Sofia Zetterlund's Apartment

Victoria Bergman is sitting on the wide windowsill in the kitchen with a cup of coffee and her mobile phone in her hand. The morning sun is strong, casting razor-sharp shadows on the street below.

The shadow play looks like a cubist puzzle, where the edges of the pieces are like shards of glass, and she contemplates her own internal puzzle, now so close to completion.

Can she go on working as a psychologist? She doesn't know, but she knows she must accept for the time being that she is Sofia Zetterlund, a psychotherapist with her own private practice in rented premises on Mariatorget.

Victoria Bergman unofficially, she thinks. And Sofia Zetterlund on paper. This has been the case for a long time, but the big difference is that now the Sleepwalker is dead, and I'm the one making the decisions, feeling and acting.

No more memory lapses. No nocturnal walks and visits to bars, no more staggering through dark parks drunk. She no longer has to remind Sofia of her existence that way. Once she had even fallen in the water, down by Norra Hammarbyhamnen, and she remembers Sofia sitting in the kitchen the day after with her wet clothes, desperately trying to work out what had happened. The answer was both simple and extremely tasteless. She had gone to the Clarion Hotel, went with someone to his room, fucked until she felt sick, then walked down to the water with two bottles of wine, got too drunk and fell in.

Victoria jumps down from the windowsill, puts her cup on the draining board and goes into the hall. Just the bags to sort out.

Now she knows what she's going to do with them and where she's going to take them. The logical place.

She calls Ann-Britt and says that she's thinking of closing the practice for the foreseeable future. She needs a holiday, needs to get away somewhere, anywhere, and doesn't know how long she'll be gone. She might stay a month or two, or she might be back in a few days. But the rent for her office has already been paid a year in advance, so that won't be a problem.

She promises to get in touch with more definite information later, and ends the call.

Another phone call, this time to a van-rental company.

She books a light van with a capacity of twenty-two cubic metres, and is told she can pick it up in an hour. Which is good, because she's got a fair distance to drive, and it's also going to take her a while to carry the bags down to the van.

She stops.

An idea is starting to form in her head.

When you feel that you have always made the wrong decisions in life, sooner or later there has to come a time when you make the right one.

This is one of those times.

Victoria Bergman gets her phone out again and calls her bank.

She is put through to a woman who helps her conduct the transactions. It's rather more complicated than usual, and at first the woman advises her against it.

But Victoria is certain. Unshakeably certain.

And Sofia doesn't object.

The next call is received without any attempts to dissuade her. On the contrary, her idea is welcomed by the young man at the Audi centre in Smista.

When she hangs up everything feels lighter.

She's put an end to her life in Stockholm.

And now she's going to a place that still means something to her.

A place where she will be on her own, where the houses are all empty at this time of year, and the starry sky is as high and clear as it was when she was really small.

Kiev

It's said that the two industrial cities in the east of Ukraine, Donetsk and Dnipropetrovsk, are the only cities in the world where the snow is black. But now she knows that's wrong. Black snow also falls on the capital, and a swarm of ash flakes is hitting the car's windows.

Madeleine is sitting in the back seat and the driver's face is reflected in the windscreen against the dark backdrop of tall cranes, chimneys and factory buildings. His face is pale, thin, unshaven. His hair is black and his eyes bright blue, cold and agitated. His name is Kolya.

The streets disappear behind them in the night haze, and they drive out across one of the bridges crossing the Dnieper River. The water glints black and she wonders how long she'd survive if she jumped in.

On the other side of the river the road is lined with industrial buildings, and Kolya slows down at an intersection, then turns right. 'It is here . . .' he says, without looking at her.

He pulls into a smaller side road and parks by the pavement next to a high wall, then gets out and opens the door for her.

The night is glitteringly cold, and the wind makes her feel frozen.

Kolya locks the car, and they walk along the wall. They stop at a shabby wooden barrier, flaking with red and white paint, beside something that looks like a small sentry box. Kolya raises the barrier and gestures to her to go through. She does so, and he follows her and lowers the barrier behind them. Then he unlocks the gate to the main building.

'Fifteen minutes,' he says, looking at his watch. A short, thin man in black steps out of the darkness and indicates that they should follow him.

They make their way to an internal courtyard and the man unlocks one of the doors to the building while Kolya stops and pulls out his cigarettes. 'I wait outside.'

Madeleine goes into a corridor where the only window is completely covered with plywood. To the left there's an open door, and she glimpses a large table inside with a row of guns lined up on top of it. The thin man is holding an automatic pistol and nods to her.

She goes in and looks around the room. Someone's stripped off the wallpaper, scraping and plastering the wall ready for repainting, but evidently never started the work. Electrical cables hang diagonally across the walls, as though they were too short and had to take the most direct route to a socket.

The man passes her a gun. 'Luger P08,' he explains. 'From the war.'

She takes the weapon, weighs it in her hand for a moment, and is surprised at how heavy it is. Then she pulls a bundle of notes from her jacket pocket and hands it to the man. Viggo Dürer's money.

The seller shows her how the old gun works. She can see rust on it and hopes that the mechanism isn't going to stick.

'What happened to your finger?' he asks, but Madeleine doesn't answer.

As Kolya drives her through the night she thinks about what awaits her.

She's sure Viggo Dürer is going to keep his part of the bargain. She knows him so well that she can trust him on that.

For her part, their agreement means that she can draw a line under the past, leave it behind and continue her cleansing process. Soon everyone who has ever owed her anything will be dead.

Apart from Annette Lundström. But she has already been punished enough. Losing her entire family and ending up in a state of psychosis. Besides, Annette was never more than a passive onlooker to the abuse.

Now Madeleine just wants to get back to her lavender fields, and there she'll stay for the rest of her life.

Kolya slows down, and she realises that they're almost there. He pulls over onto the pavement and parks next to a bus shelter.

'Syrets station,' he says. 'Over there.' He points at a low, grey concrete building some distance away. 'You find the way to the monument? The menorah?'

She nods and feels in the inside pocket of her jacket. The rusty old gun is cold to her touch as she feels the ridged butt.

'Twenty minutes,' he says. 'Then the area will be safe.'

Madeleine gets out of the car and shuts the door.

She knows she has to turn right at the station to get to the monument, but first she goes down the steps to the little shops beneath the building. Five minutes later she finds what she's looking for, a small fast-food place, and asks for a cup of ice cubes.

She goes back up the steps and turns off towards the large park. Her teeth ache as she crunches the ice, and she remembers the feeling of losing a tooth as a child. The stinging, chill sensation of having a hole in her gum. The taste of blood in her mouth.

The path leads to a small open area before continuing into the park. A paved circle with a statue on a plinth at its centre. The sculpture is unassuming, and represents three children. A girl with her hands raised, and two smaller children resting at her feet.

From the inscription on the plinth, she reads that the statue was erected in memory of the thousands of children who were executed there during the war.

Madeleine chews her ice cubes, leaves the statue behind and continues along the path into the park. For the time being the scream is still inside her, but soon she'll be able to let it out.

Village of Dala-Floda

It had started snowing somewhere near Hedemora, and she's long since given up all hope of a clear, starry sky above the lake by the cottage in Dala-Floda.

But the sky is probably never as clear as it is in childhood memories.

The forest gets thicker, and it's not far now. The last time she came this way her dad was driving and she remembers the journey as a haze of arguments. It was just before the cottage was sold, and Mum had got the wrong idea about the sort of price they could expect.

She remembers other trips as well, and is grateful that the place where he used to stop so that she could make him happy is no longer the same. The road has been widened and the lay-by is gone.

She passes all the familiar places. Grangärde, Nyhammar and, a bit further on, Björbo. Everything looks so different, uglier and blacker, even though she knows that can't be right.

How can she have such bright memories, considering everything she went through up here?

Maybe it's because of that summer when she was ten and met Martin and his family. A few weeks without Dad, with just Aunt Elsa in the next house as a babysitter.

One more bend, then the cottage, on the left-hand side.

She sees that the house is still there, stops the van next to the hedge and switches the engine off. The wind has dropped slightly, unless the forest is providing a bit of shelter, and the snowflakes are big, falling softly in the darkness as she heads towards the gate.

Like the other houses up here, their old cottage is still a holiday home and is deserted and shut up. But it's changed beyond recognition. Two outbuildings, and a terrace running right along the front and round both ends, modern windows and doors, and a new roof.

The mixture of old and new is provocatively tasteless.

She goes back to the van and sits in the driver's seat. She can't be bothered to start the engine, and just sits there for a while. The snow is falling gently on the windscreen, and her thoughts drift off, back in time. She ran along this road so many times to get to the cottage Martin's parents were renting. The house isn't visible from here, and perhaps that's why she can't summon up the energy to start the van and drive on. She's afraid of her memories.

I have to go down to the lake, she thinks, finally starting the van and continuing along the road. The cottage is visible from a bend and she casts a quick glance at it, enough to see that it too has been extended and adorned with a large terrace. It's just as deserted as the rest of the village. From here the road slopes down, and now she can just make out the lake a short distance ahead. The road is like glass, and she has to drive with two wheels on the edge of the snowdrift to get any sort of grip. One final bend and she passes between two wooden posts and a sign indicating that this is a designated swimming beach.

She gets out and opens the back doors of the van.

Twelve bags containing fragments of her life, millions of words and thousands of pictures that all, somehow, lead back to her.

Getting to know yourself can be like trying to decipher a cryptogram.

Twenty minutes later she has unloaded all the plastic bags onto the snow-covered beach.

The ice hasn't yet formed, and she crouches down by the water's edge and runs her fingers through the ice-cold water.

Her eyes are used to the darkness now and the white snow gives enough light for her to be able to see a fair way out across the lake. The snow is still falling gently and somewhere out there, beyond the speckled white pattern overlaying the lake, she knows that there's a large rock.

When she used to swim here as a little girl, the dark water would close around her and protect her from the world outside. There was security under the water, and she used to swim four lengths between the jetty and the diving rock, four times fifty metres, then lie on the beach to sunbathe. It had been on one of those occasions that she had first met Martin.

He had been just three years old then, and she had been his Pippi throughout that long, light summer. A Pippi Longstocking, a child yet somehow a grown-up, someone who had been forced to look after themselves.

With Martin she had learned to take care of others, but everything fell apart six years later when she left him alone by the Fyris River in Uppsala.

She had been gone five minutes. But that was enough.

Maybe it had been an accident, maybe not.

Either way, it was down by the river that Crow Girl got her name. She had been inside Victoria before that, but more as a nameless shadow.

Now she's sure that Crow Girl isn't one of her personalities.

The flickering she had felt under her eyelids, and the blind spots in her vision suggest that she was something else entirely.

Crow Girl is an immediate stress reaction to trauma. An epileptic disturbance of the brain, which when she was younger she had mistakenly interpreted as having an alien being inside her.

She walks back to the van and gets a towel out of her bag. Then she returns to the shore, takes her shoes off and rolls her trousers up over her knees.

Even after the first cautious step out into the water she feels numb. As if the lake itself had hands, gripping her ankles and squeezing them tight.

She stands there for a while. The numbness is replaced by a strong stinging sensation that almost feels like heat, and when it starts to feel pleasant she goes back up to the beach to get the first bag.

She pulls it behind her, letting it float on the surface. Once she's ten metres out and the water reaches up to her thighs, she carefully empties the bag into the water.

Words and pictures drift slowly out across the black water, like little ice floes, and she wades back to the beach to get the second bag.

She works hard, bag after bag. After a while she forgets the burning sensation and takes off her trousers, jacket and top. In just her vest and pants she wades further out. The water soon reaches her chest, and she doesn't notice that she's forgetting to breathe. The lake's cold embrace is contracting her muscles, and she can't feel the bottom beneath her feet. The water around her is white with paper, and it sticks to her arms and hair. The feeling is indescribable. Euphoric, perfect. And somewhere beneath the elation she's in control.

She isn't scared. If she gets a cramp she can touch the bottom.

Everything will fade, she thinks. All these papers will lose their ink and print, the words will dissolve into the water and become one with it.

The light breeze is carrying the contents of the bags out into the middle of the lake. Little sinking icebergs, disintegrating as they disappear from view further out in the water.

Once the last bag is empty she swims back to shore, but before she climbs out she lies on her back for a little while, looking up at the falling snow. The cold is warmth and she feels an intense sense of freedom.

Kiev – Babi Yar

Babi Yar. The women's ravine. This was where the city boundary once ran, and it was an inhospitable place, so the guards livened things up by asking their wives and lovers to come out.

The women's ravine used to be a symbol of love. But she remembers the place the way it looked that autumn day almost seventy years ago, and can almost hear the ground moaning.

In less than forty-eight hours the Nazis exterminated the Jewish population of Kiev, more than thirty-three thousand people, and turned the ravine into a mass grave that was covered with earth and is today an attractive, verdant park. The truth, as always, is relative. It hides as a deep evil in the ground, under the beautiful surface.

A tiny wooden vice. A thumbscrew. One more turn. Then another.

It needs to be felt. The pain must be physical. It must spread from the thumb to the heart, carried in the blood. The thumbscrew controls pain, which becomes meditation.

Her finger is starting to turn blue. One turn, then another, then another. The screams of the dead pulse in her finger.

Viggo Dürer, born Gilah Berkowitz, has ten minutes left to live, and she falls to her knees in front of the memorial, a menorah, a seven-armed candelabra. Someone has hung a garland of flowers on one of its sturdy arms.

Her body is old, her hands gnarled, her face pale and watery.

She is wearing a grey coat with a white cross on the back.

The cross is the sign for a liberated prisoner from the concentration camp in Dachau, but the coat isn't her own. It was meant for a young Dane whose name was Viggo Dürer. In other words, her freedom is false. She has never been a free person, neither before nor after Dachau. She has been in chains for over seventy years, and that's why she has come back here.

Her agreement with Madeleine will be concluded.

At the bottom of the ravine she will finally find peace together with those she once sent to their deaths.

She turns the thumbscrew once more. The pain in her finger is almost mute now, and tears are clouding her eyes. She has seven minutes left to live.

What is conscience? she thinks. Regret? Can you regret an entire life?

It had begun when she betrayed her family during the occupation. She had revealed their roots to the Germans and they had set off for the Jewish cemetery near Babi Yar with all their belongings loaded onto a wheelbarrow. It was envy that had driven her to inform on them.

She was a *mamzer*, an illegitimate child who didn't belong.

That autumn day she had made up her mind to live the rest of her life as someone else.

But she had wanted to catch a last glimpse of her father and two older brothers, and had come out here. Not far from where she is now there was a clump of trees surrounded by tall grass. She had lain hidden there, barely twenty metres from the edge of the ravine, and witnessed the whole thing. The pain in her finger throbs as the memories come back to her.

One of the Germans' Sonderkommandos and two Ukrainian police battalions took care of the logistics. Because it had been a systematic, almost industrial process.

She had seen hundreds of people led up to the ravine to be shot.

Most had been naked, stripped of their possessions. Men, women and children. It hadn't made any difference. A democracy of extermination.

Another turn of the thumbscrew. The wooden screw creaks as she turns it, but the pain has disappeared. It's just a strong pressure that feels hot. She has learned that mental pain can be driven out with physical means, and she closes her eyes and can see it all before her once more.

A Ukrainian policeman had walked up with a rusty old wheelbarrow full of screaming babies. Another two policemen had joined him, and together they had thrown the tiny bodies into the ravine.

She hadn't seen her father, but did see her brothers.

The Germans had tied a group of young boys together, two or three dozen tied up with barbed wire that cut deep into their naked flesh, and those who were still alive were forced to drag their dead or unconscious comrades.

Both of her brothers had been in the group, and had been alive when they fell to their knees at the edge of the ravine to be shot in the back of the head.

She has five minutes left to live, and at last she undoes the little wooden thumbscrew and puts it in her pocket. Her finger throbs and the pain returns.

She kneels down, the way her brothers had in the same place, and she is both now and then at the same time. She had turned her own family in, and everything had started with that.

Everything she has done in her life can be traced back to what happened on those autumn days.

She had been part of the informant community. Stalin's dictatorship turned friends into enemies, and not even the most dedicated Stalinists had been safe. When the Germans came it continued, but with the roles reversed. Then you had to inform on Jews and Communists, and she had only done the same as everyone else. Adapting and trying to survive. That was impossible as a Jewish girl, *mamzer* or not, but perfectly feasible as a strong young man.

It hadn't been easy to hide her physical gender from others, and hardest of all in Dachau. It would probably have been impossible if it hadn't been for the protection of the guard commander. To him she had been an *Ohrwürmer*, an earwig, both male and female.

Mentally Gilah Berkowitz is both male and female, or neither, but outwardly the social advantages have made it most practical to perform as a man.

She had even married one of the young girls from Sigtuna College, Henrietta Nordlund, and the marriage had been ideal. She had provided for Henrietta in exchange for her silence and regular appearances as a wife.

She couldn't have wished for a better wife. But in recent years Henrietta had become something of a burden.

The same applied to Anders Wikström, and it had been necessary to arrange an accident.

It's a quiet night, the tall trees shut out all noise from the city, and she has just three minutes left to live. She identified her executioner ten years ago, when Madeleine was just ten years old.

The same age she was when she betrayed her father and brothers.

Now Madeleine is a grown woman with many lives on her conscience.

Gilah Berkowitz listens for footsteps, but it's still quiet. Only the wind in the trees and the dead in the ground. A low moaning.

'*Holodomor*,' she mutters, pulling the coat with the white cross tighter around her.

Images flood through her. Dried-out faces and emaciated bodies. Flies on a pig's cadaver and the memory of her father at the dinner table with the silver cutlery in his hands. On the white plate is a pigeon. Father had eaten pigeons and she had eaten grass.

The Holodomor was Stalin's stage-managed famine, and that act of organised mass murder had taken the life of her mother. They had buried her outside the town, but the grave had been plundered by the starving masses because the recently dead were still edible.

And during the war the Nazis made gloves of human skin and soap out of an entire race, and both have now become exhibits on show for the price of a museum ticket.

Everything sick ends up in museums.

If she is sick then everyone is sick, and she wonders if it was a coincidence that she arrived in Denmark, which has the most embalmed corpses in the whole world. The skulls of the dead had holes drilled in them to let out evil spirits, then they were lowered into the bogs.

Not far from Babi Yar is the Monastery of the Caves, containing the mummified bodies of monks who shut themselves in cramped holes to get closer to God. Now they're in glass cabinets and their bodies are like little children's. They're covered in fabric, but their shrunken hands stick out, and sometimes a fly manages to get behind the glass and crawl on the fingers, eating whatever's left. The corpses in the dark caves are exhibits, and the price of crying over them is the same as for a thin wax candle.

Now she suddenly hears steps, heels striking stone, slowly but purposefully. Which means that she has just a minute or so left to live.

'*Konets*,' she whispers. 'Come to me.'

She thinks of the art she has created, and she has neither an explanation of what she has done nor any answer as to why she has done it. Art creates itself, because it is inexplicable and primitive.

It is Gnosis, child's play, liberated from express intentions.

If she hadn't seen her brothers die at Babi Yar, and if her mother had lived and not died in the great famine, then she would never have forced two Kazakh brothers to kill each other with their bare hands while she looked on dressed as her mother, a true Jewess.

Mamzer is the word for what she has done. *Mamzer* is regret and exclusion and it is life and death at the same time, frozen moments of what has been lost.

Becoming an adult is a crime against your own childhood and simultaneously a denial of Gnosis. A child has no gender and being genderless is closer to the primitive, the original. Discovering your gender is a criminal act against the original creator.

I am an insect, she thinks, as she listens to the steps behind her. They slow down and stop. I am a centipede, a myriapod, and I cannot be explained. Anyone who understood me would have to be as sick as I am. There is no analysis. Commit me to the moaning earth.

She thinks no more as the bullet drills through her bowed head, but her brain has time to register a bang and the flapping of birds escaping into the night sky.

Then darkness.

Dala-Floda

Once she has dried herself and got dressed, she sits beside the lake for several hours. What had once fitted into a small, enclosed room is now spread over an area of at least a hectare. At first it had looked almost like water lilies, but now there are just a few grey stains in the darkness.

A few of the sheets had drifted back to shore. A few incomprehensible lines from a book, maybe a photograph from a newspaper or a note about Gao Lian or Solace Manuti.

Then spring will come and all these papers will rot into the sand or at the bottom of the lake.

As she drives back through the village it has stopped snowing, and she doesn't so much as glance at the cottages. She just concentrates on the road winding its way south through the forest.

Soon the snow disappears from the surface of the road; the conifers become mixed forest with birch and maples interspersed with pine and fir. The landscape becomes flatter and the van feels as light as a feather on the tarmac.

The weight she has left behind makes the wheels turn faster. She no longer has any baggage to drag around, and it occurs to her that the van-rental company has branches all over the country, and that she could return the van in Skåne if she wants.

She sticks just above the speed limit on main roads, but not because she's in a hurry to get anywhere. One hundred kilometres an hour is a meditative speed.

She actually has everything she needs with her. In her bag is her purse, driving licence and bank cards, as well as a clean set of underwear. The damp towel is draped over the passenger seat, steaming gently from the seat warmer.

She doesn't have to worry about money, and the payment to the housing cooperative is through direct debit.

She's approaching Fagersta. If she continues along Route 66 she'll be back in Stockholm in a couple of hours, whereas Route 68 heads south towards Örebro.

She stops in a lay-by a kilometre or so from where the road splits.

Straight ahead is home, back to the past. If she deviates from the planned route it will take her towards something new.

A journey without a goal. She switches the engine off.

During the past few weeks she has effectively shaken off her previous life. She's torn it down, dismantled it into small pieces, and thrown away those parts that don't belong to her. False memories have been deconstructed and hidden memories brought out and crystallised. She has reached clarity, a cleansed state.

Catharsis.

She will no longer give names to her characteristics, will not distance herself from her being by inventing other selves. She has freed herself from all the names: Gao Lian, Solace Manuti, the Worker, the Analyst and the Moaning Minnie, the Reptile, the Sleepwalker and Crow Girl.

She will never again hide away from life, letting unknown parts of her deal with things she finds difficult.

Everything that happens from now on happens to Victoria Bergman, no one else.

She looks at her reflection in the rear-view mirror. At last she recognises herself; it's not the contorted and cowed face she wore when Sofia Zetterlund was the one in charge.

It's a face that's still young, and she can see no regret in it, no traces of a life full of painful memories. That must mean that she has finally accepted everything that has happened.

Her childhood and adolescence were what they were. A living hell.

She starts the van and pulls out onto the road again. One kilometre, two kilometres, and then she turns right, towards the south. The last of her doubts leave her and the black forest rushes past outside the windows.

From now on she's not going to have any plans.

Everything that belongs to the past no longer has anything to do with her life. It has made her who she is today, but her past will never poison her again. Never influence her life choices and future. She has no responsibility for anyone but herself, and she realises that the decision she is making right now is definitive.

A new sign with a new place name, but she continues straight on as she thinks about Jeanette. Are you going to miss me?

Yes, but you'll get over it. People always do.

I'm going to miss you too, she thinks. I might even love you, but I don't yet know if it's for real. So it's better that I leave.

If it's genuine love, I'll come back. If I don't, then that's fine. Then we'll know it wasn't worth gambling on anyway.

It starts to get light as she's driving through the forests of Västmanland. Forest, and more forest, with the occasional break where a patch of woodland has been felled, or for the odd meadow or field. She passes through Riddarhyttan, the only community along this stretch of road, and when the forest takes over again she decides to take things to their natural conclusion. Everything must be removed, everything must go.

She looks at the time. Quarter past eight, which means that Ann-Britt ought to be at work. She takes her mobile out and calls the practice. Ann-Britt answers after a couple of rings. Victoria gets straight to the point and explains what she's decided to do, and how the practical concerns ought to be dealt with. Slightly curious about Ann-Britt's reaction, she asks if she has any questions.

'No, I don't know what to say,' the secretary replies after a few moments of silence. 'It's all very sudden, of course.'

'Are you going to miss me?' Victoria wonders.

Ann-Britt clears her throat. 'Yes, I am. Can I ask why you're doing this?'

'Because I can,' she replies, and that answer will have to do for the time being.

When they hang up and she's about to put the phone back she feels the keys in her pocket.

She takes the key ring out and holds it up in front of her. It's heavy, and contains all her keys. To the practice, and all the ones for the building on Borgmästargatan. The key to the apartment, the storage compartment, the laundry, as well as another key that she can't remember the purpose of. The bicycle store, perhaps.

She winds the window down and throws the keys out.

She leaves the window open, and the cold air spreads through the cab.

She hasn't slept for almost two days, but doesn't feel remotely tired.

Victoria looks at her phone. What does she really need it for? It only contains a mass of obligations, distracting phone numbers, and a diary with far too many appointments that Ann-Britt is now going to have to cancel. It's pointless.

She gets ready to throw her phone out as well, but changes her mind. With one hand on the wheel she struggles to tap in a short text message to Jeanette with the other. 'Sorry,' she writes, as she heads out over a bridge.

The last Victoria Bergman sees of her phone is as it hits the railing of the bridge with a clatter, before disappearing into the dark water below.

Kiev – St Sophia's Cathedral

Madeleine Silfverberg is sitting on a bench in the thin shadow of some trees full of blackbirds. The sun is warm even though it's late autumn, and the gold cupolas of the vast monastery complex in front of her are glinting against the blue sky.

A quiet, colourless stream of people is passing along the path below the cathedral, whereas the building itself is primarily white, green and gold.

She puts her headphones on and tunes the radio. A faint crackle before the receiver finds a frequency with some Ukrainian voices, then an accordion followed by brass instruments and a drum that soon develops into a hybrid of klezmer music and hysterical Europop. The contrast between the music and the stillness of the monastery precinct is like her own life.

Her frantic inner life, unknown to anyone.

People just keep walking past, absorbed in their own concerns. Outside her, shut up inside themselves.

She leans back and looks up at the fractured pattern of branches. Here and there she can make out the shape of birds, shades of grey and black standing out from the trees in relief against the clear blue flatness of the sky.

On a summer's day ten years ago Viggo had taken her to the red-and-white lighthouse at Oddesund, she had sat in his lap for several hours while he talked about his life, and the sky had been the same then as it is now.

She gets to her feet and begins walking towards the white walls that shield the area from the hubbub of the city. The music on the radio fades away and the voices return, just as excitable and present as the drums, accordion and horns.

When she was ten years old Viggo had told her about this place, and he had explained why the monks locked themselves inside the caves beneath the Pechersk Monastery. He had also told her that there is nothing worse in life than regret, and she had known even then what was tormenting him.

Something he had done as a child, when he was neither man nor woman.

And now she's done as he wanted and everything is over.

He had selected her as his most trusted confidante, and she had never forgotten that. As a ten-year-old she had been proud, but now she realises that she has simply been his slave.

She walks out of the gate beneath the tall clock tower and the voices in her headphones fall silent as the music comes back, in just as fast a tempo as before, but this time with a female singer and a tuba in the background. She hears her heels strike the paving of the square at the same rapid pace, and when she reaches the other side and crosses the street she stops and takes off her headphones.

There's an old man sitting at a small table at the street corner. He reminds her of Viggo.

The same face and posture, but this man is dressed in rags. On the rickety little table stands a mass of glasses, all different shapes and sizes. At first she thinks he's trying to sell them, but when he catches sight of her his face cracks into a toothless smile and he moistens his fingertips with his tongue and gently rubs them on the rim of one of the glasses.

The man's fingers move to and fro, notes begin to ring out, and she realises that each of the glasses is filled with a different amount of water. They're set out like three octaves on a piano, thirty-six glasses in total, and she stands in front of him, transfixed. All around her is the sound of traffic and people, and from the headphones around her neck comes a hissing chatter of voices, but the glasses on the table are making sounds she has never heard before.

The old man's glass organ sounds like something from another world.

Only a few minutes ago, inside the monastery grounds, music had seemed like chaos in contrast to the calmness within the walls.

Now the reverse is true.

The notes from the glasses merge together, conveying a swaying sensation, like floating through the air or being gently rocked back and forth by waves in the sea. The ringing, whistling sounds flow out into the chaos of noise all around, and everything becomes a bubble of calmness.

On the pavement there's a little metal can containing some crumpled notes, and under the table, beside the man's battered shoes, she can see a bucket of water.

She realises that the water is there to keep the glass organ in tune, to replace water that evaporates from the glasses, and now she also notices that there are large chunks of ice in the bucket.

Frozen water with cleansing isotopes, just like inside her own body.

Kronoberg – Police Headquarters

After ending her call with Ivo Andrić, Jeanette Kihlberg sits quietly at her desk, while Jens Hurtig sits in the chair facing her, saying nothing. They've just listened to the pathologist's description of what Ulrika Wendin suffered before she froze to death, and his account has left them speechless.

Ivo Andrić told them about living mummification, an ancient technique practised by, among others, certain sects within Japanese Buddhism.

His thoughtful, slow voice had described the procedure itself, which needs no more than a dry space with a limited supply of oxygen. Body fat is burned off with a diet of seeds, nuts, bark and roots, and bodily fluids are reduced by drinking sap. In Ulrika Wendin's case, a form of downy birch had been used.

The pathologist also explained about sensory deprivation, and the effect of being denied all sensory information in an enclosed space insulated against light and sound. He stressed that it is extremely rare for a victim to survive more than a few hours in such a state. The lack of stimulation also affects the body, and it had been a miracle that the girl had survived as long as she had, and even more so that she evidently managed to escape and get away under her own steam.

Jeanette studies the ravaged look on Hurtig's face, and knows they're both feeling a sense of impotence, failure and self-recrimination.

Hurtig is looking straight at her, but he might as well be staring straight through her at the bookcase behind. It's their fault.

To be honest, it's mostly my fault, she thinks. If I'd acted more quickly and followed my gut instinct instead of being rational, we might have been able to save Ulrika Wendin's life. It's as simple as that, really.

Jeanette knows that right about now the girl's grandmother will be hearing of her death from two police officers accompanied by a priest. There are some people who have a gift for that particular task, and Jeanette knows that she isn't one of them. Truly loving someone can be terrifying, she thinks, and her thoughts go to Johan, who will soon be sitting in a plane on his way back from London. In a few hours she'll see him again, and he'll be happy after a successful weekend away with his dad. She understood that much from the text message she received just after they had found Ulrika Wendin's body half covered with snow under a ragged pine tree. She had had a terrible death, and Jeanette will never be able to stop thinking about how frightened she must have been.

She brushes a few tears from her cheeks and looks at Hurtig. Has he got anyone to fear losing? His parents, of course. They seem to get along well, and have managed to come to terms with the loss of one member of the family. Someone who'll never be coming back.

Perhaps Ulrika Wendin's grandmother has no one she can share her grief with. Like Annette Lundström, the only survivor among all the people caught up in this horrible mess.

She finds herself thinking about a family from Sierra Leone who have also lost someone, and will soon be getting confirmation from the police.

In addition to the Polaroids in Viggo Dürer's cellar out at Hundudden, forensics found a video recording.

Samuel Bai, chained up and fighting for his life against a half-naked man whom both Jeanette and Hurtig recognised as the man they found dead in the cottage up in Lapland.

On the desk, next to the film of Samuel's death, are dozens of files and a heap of folders, one of them containing copies of Viggo Dürer's photographs of the bodies from Thorildsplan, Svartsjölandet, Danvikstull and Barnängen. It's now almost incidental that Dürer spent several years being treated for cervical cancer, or that the car that scraped the tree where the body was found out in Svartsjölandet is the same one parked under a tarpaulin at Hundudden.

But the investigation isn't over just because their four cases have been solved. There's evidence of another forty bodies, and all the files will be passed on to Europol.

None of that really makes any difference, though, Jeanette thinks, since everybody concerned is dead. Including the murderer.

The bodies that ended up cremated on Viggo Dürer's boat were, in all likelihood, Henrietta Dürer and Anders Wikström.

And Dürer has been found dead in a park in Kiev, shot in the back of the head. A murder that Iwan Lowynsky will have to deal with until Europol takes on the case.

It's over, she thinks. But I'm still not happy.

There's something that isn't right, something that can't be properly understood, leaving unanswered questions. All investigations include some degree of anticlimax, but she's found it impossible to get used to that and accept it. Like the fact that she never managed to find Madeleine Silfverberg. When it comes down to it, maybe she was just a phantom anyway. Maybe the murders of the former Sigtuna pupils really were Hannah and Jessica's work. She's never going to know, and that's just one part of everything she's going to have to live with.

What would I do if I didn't have Johan? she thinks. Resign and just take off somewhere? No, I probably wouldn't dare. Maybe apply for a leave of absence and do something else. Mind you, I'd probably return to work after a week, since police work is all I can do. Or would I?

She doesn't know, and is reminded of the fact that her personal life is as full of unanswered questions as her investigations. Does she even have a personal life? A relationship?

'What are you thinking about?' Hurtig suddenly asks.

They've been silent for so long that Jeanette had almost forgotten that he's sitting on the other side of the desk.

In relationships with other people you only see a fraction of each other, she thinks. Most of your real life takes place inside your head, and can't be translated easily into verbal communication.

'Nothing,' she says. 'I'm not thinking about anything at all.'

Hurtig gives her a weary smile. 'Me neither. And it feels very nice, actually.'

Jeanette nods, then hears footsteps out in the corridor followed by a light knock on the door. It's Billing, who gives them a concerned look as he shuts the door behind him. 'How's it going?' he asks quietly.

Jeanette gestures towards the piles on her desk. 'We're done, we just need von Kwist to come and get what we've put together.'

'Good, good . . .' the commissioner mutters. 'But, if I've understood correctly, as soon as this is made public it's going to cause . . . problems?'

Billing looks troubled, and Jeanette suddenly realises why he's there.

'Yes, that's probably unavoidable,' she says. 'It's not really possible to remove Berglind from the case.'

'This is the last thing we need right now.' Billing sighs. 'The press are going to crucify us.' He shakes his head and leaves the door open when he leaves.

The press? Jeanette thinks. So the worst thing about all this is what the papers are going to say about us?

She glances at the stacks of evidence on the desk, in which the fact that Billing's predecessor, the former police commissioner Gert Berglind, was involved in financing child pornography is revealed in macabre detail. Crucifixion probably isn't the right word for how the press is going to react.

More like slaughter.

The phone rings once Hurtig has left her office.

A call that, if it doesn't turn her entire life upside down, certainly changes the future forever.

Miracles rarely happen. That's in the nature of things.

But occasionally they do.

The call is from her bank. An impersonal call in every way, were it not for its highly personal import.

Someone has paid off the outstanding balance of her and Åke's mortgage.

Two million, four hundred and fifty-three thousand kronor.

'What did you say?' is all Jeanette can manage.

'It's quite true,' the voice at the other end says, making it sound like some sort of punishment. 'The individual in question has also transferred another two million into your personal account.'

Jeanette feels dizzy.

The coffee machine out in the kitchen rattles. Ice crystals have started to form on the window. The rain will soon turn to snow.

'There must be some mistake –'

'No, there isn't. I spoke to the person who conducted the transactions myself, and she was very clear.'

'She?'

'The donor wished to remain anonymous, but she asked me to let you know that Victoria Bergman is alive and well. Is that someone you know?'

Six months of events pass through her mind. The picture of the defiant schoolgirl in the yearbook, the only one not smiling. Sexually abused by her father. Jeanette has seen the film of the assault at the boarding school in Sigtuna.

Jeanette remembers Victoria's voice on the phone.

'Yes,' she replies after a few moments' reflection.

Gamla Enskede – Kihlberg House

By the time Hurtig drives Jeanette out to Gamla Enskede, the weather from Lapland has reached Stockholm and it starts to snow.

She hasn't told Hurtig about the bank transactions. And she hasn't told him about Victoria Bergman either.

She needs to think.

Probably for quite some time.

If things are the way she imagines, she might never tell anyone.

They sit in silence the whole way, and part with a hug. Large, light snow-stars are drifting across the street like cotton wool as she gets out of the car.

She empties the mailbox of its advertisements and bills, and as she walks round the hedge and enters the drive she sees something that erases any last traces of doubt.

A brand-new Audi is parked in front of the garage.

The same shade of red as the one she recently sent to be scrapped.

Detective Superintendent Jeanette Kihlberg stands beside the car for a long time. She feels drained of all rational thought, and when she finally reacts, it comes in the form of a smile.

Then relief.

A wonderful, liberating sense of relief.

In another time, another place, she has time to think before her mobile vibrates.

A text from Johan, saying that they've landed, and that the first thing Åke did was call Alexandra and argue about money he hasn't received.

After she's read it she notices that she's received another message without realising it. Probably while they were on their way back from Ånge.

It's a message from Sofia.

Sorry, it says.

It's always too late, Jeanette thinks.

A NOTE ABOUT THE AUTHORS

Erik Axl Sund is the pen name of the Swedish writing duo Jerker Eriksson and Håkan Axlander Sundquist. Håkan is a sound engineer, musician and artist. Jerker has been the producer of Håkan's electro-punk band iloveyoubaby! They currently own an art gallery in Stockholm.